TRAPPED

Camilla Lackberg is a worldwide bestseller renowned for her brilliant contemporary psychological thrillers. Her books are sold in over 60 countries and have been translated into 43 languages.

www.camillalackberg.com

Henrik Fexeus is one of Sweden's most sought after lecturers and a prize-winning mentalist. He has done astounding psychological experiments on SVT and TV4 and became a household name in 2007, with the debut book *The Art of Reading Minds*. Fexeus books have won several prizes, sold over a million copies and are translated into more than 30 languages. Henrik made his debut as an author of fiction in 2017, with YA Novel *The Lost*, the first part in his critically acclaimed Final Illusion Trilogy.

www.henrikfexeus.se

TRAPPED

CAMILLA LACKBERG

& HENRIK FEXEUS

Translated from the Swedish by Ian Giles

HarperCollins*Publishers*

HarperCollins*Publishers* Ltd
1 London Bridge Street,
London SE1 9GF

www.harpercollins.co.uk

HarperCollins*Publishers*
1st Floor, Watermarque Building, Ringsend Road
Dublin 4, Ireland

Published by HarperCollins*Publishers* 2022
1

Originally published in 2021 by
Bokförlaget Forum, Sweden, as *Box*

ISBN: 978-0-00-846418-9 (HB)
ISBN: 978-0-00-846419-6 (TPB)

Typeset in Sabon LT Std by Palimpsest Book Production Ltd,
Falkirk, Stirlingshire

Printed and Bound in the UK using 100% renewable electricity at CPI Group (UK) Ltd

1

Feeling stressed, Tuva drums her fingers on the cafe counter. She's still at work at the cafe at Hornstull, despite the fact that she shouldn't be. A customer who has just sat down in the corner looks at her in irritation and she fires him a murderous gaze in reply. She memorizes his face, while making a mental note not to give that customer a heart in his cappuccino next time. Perhaps she'll opt for an extended middle finger instead.

Not being on time always leaves her in a bad mood. And right now she is really late. She tucks her blond hair behind her ear without thinking about it. Linus was supposed to have been picked up from nursery half an hour ago. She's immune to the forbidding expressions of the staff – she's seen them far too many times for them to have an impact on her anymore. But her three-year-old son will be upset. And Tuva isn't the kind of person to upset kids. Especially not Linus. She has no idea how many times she has said she'd die for him – but in reality it's not always quite so straightforward. Although God knows she is trying. So damn hard. She takes off her apron, opens the cleaning cupboard door and slings the apron onto the precarious heap of items to be laundered. She can't leave until relief arrives. Where the hell is he?

Martin, Linus's dad, was away the day his son was born. Tuva didn't blame him for that – she'd been rushed to the maternity ward by ambulance a fortnight ahead of her due date. On the other hand, she'd thought it was weird when Martin didn't come to visit her in hospital over the subsequent days that she was there. The birth had not been without its complications. She had been too groggy to commit it all to memory – all she had were faint recollections of doctors who had come to check her vitals and those of her baby over and over again before noting that everything was fine. Just like Martin did in the short text messages he sent her during that hospital stay. He was coming, he said, but first he needed to sort out a few things. However, while her days in the maternity wing might have been fuzzy, she could remember with razor-sharp clarity the empty flat waiting for her and Linus when they came home. While she had been giving birth to and fighting for their son, Martin had taken his stuff and gone. That was apparently what he had needed to 'sort out'. She hadn't seen or heard from that cowardly shit since. Just as well – she would likely have murdered him if he'd shown up.

Since then, it's been her and Linus against the world. Though the world was forever trying to come between them. Like right now. Daniel, who is supposed to be working the afternoon shift, should have been here an hour ago. But he still hasn't turned up. She'd had to call him and wake him. At half past one in the afternoon. Was she ever that irresponsible when she was twenty-one? Probably. No wonder things didn't work out with Martin. She checks her wristwatch.

For. Heaven's. Sake.

She puts on her quilted jacket and hat, and then makes two double espressos. One in a porcelain cup. The other in paper.

No doubt it will be Matti who has once again had to stay late at the nursery and wait for her. Matti, the member of staff who her son has started to refer to as Dad. Each time it happens, Matti gives her that look. The one that says she ought to spend more time with her son instead of at work. Well, thank you very much for the guilty conscience. As if it isn't bad enough having to deal with Linus's tears over not knowing when Mum is coming.

The espresso is ready by the time Daniel saunters through the door, his hair standing on end. The bitter February chill enters the cafe with him and some of the patrons make a performance of shivering, but Daniel doesn't seem to notice. Or perhaps he doesn't care. Good God, how did she ever think he was even a little attractive?

'Here,' she says with all the iciness that can be contained in four letters, pushing the porcelain cup towards him. 'You look as though you need it. I'm off.'

She doesn't wait for a reply, grabbing the paper cup and rushing out into the snow, which shows no sign of melting. She isn't paying sufficient attention and walks straight into a decrepit-looking old couple.

'Sorry, I'm late – have to do the nursery pickup,' she mutters hastily, without looking at them.

2

'Ah well, children can be surprisingly resourceful, left to themselves.'
The voice is kind rather than reproachful.

Tuva doesn't answer, but is relieved that there doesn't seem to be a row brewing over her clumsiness. People can be so touchy. On several occasions, patrons have demanded not only reimbursement of their dry-cleaning costs but financial compensation after she has accidentally spilled a little coffee on them. She smiles apologetically at the couple. Tuva hears the coffee swilling around in the cup in her hand and realizes she doesn't have time for this. She manages to blurt out yet another apology and begins to jog towards the underground station while knocking back the espresso on the go. The hot coffee burns – first her tongue and then her stomach. It tastes chemical. Almost like medicine. She needs to clean the machine. The contrast with the cold outdoors makes the coffee seem even hotter.

After picking up Linus, she's going to bring him back to the cafe. Daniel can give him all the buns and cakes he wants. It's only right. To hell with the macaroni and meatballs on the meal plan for the day. Tomorrow she's going away, but tonight it's just her and Linus.

As she reaches the stairs to the underground station her legs suddenly give way beneath her. She cries out and at the last second manages to grab the handrail to save herself. She must have tripped. She's not in that much of a hurry. No need to arrive at the nursery black and blue.

She tries to stand up again, but it's as if the bones inside her legs are gone. Her feet fold over. She feels dizzy. Nauseous. Almost as if she's going to faint. The same feeling she had when they gave her all those drugs in hospital. For the birth.

Linus.

I'm coming.

She tries to pull herself up with the support of the handrail, but her arms are now several kilometres long. The bannister floats high above her head and she no longer has any idea how it works. Dark patches are dancing in the periphery of her vision. The world is spinning in giddy revolutions and a small voice inside her tells her she's falling down the stairs. She can't feel it at all.

The first thing Tuva notices when she comes to is that her joints hurt. She's lying in an uncomfortable position. She licks her lips and clears her throat. Her mouth is completely dry. There's an unfamiliar taste lingering. It takes a few seconds to regain full consciousness and then she realizes that she isn't lying down, she's on her knees, leaning forward

3

slightly. Walls are pressing against her from all sides. Even from above – she can feel the pressure against her neck.

It's as if she's inside a box with no room to move.

It hurts too much to be a dream. But it can't be for real either. It can't be. And yet . . . The smell of wood is far too real. Light seeps in through short, narrow cracks, creating rectangles on her bare arms and legs. Her *bare* . . . Where are her clothes? It's not just her coat that's gone, but her hoodie too. And her jeans. Someone has undressed her. She's sitting there in her vest and knickers, and this can't be happening.

She licks her lips again. That chemical taste is still there. There must have been something in the coffee. Someone put something in it without her noticing. And she was too stressed to notice. She drank the lot.

Her skin begins to prickle as adrenaline floods her body. She needs to get out. She screams and pushes against the sides of the box as hard as she can. The wood is springy, but there isn't enough give for it to crack or for the box to open. She can't kick since she's on her knees – she has to make do with pounding the walls with the palms of her hands, yet they are far too close for her to achieve any force in her blows. The light on one side of her is suddenly blocked out. Someone is outside the box.

'Let me out!' she yells. 'What are you playing at?'

No one replies. But she can feel the presence. Hear breathing. She cries out again, but the silence remains just as dense, just as threatening. The prickling feeling spreads all over her skin. She strikes the wooden walls with renewed force, but the cramped space refuses to lend her the strength she needs.

'What do you want?' she screams, blinking her eyes as tears fill them. 'Let me out! Please! That way we can talk. I need to pick up Linus!'

She glances down at her arm. The glass on her wristwatch is smashed and the hands have stopped at three o'clock on the dot. Matti must have called and tried to get hold of her by now. Perhaps he's started to wonder where she's got to, perhaps he's come looking and he'll find her in the box any moment now . . . Perhaps she's often even later than this for the nursery pickup.

No one is searching for her.

Because no one has missed her yet.

No one knows she's been kidnapped.

Kidnapped. The meaning of the word sinks in and it becomes difficult to breathe. A metallic sound is audible near the box – it makes her shudder.

4

'Hello?' she calls out.

Through one of the lower cracks on her left-hand side, something sharp and silver is stuck in. It resembles the tip of a sword. The metal blade continues to slowly penetrate the box. She tries to move her thigh out of the way but it's too tight. She has nowhere to go. The tip of the sword reaches her thigh and is pushed hard against her skin. It hurts, although it isn't quite as sharp as it looks.

'Ouch, what are you doing?' she shouts. 'Stop it!'

The sword blade continues to press against her thigh until it punctures the skin and a drop of blood appears. The movement is tentative. As if the person outside is engaging in trial and error. Tuva screams again but can barely hear her own words. Then, without any warning, the pressure stops and the blade is pulled back a centimetre or two.

There's the sound of an engine starting. The sword blade begins vibrating and moving forward again, and this time it doesn't stop when it reaches her leg. Tuva screams as it cuts into her thigh muscle. The sword continues into the tissue as her screams are drowned out by the engine. The pain is incredible. Explosions of colour drench her field of vision as her nerve endings are set on fire. The world is disappearing – all that exists is pain. The sword reaches the femur and the vibrations of the blade are propagated throughout her skeleton, making her entire body vibrate. Tuva involuntarily throws up, covering herself and the bloodied sword in vomit. The blade eventually glides over the bone inside her leg and continues on its way out through the muscle on the other side. The point of the sword looks bordering on obscene as it presses out through the skin. Blood immediately begins to pulse from the new hole, tracing the rounded contour of the leg and collecting beneath her in a puddle. And the sword doesn't stop. It continues moving through her thigh on the way towards her other leg. She still can't move.

'Please stop. Please,' she begs through tears. 'I have to pick up Linus. I'm late. He's alone.'

When the sword enters her other leg, Tuva is ready for the pain. But it is impossible to be ready. She lets out a loud cry and wishes she could lose consciousness, go mad, anything not to feel any more. It takes a few seconds. An eternity. She can no longer see. The blade eventually ends up running through both her legs and out a crack on the other side of the box. The sword finally stops vibrating.

But the sound of the engine is still there.

Something stings her on the back of her shoulder and the part of

Tuva that is her sense of reason dies. She can feel it in purely physical terms – how part of her brain collapses. Because there are also cracks in the box behind her. Of course. She tries to lean forward to escape the sword at her shoulder, but the movement makes her thighs burn even more. And Tuva is no longer there. She's in the maternity ward, fighting for her son. She is in the cafe where she managed to get a job through sheer luck, she's kissing Daniel, she's with Martin and he's telling her that he loves her. She hears the sound of cartilage and tissue being decimated in her back and she thinks about how Linus always calls Matti Dad.

Then she looks down and sees the skin below her collarbone bulging outwards before it cracks and the sword comes out of her front. Like a magic trick. She's the magician's assistant and soon she's going to be taking the applause. She's seen it on TV. The blood from her chest stains her vest red as the sword continues on to one of the cracks in the wooden wall. The smell of iron is overwhelming.

Linus's blue eyes are in front of her.

Are you leaving me too, Mum?

A squeaking sound emerges from her throat when she tries to speak. 'Please. I'm late.'

Outside the box, someone moves something. One of the cracks in front of her face darkens. A third sword. The distance to Tuva's head is merely inches. The two swords already penetrating her are holding her in place.

'No more,' she whispers.

The sword moves slowly but the distance is far too small. She can see the tip glittering until it gets too close for her eyes to focus on it properly.

Linus. Sorry. Mum loves you.

She shudders when the tip grazes the spot between her right eye and the bridge of her nose and then it continues on, puncturing the eye. Something moist runs down her cheek and Tuva is blinded on her right side. But it doesn't hurt. At least it doesn't hurt any more.

Tuva's final thought is to wonder why it smells of burning.

Then the sword cuts into her brain.

2

Vincent slammed the palm of his hand against the table in front of him with all his might. The people in the theatre gasped audibly. He frowned, paused for dramatic effect and then gazed at his audience while raising his hand. Beneath it a crushed white paper bag was visible. Nervous ripples of laughter began to spread through the auditorium as he brushed the remains onto the floor.

'It's not under bag number five either,' he said.

The stage was dark save for a single spotlight. It was directed at him, the table and the woman standing beside it. The bare light emphasized the gravity of the final number in his set. The silence was absolute. His final number didn't feature music. That made it even more uncomfortable. To begin with, there had been five upside-down, numbered paper bags. He had already crushed two of them with his hand.

'*Three* left,' he said, looking at the woman. 'Magdalena, don't look at the *three* bags – that means I can follow the movements of your eyes. But keep in mind which bag the big nail is under. Only you know. The audience didn't see where you hid it and I didn't see it either. *Three*. Remember how sharp the nail was when you touched it. Just hold that in your mind.'

The woman was sweating profusely. The spotlight was warm, but she was also nervous. Even more nervous than the rest of the audience. Vincent studied her closely.

'You didn't react to *three* despite the fact that I said it three times,' he said. 'So it's probably not there.'

She slammed his hand down hard on bag number three before the audience had time to react. The sound made someone in the auditorium cry out.

Two bags left. A 50 per cent chance of doing himself real harm. He

7

really did not understand why he still did this one. Everyone who did it hurt themselves sooner or later. It was inescapable if you did it enough times. But the audience couldn't be allowed to see that he was genuinely worried. A big part of the trick was to appear to be more in control than he actually was.

'Number two and number four left,' he said to the woman. 'Visualize the nail in front of you – all twenty centimetres of it.'

She closed her eyes and nodded unhappily.

'Do you remember it gleaming as you stood it on end? Under one of these two bags. The one we *don't* want me to hit.'

'But I don't know whether I remember for sure,' she whimpered.

He raised an eyebrow. The atmosphere in the theatre was so dense you could cut it with a knife. Two bags. He raised his hand over one of them. Then he moved his hand to the other one. One of the bags would see the show end in a standing ovation. The other would result in a penetrative wound and a trip in an ambulance.

'Open your eyes,' he said.

The woman reluctantly opened them and squinted towards the bags. He looked at her. Then he raised his hand to strike down on one of the bags, before noticing her eyes widen in panic as his palm was on the way down. He changed midway and instead slammed down hard on the other one. The woman cried out as his hand struck the table. He waited with his head bowed for a few seconds. Then he triumphantly swept the crumpled but empty bag onto the floor before lifting the final one. The nail underneath it was pointing straight up like a rocket, with a deadly glitter in the cold light. The audience roared and got to their feet as the music began. He signed the nail with a sharpie, put it in the bag and gave it to the woman, who was helped offstage, visibly relieved.

Vincent stepped to the very front of the stage and held out his arms. There was no need to fake his relief.

The applause was deafening. The performance at Gävle Theatre was over. He bowed dramatically and then fixed his gaze on a distant point in the auditorium. The roving beam of light during the applause blinded him so that he couldn't see his audience, but he behaved as if he could. The knack was to look straight ahead and pretend to make eye contact with someone. He laughed into the darkness in which he knew there were now 415 people standing up and offering their tribute to Vincent Walder, the Master Mentalist.

'Thank you for coming,' he shouted through the torrent of applause. The volume of the clapping and whistles increased. The theatre was sold out. It had been a good night. A very good night, in fact. She hadn't been there. The one who was a worrying factor. The nights she didn't come were a greater relief to him than he was willing to admit, even to himself.

He resisted the temptation to shade his eyes to see the standing ovation. He had worked hard for it – this was his moment to enjoy. At the same time, pure adrenaline was all that was keeping him upright.

It had been a close-run thing with that damn nail today. And it was the very last number in a two-hour set. The sweat was pouring down his back and his brain felt like it was boiling over:

. . . 415 seats. 41 plus 5 was 46. The same as his age. At least for a few more weeks.

Stop.

Of course, the big secret was not in being able to predict the behaviour of the audience or making it seem as if he could read their thoughts. The illusion was to make it look easy while his brain was in overdrive. The poster in the foyer bragged that he was 'The Master Mentalist', but he wished he hadn't gone along with that when they suggested it. It was too . . . unsophisticated. Vulgar. Although it was useful to hide behind it. It made it sound like he was an invented character. Rather than someone who more than anything wanted to lie down in his dressing room and spend ten minutes catching his breath. And now, with the performance over, it was important to regain control of his thoughts before they careered off in their own direction. It took longer than usual tonight.

Composed. An eight-letter word. The same number of rows he knew there to be on the balconies.

Stop.

Vincent raised his gaze towards the first balcony, where he had persuaded four people to forget their names during the first act; 23 seats on each row on the balcony, a total of 184 seats . . .

Someone wolf-whistled from the balcony.

Take a deep breath. Don't follow that thought.

. . . 184 seats. The eighteenth of the fourth was also the final date on the tour.

And 23 seats per row, 8 rows, 2 plus 3 plus 3 was 13, which was how many shows there were left until then.

Stopstopstop.

He bit his tongue hard. Then he walked offstage. He stopped behind the velvet curtain facing one of the wings and began to count to himself silently. One. If the applause continued when he reached ten he would run back onto the stage for a final bow. Two. A shadow emerged from the darkness of the wings. It was a woman in her thirties. Three. He went completely cold. She had come after all. Four. But this time she hadn't even waited until the performance was over before she ran to the stage. Five. How had she managed to get backstage? No one was allowed to be there when he was performing. The person who had let her in would have him to deal with. He had asked them to keep an eye out for her. But that was to prevent her getting close, not to help her. Six. Now he would at least see what she looked like. Dark hair in a ponytail. Polo neck. Black jacket. Seven. Eyes that widened slightly as she prepared to speak. He had no idea how dangerous she was. Eight. He signalled to her to be quiet and pointed at the stage with his thumb to indicate that he wasn't done yet. Perhaps there was another way offstage after he'd taken his bow. Nine. Try not to think about her. A deep breath and switch on the smile. Ten. He ran back into the spotlight again.

'Thank you, thank you! You're too kind!' he shouted. 'I can well understand that you'd prefer to stay here, but I'm afraid that reality awaits you. It's time to head back into it. And if you find yourself tossing and turning over something you've seen here tonight, then remember this: it's only for fun.'

He paused.

'Perhaps.'

The audience laughed loudly. And a little nervously. He couldn't help smiling. It worked every time. Vincent hurried offstage before the audience began to stand up, even though it was the last thing he wanted to do. It never looked good for the artist still to be there as the audience started to leave. And if they had their winter coats to retrieve from the cloakroom – as they would today – then they always began to get up earlier in a naive attempt to avoid the inevitable queue. The woman was still standing in the wings offstage when he returned.

'She's here,' he said quietly into his microphone. 'Bring the bouncer here. Now.'

He was taking a chance, but with a little luck the sound desk would still be listening to him even if they had the audio turned down. Most fans who sought him out were nice, but he didn't want any surprises during a performance. Especially not a woman who had become known for rushing up on stage when his show was over. That kind of behaviour was not acceptable. However, he had succeeded in avoiding meeting her. Until now.

It was hard to think straight. After the show he needed time to decompress and get his brain back to its normal temperature. He couldn't analyse the situation as well as he needed to. But he had no choice but to be pleasant while waiting for the bouncer to show. And to keep his distance.

He pointed at the small flight of stairs down to the green room to buy himself time. She walked ahead of him. It turned out there were seven steps. Aargh! Vincent did the last step twice just to finish on an even number. The woman in front of him didn't seem to notice.

Vincent and the woman entered a room furnished as a living room. Where the hell was that bouncer? Four unopened bottles of mineral water were standing on the coffee table. Vincent took off his jacket and threw it onto a sofa. He adjusted one of the bottles so that they all had their labels pointing the same way. The woman kept her jacket on. He wiped his face with wet wipes to remove the make-up. The woman wrinkled her nose almost imperceptibly. Good. Anything that put her off was to his advantage. Hopefully he smelled sweaty too.

'Look, I don't want to be rude,' he said, 'but no one's really allowed back here.'

He opened one of the bottles of water and poured it into a glass. He regarded the bubbles with suspicion.

'You can't go on like this,' he said. 'The stage and wings are off limits to everyone except the production and—'

The woman cut in to introduce herself.

'Mina,' she said. 'Mina Dabiri. I'm from the police.'

Then she quickly adjusted the bottle that had been knocked slightly as he took his, so that all the labels were once again pointing in the same direction, before proffering her hand to him. Vincent fell silent and shook her hand. The Master Mentalist suddenly had no idea what to say next.

3

Mina looked at the man who was sitting opposite her across the small dark brown table. Vincent Walder. She'd had to wait for him while he changed out of his stage costume, an elegant but sober blue suit with a black shirt. He was now decidedly more casually dressed in a white T-shirt and black jeans. Despite the fact that it was still only March and winter had Gävle firmly in its grip, Vincent hadn't put on a coat.

To her surprise, she found him attractive. It was rare that this happened. And the word that actually came to mind was 'handsome'. There was something reserved about him, a slightly old-fashioned elegance, even when wearing jeans and a T-shirt. When she had seen him in a suit earlier it had been even more apparent.

Mina had wanted to speak to him in private, but Vincent had insisted that he needed food. Changing a plan was never ideal, but she resigned herself to letting him have his way. After all, she had come to him. Which is why she now found herself obliged to discuss sensitive police business in a branch of the Harrys pub chain, one of the few places in Gävle where the kitchen was still open after ten o'clock.

Vincent looked more worn out following his show than she would have liked. Hopefully, the food would help. She needed him sharp. She was already distracted by the cluster of patrons standing at the bar, speaking in broad Skåne accents and wearing white paper rectangles dangling around their necks. Presumably they were delegates from some conference at one of the surrounding hotels. They reminded her of overgrown schoolchildren with latchkeys hanging at chest height.

The smell of beer and hopeful pheromones lingered in the air and made her want more than anything to put on a mask, but she suppressed that feeling and focused on Vincent. There had been nothing on him in the police records, so she'd had to find out what she could by other means. Wikipedia and a fair amount of googling had told her that he was due to turn forty-seven in a month's time, that Walder was an assumed name and that his profession was 'mentalist'.

According to the website, a mentalist was someone who used psychology, personal influence and secret tricks to create the illusion of having psychic abilities or the capacity to read minds. He also seemed to be well versed in ordinary magic, judging by the interviews she had read. Although she was here for his knowledge about how people functioned, some insight into magic would do no harm, given the photos she had in her file. She hadn't found any information about what he had done before or where he had been born. His Wikipedia entry stated that Vincent had been working professionally for fifteen years, but it was only of late that he had come to the public's attention, thanks to a primetime series on TV4.

In one of the programmes, he had conducted a psychological experiment using hidden cameras. Vincent had randomly selected a man whose daily life he began to fill with imperceptible suggestions and hypnotic commands without the poor participant realizing that anything was happening. In the end, the man had headed out one night to an industrial park where he had spray-painted VINCENT WALDER on the walls. One hundred times. It had taken him hours.

The security team on site hadn't been given a heads-up. When they apprehended the man and asked him what he was up to, he replied that he had no idea what they were talking about. He had no clue what he had been doing for the past few hours and was genuinely surprised when he saw the paint stains on his hands and clothing.

Mina hadn't seen the show, but she remembered everyone talking about it. There had been a real to-do. Many commentators had questioned the ethics behind it. Vincent had explained that it was about fanaticism and that he wanted to show how even the most absurd ideas could take hold of our subconscious and govern our behaviour without us realizing it. The whole thing with painting the walls was apparently a tribute to a Monty Python film, and when he was asked about the message being spray-painted, he said it was the least objectionable thing he could think of. What was more, he had added, an artist always signed his works. That quote had quickly morphed into a meme on Instagram before it all died down a few months later.

The scent of frying oil and grilled meat reached Mina's nostrils seconds before a server set down a hamburger in front of Vincent. There were open bowls of mayonnaise and ketchup. Mina was taken aback. They could have been interfered with by just about anybody on the way from the kitchen. It was incredibly unhygienic. She retrieved a recently purchased bottle of hand sanitizer from her pocket on reflex and squirted a dollop onto her palm before rubbing her hands together.

'I need carbs after a performance,' the mentalist said apologetically. 'Otherwise I can't think clearly.'

He took a fry from the plate, dipped it in the mayonnaise and then put it into his mouth. Mina watched him closely. If he was going to double-dip then she would have to consign him to the section of humanity that she wanted nothing to do with. Fortunately, he only dipped once. There was hope.

'And I really must apologize for my behaviour earlier,' he said. 'I thought you were someone else. We've had problems with a some-what . . . over-enthusiastic . . . admirer. I thought you were her. I didn't mean to be rude.'

She waved her hand dismissively. The server set down a beer in front of Vincent and a Coke Zero in front of her. She took a disposable straw out of her pocket, removed the paper wrapper and inserted it into the glass. Vincent looked at it but said nothing.

She waited until the server was out of earshot before she began to speak.

'I was advised to speak to you,' she said in a low voice. 'From what I understand, you're an expert in the human psyche. But you also seem to know plenty about regular magic too. And we need someone who understands both.'

He nodded and sipped his beer.

'I did a lot of magic when I was younger,' he said. 'But when I was twenty, I realized that card tricks were possibly not the best way to chat up women. So I quit.'

'Did that help?' she said.

'I'll let you judge. I met my first wife a month later. My interest in it has only been as a hobby since then. But why do the police want to know about that?'

Before she could reply, Vincent checked the time.

'Good Lord, I must apologize,' he said, 'but speaking of wives . . . It's a quarter to. I need to call home. We always speak at around this time. It'll only take a minute.'

She was beginning to get impatient and wanted to get to the point. She'd already had to wait for him. Her colleagues usually said she was too pushy, that she needed to work on her social skills if she wanted

14

others to respond positively to her. She was sceptical. In the ten years she'd been a police officer, she couldn't think of a single investigation where the outcome had been dependent on how pleasant she was. But whatever.

'No problem,' she said, discreetly changing position on the hard chair.

She stared down into her Coke and shut out Vincent's voice as he spoke to his wife. Instead, she pictured the box they had found a week earlier. The box that had looked like it ought to be covered in glitter and featured in a magic show in Las Vegas. She imagined a sequinned assistant (a woman obviously; it was always women who were degraded in magic tricks) crawling into the box and a magician (a man, naturally) inserting long swords through the openings in it while the audience ooohed and aaahed. She had googled it. The woman-hostile stage trick was known as the sword box illusion, or sometimes as the sword cabinet, sword casket or sword basket. Apparently the thing had a plethora of names. In the original version, it hadn't even been a box – just a small basket. With a child in it. Awful. Yet the illusion was considered a classic. Women and children. Always its victims.

But she wasn't sitting in a Harrys in Gävle on a freezing cold night waiting for Vincent Walder because her colleagues had found some magician's home-made equipment. She was there because of the body they had found *inside* the box. A body that they still hadn't been able to identify. And she was there because they had hit a dead end. They had followed standard procedure in pursuing every lead and it had got them nowhere. In the end, she and her boss, Julia, had concluded that if they were to have any hope of solving the case they would have to resort to less conventional methods.

Mina sucked the fizzy drink through her straw and fixed her gaze on the conference delegates at the bar – anything to stop the gruesome images flashing through her mind. She didn't want to be reminded of them, but they were there, as vivid as the first time. It was rare that a case got to her this badly, but then she'd never dealt with a murder as sadistic as this one.

The box had been found with sword hilts sticking out of the top and the left-hand side, with the tips of the swords protruding from the bottom and right-hand side. Inside the box, suspended on the sword blades like a grotesque marionette, was a young woman. Mina screwed up her eyes. Too late. It was always too late.

A week had gone by and they still hadn't established who the woman was. They had no suspect either. Milda Hjort had been as thorough as ever, but the autopsy results contained no revelations that would help them solve the case. Forensics were still working on the box, but Mina didn't hold out much hope of them finding some vital clue that would unmask the killer. The method was the key to this crime – she was convinced of it.

Suddenly aware that Vincent had finished talking to his wife and was now looking at her, Mina cleared her throat and pushed the images out of her head.

'Sorry about that,' he said. 'But now I'm all yours. I can tell you're not from around here. I guess you work in Stockholm? And yet you're here in Gävle. Late on a Thursday night. And you want to talk about magic and the human psyche with a mentalist. You said that someone advised you to talk to me? I'm very curious about what that means.'

Vincent leaned forward, as if to demonstrate his interest. She decided to let him wait. She needed to get him properly engaged.

'I saw you pulled the autograph stunt at the end of the show,' she said, smiling as warmly as she could. 'An artist apparently signs all his works.'

He looked confused and then laughed.

'You mean the nail? I know, it's so clichéd. But what can I say? The audience expect me to sign – ever since that TV show. And I don't want to disappoint them. After all, they've invested both their time and money in the evening.'

Vincent's shoulders sank as he relaxed. If he'd had his guard up, it was now lowered. For the time being.

'You were right, by the way,' she said. 'I wouldn't be here if it wasn't important. You see, we have a case I don't understand. We've managed to keep it out of the press so far, but it won't be long before you read about it in the papers.'

He cut a piece of the hamburger. She was beyond relieved to see him eating it with a knife and fork. If he'd picked up the greasy burger in his hand she would have got up and left.

'Sorry,' said Vincent, waving a chunk of hamburger on his fork, 'but what's that got to do with me?'

Instead of answering, Mina pulled a manila envelope out of a folder and took out the photographs. She thumbed through them until she got to one that didn't show the lacerated body but only the box it had been found in, along with the swords. She put the photo on top and then put an elastic band around the bundle. Vincent really didn't need to see the other photos.

16

'Do you know what this is?' she asked, pointing at the picture.

Vincent's fork stopped a centimetre from his open mouth.

'Sword casket,' he said. 'Sometimes they call it a sword box. But what . . . how . . . I don't understand.'

The hamburger chunk entered his mouth.

'Nor do I,' she said. 'Well, rather, we have a perpetrator that I don't understand. But I think you might. Given . . . well, your particular skills. So I want to ask for your help. Let me put it like this: the box was not empty when we found it. It took time to free her from the swords.'

Vincent stopped chewing and visibly paled.

'We haven't got anywhere with identifying the victim,' Mina added. 'I think the only way to find the person who did this is to know how he or she ticks. I wish I could tell you that mutilated bodies were a rare find, but I'm afraid that's not true. At least, not as rare as I'd like. But in a magic box? That's new. Who would even come up with such an idea? And *why*? That's where you come in. I saw your show. You know how people think. More than most people. So help me to understand who this is.'

Vincent leaned back and looked surprised.

'But surely you've got your own criminal psychologists for that kind of thing,' he said. 'What do you think I'll bring to the table that they can't offer? Profiling criminals isn't exactly my nine-to-five.'

He dipped a few fries in the mayonnaise before popping them into his mouth.

'As I said, you are familiar with the psyche and with magic. Our criminal psychologist isn't. What's more . . .'

She looked around before continuing in a low voice.

'What's more, the most recent profile compiled for us by our criminal psychologist told us we were looking for "a middle-aged Greek man accustomed to mixing in high society". It turned out the perp was actually a young Swedish woman who worked in a warehouse.'

Vincent managed to put a napkin to his mouth before laughing the fries out of it.

'It still sounds like a weird setup,' he said. 'From what I know, the police don't usually look too kindly on civilian involvement. And I don't have any training in profiling. I've learned a lot about how people function, but I base my conclusions solely on basic psychology, my own observations and general statistical probabilities.'

'And what do you think criminal psychologists do?'

17

'But I'm an entertainer. No one gets hurt if I make a mistake in a performance.'

'Except you,' she said. 'You trust your own ability to read other people enough to risk sticking a nail through your hand.'

He smiled weakly.

'Which I really shouldn't,' he said. 'But OK. Although I don't quite get what my role in this would be and why you've come to me.'

'We . . .' Mina hesitated. 'Our team is in a somewhat unusual position in the police. We're outside the regular organizational structure.'

'Why?'

'Well, our boss Julia is the daughter of the police commissioner and . . .'

'Nepotism?'

She flared up at that.

'Absolutely not! Julia is incredibly competent, a natural leader, and I wouldn't be surprised if she becomes police commissioner herself someday. But she's as frustrated as the rest of us about the rigid and unwieldy organization we have to work in. And it's actually more *in spite* of the fact that she's the commissioner's daughter that she managed to persuade the chiefs to appoint a more . . . independent team, which she leads and serves on.'

'The best of the best?'

'Hmm,' Mina said drily. 'That might be pushing it a bit. More like, beggars can't be choosers.'

'A specialist team without specialist expertise?' Vincent said, somewhat surprised.

Mina could understand where he was coming from, but couldn't quite see how to explain. She made an attempt:

'Everyone has their particular talent. But people are people and there are a thousand reasons why a police unit would willingly allow a member of personnel to be seconded to a new team.'

'And why are you on secondment?' Vincent said, the corners of his mouth twitching.

'I don't actually know why. I know what my assets as a police officer are. I'm stubborn, driven and dare to think laterally.'

'But . . .?' said Vincent, reaching for another fry.

'But the team I was on before seemed to have a hard time dealing with me. I've no idea why. I didn't have a problem with them. I don't have a problem with any team. It's teams that have problems with me.'

She cleared her throat before carrying on.

18

'Anyway, my boss has approved us taking on an external consultant on this case. I'm afraid we can only pay a modest fee. But you'll be involved in something that could make a difference.'

'Unlike being on stage, you mean?' he said, pushing the photographs back to her. 'I think you've got "The Master Mentalist" confused with reality. I'm sorry you've had a wasted trip. But there's something you have to understand: I'm an entertainer. My job is to amuse people. "The Master Mentalist" is a character, nothing more. What I do on stage . . . it stays there. It's not for real. It might seem as if I have unique or special abilities, but the truth is that anyone can learn them. You're talking about compiling psychological profiles. Of murderers. I don't know anything about murderers. Once again, there are people who do that for a living. People who – what did you say? – want to "make a difference".'

He didn't return her eye contact. This wasn't what she had been expecting. She had thought he would say that he didn't have time or that he had more important things to do. She had been prepared to stroke his ego. But she hadn't thought he would lie to her.

'I understand,' she said, getting up.

Time for a new strategy.

'I must have been mistaken. You're just so very convincing on stage. I'm sorry. It was only an idea. I'll pay the bill on my way out – I think I left it on the bar by those guys from Skåne.'

'Helsingborg,' he said wearily, resuming his prodding of the hamburger. 'They're from Helsingborg. Here for a conference on electrical safety. You can see the logo on their name tags. And I wouldn't bother them if I were you. The tall woman with her back turned to us has just started talking to a man – it's the first conversation tonight where she hasn't had to hunch her back to make herself smaller so that the man dares to stick around. Pity that he's married. I don't get men who think they look single simply because they've taken off their ring. As if you can't tell from a mile off that they're married anyway. I digress. I don't think those two want to be interrupted and she looks like she needs it.'

Mina struggled to hide her smile. Vincent didn't seem to be conscious of what he'd said.

'And there's no need for you to pick up the tab,' he said. 'I've already paid.'

'How many steps from the stage down into the green room at the Gävle Theatre?' she said briskly.

19

Vincent looked up with a puzzled expression.

'Eight,' he said. 'But why do you ask?'

'It's actually seven. If you don't take an extra step to finish on an even number.'

Vincent's jaw dropped. She had his attention. He wasn't used to other people noticing his predilections. She sat back down again and smiled openly this time.

'So,' she said, pushing the photographs back towards him. 'Any ideas?'

'OK,' said Vincent. 'You win. At least for now.'

The top photo had slid to one side, revealing part of the photograph underneath. She wasn't quick enough to stop Vincent pulling out the picture.

'Jesus Christ!' he said, grimacing.

'Yes. That's the entirely appropriate reaction.'

Vincent squinted at the photo, as if gradually growing accustomed to seeing the horror of it.

'What's that?' he said, pointing to an object in a plastic bag positioned by the body.

'The victim's watch. The clock face was smashed with the hand at three o'clock, and that seems to correlate with the time of death. Three in the afternoon, that is.'

'No, not the watch. *That*.'

He pointed at the lines that had been carved into one of the woman's thighs just below the hole where the sword entered. Two longer lines connected by three shorter ones, all at an equal distance. Mina thought it resembled a ladder.

'Cuts,' she said. 'A knife or something like it. Probably to terrorize the victim. A taste of what was to come.'

'It's been very carefully done,' he said, 'and it's completely at odds with how violently the body has otherwise been penetrated. I don't think it's torture. I think that "ladder" is a symbol.'

'For what?'

'Hmm, well, several religions have ladders. In the Bible, Jacob's ladder goes up to heaven. Freud thought the ladder was linked to the sexual act itself. Don't ask me why. But I think this is something more straight-forward.'

He turned the photo ninety degrees and pointed at the carved ladder, which was now on its side.

Mina realized she was no longer looking at a ladder.

She was looking at the Roman numeral III.

They were both silent for a long time. The hum of the group at the bar drowned out her own thoughts.

After a while, Vincent said: 'I don't really want to ask, but . . .'

Mina nodded.

'I know what you're thinking,' she said. 'If this is three, then where are one and two?'

4

Vincent always struggled to orient himself in the morning. Those seconds between sleep and wakefulness when all he knew was the feeling of the sheets against his skin, a ray of sunshine dazzling him, the stale aftertaste of the sleeping tablet. No room, no space, no perception of time or where in the universe he might be. A vacuum of a few blessed seconds in which he could simply exist.

Then reality slowly began to make itself known. The sound of clinking crockery. A bird defying winter to twitter on the bird feeder that Maria had built. The voice of his son Aston rising and falling, switching from delight to fury within an interval of a few seconds.

Vincent sat up and pulled away the duvet. He set his feet down on the floor. Left foot first. He put on his trousers and yesterday's shirt – he had only used it in the evening and was going to put it in the wash later. He ignored the top button as if it didn't exist and buttoned up the other six. Just as it was supposed to be. He didn't understand why all shirts came with seven buttons sewn on. They must be designed by psychopaths.

When he emerged into the kitchen, everyone was sitting at the table. Everyone except Rebecka.

'Go and tell your teenage daughter that it's time for breakfast,' Maria said, without looking at him.

Vincent tried to remember a time when the words passing between them hadn't been filled with unspoken meaning and hidden significance. He failed. Life, the daily humdrum, the rows and the suspicion had slowly and reticently eroded what had once been there. It was impossible to set an exact time for when that had happened.

Maria cut up pieces of apple for Aston, who was stirring a spoon in his yogurt with great intensity. The green tea in the mug beside her

22

had gone cold long ago. Benjamin was slowly peeling his two eggs while doing his best to look as if he were still asleep. One side plate for the eggshells, another for the eggs. Vincent went to knock on Rebecka's door.

'Rebecka? Come out and eat!' he shouted at the door.

He already knew what the answer would be.

'I'm not hungry!' said Rebecka's voice from the other side of the door.

'You've got to eat. Come out now.'

He returned to the kitchen without waiting for a reply. As he sat down at the kitchen table, he heard the door open behind him. And then close with a slam. Benjamin looked towards Rebecka in irritation but said nothing.

'Muuuummmmm!' Aston suddenly shouted. 'The bits are too big! You've made the bits too big!'

Aston pushed the bowl towards Maria so hard that a little yogurt splashed onto the table.

'No, I haven't, sweetheart, they're just the same as usual. See for yourself.'

Maria picked up one of the pieces with her fingertips, which became covered in yogurt. She looked annoyed but Aston burst into laughter.

'Mum, you can't eat yogurt with your fingers!' he said. 'That'd take a hundred years!'

'They are actually a bit bigger,' said Vincent, reaching for the bowl.

He took a knife and began to cut the messy chunks of apple into smaller pieces. Vincent glanced at his wife. She still looked annoyed as she licked her fingers. He weighed up whether to say something. With Maria, it always came down to whether she was receptive in the moment. Whether it was her sender or receiver that was plugged in. Sometimes he guessed right. Sometimes not.

'Pick your battles,' he finally said to her. 'Your tea's going cold.'

He received a devastating look in reply. He had apparently guessed wrong.

'I want Mum to cut,' said Aston, slamming the palm of his hand on the table. 'She makes prettier pieces.'

'You're big enough to cut your own apple,' he said to Aston. 'That way it'll be the way you want it. If we cut it then it'll be how *we* want it.'

'But it's your job to make breakfast,' said Aston.

'You're such a baby,' Rebecka snorted at her little brother.

She sat down at the table with her arms ostentatiously folded.

'No way!' Aston yelled, his face flushing bright red with anger. '*You're a baby!*'

'I'm fifteen, you're eight. I'm almost twice your age. So you're the baby.'

'Noooo!'

Aston half rose but Maria put her hand on his shoulder.

'Rebecka is actually older than you,' she said. 'But all that means is that she has to cut up her own apples. In fact, she has to do everything herself. But you don't have to.'

Aston grinned broadly when Maria winked at him. Vincent knew that his son worshipped his mother and nothing made Aston happier than the feeling that it was him and Maria against his older siblings.

'Who even eats apple for breakfast?' said Rebecka. 'That's so whack.'

Vincent focused on the apple. Nineteen pieces, which meant thirty-eight pieces of apple if he halved them all. Odd to even. He was filled with calm. He liked the symbolism. That things that were odd had the chance to be made uniform. There was hope. He loved his family, but the chaos it created was tough for him to cope with. He liked order. Structure. Even numbers.

'Here you go, brat.'

Vincent pushed the bowl towards Aston, who for a moment seemed to consider whether he had anything to add about the apple pieces. But he didn't seem entirely certain what brat meant, so with a defiant glance at his father he began to eat.

'Have a sandwich,' Maria pleaded with Rebecka. 'Or yogurt. Or anything. But eat something.'

'I don't have to eat breakfast when I'm at Mum's,' Rebecka said, her arms still folded. 'She doesn't eat anything herself before noon. Periodic fasting. It's good for the body to rest its digestive system – our bodies aren't built to eat food all the time. We eat far too often. In the Stone Age, they only ate every now and then – they sometimes went days without eating.'

'Those are your mother's words, not yours. And we don't live in the Stone Age. Vincent, tell your daughter.'

'She's actually right,' said Vincent, pouring himself a coffee. 'Our bodies aren't designed for the modern diet and recent studies have shown that . . .'

Maria got up abruptly and picked up her side plate with half an avocado on rye sandwich on it. With organic coconut sprinkles on top, as always. That stuff had a price per kilo akin to gold, but it was an anti-inflammatory, which Maria considered to be the elixir of life.

'Good God, you'd think you might help out every now and again,' she said. 'Of course Rebecka has to eat! She's a growing teenager, there's lots developing in her body, girls can miss their period if they don't eat—'

'Bloody hell,' Benjamin interrupted. 'Do you really have to talk about periods? I'm *eating*.'

'You're nineteen years old, Benjamin,' said Vincent. 'You can't still be sensitive about bodily fluids.'

Benjamin stared at his father. Then he got up, carrying the final egg in his hand, and went to his room shaking his head.

'Dad, you're such an aspie,' Rebecka drily observed.

'We don't say that nowadays, Rebecka,' Vincent said sternly. 'I think it's called ASD these days.'

Maria ignored them and continued on her own beaten path.

'And constantly going on about what your mother does,' she said. 'Rebecka, you have to understand that in this home and in this family we have *our own* rules and routines. What you do at Ulrika's is of no relevance to our family.'

'Yes, Aunt Maria.'

Rebecka got up, taking a slice of bread from the basket. She pointedly held it up in front of Maria before returning to her room and slamming the door behind her.

'Done! Thanks, Mum! Now I'm going to feed the pets.'

Aston pushed his chair away from the table and ran off to the aquarium in the living room.

'The *fish*,' Vincent called out after him. 'They're central mudminnows.'

'I know that,' Aston replied while blanketing the surface of the water in fish food. 'Eat up, everybody!'

Then he came back to the kitchen, retrieved his iPad, which had been charging on the counter, and ran off to his room.

'Five minutes, Aston!' Vincent shouted to his back. 'Then we need to be dressed and leaving for school. Five minutes!'

Maria leaned against the kitchen counter and crossed her arms, an unconscious copy of Rebecka.

'That "Aunt Maria" stuff . . . she only does it to provoke me.'

Vincent looked at his wife in puzzlement.

'But you *are* her aunt,' he said. 'You're sisters – you and her mother. How can you be angry at Rebecka for pointing that out? It's true . . .'

25

He couldn't understand why she was expending energy on questioning an objective fact. He reached for a slice of rye bread and began to spread butter carefully on one side. No lumps, right to the edges.

'Of course it's not about that,' Maria said. 'Do you seriously not get it? Jesus Christ, what kind of robot am I married to? She's only saying that stuff to screw with me.'

He frowned. He really did want to understand. But the logic behind Maria's reaction was incomprehensible. Facts were facts. What you felt emotionally about those facts was another matter altogether. But the fact itself couldn't be overlooked.

'By the way, who did you take out for dinner the night before last?' she said, her tone changing. 'Was it Ulrika?'

Vincent looked up in surprise. He had just taken a bite out of his sandwich and had to finish chewing it before he could reply. Ten chews. It was almost eleven, but he caught himself at the last moment.

'Why would I have dinner with my ex-wife?' he said.

'I saw the total from the restaurant in my banking app. And then I checked the receipt that was in your wallet. You took someone out for dinner in Gävle. Did she sleep over in the hotel room? Did you fuck her?'

Maria's voice had risen to a falsetto. Vincent swore silently. He should have known this would happen. It was a dance they had performed many times by now. Maria's unfounded jealousy could strike at any moment – and it was doing so more and more often these days. It was one of the many things that was slowly dissolving their so-called marriage.

'It was a police officer who had tracked me down,' he said. 'She wanted to discuss a murder she's working on.'

'Ha!' said Maria, emitting a high, forced laugh. 'A *police officer*? And a female officer at that. How fitting . . . Come on, Vincent, how stupid do you think I am? Can you really not think of anything better than a *police officer*? Who wanted to talk to *you* about a case? Why would a cop come to you about a murder?'

'Because it's to do—'

Maria interrupted him by holding up a hand.

'You can confess to what actually happened later, but you need to take Aston to school now.'

'But . . .'

He stopped talking when he saw that Maria was already heading for Aston's room.

'Aston!' she shouted. 'You've got to hurry! Drop the iPad now! You're leaving in five seconds.'

Then she moved on into the house, heading for the bedroom.

Vincent looked at his sandwich. The policewoman. Mina. She'd been in his thoughts since they had met. Part of him hoped she'd be in touch again. His teeth had made the edges around his bite form small walls of butter. He picked up the butter knife, levelled out the butter and took another bite – equivalent to a sixth of the sandwich. Six pieces was good. Although now there were only five left. Less good.

In the hours they had spent together, Mina had possessed an almost uncanny ability to see right through him. He'd done as usual and tried to play the Urbane Artist. It was a well-practised mask, a good shield when meeting journalists and others. More often than not, that kept them happy. It was the person they thought they were going to meet and that meant they didn't question it. But she had seen him counting the stairs. She had noticed and adjusted the bottle labels in the green room. And she had tricked him into analysing the patrons in that bar.

That was more than Maria or Ulrika had ever understood about him, and he had spent years living with the two of them.

He ate the rest of the sandwich while counting each part. Parts three and one were eaten with particular speed.

Mina had to be a very talented detective. But it wasn't just her attentiveness that this was about, even if it was flattering and worrying at once that she so easily saw things he thought he was concealing well. It was about the fact that he had also understood her. Which was far from ordinary – something that Maria would be first in line to testify to. Reading and controlling people on stage was one thing. In that setting, he was in control of all the parameters. But in real life, other people were still a mystery. Sometimes it felt as if there had been a day at school when the tools for social mixing had been handed out and he'd been off sick. That was why he played the role of the Urbane Artist as often as possible. The artist knew how to deal with other people. Personally, he had no idea.

'Aston!' he shouted.

His son came out of his room with a slightly startled look, the iPad in his hand. He seemed to have forgotten that he was going to school.

'We're off. Put on your coat and shoes.'

Vincent pulled on a light grey knitted hoodie while Aston gave his mother, who had hurried into the hallway with his backpack, a big hug which was met with a kiss in reply.

But Mina hadn't been a mystery. At least, not as much of one as other people. He'd seen her rituals. The way she always brushed her hair off her face with her right hand. How she avoided touching any surfaces unless absolutely necessary. And he had caught sight of a Rubik's cube in her coat pocket. Not just any old one either – it had been a speed cube. They were pre-lubricated and easier to turn.

So, it would definitely be interesting to meet her again. At the same time, he hoped that she *wouldn't* get in touch. He wasn't all that keen to get involved in something that would be guaranteed to give him nightmares. His world was fragile enough as it was. He didn't need it to be populated with mutilated bodies as well.

5

As ever, the shower jet was so hot that it almost scalded her skin. Mina's body reacted by turning an angry shade of flame red, but it allowed her to feel clean and unsullied, as if the hot water was killing all the microorganisms, transforming her into a blank canvas without impurities, without blemishes. It was a wonderful feeling.

In the shower, she felt strong. On her days off, she could end up standing there for hours, until her skin was like a blazing red raisin. But today she didn't have more than ten minutes to spare. Her thoughts refused to settle down.

Vincent Walder. Mina still didn't know whether she needed his expertise, whether he was better than their in-house criminal psychologist, or whether he'd turn out to be nothing more than a drain on police time and resources. In which case she'd be branded an idiot by the rest of the team. It had been a long shot, uncharacteristically risky for her, but it was done now and she'd just have to wait and see whether it paid off. In the meantime, her curiosity was piqued; from what she'd seen of Vincent she could tell there was more to the master mentalist than met the eye. She could have done without his condescending attitude, but she'd seen the way he registered that she'd brought her own drinking straw. What else had he noticed? He'd made no comment, so she shouldn't assume that she knew what he was thinking. But if he began to take pity on her or display empathy – like all the others – then she wouldn't want his help. Julia could go find someone else herself.

Mina switched off the water, gingerly stepped out of the bathtub and dried herself thoroughly with a clean towel. The towel had been washed at ninety degrees with both detergent and stain remover, and it smelled as clean as her skin. But she knew that feeling of cleanliness was only temporary. If she stayed in the flat, it could last up to twenty-four hours.

But as soon as she stepped out of the door, the wider world enveloped her in its dirty embrace.

She put on the clothes she had laid out before getting into the shower. Knickers, white sports bra, jeans and black socks. The knickers were brand new – the ones she'd been wearing had already gone in the bin. There was no point even trying to wash knickers – no stain remover on earth would make her feel fresh in a pair of used knickers. But she had found a place where she could buy large consignments of basic cotton underwear for ten kronor a go, which she considered a justifiable expense.

She had woken up early and had a whole hour before she needed to leave for work. Her tummy rumbled. She opened a kitchen drawer and looked at the box of thin single-use gloves inside. She knew she didn't need them. No one ever ended up at death's door from touching a yogurt pot. She *knew* that. But the mere thought of opening the fridge without any protection whatsoever between her and the food tied her stomach in knots.

Sighing, Mina took out a pair of gloves and put them on – carefully, to ensure that they didn't tear. Her colleagues at the police station would laugh at what they thought were her foibles. But when they had all gone down with norovirus at Christmas she had been the only one who'd stayed healthy. There hadn't been anyone laughing then.

She opened the fridge, quickly scanned the options and decided to have the vanilla quark. Having scrutinized the packaging to ensure the seal was intact, she opened it cautiously. After putting it on the table, she got out a clean teaspoon, washed it, got a bottle of hand sanitizer from the counter and squeezed a drop onto the spoon, ensuring she covered every millimetre. She visualized the disinfectant killing everything. Bacteria. Viruses. Disgusting particles that could make their way into her body.

You don't need to. It's clean. You just washed it.

Yes, but how could she *know* that she had removed all the bacteria if she didn't disinfect it? After all, she was going to put it in her mouth. That thought made her grasp the hand sanitizer a second time.

Let go of the bottle. You're manic. The spoon. Is. Clean. Let. Go.

But she couldn't. She felt the tears coming at the same time as she opened the little plastic lid and squeezed out a new drop. She didn't want to. But she had to. She rubbed the new blob of gel onto the spoon as if she were trying to make a hole in it.

After finally sitting down at the kitchen table, she stared at the small plastic tub of quark for a long time, trying not to think about all the people who had handled the packaging, touched the contents inside the plastic tub. She tried not to think about the billions of germs crawling all over those people's hands and she tried to persuade herself that the factory had been as careful as she was when it came to cleanliness. Although she doubted it.

Still, she had to eat something, so might as well get it over with. Disgusted, she grimaced as she dipped the spoon in the quark and raised it to her mouth. After a couple of mouthfuls the taste of alcohol was gone and she could only taste the quark. She was pleased with herself when she had finished it all. Every mealtime, every time she consumed food was a victory.

After throwing away the quark packaging and plastic gloves, she brewed some coffee. That was always easier – she didn't know why. But she still sanitized the coffee mug before using it.

There was half an hour left until she needed to set off. She had time to do some cleaning. It wasn't a mania, merely common sense. She hadn't cleaned since yesterday. She got a big bucket filled with cleaning fluids and equipment out of the cupboard under the sink. It had everything. Window polish, liquid soap, caustic soda, general cleaner, kitchen cleaner, washing-up liquid, more sanitizer, toilet gel, wire wool, dish-cloths, microfibre cloths, brushes, sponges . . . Things like cloths and brushes obviously only got used once before being thrown away. But she had also found a place that would let her buy large batches of those at wholesale prices. She had a stash of boxes filled with new items in the small room that was supposed to be her study but instead served as a storeroom.

By the time she'd finished cleaning, she was warm and sweaty. She sniffed her armpits and immediately wished she hadn't. Ten minutes until she needed to leave. She'd intended to give the Master Mentalist a few more days to make up his mind, but Julia had asked her to introduce him to the rest of the team as soon as possible. Mina hoped he would agree to help her. Help them. Now that he'd awakened her curiosity, she wanted the chance to observe him.

She checked her watch. There was still enough time for another quick shower. And a change into clean clothes.

6

'Can I choose whatever I want?' said Steffo Törnqvist, pointing at the objects in front of him.

Vincent nodded. He blinked, dazzled by the bright studio lights. He ought to be used to them by now – it was hardly his first time on TV4's *Nyhetsmorgon* breakfast show. But they always managed to shine right into his eyes.

He leaned back on the sofa, trying to look relaxed, trying to forget the pictures that police officer, Mina, had shown him a week ago. They hadn't been in contact since then. Perhaps she'd already written him off. He'd done all he could to explain how unsuited he was to assisting them in a murder inquiry. It was too much responsibility. At the same time, he couldn't help but wonder which method she usually used to solve her Rubik's cube.

Focus, Vincent.

He needed to be here. In the now. After all, this was going out live.

'Whatever you like – provided you do it without thinking too much. It's important for it to *feel* good.'

Steffo looked at the items on the table. There was Jenny Strömstedt's car key, a pastry that Vincent had borrowed from the green room breakfast spread, Steffo's mobile phone and a battered leather wallet adorned with an image of Che Guevara. The final item had been added to the mix by Vincent.

'I'm going to take this one,' said Steffo, picking up the wallet. 'It feels . . . Somehow it makes me happy.'

'So, the wallet it is,' said Vincent. 'Would you say that you acted using your own free will?'

'Absolutely,' said Steffo, laughing. 'I could have picked anything.'

'I'd have gone for the pastry – it looks delicious,' Jenny interjected, winking at the viewers through the camera lens.

'Anything – of course,' Vincent said with a wry smile, nodding at a scrap of paper on the table.

He had given it to Steffo before the experiment began. Steffo unfolded the note and looked at it. Then he frowned and cleared his throat. He touched the microphone with his hand, making the sound crackle.

'Read it out,' said Jenny.

But Steffo gave the note to her instead. Jenny read out the message in her clearest TV presenter voice.

'*My actions will always be governed by two things: my own preferences and values, and the influence of others. These in combination mean there is a ninety per cent degree of probability that I will select the wallet, even if I do not know why.*'

Jenny glanced at Steffo, who looked very troubled. Vincent took a sip of water. Jenny turned towards the camera, behind which there was a baffled cameraman shaking his head.

'For those of you just tuning in, we're joined on the sofa by Vincent Walder, who is here to tell us about our brains – or possibly make us even more confused about them.'

Vincent saw himself on a monitor by the camera. Underneath it there were glowing red numbers counting down. It read 04:14, which meant he had around four minutes left to explain how he had predicted which item Steffo would choose; 414 – the fourth, first and fourth letters of the alphabet, which spelled DAD. As a dad, he probably shouldn't have brought Aston to the studio, but the eight-year-old seemed quite contented with the pastries and orange juice in the green room. Hopefully they wouldn't be that late to school.

'So you're saying that our actions can be controlled by things we're not aware of,' said Steffo. 'How is it possible that I'm not familiar with my own preferences and values?'

There was a trace of agitation in his manner. Vincent made a conscious effort to return his thoughts to the studio.

'You don't necessarily know *all* your preferences and values,' he said. 'For example, a trauma suffered in childhood will mean that a person can't help behaving in a certain way in adulthood. They may be completely unaware of it, but their behaviour can be predicted.'

'But is it really that simple?' Jenny interrupted. 'If I fall off my bike, surely I won't hate bicycles for the rest of my life?'

'Hopefully not,' Steffo chuckled, 'given how often you do yourself a mischief on the furniture in the studio. You even came close to burning the whole studio to the ground once!'

Jenny threw an icy look at him. Steffo was referring to the time she was meant to fry some cheese puffs live on air and instead they caught fire. The clip had gone viral all around the world.

'But if someone runs you over in a blue Audi, you're likely to experience elevated levels of stress for a long time afterwards whenever you see a blue car,' said Vincent. 'Of course, it doesn't have to be that dramatic. It's enough for there to be powerful emotions aroused.'

One minute left. He needed to hurry.

Focus.

'Like when I was on *Strictly*,' said Steffo. 'Those were powerful emotions, all right! Especially the final number. I remember it like it was yesterday.'

'Not again,' said Jenny, rolling her eyes.

Vincent realized he had Steffo where he wanted him.

'Now we're getting to the crux of the matter,' he said. 'Strong, positive emotions, connected to details from the memory of your experience. Details that can still trigger those happy emotions and thus draw you to them. Steffo, do you remember what you were wearing in that dance number?'

'Absolutely. A white T-shirt with . . .'

Steffo fell silent and his eyes opened wide.

'You're kidding.'

'What?' said Jenny. 'What is it?'

The clock under the monitor showed 00:10. Ten seconds left before they cut to the ad break. Vincent had timed it to perfection.

'A white T-shirt with Che Guevara on it,' said Steffo, holding up the wallet to allow the camera to zoom in on the sticker of the Cuban revolutionary for its final shot.

'But is it really that easy?' said Jenny in astonishment.

Vincent smiled.

'Sometimes.'

They cut to ads a second after he fixed his gaze on the camera. There was no denying it: he knew how to do TV.

'Thanks, guys,' he said with a smile, putting his hand on Steffo's upper arm. 'You can keep the wallet.'

He left the presenters laughing behind him. He only hoped that Aston had left at least half a pastry for the other guests that morning. On his way back to the green room, he pulled out his mobile to take it off silent. There was a notification on the screen. Three missed calls. All from Mina.

7

She walked down the narrow staircase and emerged into a short corridor. On one wall there were mirrors with small make-up tables in front of them. The passage opened up into a bigger room dominated by two sofas around a table with bowls of fruit and sweets on it. A refrigerator with a glass door was full to bursting with bottles of sparkling water.

'I thought you said last time that backstage was off limits?' she said.

'It is, to people I don't know,' Vincent said. 'The long arm of the law is another matter.'

Mina looked around the room.

'This is cosy,' she said. 'I thought dressing rooms were way tattier – I'd expected graffiti on the wall and the smell of stale beer.'

In truth, she had initially considered declining when Vincent suggested they meet in his dressing room at the Rival Hotel theatre, where he was due to perform in Stockholm. She had plastic gloves and a seat cover with her, ready to be produced at a moment's notice.

'The Rival Hotel's dressing rooms are among the best in town,' he said. 'And since we're basically *under* the stage there's no danger of anyone overhearing us.'

He was right. The dressing room was pristine and appeared to have been recently refurbished. She let out a sigh of relief and sat down on one of the sofas, which seemed to be brand new. As yet, no groupies had made out with the band's drummer on this sofa. She wouldn't need the seat cover after all.

'Thank you for agreeing to see me,' she said. 'Have you decided whether you're going to help us? I'd like to introduce you to the other members of the team as soon as possible – preferably tomorrow. I thought you could tell them about those cuts that you identified as a number.'

Vincent looked at her in surprise.

'But surely you'd realized that too?'

'We've been . . . looking for other things. Our priority has been trying to identify the victim, in the hope that will lead us to the perpetrator. But as I said last week in Gävle, so far we've drawn a blank. The discovery that the victim has some kind of symbol on her seemed . . . surreal.'

Vincent sighed. Something crossed his face. As if he were retiring into his shell.

'I did warn you that I don't have the right expertise,' he said. 'Surreal. Hmm. You're probably right. That means you don't need me. Would you like a sweet?'

He pushed one of the bowls towards her. She noted that all the pieces of candy were in paper wrappers. Even if a stranger's unhygienic hands had been digging through the bowl, the sweets themselves were still protected. She wondered whether Vincent had requested wrapped sweets on purpose. If he had analysed her that closely and knew about her foibles, it probably wouldn't be long before the jibes started. Most people couldn't resist cracking jokes about it. She hoped he wasn't like most people. It was bad enough that a complete stranger seemed able to read her like an open book.

Lying at the bottom of the bowl was a Dumle toffee. Her favourite. But it was too far down. Her hand would have to touch far too many other sweets that others might have touched before she reached it. She looked longingly at the wrapped Dumle. Then she shook her head in reply to his offer.

'I don't think you're wrong about the cuts,' she said. 'That's why I'd like you to meet the others. Because I think you're right. Perhaps we should have spotted the numbers ourselves. But we didn't. We need you.'

He looked at her silently. She could hear the hum of the audience as they began to filter into the auditorium above them. In twenty minutes the curtain would rise. Then Vincent would charm and shock eight hundred people in the guise of the Master Mentalist. He would manipulate their thoughts and their behaviour with aplomb, and he would appear to be in complete control. It was hard to believe that the man sitting opposite her was the same person. Sitting there on the sofa, he seemed almost nervous.

'I'd like to help you, if I can,' he said finally. 'But I'm not great with groups. Just so you know.'

No? Well, who was? A group at work was merely a bunch of strangers

36

who thought they knew you because you worked in the same place. Mina had never understood why people insisted on talking about what they did at the weekends or how many teeth their kids had. As if it were of interest . . .

'The meeting is at nine o'clock tomorrow morning at police head-quarters,' she said, getting up. 'I'll meet you at the main entrance. I'm going to leave you to your audience – they sound a little impatient.'

'I'll soon lick them into shape,' he said. 'Oh, by the way. Here you go.'

He fetched something lying on top of the fridge and passed it to her. An unopened bag of Dumle toffees.

'See you tomorrow,' he said.

8

Police headquarters was located on Polhemsgatan in the Kungsholmen neighbourhood. The air was crisp and the sky grey, as if threatening precipitation. Sleet that would be transformed to rain before it reached terra firma. March was not Vincent's favourite month. While hugging himself to keep warm, he scrutinized the people coming and going through the main entrance. He was disappointed each time it wasn't Mina. The butterflies in his stomach refused to settle. He didn't know what sort of welcome he'd get from her fellow officers. Or whether he'd be welcome at all. The risk of being excluded before he had been included had the butterflies dancing some kind of war dance in his lower intestines.

Eventually, Mina emerged through the glass doors. Today she was wearing a red polo neck. He couldn't help but notice how well that colour suited her. It was dramatic yet restrained. Naturally he understood that part of what he was feeling was because the colour red automatically triggered a shot of adrenaline inside him, in the same way it had done in humankind for hundreds of thousands of years. Blood was red. Angry faces were red. More adrenaline in your body made it easier to escape those situations.

'I was wondering where you'd got to,' she said. 'Why are you standing out here? Thinking about escaping?'

'Among other things.'

She gave him an amused look, which he noted kickstarted a dose of both the stress hormone cortisol and the 'feel-good juice' dopamine in his body, while also increasing his serotonin levels, which meant his brain was turning at top gear while his testosterone levels increased by 40 per cent. It was a hormonal cocktail, which when experienced by two people, was known as 'having chemistry'. If only people knew how

38

accurate that description was. Researchers didn't know why it happened, but they all agreed that it existed. He wondered whether Mina felt the same thing. Because in truth, flight had never been on the cards. She was far too interesting for that.

'You've talked in front of strangers a thousand times,' she said. 'This is exactly the same. Come on.'

Vincent looked around in curiosity as Mina guided him along the corridors of police headquarters. It looked more or less as he had expected. Public sector. Small offices with stacks of papers and binders lined up in rows, as well as a large open-plan office with partition dividers between the desks, and mugs with the inscription *Polisen* on the desktops.

When they reached a large glass door with a curtain on the inside, she paused.

'So, what do you say? Ready to enter the lion's den?'

Think of it as a performance, he told himself. Nothing to worry about. This bout of the jitters could be blamed on Mina's red top and the increased production of cortisol.

Vincent suddenly spotted that she was also nervous. He guessed that it was because she still wasn't 100 per cent sure what role he would play or what he had to offer, and was therefore unsure what to tell her colleagues. A highly plausible concern. But it wasn't necessary for them both to be nervous. He tried to find the words to placate her.

'You're right about this being a talk like any other,' he said. 'But it's really about the group dynamic. Established groups always react to the introduction of a new element. Freud spent a lot of time studying what he referred to as "group spirit" – a kind of collective consciousness that emerges over time. The theory is that a group tends to act differently to how its members would individually.'

Mina stared at him.

'And why are you telling me this?' she said.

'Well, I often make use of group psychology when I do my shows,' he said. 'A big audience will react differently to a single person, and that's a factor I can use to control the audience and get them where I want them. I mostly rely on Kurt Lewin's field theory. It's based on three key variables. Energy – ergo what causes and motivates actions. Tension – as in the difference between someone's goals and their present state. And Need – the physical or psychological requirement that awakens that inner tension.'

Mina was still staring at him, shaking her head. But he noted that she no longer looked nervous. Diverting someone's attention was the simplest tool in his arsenal. But it usually worked. In both directions, he realized. His own nervousness had also dissipated. Not entirely, but enough.

'What positions do the members of the group have?'

'It's irrelevant,' said Mina curtly. 'The police organizational structure is complicated and it would take me an age to explain it to you. Besides, this particular group was formed to cut through the usual hierarchies. Julia's in charge – that's all you need to know.'

She opened the door and they went in. Three pairs of eyes turned towards them. There ought to have been four, but one of people in the room was asleep.

'Hi, everyone. This is Vincent Walder. I know that Julia has told you that Vincent will be consulting for us on aspects of the investigation.'

Heavy silence. A gentle snore from the sleeping man. Vincent noted the oddity of sleeping in the middle of a workplace meeting and reviewed the possible explanations in his head. At a guess, the man either suffered from narcolepsy or he was a new father. The latter was statistically far likelier. A vomit stain on his shoulder provided the final clue.

'Hello,' Vincent said tentatively.

From the corner of his eye, he saw Mina anxiously shifting her weight from foot to foot. Personally, he now felt completely at ease. He was in work mode. This was his field. All he had to do was find the key to each person sitting around the table, while at the same time finding his own place in the group dynamic. Then it would all be fine.

'As Mina said, my name is Vincent. And I'm a mentalist. This means I've made it my job to find out how we can manipulate the human psyche and people's behaviour. Of course, that's only possible if you actually have a good grasp of how people function in the first place. I am not, however, a psychologist or therapist – I primarily use my skills as an entertainer.'

A somewhat over-tanned man with discreet streaks in his hair snorted. His shirt was undone one button too far, exposing a red rash, the legacy of a recent waxing. He looked good in a way that suggested a certain desperation about growing older. There was an air of self-confidence about him that suggested, despite his over-inflated ego, many women found him attractive. No doubt the well-developed *pectoralis major* helped. It was funny how both sexes were drawn to big chests, albeit for completely different reasons. Big breasts on a woman indicated a good ability to feed offspring. Well-developed chest muscles on men indicated strength and the ability to provide protection. Moobs, however, were an entirely different matter.

'Sorry,' said Mina, interrupting his train of thought. 'I haven't introduced everyone.'

She began with the man with the over-inflated ego:

'This is Ruben Höök. And that's Christer Bengtsson, our grand old man.'

'I'm not that fucking old,' Christer muttered.

Vincent hid a smile. Christer was clearly a glass-half-empty kind of guy. He didn't know what disappointments had shaped the older policeman's view on life, but he guessed it had been a self-fulfilling prophecy. No ring on his finger. Most likely lived alone. A considerable waistline and slightly laboured breathing indicated a penchant for junk food and little exercise. No pets at home that needed walking, then. Newspaper ink on his fingers – so he still read his news in the papers rather than online. Vincent was willing to bet there would be an obsolete Bakelite telephone with a rotary dial in Christer's home.

'Would someone mind waking up Peder?'

Mina said it without any trace of negativity. Peder was clearly well liked by his colleagues, otherwise they wouldn't have tolerated him sleeping during the meeting, no matter how many kids he had at home.

'Peder! Wake up!'

Ruben shook Peder, and he sat up groggily.

'What? Who?'

'Here,' said Mina, placing a Red Bull in front of him.

He gave her a grateful look.

'And this is Peder Jensen.'

Mina couldn't help but smile as she pointed at him.

'I'm not actually Danish even though it sounds like I am,' said Peder in a surprisingly alert voice. 'Dad is, but I was born and raised in Bromma.'

Peder Jensen radiated friendliness and openness, which confirmed Vincent's analysis. Most of all, he radiated exhaustion.

'Peder and his wife had triplets three months ago,' said Mina.

Vincent whistled. Triplets. No wonder the guy was asleep on the job.

'And then there's me,' said the woman sitting at the head of the table. 'Julia Hammarsten. I'm in charge of this motley crew in my capacity as lead investigator, but I'm also active in the field. We all are. We're not that obsessed with titles here.'

Julia gestured towards her colleagues.

'We come from different police units and this team is a kind of experiment – I'm not going to deny that. My father is – as Mina may have told you – the Stockholm police commissioner, and he has agreed to the formation of this group as a way of meeting the need for greater flexibility and dynamism within the force. This investigation is a real test for us; if we don't deliver results, the experiment might be judged a failure and the opportunities afforded to us will very quickly disappear.'

Her tone of resignation and controlled body language suggested a woman who had erected impenetrable walls around her innermost, private self. There was also an aura of sorrow about her. Something was weighing her down, something that was in her thoughts most of the time. Vincent was fairly certain that it was personal and had nothing to do with the responsibility of making a success of the team. Most people didn't think about the upper portion of their face when trying to control their expressions, which was why it was always easiest to find the genuine expressions on the forehead, eyebrows and even the eyelids. But Julia had full control over her entire face, which made it difficult for him to go on more than a vague feeling that she would prefer not to let anyone into her life.

He realized that the room had fallen silent and the others appeared to be waiting for him to say something. He cleared his throat.

'I'm guessing that's where I come in,' he said. 'I gather that my specialist skills could be of use to this case. I was unsure to begin with, but in our brief time together Mina and I have already come up with a few . . . observations.'

He exchanged a glance with Mina, who nodded.

'Before we continue, I suggest we all stretch our legs,' said Julia. 'I want everyone alert. Peder, you'd better crack open another Red Bull.'

Christer's joints creaked loudly as he stood up. Ruben began shadow-boxing out in the corridor, which looked rather absurd, while Peder grabbed the second can of Red Bull he had been prescribed and opened it with an audible hiss.

It occurred to Vincent that Kurt Lewin's field theory was proving staggeringly accurate. Within himself he could feel the three variables at work: his desire to get Mina's attention had given rise to a tension, which in turn was motivating him to act. The fact of the matter was, he wanted to get her to like him.

9

The short break was over and they'd returned to their seats. Ruben was impatiently drumming his fingers on the table, making it clear he wasn't impressed by Julia's latest initiative. Seeking expert help was one thing, but bringing in a *mentalist*? They would be the laughing stock of the force if this got out.

Many within headquarters had predicted this new team initiative would be short-lived. If Julia and Mina were going to resort to this kind of hocus pocus, they might as well abort the experiment now. That was the problem when you worked with women. There was no knowing what they'd try next. Probably drag in some crackpot psychic who'd lay out tarot cards and get the spirits to tell them who the murderer was. Absurd.

'I've seen you on TV,' Peder said cheerfully to Vincent. 'It was impressive, what you did.'

'I'm familiar with your work too,' said Christer, but in a much more sceptical tone. 'Don't take this the wrong way, but aren't you just a magician? And don't we have our own criminal psychologist?'

'Mentalist,' Vincent corrected him. 'And as for the psychologist, I heard something about Greek men . . .?'

Julia coughed and Peder began to laugh.

'Oh my God, yes. Jan really was talking through his hat on that one,' he said with a shake of his head.

'I want to point out that I'm not a magician,' Vincent told them, 'although I do make use of illusion, and I have a working knowledge of magic having performed various tricks in my youth. Nowadays, the most I can manage is a false shuffle of a deck of cards. I'm more interested in what goes on inside people's heads.'

'In addition to his knowledge of human behaviour,' said Mina, looking at her colleagues, 'Vincent is also good at identifying patterns.'

43

She crossed her arms as if readying herself to go into battle to defend Vincent and his abilities. For some reason, that bothered Ruben. Why was she so invested in this mentalist? What did he have going for him? Ruben prided himself on knowing what women wanted. His superpower was appealing to women. All women loved him, regardless of age, appearance, background, political affiliation or culture. There wasn't a woman in Ruben's life that he hadn't succeeded in charming. Until Mina came along. It wasn't that she disliked him. She was just . . . indifferent. Which in his world was even worse.

To begin with, he'd tried to hit on her. Tried to get her to fall for him with every trick in the book. Not because he was in the slightest bit attracted to her – he preferred buxom blondes. It was more an exercise, seeing whether he could. That was Ruben's main driving force. The pursuit. The reeling in. The actual sex was usually pretty uninteresting – he would soon weary of each conquest and move onto the next. But having snared his prey, he always followed through. It was a question of honour. He couldn't understand fishermen who caught their fish and then threw them back into the sea. That wasn't the way the hunt was supposed to end.

But Mina had been entirely immune to all his tricks.

Today he was particularly worked up about her. Right now she was standing by the whiteboard writing things and attaching photos with a magnet. She was wearing navy jeans, a red polo neck that betrayed no hint of her bra underneath, her hair was pulled back into a ponytail with not even a strand of hair out of line, and as ever her face was clean and clear of all make-up. The only thing that wasn't perfect about Mina was her hands, which were red and chapped from cleansing with all the litres of hand sanitizer that she kept on her desk. Ruben wondered about that neat outer shell. He was a master at guessing women's underwear. He could always tell straight away what type they were. Expensive silk lingerie in a shade of mother-of-pearl from La Perla. Cheap and sexy red lace from Victoria's Secret, or slutty, either a black thong or those ones with the opening at the crotch ordered online from some porn mail-order site . . .

He sighed. Mina was probably wearing practical cotton pants.

'When I showed the material to Vincent, he made certain observations,' she said. 'Things that we missed.'

Mina fell silent and turned to Vincent, who took a step forward.

'Judging by the photos,' Vincent said, 'I'd say the cuts found on the victim were not random, as was conjectured. I believe they are intended to be a Roman numeral. The number three, to be specific.'

'Numbers?' Christer said in surprise.

Ruben snorted out loud. Mina turned to him with her eyebrows raised.

'Ruben?' she said, her voice ice cold. 'What do you think?'

Ruben pretended not to understand what she meant.

'About what?'

His tone was slightly more aggressive than he'd intended. Julia looked at him reproachfully. Peder leaned forward in interest and Christer muttered something inaudible while scratching his scalp, which was visible through thinning grey hair.

'About what Vincent's theory that the cuts are intentional – possibly even representing a number. What's your professional view on the matter?'

He shrugged. This was first-class nonsense.

'It seems far-fetched,' he sighed. 'If you hear the sound of hooves then you guess horses, not zebras. We've seen perps before who got caught up in the moment and did a little extra carving. It's nothing new.'

Vincent leaned forward and put the tips of his fingers together. His entire body was itching with irritation. The guy couldn't look more conceited if he tried. Was Mina really buying this? Women . . . Who could make sense of them?

'Well, that's the point, isn't it?' said Mina. 'Everything else has been done so very meticulously. Someone went to the trouble of building a carbon copy of something that would be used by a magician. And consciously staging a classic magic trick – minus the happy ending. We're talking time. Planning. Patience. Does that feel like someone who gets "caught up in the moment and does a little extra carving"?'

Ruben shrugged.

'Yes, noooo, hmm, maybe not . . .'

'I don't think it looks slapdash,' said Julia, getting up and going over to the whiteboard.

White La Perla, Ruben thought to himself. But in this case it was no guess. He'd been familiar with her underwear and its contents since the police Christmas party had been staged on a Baltic cruise five years ago. She'd been shitfaced and had fucked him like an animal in his cabin. That was before she'd met that bore of a husband, Torkel. They were doing missionary only, guaranteed. On the cruise she'd been on her period, so the place had looked like an abattoir the next morning when he'd woken up, and she'd already sneaked off. Oh well – that was the kind of stuff that happened at parties. Julia being his boss could

45

have been a concern, but they had never mentioned that one-night stand. And Torkel was definitely no threat. Not that Ruben was even the slightest bit interested in Julia, but still. It was always a nice feeling to know you'd been there.

Mina stepped to one side to give Julia space at the board. Julia happened to graze Mina's elbow and Ruben saw Mina jump as if she'd had an electric shock.

'The cuts are perfectly symmetrical,' said Julia. 'They definitely look intentional. On the other hand, they're not necessarily a number. There's no context.'

Julia turned to Peder and Christer. Peder looked tired again and had started to nod off.

'What do we know about the place where she was found?' said Julia.

Silence. Ruben chucked a pen so that it landed on the table right in front of Peder, who started.

'What?' said Peder, looking around dozily.

'The place where the body was found,' said Mina, repeating Julia's question. 'What do we know about it? What do forensics say?'

Peder shook himself like a wet dog to make himself more alert and then reached for the sheet of paper lying on the table in front of him.

'She was found outside the main entrance to the theme park at Gröna Lund. But that's in all likelihood a secondary crime scene. Not enough blood for her to have been murdered there. The box was transported there and then staged.'

'Witnesses?' Vincent asked.

'There's no one who lives right there. But we checked with the staff working at the Abba Museum and the adjacent restaurant. No one saw or heard anything.'

'And do you know who the victim is?'

Christer gloomily shook his head. That didn't have to mean anything in itself – Christer did everything with a gloomy demeanour.

'Not yet,' he said. 'We're in the process of going through missing women of about the same age, but so far no one has matched the description. There's a risk that she hasn't been reported missing. And that's the problem. If no one reports her missing, finding her will continue to be almost impossible. Blonde woman in her thirties. There are a few of them around.'

'We'll keep looking nevertheless,' said Julia, without hiding her ironic tone. 'It seems a bit unnecessary to give up all hope of identification just because she doesn't have a distinctive mole on her chin.'

Christer shrugged in resigned affirmation, and Julia turned back to the group. She moved towards Mina, and Ruben noticed how Mina darted out of the way to ensure Julia didn't graze her again. He wondered how it worked when Mina fucked someone. Was she one of those who took care of everything herself so she didn't have to get anyone else involved? With a little sterile battery-powered thing? Or did she force the guy to wash in caustic soda first? Maybe he had to wear one of those rustling whole-body plastic overalls from hospital, with a little hole on the front for his cock . . . Ruben tittered aloud and got a sharp look from Julia. He hurriedly composed his face but couldn't remove the image from his mind of Mina being taken by a man in whole-body plastic overalls. For some reason the man in the overalls had acquired Vincent's face.

'Christer, I want you to carry on trying to find out the victim's identity. Peder, you go through the work done by forensics with a fine-tooth comb – even the smallest detail may be important. Well, you know that.' Julia turned to Vincent to explain: 'Peder's our virtuoso when it comes to analysis. He can review lists that would take the rest of us weeks to get through in a fraction of the time without missing any details.'

Peder blushed a little, but seemed to be pleased by the compliment.

'Ruben—' Julia continued.

'I'll take the box,' he cut in.

'Exactly. See what you can find out about the manufacturer, materials, structure – anything that might give us a lead on who built it or bought it. Check out where those swords are from. And stop staring.'

Ruben averted his gaze upwards and smiled roguishly, picturing Julia. La Perla.

'Mina, talk to the medical examiner and see what we can find out about the cuts and other things that have turned up. I've already spoken to someone in forensics about analysing the damaged glass from the watch. And Vincent, it would be useful if you tried compiling a profile.'

'Try is the operative word. Like I said, I'm not a trained profiler – I've just got another skillset that allows me to make pretty accurate observations about people.'

'I'd appreciate it if you would give it a go anyway.'

She was quite seriously going to put the mentalist to work. Give him access to confidential police files. This was the last straw. Ruben couldn't contain himself any longer.

'That's enough,' he said. 'The guy's an entertainer. An entertaining buffoon. We're the *police*. Surely you're not going to listen to him?'

47

The others fell silent and looked at Ruben. You could cut through the atmosphere with a knife.

'We've still got a little time before this leaks to the press, we have to exploit that,' said Julia through gritted teeth. 'In every way possible.'

Ruben held out his arms. He gave up. This was what happened when you left the women in charge.

'I'm off to forensics,' he said, standing up. 'Just going to requisition a crystal ball first.'

Peder, Christer and Ruben trooped out of the room, followed by Vincent, who had a prior engagement. Julia stayed behind with Mina. They were standing by the whiteboard with the photographs. Mina felt dirty from just looking at them and wished she hadn't left the hand sanitizer on her desk.

'How do you think that went?' Julia asked.

'I don't know,' said Mina, looking at the photos. 'It wasn't exactly a standing ovation from the group.'

She rubbed her forearms to remove the top layer of dead skin that she knew was there by this stage of the day.

'But do you think he can build a profile?' said Julia. 'He didn't sound too convinced.'

Mina shrugged.

'I think he's able to do things we've not seen him do yet. And it's not like we've got anyone else, unless we want to end up on another Greek high society wild goose chase. I'd like to carry on working with Vincent and give him a chance. We need a straw to clutch at. He's our straw.'

'You need to be one hundred per cent certain he's the right person for this,' said Julia. 'Because, as you might have noticed, you've got a room full of sceptics to convince. Well, maybe not Peder, but Ruben and Christer aren't climbing aboard this particular train. Ruben isn't even standing on the platform yet.'

Julia left her there alone. Mina let out a deep sigh. The meeting had been a disaster – it couldn't be regarded any other way. Though Vincent had been tasked with compiling a profile, she didn't think they'd pay any heed to what he had to say. His performance in the meeting had been less than stellar. She couldn't blame him; he'd warned her that it was all a matter of group dynamics. It was a pity his efforts to fit in with the team had come to nothing. Faced with Ruben and his preconceived notions, what hope did he have? She'd known since seeing him in action at the theatre that she wanted to work with him. But apparently that would have to be outside the conservative walls of police HQ.

Her gaze lingered on the photos on the board. The bloodied body hanging between the swords running straight through the box. Nothing but white knickers and a vest. She didn't want to look. But she had to. One of the swords had gone into the woman's eye and out the back of her head. *A classic illusion.* Anyone who thought magic was entertaining must be sick.

10

Kvibille 1982

Jane scraped the mud from her shoes onto a rock. She hated this. *Hated* it. It hadn't been her idea for them to move to the country. But she was the one who had to suffer as a result.

'Hurry up, Jane!' shouted her little brother from the lawn. 'We can't start on the cake until you're here!'

Mum was already there, wearing – as usual – one of her own dresses. Surely someday Mum could go out and buy some clothes instead of making them herself? At least she'd put on her best-looking one – the one with a leopard print. How she had got hold of leopard print fabric was a mystery, but when it came to textiles, Mum had an almost supernatural ability. The dress almost made her look sophisticated, even though it was home-made. If it hadn't been for the bare feet . . . In honour of her birthday, Mum had also put a wreath of flowers on her head. Jane sighed and pretended not to hear her brother.

Jane would soon be sixteen years old and had lived on this farm for half her life. She and Mum had been the first to arrive. In the summer of 1974, her mother had quit her job in Stockholm. They had moved out of the city centre flat and away from all of Jane's friends because her hippy mum was going to set up a commune with her chums on a farm outside Kvibille – a village in Halland county that was so small that, had it not been for the big cheese factory, no one would have heard of it. Cheese was where people's awareness of the village started and finished.

Jane didn't even live in Kvibille. She lived *outside* it. Where you could never wear anything nice since there was mud everywhere.

She inspected her shoes. The white soles were beyond salvation. She hated it. Again.

Jane went up to the house, took off her shoes and jammed her feet into a pair of wellies, sighing. Just because Mum chose to stay didn't mean *she* had to. She went down to the lawn, where Mum and her little brother were waiting.

'Mum, when are we moving?' she asked as she sat down on the blanket, just as she always did.

'And hello to you too,' said Mum.

'Erik got out,' Jane muttered. 'So why not us?'

Erik had been the only one of Mum's acquaintances who had actually put in an appearance. But he'd only managed six months. When Mum fell pregnant, it was apparently no longer quite as far out to be at one with nature. So Erik had bounced. They'd heard on the grapevine that he worked at a bank and had only taken a leave of absence for a few months. Another time they heard he was a travelling salesman for a sports equipment store. They didn't know what to believe. Mum didn't even know where he was any longer.

'You know why,' her mother said. 'It's hard to find work out here in the country. At least our costs are low, here on the farm. And, sweetheart – you've lived here for as long as we lived in Stockholm. Besides, the city's not the way you remember it – you've built up some fantasy about what life was like for us there. It wasn't that good. We're better off here – much better. I promise. But that's enough talk about that. Time to eat cake – once your brother has done his magic for us.'

Mum looked tired. It was one of those days. There was no point causing any more fuss. She might as well be left to be happy.

'It's a birthday present,' said her little brother by way of explanation for the imminent magic display.

He was wearing the cape that Jane had made for him on his last birthday. He was already outgrowing it.

'I got you a present,' said Jane, proffering a small parcel to her mother. 'But you can only open it if you can read the card.'

Hanging below the package was a piece of paper on which she had drawn lines. Some were dashed and others solid. Fragments of letters were also visible here and there, interrupted where they encountered the lines. Mum twisted and turned the piece of paper.

'How am I supposed to . . .?' she muttered in confusion.

Jane sighed. It was annoying when people didn't even try.

'Think origami,' she said, by way of a clue.

Mum looked at her uncomprehendingly.

'Good God, Mother. Think paper plane.'

'You mean I'm supposed to fold it?' said Mum with a laugh. 'Fun!'

She stuck the tip of her tongue out of the corner of her mouth as she folded the paper, following the lines. A twig under the blanket pricked Jane's thigh. She tried to find a more comfortable position without success. It seemed everything in this place was out to get her.

'Done,' said Mum in a concerned tone. 'But I think I may have got it wrong.'

She was clasping a crumpled little ball of paper on which half an F was visible on the top. Jane, her little brother and their mother began to roar with laughter all at the same time.

'That's how a cat would fold it,' said her little brother, tugging meaningfully at the leopard print dress his mother was wearing.

Jane laughed even more.

'She said like a paper plane,' he explained. 'You fold the dashed lines inwards, the solid ones outwards.'

Mum unfurled the paper and refolded it according to his instructions. The result was a perfect hexagon with a clear message on the top.

'*Happy birthday*,' Mum read from the hexagon. '*Your last one in Kvibille!*'

'We can always live in hope,' Jane said, when her mother glowered at her.

'OK, Sis,' said her little brother. 'Now it's my turn.'

He got out a deck of cards and waved it flamboyantly, as if it were a living thing.

'Remember this day: three o'clock in the afternoon on the eighth of July,' he said dramatically, 'because you'll be telling your grandchildren about it.'

'Do you even know where grandchildren come from?' said Jane, rolling her eyes but also smiling in spite of herself.

'Take this deck of cards,' he carried on as if he hadn't heard her. 'Cut it, shuffle it and take a card. Look at it but don't tell us what it is.'

It was so unfair: her little brother always seemed to be happy. Sometimes he verged on manic. But he had spent all his seven years on the farm and didn't know anything else. He was happy as long as he was left to do woodwork in the barn and practise his magic tricks. He was actually starting to get really good at the magic. The fact that Jane was nearly always able to work out how he had done it wasn't his fault. She'd always found it easy to calculate logical consequences, ever since she could remember. When the trick was over, she had no difficulty looking back and working out what must have happened. Of course, she always pretended to be surprised.

She took the cards, shuffled them, looked at one and then replaced it in the deck. Eight of clubs. Without being able to help it, she noted that the card ended up in eleventh or twelfth position in the face-down deck.

'Was I supposed to remember it too?' she said teasingly.

She received a dark look in reply. Magic was serious for her brother.

'Mum, now it's your turn,' he said, taking the deck of cards from her and handing it to her mother. 'Shuffle it and pick a card – any card.'

Mum concentrated as she shuffled and then selected a card.

'You were able to select any card at all, right?' he asked in a serious voice.

'Yes,' Mum replied, just as seriously.

She raised an eyebrow and tried to look earnest. Jane couldn't help laughing.

'And now, for the first time,' he said, turning back to her, 'would you be good enough to tell us which card you're thinking of, miss?'

'I'll show you "miss"!' she said. 'But OK, I saw the eight of clubs. Not that you can know that.'

'And what do you have in your hand, madame?'

He gesticulated towards Mum, indicating that she should show the card she'd removed from the deck. It was the eight of clubs.

'Bloody hell!' Jane exclaimed, bursting into laughter.

'Jane!' her mother said.

Her little brother had pulled the wool over her eyes. It was an unusual but wonderful feeling. She might be able to work out how he'd pulled it off, but she had absolutely no desire to. Not today. He bowed and she and Mum applauded him enthusiastically. As they always did.

Everything was as it should be.

But it wouldn't last for much longer – she knew that. This summer everything was going to change. She needed to tell Mum that she'd be leaving as soon as the holidays were over. That her life was going to take a new direction. She was going to tell her soon. Soon.

11

Vincent bent down and adjusted the shoelace on his right-hand shoe. The loops had been bigger on the right than the left. He wasn't usually so careless. But his thoughts weren't as collected as he'd have liked them to be. He stood up and took his coat off the hanger.

'So you really think I should go there on my own?' said Maria from the kitchen behind him.

She had a book about research methodologies open in front of her. She was training to be a social worker, but didn't seem to have fully grasped what this involved in terms of study, and she was constantly muttering 'Christ, I thought this was going to be about *people*' whenever she was forced to take the more theoretically demanding courses. But now there was something else on the agenda. Vincent could feel the knot in his stomach growing.

'You've known about Dad's seventieth for months. Given you're "The Master Mentalist", you're useless at planning sometimes. You'll have to call Umberto at the agency and ask them to cancel your show. There's more than a month to go, so it shouldn't be a problem.'

He turned around and looked at his wife sitting at the table. Maria was clenching her mug of tea so hard her knuckles were white. He had been so close to getting out of the door. He was reluctant to take off his shoes now – it was doubtful whether he would get the knots as symmetrical again. Vincent stared at the words on the ceramic mug: *Glitter Pussy*. There wasn't much glitter to Maria right now. Rather, she was surrounded by a thunder cloud. And the storm was heading his way.

'You know that it's not up to me to schedule shows,' he said, hoping it was one of those days where Maria accepted straightforward explanations and that the thunder would pass by without any lightning strikes.

The even tighter grasp on *Glitter Pussy* quickly dashed that hope.

'So you're telling me . . .' she said, inserting an ice-cold dramatic pause, 'you're telling me that if you had told your agent when the tour was being planned four months ago that they couldn't schedule a show on the date my father was having his party – *a party you've known about for six months* – they wouldn't have paid any heed to that?'

Vincent could feel the door frame cutting into his shoulder while he thought. This was funny. He could win arguments against anyone with clever rhetorical devices. It wasn't even sporting. But Maria, with her frankly simplistic analytical skills, always managed to put him on the spot. None of his usual tricks worked on her. Granted, they hadn't worked on Ulrika either. Perhaps it was hereditary. And she was right. Even if he couldn't do anything about it now, it didn't mean that he couldn't have done something about it earlier.

'Are you going to say anything?'

Lightning was beginning to flicker in the dark clouds around Maria. He realized that he'd allowed his moment of thought to extend for too long.

'I may have forgotten to mention it,' he said. 'But now things are how they are.'

He realized his tone was too untroubled. Big mistake. He sighed, bent down, untied the perfect shoelaces and took off his shoes.

'"Things are how they are"?' his wife mimicked. '*Things are how they are?* How can you be so insensitive?'

Maria's voice rose to a falsetto and he could hear that she was verging on tears. He would have preferred the lightning strike. Her tears left him defenceless. He went into the kitchen and sat down opposite her. The pattern of small eddies on the wooden table reminded him of fingerprints. He began to trace the waves and meanderings with his index finger.

Vincent wondered whether to take Maria's hand in his. It lay there in front of him, the wedding ring glimmering on her ring finger. But just as he was about to put his hand on top of hers, she pulled it out of the way and placed it in her lap. He avoided meeting her gaze, knowing that he would see eyes shiny with tears and a trembling lower lip.

'I don't mean to be insensitive,' he said, his gaze glued to the table. 'But no matter how stupid it was of me not to say anything – and I admit it was stupid – it doesn't change anything now. Of course I should have put Leif's seventieth in the diary back in the autumn, but I made a mistake. And now we have to adapt to the circumstances, no matter how stupid we think they are.'

Maria let out a sob. She took a big gulp of her green tea and grimaced. Vincent had never understood why she continued to drink litres of the stuff on a daily basis when she didn't even like it. But green tea and its health benefits were one of Maria's many hobby horses. For a while, she had tried to force him and the kids to drink the crap too, but that had almost descended into outright war and she'd had to give up after a couple of days.

He got up, went to the kitchen cupboard above the draining board and got out a mug. It matched Maria's, but the difference was that it said *Festive Farter* on his. He shook his head. The alliteration appealed to him and there was something amusing about how the consonants in the words slipped off the tongue, but it massively bothered him how unevenly the letters were positioned. How hard was it to stay in one line?

The teenagers had been suitably scandalized by Maria's sense of humour, but all objections had been met with a long lecture on how bodily functions were perfectly normal and everyone should learn to be more comfortable with their bodies. Which was ironic, given how uncomfortable she was when it came to her own body. She could now only have sex if the lights were off, the curtains drawn and neither of them said anything. It hadn't always been like that, so he suspected that it was because it was him she had to have sex with.

The aim for openness was naturally the correct one, on principle – that much he realized. And he didn't require his wife to practise what she preached. But it could be annoying when she managed to convince herself she was doing so. There had been another time. Another Maria. A snapshot flashed through his memory of Maria, wild and sweaty beneath him on the kitchen table – the same table whose surface he was now tracing with his finger.

His thoughts moved on to Mina. He wondered whether the detective had found any fingerprints on that sword box. Probably not. He ought to ask her how they did that kind of thing the next time he saw her.

'So what do you think we should do?' she said. 'About the party.'

He got up, poured a mug of coffee and sat back down again. Vincent looked carefully at her face. He had hoped that Maria's rush of adrenaline would have dissipated a little before they continued their discussion, but she was still bright red with rage and there were tears in her eyelashes.

'I'm not really sure what Umberto can do. Seven hundred people have bought tickets to the show. I can't move it or cancel. It's up to you what to do about the party – whether or not you're going.'

He sipped the coffee. It was over-brewed.

'Whether or not I go?' said Maria, knocking back a big swig of green tea. 'What on earth are you like? Why wouldn't I go to my own father's seventieth birthday party?'

Her voice cracked. He didn't know what to say. They always ended up at this point eventually. The logic was perfectly clear. He couldn't go to the party. Maria would have to take the kids by herself. Maybe she could see the party as time to herself? After all, Aston loved his grandfather. Or she could choose to stay at home. But he knew that Maria had seen through him.

'You know how it usually goes when I come along,' he said, in an attempt to head her off.

He wiggled his toes under the table. This topic always made him jittery. He had put it behind him; the fact that everyone else stubbornly insisted on dwelling on it wasn't his problem. But it galled him that they still brought it up at every family dinner.

'I don't want them to think we're having problems,' said Maria.

And there it was. The root of this entire discussion. The facade was important to Maria. Especially in front of her family. It had been a scandal without parallel when he had left his then wife for her sister Maria, who was eight years younger. It hadn't been taken well, which was altogether understandable. But not indefinitely. After all, it had been almost ten years ago – the family had had plenty of time to calm down. It wasn't rational for them to still have so many views on the matter a decade later. Views on things that were none of their business in the first place. Their attitude was illogical and unreasoning and that meant he struggled to relate to it. So he hadn't told his agent about the date. Sometimes the most logical thing to do was to avoid an illogical and complex situation.

'Oh, wouldn't Ulrika be pleased if she thought we were having problems,' Maria said. 'She's been hoping for it all these years. For us to separate, for you to leave me, preferably for someone else. Or to come back to her. She even said as much—'

He'd heard this many times before. Dwelling on the past.

'So what?' he said, interrupting her. 'She only has the power over you that you give her.'

'And you're saying she doesn't have any power over you? You're in touch several times a month.'

'Maria, your sister and I have kids. But it's you and I who live together.'

'You and I have a child together too,' she said.

'Yes, although sometimes I wonder whether Aston knows that he has a dad,' he said. 'I think Aston would marry you if he could.'

A microscopic smile appeared at the corner of Maria's mouth, but it quickly vanished, to be replaced by the same bitter expression as before. She opened her mouth to say something else.

He didn't feel up to listening and stared at the mug in front of him. *Festive Farter* – 13 letters . . . 8 consonants and 5 vowels: 13 8 5. He took out his mobile phone under the table and looked up 1385 on Wikipedia. In 1385, King Olof of Norway had proclaimed himself King of Sweden. Well, there you had it. And Olof was Benjamin's, his son's, middle name. Him – the mug – *Festive Farter* – 1385 – King Olof – Benjamin – him. A closed circle. Vincent realized too late that Maria had just said something about Benjamin.

'And tell your teenagers that they're definitely not allowed to call me auntie at the party. Ulrika loves it when they do that.'

The tears had dried up and he could see that she was now more angry than upset. Which was in many ways easier to deal with.

'I promise I'll speak to them,' said Vincent.

He put the phone in his pocket and stood up.

'On the subject of leaving me, when are you going to say something about that cop?' said Maria.

He sat down again. The tone betrayed that she had deliberately waited until he had his guard down.

'What do you mean?' he said.

'I know you saw her at the Rival,' she said.

'Yes, I told you I had a meeting,' he interjected.

'Don't interrupt me!' she hissed.

The new subject didn't seem to make her any less angry.

'You're not truly present when you're here. What is it you're thinking about, Vincent? Where you're going to fuck her next time? How good it was last time? Or weren't the sofas at the Rival the right height for taking her from behind? I suppose I'm meant to be grateful that you're not bringing her here. Yet.'

He put his face in his hands in an attempt to calm down. The first few times Maria's jealousy had reared its head, he'd been thrown into a rage. The jealousy hadn't been there from the beginning, but it had grown as their relationship had deteriorated. Soon enough, he had learned to rein in his reactions, but it still provoked a strong response within him. He couldn't help it. The accusation of betrayal triggered something primal, something deep down, even though he knew the jealousy wasn't about him. It was about her. Like everything else.

'Darling,' he said, controlling his breathing in an attempt to subdue the adrenaline that was flooding through him, 'if that's what you think then it's lucky for you that you're studying with a bunch of twenty-five-year-olds. All you have to do is pick and choose. But the last time I saw Mina was at police headquarters. I'm helping her. Them. The police team. On an investigation. If you're going to be like this every time, then it'll be impossible for me to do it. What do you think I should tell them?'

Maria looked at him and sobbed again.

'I want a phone number for this team,' she said.

'Good God— OK. Phone number. Fine. Now I really do have to go. I'm sorry I messed up about the party. I'll make it up to you somehow.'

He got to his feet and patted her awkwardly on the cheek. She let him. Vincent went into the hallway, put his feet in his shoes and bent down to tie the shoelaces again. Naturally they weren't as perfect as last time. But it would have to do. He went outside and managed to get almost all the way down the path through the snow blanketing the grass before he stopped to undo the laces and tie them again. Some things had to be done right.

12

Mina was in a taxi on the way to the National Board of Forensic Medicine, which was otherwise known as the RMV and was based in Solna. She wasn't coming straight from police headquarters but from a private meeting. None of her colleagues were aware that once a week – or whenever the need arose – she went to AA: Alcoholics Anonymous. There was no reason for them to know about it, especially since she wasn't an alcoholic. For her it had been about something else. For a period. A long period which had cost her a lot. And she was still paying the price for her mistake every single day. But that was her business.

The venue was in Kungsholmen, a few hundred metres from head-quarters, and that was why she opted to go to AA instead of . . . the other place. The other location wasn't as convenient, and for her they fulfilled the same purpose. The ideology was effectively the same. And if she bumped into a colleague en route then she could just say she was on her way home from work.

When she got out of the taxi, she wrapped her coat even more tightly around her to ward off the chill. There was no reason why her colleagues should know anything about her – she found it incredibly difficult to get to grips with the sharing of snippets of personal life that some people engaged in simply because they worked together. And her colleagues had learned after a few initial attempts that it wasn't worth asking her questions about anything other than work.

She was admitted into the forensic premises, put on her protective overalls and face mask and stood expectantly outside the autopsy room. She knocked on the door and heard 'come in' in response.

Milda Hjort didn't look towards Mina as she came through the door – she knew Mina was on her way and she was fully focused on the body in front of her. Mina went over and stood by her. She took in the box beside the body on the shiny, sterile table with fascination.

The box itself, however, was far from sterile. Blood, tufts of hair, brain matter and a string of other human materials were to be found here and there on the pale wood. A man in his fifties whom Mina assumed to be a forensic specialist was working on it in deep concentration. He was documenting and examining the box, while Milda was focusing on the body. The RMV was merely the first port of call for the box; it had been brought here because it would have been impossible to extricate the body without destroying evidence. It should really have gone straight to the National Forensic Centre, NFC, in Linköping via the police. As if he could hear her thoughts, the man nodded and took a step back from the box.

'I'm done. I'll make sure it's picked up and sent on to Linköping.'

'Thanks,' said Milda, without looking up from the body.

The man left the room, leaving the two women behind with Milda's assistant, Loke, an extraordinarily inhibited young man with whom Mina had never exchanged a single word, despite years of attending autopsies.

'This is a complete mess,' said Milda. 'It wasn't the easiest job getting her out of the box. The body had stiffened in position. Do you know who she is yet?'

'No, but we're working on it. Worst case, we'll have to put out an appeal in the media, but I'd rather avoid setting off that circus for as long as possible.'

'Understood.'

Milda turned her eyes towards the box. Mina slowly walked around it and took it in from every angle.

'Have you ever seen anything like this before?' she said.

'I've seen a lot in my time,' said Milda, 'but this is something new to me. Your colleague Ruben also stopped by earlier.'

'What did forensics say about the box itself?'

'Not much. Plywood. Nailed and glued into a cube. A few odd details about the structure – it seems it ought to have been built differently. I'm afraid you'll have to ask them, because it made no sense to me. Apparently the small slits in the sides are a precise fit for the width and thickness of the swords. And then of course there are the swords themselves.'

Milda nodded towards a different table where a number of see-through plastic containers were lined up in a row with a sword inside each one. Mina went over and looked at them in grim wonderment. All the swords were identical. They were made entirely from metal, with a long blade and a handle equipped with a shield to prevent the hand from slipping onto the blade. The swords were bloody and stained with various substances from the victim. Mina took out her phone and photographed them. She tried to capture them both as a whole and with as many individual details as she could through the plastic. She then returned to the body and proceeded to photograph it from every angle.

'Does it take a lot of force to drive a sword through a body?'

Milda nodded.

'Granted, the swords are pretty sharp. But still, driving them through the body so precisely that they lined up with the hole on the opposite side . . . Well, that would have taken both strength and precision.'

'There's nothing out of the ordinary? Apart from the obvious, that is? No detail on the box or swords that might prove useful?'

'Dead bodies are my department,' said Milda. 'You'll have to ask forensics about the box once NFC have taken a look. But if you're careful you can take a look now – it'll be here until it's picked up.'

Mina nodded and looked around the room. She shivered with delight at the sterile setting – cleanliness everywhere. Other than the box, there was no clutter, no dirt, no bacteria. The smell of disinfectant lingered astringently and delightfully in her nostrils. She would quite happily have lived in this room. The ever-present anxiety in her breast gave way and instead a relaxing warmth spread throughout her body. Was this how normal people felt when wandering around the dirty outside world?

She pulled up the photos she had taken of the swords on her phone and looked at them. It was easier than dealing with the containers. One detail made her zoom in.

'Where are the marks from?' she said.

'Sorry?'

'The marks?' she repeated. 'There are marks on the hilts of the swords. Where you hold them, I mean.'

Milda joined her alongside the containers and bent down to look at the hilts close up. Mina had opted to ignore the body on the autopsy table, but out of the corner of her eye she could see Loke continuing his work.

'You're right,' said Milda. 'It looks as though they were attached to something. No idea what it could be.'

'You don't have a theory?'

'No, like I said: dead bodies are my department, not objects. You'll have to wait for the report from Linköping.'

Mina took a few final pictures of the box.

'Will you call me if they find anything useful?' she said.

'Of course.'

'How long do you think the box will be here for?'

'A few hours. They need to find someone to drive it down.'

Mina nodded.

She trusted Milda. Reluctant as she was to admit it, even Ruben, who had been tasked with gathering information about the box, was good at his job. He had an almost photographic memory, which had on many occasions proved an invaluable asset. The reason for his assignment to the team had nothing to do with incompetence. It was all to do with #MeToo. But both he and Milda lacked a crucial frame of reference. To them, the box and swords were merely murder weapons. Vincent could tell them something important about its connection to magic. They'd had him in the meeting and not even asked him. But she trusted Vincent's expertise more at this stage than anything that Ruben might come up with. Ruben could say what he wanted – she needed to get Vincent in the same room as the box before it vanished off to NFC.

Taking a deep breath, she grasped the door handle and turned it slowly. Part of her didn't want to leave the lovely sterile environment and head out into the grime. But she knew she had no choice. This shit couldn't be avoided.

13

The taxi meter stopped at 437 kronor.

'Sorry,' said Vincent, leaning forward to speak to the taxi driver. 'Would you mind driving another few metres?'

'But I've stopped right outside the entrance,' said the cabbie a little sullenly.

'Yes, and that's great. But I'd like you to drive another few metres.'

The driver, whose name was Yusuf according to the official ID stuck to the windscreen, shook his head and did as Vincent asked. He pulled forward a few metres. When the meter moved up to 444 kronor, Vincent told him he could stop. Yusef shrugged, shook his head, and pulled to a halt.

'You're the customer. Happy to do it your way. Is this better?'

'This is perfect,' said Vincent, before paying.

He got out and took a big step to avoid the puddle of slush that the taxi had stopped in.

Mina was visible through the glass inside the entrance of the forensics lab. She met him with a nod. No handshake. Presumably she didn't have wet wipes with her.

'Thanks for coming so quickly,' she said.

'Not a problem,' he said politely. 'Where's the box?' he asked, looking around. He had never been here before. 'And is Ruben meeting us, given that he's the team member responsible for checking out everything to do with the box?'

'Ruben's back at HQ, following up on leads. I wanted you to see the actual box, not just photos, so you can examine it properly. It might even give you some data for that profile Julia asked you to compile.'

As they took the stairs to the third floor, Vincent glanced at Mina from the corner of his eye. She was the most interesting person he had met in a very long time – mutilated bodies or not.

'Over here,' she said.

They entered a long corridor. Mina led the way and he followed her dark ponytail with his eyes as it swung from side to side, almost as if it wanted to hypnotize him. They went into a changing room where they put on overalls, and then she opened the door into a sterile space with shiny metal tables inside. It was clean, deserted, and looked like forensic labs did on TV. And at the very rear of the room was the box.

Vincent stopped in his stride. It had been a long time since he'd seen one in reality. Mina was right: it was completely different to seeing it in photographs. It awakened memories – memories he had thought were long gone. Although in practice he knew better than that. He of all people knew about the brain's capacity to retain information. Nothing disappeared. Everything was still there in the convolutions of the brain, waiting to resurface when you least expected it. He had simply not believed that these particular memories would ever need to resurface.

'It looked smaller in the pictures,' he mused. 'But that's also part of the illusion. The box is meant to look smaller than it actually is because it's supposed to seem impossible for the assistant to avoid the swords. Not that it made any difference this time around . . .'

The box was positioned on a fairly low metal table and he crouched in front of it.

'Can I touch it? Or will I destroy evidence if I do?'

'That depends on whether you want us to find your fingerprints when it undergoes another round of analysis by the defence team's forensics experts,' she said.

'Good point,' he said, taking a step back. 'Someone has done their research at any rate. The sword box is considered to be one of the earliest stage illusions out there. Colonel Stodare performed with one at the Egyptian Hall in London in 1865, and published details of how it worked a year later. Although in his version it was of course a basket. The box came later. But Jesus Christ, imagine having to crawl into something like this.'

'You don't like confined spaces?'

'You could say that. Inherited from my mother. The mere thought of it gives me nightmares.'

He stuck his head in the box and carefully examined the slits for the swords without breathing too hard through the mask. The holes were in completely the wrong places. Assuming you wanted the assistant to live, that was.

'Some conclude the illusion by showing that the box is empty,' he said. 'And then the assistant pops up somewhere in the audience. Personally, I've never seen the point.'

He'd been afraid that the box would smell. Bodily fluids. Blood, sweat, maybe even piss. But thanks to the mask he was wearing it was completely odourless, despite the large bloodstains that had permanently marked the untreated timber.

'I don't get it, surely that's an even better trick?' said Mina.

'Think about it. The illusion is based on the assistant being penetrated by swords and surviving. But if the box is then shown to be empty because she's somewhere else, that eliminates the first effect. She was never in the box. Hence the swords were unnecessary. No chance of doing that with this box, obviously,' he said, pointing at the back, where there would ordinarily have been a secret door. 'There's no way out of this one.'

He stood up and stretched his legs.

'Aren't you overthinking it?' said Mina. 'It's only magic.'

'Exactly. It's when you don't think about it that it becomes "only" magic. Nice to look at, but you're not really sure whether you understood what it involved. Where are the swords?'

'They're here,' said Mina, pointing to some transparent plastic cylinders on a nearby table. 'The swords are inside the containers to preserve evidence and to prevent anyone cutting themselves on the blades. NFC are running DNA checks and they've lifted a few partial fingerprints. But it may take time to get the results.'

'NFC?' said Vincent.

'National Forensic Centre. The building we're in,' Mina clarified.

'I don't think this is going to get us anywhere much in pure profile terms,' he said, picking up a cylinder. He examined the sword inside carefully from every angle. 'It's a Condor Grosse Messer. At first I thought it might be a Falchion – they've got quite small blades – but unlike the Falchion, the Messer has a scaly structure on the hilt. Take a look.'

He held up the cylinder towards Mina so that she could see better. She leaned forward, studied the sword intensely and nodded. Then she looked at him.

'Dare I even ask how you know this? Illusions are one thing – that's pretty much your world. But this?'

He laughed.

'I had a period of LARPing in my youth.'

'LARPing?'

'Live Action Role Playing. There was a bunch of us who got together and played a medieval LARP game.'

'Hmm, you can't have been getting much action as a teenager.'

Taken by surprise, Vincent let out a laugh that echoed uncomfortably in the sterile space.

'More than the guys with the foam swords got. Anyway, what woman doesn't love a valiant knight?'

'True – I can see how valiant you were,' said Mina, and he felt himself beginning to blush. 'But OK. So it's a . . .?'

'Condor Grosser Messer. Manufactured in Ecuador. Weighs about two kilos. The blade is 1075 carbon steel, the handle is made from hickory and walnut.'

'OK, so now you've gone from LARPing to being a living version of Wikipedia . . . What makes you so sure it isn't going to help with the profile?'

Vincent balanced the cylinder in his hand. He felt the weight of the sword. Then he placed it back on the table next to the other identical swords in their cylinders.

'It's not an unusual sword in any regard. There are loads on the market. And in addition to new ones, there's also a big second-hand market – they may have been bought used. So it'll probably be difficult to trace them back to a specific buyer or seller. Anyone who does something this thoroughly isn't going to fall on their sword over that.'

'Cool. How long have you been waiting to drop that pun in?' said Mina with a smile in her eyes.

'A bit too long, apparently.'

'And the box? What do you make of the box itself? Does it take expert knowledge to build something like this?'

He crouched in front of the box again and stuck his head back in.

'The box is a better piece of evidence, I'd say. How many people would even know what it is?'

'Do you think it's home-made? Or can you order these from a manufacturer?'

His knees creaked as he stood back up.

'Could be either or,' he said. 'If you order one from a manufacturer then it still has to be customized to fit the person who is going inside the box. There are also designs available to purchase if you want to build your own. You only need to know where to look.'

'It'd be interesting to see what these designs look like,' she said.

'Whoever built this has at least used something to guide them, which

67

means he or she must have been in contact with someone in the industry. It may even have been commissioned. I can start by checking out the manufacturers I know, if you like. It's not a long list. I'm off to see my agent next, but after that I can get started.'

'Please,' said Mina, nodding and making her ponytail swing about. 'We need all the help we can get.'

They began to walk towards the door.

'I hope I was right – that this gave you a bit more material for your profile,' she said.

He stopped and turned to face her.

'It takes time to build a box,' he said. 'So this is someone who has planned every detail. At the same time, it feels too aggressive not to be a crime of passion. There's a conflict in how it was executed that leaves me confused. I daren't say anything yet in case I come out with a false diagnosis of the murderer's state of mind. I need to digest it all for a bit. By the way, have you got any further with the lines? The number carved into the body?'

'No. Not yet. But I asked the pathologist to check her records to see whether there were any other cases like it. Although we don't yet know whether it is a number. At the moment that's just a hypothesis. Your hypothesis.'

'Still, it's worth checking. I've been giving it some more thought and I'm convinced a number is the most likely explanation. Even if Julia doesn't agree. Perhaps that's all you need to find your murderer, rather than a profile from me.'

The door opened before they'd made it all the way across the room and they had to step aside to avoid it hitting them in the face. Standing in the doorway was Ruben, looking like thunder at the sight of Vincent and Mina.

'What's he doing here?' he demanded, glowering at Vincent.

'Julia's orders,' she said, shrugging her shoulders as nonchalantly as she could. 'Where have you been?'

'There are some . . . nice lady lab technicians that I always get a coffee with,' said Ruben, sweeping past them.

When Vincent and Mina emerged into the corridor and the door closed behind them, he scrutinized her profile.

'Why did I sense a degree of tension there?' he said.

'Let me put it like this,' she said. 'Julia did ask you to compile a profile. But to avoid creating conflict and unrest within the team, she asked me to "handle you" and . . . well, that's a direct quote. We're also bringing in Jan Bergsvik, our usual criminal psychologist. Sooner or later.'

Mina grimaced before continuing.

'Julia gave me the OK to bring you in, but she's only half-convinced. And the others . . . As far as they're concerned, you're not part of the team. Vincent, I really want your help, but I'm worried they won't listen to us. Ruben especially. You and I are going to have to sort this out by ourselves.'

'Perhaps I should try and charm them with my suave personality?' he said.

'Yes, because that went so well last time,' she said drily.

Vincent didn't take it badly. The social graces didn't come to him as naturally as they did to others. He'd had to learn them consciously – that was why he'd got so good at controlling people on stage. He'd had to find out exactly what you needed to do. And yet it still only worked there – on stage. His family life was proof of that.

In a way, it was good that Mina knew. It made things easier.

'That profile,' she said. 'How's it going?'

'I've not worked up my analysis yet; there are still too many variables. As I said previously, there are aspects both of organization and disorganization. In one and the same person. That's unusual. Not impossible, but unusual.'

Mina furrowed her brow.

'Sorry,' he said. 'I'll try to explain that better. First though, I need to gather my thoughts a little. But thanks for showing me the box. That suggested a lot to me. As regards analysis, you know that Ruben wants to sleep with you, right? His body language when he leaned in towards you, the way his pupils dilated—'

Mina interrupted him.

'Good God, Vincent. It doesn't take a mentalist to know that. Ruben wants to sleep with everyone.'

'And if he'd been a medieval LARPer he would have got to as well. Unless he was one of the guys with a foam sword. Is he a guy with a foam sword?'

Mina's laughter echoed down the corridor. It was a good sound – a sound to make anyone happy. Vincent didn't even count the number of laughs.

14

Practically impossible. He knew it. Christer Bengtsson sighed as he sat there at the computer. Going through all the missing persons reports was slow and monotonous. People would be surprised if they knew how many people went missing in Sweden every year. Albeit most of them did so of their own volition.

They had estimated the victim's age to be between twenty and thirty. But it was hard to judge a person's age in life, and even harder in death. Christer looked at the photo he'd been given by the pathologist to compare to photos of missing people, then shifted his gaze back to the screen and continued scrolling. Sweden was full of blue-eyed blondes, many of them with shoulder-length hair, but there were none that he felt really matched the photo on his desk.

Christer had never dated a blonde. The few relationships he'd had were with dark-haired women. There was doubtless something Freudian about it, connected to his blessed mother's raven-black hair. But none of them had stuck around. Eventually they'd move on and he'd find himself living alone again. It came as no surprise to him. Right from the beginning of a relationship, he always expected it to end sooner or later. It never felt right. Love wasn't forever. Nothing was forever. Only the weather. Well, actually, not even that was forever if bloody Greta Thunberg was to be believed.

He returned to the display, absent-mindedly reaching for his coffee cup and drinking a mouthful before spitting it back into the cup with a grimace. Jesus, cold coffee was the worst. Face after face passed by on his screen. They looked young and hopeful. But it would only be a matter of time before life would squeeze the hopefulness out of them. Christer was glad that his mother had taught him from an early age that life offered nothing but disappointment and despondency. If more

70

people realized that earlier on, then life would be easier for them. All these depressed people suffering from burnout – he was convinced that their problems derived from excessive expectations of what life had to offer and the inevitable disappointment that followed.

The faces continued to pass by on his screen. He raised the coffee cup to his lips again without thinking, took another gulp and swore when he realized yet again that the coffee was cold. Christer spat it out and stared glumly down into the cup. Life. Fucking hell. Life.

15

Vincent adjusted the biscuits on the plate so that there were two rows with four biscuits in each. He was visiting the agency who represented him, ShowLife Productions, in their office on Strandvägen. Ever since leaving the National Forensic Centre, he'd been unable to shake off thoughts of the box with its creepy holes. He could see it now in his mind's eye. And Mina standing beside it. With her glossy ponytail.

Pull yourself together.

In the early days of his partnership with ShowLife, they'd laid on fancy cakes, pistachio biscotti and squares of dark chocolate at every meeting. But the longer they had worked together, the less need the agency felt to impress Vincent – at least, in such superficial ways. The fact that the plate in front of him was piled with biscuits from the Tösse bakery was an ominous sign. Not that biscuits from Tösse were to be sneered at. But it meant that Umberto had something on his mind.

Umberto had come to Sweden fifteen years ago, but his Italian accent was still pronounced. Vincent suspected that Umberto thought – without any justification – that it made him sound sophisticated. If they needed to have biscuits at all, a regular pack of Ballerinas from the supermarket would have been Vincent's preference. Artisan was obviously tastier, but Ballerinas were made in a factory, which meant they were all exactly the same size. No biscuit differed from any other, none of them stood out, they were all the same. It was also easier to line them up.

'Has she turned up again?'

Vincent shook his head. 'No, not for two shows. But it's only a matter of time.'

'I still think we should consider hiring a couple of security guards.'

'No, no. It's an unnecessary cost. I think the theatres can handle it. It'll be fine.'

'I expect that's what John Lennon said about Mark Chapman,' Umberto muttered.

'That's enough of that,' said Vincent dismissively. He picked up a biscuit. White chocolate and walnut. It really was delicious despite its asymmetry.

'Vincent, we've had some complaints,' said Umberto in a troubled tone, stroking his meticulously trimmed beard. 'Last week you were at the Linköping Konsert & Kongress and at Slagthuset in Malmö.'

'One thousand one hundred and ninety-six seats in Linköping and nine hundred in Malmö,' Vincent said with a nod. 'Fully booked. Standing ovations. Someone's complained about the show?'

Umberto sighed.

'No, not about the show. But, Vincent . . . you can't lie flat out on the floor in your dressing room after shows. The cleaner almost had a heart attack. At both venues.'

Vincent helped himself to another biscuit. To even up the rows.

Umberto put his hand into a paper bag to lay out more biscuits. Vincent stopped him with a look. The rows would end up all wrong.

'Umberto, how long have we been working together?' he said. 'Ten years? I pay a price for these shows. It's not as easy as I make it look. My brain needs to recover afterwards. And the best way to do that is to lie down. You already know this.'

'But for *an hour*? Also, the techies in Karlstad got very worked up about the fact that you sorted their cables according to colour.'

'OK,' said Vincent. 'Tell them sorry from me. I'll try to be more considerate. In Karlstad I had some problems with the nail number. I almost put my hand through it. So I needed something to distract myself afterwards.'

Umberto screwed his eyes shut and shook his head. Then he opened them again and looked out of the window. Vincent followed his gaze. Still a week to go until Easter, yet the sun was making the water in Nybroviken bay glitter like it was summer.

'I'd prefer it if you didn't do numbers like that,' said Umberto, without looking at Vincent. 'What happens to the tour if you injure yourself? What would Maria say?'

'She'd say it was the best thing that could have happened,' he said. 'Because then I'd be able to come with her to the party.'

'Party,' echoed Umberto, without really listening.

Instead, he was looking at two young women in short yellow skirts who had just appeared on the other side of the street and were now pointing out across the water. Presumably they were tourists who had overestimated the Stockholm spring climate.

'You know what, I'm not going to let you have your own way this time. I'm going to hire a guard for the next show.'

'That's ridiculous,' said Vincent. 'I'm hardly Benjamin Ingrosso. Or John Lennon, come to that. But I know it's not worth arguing with you once your mind is made up. So thanks.'

Umberto turned back to face Vincent.

'Are you still signing the nail, by the way?' he said.

'The nail, photos people have brought, their T-shirts . . .' said Vincent, running a hand over his face. 'If only you knew what people want me to autograph.'

'An artist always signs all his works,' said Umberto with a laugh. 'You dug a hole for yourself with that one.'

'Yes, yes. But if we're talking about the show, could you ask the venues to stop putting fizzy water in the dressing rooms?'

'They just want you to feel welcome,' said Umberto, whose gaze was once again glued on the window. 'As per your instructions, there's no contract rider on what has to be in the dressing room. If they've supplied fruit or sweets or water, then it's on the theatre's own initiative. We've discussed this already.'

'Yes, but they should know that it's impossible to drink carbonated water before a performance. I use my diaphragm to project my voice. Fizzy water in my stomach makes me burp. Tap water is better.'

The women across the street moved on and Umberto looked at Vincent with a slightly worn-out expression.

'Vincent. It's a gesture on their part. Let them do it. You can always drink the water after the performance.'

'But I can't deal with—'

Umberto held up his hand in a gesture of impatience.

'I can't believe we're even discussing this,' he said. '*Adesso basta!* Sometimes you're like a child. Drink the water. Or don't. No one cares. OK?'

Vincent shrugged his shoulders. He just thought it was unnecessary for the venues to throw money away. Plus more bottles meant more labels on the bottles to set in order.

'Do you remember the magician you used to work with?' he said, changing tack. 'The one with all the boxes. The sawn-in-half woman.

Zigzag lady. Water torture cell. All very old school. Do you know what happened to his props?'

Umberto picked up a biscuit and thought about it.

'Do you mean Tom Presto? Now that was quite a production: eight dancers, three trucks for the rig, one massive ego – cost a fortune to keep that guy on the road. Why do you ask?'

'I was wondering whether his stuff was accessible, should someone want to buy something from him. A sword casket, for example.'

Umberto inserted the rest of the biscuit into his mouth, wiped the crumbs from his beard and shook his head.

'We sold the lot when the show ended,' he said. 'To a French collector. As far as I know, it's all locked up in a warehouse in Nice. Except for that water thing you mentioned, actually. The collector wouldn't touch that with a bargepole. I don't know if you ever saw Tom Presto's show, but he liked taking risks.'

'He struck me as someone who needed to be in complete control.'

'I thought so too. I assumed the act wasn't as dangerous as it appeared, until that collector explained how the magic works. Apparently, that giant fish tank Tom would climb into and be locked inside—'

'Houdini called it a water torture cell,' Vincent interjected, but Umberto waved him away.

'—it's meant to have a secret lever on the outside. A panic lever. So if the trick goes wrong and the magician can't get out, then the assistant can pull the handle and drain all the water in a few seconds to ensure the magician doesn't drown.'

'Seems a smart addition.'

'You'd think so, but Tom Presto's tank didn't have one of those. I guess he considered it a sign of weakness. The Frenchman refused to have something that dangerous in his collection. *C'est trop extrême* were his exact words. I don't know where that tank is gathering dust now – but if you're interested I can try to find out.'

Umberto suddenly slapped his forehead.

'On the subject of things gathering dust,' he said, 'you received a Christmas present! Just a second.'

He vanished out of the room before Vincent could say a word. After thirty seconds or so he returned with a large object in his arms.

'Christmas was months ago,' said Vincent. 'It's almost Easter, in case you hadn't noticed.'

Umberto handed over the item. It was a thick book with a red ribbon artfully tied around it. There was a card hanging from the ribbon.

75

Dear Vincent, it said on the card. *Perhaps not really your field, but it may be more interesting than you think. From an admirer.* Old-fashioned, ornate handwriting. Beautiful. Feminine. He thought he vaguely recognized it, but he couldn't place where from. Then again, it might just have been his imagination.

The book, which was called *Mammals of Mexico* and had a photograph of a leopard baring its teeth on the cover, appeared to be at least a thousand pages long.

'Thanks,' said Vincent. 'Exactly what I want to drag around all day.'

Umberto laughed.

'They're your crazy fans,' he said, 'not mine. I put it to one side because it was too big to send over with the rest of your mail, then forgot all about it. Anyway, never mind that – what are we going to do about your show? You can't keep giving the crew heart attacks.'

'There's no need for you to worry,' said Vincent. 'The rest of the tour is going to be free of complaints. I promise. Provided you promise to keep the cleaners away for an hour every night.'

Umberto laughed and proffered his hand.

'Deal, *amico mio*.'

'Deal,' said Vincent, shaking his hand.

Then he stood up, tucked the heavy book under his arm and grabbed the bag of biscuits on his way out.

16

Mina had her work phone pressed to her ear. It was lucky she'd cleaned the receiver thoroughly with sanitizer right before she picked up. She was listening quietly while feverishly taking notes on the back of a bill, the nearest piece of paper she'd been able to find on her desk. She asked a few quick questions in return. Thirty seconds later, she checked the time and hurried to the canteen.

Ruben had his back to her and was working his way voraciously through meatballs and salad. He'd dropped carbs since the first hint that he was beginning to pile on the pounds around his belly. A fact that he often shared at lunch.

'You handled a suicide two and a half months ago,' Mina said to his back. 'Thirteenth January. Agnes Ceci. Twenty-one years old.'

Ruben stopped with the fork halfway to his mouth.

'Er, yeah. Rings a bell. What about it?'

He raised his eyebrows when she pulled out a chair and sat down opposite him. He rolled his eyes and put down the fork. She tried not to think about how dirty the canteen chair must be. All the things now crawling over her trousers. She had to master herself at work in order to function, but it took so much of her strength that when she got home of an evening she usually collapsed from exhaustion. She couldn't resist the urge to discreetly pull down her sleeves so that her skin didn't have to come in contact with the tabletop when she leaned towards Ruben and stared at him hard.

'Tell me about it.'

'Wellll . . . there's not much to tell. It was me and Lindgren, one of the younger lads, who were first on the scene and it was pretty obviously suicide from the word go.'

'Why?'

77

Ruben sighed again. He looked longingly at his meatballs, which were slowly going cold and beginning to look gelatinous. Mina ignored his hunger. He really shouldn't eat that – she was very dubious about the food hygiene procedures in the police canteen. She was actually doing him a favour.

'One shot in the mouth. Weapon right beside her. Her fingerprints. No coat, even though it was winter. All signs that she wasn't completely in her right mind.'

'Was there a note?'

'No, no note. But Agnes had a long history of depression and mental illness. She'd been in St Göran's hospital several times and none of the people we spoke to seemed all that surprised. Not even the friend she shared her flat with.'

'Was the flatmate considered a potential suspect?'

'Initially, given that there was no suicide note. People who are so dramatic that they shoot themselves often leave a message. Plus he was the one who called it in, which always rings faint alarm bells. We pushed a little during questioning, but it was pretty obvious that it was suicide. Probably a spur-of-the-moment thing – if you were planning on killing yourself, you'd do it at home rather than on a park bench. Why are you asking?'

'Do you have any photos? From the autopsy? The crime scene?'

'Crime scene? Like I said, it was a suicide.'

Mina ignored him. She would explain in due course. Right now she wanted to see the pictures.

'Come on,' said Ruben, getting up with a sigh.

She noted that he didn't return his tray. She considered asking whether his mother worked there, but decided to refrain. Men rarely seemed to appreciate that comment and Ruben was slightly more easily riled than the average bloke. What was more, she needed his help. He headed for the lift and she followed. What she'd been told over the phone had piqued her interest, but the pictures would give her more to go on. If she was right, it would change everything.

17

'What is it that's so urgent?' Julia came into the room with a coat over her arm. 'I was just heading out when I got the message, but there were no details.'

'No idea,' said Christer sullenly, a coffee cup in one hand and a big bun in the other.

'You didn't happen to bring any more buns, did you?' said Ruben in a longing tone.

Mina ignored them and concentrated on attaching the contents of the file to the whiteboard alongside the existing items.

'Where's Peder?' she said once she'd turned around. 'I want everyone to be here.'

Ruben shrugged. He took an apple from the fruit bowl on the table and bit into it loudly. Mina couldn't look at him when he was eating. The apple had been there for days. In her mind's eye, she pictured germs crawling all over the apple, enveloping it, and now it was disappearing straight into Ruben's mouth. She didn't want to think about where Ruben's mouth had been either. Or on whom. No doubt that would be a bacteria-fest of monumental proportions. She swallowed, trying to suppress the nausea. Somehow she needed to try to pretend everything was fine.

'He didn't pick up,' said Ruben, taking another loud bite.

'Did you check his desk?' she asked, unable to conceal her irritation. Ruben shrugged.

Mina put down the folder, which was now empty. She left the meeting room and found Peder at his desk, fast asleep. His head was tipped back against the headrest and he was snoring gently. Some joker had drawn a moustache on him.

'Peder!'

She shook him hard. He jumped and looked around drowsily.

'Come on, we've got a meeting,' she said.

She returned to the meeting room without waiting for him, but she could hear his shuffling footsteps behind her. When she got back to the team, she saw that they were all intently examining what she had put up on the board. She knew they wouldn't see what she'd spotted without her help. It was only thanks to the call from Milda, who'd carried out the autopsy, that she'd found it. That and Vincent's clue. She knew that the group were still sceptical about him. But hopefully not for much longer. He'd already shown himself to be invaluable.

Peder entered the room and collapsed into a chair, exhausted. He rubbed his eyes, but mostly seemed to be moving the bags under them around. His colleagues giggled at the moustache, but no one told him it was there.

Mina turned to them. She fixed her gaze on each one in turn. She needed to persuade them all of what she now believed. She took a deep breath. Then she pointed at the board.

'I think Vincent was right. We're dealing with a serial killer.'

Silence. They were doubtful. But she'd expected that.

'As you know, I was pretty much convinced that the symbol carved on our victim's body was a Roman numeral three,' she continued. 'Hence it was natural to consider whether there were any other numbers on previous bodies that we might have missed. I checked with Milda, who couldn't remember anything like that offhand but agreed to go through her recent cases. She called an hour ago to tell me about Agnes – Agnes Ceci.'

Mina pointed at the photographs she had put up on the board. The photo she was pointing at depicted a young, red-haired woman, slumped on a park bench, with blood forming a red shadow in the snow around her feet. Despite the fact that it was the middle of winter, she wasn't wearing a coat. There was a pistol lying beside her right hand as if it had fallen from her grasp.

'This was taken at Berzelii Park, right outside the China Theatre,' she said.

'Doesn't exactly look like a musical,' Christer quipped.

His other colleagues looked at him in surprise, but he merely shrugged.

Mina moved her finger to another picture showing the sterile, grey surface of the autopsy table. The woman who had been sitting outside the theatre was lying on it, naked. On her right thigh there were three lines clearly visible. One straight one and two leaning into each other to form a V joined together by horizontal lines at the top and bottom.

The Roman symbol for four.

'A Roman numeral. Just like Vincent said,' she clarified. 'The thing you didn't believe. And that we simply missed.'

Her colleagues leaned in. Interested. But still not wholly convinced. Ruben's raised eyebrow indicated scepticism. Peder blinked his eyes and tried to focus. She drew their attention back to the photo of Agnes on the autopsy table.

'The marks were noted during the autopsy and are in the report, but due to Agnes's history of poor mental health they were written off as signs of self-harm. Something she'd done to herself.'

'Which is still a likely explanation,' said Ruben dismissively, leaning back in his chair again.

He crossed one leg over the other and swayed gently on the chair.

'Certainly. It could very well be. Stranger things have happened,' said Mina calmly. 'It might not be a serial killer – if it weren't for this.'

She pointed at another photo. And then another at the far end of the whiteboard where the photos of their first victim were pinned up. She said nothing else, letting the photographs speak for themselves. Julia stood up. She went over to the board. She carefully studied the pictures that Mina had pointed out.

'Smashed wristwatches.'

Mina nodded.

'Yes, exactly. Both victims had watches that had been smashed so that they stopped right on the hour. Our first victim had a watch that had stopped at three o'clock – 15:00. And Agnes's watch had stopped at 14:00. I'll buy one random coincidence, but not two.'

Silence descended on the room. Everyone seemed to be taking in what Mina had just shown them.

'Do you think it's the same person?' said Ruben.

He now seemed to be reluctantly open to Vincent's theory.

'Do you think that it *isn't*?' Mina countered.

Ruben was about to say something but then shut his mouth. Julia's face was grave as she took in everything that Mina had put on the board.

'We need to review everything from the start,' she said. 'Every single detail. We're in this for the long haul. Call home if you need to let them know you'll be working late. Mina – good job.'

Everyone nodded. Then Peder cleared his throat.

'If there's a victim marked with a three,' he said, his voice thick with tiredness, 'and a victim marked with a four . . . Does that mean this serial killer has been at it for a while without us realizing?'

'That's exactly what I'm wondering too,' said Mina.

She fiddled with the folder. There was something about this case that bothered her. Something that she ought to see but that slipped away when her consciousness tried to grasp it. She shook her head. It would come to her sooner or later.

She removed a pack of wet wipes from her pocket. She pulled out several and passed them to Peder.

'Here. There's something around your mouth – wipe it off with this.'

18

Vincent opened his eyes with an effort. He had been up for most of the night searching for information on the manufacture and sale of both the box and the swords that had penetrated it. The task seemed overwhelming, but he'd been driven to work on through the night by the pressure of needing to live up to Mina's expectations and deliver something new.

Now, after far too few hours' sleep, he had been woken by a sound that he couldn't identify. It seemed to be coming from far away. There was a clear dissonance. Singing. But in different keys. It was so off that he wished he was tone deaf. It annoyed him that the term was mostly used jokingly, even though it was a genuine phenomenon. It described someone who was unable to identify differences between sound frequencies. The direct opposite of tone deaf was absolute pitch, which was the ability to perceive and state the exact key without a reference point. A variant of this was relative pitch – the ability to perceive intervals between keys, but unlike absolute pitch being unable to recognize a specific key unless you had something to relate it to. Right now he was indescribably pleased that his sense of pitch was decidedly under-developed.

'. . . tooooo yooouuuuuuuuu . . .'

The song finally ended. He sat up and squinted. The whole family was standing at the foot of the bed. Maria and Aston shared the same expectant expression, while Benjamin and Rebecka looked like they were en route to their own execution. Vincent spontaneously felt more sympathy with his two eldest children. He hated birthdays. Well . . . Not birthdays as such. The kids' birthdays were fun. It was *his* birthdays that were the problem.

'Three cheers – hip-hip . . . *ow!*'

Aston yelled and grabbed his leg. He turned around angrily and glowered at Benjamin, who shrugged and pointed at Rebecka. Aston stared at her as angrily as he could but eventually gave up. The family hierarchy was clear to Vincent's youngest son. Rebecka was crueller than Benjamin – she was both capable of and prepared to inflict pain if he didn't do things her way.

'Happy birthday, darling!'

Maria placed a large, home-made gateau on a silver platter on the bed. Vincent felt the nausea rising. Cream in the morning wasn't a favourite of his. But it was a tradition in Maria's family. Which meant he hadn't avoided the mandatory stodgy cake in the morning in his years with Ulrika either. He realized the cake was intended as a sign of affection and wasn't meant as an attack on his digestive system, so he forced his mouth into a big smile.

'Aston! The parcels!'

Maria's eyes were glittering as she carefully sat down on the bed. She loved birthdays. Primarily her own, but those of others too. With a heavy thud, Aston leapt up onto the duvet with two parcels in his arms, nearly making the cake topple off.

'Mum and me made the cake last night!' his son said, bursting with pride. 'We were like pros at making cake. I ate soooooo much cream!'

Aston's pronunciation of 'pros' was in cocksure American. Definitely something he had picked up from YouTube. Vincent looked at the cake. For a moment, he wished it would simply slide off the platter onto the floor and meet an early demise. But he knew that the cost of an incident like that would be dearer than the pleasure it brought. Maria would consider it an omen and regard the rest of the day as doomed, which would mean one disaster after another in a self-fulfilling prophecy.

'Here, Dad,' said Aston cheerfully, handing over the parcels while continuing to bounce up and down in excitement.

He kept glancing joyfully at his mother.

The first parcel had been carelessly wrapped with pieces of tape that were coming off and scrunched-up wrapping paper that looked like the contents had found their way inside by accident. Monster Trucks. Leftover paper from Aston's birthday in February. Vincent grinned and hugged his son. Who didn't love Monster Trucks?

'Oh, thank you!' he said, pulling out a tie.

Maria ruffled Aston's hair proudly. Vincent noted that it was the third identical tie he had been given. The children had no doubt been given money to shop for a gift for him and children's reasoning could be so straightforward. If their parent liked the present last year, they would surely like it again this year. There was something loving in that which he was completely able to embrace. What was more, he had the perfect riposte. He was going to give them all a tie each when they turned twenty.

'Next! Do the next one!'

The cream began to slide off the top tier of the cake as Aston bounced again.

'Take it easy, sweetheart,' said Maria, putting a firm hand on her son.

She still had her eyes fixed expectantly on Vincent. It was a thin, flat parcel. This one had been more thoroughly wrapped, so he guessed it had been done by Maria. This was confirmed by the glittery sticker – a peace symbol in the shape of a heart on the top. He undid the paper.

'We're going on a boat, Dad! All of us!'

Vincent looked at the card: his worst nightmare was about to be realized. A Baltic cruise to Finland. Fifty thousand tonnes of anxiety with a stench of beer to boot. He looked up at Benjamin and Rebecka. The same pain that was probably written all over his face was reflected in theirs. They exchanged a look of understanding. All three of them knew that once Maria had decided something was going to be 'amazing to do together as a family', there was no turning back. In the near future, they would spend twenty-four hours trapped inside a steel vessel with an unsafe bow door. He checked the back of the folder. The gift card was valid for a year. He had twelve months to flee the country.

'Have some cake, darling,' said Maria warmly, proffering a side plate with a huge slice that she had just cut. 'Aston is right. We are total pros at cake. And there's loads of cream.'

Vincent swallowed and smiled. He knew that it was all done out of affection. And meant well. He tried to play along as best as he could.

'Thank you, darling. Perhaps we can all eat cake together at the kitchen table?'

They gathered up the presents, paper and cake and headed into the kitchen. On the way, he retrieved his birthday present to himself. The double album *Xerrox 4* by Alva Noto. He untied the red ribbon he had attached himself, carefully opened the cellophane with his nail and removed the first vinyl record from the sleeve to the gentle sound of static. He inspected the grooves carefully to establish a visual understanding of what he could expect before he put it on the record player in the living room. It looked good.

He picked up the tub of fish food, poured a little into the palm of

85

his hand and went over to the aquarium. Then he held his hand right above the water and waited. He had chosen central mudminnows for a reason. They might not be the most beautiful fish, but they were the only fish he knew of that would actually eat from your hand. He didn't have to wait long before four fish were merrily guzzling the flakes out of his hand.

'Things might get a bit noisy today,' he whispered to the fish. 'Apologies in advance. You know how it is.'

Then he went into the kitchen.

When the first track began to play, he relaxed a little. Maria, on the other hand, seemed to have the opposite reaction – he could see her shoulders tensing. Not her thing. She usually grumbled over his insistence on playing obscure vinyl records when they could be listening to Ed Sheeran on Spotify. Which also took up less space. But she'd seen the red ribbon – this was his. This was his moment. For now.

He sat down and helped himself to a slice of cake while quickly performing a calculation in his head. It was eight o'clock on the dot. Sixteen hours. Nine hundred and sixty minutes. Fifty-seven thousand six hundred seconds. Then his birthday would be over.

19

'Did you share today?'

Mina shook her head.

'Today wasn't a good day for it,' she said. 'But I've listened. And I don't usually share. You know that. How long has it been, anyway?'

'Well yes, no. True. Might as well not bother when it doesn't feel right. I only just got here, but thought I'd stick around for the second half. Then I can see how I'm feeling. Whether it's a good day for me to share or not. Coffee?'

The man with the dog, as Mina had christened him from an early stage, proffered a paper cup. She knew his real name, but her initial labelling of him had stuck. The regulars also included 'the woman with the purple shawl', 'the one from Skåne' and 'dolphin girl'. She knew their names too, but she preferred to keep them anonymous, impersonal. After all, this was Alcoholics *Anonymous*. And besides, she wasn't actually an alcoholic, which had given her a good excuse over the years to keep clear of the sense of community that otherwise so easily arose within the group.

Mina shook her head at the paper cup the man with the dog was offering to her. She suppressed the thought of what might be crawling on the cup and the pump flask on the table that had been touched by everyone. He shrugged and pushed the button to fill a cup for himself. The coffee had an oily surface and looked watery. She wouldn't have wanted to drink it even if it had been sterile.

'How come you were late?' she said, immediately feeling the urge to bite her tongue.

It was partly that she wasn't interested and partly that it might be impolite to ask. She couldn't always tell.

'I had to drive my partner to a doctor's appointment. She has to have a few check-ups after her operation. She's got severe scoliosis and has been in a wheelchair for the last couple of years.'

Mina nodded but said nothing. She deeply regretted asking. Too much personal information. Mercifully, the man with the dog broke off relaying details about his partner in order to give his golden retriever a bowl of water and a brief scratch behind the ears.

'What's the dog's name?'

Once again – not interested. Mina did not get why today of all days she seemed to have a need to fill the silence. She didn't even like small talk. But the man lit up.

'Bosse,' he said with pride. 'He's four years old.'

Mina didn't reply. Animals had never been her thing. For obvious reasons. Bosse's paws were grimy from walking through the mucky snow outside.

'Hi! Great to see you!'

The dolphin girl came over to the coffee table and smiled broadly at Mina. The dolphin girl was always excessively happy. Which almost seemed perverse, given where they were. Mina was many things at the meetings, but she was rarely explosively positive. The dolphin girl's real name was Anna, but she'd acquired her name thanks to the dolphin tattoo on her calf, that she had shown Mina the first time they had met. Mina hadn't asked whether the dolphin had any companions on the young woman's body – she was worried Anna might start undressing there and then. Mina would have been just fine not knowing about the dolphin either, but the dolphin girl had turned out to be unexpectedly very helpful. Mina smiled at her and nodded by way of greeting.

'Thanks for the tip about contacting Vincent Walder,' she said. 'My boss went for it right away.'

The dolphin girl beamed.

'Did it pay off?'

'I think so,' said Mina. 'I hope so.'

The dolphin girl beamed even more brightly. 'And you were able to get hold of him? Vincent Walder? Wow – that's so great! It was just a brainwave I had – I don't know him, but he's *so* cool. And sorry again about eavesdropping.'

Mina had been talking to Julia on the phone during the coffee break at an AA meeting a day or so after they'd found the body in the sword box. After the break, the dolphin girl had initiated contact. At first, Mina had been hesitant, but Anna's suggestion to look up Vincent had undeniably helped kickstart the investigation, and dealing with the master mentalist had made Mina's existence decidedly more interesting of late. More difficult, but more interesting. She was a person who didn't let anyone in. Who didn't let anyone get close. She had suddenly nudged the door ajar – and for a stranger at that. But as long as it was only in her thoughts, she felt OK about it. She was still in control. All that remained was for her to learn how to keep her voice down when she was on the phone.

Bosse the dog had stopped drinking his water and now approached her with his tongue lolling out of his mouth. She clenched her fists and tried to control the desire to back away, succeeding for three or four seconds, but when she felt a wet nose touch her hand she was unable to block her instincts, taking several quick steps backwards.

'He's a sweetheart,' said the man, scratching Bosse behind the ears.

Mina saw drool dripping from the corner of the dog's mouth. Mistaking her look of horror for positive attention, he cheerfully wagged his tail.

'Mmm,' said Mina, her eyes still fixed on Bosse and his dirty paws.

Silence again. The dog took a hopeful step closer.

'I'm considering getting a wolf next time,' said the dolphin girl.

Mina had forgotten she was still there.

'And some cool text – I've not quite made up my mind what though. Maybe *Carpe diem*. Or maybe that's a bit hackneyed? It still sounds good though, right? Seize the day – that's what it means. And isn't that what everything is about? We have to seize the day, live in the now, make sure we're *here*.'

The dolphin girl exposed her upper arm while she was talking by rolling up the sleeve of her sweatshirt.

'You know what I think about tattoos,' said Mina, looking at her politely. 'There's no guarantee the needle has been properly sterilized and you've got no idea how clean the ink is either . . .'

'I know – isn't it cool?' said the dolphin girl. 'It makes you feel like you're alive, right? Not knowing what's going to happen . . . What if that shit's infected and you get one of those deadly bacteria inside you – the flesh-eating kind. And it slowly starts to eat your whole arm . . .'

'Living on the edge,' said Mina drily.

'Yes! Good suggestion! Thanks! Of course I should go for "Living on the edge"! Fuck me, you're the best.'

Mina looked at the dolphin girl, now lost in enthusiasm for what had most definitely not been a suggestion, and found herself completely at a loss as to how to continue the conversation. It felt as if whatever she said might end up in shitty, infected script on the dolphin girl's arm.

'Time to come in!' a man's voice shouted from the doorway into the hall.

Mina offered silent thanks for deliverance from the dolphin girl, smiled in apology and hurried inside.

20

'How's it going?' a voice behind him shouted. 'What are you building?'

The sound made him jump – he hadn't heard anyone coming into the barn. He'd been fully concentrating on sawing a plank of wood in two without it splintering. One half broke off and fell to the floor without him managing to catch it. An ugly splinter was sticking out of the wood where it had separated. He quickly picked up the piece from the ground and put it on the pile with the others before throwing a sheet over the lot. The sheet was covered in painted-on stars and mysterious symbols. He had made up most of them himself. Then he turned around and looked at his mother.

Mum was standing in the open doorway of the barn, the evening sun surrounding her silhouette with gold. He had to squint to see her.

'I can't tell you what I'm doing,' he said. 'If I did, you'd know how the illusion works. I'll show you later when it's finished.'

A beam of light fell on his woodworking bench as Mum moved out of the doorway and came into the barn itself. Particles of dust moved languidly in the air. When the sun struck them they shone like glitter. Magical glitter. His mother picked up one of the brushes lying on the bench and waved it in the air.

'Can I at least help you to paint?' she said, attempting to look behind him. 'I still think it's incredible that you can build these things all by yourself. After all, you're only seven years old. What other seven-year-old can do this kind of stuff?'

'It's not that hard,' he said. 'I've started doing drawings. And I'm careful. Anyway, it's not like I've got much else to do. And it's going better now than it did in the beginning. But if you're going to help, then you're not allowed to peek until I'm done. And no stars this time.'

He pointed meaningfully at the sheet.

'It's meant to look like . . .'

'I know. Like Les Vargas,' she said. 'The Spanish artist.'

She did a dramatic dance movement – he had no idea what it was meant to represent.

'Las Vegas, Mum,' he said.

Then he stopped himself and looked at her. Her eyes were clear and smiling at him. The tension in his body disappeared. Today was a good day. But he also realized he'd walked into a trap.

'Mum, you . . . you were joking, right? There isn't anyone called Les Vargas, is there?'

He wished Mum wouldn't do this. It was hard for him to know when other people were joking. Like at school. Total nightmare. What if the summer holidays could last forever, so that he never had to leave the farm? Mum and Jane were more than enough for him.

His mother winked at him.

'You're right,' she said. 'Vargas was a joke. OK – one order for Las Vegas!'

Then she raised the brush as a warning.

'If you teach me a card trick. Otherwise it'll be Spanish after all.'

He laughed. No one loved magic as much as Mum. She almost loved it more than he did. But he understood her. When he was doing magic, problems could disappear. Money could be doubled. The world was different – at least for a bit.

Everything was once again possible.

He turned around and looked at the stack of wood. In his mind's eye, he visualized them being joined together in a way only he understood. When he was finished, it would be a box. And from that box he would be able to summon anything.

Anything that would make sure that Mum stayed happy.

21

Slush squelched under Vincent's boots as he walked through the park. Mina had called to say they needed to talk, and he had suggested they meet for a lunchtime stroll in Rålambshov Park. The park was within comfortable walking distance of police headquarters, so she wouldn't be gone too long. At the same time, there was little risk anyone would notice them there.

That had been the idea. But now there was a young woman in a light blue quilted jacket around ten metres down the path, staring at him. She presumably recognized him from TV and didn't know whether she should greet him or not. He helped her out by waving. She responded by turning on her heel and leaving. You couldn't win them all.

At least the weather was on his side. The sun was shining and there were dogs playing with their owners on the large swathes of grass. Most of the snow on the city streets had melted away, but in the park there were still patches of it left. Five dogs, five owners. Five plus five was ten. An odd became an even.

'Happy birthday,' said a voice behind him. 'Many happy returns.'

He spun around and saw Mina. Birthday. Bloody Wikipedia. He hoped she didn't have a gift for him too. Or plan to hug him.

'No talk about birthdays,' he said sternly.

A small smile played on her lips, but only for a second and then she was back to her usual reserved self again.

'We've got a new case. Or rather, an old one – a previous victim.'

She passed him two photos. The top one was a printout of a selfie on Instagram. A young girl with a zest for life raising a glass to the camera. At the table behind her were friends and a stack of presents. Bloody birthdays.

'Her name was Agnes Ceci,' said Mina. 'Twenty-one years old. Shared

93

a flat with a friend in town, her dad lived in Arvika, her mum was dead. The case was written off as a suicide.'

Vincent looked at the next picture. He jumped. A naked body on a stainless steel table. The picture had been cut so that the head wasn't included.

'It's her. Look at the thigh.'

Vincent could see the neat cuts very clearly. He didn't want to look at the photo any longer than was necessary.

'As you can see, she's also been marked with a number. But since the body in the box was marked with a three, I thought a previous victim would be marked with the number two. The murderer keeping count, as it were. But as you can see, Agnes is marked with the Roman numeral for four. As if he's already killed four times.'

Vincent stopped in his tracks.

'You said she was an earlier victim?' he said. 'You're telling me she died before the woman with the swords?'

'One month before, in January,' Mina said, hugging herself against the chill in the air. Her red coat didn't seem to keep out the cold – it was pervasive despite the sunshine. Vincent thought for a moment. A four and a three. Numbers in order. Numbers counting down. It was a slim statistical basis to work on thus far – the more numbers, the greater the range and probability. But his gut told him he was right.

'Are you cold?' he asked politely, handing the photos back.

'No. I love the cold,' she replied firmly.

He could tell she meant it.

'I may be wrong,' he said. 'But I don't think you're going to find bodies marked with a one and two. Not yet.'

Mina looked at him but said nothing.

'I think it's a countdown,' he clarified. 'Murders one and two haven't happened yet. Do you understand? Four, three, two, one – and maybe one more with a zero.'

'Why do you think that?' said Mina, staring at him in horror. 'You're saying there could be up to three more murders?'

'If we don't stop the murderer,' he said, starting to walk again. 'I can't find any other reason for a reverse numerical order except that it's a countdown. I can't see any patterns or combinations that it fits better. But there's another and equally important question you need to ask yourselves.'

'You mean we. And what question is that?'

'What is it a countdown *to*? What happens when it reaches zero?'

Mina was quiet for a while.

'It's completely sick.'

Vincent nodded.

'I'm not certain, just to be clear. With only two victims to go on, this is only a guess at the moment.'

'By the way, she also had a watch which had been smashed, and it was on exactly two o'clock,' said Mina.

He grunted in reply and they continued in silence. He wanted to suggest they go and warm up in one of the cafes along Norr Mälarstrand, but Mina seemed happy with the park despite the chill. Vincent rubbed his gloved hands together and tried to get his thoughts in order.

'I do like it when it's cold,' said Mina. 'It feels so . . . clean. As if nothing nasty can survive.'

'Except that you've got a murderer on the loose,' he said. 'That's pretty nasty. How did the new one die? Or rather, the previous one. The girl on the bench?'

'Shot in the face,' said Mina, and Vincent automatically grimaced. 'Don't worry, I didn't bring any more photos. But I don't get why the murderer wants to say what time the murders took place. The smashed watches, I mean. They weren't at the same time but exactly one hour apart.'

Before Vincent could reply, a frisbee came sailing through the air barely a metre in front of them, with a black Doberman in hot pursuit. It leapt up and caught the frisbee between its teeth and landed right at Mina's and Vincent's feet. The dog looked up at them happily. Then it ran off in the direction it had come from.

'I don't like dogs,' said Mina.

Vincent watched it as it disappeared with its prey clamped between its teeth.

'Bullet catch,' he said.

'What?'

'The girl who was shot. It's another classic magical illusion, same as the sword box. Well, it's actually more a trick than an illusion. It's been around for a very long time, probably since the end of the sixteenth century. The first detailed account is found in a book published in 1631 by the Reverend Thomas Beard. Someone in the audience marks a bullet. The bullet is placed in a pistol and fired at the magician or his assistant. They start as if in surprise, then show that they've caught the bullet with their teeth. Or in their hand in the earlier versions.'

'How is that a magic trick? It sounds dreadful.'

'Because everyone knows that it's impossible to catch a bullet with your teeth, and that no one in their right mind would actually fire a loaded pistol at the artiste. So the question is: if we know it's not real, how does it work? The answer is that it's magic. It's a fairly politically incorrect trick to perform these days. And it can be lethal – there have been twelve deaths documented. The earliest of them was the first magician known for performing the trick – Coullew of Lorraine. He died in 1613. The member of the audience who fired the pistol got angry and beat him to death. Ironically enough, he did so with the very pistol that had been used in the trick.'

Mina kicked out at a small snowdrift.

'Is all magic based on pretending to kill someone?' she said.

'Quite a lot of it, actually.'

He cleared his throat.

'The classic stage illusions are basically all about killing or maiming a woman. For example, by sawing her into pieces, moving body parts around, driving swords through her – before eventually demonstrating that she is unharmed. The fact that it's almost always a woman is no coincidence; apparently women are slimmer and more agile than men, which makes it easier for them to fit into the boxes. Or so I'm told.'

'Women are often the victims in reality too,' Mina muttered grimly.

She bent down and gathered up some wet snow in her gloves before starting to shape it into a ball.

'I think it's mainly grounded in mysticism,' said Vincent, stopping again. 'A woman can give life. That means it's more tragic when a woman is the victim in a story. In purely symbolic terms, it's not just her being killed, it's the continuation of humankind that she represents. I believe that somewhere in our subconscious we recognize that. Men are more . . . replaceable. And when it comes to victims in reality, well . . . one way to deal with what you can't have for yourself is to break it.'

'Although pretending to kill someone doesn't sound like magic in the way I think of it,' she said. 'Setting aside the chauvinism for a minute, if I stick a sword through someone and then immediately reveal that my "victim" isn't injured, then all I've done is prove that the sword was fake. Surely no one's impressed by that?'

She stood up with a perfectly round snowball in her hand. Of course she hadn't done it in half measures.

'Once again, you're missing the symbolic element,' said Vincent, backing away cautiously with an eye on the snowball. 'If I saw someone in half, then I'm killing that person, right? If I then show that person to be alive and unharmed once again, I have resurrected her from the dead. That's the magic the classic illusions lay claim to – no matter how silly we may find them today. The power over life and death. And with a female assistant, that's also power over the divine.'

He discreetly checked the time. Mina's lunch hour had ended some time ago. He hoped she didn't realize that. They continued walking and before long reached the shrubs down by the water. The boats that were usually tied up by the jetties hadn't yet been brought out for the season and the water was glittering in the sunlight. Vincent brushed his hand over the leaves of the bushes. Drops of melted snow clung to his gloves.

'So we're looking for someone with a God complex?' said Mina. 'Someone who took their magic too far and ended up killing them for real? Is that your professional view on the person we're looking for? Someone who is power hungry and wants to play God?'

'Not at all. The two victims you've found aren't illusions gone wrong. They lack the final step – resurrection – on purpose. I believe we're looking for a complete madman. But at the same time not.'

Mina looked at him with a furrowed brow.

'I touched on this before. This is someone whose personality, on the one hand, allows him to be sufficiently rational to build boxes, plan kidnaps and leave cryptic messages,' he said. 'While on the other hand, he is sufficiently unbalanced to act with violent impulsiveness. Neither of the murders appears to have been carried out with surgical precision. The preparations, yes. But not the deeds themselves.'

'Although the murder in the box must have been carried out with a degree of precision?'

'Yes, absolutely. But it gives the impression of someone who is thorough rather than skilled. And I sense that there are strong emotions at play here rather than cool distancing, and— Sorry, I've got to ask. What's the snowball for?'

'In case the dog comes back,' she said, weighing up the ball in her hand.

Vincent tried to seem unaffected. However, Mina's words had brought unwelcome thoughts to life. Thoughts about magic and death. Sweaty palms.

Hoping she wouldn't notice what he was doing, Vincent put his glove against his cheek and squeezed the ice-cold drops from the bushes against his skin in an effort to clear his mind.

'The only thing we can do right now is to try and prevent the next two or three murders,' he said. 'Regardless of what your colleagues think of me. I don't like the fact that the murderer is telling us they will strike again through that countdown. If that is what it is. But we've got nothing else to go on. Now you've got me emotionally involved in this. Given that there was only a month's gap between the two you've found, I don't think we've got very long. And . . .'

He hesitated.

'I'd like to see where the box was found,' he said.

'The crime scene has already been examined by forensics. The cordon has been removed. It's highly doubtful there will be anything left that hasn't been documented.'

'I'd still like to see it. I haven't compiled a profile like this before, but I believe in the concept of walking in the killer's footsteps. Trying to get a feeling not only for how or why he acted, but also where. Have you been to the scene?'

'No, Peder was the one who got the call when they found the body. But . . . but I assume I can ask him to take us there. I expect that would be fine. He's a bit like a Labrador – loves everyone. Including mentalists.'

'Thanks,' he said.

The young woman in the quilted jacket was suddenly back. She was standing a short distance away behind Mina, still too far away for him to see who it was. This time she waved at him. He pretended not to see. It might be impolite, but he wanted to focus on Mina.

'I've got you emotionally involved, you say?' she smiled before quickly lobbing the wet snowball at him. 'Good.'

It struck his arm with a wet sound and fell to the ground.

'I think so too,' he said. 'Well, I mean . . . the investigation is . . .'

The words died away in his mouth as he looked her in the eyes. He knew nothing about Mina's personal life. He'd only met her a handful of times. And yet, her presence already felt so natural. So simple. Even when they weren't together it was there, in the background, in the same straightforward way that he breathed in oxygen or that blood circulated through his body without him thinking about it. That wasn't how he usually related to new people. On the contrary, it could take years for him to let people in – and she seemed to be the same. But it really was different with Mina. He was already so comfortable with her.

Mina was . . .

Blood circulating in his body.

How could he not have thought of that? That was the difference between him and a real cop.

'By the way, the girl who was labelled a suicide . . .' he said.

'Agnes. Agnes Ceci.'

'Yes, Agnes. Were there traces of any substances in her body?'

Mina stared at him.

'Something has been bothering me about the file on Agnes's investigation. Now I know what it is,' she said.

22

It was fine weather today. The sun was shining and the snow had begun to melt. He loved fine weather. Granted, he loved rain too. And that clean smell in the air after it had rained. Like when Mum and Dad had washed the bedclothes. He liked freshly washed bedclothes. He liked Mum and Dad. He liked liking, because when you liked things it gave you that happy feeling in your tummy that he liked having.

Sometimes he had tummy aches. He didn't like that. It didn't happen often. But when it hurt, it always hurt very, very much. Mum and Dad said it was because he'd chewed on the wrong things. And he knew from experience that they were right, but he liked chewing on things. Feeling new tastes and sensations in his mouth, feeling them with his tongue, letting them roll around in his mouth – new things he hadn't tried before. He just couldn't help himself. He loved it nearly as much as using his slingshot. But only nearly.

'Hi, Billy!' he shouted cheerily.

He bent down and greeted the small cocker spaniel that he encountered almost daily when he was out and about. The dog jumped up eagerly and wanted to lick his face. It was allowed to. It was so cute. After scratching Billy behind the ears for a bit, he thanked the dog's master – as he always did – and carried on towards the edge of the forest. Saying thank you was important. Mum frequently said so, but that was a good thing because he often forgot.

Once he reached the edge of the forest, he felt behind the big tree stump with his hand. His plastic bottles were still there. Sometimes they would be gone. That meant someone had stolen them. He didn't like it when people stole his plastic bottles, but he wasn't allowed to take them to his room, so he had no choice other than to hide them here.

He carefully and methodically lined them up on the stump. Three in a row. At exact distances. Then he stepped backwards until he found the spot he had marked. Fifty paces away. The spot had got muddy. It was a good thing he'd worn his boots. It was important to train from exactly the same place and over the exact same distance. How else would he know whether he was improving?

The stones he used as ammunition were carefully selected. He could spend hours lying on the gravel path outside the house searching for the right kind of stones. He would put some of them in his mouth too. He loved to suck them – the feeling of the rough stone against his tongue. The stones that he selected now were the best he had. His favourites. He weighed them up. He picked one – it had a little glitter in it that flashed in the sun.

He pulled the slingshot from his back pocket. It was well-used, and the wood was the worse for wear, but that was how he wanted it. It had been shaped for his hand. It was as if they became one – he and the slingshot – as soon as he wrapped his hand around it. He carefully placed the stone in the sling. He closed one eye, took aim . . . and fired the stone. It hit the bottle dead on, so that it tipped elegantly backwards.

'Bravo! Nicely done!'

He jumped. He hadn't seen anyone coming. But he was happy to have an audience. It was more fun taking shots when someone was watching.

'Watch this then!' he said, stretching happily as he inserted the next stone into the sling. 'This time I'm going to aim at the cap!'

He once again closed one eye and took aim. Fired. The stone hit the bright green cap, making the bottle fall straight backwards.

'Wow! You're really good!'

He received applause. He loved applause. It made his whole body tingle. He pulled out a third stone. He hurried to take aim and fire. He wanted to make the most of it while someone was willing to watch him – he'd soon have to practise alone again. No one ever stayed long. The third bottle fell backwards just as neatly as the first two.

'Wow, you deserve some kind of prize! You must be world champion at this! Come with me! My car's right over here. I think I've got a prize to give you!'

His whole body was warm with joy. He loved prizes. But he'd never won one in his entire life. He would have liked to. But no one gave prizes to people like him.

He happily followed. The car was big. Good. Perhaps it was a big

101

prize then. As big as those giant cuddly toys that he never won at Gröna Lund. Imagine if it were that big!

'Go inside, right to the back. You'll see the prize there. You'll know it when you see it.'

His heart was pounding hard as he got into the car. Finally. A prize. A really, really, great big prize.

23

Milda Hjort felt anxiety tearing at her breast. She had picked up the phone several times to make the call, but had instead ended up sitting behind her desk, phone in hand. More than twenty-five years in the profession. And she reckoned she was pretty certain she had made very few mistakes. She was thorough. She took her work seriously. She felt a responsibility to both the victims and their families to make sure that they got the answers they deserved. She also had a responsibility to provide the police and justice system with the tools they needed so they could punish those responsible for the actions whose consequences she had to deal with.

But things had been topsy-turvy for a while. Not at work. It was at home that life had been shaken up. She hadn't thought she'd let it affect her work. Yet now she had evidence in black and white that the chaos at home had leaked into her professional life. She'd made a mistake. A big mistake.

Milda reached for the photo standing on the desk. It was one of the few personal belongings she had in her office. She believed in tidiness and orderliness. At home, she had fully accepted the Marie Kondo approach and had got rid of everything that wasn't necessary or that didn't 'spark joy when she held it'. After the divorce, she had basically looked after the kids single-handed for more than fifteen years, so her ex-husband could hardly object to the strict order in place.

The picture had been taken a few years earlier, on a beach in Falkenberg. Vera and Conrad were happy, tanned, with hair that was slightly too long, and covered in the freckles that they acquired every summer. When the kids had been little, she had come up with names for the freckles. New names every day. The kids had loved it. Obviously it hadn't always been a walk in the park being their main carer while at the same time dedicating so much energy and passion to her job.

Their father did the best that he could. Based on what he thought was appropriate. But she would have preferred that he didn't bother. It was very clear where Conrad's complexes came from. She intended to do everything in her power to ensure that he didn't end up like his father, who hadn't worked since he'd been the entertainment in that seedy Swedish bar in Las Playas on Gran Canaria.

But somehow, she'd pulled it off. At least she thought so. They'd had it good – she and the kids. They'd got what they needed.

With the benefit of hindsight, maybe she'd still not been good enough. Or maybe it was just chance. The gene lottery. It hadn't been easy. And it had taken time. Stolen focus. She'd gone without sleep many nights, instead heading out to search for Conrad. When she'd then gone to work with the baggage of all those night-time worries and a lack of sleep, she had lacked that sharp perspective on her work that she had always been so proud of.

There were no excuses. The mistake was hers.

Hers alone.

She picked up the phone again to dial, but was interrupted by a knock on the door. She cleared her throat.

'Come in.'

The door opened and Mina was standing in the doorway. In her hand she had the files for both the victims. Milda had seen the worn-out paper covers too often not to be able to recognize them immediately. She nodded and put down the phone. At least she wouldn't have to make that call.

24

Peder was thinking over the conversation he'd just had. Mina had asked him to do her 'an enormous favour' and give Vincent Walder a tour of the crime scene.

Ordinarily, he would have been hesitant; it came as a surprise to him that Vincent was still on board as a consultant. But Mina was good. He liked her. What was more, her request meant he had an excuse to leave the house for longer today. Of course, that was disloyal towards his wife, who would have to take care of the triplets by herself. But his baby-fuddled brain was doing pirouettes of joy.

'I'm off to work,' he said, kissing his wife on the cheek. 'Call me if you need anything.'

She looked as tired as he felt. Neither of them had slept more than an hour at a time since the triplets had been born. They'd arrived the day before Christmas Eve. He didn't dare contemplate the present chaos at future Christmases. Molly was whimpering in Anette's arms, and he saw before Anette did that the teat of the bottle had come out of her mouth. He carefully guided the bottle back into his daughter's mouth again, and she hungrily began to suck on it.

'Those two are asleep at least. Hope they stay that way for a while.'

He looked tenderly at Meja and Majken each lying in a pram insert on the floor.

'No wonder they're asleep now, given they were up all night,' said Anette irritably.

Peder caressed her cheek.

'Hey, we're doing this together. We'll survive. It'll whizz by and we'll be able to look back at this time and laugh.'

'Whizz. Nope, didn't work. I'm not laughing.'

'Grit your teeth for a couple of hours and I'll be home as soon as I can to relieve you. And your mother's coming next week to help out. Another pair of hands will work miracles.'

'I never thought I'd look forward to my mother coming. But I don't think I've ever longed for something so hard in my life.'

'One day when we're not so tired, we'll appreciate how lucky we are. In the meantime, I'd best get going. Give me a bell if anything comes up.'

Without waiting for an answer, Peder hurried out to the car. Terrified of falling asleep at the wheel, he opened the bottle of Nocco he'd got out of the fridge. He was probably their single biggest customer right now. Energy drinks were the only thing that kept him going, albeit for brief spells. He only wished they could squeeze double the amount of caffeine into the cans; 180 milligrams didn't go far in a parent to triplets.

On the radio, they were appealing for help finding Robert, the missing kid his colleagues in CID had been out searching for. Apparently he had learning difficulties. Probably not a crime, Peder told himself. With luck, young Bobby had just wandered off into the woods or into town, and got himself lost. Before joining Julia's team, he had once spent several days combing the countryside for a five-year-old who it transpired had got on the train to Copenhagen to pay a visit to Granny. No one had stopped him. He'd even got a lift from the station to his grandmother's with the Danish police. The old lady had in turn called the Swedish police as soon as the boy turned up at her door. Hopefully this missing child case would have a happy outcome too, but in the meantime Peder switched to Lugna Favoriter, a radio station that played nothing but chilled, calming music. Since becoming a father, he'd grown far more sensitive about news involving youngsters.

When he pulled into the car park opposite Gröna Lund, Mina and Vincent were already standing there waiting. In spite of himself, he was curious about Vincent Walder. He and Anette had gone to one of the master mentalist's shows three years ago. It had been impressive and frustrating, and he still didn't understand how the guy had been able to do what he had done.

Vincent's black coat was fluttering in the wind. Classic was the word that spontaneously sprang to mind when he saw Vincent. Like he'd stepped out of a black-and-white movie. He'd had that thought back at police headquarters – and also that he wouldn't mind looking like that himself. Some hope, with three loud babies at home.

25

Peder parked and hurried towards them. Vincent saw him shudder when the strong wind hit him right in the face.

'Hi, Vincent,' he said, reaching out to shake his hand.

Vincent held on for a moment to gauge the handshake. Surprisingly powerful, given how tired Peder otherwise appeared to be.

'You look . . . steamrollered,' said Mina, and Peder nodded in agreement.

'Last night they were awake in shifts,' he said.

Vincent couldn't help but be wide-eyed. Dear God. His own three kids had been hard work, and that was with a ten-year gap between the eldest and youngest. It was impossible to imagine what three at once must be like. He doubted he'd be on his feet.

'I'm impressed that you're even here,' he said. 'Sleep is a fascinating topic. For example, did you know that it was only very recently that we found out what it is that makes us fall asleep?'

'No . . . no, I didn't know that.'

Peder began to walk towards the main entrance to Gröna Lund. Mina and Vincent followed.

'Two research teams have identified what they call the sleep button,' Vincent continued. 'They named it Nemuri, after the Japanese word for sleep.'

'Oh right, I—'

'They studied twelve thousand fruit flies and examined their sleep patterns, and discovered a gene that controls this sleep button.'

'Fruit flies, you say . . .' Peder mumbled, pointing towards the entrance.

He didn't seem entirely receptive, which struck Vincent as odd. Peder of all people ought to have sleep at the forefront of his mind right now. No doubt fatigue was making it difficult for him to process information.

'Vincent,' said Mina in a low voice behind him. 'Consider this a Wikipedia warning.'

He nodded and fell silent.

The theme park felt weirdly abandoned now that it was closed for the season. There were no screams from the free-fall tower. No music from the main stage. No creaking from the rides nor the hubbub of thousands of people.

'The box was here.'

Peder indicated a point in front of the main gate. He'd even brought along the photos taken by the crime scene investigators, which he handed to Vincent, who examined them in silence.

'Did you find . . . did forensics find any leads?' he asked. 'Anything that might be related to the murder?'

'Not as yet,' said Peder, rubbing some grit out of his eye. 'Obviously they took loads of samples, but it can take a while for the results to come through. In a location like this it's very difficult to know what might be connected to the box and what was already here when it arrived.'

'Of course,' Vincent said pensively, walking around with his eyes fixed on the ground. 'You know that if you sleep badly for long periods it can have serious side-effects. The risk of various diseases increases, your memory deteriorates and your immune system is weakened.'

'Yes,' said Peder with a cough. 'I . . .'

'It also increases the risk of Alzheimer's, alcoholism and obesity. Without enough sleep, we risk overwhelming the brain – sleep helps us to forget things that are unnecessary.'

'Yes, I can't help but notice that I'm not firing on all cylinders right now,' Peder said. 'And that seems to apply to more than just me.'

He had added the last bit quietly while throwing a look at Mina, but Vincent heard him. So much for trying to share a little useful information. He always found it a struggle to calibrate what was the 'right' level; presumably he'd got it wrong and said one or two things too many.

He crouched and examined the ground where the box had been. A small piece of police tape that had been left behind was fluttering in the wind as if it wanted to blow away. Mina was standing next to him, watching with her arms crossed, her teeth chattering slightly. The cold made her pale, except for her lips, which remained red. He knew that she didn't wear make-up, but it felt like they were very red. Not that he knew what her lips felt like . . . He cleared his throat and concentrated on the ground.

'In the old days, people often sat up to sleep rather than lying down,' he said, still crouching.

He brushed a gloved hand over the cobbles. When the box was found, there had been snow there. Anything that hadn't been swept up by forensics in their pursuit of meaningful evidence had probably disappeared along with winter. This was giving him less than he'd hoped for. He would have to rely on his brain subconsciously picking up something that he hadn't registered.

'That's why you often find beds in museums that are so very short. Doctors in the seventeenth century thought it was harmful to sleep lying down – they claimed that food could move from the stomach up the trachea and into the head. Jesus Christ, it's windy today.'

He stood up and his knees creaked loudly.

'But what you're experiencing now is an extreme version of what is known as biphasic sleep. Sleep that's divided. It used to be common to go to bed at eight, get up at midnight, be awake for two hours, then go back to bed for another few hours' sleep.'

He looked at Peder meaningfully – the man looked like the human embodiment of a question mark.

'Too little sleep is driving you crazy and making you fat,' Mina translated.

'Oh, right. Thanks for telling me. I'll be sure to let my wife know,' Peder laughed.

'Any idea how long it took for the box to be found?' said Vincent, looking at the ground again.

'We think it was placed here in the night and found early the next morning. Passengers from the commuter ferry from Södermalm pass right by here.'

'That must have been the intention,' he said. 'For her to be found quickly. I assume she wasn't murdered here?'

'That's right – we would have found more blood if it had happened here,' Peder said. 'The pathologist was certain that the box was moved here after she was dead.'

The choice of location was as spectacular as the box itself. An open spot with passers-by. The murderer wanted it to be visible. And for the body to be found immediately. The question was why.

'This person doesn't leave things to chance,' Vincent said, turning to

Mina. 'Every move is calculated. Yet he takes the risk of transporting the box here. We need to understand why.'

The spring storm felt like it was blowing straight through him. Mina looked as if she was even colder. He would more than happily have offered her his coat, but he knew she wouldn't accept it unless it was sandblasted and dipped in caustic soda first. Better to get her into the warm instead. They were done here.

'I've seen what there is to see,' he said. 'Thanks, Peder.'

It looked as if Peder was suddenly hit by the full force of his exhaustion. He swayed.

'Have a nap in the car before you go home,' Vincent said, putting a hand on Peder's shoulder. 'You don't want to risk an accident. Both your cognitive abilities and your reactions can be reduced by up to eighty per cent by fatigue.'

Peder shook his head. 'I need to get back . . .'

'Sleep for an hour. You've got kids to get home to. They don't need to grow up without their father. The statistics for accidents where the driver has fallen asleep at the wheel are—'

Peder held up a hand to ward him off.

'You've convinced me. An hour's nap it is. Thanks.'

'No – thank you,' said Vincent cheerfully.

'Just don't tell my wife.'

Peder bent into the wind and made his way unsteadily back towards his car.

26

Mina and Vincent walked towards her car. She unlocked it but at the very moment she heard the shrill beep from the locking system she had an idea and turned to Vincent.

'Are you in a rush?' she said. 'Or have we got time for a coffee?'

She held her breath. Maybe it was a stupid suggestion. But she didn't want to part yet. She thought she caught a happy glint in Vincent's eye but it might have been the morning sun reflecting off a shiny surface. The sun made his hair even paler, almost white, and she found herself wondering whether he dyed it or whether it was that light naturally. Regardless of which was true, she liked it.

'Sure. I expect Hasselbacken is open.'

He nodded towards the beautiful building sitting in state a little further up the hill above the car park. Mina nodded, locked the car with another shrill beep and put the car key in her coat pocket.

'Don't you ever carry a handbag?' said Vincent.

'Is that strange?' she said, realizing as she asked that it probably was unusual for a woman.

They began to walk towards the hotel.

'I find handbags unhygienic,' she continued, shrugging her shoulders. 'You gather all sorts of stuff in them, which then stays there for ages and gathers bacteria.'

'Don't pockets do that too?' said Vincent.

Mina shuddered.

'Shush,' she said, hurriedly removing her hands from her pockets. 'Don't give me any new ideas. I've quite enough of them as it is.'

He laughed.

She liked that she could talk so easily about the thing that controlled her life. It felt as if he understood. Of course, she couldn't talk about it properly – she could only brush past it in a joking tone that implied it wasn't so bad. As if she was a little eccentric but actually in full control. Nevertheless, she was able to brush closer to it with him than with anyone else.

Vincent had been right. The hotel was open. They sat down in a corner of the lobby and ordered a cup of filter coffee each. Mina noted that Vincent was observing her closely when the cups arrived. And that he noticed the quick, discreet wipe around the rim with the napkin – the one she had perfected down to a tee. It had taken her colleagues at police headquarters far longer to notice it, but with Vincent there was nothing that escaped his attention. She automatically steeled herself for the jibes she usually got at work.

Vincent picked up a napkin and wiped his cup the same way.

'You never know where these things have been,' he said in an apologetic tone, blowing on the hot coffee.

She searched his eyes for something indicating that he thought she was mad, but found nothing. Instead he was looking at her with an innocent expression. She took a few sips of her own coffee. It warmed her pleasantly after being out in the wild spring weather. Vincent made her feel like she belonged. Or, if she was an outsider, then he was an outsider with her. It was . . . an unusual feeling. But a good one, nonetheless.

'Did you get anything out of this visit?' she asked.

'Yes and no. As you say, there's no evidence left – too many people pass by there each day. But yes, it gave me a feeling of what kind of murderer we're dealing with. Above all, there were two things that struck me. The audacity of placing the body in such an open location. And the fact that no one noticed anything out of the ordinary, which makes me think the person we're looking for is someone who blends in.'

'Mmm,' Mina said thoughtfully.

'How familiar are you with the history of Gröna Lund?' Vincent asked, sipping his coffee.

'Not at all,' she said, shaking her head at the waitress who was approaching their table.

'It's Sweden's oldest amusement park,' said Vincent. 'Opened in 1883. But in 1924 it faced competition when a travelling fair called Nöjet set up shop right across the street.'

'I do remember hearing about that. Wasn't there some sort of love story mixed up in it all?'

'That's right. The son of the family that owned Nöjet and the daughter of the family that owned Gröna Lund fell in love. They married and ran Nöjet together, and later on Gröna Lund. Their daughter, Nadia, was the park director at Gröna Lund until 2001.'

'Romantic,' said Mina, but she could hear how false she sounded.

She hadn't meant to sound ironic. Romance wasn't her thing. It disturbed order. Anyway, it was always messy – sooner or later.

'What I find most interesting are the human attractions of the 1920s,' Vincent said, looking out of the window towards the silhouette of the theme park.

'Human attractions? As in a freak show?'

She frowned. The thought of displaying people for a fee simply because they were different made her angry. What would they have called her? *Mina – the bacteria-free woman! See how she washes! Smell the scent of her hand sanitizer!*

'At Gröna Lund, you could see an African tribe,' said Vincent, turning to face her. 'And a group of German dwarves in the Lilliput village. And there was a striptease.'

'Oh, how family friendly!' she said sharply.

His eyes narrowed as he looked at her.

'People find the things they aren't used to strange,' he said, carefully setting down his coffee cup on the table. 'People believe their own norms apply to everyone else, and are worried by anything that doesn't adhere to their rules. Standing out from the crowd can attract admiration but also pointing fingers. Sometimes both at once. People pay to look at me too, you realize. Surely you don't believe that I'm in anyway considered normal? That I'm the kind of guy you invite to a casual drinks party? We're unique, Mina, and we pay a price for that. But always remember one thing – the only power others have over your life is what you give them. Let them look if they want. Why not let them pay for the pleasure if they're willing? And let them talk. It's nothing to do with you.'

She looked back at the amusement park at the bottom of the hill to avoid meeting his gaze. She blinked several times. He made it sound so easy. But it wasn't easy. It was hard. She considered telling him about the AA meetings, but they didn't know each other well enough for that. They were *never* going to know each other that well.

'Geniuses like us are always misunderstood,' Vincent added with a wry smile.

'I appreciate you being so humble,' she said, smiling back. 'By the way, this genius spoke to Milda Hjort earlier today.'

'Milda who?' said Vincent, looking confused.

'The pathologist. The one who performed the autopsy on Agnes Ceci. She was the one who got in touch with me about the marks on the body. Do you remember asking me about substances in the body?'

'I can tell there's a "but" coming here,' said Vincent, leaning in.

'She missed something,' she said, also leaning forward. 'She didn't run a tox screen on the victim. Didn't take any samples. Didn't request any tests. Even though it's routine.'

'Oh dear,' said Vincent.

Mina nodded. Milda's despair had been palpable. She was going to be investigated. And there might be consequences.

'The human factor,' Mina said. 'She's . . . she's had a tough time.'

Vincent drummed his fingers on the table. The same rhythm over and over. Mina noticed that he had begun to move his foot in time with his drumming. She forced herself to keep still. She waited while he processed this information.

'So what happens now?' he said slowly, stopping his drumming.

'Milda has contacted the prosecutor and I've notified Julia. We'll request an exhumation as soon as possible, and given the circumstances I should think we'll get a decision immediately. We may even be able to get it today if we're lucky. Bodies decompose rapidly. The longer the delay before samples are taken, the greater the risk that evidence will be lost. All we can do in the meantime is focus on the practicalities. Excavators. Personnel to do the digging. Clergy. CSIs. The problem is that we may have to wait weeks for everyone to be free.'

Vincent stood up and got out his phone.

'I think I can help you on two of those points,' he said. 'If you speak to the church where she's buried and deal with the forensics staff, I'll see what we can do about diggers and equipment.'

'It doesn't work like that. Services have to go out to tender. It takes time.'

'For you, maybe. But I don't work for the police. Just pretend you don't know who I'm calling. Aren't you in the middle of trying to apply for some permit or other?'

The tables in the lobby had filled up with people while they'd been talking, so he headed towards the reception area to make his call undisturbed.

'I would never have guessed your networks included digger operators,' she shouted to his back in amusement.

114

'There's a lot you don't know about me,' he called back, half turned away.

It was true. Vincent was still an uncracked nut. A wrapped gift, she managed to think before stopping herself. But he made her happy. It had been a long time since anything or anyone had done that. She rolled her head and then her shoulders and realized that they weren't tense. She was often so tense during the day that she had a migraine when she went to bed at night – but now, for the first time in ages, her entire body was relaxed. She let out a contented sigh and drank a little more coffee while waiting for Vincent to return.

When the waitress walked by with the coffee pot offering refills she said yes. She carefully wiped the rim of the cup with a new napkin before raising it to her mouth. This time she made no attempt to conceal it. She could hear Vincent's voice from reception, but was unable to make out the words. She smiled. And persuaded herself that the warmth in her stomach was from the coffee.

27

They hesitated outside the entrance to the police station. Gunnar tenderly took Märta by the arm. He could feel her trembling through her brown woollen coat, which was really far too warm for the time of year. The spring weather meant business. Neither of them had attached any importance to what they had put on. The only thing they could think about was the gnawing anxiety, the feeling that something was wrong.

'We might as well get it over with,' he said softly.

Märta was still hesitating, but he gently pulled her through the entrance. He knew how her mind worked. After sixty years of marriage, he knew her innermost thoughts and now he knew that she was fighting the instinct to stick her head in the sand – for as long as they didn't know anything had happened, nothing had happened. But Gunnar knew better. They had been monitoring their phones, had called around, searched, scoured their memories for friends they didn't really know, people she might have mentioned in passing. Some name they hadn't perceived as important at the time, but which they now wished they'd committed to memory. Someone in the organization. No one knew anything. It was as if the earth had swallowed her up. And there were only a few days left until Easter – which they always celebrated together.

Gunnar had been a priest for more than forty years, but in his old age he had practically ceased speaking to God. Not that he no longer believed – his faith was stronger than in his youth, when he'd been an enthusiastic newly ordained priest. No, it was more that he had begun to take Him for granted, assuming that He was there by his side, following his footsteps, watching over him, without Gunnar needing to do anything in return. Perhaps it was his arrogance that was now being punished. He didn't know. All he knew was that he hadn't stopped praying since the boat had come back without her. Even then he'd known that she had somehow been lost to them.

'Excuse me,' he said, stepping diffidently up to the window.

A young woman with kind eyes was sitting behind the glass. Ordinarily, her smile would have warmed his heart – other people's happiness sustained him and he had always tried to spread as much hope and joy around him as he had been able to, in both his professional and private life. But today there was no space in his breast for any joy. Or any hope. He knew that Märta still harboured hopes, and he wished so deeply that she would turn out to be right and he would be wrong. But he had felt the silence strike him when he had cried out his despair, his prayer for assistance. For the first time, God had not answered his prayers. He could no longer feel God's presence, no matter how much he prayed. He felt only emptiness.

'We want to report someone missing,' he said, drawing Märta closer so that she was also within the receptionist's field of vision.

'Who do you want to report missing?' said the woman, her friendly smile replaced by warm sympathy.

She must be used to cases like this, Gunnar thought to himself. What misery didn't she see and hear on a daily basis in her work? Even so, she couldn't understand how deep the pit of their despair was. And what if she didn't take them seriously?

Märta stuck her hand in her handbag and pulled out a photo that she slipped through the slot at the bottom of the window without saying a word. They had picked it together. Gunnar had taken the photo in the park near their terraced house in Upplands Väsby. She was sitting with the boy in her arms on one of those wooden horses that rocked back and forth on a huge spring. She had been so happy that day.

Her eyes shone – both due to the sun and because of what was inside her – what he had always described as God's light. She hadn't been a believer. Not in the way that he and Märta were. Perhaps a childish faith, diluted to no more than a Christmas service and their Easter celebrations together. But she had still liked it when he said it – even when she was little. That she bore God's light within her. He hoped that the woman behind the glass could see it too. That she would understand that no one with light like that, and with a boy like that in her arms, could go missing of her own free will.

'This is our granddaughter and our great grandchild. She was meant to go travelling on a boat for a few weeks but she never came back from the trip. And now we've found out that she never left. That means she went missing a month ago. Linus, that's her son, has been staying with us all along. But he needs his mother.'

'And there's nothing to suggest she may have gone missing of her own volition?' said the woman.

Now she had a deep frown between her eyebrows and a soft expression in her eyes that he thought might be empathy. Thank God. She was taking them seriously.

'We need to speak to someone. In the police,' said Märta in a fragile voice, swaying.

Gunnar instinctively held out his arm and caught her. The relapses had got worse in the last twenty-four hours. Anxiety and MS were uncomfortable bedfellows. He supported his wife while the woman looked at the photo.

'You can speak to one of our officers,' she told him. 'What's your granddaughter's name?'

'Tuva,' said Gunnar. 'Her name is Tuva.'

28

At least they hadn't opted for a security guard who resembled a body-builder. He had to be satisfied with that. For his show to work, the audience needed to relax. More than that, he needed a pliable audience. Comfortable and in a good mood. A muscle mountain with arms folded at the side of the stage would have the opposite effect. But Umberto didn't think they had any choice.

He greeted the guard, whose name was Ola.

'She always comes after I've gone off,' Vincent said. 'So I don't know exactly what happens. But apparently she gets up onto the stage as soon as the curtain falls, to try and find the backstage area and me.'

'What is it she wants?' said Ola.

Vincent shrugged. He stepped onto the stage and inspected the props for the evening's performance.

'I've never met her,' he said. 'The stagehands always catch her when she tries to cross the stage. She hasn't acted threateningly towards them, but that doesn't mean anything. She's extremely focused. Last week we tightened the security. She still managed to get through. I'm mostly worried that she's going to break something. Or hurt herself.'

Vincent adjusted a stack of Rubik's cubes and a few decks of cards with pictures of celebrities on the back.

'Doesn't sound right,' said the guard.

'That's why you're here.'

'But I don't get it,' said Ola, folding his arms. 'I mean, I'm happy to stand here for the rest of the tour and make sure no unauthorized persons get up here during or after the show. That's my job. But if she's so keen to meet you, why doesn't she go to the stage door and wait for you there? Sooner or later, you've got to come out.'

Vincent wished Ola hadn't folded his arms across his chest. Nothing said 'guard' like that did. What was more, there were studies showing that people got worse at taking in information from the outside world, such as what others were saying to them, when they folded their arms. The gesture was so strongly associated with thinking that the brain automatically retreated inwards whenever the arms were folded. And Ola needed to understand.

'Could you hold this for a second?' he said, passing the guard a deck of celebrity cards.

That was all it took to get Ola to unfold his arms.

'I had the same thought,' said Vincent. 'Why doesn't she just go to the performers' entrance? The only reason I can think of is that the action isn't planned. Despite it being repeated. She sees the whole show – tonight it might be the tenth time – and when it ends she has such a strong emotional impulse to get up onto the stage that it takes over completely. She can't help herself. It's completely spontaneous. Suddenly she's convinced that *this time* it might work.'

He looked at Ola gravely.

'The definition of madness is doing exactly the same thing over and over and thinking you'll get different results to last time. I can't see that it's anything other than her having certain mental . . . challenges. What's more, I received this.'

He pulled a crumpled envelope from his jacket pocket.

'A letter?' said Ola in surprise. 'Do people still send those?'

'It's often older people who do it,' Vincent said. 'But not this time.'

He unfolded the first half of the letter so that Ola could read it. While it was passionately written, the hand that had held the pen had been anything but shaky. On the contrary, the handwriting was almost chilly.

I saw you on Nyhetsmorgon, it said. *You were there with Jenny and Steffo. And as ever, your signals to me were clear. I only wish I'd understood them sooner. You're right – you and I belong together.*

'Wow,' said the guard, shaking his head.

'So far, it's just a confused person projecting their needs onto someone they saw on TV,' said Vincent. 'It's a well-known psychological phenomenon. It's not uncommon for people to become convinced that people on TV, even fictional characters in TV series, are their actual friends in real life. And these days, with streaming services making it possible to binge whole series in one go, it's getting more and more common. The brain is simply not built to distinguish between real and made-up relationships. If you also happen to be a bit depressed, a one-way relationship like that can become vital. It may even be perceived as bidirectional, as the letter writer says.'

'Do you think this is from the woman who comes to your shows, then?'

'I don't know. Perhaps. If it had just been this, I wouldn't have been worried. But this is the second letter I've received from the same person. One letter can be sent in a state of temporary confusion. But two letters feels like a plan. You haven't read it all yet. It's what comes next that leaves me struggling to sleep at night.'

He unfolded the bottom half of the letter. Ola's eyes widened.

But since then you haven't been on Nyhetsmorgon *again. It's been too long for it not to be on purpose. At the very moment that I realize we belong together, you turn your back on me. I won't tolerate this.*

'No explanation of what she means with that last bit,' he said. 'Or how serious the threat is. I know I sound like a self-obsessed artiste climbing onto his high horse, and I don't know for sure that it's dangerous. But this is not a person I want to meet. And I can't have anyone going near the props I use onstage when I'm not there.'

Ola handed back the deck of cards.

'Don't worry about sounding OTT,' he said. 'People are weird. And I've done security for Sannex gigs. Talk about crazy fans! Your little stalker is a sweetheart in comparison.'

29

Julia stuck her head into Ruben's office.

'Drop whatever you're doing and come to the meeting room now,' she said, and vanished before he could react.

He looked at the message that he had been deftly crafting.

Sofie, it was great to meet you yesterday. I'm afraid I've just been summoned to report for a secret assignment abroad and will be gone for six months. But I'd love to get in touch when I'm back home again, he'd written thus far. It was important not to be too available to begin with. If they had to work for it, they always came running. It never failed. He just needed to sign off with something sexy. Perhaps something about not being sure he'd survive?

'Ruben!' Julia yelled sternly from the corridor.

He sighed and held down the delete key until the message was gone. Not answering at all was an effective strategy too.

Waiting in the meeting room were Mina, Christer and Julia. Peder was probably napping in a corner somewhere. Julia's cheeks were slightly flushed, as if she had been running. Which in fact she had been. But Ruben still couldn't help fantasizing about other reasons for the pink cheeks. He'd seen her blush before. When she'd been wearing rather fewer clothes and he'd been lying underneath her with his hands on her hips . . . He sat down and flashed a smug smile at Julia, who ignored him completely.

He wondered what the meeting was about and why it was so urgent. After all, there had been a brief catch-up only an hour earlier, in which Mina had informed them about the request to exhume Agnes Ceci's body.

'We've confirmed the identity of the woman in the sword box,' said Julia, standing at the head of the table. 'Her name was Tuva Bengtsson, she was twenty-five years old and lived in Hägersten. Her closest relations were her maternal grandparents and her three-year-old son Linus. Tuva's parents aren't in the picture and haven't been for a long time,' she added, in reply to Christer's quizzical expression. 'We've just had the grandparents here and they were able to confirm that Linus's father, Tuva's ex-boyfriend, is in London and has been for the last three years. Of course, we'll double-check that. We haven't been given any contact details for friends, but she worked at a cafe called Fab Fika in Hornstull. Closest colleague is called Daniel. No last name.'

'I'll go to the cafe right away,' said Mina, before Ruben even had time to open his mouth.

Julia looked doubtful. She leaned on the table with her hands and Ruben couldn't help but notice how good the curve of her behind looked when she leaned forward. He tried to glimpse a trace of the edge of her panties through the denim but could see nothing. She was probably wearing a thong today. It wouldn't surprise him if it was for his benefit.

'Are you sure?' Julia asked Mina. 'You're great at a lot of things, but new contacts are perhaps not your strongest suit? You'll need to speak to people who don't know that Tuva is dead, and you can't tell them that she is, either.'

'What can you possibly mean, Julia?' said Ruben, leaning back with his hands behind his head. 'Mina's always so warm and fluffy. But I'd be happy to go instead. I can get anybody to open up. As you know.'

He looked meaningfully at his boss.

'Ruben, you've just convinced me,' said Julia. 'Mina's going.'

Mina nodded, got to her feet and left the room.

'You two see what else you can find out about Tuva Bengtsson,' said Julia to Christer and Ruben. 'You'll find her social security number and other details in the DurTvå database.'

Ruben made to leave, but Julia stopped him with a hand on his arm. She waited until Christer was in the corridor.

'Ruben,' she said in a low voice. 'I know you think you're God's gift to women, but one more comment like that and "working from home" will take on a completely new meaning – assuming you still have a job. You've been given a lot of chances already. This team might be your last. I don't believe the Swedish Police Authority has any further training courses on equality it can offer you.'

With that she let go of his arm and walked ahead of him into the corridor. He stared at her receding back. Suddenly he had no desire at all to look at her arse. Aggressive women were so damn unsexy.

30

Hornstull lay just across the Västerbron bridge, practically within walking distance of police headquarters. Nonetheless, Mina took the car. She immediately spotted Fab Fika on the right-hand side. The sun was reflecting off the windows, making it impossible to see who was inside. She drove on, away from the cafe and towards Gullmarsplan, where she'd arranged to pick up Vincent. She'd called him as soon as the meeting had ended and asked him to come with her when she went to meet Daniel. It was always a smart move to have an observer in interview situations and she needed someone who would spot things in Daniel's behaviour that she might miss. She couldn't see Ruben filling that role. Besides, work was a lot more fun when Vincent was around.

She pulled over in the square at Gullmarsplan and there he was, wearing his black jacket and black polo neck. Brown shoes. She smiled to herself. He couldn't look more like a mind reader if he tried. Or an undercover cop, she realized. The TV version, that is. She would have to suggest that he change channels. He caught sight of her and grinned.

'So this guy we're going to meet,' he said as he got into the car. 'Is he a suspect?'

'Hello to you too,' she said, with a meaningful look. 'How are you? And are you OK with me driving?'

At first he looked completely thrown. Then he frowned.

'Sorry,' he said. 'Of course I want to know how you are. You just sounded so enthusiastic on the phone. It was infectious. But hello. Hello, Mina.'

'Hello, Vincent.'

She pulled out of the square and drove towards Södermalm. He shifted in his seat, which rustled underneath him.

'Do you have . . . is there plastic on the seat?' he said.

124

'It's so that I can murder people in the car without leaving any stains. Guess why you're sitting there.'

Vincent burst into laughter while she concentrated on the traffic.

'Sorry,' he said. 'So, what do you think we'll find out from Tuva's workmate?'

'I doubt we'll learn much about Tuva. When we question friends and acquaintances, it's surprising how little they know about the life of the victim. Despite being close to them, often they can't even tell us what the victim was like. Their accounts rarely correlate with what we discover when we search the victim's home.'

'What do you look for there?' said Vincent, gripping the edge of his seat as Mina rapidly changed lanes.

'Well, if there's not much in their fridge then it means they often eat out. Which forms both a predictable pattern and an occasion to meet strangers – such as the murderer. And if we look at what's missing from the fridge, we also get an idea of whether it's breakfast or dinner that they eat elsewhere. You have to develop a sense of what's significant. Musical instruments and half-finished paintings might suggest a hobby. Tuva and Agnes might have been members of the same club or taken a course together where they met the murderer. Sex toys are also a good indicator.'

'Sex toys?' Vincent said in surprise.

She shrugged. She'd long ago stopped being surprised by what you found in people's homes. You had to steel yourself before looking under the bed or in the headboard cavities. The worst time had been when they'd found nothing but a toilet roll. That meant you could be sure there were other things hidden elsewhere.

'We know that Tuva was single,' she said. 'We haven't been told that Agnes was in a relationship. If we find sex toys with a domination theme, it could indicate a lifestyle that played out in particular clubs. Places where they may have met each other as well as the murderer.'

Vincent nodded thoughtfully.

'Sherlock Holmes's skills may have been exaggerated,' he said. 'But in 1956 Brunswick formulated a model for the link between the items we choose to have around us in our homes and the way others see us. Since then, Baumeister and Swann have explored the way we communicate with symbols when we decorate, and in 1997 Sam Gosling began to map the link between different personalities and specific objects in people's bedrooms. Fascinating stuff.'

Mina glanced at him quickly.

'And it's at this point that I identify a link that explains why you didn't get much action when you were younger,' she said, pulling on to Ringvägen.

She got stuck behind a Volvo with learner driver plates doing 30 kmh. Typical.

'Regardless of what we find,' said Vincent, 'there's another piece of the jigsaw that indicates they had similar lifestyles. The murders took place at about the same time of day – two and three o'clock. I think this means they also occurred in the same kind of place. Tuva and Agnes might simply have eaten lunch at the same restaurant.'

She nodded. Vincent would make a pretty decent policeman, despite his black attire.

'I've had that thought too,' she said. 'Peder's going to check the takeaway menus that are bound to be in their kitchens. If we're lucky, we might find the same one in both.'

Out of the corner of her eye she saw Vincent opening his bag and taking out the files she'd given to him, unbeknownst to her colleagues. He began to read Milda's autopsy reports.

'I can't quite make it add up,' he mused. 'This profile. It's so contradictory.'

'How are they taking it at home?' she said. 'That you're helping the police in secret, I mean.'

He closed the file and looked at her for a while. She pulled onto Hornsgatan. The Volvo went the other way. Finally. They'd be at Fab Fika in a minute or two.

'To begin with, I'm not helping the police,' he said. 'Your colleagues on the force have been quite clear about that. I'm helping *you*. And I'm happy to. But my family . . . Let me put it like this: Benjamin thinks it's really exciting. Rebecka thinks I'm an embarrassment, regardless of what I do. Aston is uninterested in anything that isn't Lego. And Maria . . . is Maria.'

'Can I take a guess? She won't be inviting me round for a coffee anytime soon.'

Mina began to search for a parking spot. She'd taken a marked police car, so she could stop anywhere she liked. However, an unmarked car would have been better in this situation. She didn't want to unduly frighten Daniel. She found a spot and switched off the engine. Fab Fika was a hundred metres ahead of them.

'That's one way of looking at it,' said Vincent. 'This Daniel guy . . . What's the strategy?'

'I talk. You watch. But be prepared for anything.'

126

31

Daniel squinted out through the windows of the cafe in Hornstull. When the spring sunshine shone straight in, like it was doing now, you could really see how dirty they were. Tuva made it a rule to turn down all window cleaners who came in on spec – she preferred to do it herself. And Daniel had nothing against it, so long as he didn't have to do it. But Tuva hadn't cleaned the windows in ages. She hadn't been able to do anything for a while, since she hadn't been there. He sighed. He'd seen the patrons looking disapprovingly at the dirty windows. It was going to be his job – he knew it. The dirt would only become more visible the more spring sprang outside. He rinsed a well-worn cloth and began to wipe down the crockery that separated him from the customers. He saw his bleached hair reflected in the glass counter and smiled in satisfaction. He liked it that way.

The door opened and a man and a woman came in. He could see right away that they weren't regular customers. He recognized the man from somewhere, but couldn't place him. Definitely not a regular. Maybe off the TV? Online?

The woman came straight up to him while the man lingered in the background.

'Are you Daniel?' she said.

He nodded. She was good looking, in a restrained kind of way. His form-fitting black T-shirt seemed to have no effect on her at all. Instead, she stared at the dish cloth in his hand. She appeared to be struggling to swallow.

'Mina Dabiri. I'm from the police,' she said. 'Are you Tuva's colleague?'

Shit. Fuck. Damn. The police. This could not be good in any way whatsoever. He dropped the rag and reached out to shake her hand, but she stepped back lightning fast, as if she thought she might get burnt. Weird chick. He glanced at the other patrons. Then he gestured for the hot cop to follow him to the far end of the counter and he lowered his voice. The man followed them. Meh.

'Is she in trouble?' he asked as neutrally as he could.

It was vital he didn't say anything wrong. Every word had to have the right impact. Exactly right. His tone couldn't be off either.

The woman exchanged a quick look with the man. They knew something.

'Hi, by the way,' he said, offering his hand to the man. 'Daniel.'

'Vincent,' said the man, shaking his hand.

There was something practised about the way the man did it, as if he was thinking very carefully about how they were greeting each other. Daniel didn't have time to think about it. He needed to find out what they knew. He wouldn't have a chance otherwise.

'Tuva's been reported missing,' said the hot cop. 'I'm speaking to everyone who was – is – close to Tuva. Her grandparents said she worked here and gave us your name. I can't tell you any more than that. What have you heard?'

'Missing,' he said, exhaling while hoping it wasn't visible. 'The only thing is, Gunnar and Märta called here a few days ago. Do you want a coffee?'

The cop shook her head, but the man gratefully accepted an espresso.

'So you know Gunnar and Märta?' said the cop. She looked surprised.

'Sometimes they come here for a coffee with Linus,' Daniel explained. 'When Tuva didn't show up to collect Linus and no one could get hold of her, the nursery called Märta – that's Tuva's grandma – who came and picked him up. Apparently, Tuva was meant to be going to a Greenpeace demo. Märta thought she and Gunnar might have got the wrong day and that it was their turn to pick up Linus. Tuva didn't mention it, but it wouldn't be the first time that had happened. Anyway, they've been here for coffee with Linus every week since then. Meanwhile I've had to look after the cafe all by myself. It's knackering. And my girlfriend's not very happy about it – all the evening work since Tuva went off. Plus it's messed up our Easter travelling plans. But . . . missing? That doesn't sound like Tuva.'

He didn't like the way the man, Vincent, stayed in the background and watched him without saying anything. It felt as if he had a searchlight trained on him, and that nothing could be hidden from its light.

'And you have no idea about what might have happened to her?' the cop asked, clearly not interested in the fact that he'd missed all those nights with Evelyn because he'd had to cover for Tuva.

'She'd never leave Linus like that of her own free will,' he said. 'Presumably you've checked the hospitals?'

The cop hesitated for a split second. That was the opening Daniel needed. He flashed his most charming and innocent smile. He needed her on his side, he needed to know. Things had been close to going south the last time he'd been questioned – really far south. He didn't want the same issue a second time. But the opening he'd identified closed just as quickly.

'So far we've heard nothing,' she said, passing him a business card. 'If you hear anything or think of something, please call me at any time. Don't bother with the switchboard. This is my personal mobile.'

Personal mobile. Was she flirting with him? He smiled wryly to see whether it was reciprocated. She glowered back at him.

'By the way, do you have CCTV? Is there any footage from the time before Tuva went missing?'

Daniel shook his head. CCTV – in this shithole of a cafe? The police-woman looked at him in disappointment for a moment. Then they said farewell and the man opened the door for her and they left. He watched them go through the dirty windows. He waited until they were out of sight. Then he grabbed his jacket and ran out of the door, heading in the opposite direction. The cafe was the least of his worries right now.

'Well?' said Mina once they were back in the car.

She didn't start the engine, turning instead towards Vincent.

'I can tell there was something. Care to share?'

Vincent didn't reply at once, but began to search his bag.

'He's not lying,' he said. 'But that doesn't mean he's telling us every-thing. Did you notice that he never used the word "I" the whole time he was talking about Tuva? It only cropped up once, and that was in a sentence about how he'd been working lots. Removing yourself from the conversation is a distancing technique – it often occurs when some-thing becomes too emotional or you're lying.'

He pulled out the two files again.

'So the question is,' he said, 'why would a conversation about Tuva be so emotionally uncomfortable? What is it Daniel's afraid we're going to discover about him?'

He handed the files to her.

'You remember that both Tuva and Agnes were single,' he added. 'No steady partners. Tuva lived alone with her son Linus, her ex-boyfriend has been out of the picture for three years and her parents

129

have been living abroad too. Agnes shared a flat with a male friend who was questioned a few months ago.'

Mina nodded. She'd been through the files Vincent had handed to her at least a hundred times.

'I didn't say anything back there in case I was wrong,' he said. 'But I wasn't. Mina, can you describe the friend that Agnes lived with to me?'

She didn't have to search far in her memory to recall the description contained in the file.

'Brown hair,' she began. 'Big, ruffled hairstyle, early twenties, thin but athletic build. Briefly came under suspicion when we found out the friend she shared a flat with was a man rather than a woman, but no romantic connection so far as we know. He was the one who found Agnes. And his name was . . .'

Her eyes opened wide when the realization dawned upon her.

Vincent nodded in confirmation.

'Hair can be cut and it can also be bleached,' he said.

'Agnes's flatmate was called Daniel Bargabriel,' she said. 'And we just spoke to him.'

She threw herself out of the car and began to run towards the cafe.

32

Vincent knocked on the door of his eldest son's bedroom.

'Benjamin?'

No answer. He probably had his headphones on. Vincent opened the door unbidden, aware that he was intruding. As expected, Benjamin had his headphones on and was wearing nothing but a dressing gown. When he spotted his father, he took off the headphones and paused the game. A logo with the words *Path of Exile* appeared on the screen. Benjamin gave his father a quizzical look. Words were to be avoided insofar as it was possible.

'Come on,' said Vincent, when he saw the dressing gown.

The role of parent took over, even though Benjamin was nineteen and smart enough to have skipped a year in primary school. He was allowed to control his own life. Almost. There were certain rules in place as long as he was still living at home.

'It's almost half past five in the afternoon,' said Vincent. 'And you're not dressed yet. When exactly did you get up?'

'Don't know,' said Benjamin. 'Two hours ago?'

'You slept until four o'clock?! That's seventeen hours! What about school?'

Benjamin looked at him with the gaze of a son who considers himself to have outgrown his father. Vincent had never been able to use that look – he'd never had a father in that way, but he still knew what it meant.

'I'm at *university*, Dad. And it'd be a waste of time and money to go all the way to Kista when they put all the lectures online. I watched today's lecture ages ago. And memorized it.'

Vincent wanted to ask when Benjamin had last aired his room, given that the smell reminded him of dead animals. But he wanted Benjamin's help and he was already risking being thrown out of the room.

Vincent needed to find a connection between the two murder victims. A pattern they hadn't seen. What he needed from Benjamin that he wasn't able to provide himself was an understanding of young people's patterns of life. While both Tuva and Agnes were a few years older than Benjamin, he guessed that their worlds had been decidedly more akin to Benjamin's than his own.

The numbering of the bodies and the smashed watches made him think there was more to discover. A message hidden in the circumstances around the murders. He was good at that kind of thing, but Benjamin was the expert. It was Benjamin who could read binary code without breaking sweat and who could write the computer programs they might need to figure it all out. He'd already given Benjamin what little information he'd received from Mina and was hoping for the best.

'Did you actually want anything?' said Benjamin, nodding meaningfully at the paused game.

Vincent closed the door behind him. The rest of the family didn't need to hear.

'I want to know how it's going,' he said, moving a thick volume on Java and the rulebooks for *Warhammer 40,000* from a chair and sitting down.

'I haven't exactly got loads to go on,' said Benjamin, who understood him right away. 'Are you sure you don't have any other information you can give me?'

'Afraid not,' said Vincent, shaking his head. 'We've got their names: Tuva Bengtsson and Agnes Ceci. We know what they look like, what they did and where they lived. We know when they died from their smashed watches. We're guessing that's important. But that's it.'

There were clothes strewn across the floor – it was unclear whether they were clean or not – and Vincent had no choice but to put his feet on them.

'And,' he added, 'that they were marked with the Roman numerals for three and four.'

'Or they could just be random cuts.'

Benjamin gathered up the books that Vincent had moved and put them on the bookcase. He was clearly more worried about them than his clothes.

'Absolutely,' said Vincent. 'The police team aren't convinced that they were numbers. But let's assume they aren't a coincidence.'

Benjamin scratched his head. Vincent was still waiting for the day when he might see his son run a comb through that mop of hair.

'It'd be good to know whether they knew the murderer or not,' said Benjamin.

Vincent laughed.

'Yes, that would solve a lot. But at present we have no idea. Well, there is one guy who knew them both.'

'Well then.'

'I thought that too. But I met him at the cafe where he works. I wish he'd given off psychopath vibes, but I didn't get that feeling. He's odd, but I think there's something else behind that. Although, of course, everything is possible when we know so little. There are too many options, too many assumptions still to be made, and all on the basis of too little data.'

'Dad, you're familiar with Occam's razor, right?'

'When several explanations for a phenomenon exist, you should choose the most straightforward.'

'So . . .?'

'He's not the most straightforward explanation. He just looks like it. He's possibly part of the explanation, but not the whole thing. Forget about Occam for now and pretend I didn't say anything about this guy.'

'OK. Let's look at it systematically.'

Benjamin opened a program that was reminiscent of Excel, but the screen displayed photos of the two murdered women. Tuva and Agnes. Benjamin clicked on the faces, which enlarged them until they filled the screen.

'In terms of appearance, they're completely different,' he said. 'So we can drop that idea right away. We need to find something else that unites them. Apart from the incredibly obvious fact that they have a male friend in common, that is. Did you check their movements in the months prior to the murders?'

'You mean the GPS on their phones? I would assume it's standard procedure for the police. That's not the kind of thing Mina needs me for.'

His son gave him a funny look.

'Good. Because even if they weren't in the same place, they may have been to similar places. Which may in turn offer us a clue. And even if they haven't been, it's worth cross-referencing the GPS with that fitness app that's always running these days. They might have worked out. In which case they had predictable patterns of movement.'

'The fitness app?' said Vincent thoughtfully.

He hadn't thought of that. It was a clear demonstration of the differences between the generations – at Benjamin's age it was a given that your mobile phone was tracking everything you did, even when it was in your pocket. Perhaps the police hadn't thought of that. He sent a brief message to Mina. The reply notification pinged in his hand before the phone had returned to his pocket.

'What does she say?'

He hadn't told Benjamin who he was messaging. But he didn't have his feet buried in dirty laundry because his son was dim. He read the message and laughed.

'She says of course they check that kind of thing. "People who go out running are easier than ever to waylay because everyone listens to podcasts these days." Then she writes that it would have helped if they had Tuva's phone. I think this sort of smiling emoji at the end is meant to be sarcastic.'

Benjamin looked at him in surprise.

'Tuva didn't have her phone on her?'

'No. She was found stripped to her underwear.'

His son shook his head. It was quite possible that the thought of losing your mobile was worse than being found undressed and maimed. Aston's voice suddenly penetrated the door.

'*I want three scoops of hot chocolate in it!*' he shouted furiously. '*Not two!*'

Vincent smiled. Someone in the family was going to get his way tonight. He looked back at the two faces staring at him from Benjamin's monitor. Two young women who no longer existed. Women who had been subjected to terrible violence. And here he was, wondering whether they'd gone jogging. It was downright absurd. He shifted his gaze to the shelf where the Warhammer figurines that Benjamin had painted with such care a couple of years earlier were standing. He couldn't bear to look at the unspoken question in the two pairs of eyes on the screen. The door opened and Aston ran into the room with chocolate milk around his whole mouth.

'What are you doing?' he hooted cheerfully. 'Mum and me just had a snack and you missed it.'

'Knock!' Benjamin shouted.

Aston threw himself towards the screen where Agnes and Tuva were staring back out at him with gazes that didn't know they were dead.

'Who are they?' said Aston. 'Are they your friends, Dad?'

Maria appeared in the doorway.

'Who are Dad's friends?' she said, squinting towards the screen. 'Vincent! Give me strength! They can't even be thirty!'

'Maria!' Benjamin shouted, his face bright red as he tugged the dressing gown tighter around his body. 'We're doing something!'

Vincent leaned back on the chair and closed his eyes. They weren't going to make any further progress today.

'Well dinner's ready, anyway,' Maria snapped. 'When you're done with your dating site.'

'So you had a snack right before dinner?' Vincent said meaningfully.

Maria glowered at him without saying anything. Both of them knew that Aston had his mother wrapped around his little finger. Both of them also knew Vincent had never had a relationship with Benjamin and Rebecka that was as close as his wife's with Aston.

'Was she like that before?' said Benjamin when Maria had left. 'When you met?'

'I don't think she's aware of it,' said Vincent. 'I think she wants to be loving and tolerant, actually. But it's as if she can't do more than that.'

'She spends too much time laying out tarot cards with her pendulum,' Benjamin snorted. 'Mum still laughs every time I tell her about it.'

'Try to be nice. She means no harm.'

Benjamin shrugged and turned back towards the computer, resting his hands on the keyboard. Vincent got up to leave.

'There's one more thing, Dad. The dates of the murders. The times. Have you tried translating them into something else? Letters, for instance?'

Vincent nodded. He'd already thought of that. He'd thought that he'd been onto something when he realized that the first murder – Agnes – had taken place on 13 January at 14:00. Translated into the thirteenth, first and fourteenth letters of the alphabet, that spelled M-A-N. Peculiar, since Agnes was a woman. He'd wondered whether the murderer was trying to say something about gender. But it was a strained inference and had been crushed by the murder of Tuva on 20 February at 15:00: the twentieth, second and fifteenth letters spelled T-B-O. Which stood for *To Be Ordered* . . . *Turbo* . . . *To Be Honest* – nothing that had any significance.

'I tried, but drew a blank,' he said.

'OK, I'll keep at it, see what happens when we translate to binary. All the numbers are palindromic, but in different counting systems. Who knows, there might be some number sequence that 13-1-14-20-2-15 is part of. Might even be coordinates for somewhere – like on a map.'

'That sounds logical,' said Vincent. He didn't have the heart to stifle his son's enthusiasm by telling him he'd already tried those options. And about a million others.

'Am I being paid for this or what?'

'On the subject of maps, I think you need to stop staying up late to watch *National Treasure*,' Vincent said with a wry smile before getting up. 'But by all means, keep trying. Let's have dinner first, though. Maria will so disappointed otherwise.'

'Sure. But like I said: Occam's razor.'

'Your point has been communicated with the utmost clarity,' Vincent said. 'But you didn't see Daniel at the cafe. He could barely wipe the counter. I'm not saying he isn't a suspect. Right now he seems to be in the thick of it, but he isn't going to talk. Which suggests there's more behind it all. We need to find out what.'

Vincent stifled an impulse to tousle his son's hair. By the time he walked out of the door, Benjamin had already put his headphones back on and resumed playing *Path of Exile*. There was no point in reminding him about dinner.

33

Kvibille 1982

Jane stopped on the threshold to the kitchen. Her little brother was sitting at the kitchen table in his pyjamas eating yogurt for breakfast. She could smell strawberries from the doorway and the quantity of jam that had ended up on the orange wax tablecloth revealed that he had made his own breakfast. Between mouthfuls, he was fully occupied shuffling a tattered deck of cards. Half of the cards had ended up on the floor. She couldn't help smiling. It was presumably a new magic trick that was not yet going the way he wanted it to.

Mum was sitting next to him still wearing her dressing gown and with her head buried in her arms on the table. Jane's smile disappeared. Today was apparently not one of Mum's better days.

She shivered as a cool morning breeze brushed her bare legs and she tugged the bottom of her T-shirt down in an attempt to cover her thighs. The window must have been open all night. The question was whether Mum had slept at the kitchen table. It wouldn't be the first time if she had.

'Come on,' she said in a low voice, waving her little brother over.

So far, Mum was quiet, but she knew it was only a matter of time before the usual sequence followed. Her little brother didn't need to hear the spiel about not wanting to live any longer, that she was good for nothing and how she couldn't even make a relationship stick or even get a damn job. That part of the adult world wasn't something he needed to participate in as yet. His mother was still his best friend. Sometimes Jane envied him that, but she knew it was merely the difference between being almost sixteen and still being a child. She had a responsibility, even if she had never asked for it. At least for another week or so.

'I tried to make Mum's triangular toasted sandwiches, but they broke,' her little brother said unhappily.

'It's OK. Come on. Mum just needs to rest a bit. You know how she gets tired sometimes.'

'I didn't want to wake her,' he said, scraping the bottom of his bowl of yogurt.

Then he set it down on the draining board with the rest of the washing up and walked over to Jane.

Mum didn't move an inch.

'Are you doing a new card trick?' she said, leading him out of the kitchen.

'Yes, but it's not done yet,' he said.

'Maybe you could call the Girl Trio, and see whether they fancy doing anything?'

Her brother groaned.

'They're actually called Malla, Sickan and Lotta,' he said. 'You make them sound like some dumb gang in a story. And they're not at home today.'

'I'm on my own today too,' she said. 'Although that's always the way. At least you've got your friends here. I miss my three Ts in the big city.'

She noticed that he didn't take the bait.

'Theatre, Theme-parks and Traffic,' she continued. 'My three friends in the city. None of them are here.'

'Ooooooh right,' her little brother groaned. 'You're just trying to sound grown up. You were only a bit older than me when you and Mum moved here. How often did you go to the theatre before that? And if you want traffic there are plenty of trucks outside the dairy. Three Ts. Haha. You read that in a book, didn't you?'

'Maybe,' she said. 'But I still miss it.'

She paused and pulled out a plastic object from her pocket.

'And if it's only you and me today, bro, then I've got a challenge for you.'

Her little brother's eyes lit up. He loved her challenges.

She handed over the small square plastic frame. Inside it were fifteen smaller plastic squares numbered 1 to 15. The space where the sixteenth should have been was empty. That allowed the other pieces in the frame to be moved around in order to change the sequence of the numbers.

'Dead easy,' said her little brother when he saw the number puzzle. 'I'm quick at solving those nowadays.'

'I didn't say what the challenge was,' she said. 'You have to put all

138

the numbers in order except the last two – fourteen and fifteen. They have to swap places with each other.'

Her little brother took the puzzle from her and looked at it.

'Easy,' he said, running upstairs to his room.

She watched him go with a pang of guilty conscience for being devious. But she needed to talk to Mum alone. She would go and find him in an hour. The stairs had creaked good and proper as he'd run up them, but it didn't matter now whether Mum woke up. In fact, it might be for the best if she did.

Jane returned to the kitchen. Mum was sitting up but her face was still hidden in her hands. Her hair was lank and unwashed, and her dressing gown had slipped open. Jane was filled with empathy and contempt at the same time. It wasn't Mum's fault that her emotions were an ever-revolving carousel that wouldn't stop. Not really. Jane had borrowed a book about psychiatry from Barbro, the school nurse, on the pretence that it was for a school project. She'd read about genetic risk factors that you could do nothing about, and her mother clearly fit the profile.

She'd also read about treatments for the condition. Like lithium. But Mum wasn't taking tablets. She didn't even know she was sick. That made Jane a captive, even if it wasn't intentional. She always needed to be standing by, whether to protect her brother or take care of her mother. As if she had no life of her own.

But she intended to start having one.

Jane sat down at the kitchen table, taking care to avoid the patches of jam.

'Mum, do you want breakfast?'

They really needed to talk. But she could see that it wasn't going to happen today.

139

34

Reception at police headquarters was full of schoolchildren. They looked like sixth formers. Mina realized it must be a school trip – thirty seventeen-year-olds would hardly come in just because it was cold out. They usually preferred to gather at the 7-Eleven a block away, and they could stay there, as far as she was concerned. Yet here they were, along with a teacher who was handing out visitor badges and trying in vain to get her pupils to attach them at chest height.

'Come on then, pig, here I am,' shouted someone who was clearly the Cool Guy in the class. He was duly rewarded with his classmates' laughter.

She didn't know how Vincent would react when he was forced to make his way through this heaving mass of teenage hormones. If they recognized him, it was bound to be uncomfortable for him. But she could hardly bring him in through a side entrance. And there was no way she could usher him through the crowd of unruly youths – she felt grubby just looking at them. Maybe if she wore gloves. And a visor. Although perhaps not even then.

She could smell the stench of teenage sweat all the way from where she was standing at a safe distance on the other side of the barriers; it seemed to envelop her, coating her entire body. Vincent would have to manage on his own. The police might benefit from a bit of celebrity glamour. Even if it was provided by a forty-seven-year-old mindreader.

Vincent appeared on the far side of the sea of schoolchildren. His eyes widened when he spotted them. Then he lowered his head and ploughed through the throng.

'Ey, Vincent!' someone shouted.

Mina was impressed. She hadn't been sure they would recognize someone who wasn't big on TikTok.

'Shit, Vincent! Are you with the mind police now?' yelled the Cool Guy. 'That means we've got no chance!'

Vincent stopped and sought out Cool Guy's gaze.

'Exactly,' he said loudly, with a knowing smile. 'I already did your mum this morning.'

Cool Guy was taken aback. Then he exploded with laughter and offered Vincent a fist bump. Mina smiled to herself. Vincent Walder the private citizen had clear social issues. In fact, he was socially handicapped. But when playing the role of the Master Mentalist, he most clearly did not.

Finally, he reached the near side of the horde and the barriers. He waved to her and she let him through.

The school group appeared to have already forgotten about him. The teacher raised her voice, trying to get her pupils' attention, once again in vain.

'Junior officers keep getting younger, I see,' said Vincent.

'You'd be surprised,' she said. 'The tough guy you just spoke to will probably apply to the police academy the moment he finishes sixth form.'

Vincent nodded with a smile and they began to walk to the lift.

'How come you wanted to meet at police headquarters?' he said. 'I thought my presence wasn't appreciated here.'

'Surely I can meet whoever I like on my lunch break?' she said. 'Anyway, the rest of the team aren't here. We've initiated a search for Daniel Bargabriel after our visit to Fab Fika. He hasn't been home since he did a runner from the cafe, so Ruben's gone over there with a locksmith. He insists on calling him Daniel Gargamel.'

They reached the lift, where there were already three people waiting. Without missing a beat, Mina changed course and headed for the stairs instead. No way was she going to squeeze into a bacteria box with that many people. There were limits.

'Bargabriel means Gabriel's son,' said Vincent, who had been about to stop, but corrected his movements mid-step and continued to follow her. 'Ruben basically means son. You can tell him that from me. Where are we going, by the way?'

'I need to fetch my wallet from the office – I thought we could get lunch,' she said.

She bounded up the stairs in big steps, talking all the while.

'Ruben is convinced that Daniel is our murderer, that the three of them were in some love triangle. Or, as he so charmingly put it, "so

141

much for theories about serial killers and Roman watches and all that shit. Daniel was fucking them both. Simple as." He pointed out that when you have his kind of professional experience, you know which solutions are the right ones.'

'How much experience are we talking about?' Vincent said, slightly short of breath – but then again, he didn't climb the stairs at police headquarters on a daily basis.

'He was a year ahead of me at the police academy.'

Vincent laughed so hard it echoed in the stairwell.

'So I've been wrong about everything, in other words. What do the others say? And must you take the steps two at a time?'

'Sorry. Do you need a stick?'

'Remember that it's my brain you're impressed with,' he said. 'Not my elite physique. How many more floors to go?'

'Two. Probably best you have a rest, Grandpa.'

Vincent stopped and leaned against the wall.

Mina backtracked a few steps and stood next to him.

'The others aren't convinced either,' she said. 'We encounter a lot of strange things that end up being nothing more than that – strange things. Random details.'

'I don't agree. I'm more and more certain that it's a countdown. Daniel might be a way in. But he didn't come across like a murderer. This is far from over.'

Vincent sat down on the step and she sat next to him.

'Pity there wasn't any CCTV at the cafe when Tuva was last seen.' She sighed. 'No witnesses have come forward who saw her anywhere else. I would have liked to see who was coming and going on the day she disappeared. And for a few days before that. Jesus.'

'The cafe might not have had a camera, but . . .' Vincent furrowed his brow in concentration. 'Do you remember what it looked like around the cafe? Any details?'

His gaze was focusing on something that wasn't there. His eyes were moving back and forth as if he were looking around and he continued to talk:

'There was a 7-Eleven, the exit at the corner of the building. Round bench around the trunk of a tree. Overfilled bike rack. Two restaurants. More people in one of them, the other almost empty. The hotdog stand. Five people in the queue. And on the other side of the street . . . Yep. There was a bank opposite. I'm almost certain it was a branch of Nordea. They usually have high levels of security. With a little luck—'

142

'You're a genius,' Mina said, perking up. 'Julia will have to ask Christer to get hold of the footage from Nordea's cameras. He's got a flair for that kind of thing.'

'Christer?' Vincent said in surprise.

Mina smiled.

'I've tried to tell you. I realize that our unit falls some way short of those super sharp specialist forces on TV,' she said. 'But everyone has their strengths. Christer's is an uncanny ability to spot patterns where no one else can.'

'I can relate to that,' Vincent muttered.

'So my hope is that Christer will notice if something is out of the ordinary,' she continued. 'Someone who's there too often. Someone who usually comes regularly and then doesn't. Well, I don't know. But it's exactly what Christer is good at.'

Vincent nodded.

'Two floors did you say?' he said suddenly, smiling teasingly.

Then he leapt to his feet and raced up the stairs. He vanished from sight as he turned at the next switchback. She heard him carry on up, taking two steps at a time. There was absolutely nothing wrong with his fitness. He'd got her to sit down on purpose. And she'd gone along with it.

'Vincent?'

No answer. He was too far up the stairwell. Mina dug her hands into her pockets and felt a square object in one of them. Her wallet. She had completely forgotten that she'd brought it with her. She looked up the stairwell and a smile played on her lips. She would just have to wait for Vincent to come back.

35

The small, terraced house in Upplands Väsby reminded Christer of his mother's house. The tidiness, the knick-knacks everywhere, the well-pressed curtains, the thoroughly wiped down surfaces. A clock ticking loudly in the living room. Two armchairs with visible indentations and a sofa that appeared to have had barely any visitors. A posh sofa. Too posh to use. His mother's had been green with purple flowers. On sunny days, his mother had thrown a sheet over it to make sure the upholstery didn't fade in the sun.

'Would you like coffee, officer?'

Märta, the victim's grandmother, looked at him pleadingly. He wasn't at all keen on coffee. It made him feel wired and edgy. And he didn't like the clarity of thought that it gave him – it was far more comfortable to be enveloped in a sleepy haze. But at the same time, he knew that work sometimes demanded coffee. Relatives took comfort in the familiarity of serving freshly brewed coffee in china cups. It made them talk more easily. And he could always stick to sipping it. If he was lucky, there might be something sweet to go with it.

'I'd love a coffee, thanks,' he said, looking around the kitchen.

Gunnar was already sitting at the table. His gaze was fixed on the surface. He didn't seem altogether present, which was something Christer had seen many times in the relatives of victims. That first phase when what had happened hadn't quite sunk in but was still lingering in the borderlands between reality and unreality.

The kitchen was cosy. That was the best word to describe it. Lingonberry-print curtains. A wax tablecloth to match. Purple begonias in the window. Twigs on the table to mark Easter. A beautifully framed pen-and-ink drawing of some kind of bird. A falcon, Christer guessed.

'Majestic.'

He pointed at the picture. The silence in the room was beginning to get under his skin, but he didn't want to start questioning them until Märta had finished making the coffee and joined them.

'Peregrine falcon,' Gunnar said in a muffled voice, raising his gaze to look at the drawing. 'The county bird of Halland. The Falcon brewery, you know. It's one of the world's fastest animals – can reach speeds of up to three hundred and twenty kilometres an hour when diving. It's an incredible hunter. It can spot a pigeon from eight kilometres away.'

'You know your birds?' Christer said without any enthusiasm.

He found it hard to cultivate any interest in fowl. In fact, he didn't much like animals in general. All they did was disappear or die on you. When he'd been little he'd been given a kitten by his uncle. He'd loved that kitten. But one day when he'd come home from school it was gone. Mum had said he must have left the door open and it had escaped. He had cried for weeks. A couple of years later he'd been given a rabbit by one of Mum's boyfriends. And funnily enough the same thing had happened. Ever since, he had taken particular care to close the door behind him. And he'd learned it wasn't worth getting attached to anything, whether it was animal or human.

'I'm a semi-professional birdwatcher in my free time,' said Gunnar with a tad more energy. 'Have been for many years. I've seen four hundred and thirty-two Swedish species of bird. I'm hot on the heels of Bertil Svensson in Skåne. He's seen four hundred and fifty-nine.'

'How many are there?' Christer said in astonishment.

He couldn't for the life of him understand the pleasure in trudging around in the woods and countryside with a pair of binoculars, hunting for birds.

'Five hundred and seven,' said Gunnar, falling silent again.

Christer didn't know how much more small talk on birds he could take. To his relief, Märta appeared with the coffee. And a plate of oat cookies. She sat down on the chair next to her husband's.

'I need to ask you some questions about Tuva,' he said as gently as he could. 'But first of all, I'm wondering why it was you who reported her missing rather than her parents?'

Märta gave Gunnar a pained look.

'Tuva's parents – that's our daughter Malin and her husband Carl – moved to a small house in France when Tuva was sixteen. They said they were in the autumn of their old age,' she snorted. 'They're actually just kids. They haven't been back since. Tuva was left all by herself. And Linus's dad disappeared around the same time Linus was born. God knows, she didn't have much luck with her family. But she got Linus. Wonderful Linus. And she had us. She and Linus have always had us. You have to make the best of things.'

Märta fiddled with the buds on the twigs while Christer nodded and silently took notes in his notebook.

'I'd like you to tell me more about Linus's father – and I'll need contact details for Tuva's mother and father. But first I need to know why you waited so long to report her missing. Something about a trip . . .?'

Gunnar looked at Märta with renewed energy in his eyes.

'Tuva's an environmental activist,' he said.

'What does that mean exactly? Is she one of those protestors who blocks traffic?' said Christer.

He couldn't conceal how unimpressed he was.

'Greenpeace,' said Märta, her voice a little sharper.

'Oh wow. Old school.' Christer raised his eyebrows in surprise. 'I didn't think anyone still did that. Stopping them from catching whales and stuff?'

'And stuff. Tuva's very active. She – well . . . she probably got that from us.'

Märta patted Gunnar's arm.

'We were very active in the movement back in the seventies. Before we got too old.'

Christer tried to imagine the old couple laying siege to a Norwegian oil rig in a stormy sea. Fifty years before twigs and peregrine falcons had taken over their interests. To his surprise, he realized he could. Gunnar and Märta might be decrepit now, but there was clearly fiery passion within. Not that that kind of activism actually made any difference . . . Everyone would die in the end anyway. The ice caps would melt. The ozone layer would disappear. A deadly virus would be spread from some damn meat market in China. The earth would be destroyed. Destiny couldn't be changed.

'Tuva was meant to be going to a demonstration,' said Gunnar. 'She's usually gone two or three weeks, and we're not always in touch while she's gone because their operations tend to be secret. Or in the middle of the sea. So we didn't miss her at first.'

'But what about Linus?' said Christer.

'Linus is used to it. He's got his own room here with us. Tuva is an otherwise very present parent – but she sees her environmental work as her way of helping to provide Linus with a future. So when they

146

called from the nursery to say that Tuva hadn't come to pick up Linus, we thought we must have got our days mixed up and that she had already gone and we were the ones who were meant to pick up Linus. So we didn't miss her until the boat came back. And then we found out she'd never boarded in the first place.'

Märta's voice failed her and she grasped Gunnar's hand hard.

'Do you know whether Tuva had any enemies?' said Christer as gently as he could. 'Has she ever said anything about someone called Daniel Bargabriel?'

Märta and Gunnar exchanged another glance. Then Gunnar sat up straight. The peregrine falcon from Halland was right above his head and it looked like the huge bird had landed on his crown.

'Tuva was unlucky with men,' he said, his voice trembling. 'We knew about Daniel, but she didn't want to talk about him. She said several times that he was going to hurt her.'

Märta took his hand.

'How badly did he hurt her?' she said.

Christer took a bite out of the oat cookie to avoid answering.

36

Daniel adjusted the lowered blind. Opened it. Closed it again. He couldn't make up his mind what was best – preventing people from seeing in or quickly being able to spot the police coming. It was just as well to be alert. He opened it halfway and looked out at the car park beyond the window. The flat in Märsta was actually Josef's, but he had borrowed it for the time being. Josef didn't need it and Daniel didn't dare go back to the flat in Hornstull in case the police were watching it. But it was impossible for them to know about Josef's one-bedder.

The flat was spartanly furnished to say the least – there wasn't even a bed, just a mattress on the floor. Not that sleep comfort was a priority right now. Daniel didn't know when he would dare to fall asleep again. If he ever would.

Since he had left the flat he'd been sharing with Agnes, he'd moved around, staying with Evelyn and then various friends. The cops handling the investigation into Agnes hadn't even asked him for his new address. Of course they were keeping an eye on him – that was a given. Granted, he'd heard the police in Sweden weren't like the ones back home in Syria. But these cops, these *Swedish* cops, had still almost managed to put him away for murder.

At first they hadn't believed the story that he'd had nothing to do with Agnes's death. He'd tried to play his most charming, innocent self but they had been convinced that he'd been mixed up in it. At least one of them seemed to think that he had been the one who'd fired the shot that had killed her. In the end they'd had to let him go because they had no evidence. And after all, Agnes had been depressed . . .

He had promised himself that for the rest of his life he'd avoid the police as much as possible, no matter where he was. They couldn't be trusted. And yet he'd been careless. So goddamn careless.

Barely a month had gone by between finding Agnes dead and Tuva going missing. He should have been the one to call the police about Tuva rather than her grandparents. That way the suspicion might not have been aimed at him. Now it was too late. And if those two cops who came to visit him at the cafe didn't already know who he was, then it wouldn't take long before they found the connection. The hot cop didn't seem to have understood a thing, but that man had looked like he recognized Daniel at once. The man he had seen before but couldn't place.

The question was whether he should call Evelyn. Whether he should explain what had happened. She must be wondering where he'd got to. And he missed her so much that his stomach ached. He wanted nothing more than to sit in her kitchen drinking wine, see her light up a ciggie and talk about everything and nothing. Or do something more fun than talk. He pictured her in front of him, thinking about how she would teasingly blow smoke into his mouth when she kissed him.

But it wasn't a great idea to get her mixed up in this too. He had to deal with this on his own. He had briefly considered calling Samir. Samir had had a worse time of it than he had – he'd actually gone down for real. For something he said he hadn't done. Daniel didn't know what to believe, but Samir might have a few handy tips.

Then again, if the police checked his phone that call wouldn't look good at all. No, he had to deal with the situation by himself.

Daniel fingered the business card in his pocket. If the police were looking for him, which he had to assume they were, it would look really bad if he remained a fugitive. So far, he could explain away his disappearance by saying he'd got frightened. An innocent person wouldn't wait too long before contacting the police. Tuva was his workmate; of course he ought to be worried about her. He ought to want to help. The best way to avoid prison might be to pre-empt them and go to the police himself.

In Syria, the only way to avoid the police was to start running and hope they didn't have motorbikes. But in Sweden, perhaps the best way to avoid the police was to go to them. The way an innocent person would.

He opened the blind.

Closed it.

Fingered the business card in his pocket again.

Perhaps.

149

37

Schoolchildren were pouring into the playground. Mina knew exactly where to stand to avoid being seen. Most of them dressed so similarly that they might as well have been wearing uniforms. It made the few kids who stood out look even more striking. It was the first day back at school after the Easter holidays, so energy levels among the shouting and laughing children were significantly higher than usual.

She blended in well, but Mina had no difficulty finding her in the cluster of children. If you could call them children at that age. Half children, half adults. Her dark hair was in a ponytail. Jeans. Thin green army jacket and white trainers. A dark blue Fjällräven Kånken backpack. She was beautiful. So incredibly beautiful.

Mina jumped when the girl turned around. Mina knew that she was invisible in the spot where she stood on the platform at Blåsut metro station, with its view of the entrance to Drottning Blankas sixth form. But she wanted to imagine that they were looking at each other. That they could *see* each other. The girl looked like she was searching for something, then she turned her gaze away again.

Mina only had a few minutes with her before she was gone. She vanished through the door, on the way to a classroom somewhere inside the building. For lessons in Swedish, Spanish, Maths, Economy. Or whatever she was studying.

The metro train was approaching. Mina turned around as it pulled into the station. People stared listlessly at the ground as they got on, avoiding meeting each other's eyes. Mina began to head for the station exit. Her car was parked nearby. She would never dream of getting on the metro. The cloud of bacteria floating around the people crammed into those coaches was so thick that it was almost visible to the naked eye.

The train pulled away, leaving her alone on the platform. With a great effort, she stopped herself from turning around and looking at the school building one more time. She didn't need to see the closed door to be reminded of the insurmountable wall between them. The loss ached throughout her whole body.

On the way out, she passed a newspaper stand. Every front page told of the tragedy of the missing kid, Robert. New discoveries, promising trails. Right? A new level of cynicism, more like. But she wasn't surprised. She didn't even have the strength to meet his happy, inviting gaze as she walked past the yellow boards. The world could be an awful place.

The phone rang in her pocket. At first she considered not answering, then she pulled it out after allowing herself one last glance at the school. It was a brief but useful call. Tomorrow they were going to exhume Agnes Ceci's body.

38

Vincent was absent-mindedly reading the safety card in the pocket of the aircraft seat in front of him. The flight to Sundsvall was being operated by an ATR 72-500, which could carry 72 passengers, according to the card. Vincent had only counted 30 passengers when he'd boarded, so in purely mathematical terms everyone should have had their own pair of seats, free from annoying neighbours. But of course someone had sat down in the vacant seat next to him. Someone who happened to be playing music so loudly that a mechanical backbeat rhythm was leaking out of their headphones.

The man next to him started singing in time with the music.

Vincent hated small planes. It felt like travelling in an oversized coffin. He began to breathe in a controlled fashion. The trick to keeping claustrophobia at bay was to assign a task to the rational part of your brain. Preferably a difficult one. That way, the hippocampus – the part of the brain controlling his emotions – would be deprived of the resources it needed to make him panic.

He studied the safety card again: 72 seats plus 30 passengers came to 102. If 1 was A and 2 was B, 0 would have to be O. So 102 made AOB. Ace of Base – who had recorded the hit single 'All That She Wants' in 1992. He looked out of the window in disappointment. Sometimes it was too easy. But at least it was keeping the claustrophobia at bay.

He was on his way to Sundsvall to meet Sains Bergander, Sweden's foremost builder of illusions and magic props. With him he had the photos that Mina had secured for him. Presumably she didn't have permission to give him the photos since he was officially an outsider, but if anyone could help them understand the sword box it would be Sains. Vincent had known him for about ten years. What Sains didn't know about constructing illusions wasn't worth knowing.

An hour later, Vincent stepped into the arrivals hall at Midlanda airport and looked around. There were four people waiting for passengers. One of them was a middle-aged man in unassuming clothes. If anyone even noticed him, they would think he worked for the local council. Vincent knew this was exactly the way Sains Bergander wanted it to be.

'Hello, old man. Good to see you again,' he said, extending his hand.

Sains squeezed Vincent's hand with both of his own. The illusionist's best magic trick was to make himself invisible. There were few people outside his own family who knew of his existence, let alone what he actually did. Sundsvall was a small town and Sains Bergander was more than happy to fly under people's radar.

They got into Sains's Subaru Outback and he pulled out of the car park.

'What did you want to talk about?' he said. 'You were very secretive on the phone.'

'I'm not really allowed to show you what I'm about to show you,' said Vincent. 'Probably not even allowed to talk about it. But I know you can't resist a secret. Anyway, it's been far too long since we last met.'

'You're right about that. And I've got nothing against visits – it's not often someone stops by and physically knocks on my door these days.'

Sains pulled over and parked outside the house that served as his workshop.

'Welcome to the heart of the magic,' he said as they stood on the doorstep.

Vincent entered a room that was reminiscent of both Santa's workshop and a woodwork classroom. Machines whose purpose he could only guess at lined the walls – the only ones he recognized were two circular saws and an industrial-sized 3D printer. Thick pipes ran away from the machines, presumably to extract dust and wood chips, but that didn't prevent the room from being overwhelmed with pieces of wood, hinges, paint and clusters of thin magnets, in the midst of finished boxes and frames whose destiny was as yet unclear. Vincent stopped in front of a sheet of wood fixed to a rope suspended from the ceiling. The board was hanging upright at head height and had two obscenely thick bolts screwed into either end.

'What's this?' he asked.

'Personal project that I'm working on,' Sains said proudly. 'I'm not accepting orders for it, just to be clear.'

He stood in front of the board and put his hands to the sides of his head so that they were lined up with the bolts.

'It's a cross,' he said. 'The bolts go right through your hands. It's incredibly realistic. Two hundred millilitres of blood pour out of each wound. I've even tailored a monk's cloak to enable someone to play the role of executioner. It's the business. Want to see it?'

Vincent shook his head. He wondered what Mina would make of it. Illusion or not, he had enough blood and mutilation in his life right now. Instead, he pulled out the plastic folder containing the printed photos, shifted a stack of metal clamps from a workbench and laid them out.

'What do you make of this?' he said.

Sains leaned over the photos.

'It's a sword casket,' he said. 'Or sword box, depending on who you ask. But surely you don't need me to tell you that?'

Vincent shook his head.

'Have you seen one like this before?' he said.

'No, not exactly. Who built it?'

'I hoped you might be able to tell me that. Has anyone ordered parts for a box from you, or do you know if anyone else in the game has sold one recently? Maybe even just the design?'

Sains snorted and pointed at the photos.

'Do you think I'd be involved in a shoddy piece of work like this? You should be ashamed, Vincent. You know I'm the best in the business. But even my rivals can do better than this piece of crap.'

'So it's definitely a home-made job?'

'Hmm, it's not quite that simple. In terms of design, it's not as easy as you'd think.'

'How do you mean?'

Sains went over to a bookcase and searched for something. After a while he returned with three spiralbound volumes.

'Paul Osbourne's *Illusion Systems*, volumes one, two and three,' he said, laying them out in front of Vincent. 'Probably the foremost modern source of designs for illusions. Take a look. Could you build this?'

Vincent opened one of the volumes and leafed through the drawings. 'I could have a go,' he said.

'And you'd get it wrong. The people who buy the drawings are magicians, but it's better to get a cabinet maker to build them. Having the machinery isn't enough; you need to understand the materials too, else the illusion will end up too heavy, or you'll use the wrong screws, or make some other stupid mistake. Which isn't difficult to do, considering many of the classic design blueprints contain deliberate errors.'

Vincent didn't understand.

'Why would anyone sell dodgy drawings?' he said.

'Because it allows them to publicize an illusion and claim copyright, while at the same time ensuring that no one else can pull it off. You must have heard about the many feuds between magicians that started because one claimed credit for the other's creation. The traditional way to claim an invention as your own is to publish it. But at the same time, you don't want other people to copy it and start doing the same trick you came up with. All magicians want to be unique. So you publish, but with a few small mistakes.'

'And what happens if someone tries to follow the blueprint, errors and all?'

'It simply won't work – either the trapdoor won't open, or the walls won't stay together, or the whole thing will collapse. My point is, if you're going to build an illusion, you need to understand what to change from the blueprint so that it actually works. And that has a positive impact, because in the process you will be putting your own mark on the illusion. Someone else will change it in a different way.'

Otherwise the trapdoor won't open. A memory shifted at the back of Vincent's mind, but he immediately suppressed it. Instead, he drummed his fingers on the photos in frustration.

'OK, so this box hasn't been made by a pro,' he said. 'Can you take another look and see if there's anything else you can tell me about it.'

Sains squinted at the photos more closely.

'Hmm. Is it an old photo? Because the model is. Old, that is. The structure has changed quite a lot over time – this one reminds me of how they used to be made in the 1960s. But . . .'

Sains picked up one of the photos and frowned. Then he let go of it and put his hand to his mouth.

'Vincent, who built this?' he said in a faint voice through his fingers.

'That's what I was asking you.'

'But surely it hasn't been used?'

Sains leaned against the bench. His face had acquired a green tinge.

'What is it?' Vincent said anxiously.

Sains seemed to pull himself together a little and reached for one of the books.

'As it happens, there are actually good drawings available for sword boxes and sword caskets,' he said, leafing through until he found what he was looking for. 'And they're also easy to build. Take a look.'

He pointed at a design in the book.

'The magician's assistant sits in a very precise position in the box in relation to the sword holes. The holes are distributed to make it look like they cover the whole outside, but in reality the positioning of the swords means that they leave a perfect gap for the woman inside the box – as long as she doesn't budge an inch. There are some who have taken this to the extreme – a magician in Germany apparently broke seven ribs and the jaw of his assistant in a performance a few years ago. It's on YouTube. But there's always *some* space for the assistant in the box. But Vincent . . .'

Sains picked up one of the photographs that Vincent had brought and pointed out the obvious.

'In this box there is no space. If someone sat in this box, she'd be penetrated by the swords. There's nowhere to go. And yet . . . I can see it's based on a proper drawing, even if it's old. They've just removed . . . the actual illusion.'

Sains stared at him.

'Vincent. What *is* this?'

'That, my friend, is what we need to find out.'

39

Watching CCTV footage was about as painfully dull as watching paint dry. Christer blinked his eyes. Dusk was falling and the office was emptying of people. It never emptied entirely – it was always staffed – but the workforce decreased significantly in the evening and overnight. People wanted to get home to their families. Though there was no one waiting at home for Christer, he still wanted to head off soon. He was used to the solitude. Had accepted it.

He had retrieved the footage for the three days leading up to Tuva's disappearance. Which was odd really, since that kind of material was only allowed to be kept for twenty-four hours, and should have been deleted long ago, as the bank had diligently pointed out when he had got in touch. But when he had told them what he wanted the footage for, they had discovered – with mock surprise – that some IT technician had been careless and that all of it was still on a server. They could come up with any excuse they liked. No one was more pleased than he was that it was still in existence.

At least, that was how he'd felt before he began watching the monotonous footage. The camera was obviously pointed at the bank's own entrance, but he could see the cafe on the other side of the street. Unluckily, the actual door wasn't visible as it was out of shot. But he could see the pavement, the road, and a little way inside the cafe through its large windows. Most people passing by weren't alone. There were laughing couples. Two blokes who seemed to be having a row about something. A dogwalker with a big dog. An old lady and a child – presumably a grandparent and grandchild.

Two women, each with a small chihuahua. He'd never wrapped his head around the trend for those bloody tiny dogs. Rats on a leash as far as he was concerned.

Christer blinked and took another few gulps of coffee. He grimaced. Cold. Of course it was cold. Life rarely served him hot coffee.

He carried on watching. A solitary man he'd observed drinking coffee inside Fab Fika emerged onto the pavement. He had clearly just left the cafe. Christer leaned forward. There was something familiar about him. The footage was too grainy to really see much, and it was impossible to make out any facial features. The man had a slight limp, which triggered something in Christer. But for the life of him he couldn't come up with any more information in the byways of his brain. The gait was so familiar, but the more he reached for the information, the further away it got.

Sometimes when he didn't come up with something right away or was fumbling for some word he knew he ought to know, he got worried. His mother had passed away with dementia, and it had been a long twilight that had lasted almost a decade. It wasn't a fate that Christer wanted to share. His greatest fear was that he'd end up with some gum-chewing twenty-year-old changing his nappies and wiping his arse. So just to be sure, he'd hidden away a little capsule in a box his mother had kept her fine jewellery in. There it was, waiting for the day when it would be needed. A quick death. And a dignified one.

He rewound and watched the man with the slight limp again. No. His memory was going to be of no further assistance whatsoever. Christer sighed, closed the file, got up and put on his coat. That was enough for tonight.

40

Mina dropped into the meeting before work. Actually, she often got there early, but on the days after she'd seen the girl she could never quite bring herself to jump straight back into reality at work. She needed to find a way to chill out a bit first. She had considered calling Vincent, but the girl was another secret she would struggle to explain. Better to numb the feeling of loss using another secret.

Everyone had already sat down when she arrived. She crept in and took one of the empty chairs. There were always too many chairs. No one should ever feel like there wasn't space for them and that they weren't welcome. Far too many of them were there because they hadn't fitted in, hadn't been welcome. She nodded at Skåne and the woman with the purple shawl.

Dolphin girl had her sleeve rolled up and clingfilm around her arm. A tattoo with the words *Living on the edge* was visible underneath it, and the skin around it was an angry shade of red. Mina couldn't help picturing the murderous bacteria now thriving under her skin, eating their way in towards the bone, ruining all living matter. She rubbed her hands against her trousers and then pinched her thigh hard but discreetly to stop her train of thought. Dolphin girl raised a hand in greeting and smiled at her. Mina tried to smile back, but it felt stiff and unnatural.

The man with the dog was sitting opposite her. Technically, she ought to stop calling him the man with the dog and say the man with Bosse instead. A woman in a wheelchair was sitting next to him, and Mina made the plausible assumption that it was the partner he had mentioned.

Bosse's ears pricked up when he saw Mina, and before his master could grab the lead the dog had run over and leapt up, placing his front paws in her lap and feverishly attempting to lick her face. Mina stood up in a panic and began to frantically brush her trousers. At least it had been dry outside so his paws weren't wet, but she would still have to throw them away. And now it was on her hands too. The man with the dog ran over and grabbed the lead.

'Sorry, I thought I'd tied him to the chair leg.'

'No need to apologize,' Mina said stiffly. 'I'm just . . . a bit afraid of dogs.'

'I completely understand – he's such a big boy. But he's a sweetheart, honestly. It looks as though he's taken a real liking to you.'

She squeezed out a weak smile and sat down on the chair again while Bosse was led away. Her pulse slowly began to calm. Everyone was looking at her. She looked at the floor. She would have preferred to be invisible. She didn't want to be seen, didn't want to take up space. Not there. She wanted to listen, watch, learn. So far, she hadn't chosen to share even once, even though she'd been going for three years.

The woman in the wheelchair smiled at her sympathetically. Mina pretended not to see. Bosse had lain down under his master's chair with his big head settled against his paws, and his moist brown eyes fixed on Mina. Sad, rejected, betrayed.

In the break, Mina stayed to one side of the group. Most of the others were standing or sitting together in small clusters, drinking coffee, eating biscuits, chatting. Mina sat in a corner and pulled out her phone. No messages. She opened Candy Crush – she was on level twenty. It had taken her countless hours to reach that level, but it was the perfect way to unwind. Her whole brain relaxed when she was staring at the colourful sweets moving, being erased, being refilled. There was a beginning, but no end.

'I also want to apologize on behalf of Bosse.'

The voice made Mina jump – it came from her left.

'He came to us when he was grown up – he's a rescue. And I'm afraid we haven't been quite as successful in training him as we would have liked.'

The woman in the wheelchair smiled apologetically at her. Mina sighed silently and put her phone in her pocket. It seemed she couldn't avoid small talk, no matter how hard she tried. People were hopeless when it came to reading body language. Sometimes she dreamt of a world in which people had learned to wash their hands properly and used plastic gloves and face masks, and where big signs saying 'keep your distance' were installed all over the place.

'Really, it's nothing,' she said, hoping the woman would get the hint and trundle off in her wheelchair. But she stayed put, taking Mina in with a gentle smile. The man with the dog came towards them with two cups of coffee in his hands. He handed one to the woman in the wheelchair and smiled apologetically at Mina.

'Sorry, I didn't bring you a cup. But you don't usually drink . . .'

'No, no, it's fine.'

Bosse remained obediently at heel, but looked as if he would leap on Mina and lick her face at the first opportunity. She carefully shuffled backwards.

'Don't worry, I've got him on the lead,' the man said, sitting down opposite Mina.

She fought an impulse to get up and leave. She didn't want to get acquainted with them. Didn't want to know their first and last names. Didn't want to know where they lived. Didn't want to know what their jobs were or had been. Didn't. Want. To. Know. They were dangerously close to penetrating her sphere. They were strangers. She only spoke to strangers when her job required it. When she wasn't at work, she saw no need to talk to people she didn't know. To be honest, she saw no need to talk to people she knew either. And that was a rather short list which was growing ever shorter as people grew tired of her never getting in touch.

'Kenneth told me you're a police officer,' said the woman.

'Yes,' Mina said tersely.

Bloody hell. Names. She already knew from the sharing sessions that he was called that, but names were too personal. Too intimate. She didn't want to talk about work with strangers, either. The fact that Kenneth – for fuck's sake, now she was thinking about him by name – and the others had happened to hear her talking to Julia about the investigation had been an accident. It hadn't happened again. It wouldn't happen again. There were firewalls between the different compartments of her life. It was the only way she knew to handle it. The only way she could handle it.

Mina looked around the room. Wasn't it time to get started again? Granted, there was no need to stay for the second half of the meeting. It was voluntary. She could leave at any time. But eventually the silence was too oppressive. Without being able to stop herself, she pointed at the wheelchair.

'Why are you in a wheelchair?' she asked.

'Scoliosis,' the woman said matter-of-factly.

'Oh yes, right. He . . . Kenneth mentioned it.'

Silence again. Mina gritted her teeth. Bosse felt closer now. It was as if he were trying to sneak up on her, centimetre by centimetre. She pushed her chair back. Far enough that the dog's uncleanliness wouldn't manage to jump across to her. The silence covered them like a wet blanket, and Mina considered once again whether to leave. Or at least change seats. Perhaps her excuse could be asking dolphin girl a question about the tattoo. But she preferred to stay as far away from that arm as possible.

There was a buzz from her mobile and she gratefully took it out of her pocket. She read the message, thought about it, and then quickly wrote a reply and sent it. When she looked up she saw that Kenneth and his wife were watching her with curious expressions. She rose and picked up her coat, which was hanging on the back of the chair.

'Sorry – duty calls. Nice to meet you.'

She nodded at the woman in the wheelchair. Bosse followed her with disappointed eyes as she hurried past. She passed the toilets on her way out of the building, but deliberately avoided going in to wash her hands. She would only pick up more bacteria than she already had on her. There were wet wipes in the car. And hand sanitizer. They would have to do.

41

Christer sighed. Yet more pointless hours spent watching Nordea's CCTV footage. He was almost at the end of the material they had been given – seventy-two whole hours, right up to the time they knew Tuva had gone out the door and disappeared. Heading off to what they now knew to be her death. But the camera hadn't captured an ominous black van that might have kidnapped her or any masked assailants suddenly running up behind her. No patterns. Nothing that stood out.

He hadn't found anything worthwhile. There was something about that faintly familiar man with a limp that was still gnawing at him, but there wasn't much he could do except leave it to stew. If you couldn't remember something, then you couldn't remember it. Simple. He was no bloody magician. If that was what they needed then they should have kept Vincent on board.

Christer closed the CCTV file and sighed again. His next task was no more tempting. When Agnes had been found dead in an apparent suicide, he had been the one tasked with calling Jesper Ceci. The father. Charlotte Ceci, the mother, had died when Agnes had been little. Jesper had moved to Arvika to start a new family as soon as Agnes had been old enough to get by on her own.

Christer was the one on the team with the most experience of talking to families, which was why he was always the one who handled them. His colleagues didn't seem to get that he disliked it just as much as they did. He was probably also worse at it than most of the others. He could be calming when it was called for, but that comforting thing wasn't exactly his forte.

He remembered the conversation with Agnes's father very well. He hadn't always been a murder investigator, so he'd had all sorts of conversations over the course of his career. Some family members would break down the moment he said he was from the police. Even if he was only calling about a missing cat that had turned up dead. The fact that pet owners always took it so hard never ceased to surprise him. They ought to know that animals always disappeared. Others would react angrily and accuse him of professional negligence. Like that woman whose Michael Kors bag had been found in perfect condition but the mobile phone had been gone. Eventually he'd had enough and asked her which mobile phone she was using to talk to him . . . People. What the hell was wrong with them?

It was harder when he had to notify family members of a death, especially over the phone. It made you feel so powerless, hearing them going to pieces at the other end of the line when there was nothing you could do to help.

Jesper Ceci, however, belonged to another category. He had sounded almost . . . polite. Which might have been his way of being shocked – it wasn't unusual for relatives to distance themselves emotionally in order to cope with bad tidings. But when it came to Jesper, Christer didn't think that had been the case. Jesper had a new wife and a five-year-old son in Arvika. He'd had very little contact with his daughter in Stockholm since moving away. When Christer had called, Jesper had talked about Agnes as if she were a distant relative. Someone he had met at a dinner a few years ago. It had sent shivers down Christer's spine.

And now he had to call Jesper again, to ask a lot of questions that he knew Jesper had zero interest in answering. Jesus Christ. But it was best to get it out of the way so that this day could end. Like they said, tomorrow was another day. As if it would be any better . . .

He got up from his desk and opened the door into the corridor.

Some people liked to shut the door when having a difficult conversation. Christer preferred it open. The sight of the corridor and the sounds coming from it provided a link to reality. A far from ideal reality, but better than his little office. If nothing else, it was bigger.

Due to the new data protection rules, all details of Agnes's relatives had been erased as soon as any suspicion of a crime had been discounted. The police were now only allowed to retain personal data as part of crime prevention efforts, and Agnes's suicide hadn't fallen into that category. Until now. If anyone had asked Christer, which no one ever did, he would have pointed out that General Data Protection Regulation was a crock of shit. Surely it had never done any harm to keep records of necessary information about people? He couldn't understand why everyone suddenly needed to be so goddamn secretive. If someone wanted to know the last four digits of his social security number, he was happy to tell them.

Presumably someone from the National Board of Forensic Medicine could have given him the number, because they'd had the unhappy task of notifying Agnes's next of kin of their intention to exhume her body. But rather than go down that route he decided to google the phone number for Jesper's employer.

While on Google, he'd also found a recent article on the *Arvika Nyheter* website. Jesper was active in Sweden's Future, a political party strongly influenced by the Progress Party in Norway but even more right-wing. They had begun to gain popularity when they declared that people who didn't pay taxes shouldn't receive benefits. They'd shown no hesitation in calling it 'the immigration issue'.

Christer looked at the photo of Jesper used to illustrate the article. Agnes's father was smiling coldly at him with his thinning hair combed back and his blue jacket accentuated by a red scarf around his neck. It looked as if he was going out sailing. Jesper was on the local council in Arvika and the article was about changes he hoped to see in the coming year. Christer had no difficulty imagining Jesper happily announcing that immigrants must in future wear armbands.

He couldn't bring himself to read any more. Instead, he dialled the number for Arvika municipality and got through to someone on the switchboard. After three attempts, he was put through. Jesper picked up on the first ring.

'Enough,' he said into Christer's ear. 'I've told you not to call here, it doesn't look good.'

'Er, hello. This is Christer Bengtsson from the Stockholm police.'

'Oh! Sorry,' said Jesper in an entirely different tone of voice. 'I do apologize: I thought you were my wife.'

'No, it's Christer Bengtsson, as I said. We spoke once before when—'

'I remember,' Jesper cut in. 'It's not a conversation you forget in a hurry.'

Christer was surprised to hear that Jesper didn't have a Värmland accent, despite the fact that he had spoken to him before and surely ought to have remembered that. What was more, he'd just read in the article that Jesper had been born and raised in Halmstad. Memory could be spotty sometimes. The voice in his ear had a clear Halland lilt to it. 'Not a conversation you forget in a hurry.' Funny, Christer could have sworn that that was exactly what a man like Jesper would have tried to do.

'I'm sorry to call you again,' he said. 'But as you're aware, the investigation into your daughter's death has been reopened and her body has been exhumed in light of new information that suggests she may have been murdered.'

Jesper was silent.

Christer waited a moment and then continued: 'I need to ask whether Agnes had any enemies, if you're aware of anyone having threatened her? Was she in debt, or involved in criminal activities—'

'How dare you suggest that my daughter was a criminal!' Jesper shouted so loudly that Christer's ears rang. 'One more word and I'll sue you and the entire Stockholm police force for slander! You're a bunch of incompetent morons! I *never* believed it was suicide! As if she would take her own life in a park, in front of a bloody *theatre*! As if she was in a scene from a play!'

There was something contrived about Jesper's voice. Christer slammed the receiver against his forehead in frustration. He had called Jesper at the local council. If someone could hear their conversation then Jesper needed a line of retreat open to him. It would look bad if a politician from Sweden's Future had had a daughter who mixed with the wrong crowd. Christer didn't believe for one second that Jesper cared. He was yelling because he had an audience and wanted to sound like a devoted father.

'I didn't mean to be insensitive,' Christer said patiently. 'I realize you didn't know anything about her life in Stockholm, given the distance and how long it had been since you'd seen her. I understand you're very busy with your career in Arvika – and congratulations on the new family, by the way.'

'Be careful what you insinuate,' Jesper said icily.

The soft Halland accent was in sharp contrast to the cold tone. Something was shifting in Christer's subconscious. Something that was crying out for his attention, a pattern he ought to spot. But it slipped away as soon as he tried to catch it. He replied to Jesper matter-of-factly:

'I'm not insinuating anything. Agnes was a grown woman with her own life. My objective in calling was simply to inform you that we have reopened the investigation.'

Jesper fell silent again. It sounded like he was moving, perhaps into another room.

'That . . . terrorist,' Jesper said in a low voice. 'If I were you, I'd start with him.'

'Who are we talking about?' Christer asked, the adrenaline kicking in.

'The one she lived with. From Iran or Syria or wherever it was. Barely making ends meet. Wouldn't even have had somewhere to live if Agnes hadn't taken pity on him. I'll bet he was desperate to have that flat to himself.'

'What makes you think he's a terrorist?'

Christer was searching feverishly for a pen to take notes.

'Maybe not him personally. But his kind. They'll do anything to get ahead. Even killing my daughter.'

'I got the impression they were good friends,' Christer said, giving up on his search.

He wasn't sure the conversation was worth noting down.

'Agnes, friends with someone like that?' said Jesper. 'Never. It's precisely that kind of naive attitude that has got the country into the state it's in today. Unregulated. Unguarded. I thought if anyone knew that, it was the police. But you haven't been out into the real Sweden – I can hear that much. You should be ashamed. Get in touch once you've caught him.'

Jesper hung up. Christer sighed and looked at the photo in the *Arvika Nyheter* article again. Ordinarily, he wouldn't condone a father abandoning his daughter on her eighteenth birthday. But perhaps it had been the biggest favour Jesper had ever done Agnes. At least she'd had a few years without having to listen to him day in day out.

And then she'd died.

Daniel Bargabriel had already been questioned and released. It hadn't seemed as if he was guilty. Not then. But Mina had reported how he'd fled the cafe after her visit, and now he was missing. It didn't look good. Far from it. And Tuva's grandparents had said that Tuva thought Daniel would hurt her. Bloody hell.

He sat down in his seat and rubbed his eyes. It had been a long day. And not one of the most positive ones, at that. He didn't want to belittle the dreadful things that had happened to Agnes and Tuva, but at the same time, everybody had to die sooner or later. You could never know whose turn it was or when it might happen. That was the way it was. Sometimes Christer imagined a black-robed figure with a scythe darkening his door. Not necessarily because he wanted to die. He was pretty sure he didn't. But a bit of variation might be nice. Death. Life. Fucking hell.

He started up the CCTV footage on his computer with a sigh. Not that he had been planning to watch it again. But if he had it up on the screen playing, it would look like he was working. He clasped his hands over his stomach, leaned back against the backrest and closed his eyes, hoping it wouldn't turn out to be Daniel – he didn't want to add grist to Jesper's mill. But right now everything was pointing that way. Christer sighed. Regrettably, even racists were occasionally right.

42

In Srebrenica, he'd been a carpenter. He'd made things with his hands. He'd inherited his profession from his father and his father's father, and it was as if all their accumulated knowledge had been refined into him. At least, that was what his grandmother had always said. He could look at a piece of wood and see what was within it, what it wanted, what it *ought* to be shaped into. He had created so many beautiful things with his hands. He'd never let go of anything that wasn't exactly how it was meant to be.

Now he was no longer a creator. The war had taken away the desire to create. Death had dimmed his eye for beauty. Where previously there had been joy, there was now only a black mass comprising the collective weight of the war. All its sorrows could be found inside him. All the pain gathered in his joints, making his hands clench at the very thought of creating something.

But the war had left him with a different talent. Digging. Digging to bury the dead. He had lost count of how many people he had buried. Now he dug holes for coffins. People buried one by one. Under the auspices of the church.

Then.

Then they had simply heaved in heaps of people. Mostly men. And boys. Deep graves filled with people toppling in like animals. The sound of flesh landing on flesh. Bodies being stripped of those few valuables they had. Most had nothing worth stealing. They were poor. Insignificant.

Sometimes he wondered whether Mladić could hear the heavy thudding of bodies from inside his cell. Probably not. The sound of eight thousand Bosnian Muslims being tipped into graves ought to be echoing between the cell walls, but no doubt that bastard was sitting pretty with food, heating and a TV. It took a particular kind of monster to murder eight thousand people.

'All right, mate. I'm Ove – the man with the digger. You've gotta tell me how to dig.'

Nikola shook the proffered hand. The man was in his fifties. He was stocky, bald and had tattoos covering his head. A company decal, *Ove's Mini Excavation,* was visible on the small digger. Nikola looked at him suspiciously. In Srebrenica, the tattoos would have indicated that he was a criminal who had spent at least ten years inside. He wasn't sure what they meant here, but he decided that he would at no point turn his back on the man.

'If you start by digging carefully through the top layer,' said Nikola, 'then Emil and I will take over as we get closer to the coffin. They're usually two or three metres down, so don't go further than one and a half, just to be safe.'

The man with the tattooed head nodded and headed back to his digger. Nikola followed him suspiciously with his gaze.

A man and a woman were approaching and close behind them were another man and woman. The two at the back were wearing protective overalls.

'Mina Dabiri. I'm with the police,' said the first woman. 'This is Vincent Walder.'

'It was me who brought in Ove,' said the man next to the police-woman. 'He's good. And my neighbour. Well, the nearest house at any rate. I assume he called you?'

'Is he a criminal?' Nikola asked.

It was best to be upfront. You needed to know where you were with people. The man stared at him.

'A criminal? I don't think so. Why . . . why do you ask?'

Nikola nodded curtly in reply.

'Good,' he said. 'He seems good.'

'We've also got forensics here,' Mina added, nodding at the couple behind them. 'They will take over and deal with the coffin as soon as it's been exhumed.'

Nikola nodded again. He was never one for words, preferring just to get on and do his job. The Swedes were far too talkative sometimes. It was as if they couldn't bear the silence and were always striving to fill it. Personally, he loved the silence.

Nikola and Emil took a couple of steps back to keep out of the way of the digger. They didn't need to talk to each other. They were brothers.

170

Not by blood, but ever since they had dug graves in Srebrenica, they hadn't left each other's sides. They had both lost everything. Their families were somewhere in the anonymous mass graves. Never found. Never identified.

They had come to Sweden together and shared a small two-bed flat in Rinkeby. Nikola cooked. Emil did the washing up. They existed. It would be too much to say they lived.

The digger was being deftly operated by the man with the tattooed head, and it didn't take long before the upper layer of soil was carefully peeled away. He squinted at the man who had come with the police-woman and the way he was attentively watching the process with the digger. Somehow, the man reminded Nikola of his brother. Nermin had been the intelligent one of the two. When Nikola had been creating with his hands, Nermin had been creating with his brain.

Before the war, his brother had been a Maths lecturer at the university. Nikola often missed him. He didn't understand why he had been spared while Nermin had been dust and bones for decades.

'What did you tell forensics about me?' the man said to the woman.

Apparently he had forgotten Nikola was there.

'Nothing,' she said. 'Julia's team is fairly new, so they're not that sure who's on it or what consultants have been drafted in to assist. Just play along as if you're one of us – it's unlikely they'll be any the wiser.'

Nikola shook his head. Everyone had secrets, even here. Too many secrets were a bad thing. It was when you didn't trust everyone that things could come tumbling down. The digger reversed and stopped. The cab door opened.

'Is that about right? Or should I keep digging?'

Nikola took the spade in his hand and went over to the grave. Emil followed close behind. They peered down. He assessed the distance from the surface to where the soil had been dug up. He looked at Emil, who nodded.

'We'll take over now,' he said.

They climbed down into the pit and began to dig with their shovels. In his breast ached the memory of another soil, another death, too long ago.

But he felt it now too.

Always now.

43

At first he didn't hear the phone ringing. Not until Maria kicked his foot.

'Are you going to answer?' she said.

He had been deeply absorbed in a book on behavioural patterns and age-related crises. The author was outlining which views, values and actions were most common in various phases of life. People weren't as different as they thought. In the beginning, he'd bought the book to help him understand his family. He didn't want to make the mistake of believing that an eight-year-old, a fifteen-year-old, a nineteen-year-old and a forty-year-old all thought the same way. But he had begun to suspect that the data the book was based on didn't cover his family.

This time he was reading it to try to understand the murderer. Perhaps by assessing the actions they were aware of, he could try to calculate age, gender and background. That would be something at least. But he had got hung up on the fact that the murderer's actions were so contradictory.

'Vincent?' Maria said again in an irritated tone of voice. 'Your phone is ringing! Or don't you dare answer because I'm sitting here and can hear?'

He closed the book and looked at his mobile lying on the coffee table. Mina's name was glowing at him. He quickly picked it up to answer while Maria pointedly turned up the TV.

'Give my best to your lover,' she said. 'Just don't wake Aston. He's had a rough day at school.'

He went into the study. It was that or compete with the sound from *Let's Dance* on TV4 Play.

'Hi Mina,' he said, pulling the door to.

'Christer has spoken to Tuva's grandparents – I just read the report,' she said.

He sat down at the desk and slowly spun in his chair. Mina wouldn't want to put a phone that had been lying on a table or in her pocket against her ear, not without cleaning it thoroughly first, so she was either using headphones or Airpods. Which would also have to be cleaned before use. How many times would she use them before having to buy new ones? He decided that if he ever bought her a Christmas present, it was going to be an extra pair of Airpods.

'Christer has also spoken to Agnes's father, Jesper,' she continued. 'Guess who all three mention?'

'Daniel Bargabriel.'

It was a guess, but it was all he had.

'Well done, Master Mentalist. Granted it's all circumstantial. Märta and Gunnar said that Tuva didn't dare talk about him she was so afraid he would hurt her. Jesper claimed that Daniel wanted Agnes's flat. While he may have said that because he's a racist—'

'Daniel fled the cafe for a reason.'

Mina fell silent. He could hear voices in the background. They grew louder and then fainter again. She was obviously at work and no one knew that she was calling him. He waited for her to continue talking. He liked listening to her.

'So what does your profile tell us?' she said, once the voices in the background were gone. 'Is Ruben right? Could it be him?'

He considered what he had seen when he had observed Daniel during their brief visit to Fab Fika. Through the wall of the living room, he could hear Tony Irving saying something about a perfect slow foxtrot. Maria must have turned up the volume even more when he didn't come back. Doubtless she was going to make him pay for this later, but he would have to cross that bridge when he came to it.

'When we met Daniel, he showed signs of both nervousness and of hiding something,' he said. 'But nothing more than that. It's possible that he may turn violent if he is pushed harder. But I didn't see any signs of repressed anger. If there had been, he would have been more sarcastic or cynical, rather than activating his *orbicularis oculi*—'

'Orbi-what?' Mina interjected.

'He wouldn't have been smiling with his eyes. And the stress we subjected him to would have led to some form of tic in his hands or face. None of that happened. At the same time, it's dangerous to generalize from one single encounter. Just because Daniel wasn't violent with

173

us doesn't mean that he can't be in other situations. But I've also said that the murderer seems to have two sides. There's an explosive and violent side, but also one that is calm and capable of planning. It remains to be seen whether Daniel possesses both.'

Mina swore.

'It sounds like our priority is to bring Daniel in right away,' she said. 'Even if he's innocent of the murders, he may need protection from the supporters of Sweden's Future. Agnes's father is a high-ranking member of the party and he is very angry. I doubt he'd risk getting his hands dirty by attacking Daniel himself, but I wouldn't put it past him to reach out to the party faithful by putting Daniel's picture on his Facebook page and encouraging them to "do the right thing". It's been done before.'

Vincent groaned and did a spin in his chair.

'Sweden's Future. God, they're muppets,' he said. 'Are we going to have to deal with them too?'

'Muppets?' Mina said. 'I think you must have been watching a different version to me. But thanks. See you soon.'

She ended the call.

He stayed there for a while with the phone in his hand while gathering the strength to go back to Maria. At least *Let's Dance* seemed to be reaching its end – he could hear the presenters summarizing the evening. He looked at the mobile display, trying to make it light up again with Mina's name. It remained blank. He took a deep breath, opened the door and went back into the living room.

'I'm sitting right here and can hear everything,' Maria exclaimed. 'And you're having phone sex in the next room. It's so disgusting! You should be ashamed!'

He looked at his wife. Hundreds of cutting replies whirled around his head, each better formulated than the last. Each worse for their relationship than the last. In the end he said nothing at all.

44

Daniel had waited as long as he could to leave the flat in Märsta, but he couldn't wait any longer. He needed groceries. Toilet paper. And to be outside for a bit. He studied his reflection in the bathroom mirror. Instead of sexy stubble he sprouted pathetic wisps of hair that formed an uneven patchwork over his chin, which was why he always tried to ensure he was cleanshaven. His hair hadn't been washed for a week and was sticking to his head like a greasy helmet. The dye had grown out so that it was brown at the roots. In short, he looked a mess.

It was a good thing Evelyn couldn't see him – she would have told him he looked like a homeless guy with cancer. She had a way of saying whatever would hit people the hardest at any given moment. He missed her more than ever. But she would probably break up with him on the spot if she saw him now. It wouldn't surprise him if he smelled bad too.

The question was whether they knew. If the police knew where he was. He had been stupidly careless. And he'd had to lie about Tuva. Well, maybe not straight-up lie, but he obviously hadn't told them everything. And that could come back to get him. It had been a close-run thing twice now. He couldn't afford any more mistakes.

Daniel looked in the mirror again. For starters, he needed to put on more than just the T-shirt and pants he'd been wearing day in day out, then he needed to get out of the door. But he couldn't shake off the sense that the police were waiting to jump him the second he came out of the flat. Then they'd beat him senseless. Or someone would see him and call in a tip about where he was. His face was probably on wanted posters hanging from every single lamppost from the flat as far as the supermarket. And not without cause.

'Pull yourself together,' he said out loud.

But it was no good. He was too afraid to go out. And the longer he left it, the more the fear would paralyse him.

He looked at his reflection in the mirror for a third time. Ran his hand over his straggly beard. Scrutinized his stained T-shirt. Maybe he could call Samir, ask him to come by with food and clothes. But Samir would bring a bunch of other problems with him. He'd be over the moon to have somewhere to sell his little bags from. And Josef, who owned the flat, wouldn't be happy about that. No, Samir was not an option. Daniel hadn't talked to Evelyn since he'd fled, but she'd dump him if he got mixed up with Samir. And he didn't want to lose her – nothing was worth that.

Evelyn decided matters.

He couldn't be the prey any longer – he needed to go on the offensive. And that meant making contact with the police instead of waiting for them to find him. And he had to be so convincing that they would forget him for a long time to come. Forever sounded like a good amount of time. He took down the business card that was stuck to the mirror, fetched his phone and dialled the number.

Someone picked up at the other end but he didn't quite catch what she said. The maelstrom of his nerves was too loud inside his own head.

'Hello,' he said. 'You came to my work a while back and wanted to talk. It's about Tuva. Tuva Bengtsson.'

45

Kvibille 1982

He unfolded the drawing on the barn floor, which had been carefully swept to ensure the drawing didn't get dirty. It had taken several days to draw, measure, change and redo, but now it was finally ready. He lay down next to the drawing and looked at it in depth, part by part, to check that he hadn't made any mistakes.

It had been a long time since there had been animals kept in the barn, but it still smelled of cows and manure. Jane thought the smell was completely disgusting and refused to set foot inside the building. But it made him feel safe.

It was his place and no one else's. He reckoned he had spent more time there with his projects than he had in the real house.

There was a knock on the door and it opened. Jane was standing in the doorway with her hand still on the handle.

'Can I come in?' she said.

'Yes, but I thought you didn't like being in here,' he replied, sitting up.

'I know, but I've realized it's only malodorous molecules. I'm working on re-interpreting them. I read about how you could do that. And I wanted to find out how you were getting on with the number puzzle. I forgot about it before.'

He took the plastic frame with the numbers out of his back pocket, stood up and went over to his sister. He had been trying to beat her challenge for several days.

'I don't understand,' he said, handing her the puzzle. 'It's as if it . . . it can't be done.'

'Bingo,' she said. 'It's unsolvable.'

He frowned. How could one order of numbers be possible while another wasn't? It didn't make sense.

'Look,' she said. 'All the numbers need to be in order except for fourteen and fifteen, which need to swap. If we start with one of the other numbers, what's the smallest number of moves you can do to have them end up in the same place they started – if you have to make at least one?'

'Two moves. First one step away – in any direction – and then back again.'

'Good. An even number of moves. That means that no matter how many moves you make, it always has to end in an even number of moves for a number to return to the same place. Don't look at me like that – it's mathematical logic. But how many moves does it require for fourteen to end up in fifteen's spot?'

'One,' he said. 'Ah! An odd number of moves.'

'You've got it. Nicely done for one so little. It's always going to take an odd number of moves for fourteen and fifteen to change places. But it takes an even number to keep the others in place. And you can't make an odd and even number of moves at the same time. So it's unsolvable.'

He shook his head. He didn't understand everything she was saying. But somehow it sounded right.

'I like evens,' he said. 'Isn't there some kind of club for people like you?'

'You mean extra smart people?'

'Nope, annoying big sisters.' Then he slowly added: 'By the way, you know those molecules you're training your nose with? You do realize they're *poo molecules*, right?'

Jane's face turned green.

'Urgh!' she yelled. 'God, you're disgusting!'

She ran out of the barn, while he laughed so hard he bent over double. He laughed even more when he saw her trying to blow her nose on her sleeve in an attempt to flush out whatever invisible contents were in there.

Then he returned to his drawing and brushed away a few pieces of straw that had ended up on it. It wasn't his first drawing. Along the walls were a number of structures – big and small – and he had built them all. His magic tricks. Some of them worked, others didn't. Allan, the owner of the timberyard, knew about his passion for construction and was impressed by how good he had got at it. So there were always offcuts, a few planks or a piece of fabric whenever he needed them. And when there weren't, he improvised with old cereal boxes instead.

The latest drawing, however, was something else. He had invented the illusions lined up against the wall after seeing magicians on TV and trying to work out what they did. He never knew whether he'd guessed right. But the drawing on the floor – it was *for real*.

With Mum's help, he'd ordered some books about stage illusions through the library in Kvibille. It had taken over a month for them to arrive. The books had mostly turned out to be biographies, with photographs of sequin-suited magicians in Las Vegas. He had hoped that it would say how they built their illusions, but apparently no one was willing to divulge that. Until he came to *Hobby Series 12: Build your own magic!* – a title so dull he had almost not bothered ordering it. To his amazement, it featured blueprints for many of the best-known illusions. He couldn't believe a book like that existed. A book with all the secrets.

It was carelessly done – the instructions consisted of photographed drawings, most of which were presumably American, because the author had changed the measurements from inches to centimetres in the margins next to each photo. But that didn't make any difference. The book contained the explanation for his favourite illusion: *The Substitution Trunk*.

Most other illusions that he had seen were based on the magician squeezing their assistant into a box and then doing something with that box. Sawing it in half, setting fire to it, sticking swords through it. Then the assistant would emerge, having changed clothes. He had always found it a bit odd. Magic tricks based on harming someone while they were getting changed. It must be some grown-up thing.

What set *The Substitution Trunk* apart from other illusions was that the magician and the assistant had to go through the same experience. Both of them were magicians. Both were assistants. The magician *became* the assistant.

He was able to change places with someone else. *Become* someone else. That was a better story.

He squinted at the picture in the open book, which was propped on the floor next to the drawing. Two people were smiling and receiving applause. He needed to find an assistant. Jane was out of the question. But with the new measurements he had calculated on the drawing, Mum would easily fit into the box. She was going to be so surprised, so proud of him. He was finally going to do his own magic. He checked the measurements one more time – just to be sure.

It was going to be his best trick ever.

46

'How did the seventieth go?'

Vincent maintained a light tone of voice. He lived in the hope that she would let it pass. Not that the odds were good. Frankly, if it did happen then today was the day to go out and buy his first-ever lottery scratch card.

You had a one in 250,000 chance of winning one million kronor but the chance of winning *something* was actually up to one in five. The odds of getting six numbers and a share of the jackpot in the main lottery were 1 in 490,860. And 1 in 50 to win anything at all. It would have to be a scratch card. On the other hand, when you played along with Bingolotto on TV, the probability of getting to play the Super Chance or the Colour Five was around 1 in 166,000. As for any kind of win at all, the probability was 1 in 7.7 tickets, so perhaps he ought to . . .

'Vincent! Are you even listening to me?' Maria hissed, her face flushed red with anger.

He blinked and returned to reality. Maria was always hopping mad after having spent time with her family. Filled with the bitter poison that her siblings and parents insisted on trickling into her ears.

Nevertheless, his heart sank a little when he realized that there would be no scratch card today. On the contrary. It was going to be conflict management, God help him. He got up and refilled *Festive Farter* with coffee before sitting down opposite her. The sun was casting a golden glow onto the table as if it were rehearsing for the summer.

'Everyone thought it was very odd that you weren't at the party,' said Maria. 'I explained that you had a performance the same evening, but both Mum and Dad took it very badly.'

'That's a pity,' he said, noting at the same moment from Maria's body language that this was altogether the wrong answer.

He could read an audience of eight hundred people down to the smallest mood-shift and nuance, and he could play them like an orchestra. But for some reason he was unable to communicate with the human minefield that was his wife. Especially not after those mines had been primed by her parents. And Ulrika.

'A pity?'

Maria's voice rose to a falsetto. She was holding her *Glitter Pussy* mug and he reflected again on how poorly the epithet suited her. There were many terms that better described his wife. Most other words, actually.

'I didn't mean . . .'

He was tapping his foot rhythmically under the table but forced himself to stop. If he seemed nervous, she would only get more annoyed. Sometimes he wondered what exactly she'd seen in him. Why she'd fallen for him. He was completely the wrong type for her. Or to turn it around, maybe she was completely the wrong type for him. How you looked at the situation depended on who had picked who. And which of them had initiated what was regarded as a betrayal of the family of such magnitude that relatives were still licking their wounds.

He told himself that she had been the one who had made the first move. She claimed it had been him. Perhaps the truth was somewhere in the middle. Maria had always been competing with Ulrika, which hadn't always been an easy task, given Ulrika's annoying habit of being perfect. Maria was the little sister who never quite got it together. At the same time, perhaps it was Ulrika's perfection that had drawn him to Maria. It was exhausting trying to live up to Ulrika's standards. Maria had no standards. At least not in that sense. She was there, in the present. Open. Immediate. Or so he had thought at the time. Only it had turned out that the version of herself that Maria had been showing the world had been some distance from her true self. But by the time he had discovered that, it had already been too late. By then, their betrayal was already public and they were side by side on the battlefield, surrounded by devastation of their own making. And if he was being honest, he probably hadn't lived up to what she had expected of him either.

However, he staunchly maintained that it had been Maria who had crossed the forbidden boundary. Regardless what Maria might say the chemistry between them had been brewing for months. Looks. Movements. Bodies that happened to brush against each other in passing. They had been at Maria and Ulrika's parents' summer house.

The others had gone out for a swim. Vincent had stayed behind with the excuse that he needed to work. He had no idea what excuse Maria had given. But it was there in that battered old country kitchen that they'd had sex for the first time. Maria had come up to him. Put her arms around him, kissed him, and then without missing a beat stuck her hand down his shorts and grasped his hard cock. He had picked her up and carried her into the guestroom where he and Ulrika usually stayed when they were visiting. Then he'd been inside her.

They had both known then and there that they were choosing a path where the only possible route was forward. This was a decision that they had resolutely stuck to – to the family's horror. He had filed for divorce from Ulrika a week later.

They had fucked like crazy that first year, mostly at Maria's initiative. She was the one who had wanted to conquer his body, occupy it like a fortress of which her sister had been the commander. And he'd had nothing against that. He liked sex with Maria. With Ulrika it had mostly been about performance. But with Maria it had felt more . . . genuine.

But whatever it had been, it had soon ebbed away. In recent years, it had been a rarity if they had managed once a month. Now he could barely remember when Maria had last touched him. And when she actually did let him come, it was with that newfound prudishness and the demand that the lights be switched off. It now felt like a distant fantasy that she had ever wanted to look him in the eyes when he had been inside her.

'Good God. Hellooooo? Where are you? Surely you can at least pretend to take some interest in what I'm saying?' she hissed.

He couldn't understand why he found it so hard to focus on what she said. Perhaps it was because he usually knew in advance what it was going to be; sometimes he muttered her lines in a low voice to himself at the same time as she said them out loud.

'I just said that you have to call Mum and Dad to apologize,' she said. 'Seventy is a milestone event. When exactly are you going to start prioritizing the family? I know you get off on coming and going as you please, but the rest of us – those of us in the real world – we don't have that luxury!'

'I don't come and go as I please,' he said in a tired voice. 'I have a job that means I travel a lot in the evenings and weekends. But it's a job.'

'And this new thing that you're so fucking secretive about? With her, that cop? Is that supposed to be a job too?'

182

He knew it didn't matter what he said. Maria didn't engage in dialogue with him – it was always a monologue. But he was tired of playing the onlooker – confined to emitting the occasional noise to show he was paying attention. Not this time.

'What do you think is going on?' he continued. 'Just because I've got a spotlight on me when I'm at work, you think it's all groupies, coke and parties every night? You know what? You're bang on target. That's exactly what my life is like. If only you knew how many TV sets I've thrown out of hotel windows after snorting lines off naked models' flat stomachs. Especially in Vara and Kalmar – you know, the smaller places – I have one hell of a fucking time! There aren't enough hours in the day to service all the horny twenty-two-year-olds who come to me begging for it!'

Maria stared at him.

'Now you're being ridiculous,' she said.

'You knew what my job involved when you chose me,' he said. 'It's tiring, I travel a lot, and yes, I'm in the public eye. But saying that I don't prioritize the family? When I'm not on tour I'm actually with my family more than the average father. Which one of us drops off and picks up Aston four days in five? Which one of us walked Rebecka and Benjamin home from school every day two hours before all the other kids? And I'm *here*, Maria. When did you last fix Aston's remote-control car? Or paint figurines with Benjamin? Or have a real conversation with Rebecka? Sitting there with your mug of tea scrolling through Facebook isn't being with your family. Being under the same roof doesn't mean you're present. And by the way, who do you think is *paying* for your personalized Christmas mugs with "witty" epithets on them?'

He paused for breath. He hadn't been meaning to go quite that far, but at the same time . . . everything he'd said was true.

Maria stood up holding her *Glitter Pussy* mug.

'I want us to see a therapist,' she said. 'What's more, you have no idea how much I do with Aston. Why do you think he won't do his reading with you?'

For once, she had managed to take him by surprise.

'Therapy?' he said tentatively. 'What kind?'

He was on thin ice. He couldn't imagine anything more meaningless than spending money and time on consulting with someone who possessed less knowledge on the human psyche than he did. It would be like a brain surgeon going to see a gynaecologist for advice ahead of their next operation. Madness. But he knew that was perhaps not the best thing to say to Maria right now.

'You choose,' Maria snorted, heading for the hallway. 'I'm late for yoga.'

Vincent waited until she had left. Then he retrieved his mobile from his pocket where it had been vibrating for the last three minutes. Two missed calls from Mina. And a message.

Can you come to police HQ asap? Daniel is coming in. I want you at the interview.

47

They showed him into a small room at police headquarters. He assumed it was an interrogation room, given that it looked exactly like the ones he had seen in the movies. A table with two chairs, one either side. A few chairs along the walls. Otherwise empty. The only difference was that the table was made of light brown wood and resembled office furniture from the nineties. It also lacked the anchor points to attach handcuffs to. Daniel had never been in an interrogation room in Syria, but he suspected they didn't feature furniture from IKEA.

The door opened and the hot cop who had come to the cafe entered. She had the same man with her as last time.

'Sorry to keep you waiting,' she said. 'My colleague wasn't in the office when you arrived.'

The man nodded at him and settled down on one of the chairs along the wall. What was his name again? Willy or something like that. Daniel had recognized him last time and now that feeling was even stronger. But he didn't know where from.

'It may be that you've seen me on TV,' the man said in reply to the question that Daniel had only posed in his head. 'And my name's Vincent.'

He was clearly an open book to this guy. Turning himself in might not have been the best idea after all.

'Vincent Walder is helping us with the investigation,' Mina said. 'He's not a policeman, but he does bring . . . other expertise to the table.'

Daniel wondered whether Mina knew that she smiled when she talked about Vincent.

'Today he'll just be sitting in and listening,' she continued. 'I don't know whether you remember, but my name is Mina Dabiri.'

'Yeah, it said so on the business card,' he said.

'You wanted to talk to us.'

Mina sat down opposite him and opened a laptop.

'Do you want to take off your jacket?'

He had rehearsed what he was going to say and above all how he was going to sound. If he seemed too well prepared, it would sound dishonest. But if he seemed too nervous then he'd sound guilty. The art was to find the exact midpoint between the two. Ensuring that he paused enough, but not too much. Making sure that he occasionally stopped in the middle of a word, as if he was uncertain about what to say. But not being flighty for the sake of it. So he had rehearsed his speech carefully. But that guy Vincent looked like he could see straight through him. He didn't dare give his speech. He needed to think of something else.

'Sorry I ran away from the cafe,' he said. 'But I panicked. And it's a thin jacket. It's warm out. I'd rather keep it on.'

'Why did you panic?' said Mina. 'Has something happened that we ought to know about?'

'Who wouldn't panic if the police came knocking?' Daniel said, trying to smile, only to abandon the attempt after glancing at Vincent.

'The last time I had anything to do with you lot, you wanted to put me away for murder,' he said. 'You know I lived with Agnes Ceci. That's why I reacted . . . so strongly . . . when you came.'

'And now?' said Mina. 'What do we want to put you away for now?'

She was smart. She was getting him to do all the talking. Daniel shrugged his shoulders and hoped it looked natural. He dug his hands into his jacket pockets. The garment was a good shield – hopefully it wasn't as easy to read him with it on. It felt like he was watching himself through Vincent's eyes. Everything he did looked suspicious. The same applied to everything he didn't do. He was overcome by nerves and blinked his eyes rapidly a few times. For fuck's sake. Blinking was probably a bad sign.

'I assume Tuva is still missing,' he said. 'Otherwise you wouldn't have been interested in talking to me. But the truth is I don't know anything. I barely knew her. It was Agnes and Tuva who knew each other.'

Mina stiffened and even Vincent over by the wall seemed to react.

'They *knew* each other?' said Mina. 'That's news to us. We didn't hear anything to that effect when we talked to the people who knew Agnes or to Tuva's grandparents. We knew that you were a common factor between them, but there's a direct connection between them? Is that what you're saying?'

186

He fidgeted in his seat. He had simply assumed they knew. If only this Vincent guy would stop staring at him.

'Well,' he said. 'Maybe *knew* is the wrong word. More that they knew *of* each other. Agnes worked at the cafe before Tuva started. That was how I got the job. Agnes got me Tuva's phone number. But I did the rest of the work myself.'

'And both of them knew you,' said Mina, typing furiously on her keyboard.

Then she glanced up, leaned over the computer and looked him in the eyes.

'First the one you live with dies,' she said. 'Shot in the face. And barely a month later your workmate . . . disappears. You must see how this looks for you. If you've got anything to say then say it now. Keep things from getting any worse.'

Daniel's mouth went dry. This was the moment. If he got the next words wrong, then he was screwed. They would eat him alive.

'I understand how it must look,' he said. 'I really do understand.'

He made sure he looked concerned but not worried.

'But what am I meant to say?' he continued. 'Stockholm isn't that big. Like I already said, the reason I worked with Tuva was simply because I lived with Agnes.'

'And that rules out your involvement how?'

She kept her eyes fixed on him.

'But you're looking at it the wrong way!' he said, a little more desperately. 'I'm not the common denominator for Agnes and Tuva – it's Agnes who is. If someone else had lived with Agnes then it would have been someone else who worked with Tuva. It's a fluke that it's me sitting here. I don't have anything to do with it. Surely you must understand that?'

'So why do Tuva's grandparents say that she didn't want to talk about you – that she was afraid you would hurt her? Why has Agnes's father identified you as a suspect?'

He hadn't been expecting that. He gulped. He would have preferred not to tell them. Evelyn would go nuts when she found out. But he had no choice.

'Agnes's dad is a racist, in case you don't know. He's suspicious of everyone who isn't Swedish forests. As for Tuva . . . Tuva didn't want to talk about me because we had a thing.'

'A thing?'

'We were together,' he said, fidgeting. 'For a while. But I was also

187

with Evelyn. Tuva knew I wouldn't leave Evelyn for her. That was what she meant about hurting her. Emotionally. Not physically. I would never . . .'

'Daniel,' said Vincent, who had been silent until now, 'describe a double lift for me.'

'A double . . . what? Is that some kind of . . . oh, no no no. I never had a threesome with Tuva and Evelyn – that would never have worked.'

Vincent looked at him with a stare that was unreadable. Daniel desperately wanted to joke about something, but realized it was best to keep his mouth shut.

'We're going to play a little game,' said Vincent. 'Try to answer without thinking. What's the first thing that springs to mind when you hear the word . . . illusions?'

'Er, Harry Potter?'

'Patterns?' Vincent said.

'Shirt.'

'Violence?'

'Ouch.'

Vincent cracked a smile. Then he nodded curtly to Mina. Whatever it had been about, it was apparently over. Mina's expression softened compared to earlier and she leaned against the backrest of the chair.

'So you're just a victim of circumstance?' she said. 'OK. Let's go with that for now. It's not unfeasible that you were simply in the wrong place at the wrong time. Is there anything you want to add to your previous statement about Agnes? Any thoughts on who might have taken her life?'

'Taken?' Daniel said in confusion.

'Murdered her,' Mina clarified.

He shook his head.

'In that case, do you know of anyone who might want to hurt Tuva? Has anyone behaved threateningly in the cafe? Was there anyone who came there regularly and talked to her?'

He exhaled and forced himself not to breathe in too quickly. Perhaps it was going to be OK after all. But adrenaline was still rushing around his body.

'People come in all the time who are high or weird,' he said. 'And sure, we've got a few regulars among them. But most of the people who come in regularly use the cafe as their office or living room.'

'What do you mean by that?' said Mina.

'The media types always have their laptops and iPhones with them.

One regular is always staring at drawings in a folder. We had a few young girls who were knitting jumpers. The board gamers come in the evening. But I can't think of anyone who was weird around Tuva in particular – either among the normal lot or the . . . stranger ones.'

'Please think about it some more,' said Mina, nodding thoughtfully. 'See what you remember. Have any of those slightly more . . . eccentric . . . customers suddenly stopped coming to the cafe? And give some more thought to Agnes.'

She turned the laptop to face him.

'I want you to fill in your details so that we can reach you,' she said, pointing to a form on the screen. 'Other than at work. An address and a phone number. In case we have more questions. We're also going to check that the details you give are correct before we allow you to leave.'

It took him a few seconds to realize what this meant.

'So we're done?' he said, quickly filling in the form.

He suddenly felt much lighter, almost giggly. They had nothing they could hold him for. Even if they wanted to. Maybe the Swedish cops were OK after all.

'Almost done,' Mina said, turning to Vincent by the wall. 'Vincent, what do you say? Have you got anything you want to add?'

Vincent scratched his throat.

'Daniel, do me a favour,' he said. 'Describe five things in your flat – but one of them has to be made up.'

'What?' said Daniel, realizing he was desperate for a piss. 'But I . . . OK. There's, erm, blinds, a kettle, mirror in the bathroom, ceiling fan and a desk. Why?'

'Just curious,' said Vincent.

Mina coughed loudly.

'OK, we're done,' she said, getting up. 'You can go. Thanks for coming in. I'll be in touch when we know more.'

Daniel nodded at Vincent.

'If you need me then I'll be at my girlfriend Evelyn's,' he said. 'I put in her number too. I've got some explaining to do to her.'

48

'That was interesting,' said Vincent.

He felt surprisingly exhilarated by the experience of being involved in questioning Daniel. It wasn't so different from what he did on stage with people, like he had done thousands of times before. But the feeling that it was for real was intoxicating.

'Why don't we take the lift? It's quite a lot of storeys to climb.'

He pointed at the steel lift doors and felt Mina's reluctance hit him strongly and palpably. Personally, he hated the cooped-up feeling of being in a lift. It was like a moving grave. But he was at least trying to work on his claustrophobia so that the world didn't end up feeling too narrow. He was uncertain whether Mina was working on this at all. And if there was anyone who deserved a bigger world, it was her.

'By the way, how come I was allowed to sit in on the interview?' he said, distracting her attention before her anxiety about the bacteria box – as he'd heard her call the lift – grew too strong.

'I told Julia what you said about Daniel on the phone,' she said, turning towards him. 'At first she was a little surprised that we were still in touch, since she hasn't heard anything about the profile she asked you to compile. But she was interested in your analysis and approved your presence when I asked if it was OK.'

The digits on the wall display behind Mina indicated that the lift was approaching their floor. It was important not to push. Not to press too hard. It had to be tiny, tiny nudges in the right direction so that she was able to reconquer her own habitat piece by piece. So far it was going well. At least, she wasn't heading for the stairs . . .

'Thanks,' he said as the lift doors slid open. 'And the profile is on the way, if she still wants it. But I thought that Jan guy had already given you what you needed?'

He nodded quizzically towards the open lift doors. Mina hesitated. Then she shrugged with feigned nonchalance.

'Well fine,' she said. 'But only so you don't run to the wrong floor again. And I'm sure Jan is going to give us loads. Most of which will no doubt be wrong.'

He entered first and held open the door with his arm. Reluctantly, dragging her feet, Mina followed. She looked around with distaste and positioned herself precisely in the middle of the lift to avoid brushing against anything.

'Can I ask a question about the interview?' Mina said. 'What were those test questions about at the end?'

'I wanted to check his behavioural change when he was lying. He doesn't have a ceiling fan.'

Vincent pressed the 'B' button and the doors closed. The lift began to travel down and he focused his thoughts on the conversation to avoid being overcome by the feeling of being shut in.

'Wouldn't it have been better to ask those questions at the beginning then?' she said. 'So that we could see whether he was lying in the rest of the interview.'

'I can draw conclusions on that anyway – after the fact. I observed his behaviour closely throughout. If I'd asked the questions at the beginning, he might have got suspicious and become more observant of his own behaviour, which would have ruined the opportunity to take note of his natural behavioural patterns.'

Mina no longer appeared to be listening to what he was saying. Her hands were clenched so hard at her sides that the knuckles were white. She was staring at a fleck of grease on the mirror. Someone who used ample product on their hair must have leaned against it.

'I . . .' he began.

The lift suddenly stopped with a shudder. But the door didn't open. They had not reached a floor. He tried pressing the button to open the door. Nothing happened. He pressed it again and again and again. In vain.

'It must have got stuck,' Mina said.

Vincent continued to feverishly press the button. It was probably just a loose contact. That had to be it. He tried to master his breathing but it was difficult – the halt had taken him completely by surprise. He couldn't start hyperventilating; he needed to control the oxygen supply to his brain. He looked around for something to distract himself with but found nothing. He was shut in.

191

'Hey, I don't think that's going to help,' she said.

He could hear her voice but was barely conscious of the fact that she was standing there. *The door wouldn't open.* They were stuck in a metal box and couldn't get out.

The walls slowly began to close in on them.

His throat went dry and the air became too heavy to breathe. He backed towards the door while his field of vision shrunk until all he could see was a narrow tunnel surrounded by darkness. The walls were still getting closer. He could almost see the oxygen being sucked out of the lift.

Air.

There was no air.

Stars and patterns were dancing across his entire field of vision. Mina was like a tiny dot at the far end of the tunnel. Her voice sounded like it was coming from far away but he couldn't focus on it. Not with the walls about to collapse on top of him.

Someone's hands were suddenly resting on his shoulders.

'Vincent. Listen to me.'

The touch stabilized him, forcing him to concentrate.

'You're having a panic attack.'

Words slowly but surely began to penetrate through the chaos in his brain.

'What you're feeling is awful, but it isn't real,' the voice said. 'It's hormones, adrenaline and cortisol rushing through your body – that's what's making you feel like this.'

He tried to take a deep breath. Couldn't. He placed his hands on top of the ones resting on his shoulders. He breathed in again. Better this time.

'You're not dying,' said Mina. 'There's no danger. It's just chemical reactions taking over your brain. Whatever you're thinking right now, it's not real.'

He still couldn't answer, concentrating on the feel of her hands under his. Her warm skin. He recognized that it was taking a big effort on her part to stay there – that she hadn't expected him to touch her. But she didn't remove her hands.

'We'll soon be out of here. I've pressed the emergency button,' she said. 'This lift gets stuck sometimes – it's one of the reasons I prefer to take the stairs. But it's never stuck for long. So breathe with me. Deep, long breaths. We'll breathe together, Vincent . . . Breathe.'

She was standing behind him and he leaned back against her and did as she said. The warmth from her body spread through him like a wave of calm. The walls were still there and they were still far too close, but they were no longer closing in. Mina had made them stop. Made him feel safe. It had been a long time since anyone had made him feel like that. A very, very long time.

The lift suddenly shook and the doors opened. He filled his lungs with air – *new* air – which was more than welcome. Mina was now standing at his side. He turned towards her.

'Sorry. That was . . . undignified.'

Mina shrugged.

'Next time, why don't we take the stairs? You can practise your cognitive behavioural therapy on me in places other than the shitty lift at police headquarters. OK?'

Vincent took a deep breath. Then he smiled weakly.

'Ah, rumbled. OK. Deal.'

49

Vincent looked at his daughter. As usual, she hadn't touched her breakfast. He couldn't understand how she survived. He was always as hungry as a wolf in the mornings – a quality that both Benjamin and Aston had inherited. Granted, Rebecka's mother Ulrika was fussy and he had sometimes wondered whether Rebecka might be predisposed to eating disorders. But in Ulrika's defence, she insisted that it was important to eat. Just not whatever you liked anytime. *Fitness and figure* had been her mantra. A mantra that Rebecka had presumably heard slightly too often during her childhood.

The mobile lying next to his daughter was flashing with constant updates from WhatsApp and Snapchat. Apparently Rebecka's friendship group needed to be in permanent contact with each other – even when eating breakfast. Vincent sighed. He would never understand it. Deliberately not giving yourself time to think your own thoughts or develop your own ideas. Simply basing your views on what others had thought in the last ten seconds. But he had probably been the same himself at her age. Well, no . . . actually he knew with some certainty that he hadn't. But that had been a different era. And different circumstances.

'Aston, there are clean clothes for you in the bathroom,' Maria called to her son. 'Let me know if you need help with your socks.'

'Mum, I'm eight years old,' Aston said, emerging from the bathroom. 'I can get dressed by myself.'

This morning, he had put on grey tracksuit bottoms and a T-shirt with a cat on a Vespa printed on the front. Maria had bought it for him and it had immediately become his favourite top.

'But you're still barefoot,' Maria noted.

Aston forlornly handed her his socks and stretched out one foot.

Vincent couldn't remember Aston ever asking him for help with his clothes. When Maria was done, she gave Aston two slices of bread and the butter so he could apply the spread himself. They had decided collectively to give up on the slices of apple a few weeks ago.

'On the subject of clothes, aren't you a bit too warm in that?' said Maria, tugging at Rebecka's sleeve. 'It's warm out and you're still wearing long sleeves.'

Rebecka withdrew her arm.

'Leave me alone!' she snapped as she got up. 'I'll wear what I want!'

Rebecka grabbed her phone from the table and stormed into her room.

'I'm wearing long sleeves too,' Benjamin said, looking up from his bowl of yogurt. 'Am I not allowed to either?'

Maria blushed. Vincent knew exactly what she was thinking. Benjamin had never had any social self-confidence – the fact that he wanted to hide his body when everyone else was running around in swimwear was nothing out of the ordinary. He was the personification of the cliché of pale, black-clad teenagers who sat in the shade of a tree – or preferably their bedroom with the blinds down – to read a book while everyone else played beach volleyball. But Rebecka was a social professional and often the trendsetter in her own circle.

'Perhaps there's a reason she doesn't want to show her arms,' Benjamin muttered, carrying the bowl to the dishwasher where he squeezed it in between yesterday's wine-glasses. 'Maybe you should ask some time.'

Vincent filled his coffee cup and went over to Rebecka's closed door.

'Come on! I didn't mean *right now*,' Benjamin said on the way into the bathroom. 'Talk about subtle.'

Vincent knocked on the door and entered. His daughter was sitting on her bed concentrating on her mobile phone.

'Rebecka, I was wondering whether you could help me,' he said.

'I'm not going to eat something if that's what you're getting at,' she said brusquely without looking up from her phone.

He shook his head and sat down next to her on the bed. Rebecka quickly turned the phone face down on her lap and looked at him with raised eyebrows.

'You know that I'm helping the police with an investigation. Yesterday, they questioned a prime suspect. I need your help to interpret something.'

'Me? Surely you're the if-they-look-up-to-the-left-then-they're-lying man?'

195

'Firstly, that's a myth. There are no eye movements that automatically mean you're lying. But yes, I was there observing. What I want you to do is *listen*.'

He pulled out his own mobile.

'You've got a much bigger social network than I have,' he added as he began to search for the audio file on his mobile. 'And you're at an age where you're acutely tuned to spotting small variations in communications. After all, one social misstep at your age can lead to banishment for the rest of the year.'

Rebecka stared at him.

'I mean, which planet are you from?'

He looked at his daughter. Once, he had known everything about her. Now he didn't even know what her favourite flavour of ice cream was. Or whether she even liked ice cream. But he knew what was clearly visible in her concerned facial expression.

'I know it's not easy,' he said. 'If you're in the slightest bit like me then you're on tenterhooks at school because everyone else's reactions are unpredictable. You don't have to answer – I know that on the outside you're a social genius. But I remember how I felt around my friends. I just hope that yours are a bit better. At the same time, I wouldn't be surprised if they weren't that great.'

Rebecka was silent for a long time. In the worst case, he had massively overstepped the mark and was seconds from being thrown out of her room.

'So, the interview,' she said, nodding at his phone. 'Are you even allowed to play this to me?'

He interpreted that as forgiveness.

'Probably not. I'm actually surprised I was even allowed to be there. But listen to this. It'll only take ten minutes. And then tell me what you make of him.'

Vincent pressed play and let Rebecka listen to the full interview. Afterwards he stopped it and deleted the file.

'They could press charges against me for this, but I need to know . . . What do you think?'

Rebecka looked at the floor, apparently concentrating.

'He sounded frightened,' she said. 'Nervous. But I know what my friends sound like when they're lying about something that might come back to bite them, and I didn't hear that in him. Perhaps he's holding something back, but what he's sharing is probably the truth.'

'I think so too,' said Vincent, nodding. Then he nudged Rebecka with his elbow. 'Despite the fact that he was looking up and to his left throughout.'

He contemplated putting an arm around her but refrained. Neither of them would be comfortable with it. And there were other ways to show affection to your children. However, he did receive a smile by way of reward.

'But, Dad,' said Rebecka. 'That policewoman who was asking the questions . . . Is it her you're working with? What's she like?'

'You mean Mina?'

'Whatever. You know she's into you, right? It was clear as day: sickly sweet honey voice the second she talked about you.'

Vincent could feel his cheeks growing hot. He realized he was blushing like a schoolboy.

'There's nothing between us,' he replied quickly.

'Yeah, I know. You wouldn't know someone was flirting with you if they wrote it on a big sign and held it up in front of you. Although it's soooo obvious here. But I won't say a word to Aunt Maria.'

'There's nothing to say.'

'No, exactly. Right, I've got to get to school.'

Rebecka left him alone on the bed. He sat there, waiting for the blushing to stop.

50

It was still light outdoors. It was easier to see through the window from outside during the winter months – then she could see the whole kitchen and living room. It was also easier for her to avoid being seen when the evenings were dark. Now she needed to be more careful.

Not that she knew for certain she'd be recognized. It had been years now. Mina was no longer the same person. That had been a different time. A different life.

The girl she was patiently waiting for finally turned up at the window. Her dark hair fell across her face as she bent over something at the kitchen table. A light illuminated her from behind and Mina could see her clearly in the window even though it was on the fourth floor. The girl was wearing the same grey hoodie that Mina had often seen her in. It had to be a favourite. Mina watched her chewing absent-mindedly on one of the strings from the hood, but the girl was too far away to reveal any other facial expression.

A dog barked right beside Mina and she jumped. The dog was an angry little chihuahua on a lead held by a woman in a coat that looked expensive and loafers with the Gucci logo on them.

'You're in the way!' the woman hissed, forcing her way abruptly past.

Mina refrained from answering. She expected little else in Östermalm. The dog continued its mistress's scolding – it stayed where it was, yapping and growling at her while the woman pulled at the leash.

'Come on, Chloe!'

Eventually, the dog reluctantly complied, but not before it had thrown a few more angry looks at Mina, who remained where she was on the pavement on Linnégatan.

She raised her gaze to the apartment again. The girl was no longer visible and Mina felt the usual pang of pain in her heart. Longing. Guilt.

Sorrow. A mixture of all of the above and then some. She had never got to the bottom of it. And she had no intention of ever doing so. Pandora's box wasn't meant to be opened.

She wondered what the inside of the apartment looked like, and the girl's room. She had never been inside, of course. But she remembered another flat. Another room. Much smaller. A one-bed in Vasastan on the third floor. There had been a Greek restaurant down at street level. The best in town. But she had never been able to bring herself to visit the restaurant. Memories could hurt so much. It was like physical pain.

Suddenly, the girl appeared again – in the living room this time. She was gesticulating. Talking to someone. Moving back and forth. It looked like a row, but it was hard to make out. If Vincent had been there, he would have been able to interpret her body language in more detail. Mina found herself standing on tiptoe, as if that would make a difference in her attempts to see someone four storeys up. She continued to stretch upwards, nonetheless.

After a while, she could no longer see the grey hoodie in the window. Mina slowly lowered her heels back to the ground and then set off dejectedly towards the car.

51

Even though there were a few days left until Walpurgis, the weather seemed to have got the idea that it was the middle of summer. Vincent had nothing against the surprising summer heat, given that his walk might take a while. He had been wondering where to make the call without anyone eavesdropping. The easiest solution would have been to call from home, but he didn't feel up to explaining himself to Maria every time he spoke to Mina.

At first, he had considered simply getting in the car, but he needed to move around in order to think properly. And he wanted impressions. Lots of impressions. His brain needed all the blood and serotonin he could give it. Eventually he'd settled for a walk around Södermalm. Although people might be able to hear him as he walked, no one would capture more than a fragment of what he said.

He inserted his earbuds into his ears and activated the noise cancellation to kill the sound of traffic coming from Götgatan down at Skanstull. Then he called the switchboard at police headquarters and asked to speak to Mina. She picked up after two rings. As he'd guessed she would. She was like that. Dutiful.

'I've been thinking quite a lot about the murderer's psychological profile,' he said. 'Especially since we questioned Daniel. Have you got a minute?'

Next to him at the pedestrian crossing there was a man in his sixties with a ponytail and goatee. The man's eyes widened when he caught sight of Vincent, and then he pulled himself together again. Vincent had seen the reaction hundreds of times. People who had recognized him from the TV or stage but decided they weren't going to show it.

'I'm completely yours,' Mina said.

He could feel himself blushing.

'Wait, I just want to start a recording if that's OK,' she said, clicking on her computer. 'If I know you, this is going to be way too much to note down with a pen. Or even five of them.'

'OK. Try to keep up,' he said. 'As you know, I've been puzzled by how the murderer can be both a planner and as emotionally aggressive as we've seen. I thought at first you were looking for someone with a narcissistic personality disorder. Someone who thinks they're superior to other people. Others are simply of no value. They become tools that can be used any way you like.'

The light at the crossing changed to green. The man with the pony-tail passed Vincent and apparently decided to take a chance and let down his guard, because he gave Vincent a thumbs up. Vincent smiled a *thank you* to him when their eyes met. Praise cost so little. All it took was a thumb. Yet people were so bad at it. He reminded himself that he too needed to improve in that area.

'That kind of narcissistic disorder would explain the consummate planning of the murders,' he continued. 'The construction of illusions, the kidnapping of the victims, numbering the bodies, planting the smashed watches and leaving the victims in specific locations. A narcissist wouldn't have any problems with that since the murders aren't of "valid people". In the narcissist's world, there's only one valid person and it's him.'

Vincent put on his sunglasses when he reached the sunshine on the other side of the street. He had to swerve out of the way of a middle-aged woman on an electric skateboard.

People. Say what you like, but life would be boring without them. He began to walk along Götgatan, heading for Medborgarplatsen.

'Is that it?' Mina said.

'We can also add empathy deficit disorder,' he said. 'Possibly created by a physiological defect in the brain such as a shrunken amygdala or a damaged connection between the cortex and the hippocampus, which would make it even easier to commit acts of violence. It could also be that the murderer has created their own reality around the murders. Shoko Asahara – the guy who released the sarin gas on the Tokyo subway killing a dozen or so people – believed that by taking someone's life, he was assuming their sins and guiding them towards enlightenment. So according to his view of the world, he wasn't committing murders, he was helping people. And that obviously makes it easier to kill.'

Mina was silent for a long time.

201

'That sounds quite extreme,' she said at last.

Vincent had reached the metro station at Medborgarplatsen and was considering whether to divert towards Danvikstull or keep heading towards Slussen. Perhaps he could visit one of the record stores at Mosebacke. Maria would whinge if he came home with even more vinyl, but he needed some counterweight to the commercial radio stations that were always babbling away at home. Anyway, he had just paid for a TV channel that appeared to show nothing but *Real Housewives of New Jersey* and the like because that was what she liked, so Slussen it was.

'You're absolutely right,' he said. 'It's not common. Well spotted.'

He meant what he said, otherwise he wouldn't have said it. But the praise had the desired effect – he could hear down the phone that Mina was smiling. It was that simple. The man with two six-year-olds in tow next to him on the pavement wasn't smiling. One child looked troubled and the other was crying. Vincent realized that he had been walking next to them while talking for several minutes.

'Dad, I don't want to take the metro home,' protested the crying child. 'They've got satin gas there.'

The man looked like he was about to give Vincent a slap. Vincent quickly upped his pace.

'A personality like that still doesn't explain the emotional component that I think is there,' he said in a somewhat lower voice, while making sure there were no other children nearby. 'If this was a film then the murderer would have a split personality. But that's extremely unlikely in reality. Anyway, that's roughly where I'm at.'

'OK, that was . . . a lot,' said Mina. 'But do you think that Daniel fits this profile?'

Vincent came to a halt on the pavement. A couple emerging from a bookshop almost crashed into him. He pulled an apologetic expression and the couple smiled.

'No, no, not at all. Quite the reverse,' he said. 'You've met him. Daniel showed no signs like that when we met him at the cafe or at the police station. That degree of narcissism would seep through – for example in terms of the perspective that he used when talking. And Daniel used the word 'we' much more than he used 'I'. He might be self-absorbed, but my God the guy's only in his twenties. Who isn't self-absorbed at that age?'

He was almost at the first record shop. Part of his brain had begun to wonder whether there was anything missing in his collection at home and had concluded that there wasn't. He would have to confine himself to a downright indulgent purchase. Which was really more fun anyway.

'But you mentioned empathy deficit disorder,' Mina said. 'Like in psychopaths. They're good at faking empathy, right?'

'It's possible to simulate human feeling if you know you have to,' Vincent said, nodding without considering that this wasn't visible on the phone. 'And Daniel was very careful about what he said and how he reacted. But the increased pupil size when he was talking about his girlfriend isn't something you can control. Anyway, if his behaviour to date is anything to go by, I don't believe he can prepare plans that are more advanced than working out what to have for dinner.'

'So you don't agree with Ruben? You don't think Daniel is the murderer?'

'Profiling criminals isn't my main expertise, as you know. And the team knows that too. I may be completely wrong. But if you ask me, Daniel is an improbable murderer.'

He placed his hand on the door handle of the shop's entrance and paused on the step.

'Daniel's under pressure from some quarter,' he said. 'He's controlling himself extremely carefully and he doesn't like coming into contact with the police. I'd very much like to know why.'

'You know what? Me too. And thanks for the profile. I'll make sure it gets to Julia as soon as possible.'

He glanced at the vinyl records in the shop window.

'Mina,' he said. 'What kind of music do you like?'

'Erm . . . music? Why do you ask?'

'Oh, it's nothing. Just thinking aloud. Be in touch.'

He ended the call and went into the shop. It was lucky Rebecka hadn't been there to hear the final bit. She would have laughed her head off.

52

He dreamt about an old friend. He did that sometimes. Dreamt about Lasse. Why, he didn't know. Lasse was someone who had come and gone in his life. Long ago. Other people had come and gone too. He didn't dream about them. He never even dreamt about his mother. But perhaps that was because she was still so present. All her things were still around him at home in the house. Her eyes stared down at him from the photos on the walls. There was no room for her in his dreams.

Lasse was about to say something to him in the dream when another voice made him sit up straight in his chair and look around, sleepy-eyed.

'What?'

Ruben was standing next to him with his arms crossed and a grin on his face.

'Taking a nap?'

'No, no, no . . . I was just . . . Resting my eyes a little. They sting from watching that bloody CCTV footage hour in, hour out.'

'Sleep away. Peder already spends half his time sleeping . . .'

Ruben continued to smirk but looked serious.

'Anyway, have you told Julia who visited the cafe?'

Ruben pointed at the CCTV footage that was playing and Christer looked from the screen to Ruben in confusion.

'What? Who?'

Ruben leaned forward, took the mouse and clicked to rewind the footage a little. He hit play again and pointed.

'There.'

He pointed at the man with the limp and Christer felt his heart sink. He'd known there was something about that man that should have clicked.

'No need for a guilty conscience,' said Ruben, patting him on the shoulder. 'I never forget a face. Has he been there often?'

'Every day. A few hours per day.'

His thoughts were running around his brain like a stressed-out rat in a labyrinth, tearing about searching for answers he knew were in there somewhere. And suddenly the rat stopped. His brain had finally found what it was looking for. He knew who it was. White-faced, he turned towards Ruben.

'Fucking hell.'

53

Vedran rubs his hands together to stave off the cold. His gloves are still in the car. Stupid. He knows the mornings are still chilly. The first rays of sunshine have just started to make their way across the corrugated rooftops of the florist wholesale warehouse at Årsta market to the south of Stockholm. The digital watch on his wrist shows the time as 04:45. Exactly when the sun is meant to rise, according to the met institute. A good start to the day.

The florist warehouse doesn't open until five o'clock, but Aunt Jodranka taught him from an early age how important it is to be on time. And if you work with flowers, like Vedran does, then it is crucial. Vedran jogs on the spot to keep his circulation going. It's an icy-cold morning, despite the promise of summer heat later in the day. It's lucky he put on his thick oversocks. Admittedly, his florist shop in Haninge doesn't have that much competition, but he wants the people who buy from him to be satisfied. More than satisfied. They should come back. That's why he's waiting outside the door of the warehouse – to ensure that he gets the best selection.

He has worked with flowers for almost forty years – he got started before most of the people working in the warehouse were even born. In Belgrade, he even supplied flowers to Crvene zvezda, the football team, when they needed winner's bouquets. That was before the riots at Maksimir, of course. It was a shameful episode in history. But by the time it happened, he had already moved away. He had met Monica and love knew no borders. It had been a complete given that he would live with her in Sweden.

He is still alone. Vedran shakes his head. In his forty years, he hasn't had a single lie-in. He'll leave that for the lazy bones. He takes the risk of strolling a little way along the facade to keep his circulation going.

The other early risers know him. If anyone arrives they'll know he's first in line.

When he reaches the car park at the end of the building, it isn't quite empty. There's a black cabinet in the middle. It's been there for two days now – it arrived the same night that the car park was cordoned off for works. A pipe that needed laying. He's been puzzled by that cabinet the last couple of mornings. But today the car park is open again. The guys working on the digging must be done.

Vedran crosses the asphalt and approaches the cabinet. Moisture is glittering on its sides in the morning sun. He frowns. It's incomprehensible that someone has left it here. It must have been some millennial who was tasked with transporting it and abandoned it in the first deserted location they could find. He would never take on any extra help under the age of thirty. Workshy, snotty-nosed brats with their mobile phones permanently glued to their right hands. They never got any good flowers.

He completes a circuit of the cabinet. It's almost as tall as he is and about the same width. It's like a small wardrobe. It's been carelessly constructed using rough plywood and just as carelessly painted. A metal frame is visible at the edges. He runs his hand over the wood, taking care not to catch any splinters. It almost looks like the person who built the cabinet was angry. The wood has been snapped rather than sawn. Several of the nails are sticking out halfway and are crooked. Embarrassing. It seems as if there's no one around any longer who cares about doing a good job. Sweden is a great country in many ways, but far too much carelessness is permitted. This cabinet would not have passed muster back in Serbia.

When he reaches the front he sees that the cabinet door is divided into three. What he had thought was a single cupboard is actually three large boxes stacked onto each other inside a metal frame, each with a door. It appears that the middle box can be pushed out sideways from the others on rails attached to the frame. He nudges the box, but it's stuck.

Perhaps some idiot dumped the cabinet here in the car park because they were ashamed of the crappy build quality. But it can't stay there. It'll be in the way. He glances at his wrist. His digital watch says it is 04:50. He has time to drag the cabinet to the edge of the car park. A little physical work will only do him good.

Mind you, it would be stupid to put his back out. If the cabinet is full of stuff, he'll leave it be. There are limits to how much he's

207

willing to get involved. Vedran tucks his fingertips under the edge of the middle cabinet door and pulls. The panel emits a gluey sound but doesn't budge. He knows exactly what sounds like that mean. The moron who painted the cabinet left it to dry with the doors shut. Millennials . . .

Over by the entrance to the gardening warehouse, more people have begun to appear. The wholesaler will be opening soon. But a door isn't going to defeat him. Vedran pulls more forcefully, until the paint comes loose. When the door flies open, he is struck by the sharp smell of iron and decay. He automatically takes a step back with his hand to his nose.

It isn't immediately obvious what's inside the box. The animal has been cut up to fit into the box, but the pieces are all over the place. The biggest cut looks like it might be from a pig. Something without fur at any rate. The two smaller pieces look like they may be pig's legs. But he's only guessing. He works with flowers. He has no idea how to identify animal parts. But one thing is clear – it wasn't paint that made the door stick. It was blood. Both the pieces of meat and the inside of the box are covered in blood. The red stickiness is everywhere. Almost as if it's been brushed on. Who does something like that? Anyway, they don't sell meat at this wholesalers' market – as far as he knows. Only fish and vegetables. And his flowers.

He needs to get back – they'll be opening any minute now. Nevertheless, he takes a step towards the cabinet. He still has his hand over his nose. There is an object lying in the blood next to the animal body. He didn't see it at first, but someone appears to have dropped their broken wristwatch in the box. He looks more closely at the big piece of meat. There's something not right. Pigs don't have skin that smooth. Nausea rises up in his throat, but he needs to be certain. If only he had his gloves with him. Reluctantly, he tugs at the upper door until it opens with the same awful, sticky sound.

He has to know.

There's as much blood in the top box, possibly more, but Vedran barely notices. All he sees are the eyes staring back at him. A pair of chestnut brown, very human eyes.

'Jodranka, help me,' he whispers as he stumbles backwards.

The nausea shuts down his ability to think.

The boy's hair is matted with blood, which also covers his face and bare upper torso. The body has been chopped through in line with the nipples. It only just fits in the box. Vedran realizes that what he found in the middle box were the rest of the torso and arms. And there's another box at the bottom.

Horror takes hold of him.

Vedran backs away even more quickly, incapable of tearing his gaze away from the reproachful, staring eyes. Eyes asking him why. Then the enchantment is broken. Vedran turns around and runs towards the warehouse, faster than he has ever run before. Just as he gets there he begins to scream.

54

The doorbell sounded with four rapid rings. There was only one person who rang in that aggressive way. Vincent opened the door, and as expected he found Ulrika standing outside. His ex-wife. Maria's sister. As if life wasn't complicated enough. But they needed to talk.

'Come in,' he said.

'What was it you wanted to talk about?' said Ulrika, removing her sunglasses.

Straight to the point as always. No time for formalities. For Ulrika, the only thing that counted was results. As if to make that point extra clear, she was wearing her usual workout garb. At the law firm, she always wore expensive, sharp suits. But right now she was wearing a pink gym top and shorts, complemented by a belt around her waist with multiple small water bottles. He didn't even need to look at her shoes to know that they would be Philipp Pleins. Everything looked new and expensive. She hadn't changed one bit.

'Coffee?' he asked.

Ulrika removed the rubber band from her striking platinum hair, letting it fall down over her shoulders.

'You know I don't drink coffee.'

'Just wanted to see whether *anything* was different,' he said.

Ulrika ignored him and went into the kitchen. He saw that the belt had space for six water bottles. One was missing. He was convinced that she had removed it for his benefit. An odd figure to set him off balance. He would struggle to think about anything other than the gap where the sixth water bottle ought to be. It was a completely paranoid thought, but he was aware of it. At the same time, he had never met anyone who so shamelessly manipulated others and was as good at it as Ulrika. And she knew how to press all of his buttons.

'Where's my sis?' she said, filling a glass with water from the tap.

Vincent followed her and waited until she'd drained it.

'Maria isn't at home,' he said. 'I thought it would be better if you and I talked alone.'

She set down the glass on the draining board and looked at him searchingly.

When they met like this, it was easy to forget how toxic their relationship had once been. The passing of time helped to make most things seem less dangerous – at least, when there was a decade between you and what had happened.

It was easy to think that it had all been her fault, with her unattainable demands over the children's performances, how good their household finances needed to be, how shiny and clean the house always needed to be in case they received visitors. The nagging that things were never good enough. But the truth was that they hadn't been good for each other. He wasn't the man she needed. And vice versa.

It had all come to an abrupt end when he'd picked Maria instead. That had made him the bad guy. But the truth was that he and Ulrika had been living in an envenomed relationship for several years before that. And both of them knew it.

'It's about your daughter,' he said. '*Our* daughter. I think she might be self-harming. But she doesn't want to talk to me. I'd like to take her to see CAMHS.'

Ulrika frowned and looked uncomprehending.

'Child and Adolescent Mental Health Services,' he clarified.

'Out of the question,' she snorted, crossing her arms over her chest. 'Do you want to socially stigmatize our daughter?'

He should have known she would take it like this. Everything was about what others thought. What happened inside a person had never been of interest to his ex-wife. The only thing that mattered was what was on display. And she was so very good at being on display. He had long ago begun to wonder whether she had slight psychopathic tendencies. At the very least there was some kind of empathy disorder. A good quality to have in her job at the law firm, perhaps, and it had helped her climb the career ladder. But it was less helpful in her role as a mother.

'It's not about stigma,' he said. 'It's about helping her to feel better. You and I can't handle this any longer. There are other people who are pros at this kind of thing.'

'CAMHS,' Ulrika said as if tasting the word. 'Don't you get how it would look? For her? For *me*? Everyone would know!'

'Yes, it would be terrible if it came out that your daughter wasn't perfect,' he said, leaning back against the kitchen table. 'You'll probably be asked to leave the country.'

Something about Ulrika's restlessness meant he couldn't relax and sit down. She waved away his comment with a guarded hand movement. Recently painted nails, he saw. French manicure. Never anything shocking, like red. Or black, which was Rebecka's favourite colour for her own nails.

'We're not discussing this any further,' she said. 'Surely you didn't want me to come here just to talk about Rebecka?'

She raised both her arms and used both hands to put her hair back into a ponytail.

'Come on,' she said, when he seemed not to understand. 'I could have come here any time, but you wanted me to come now. When the kids aren't here. When Maria isn't at home. By the way, does she still eat scones with jam for breakfast? With the odd avocado sandwich, just to pretend to herself how healthy she is?'

The raised arms made her breasts strain clearly against the pink top. Vincent realized it was intentional and cursed himself for looking.

'My sis,' she added when she noted his temporary confusion. 'Your *wife*.'

Ulrika twitched one corner of her mouth upwards in a microscopic smile which made her look insufferably satisfied.

'Maria isn't exactly one to care about how she looks,' she said, taking a step towards him. 'Can't work out what you were thinking there.'

'We fell in love,' he said, trying to step back. 'And you and I had stopped being in love long before.'

'Perhaps. But we had other things that more than made up for it, Vincent.'

She was standing far too close.

'Good God, it's been ten years, Ulrika. How long are we going to dwell on the past?'

Ulrika ignored his question, which was largely rhetorical.

'Care to join me for a circuit?' she asked.

Her breath smelled faintly sweet, as if she'd had an energy drink.

'We can round off at mine. If you've got the energy, that is.'

He was in a minefield. No matter what he said it would be wrong. So he remained silent. Ulrika suddenly grabbed his cock through his trousers.

212

'Or maybe you've got old,' she continued. 'Maybe you're just going to stay here eating jam sandwiches with your wife instead.'

She massaged him and he felt himself hardening in her hand without being able to help it. He ought to take a step away. *Now*. But his feet wouldn't move. She took his hand and led it to the inside of her own thigh at the bottom of the short shorts. When his fingers grazed her warm skin, comprehension of what was going on suddenly rushed through him like an electric shock. He withdrew his hand as though he had been stung and took a stumble backwards, straight into the table.

'Just as I thought,' Ulrika snorted, sweeping out of the kitchen. 'Old.'

55

Mina was sitting on the corner of her bed. The sheet was new, having just come out of its plastic wrapper. It had taken five minutes to stretch it across the bed the right way so that there were no folds. She turned over the small box on her lap. On the front was a picture of a young, resolute-looking woman holding up a vibrator beneath a banner proclaiming *The Next Sexual Revolution*. On the back was something about *Air Pulse Technology*.

A small voice inside her was telling her the whole idea was a failure, a reflection of her lack of social skills. That it wasn't healthy to replace a person with a battery-operated object. Another voice said that thought was prejudiced. These were new times. A woman had control of her own sexuality; she knew that and it was nothing to be ashamed of. She didn't need any man. The young girl on the packaging was showing that very clearly. Revolution indeed.

She broke the seal on the packaging. The object inside the box was golden and looked rather like a pleasingly grippable plastic door handle. With USB charger. No chance that plastic was going to touch her until it had been cleaned. She reached for the bottle of sanitizer on the night-stand while trying to create as few wrinkles in the sheet as possible. After spraying the soft part, she ran her thumb over it. Perhaps it was too dry. She was prepared for that. She reached for the massage oil she had ordered at the same time as the vibrator and applied it to the rubber. A drop would have to do. If it got messy she wouldn't be able to continue.

It wasn't that she couldn't get a man interested in her. It was about the fact that she didn't want him all over her. The mere thought of grappling with a sweaty, smelly man's body – not to mention the organ itself . . . She shivered and pushed the picture out of her head before it crystallized too much.

214

Was it OK not to want it? At least not in the way she'd had it before? She looked at the woman on the box again and searched for some kind of answer in her eyes. But the woman was fully occupied with waving her vibrator. And Mina realized the woman was right. A sterile, good-looking golden door handle won the contest any day of the week.

The only thing she missed was looking someone in the eyes. People misunderstood her. They thought she didn't want intimacy because she didn't want them to touch her with their petri dish hands. But eye contact was far more intimate than any touch at all. Thank goodness she could look into any eyes of her choosing when she shut her own.

She put her mobile on silent and laid it on the nightstand. Then she took off her trousers and knickers, lay down on the bed and searched for the golden door handle's on button.

Air Pulse Technology. What the hell. She'd give it half an hour – any longer and she'd be late to work.

After all, it was the first date.

56

'I didn't know whether you'd still be here.'

'I'm allowed to keep working during the investigation,' said Milda. 'Thank God. I feel bad enough as it is about screwing up, and if I had to sit at home, brooding over it . . .'

She shook her head. Mina simply nodded. It wasn't for her to pass judgement or to absolve the pathologist from the guilt she felt. That was what the internal investigation was for. People made mistakes. People weren't perfect. It was also one of the main reasons that Mina preferred living alone. That and the fact that most people seemed to have a defective grasp of what personal hygiene entailed.

She noted that Julia had tried to get in touch with her several times and wondered whether she should call her right away, but she decided to speak to Milda first. She put her phone in her pocket.

'I kept up with the search for him,' said Milda.

She closed Robert's eyes, which had been open, and removed her plastic gloves.

She stepped away from the shiny table where the parts of the victim's body were lying.

'You and the rest of Sweden,' said Mina, approaching.

It was strange to see his face now, here, after having seen it on newspaper hoardings for weeks.

'Thousands of people go missing in Sweden each year. But there was something about Robert that captured everyone's interest and kept him from being just one more statistic. Not to mention the media.'

'His defencelessness,' Mina said, leaning over Robert's face.

When his eyes were shut, it looked as if he were sleeping. Nothing about the face divulged the brutality that the rest of his body had been subjected to.

'We're always particularly moved by those we perceive as helpless,' she continued. 'Robert was twenty-two years old, but he had the mental age of a child.'

'His parents' despair was heartbreaking,' Milda said, picking up the instruments she had been using.

The pathologist had put on a new pair of plastic gloves. Mina nodded quizzically towards the box and Milda held it out for her. The feeling of the thin plastic against her skin gave her goosebumps of pleasure. She would have worn plastic gloves at all times if she could, but something as idiotic as social convention had dissuaded her from that habit. If she had been born in Japan, she would have been able to wander around quite unconcerned in a mask and gloves, but in Sweden this was deemed peculiar. Personally, she considered it the only sensible approach. But it would never be accepted in her place of work. She could already hear Ruben's and Christer's remarks.

'Have the parents been informed?' said Milda, taking the box of gloves back from Mina and replacing it on the counter.

Everything was neatly lined up in straight rows. Milda applied military discipline in her sterile kingdom.

'Yes.'

Mina's answer was brief. It was the part of the job she found hardest. The fact that each victim resulted in people who would grieve. And it was their job to pass on the news.

'Is that . . .?' Mina said, pointing at one of two objects next to the body on the table.

'Yes. It was in his back pocket. The clothes were found in the bottom box.'

The object that Mina was pointing at was a slingshot. It was big, made from wood and had an elastic band sling. It had been part of the description of Robert featured in the tabloids, that he was often seen carrying a slingshot, and that he liked to show it to strangers and demonstrate how good he was at firing it. Apparently, he could hit a postcard from ten metres.

Mina tore her gaze from the object. The personal nature of it had got under her skin and she didn't want anything or anyone doing that. She was usually good at keeping it away from her – the people, their fates, the personal dimension. But something about Robert Berger had forced its way through her shell. Even now, with his body in several parts, his face was serene, friendly. It even had a hint of a smile on it.

In all the photos in the papers he had been depicted laughing heartily,

217

his eyes glittering with happiness and joie de vivre. According to an article in *Aftonbladet*, his parents called him Bobby, and she hated that she knew what the corpse's nickname had been. It was too close.

She forced herself to focus on what Milda was saying. Police work. She always had to focus on police work. Procedures. Rules. Processes. Conduct. Clean. Clinical.

'As you can see, he's been divided into three main parts,' said Milda. 'There's more if you count the arms and hands, obviously. The cuts are clean and neat – the blade that was used was very sharp.'

'Was he alive when he was cut?'

'Yes,' said Milda, pointing at the places where the body had been divided. 'He bled a great deal. His heart was presumably still beating when they cut into him. And then there's this. The reason why I called you.'

She pushed back the hair from Robert's brow. There was a clearly visible Roman numeral II carved into the smooth skin, which had risen around the deep incisions.

'The watch was loose in one of the boxes,' said Milda, pointing at the other object by the body. 'As you can see, it's set to two. The batteries have been removed, but the face has still been smashed.'

Mina gasped.

The watch. The number two on the forehead. Vincent had been right all along. It was a countdown. Ruben was going to have a fit.

'What do you think in terms of it being a primary or secondary crime scene?' she said.

'The forensics team who examined the scene will be in a better position to answer that. But if you're happy to take a guess for now, I'd guess secondary based on what I've seen.'

'Why?' said Mina.

'It doesn't look like the box was left to stand in the volume of blood that Robert must have lost. It's too clean on the underside. So he was probably moved to the place where he was found.'

Mina took a breath.

'Tox screen?' she said, hoping Milda wouldn't hate her for asking.

'I'll do it along with the autopsy. I may have to use bile, given how little blood is left in the body. But trust me, that mistake won't happen again. And I've asked them to expedite the tests for both Robert and Agnes.'

'Can you do that?' Mina asked, without any value judgement in her tone.

'Officially, no, but I had a few favours to call in. And it's the least I can do to make things right.'

'What kind of timeline are we talking about?'

Mina couldn't take her eyes off Robert's serene face.

'A few days, perhaps. With a little luck, quicker than that. But I can't make any promises. Also, I've still got to do the autopsy on Robert. I only just got him here. Do you want to stay? You can observe if you like.'

Milda took out a new pair of gloves and began to prepare the instruments neatly lined up on the table next to the body. There was also a scale standing by, which Mina knew would be used to weigh the organs. Everything from the heart to the brain and even the stomach contents would be placed on the scale. She had been to autopsies before.

'No thanks,' she said. 'I'll skip that delight today. But I will take a look at the box.'

'Of course. It's in the lab next door, waiting to go to NFC.'

She needed to get hold of Julia right away. And Vincent.

Milda nodded without looking at her and began to pick over her instruments. Mina left her to work in peace and headed for the door. When she turned around in the doorway, she saw Milda gently caressing Robert's cheek. It was a tender movement, but also one filled with sorrow.

57

Milda preferred to work alone and was relieved when Mina left. She had cheerful schlager music playing in the background at just the right volume to avoid drowning out her verbal notes. She knew it was a popular culture cliché – the pathologist listening to a certain kind of music during their autopsies. Most often opera. But all clichés arose because there was a grain of truth in them. Having music in the background provided calm and focus. It also somehow felt more hospitable towards the people she had in front of her on the table. What was more, she preferred happy music – schlager or country – to counteract the heavy presence of death. And the people who listened to and documented her voice notes had long grown accustomed to her bawling along to the music.

She sang along to 'Eloise' by Arvingarna. Songs from the Melodifestivalen song contest had a special place in her heart, and she hadn't missed an edition since she had become old enough to watch them on TV.

Singing with feeling, she carefully examined the cut surfaces where the blade had passed through.

Clean. Straight. It had taken a sharp tool to achieve that. No half-blunt swords here. But the cut didn't divulge anything else of interest. She removed the bone fragments from it and carried them over to another stainless steel bench. She lowered them into a pre-prepared solution of water, washing-up liquid and Alconox. If there was DNA to be found, this solution was the best way to avoid damaging it. The thermometer showed the water to be 55 degrees Celsius. Perfect. She needed to remove the soft tissue before she could move on.

She returned to Robert, stubbornly pushing away the thoughts that intruded with this young man on her table. It could be Conrad in a

220

few years' time, if nothing changed. If she didn't manage to change it. She carefully stroked Robert's cheek. She had to focus on him. It was her responsibility. Her duty.

Milda was still ashamed of her mistake with Agnes's tox screen. She couldn't make mistakes. It was a betrayal not just of the next of kin, but above all the victim. She had a responsibility. A responsibility to be meticulous, not miss anything, make all the right assessments, carry out all the right processes. She might not be quite up to her mother's standards, but there was no reason to miss anything in this job. She suppressed the image of Conrad lying on the table and carried on.

Milda permitted herself to pause for a moment. There were procedures to be followed, but these were somewhat complicated by the body being in several parts. Most bodies that arrived on her table were in fairly good condition and in one piece. Dismemberment wasn't a frequent occurrence.

She continued singing to herself while reaching for the shears. She usually had an assistant to help her, but she had wanted to do this alone. However, everything was being carefully documented with a video camera in addition to her verbal notes as she worked on the body.

The shears crunched as they cut through the soft cartilage around Robert's thorax. She carefully lifted away the thorax, laying bare the middle portion of his body. She had colleagues who preferred to cut higher up around the ribs instead, but she had no desire to cut herself on sharp pieces of bone. There were enough cut-through bones in Robert's body as it was.

There was hardly any blood left in the body, and what was still there had coagulated. The minimal volume of blood indicated she'd been right – Robert had been cut into pieces while still alive. The world was apparently full of monsters.

The absence of blood had given the body a pale grey tinge and meant there was an absence of clear livor mortis, which made it harder to determine when he had died. There had been no point taking fluid from the eye. While the potassium levels increased in the hours after death and could provide a pointer, Robert had been dead for days.

She put her hands into Robert's open breast. She noted the visual state of his intestines and took a few photographs. Better to document too much rather than too little. Everything looked normal except for the slightly enlarged heart, which was unfortunately common in people with Down's syndrome.

She tapped her foot gently in time to the music. Funnily enough, it helped her to stabilize her hand movements as she now carefully sought to uncover the organs. Each organ needed to be removed, measured and weighed. Only once she was completely done with the autopsy would she return them to their rightful place, before stitching him back together again as neatly as she could, ready to be delivered to some funeral director.

Heart, kidney, liver, lungs – all were weighed. Everything normal. Apart from the heart.

The stomach required a bit more work. But with a little luck, Robert's last meal might provide a clue to where he'd spent the final hours of his life.

She carefully poured the contents of the stomach into a metal bowl. The smell was sharp and unpleasant, but it had stopped bothering her a long time ago. She wasn't among those medical examiners who smear menthol cream under their nose to deal with the smells associated with a dead body. There was too much risk of missing something. For instance, cyanide poisoning could be uncovered through the faint smell of almonds when opening the stomach.

She carefully prodded the stomach contents. It would all be sent off for analysis in Linköping. She knew they weren't all that keen on stomach contents, but that couldn't be helped. However, she always made her own inventory first before handing them over to forensics. Milda frowned.

She fished a clump of something dark from Robert's stomach contents.

Then she fell silent.

Robert's stomach was full of hair.

58

He hated that he was right. He didn't want to be right. Had he been wrong, Robert would still be alive. It was almost as if he had forced Robert's murder to happen by insisting on the countdown. He knew that idea was wrong; it was only the so-called spotlight effect showing its ugly mug. He wasn't the cause of strangers' actions. But he couldn't help it – his brain wanted to think like that and so it did. It was millennia-old mind-programming that he couldn't withstand. It was there because sometimes it helped humans to survive. But today it was making Vincent feel ashamed.

He climbed the stairs with Mina.

'What kind of box was it this time?' he asked when they made it to the right floor and she reached out to open the door.

'It's better you see it for yourself.'

The news that they had found Robert Berger had left him very down. In purely professional terms, he was fascinated by the chromosome change known as trisomy 21. The fact that all it took was one extra chromosome to create a completely different type of personality. He didn't have much experience of people with Down's syndrome, but those he had met all shared certain characteristics. As their cognitive capabilities were impaired, the amygdala took over and made them incredibly emotional. But it also meant they were more honest than many other people. All their emotions were big. And all their emotions were important. There was something beautiful, something sincere about it. He knew he was guilty of gross romanticization, but neverthe-less . . .

Vincent's own impairment was in the opposite direction. He found it hard to express his emotions at all. However, he did know one thing: an individual as open and welcoming as Robert was someone to care for and learn from. You didn't break him. Anyone who could do a thing like that was a lost cause.

'Here,' said Mina, stopping in front of a cabinet about the same height as himself.

He saw right away what it was.

'Oh bloody hell,' he said, averting his gaze.

Fortunately, the doors were shut, but he had no problem imagining what had been inside. Three doors. Two blades. One cabinet. Three two one. Robert had been a countdown all of his own.

'The blades that were in the box are over here,' said Mina.

'Give me a second to gather my thoughts,' he said. 'Anyway, it's the zigzag girl – that much is clear. The illusion, that is . . .'

He paused for breath and got out his mobile.

'I've got to show this to Sains Bergander. I assume I can't take photos?'

Mina shrugged.

'Take as many as you like. You're hereby officially part of the investigation. Julia sends her regards.'

'OK? What about Ruben?'

'I don't think I've ever seen him so focused on an investigation.'

He opened the camera app and began taking pictures. It was easier to look at the unpleasantness through a screen. That allowed you to focus on the details instead of the whole picture. He ensured he included what he thought Sains needed to see. There was only one problem. He was going to need to photograph the inside too.

59

Vincent opened the pink plastic folder and spread the contents on the desk for what must have been the tenth time. He had spent all night wondering how best to persuade Julia's team, and what lay before him was what he had come up with.

It hadn't gone very well last time. But now he knew what he needed to do and how to go about it. When selecting his props he had focused on colourful, clear images that awakened curiosity. In rhetorical terms, he was going to use Marcus Antonius's old trick of starting by agreeing with them on their views of him, before using that as a lever to reverse those views. He also reminded himself that the premise was different this time. He had been right, and they knew it.

He put the photos back in the folder again. He'd had to supplement them with a few family snaps to ensure there was an even number of ten photos. He would have to be careful not to pull out the wrong photos. It wouldn't create a good impression if he flashed the photo from the holiday to Las Vegas when he'd had a stomach bug the whole time and Aston had insisted on taking his photo. Las Vegas. L was the twelfth letter in the alphabet. V the twenty-second: 1222 . . . 12:22 was known as a triple mirror hour in Christian numerology. It reminded him that he'd forgotten to have lunch an hour earlier. He checked the time. No time for food. He needed to set off immediately if he was going to make it on time.

Ten photos in the folder: 1 + 0 which made 1. One photo. One photo was the most important. But that was the one he needed to create for them inside their heads.

Julia was waiting for him in reception at police headquarters.

'Hi, Vincent,' she greeted him with a smile as she let him through the barriers.

He followed her up to the third floor into an identical meeting room to the one he'd visited last time. Although it could have been the very same room. The others were already there. Peder. Christer. Ruben. And Mina. He realized they were waiting for him. Ruben didn't meet his gaze.

'Sorry I'm a little late,' said Vincent. 'I was preparing my presentation until the last moment.'

Julia sat down next to a man he hadn't seen before. Steel-rimmed glasses, hair thinning at the temples, a knitted, moss-green waistcoat with all the buttons done up, and a serious expression. If there was an archetype for what psychologists looked like, this man fulfilled all its criteria. It had to be that profiler Mina had mentioned. Jan.

'We're going to divide this into two parts,' Julia said with a serious expression. 'We'll end with Vincent's run-through. But first Christer is going to bring us up to date on a recent development in the case.'

Julia nodded encouragingly and he saw Christer swallow hard before replying.

'Yes, well I've been going through the CCTV footage. From the bank opposite the cafe.'

He hesitated. Julia gave him another nod of encouragement. Christer emitted one of his characteristic deep sighs and continued.

'Well, as I said. I went through the CCTV footage. And there were all sorts running around the place. Men, women, boys, girls, young, old, dogs, babies, and even a chap with a polecat. But at first I didn't see anything that stood out, although I was watching intensely and closely, alertly and attentively and—'

'Get to the point,' Julia said impatiently.

Christer let out another deep sigh and looked more tormented than ever.

'Well, there was someone who seemed familiar. It wasn't possible to see people's faces, but he had a limp, and there was something . . . there was something I recognized.'

'And then I cracked it,' Ruben said, linking his hands behind his neck.

'Yes, yes, Ruben. I know. But I'd like Christer to continue.'

Julia glowered at Ruben.

'Well, at first I couldn't place the individual in question, but as Ruben quite rightly pointed out, we recognized him.'

Ruben leaned forward enthusiastically. His patience with Christer had evidently run out.

'It was Jonas Rask.'

'What the hell are you saying? Jonas Rask? Is he out?' Peder sat bolt upright in his chair.

'Who's Jonas Rask?' Vincent said, turning to Mina.

'Rapist and murderer,' replied Ruben. 'He was in Skogome Prison for twenty years. Got out in September last year – apparently he was considered *rehabilitated*.'

Ruben put air quotes around the final word with his fingers.

Vincent nodded.

'Of course, they use the national treatment model at Skogome,' he said.

Peder looked at Vincent as if he were speaking Greek.

'National treatment model?' Vincent said, looking to the others for support. 'Anyone? No? It's the moderate intensity national treatment model, which is a voluntary programme for men convicted of sexual offences. The method involves people participating in group work and one-on-one conversations with a psychologist. It's offered at five prisons, including Skogome, and it's turned out that people who go through this programme have a lower re-offending rate. Lower, in this instance, is a matter of eight to ten per cent. While there isn't enough data to ensure that's statistically significant—'

The man in the knitted green waistcoat interrupted him.

'Hello. Sorry. My name's Jan Bergsvik,' the man said, proffering his hand. 'But now we're getting into my area of expertise. I'm a psychologist and have extensive experience helping the police in their investigations, often by providing criminal profiles. I was asked to assist. Apparently you needed a profile. The investigation appeared to have been at a standstill in that regard, if I've understood correctly.'

Vincent glanced at Mina and then shook the psychiatrist's hand. It was like a dead fish. The classic handshake of an individual who considered himself superior to others and therefore couldn't be bothered to offer a proper greeting.

'I actually worked on the Jonas Rask case,' Jan added. 'It surprises me that you haven't heard of it. There was a lot of media coverage in the nineties. Jonas was a truck driver for one of the big hauliers. He drove up and down Sweden and even in Norway.'

A memory began to float to the surface of Vincent's mind.

'Was he the one who kidnapped and raped young girls that he picked up hitch-hiking? And he murdered two of them?'

'Tess Bergström and Nina Richter,' Christer muttered.

'He raped them, strangled them, then raped them again,' Jan said.

227

'The bodies were dumped by the roadside in bin bags. In pieces. He chopped them up in his truck. No one noticed the blood. As it happened, he drove for abattoirs.'

'Come on, this is a no brainer,' Ruben said in agitation. 'Jonas fucking Rask has been hanging out at the same cafe that Tuva worked at. Which means he was able to find Agnes too. Of course it's him!'

'Let's not get carried away,' Julia said with a warning tone in her voice.

Vincent cautiously raised a finger.

'Jonas Rask's modus operandi doesn't feel like it fits. How can I put it? It doesn't fit *at all* with our murderer.'

Jan in his green knitted waistcoat let out a soft laugh and shook his head as if Vincent were a child who had said something amusing.

'Sorry, who are you again?'

'Vincent has been brought in as a consultant,' Julia interjected. 'On a probationary basis.'

Apparently she didn't want have a run-in with Jan by going into further detail about what Vincent was doing there.

'Then it's probably for the best if I explain how people function, and more specifically murderers,' Jan said, looking at Vincent over the top of his glasses. 'All perpetrators develop their methods over time. But their basic make-up remains the same. Jonas Rask was a first-rate assailant. You've got three bestial murders on your hands. Women who are the same age as those Rask attacked previously. Bodies that have been grossly abused, as were Rask's victims. And you've also got a connection to Jonas Rask himself. The chances of him not being mixed up in this are microscopic.'

'You're the expert,' said Vincent. 'But I'm just thinking that Robert isn't a woman and that none of them have been sexually assaulted – wasn't that Rask's signature? And, in fact, Robert is the only one who's been cut up. What do you make of that?'

Jan was silent for a second. One of his hands unconsciously brushed over the buttons on his waistcoat from bottom to top. A clear comfort-seeking gesture. He was stressed. Vincent's question seemed to have triggered a dose of cortisol in the psychiatrist.

'Rask clearly has no sex drive any longer,' he said. 'Who knows what a few years in prison have done to him? And the absence of the sexual dimension explains why he's able to murder young men.'

'So you'd say that Rask's previous primary driving force was sexual?' Vincent asked.

'Absolutely,' Jan said complacently. 'Even his violence had a sexualized function. The actual killing, however, was secondary – a necessity to ensure they wouldn't identify him. Although we can assume he enjoyed that part too.'

'And now that his sexuality has disappeared, according to you, he's suddenly found a new driving force that compels him to commit complicated acts of violence? I'm very curious to hear your description of such a person's psychological profile. Especially since you initially said he was still driven by the same thing as before. Of course, this isn't my field, but I can't quite make it all add up.'

Vincent looked at Jan as innocently as he could. The psychologist's eyes were flickering between the other officers. Mina hid behind a notebook.

'I can clearly see that my expertise is not valued here,' he said, pursing his lips. 'Good luck dealing with the investigation on your own. The commissioner is going to hear about this.'

Jan stroked the buttons on his waistcoat again and stood up.

'And next time I suggest you teach your consultants some manners,' he said, before exiting from the room.

There was absolute silence. Vincent could see from the corner of his eye that Mina was trying to contain her laughter.

'Bloody hell, Vincent,' she said once the psychologist was out of earshot. 'Remember we only let you in here out of the goodness of our hearts.'

'Nope, I agree with Vincent,' said Ruben, crossing his arms.

Vincent stared at him. Since when had Ruben been on his side? This was new.

'Vincent never said it wasn't Rask,' Ruben said. 'All he asked was how Rask was thinking now. I'd like to know that too. It'll make it easier to catch him.'

'You're right about one thing,' said Vincent. 'A simple calculation of the probability would tell us that Rask is possibly involved. He certainly has more reason to be considered a person of interest than anyone else we've come across so far. I just can't see why.'

'We should locate Jonas Rask as soon as possible and question him,' Julia said with a nod. 'And the search is already in full swing. So let's put Jonas Rask to one side for the time being and hear what Vincent has to say.'

She looked at the pink folder in his hand with curiosity.

Vincent turned towards Julia. It was best to direct himself to the person whose attitude indicated to the rest of the group what they should think. He noted how Ruben's gaze followed his, but how it then continued down by reflex until it stopped on Julia's behind. He oughtn't to have been surprised: Mina had long ago said that Ruben wanted to sleep with everyone. But still. There was a time and a place . . . OK: focus.

'May I . . .?' he said, pointing to the whiteboard on the wall.

'It's all yours,' Julia said, waving her hand.

He opened the plastic folder, took out a few photos and put them up on the whiteboard using magnets that he had found at the corner of the board. It was no coincidence that he was doing exactly the same thing he'd seen Mina do. By putting up the photos like that, Mina had created an association in her colleagues' heads between the action and serious police work. Now that Vincent was behaving in the same way, he hoped he would awaken an unconscious association in the officers and make them feel that this was serious. He needed all the credibility he could get if they were going to buy what he was proposing. If they were to see the picture he intended to paint. This was his final chance. Peder's slightly sleepy gaze was still glued to the pink folder.

'Like candy floss,' he murmured.

Peder licked off the sugar that had stuck to his fingers and reached for another bun.

Christer offered him the plate.

'I think your brain has collapsed,' Christer said in a low voice. 'Leave half a bun for me.'

'My son's,' Vincent said, patting the folder. 'I didn't have one . . . Anyway . . .'

He cleared his throat and began.

'I've got two things I want to show you. I'll start with these photographs. Can you see what they show?'

The pictures showed smiling men in glittery sequinned costumes. Some of them were standing in front of an expensive set depicting an Egyptian temple or some other 'exotic' location, while others were in the middle of a smoke-filled laser show. They had been captured posing next to a variety of large boxes, and each of them had at least one scantily clad woman standing beside them.

'Your magician colleagues,' said Ruben. 'So what?'

He had finally shifted his gaze from Julia's behind.

'Right. But look again,' said Vincent.

Ruben squinted at the pictures and Peder leaned over the table.

'What the hell?' Ruben exclaimed after a few seconds.

230

'Those are . . .' said Peder.

'Exactly,' said Vincent. 'What you're looking at are performances featuring the bullet catch, sword box and zigzag girl. Three of the best-known stage illusions of all time. But they are also—'

'—how Agnes, Tuva and Robert died,' Julia interrupted.

She went up to the photos and looked at them curiously.

'Tuva's sword box was definitely a travesty of a magic trick,' Vincent said. 'You've been aware of that from the very beginning. Agnes's murder was most likely the same. But perhaps not. With Robert, however, there's no longer any doubt. Your assailant is someone who is thoroughly acquainted with classic stage magic – to the extent that they are building their own illusions. Which ought to reduce the number of suspects by around 99.9 per cent.'

'So we're hunting for a murderous magician?' said Julia with a shake of her head. 'Anyone know whether Daniel or Rask can do card tricks?'

'As I said, that was the first thing I wanted to show you,' said Vincent. 'I don't believe it will have come as a surprise to anyone. The second thing is this . . .'

He produced a black pen and wrote Agnes's, Tuva's and Robert's names on the whiteboard. Beneath Agnes he wrote the number 14, beneath Tuva 15, and beneath Robert 14.

'The times on their smashed watches,' said Ruben. 'Telling us when the murders occurred – this is all we need to catch the murderer. I've been trying to say that all along.'

'Have you?' said Peder. 'I thought you said the solution was that Daniel had a threesome going with Agnes and Tuva.'

Ruben pretended not to hear. He looked at the photos of the sequinned magicians.

'I mean, they're *so* homo,' he said.

Both Peder's and Christer's jaws dropped in surprise. Julia burst out in a brief peal of laughter.

'Good God, Ruben, who says homo nowadays?' she said. 'You should be ashamed.'

Vincent shifted his weight from one foot to the other. He was losing them. Right as he was about to deliver the most important part of his presentation. This was why he always declined invitations to give talks to high school students. And even their ability to concentrate was better than these police officers'.

'What are you getting at, Ruben? About the watches, that is. Not the . . . sequins,' said Peder, concealing a yawn behind his hand.

231

'I think they look fancy,' said Christer.

The last bun was long gone, but Peder moistened his fingertip and began picking up pearls of sugar from the table. He didn't appear to have slept since Vincent had last seen him.

'Check the times,' said Ruben in a satisfied tone. 'They're almost the same each time. Two identical times would have been coincidence, but not three times. Either the murderer has a set routine, where he does the same thing at a certain time of day, or the victim does. Or, most likely, they both do. Now that we've got three times, all we have to do is check where our victims usually were at around two or three in the afternoon. That's where we'll find our murderer.'

Ruben put his arms behind his head triumphantly, as if he had just solved the case single-handedly.

'What Ruben is saying is indeed the most obvious conclusion – well done for reaching it so quickly,' Vincent began.

Ruben stretched and looked, if possible, even more self-satisfied.

'In all probability, it's also completely wrong.'

Ruben's complacent smile disappeared lightning fast. Perhaps it had been cruel of him, but Vincent hadn't been able to help himself. After all, Ruben was the main reason he had been thrown out last time. All he had done was pass Ruben a shovel, shown him where he could dig, and then Ruben had dug his own hole and jumped into it all by himself.

'All right, Mister Mental Know-It-All,' said Ruben, scowling at him. 'Give me something better. But it had better be a lot bloody better.'

Vincent didn't reply. Instead, he took out a red pen and wrote two dates under Agnes's and Tuva's names on the whiteboard: *13 January* under Agnes and *20 February* under Tuva. Under Robert he wrote two question marks. One for the day and one for the month. Then he rubbed out the black numbers for the times and rewrote them in red.

'The murderer wants us to know the times of the murders,' he said. 'Hence the wristwatches. But he wants us to know more than the hour when they occurred – he wants us to know which *day*. The bodies were left in locations where they were guaranteed to be found. The murderer took a big risk moving them there. He could have avoided discovery. So it must have been important for them to be found before they began to decay, so that you could determine on exactly which date the murders took place.'

'OK, hang on,' said Christer. 'The murderer wants us to know exactly when he strikes. But *why*? Does he want to be caught?'

'That's the question,' said Vincent. 'There's no obvious pattern indicating when he will strike next time. The number of weeks between murders varies. And the times, as you can see, aren't completely identical. So I believe it's about something else.'

'I've looked into whether anything has happened on those dates at those times,' said Mina. 'But I've not turned anything up. Of course, something may have happened in the murderer's own life on those dates – something that's important to him. But if so, why go to the trouble of telling us, when we won't be aware of it?'

'I agree with Mina,' said Vincent. 'Which is why I believe the solution is a different one.'

He paused to check he had everyone's attention. Mina had been right last time. It was like a show in spite of everything. And he was now in his element.

'I believe that the dates and times are parts of a message,' he said.

'Parts? You mean they're . . . meant to go together?' Peder said slowly. 'Like jigsaw pieces?'

Vincent nodded.

'A message to whom, then?' said Julia.

'To us. To you. But we can't understand it yet because the message isn't complete. The murders are a countdown, right? The bodies are inscribed with Roman numerals. Murders four, three and two have occurred. There will be at least one more before we have the whole message.'

'*At least* one?' said Christer, horrified.

'Murder number one. We don't know what happens when we reach zero. But . . .'

Vincent paused again. He looked them in the eyes one by one. He was almost ready to deliver his final point.

'You don't need to wait for the next murder,' he said. 'You don't actually even need to know what the message means. Because the murderer has made a mistake.'

He could feel the entire room holding its breath. Even Ruben was focused. Peder had stopped with his hand halfway to his mouth; he had long since forgotten about the pearl of sugar, which now fell from his finger back onto the table.

'The final victim, Robert, was left in a location that was cordoned off for several days. His body was there for too long for you to know for certain on which date he died. You don't even know which month it happened in. He was found on the fifth of May, but he could have been killed at the end of April. If the murderer wants to give us jigsaw pieces to put together, as Peder said, then he didn't succeed this time. The date is missing. And I think he'll be eager to correct it, given how much work he's put in.'

Julia's eyes suddenly opened wide with realization. Smart girl. Almost as quick-witted as Mina.

'We'll call a press conference,' she said. 'To lure him into the open. As soon as we've spoken to the parents. We have to do something radical. I haven't wanted to burden you all with too much internal politics, but I can tell you this much – our time is running out. Patience from on high is in short supply. If we don't come up with something big soon, we'll all be back in our regular posts and we'll see this team dissolved in the very near future. I think a press conference might help to shake the tree and see whether any fruit falls out of it. We need to appeal to the public to come forward with information.'

'It'll lead to lots of disinformation too, but you know that,' Christer muttered. 'We'll be wading through shit.'

'Go to the media,' Vincent said, nodding and pretending not to have heard what Christer said.

Christer had a point. Appealing to the public was a double-edged sword, but given that their current position was akin to a blunt kitchen knife, the choice was easy.

'Explain that you're seeking information on when a black box may have been left at the wholesalers' market in Årsta. Say that you know nothing. You might even want to reveal that you're hunting a serial killer, like they do on TV. If my psychological profile is right, I think that would flatter the murderer. A narcissist wants to hear that he's the best, since that fits in with his own worldview. That will increase the chances of him getting in touch to give you that missing third piece of the jigsaw. In fact, I don't believe he'll be able to resist.'

Peder looked confused.

'But the message still won't be complete – you just said so,' he said, hiding a yawn behind his hand. 'It's got four pieces. How do we find him before he kills for a fourth time?'

'We'll set up a tip line. Then we'll just have to hope the murderer gives something away,' said Julia. 'Vincent can listen to his voice and see whether we can pick up anything from that. We can cross-reference it with the recordings of Rask to see whether it's him. We can also analyse the background noise to see whether we can figure out where he's calling from. If we're lucky, we might even manage to trace the call.

234

If he calls from a mobile we can get its GPS location. We'll start making preparations right away.'

Mina nodded towards Vincent and smiled. He had excelled himself. Julia went over to him and took his hand in both of hers.

'This was invaluable,' she said. 'At the press conference, I'd like to keep the information about Jonas Rask to ourselves for the time being. And I also want to keep your involvement secret for a while longer. If anyone asks, I've only seen Vincent Walder on TV. OK?'

He nodded in reply. It was as close to a standing ovation as he was going to get from this audience.

'There's one more thing before you all get absorbed by this,' said Julia, turning back to the group again.

Peder was half-standing at the table, visibly unsure whether to sit back down again or stand up fully.

'Sit down,' said Julia with a sigh. 'If any of you haven't yet read the file on Robert's disappearance, do so immediately. We'll have to start over with that one. Robert's parents and the staff at his sheltered housing have been interviewed several times. But not by us. And not after he . . . was found. There are questions to be asked now. Christer and I will make sure we meet the parents the day after tomorrow. And we'll head to the sheltered housing facility as soon as we can after the press conference. Right, let's all get to work.'

Christer nodded but said nothing. The others got up from the table. Julia turned back to Vincent and gave him a small piece of plastic.

'Here's your own personal pass card. You're one of us now.'

60

Julia took a deep breath before pushing the doorbell. The stairwell was beautiful. High ceilings. Black and white chequered tiles on the floor. Stucco.

She felt Christer's gloomy presence behind her. Throughout the journey to the property in Vasastan he had been questioning why he had been chosen to come with her. Just like a child. Julia had been tempted to say: 'Because.' But she had refrained. She was the boss and with that came certain obligations. She hurriedly checked her phone again before anyone had time to open the door. The search for Jonas Rask was on – she had people out looking for him at all his known previous addresses and she expected to receive a message at any moment to say they had found him. If they found Rask, they might not even have to hold the press conference.

She heard footsteps approaching. An elegant woman opened the door.

'Come in,' she said in a low voice, stepping to one side. They were expected.

They entered the hall. Julia couldn't help admiring the apartment. She would have loved to live in something exactly like this. But she and Torkel had agreed that they were best off in a terraced house with a garden, since they were going to start a family. Standing there in the *fin de siècle* hallway, she wondered whether that was really the right decision. Especially since they had been living in the terrace in Enebyberg for almost five years without anyone who might play in the back garden putting in an appearance.

'Would you like coffee?'

Robert's mother's voice was cool and gave away no emotion, but the red rims around her eyes revealed her grief. In the kitchen there was a grey-haired man in jeans and a white shirt waiting for them – he was

236

elegant too and was a number of years older than the woman. Despite the dark circles around his eyes, they made a beautiful couple.

'Coffee would be great,' said Julia and Christer, both nodding.

'Thomas.'

The man proffered his right hand and Julia and Christer shook it one after the other.

'Jessica,' said the woman, who had deftly started to make coffee using a large barista-style espresso machine that puffed and steamed. 'Sorry, I seem to keep forgetting the absolute basics, things that would come naturally ordinarily. Like courtesy. Things that seemed so important before have become trivialities . . '

Thomas sat down heavily at a large wooden kitchen table by the window and indicated that they should sit down too.

He had a slightly confused expression. As if he were in the middle of a dream. Unsure of what was up and what was down. Inside and out. Julia recognized the look from many of the loved ones she had talked to over the years.

'Thanks,' said Christer, accepting a cup of coffee from Jessica.

An oak leaf had been drawn into the crema at the top of the cup and Christer looked at Julia in astonishment. This wasn't the usual brewed-coffee-that-had-been-on-all-day that they were used to when paying visits such as this.

'We run a deli on the ground floor,' said Jessica as she made a cup for Julia. 'You probably saw it on your way in.'

Julia nodded. She had paused in front of the display window and devoured it with her eyes. Large, dried hams had been hanging in the window. Pata negra. Prosciutto. Bresaola. A huge wheel of Parmesan towered majestically over all manner of goat's cheeses, Bries and blue cheeses. She didn't know the names of most, but her mouth had been watering at the mere sight of them.

'It runs in the family,' said Thomas, shaking his head when Jessica looked at him questioningly after handing Julia her cup.

Julia's had a heart in the crema.

'Thomas's family have been a cheese family for three generations,' Jessica explained, sitting down at the table with them.

Neither she nor Thomas had a cup of coffee in front of them. Judging by their sunken cheeks, Julia doubted they had eaten or drunk anything in days.

'Yes, I always said that we had blue cheese instead of blue blood in this family,' said Jessica.

No one smiled. The joke hung on the air before dissolving and disappearing. There was no laughter left in this home.

'Have a cantucci,' said Thomas, pushing a bowl towards them.

Julia loved the small Italian almond biscotti. But it was hard to have a sensible conversation while eating hard biscuits, so she declined. Christer, however, happily helped himself to three in one go and took a loud bite. She glowered at him in irritation and he looked back at her indifferently.

'Is it true?' said Thomas, his voice trembling.

He looked down at the table as he asked the question. The wooden tabletop testified to happier times. Rings left by glasses of red wine. Bright stains from what might have been Indian dishes with turmeric or curry. Dinners. Family. Friends. Laughter.

'What do you mean?' Julia asked, although she knew what he was going to ask.

She steeled herself. She forced herself to think about something other than the boy with the broad smile who had been seen outside every single shop, petrol station and newspaper kiosk in recent weeks.

'That he wasn't . . . whole . . . when they found him.'

Julia tried to think about the flowers that were coming into bloom at home in the garden. About the bed that Torkel had made by hand that was still empty. About the feeling of injections being stuck into the soft part of her stomach. The depression that came without fail when the hormone treatment lowered her oestrogen.

Christer was still crunching on a biscotti, and outside the open window there was a crow cawing away in one of the big trees in the inner courtyard. She forced herself to answer.

'It's true,' she said, seeing how Jessica collapsed.

'And now you want to tell the whole world about this.'

'If you'll let us. But naturally we'll respect your decision if—'

'Do what you have to do to catch the sick person who did this,' said Jessica in a stony voice.

Julia was taken by surprise by the sudden change and fell silent.

'Tell us about Robert,' she said.

Jessica's face brightened. She glanced at her husband. A brief smile passed between them. Happy memories were contained in their glances.

'We married young but it was a few years before we had Robert. I was twenty-five. Our little miracle.'

She reached out her hand to her husband and he took it. Julia saw him squeezing her hand so hard that it surely had to hurt. Outside, the crow was cawing again.

'Bobby was the kindest, friendliest, most loving soul to ever walk this earth.'

Thomas's voice broke. He collected himself and carried on:

'That boy gave us so much joy every day. But . . . but when he got older we couldn't take care of him in the same way. We couldn't supervise him twenty-four seven, which was what he needed. Several times he wandered off – sometimes in the middle of the night. Well, I'm sure you know that Bobby has gone missing before. So that's why we weren't all that worried to begin with. No more so than usual. But then . . . the days passed . . .'

Christer reached for the bowl and grabbed another fistful of cantucci. Julia kicked him gently on the shin under the table. Robert's parents didn't seem to notice.

'Were you satisfied with the facility he was living at?'

It was Christer who had asked the question and Julia looked at him in surprise. He had seemed far more focused on his snack break than on what was being said.

'Very satisfied,' said Jessica. 'He's been there for five . . . no, wait, seven years. The staff are incredible. We visit him every day and he's back home every weekend. He's safe there. Loved—'

She let out a sob and Thomas squeezed her hand tightly again. The fine silver chain around her wrist jangled each time she moved her hand, and Julia saw that it had a disc with the word *Robert* engraved on it. Jessica spotted that she was looking. She let go of Thomas's hand and held up the arm with the chain.

'My Mother's Day present last year from Robert. He saved up his pocket money and asked Thomas to take him to buy it.'

'It's beautiful,' said Julia.

The thought appeared out of nowhere without her being able to stop it. She wondered whether she would ever be fêted on Mother's Day. She brushed away the thought. Her troubles were insignificant in comparison.

'Do you know of anyone who had anything against Robert?'

'No, no, no, no one,' said Thomas, shaking his head firmly. 'Everyone loved Bobby. And he loved everyone. I've never met a single person that he didn't charm.'

'Do you remember the woman whose window he managed to smash with his slingshot?' Jessica said, laughing. 'The one across the courtyard? It ended with her inviting him for buns and juice.'

'I remember.'

239

Thomas smiled and nodded. He raised his gaze and met Julia's.

'There are a thousand stories like that about Robert. He was our light. Our joy. Sure, he was born with a disability, or rather, what the world stubbornly insists on calling a disability. But believe me, the world would be a far better place if everyone was like Robert. He was perfect.'

From the corner of her eye, Julia saw a framed photo of Robert standing on the sideboard. It was the same photo that had been on the news hoardings. She wondered how she would react if she had a child with Down's syndrome. She was forty-two now. It wasn't improbable. And the probability only grew with each passing year. She wondered what Torkel would say . . .

'We're going to talk to the people who work at Robert's accommodation too. Is there anything else you'd like to add?' said Christer, looking at Julia quizzically following her sudden silence.

'He was naive,' said Thomas. 'He would happily have gone anywhere with anybody.'

Thomas hesitated before he continued:

'Do you have a suspect?'

Julia nodded. 'A violent, relapsed criminal. We're hunting him right now.'

'You . . . you have to promise you'll catch him,' he said in a low voice. 'How are we . . . how are we ever going to live otherwise?'

Julia stood up. She considered what she should say. She ought to know. She had heard the same plea so many times before. The plea for an end. The plea for deliverance. The punishment that would set everything right. But she knew that she shouldn't make promises she couldn't keep. Once she had set her coffee cup down in the sink and opened her mouth to reply, Christer beat her to it.

'I'm afraid we can't promise you that,' he said. 'But we can promise that we'll do our absolute best. And he sounds like such a lovely boy. Take solace in those moments of beauty. Your great memories. Don't let those be taken from you.'

Julia looked at him in surprise. Christer – the man who usually thought life was torment and death was liberation. She ought to discreetly check for the scent of alcohol on his breath once they were out of here.

When they left, Thomas and Jessica were still at the kitchen table. The last thing Julia saw before the door closed was that they were holding hands.

61

Kvibille 1982

Jane found Mum at the edge of the lawn, where it merged into the woods. She was sitting in the shadow of the trees, doing the weeding. Jane was tempted to ask what was the point of pulling up dandelions when they were living right next to a forest, but she knew that conversation would lead nowhere.

'How's it going?' she asked instead, crouching beside Mum.

Her mother had cleared the dandelions in a precise straight line.

'I can't say it's making much difference really.'

Mum adjusted her back, which creaked.

'Ouch. But it's good to have something to do. By the by, have you seen your little brother around?'

'He cycled off with those three girls from his class,' said Jane, tearing off one of the dandelion leaves. 'They're probably off snogging somewhere.'

'Jane!' said her mother in a shocked tone. 'They're seven years old! Anyway, "those girls" are called Malla, Sickan and Lotta. You should be happy for your brother that he has friends.'

'Surprised, more like.'

Jane examined the dandelion leaf and then bit carefully into it.

'You know that they're edible, right?' she said. 'The dandelions. If you don't want to get rid of them, that is.'

'Why would I want to eat dandelions?' said Mum, wiping the sweat from her brow with the back of her hand, and smudging a streak of soil across her eyebrows in the process.

Jane shrugged.

'They contain lots of iron, potassium and magnesium.'

'And how do you know this? You're hardly a member of the forest fan club.'

'Why *don't* you know that? Do you at least know that the French for dandelions is *piss-en-lits*, which means wet the bed? Because of their powerful diuretic properties?'

'Powerful diuretic properties,' her mother mimicked her in a pompous tone. 'Sometimes I wonder whose daughter you are. You're too smart for this place.'

And there it was. The opening she had been waiting for. Mum drove a metal tool into the earth next to the leaves of the next dandelion and began to prise it free. Jane took a deep breath. Now. She needed to say it now.

'Talking of me and this place,' she said. 'You do remember that I'm leaving in eight days' time?'

'I know.'

Mum removed the dandelion and its roots.

'You're going to visit Ylva up in Dalarna. We've discussed it. Ylva's mum seems nice. I'm not in the slightest bit worried. You'll be gone for two weeks.'

'It's not just that,' said Jane.

Say it now, say it now, say it now.

'When I come home, it'll be to pack,' she said, and held her breath.

Mum stopped mid-movement and looked up from the grass.

Jane had to carry on and say it all at once, while she still dared.

'I'm moving,' she said. 'I can't live here any longer – on this farm. I want to do things. Live in a city. Find new friends. Study. I . . . I can't bear to be here any longer. Being here is driving me crazy.'

Mum looked at her without saying anything. Jane began to blink in order to hold back the tears. She wasn't going to cry. *Wasn't*. If she did, she'd never be able to leave. If she did, Mum would win. She looked up at the clear blue sky and blinked some more. The sky was so empty. Not a cloud or plane in sight. She didn't need emptiness – she needed its opposite. And she was never going to get that here on the farm.

'Don't worry,' she said. 'I'm almost sixteen. I'll be fine. I've already sorted out somewhere to live.'

'It's not you I'm worried about,' Mum said quietly. 'It's me. You've always been the strong one. The smart one. You know things like the fact that dandelions make you wee and how to figure things out and . . . and . . . I can barely put food on the table. Without you here . . . Your brother has his own special ways . . . I won't be up to it.'

Mum looked back down at the grass again.

'If you leave I'll kill myself,' she said.

The air vanished from Jane's lungs. As if someone had punched her in the chest. She had thought Mum would get angry and forbid her and start crying and plunge into a depressive episode. Anything. But not this. Suddenly she was boiling over with rage.

'Well, fuck you,' she said. 'And you call yourself my mother? This is blackmail. I can't live your life for you. I need my own. And you won't be alone. My brother isn't as fragile as you think. And if you really can't manage on your own, then perhaps it's time to find someone who wants to stay here with you. Because I don't want to.'

Jane got up and looked at her mother, who was still staring down at the grass, down at her perfect line of weeding. She looked so small. So spineless. Jane had done the right thing in telling her. She needed to get away from here. If she stayed, she'd go under. Just like Mum.

62

Peder waited anxiously outside the bathroom door. It sounded as if his wife was dying on the other side.

'How are you feeling, darling?' he called out, his ear pressed to the white-painted wood.

A tormented mumble reached him in reply. After a minute or so Anette unlocked the door. Her face was as white as a sheet.

'Back up,' she said, waving her arms at him to make him keep his distance. 'I've got the winter vomiting sickness. Or maybe it's summer vomiting sickness. Anyway, you and the triplets can't come anywhere near me.'

Her long hair was lank and the smell from the bathroom made him quickly shut the door behind her.

'No problem, darling,' he said. 'We'll just wrap you up in clingfilm. It's good for the triplets to have their meals properly wrapped when you're breastfeeding them.'

Anette rolled her eyes and fetched a bottle of hand sanitizer from the bathroom. He held his breath. He really did wish she hadn't opened the bathroom door again. She sprayed and wiped down the door handle on both sides.

'I'm serious,' she said. 'This toilet is now off limits. It's just for me. Unless you have a desperate need to do a shit or hurl?'

Peder backed away with feigned shock on his face.

'Bodily fluids? Do we have those in this family? The triplets are so sterile . . .'

He drew her to him and stroked his wife's straggling hair. Anette was too tired to protest.

'I suggest you barricade yourself in here,' he said, leading her to the bedroom. 'I'll fetch your iPad. Don't come out until you're better or you've watched everything on Netflix. Whichever happens first. The triplets and I will take the living room. We can build a den. If they miss their mother then I'll just tell them you've left us.'

Anette smiled weakly.

'You can expect some thank-you sex later on,' she said, looking longingly at the bed. 'In a year or two.'

'I'll have to double-check my calendar then, to make sure I'm free,' said Peder, fetching a few extra pillows. 'I'd better call the station to let them know I'm going to be looking after the kids for a few days.'

He pulled out his phone while Anette carefully sat down on the edge of the bed. She really didn't look well. Perhaps he should ask Mina for a few litres of hand sanitizer. There was no way he wanted to end up as ill as his wife.

'Peder,' she said. 'Obviously I'll try to breastfeed as much as I'm able to, but what are you going to do about food?'

Peder bit his tongue. He really shouldn't. She would never forgive him. But it was an open goal.

'We'll have hamburgers dripping in grease,' he said, prolonging each and every word. 'The sort that glisten with shiny fat. Or goose giblet soup. You know, blood and salt. With some lumps in it.'

Anette stared at him. Then she rushed out of the bedroom and lunged back into the bathroom.

63

'Peder just called,' Julia told others in the conference room. 'He won't be able to help out manning the phones. Anette's sick and he has to look after the kids.'

Ruben wasn't surprised. Not in the slightest. It didn't take a genius to realize that Peder wouldn't be able to keep going indefinitely. 'Anette's sick'. Yeah, right! More likely Peder needed a break. He was probably at Riche down on Stureplan right now, enjoying an early lunch. Aww. There would be plenty of women who for whatever reason didn't need to go back to the office after lunch and would be sipping a cava or two instead. And women like that would be really turned on by the fact that Peder was a cop. Ruben had had his own experiences of that. Uniform drew them like a magnet, but it didn't look so good when out on the town. Plain clothes needed a helping hand; you had to ensure that a set of handcuffs could be glimpsed under your jacket. That made them crazy. Rings on fingers didn't make any difference at that stage. He didn't begrudge Peder that. On the contrary. After giving birth to triplets, Anette would be a no show in bed for the foreseeable.

'Is he going to look after the triplets all by himself?' said Christer, shaking his head. 'Poor chap. He'll be a shadow of his former self when he comes back. Well, he already is. A shadow of a shadow . . .'

Christer leaned back, making his chair creak, and sighed deeply.

'Maybe someone should go over there and help out,' he muttered.

If Christer was so damn fond of children then he could bloody well do it himself. Nappies were the last thing Ruben was going to let into his life.

'Anyway, we're a body short,' Julia continued.

She was wearing a jacket and a pair of wide-leg tailored trousers. He assumed those made her look more like a boss. Personally, he preferred it when she wore a skirt. Or tight jeans. But you couldn't always have it all.

'Ruben, you'll have to do your shift with Vincent,' said Julia.

'Me and the magician?' he snorted. 'A match made in heaven.'

'He'll turn on his heel before he's through the door if he hears you calling him that,' said Mina. 'Magician, that is.'

'Really?' said Ruben, adding an exaggerated tone of hope. 'I'll be sure to remember.'

Mina didn't even look at him. Jesus, she was hard to flirt with.

'Well then,' said Julia, gathering up her papers. 'We still haven't found Jonas Rask, so I'll be holding a press conference in two hours' time. I won't mention Vincent's involvement in the investigation or the fact that we're looking for Jonas Rask. After all, we don't actually have any evidence against him, it's all circumstantial. I'd also be grateful if you didn't say anything to anyone off the record – or on the record for that matter. The conference will be live-streamed via all our social media channels and covered by various other media. After that, we'll be waiting by the phone for as long as it takes. Ruben and Vincent will take the first shift.'

Ruben opened his mouth but Julia silenced him by raising a finger.

'A match made in heaven, like you said,' she told him. 'Like *I* said. Vincent is one of us now.'

64

They were standing by the stone wall high up on Fjällgatan, which offered a commanding view over Stockholm's Old Town, the island of Skeppsholmen and parts of Djurgården. When you saw the city from a distance, it was as if all the dirt, all the pollution and all the grubby people didn't exist. From a distance it glittered. They also had a good view of the theme park at Gröna Lund where Tuva had been found. But Mina tried to push away that thought and just see the amusement park for what it was.

It had been Vincent's suggestion that they take a walk and talk over the case – without the rest of the team. They had already been walking for an hour, thrashing out everything they knew or thought they knew.

'Do you have any plans for the summer?' Vincent suddenly asked, his gaze fixed on the view.

Mina stared at him.

'Plans? You do realize we're in the middle of an investigation, right?'

'Yes, but I was thinking that it's almost summer and . . .'

He cleared his throat and fell silent as if he no longer knew what he was going to say.

'Vincent, was that an attempt at small talk?'

Mina repressed a smile.

'Perhaps. It occurred to me we've talked a lot about the investigation now.'

'Good that you're practising.'

She turned her back to the view and leaned against the stone wall, but first she inserted her own plastic carrier bag from the supermarket between her back and the wall. The sun warmed her face. Her newly purchased sunglasses were being put to good use.

She thought she saw someone she recognized, but the person turned around when Mina caught sight of her and headed in the other direction. She was probably mistaken.

'A propos the investigation,' she said. 'I don't know whether it's such a good idea for you to go to the press conference. What if some journalist recognizes you and starts asking questions about why you're there? It may draw focus from the message we want to get out there. Julia was clear about not wanting to say that you're helping us.'

'I'm just curious about how a press conference like that works in reality,' he said.

She closed her eyes behind her sunglasses.

'We'll share some of the details and keep others to ourselves. Things that only the murderer knows. That way we'll be able to separate false confessions from a true one. It's more common than you'd think for people to call in and admit to all sorts of things that they haven't done. For instance, more than sixty people who have confessed to Olof Palme's murder.'

She took off her sunglasses and let the sun warm all of her. She liked it when it was cold because it felt so clean. But warmth felt . . . alive. As long as she didn't get sweaty. Currently, it was just right, with a cool breeze fanning her face.

They began to walk again.

'In that case,' said Vincent, 'I suggest that you play dumb when it comes to the "pieces of the jigsaw," as Peder described them. The murder dates and times *have* to be a code – I can't imagine they're anything else. But you don't need to divulge that you've realized that.'

'No, that's true.'

Mina fell silent for a moment. Then she looked sideways at Vincent. 'Rask? What do you think?'

'Wasn't that obvious?' said Vincent, kicking a pebble so that it bounced away across the road ahead of them. 'I think it's galling. It doesn't feel right, quite simply. Rask is a sexually driven perpetrator – I don't get the feeling that there was any kind of sexual motive around our murder victims.'

'That doesn't mean it doesn't exist. Sex isn't just about explicitly sexual acts. Many men I've met in the line of duty have got off on violence, power, dominance, pain, terror, fear.'

'As a race, we ought to be ashamed of what we're doing to the world.'

'Women can cause misery too. I've seen my fair share of that. But men perpetuate violence on a completely different scale. My point is that we can't say with certainty that there isn't a sexual element to these murders.'

Vincent nodded.

'You're absolutely right. I'm not ruling anything out. We can't afford to. But I should also say that Jonas Rask doesn't feel sufficiently . . . *refined* is possibly the word I'm looking for. So there are several factors that make me dubious about whether we should be focusing our efforts on him.'

Mina didn't answer. The conversation about sex had brought to life thoughts that she'd been trying to suppress. Sex as dominance. Sex as power. She had far too much personal experience of that. But never again. Never ever again. By comparison, her vibrator was the best lover she'd ever had.

They walked in silence for a while. It was a surprisingly comfortable silence. Then Vincent raised his hand and pointed while squinting into the sun.

'Look, that's where Maria and I got married.'

She turned around and tried to see where Vincent was pointing.

'At Gröna Lund?'

'No. Do you see that little island next to it? Kastellholmen. Her entire family refused to come.'

He laughed.

'Given what a rollercoaster the marriage turned out to be, Gröna Lund might have been more fitting.'

She saw a red oblong building on a small island below them. It must have been what he had been pointing at. It looked very beautiful. But he was right: Gröna Lund did seem more fun.

'Vincent, you know that thing about practising your small talk,' she said, standing a little closer to him. 'You're absolutely fine at normal talking too.'

'Only with some people.'

She smiled and looked back at the city again. Somewhere below them was a murderer waiting for their next opportunity. She and Vincent had no choice. They had to get there first.

65

He leaned against the wall and began by crossing his legs and then his arms. He had promised Mina he would stay in the background.

'Bunch of hyenas,' said Ruben, who was standing next to him at the very back of the room.

'They perform their role,' Vincent said matter-of-factly.

Ruben seemed to have accepted that he was on the team, at least for the time being.

'Easy for you to say. For us they're usually an aggravation. And I don't think for one moment that tip line we're going to man will give us a bloody thing.'

'I take your point, but at the same time the journalistic corps – the fourth estate – is needed to counterbalance the government and parliament. Without them we could end up with a police state . . .'

'It's not like Sweden's some bloody banana republic,' said Ruben in irritation, glowering at Vincent.

'It would be very odd if it were,' said Vincent, his gaze fixed on the podium. 'The term banana republic originally referred to Honduras, which was dependent on its banana exports, allowing the United Fruit Company of America to gain political influence. The expression later became synonymous with countries in Latin America that were dependent on a few export products, had a corrupt government or a military junta, and where foreign governments and companies exercised great influence. So it . . .'

Vincent turned around but Ruben was no longer there. He shrugged. Some people had no desire to be educated.

A murmur rippled through the room. The press conference was due to begin and the media were there in force. He could see the logos of both the major evening tabloids, the heavyweight dailies, and the TT wire agency, plus a number of local reporters, along with various new media outlets whose names he didn't recognize. There were microphones, cameras, tape recorders, mobile phones and good old notepads and pens.

Julia came in and stood at the podium. She was in uniform, which he hadn't seen her wear before. It suited her. She had a cool complexion which suited the austere police uniform, and her glossy hair looked beautiful against the blue fabric. As usual, he sensed something sad about her body language. Like a halo of sorrow around her.

She cleared her throat and the hubbub in the room died down. He suddenly noticed Mina standing in an inconspicuous spot at the right-hand side of the room. It surprised him that he hadn't seen her until now – he usually spotted her before everyone else in a room. She was good at being still.

'I'd like to welcome you to today's press conference about a series of murders that we now believe were committed by a single assailant,' Julia began. 'I would ask that you respect the rules and not to speak until it's your turn, and please let me finish what I have to say.'

No one spoke and Julia continued after quickly glancing at the bundle of papers in front of her on the table.

'We have reason to believe that the murders of Tuva Bengtsson, Agnes Ceci and Robert Berger were carried out by the same person.'

A buzz erupted throughout the room and Julia creased her eyebrows in irritation. She waited for silence to fall before she continued.

'We need the public's help to identify the killer. We're appealing for any information the public may have, but we're particularly interested in hearing from anyone who knows of a connection between the victims. We have good cause to believe that the killer will strike again.'

The buzz rose into an agitated cacophony. Camera flashes were triggered, and reporters began shouting questions and waving their hands. Out of the corner of his eye, Vincent could see Mina scowling angrily at the journalists. Determination suited her.

'Silence!' Julia roared, and the journalists reluctantly quietened down to allow her to continue. 'There is some information that we cannot disclose at this time, but what we can tell you is that they were staged as magic illusions that intentionally "went wrong". It also seems that the victims were not murdered where they were found, but were transported from the original crime scene. We have reason to believe that a vehicle with a higher cargo capacity than a regular car was required – possibly a van – but this is only speculation. We also require assistance in determining the time of the third murder – that of Robert Berger. Robert was found on the fifth of May in the car park at the wholesalers' market in Årsta here in Stockholm. But unfortunately we have been unable to determine the time of death, since the body had been in the car park for several days prior to its discovery. We are therefore seeking information on this, in case anyone saw anything. We have set up a dedicated tip line for the general public – you can see the number on the screens at the front.'

She let out a deep sigh and her eyes scanned the sea of chairs filled with reporters and photographers. Finally she nodded at a man in his forties holding a microphone emblazoned with the logo of *Expressen*.

'What makes you think that the killer will strike again? Are you saying that these murders were the work of a serial killer? Is he a known figure from the past?'

Julia didn't reply right away – she took her time to consider her words.

On the surface, she looked completely calm, but Vincent had no difficulty identifying the small signs of stress. The way she had her weight on the outside of her right foot, as if she were about to leave the room. The way she had almost stopped blinking, instead showing tiny flutters at the corner of her eye. The way her clasped hands were seemingly resting in a relaxed position on the podium, but the tips of her thumbs were discreetly rubbing back and forth against each other to pause the rush of cortisol in her body.

'That's one of the things I can't go into further detail about,' she said. 'But we have strong grounds to believe that it is the case. That's as much as I can say.'

More hands flew into the air. Julia nodded at the reporter from TT, a young woman.

'Which magic tricks have been used? There's been talk about a box in relation to the body found at Gröna Lund?'

'I can't go into that either.'

The reporter from TT added another question:

'Do you think this is someone with a personal connection to magic?'

'Have you checked whether Joe Labero has an alibi?' someone yelled, drawing scattered laughter.

'Or Brynolf and Ljung?' another joker chipped in.

The frown between Julia's eyebrows deepened. Mina looked angry. Vincent was once again struck by how beautiful she was. It was all he could do to take his eyes off her.

'We are currently unable to comment on possible suspects,' said Julia. 'But a profile is being compiled. However, I doubt that it will match Joe Labero, Mr Brynolf or Mr Ljung.'

The coarse journalistic humour didn't seem to appeal to her.

'Perhaps we're looking for some kind of Swedish Houdini . . . the Houdini killer!' shouted a young *GP* reporter to more stifled laughter.

But Vincent noted that the majority of the journalists were feverishly taking notes. The name would take hold – the fourth estate seemed intent on labelling every serial killer with a witty alias.

Julia simply continued smiling. Increasingly more stiffly.

Vincent understood. It was important to stay on good terms with the media. No matter how tasteless she thought the joke had been, Julia needed them to like her – it was the only way to retain control of the story. Otherwise they would write whatever they pleased.

'I won't be taking any further questions now. We need the general public's help, and the number to call is shown on the screens. It will also be available on the police website, as well as our Instagram and Facebook accounts.'

Cacophony again, hands in the air, questions being shouted. But Julia had turned her back on the journalists and was heading towards Mina. They vanished to the right and Vincent craned his neck to try to see Mina for as long as possible. When she was completely gone, he discreetly ducked out through the door, knowing that if he stuck around he would be recognized. And Julia didn't need to handle *those* questions.

66

'How does this work then?' Vincent asked, trying to comprehend what he was looking at on the computer screen in front of him.

The room that he and Ruben were in was full of technical equipment whose function he could only guess at. The display in front of them, however, was showing something significantly less high tech – in fact, it was rather more reminiscent of Microsoft Excel.

'We track calls with this program?' he said, trying to conceal his almost childish amusement at the whole situation.

Obviously it would have been better if one of the walls had been covered in screens showing mysterious figures and images from surveillance drones, like in the movies, but you couldn't have everything.

'Well, this is a telephone switchboard,' Ruben said. 'Everyone who calls the tip line is recorded, but you and I also listen to the tips in real time. Of course, that's impossible if too many people call at once, but there's not usually a big rush. If we hear anything that seems the slightest bit suspicious, such as someone who sounds like Rask, we flag that call. Like this. We don't do anything else for now.'

Ruben clicked on a row in the document and it went red. A telephone switchboard. It was hardly *Bourne*. Vincent struggled to hide his disappointment.

'But what about tracing them?' he said.

'In that regard we're legally buttfucked,' Ruben said, heading for the coffee.

Ruben poured a mug of coffee for himself but nothing for Vincent – he could tell from the smell that the other man would prefer not to have any. This coffee had not had a happy childhood.

'The decision to trace a call has to be made by a court,' Ruben continued, while wiping up some coffee he had spilled on the table.

'But to get that kind of permission, we have to state *who* we want to trace. And we don't know that. I mean, that's what we're here to find out. Of course, the very second we hear a suspect call we could ring the prosecutor and ask them to issue a temporary ruling so that we can trace it at once. But I'm doubtful that we'd have time to get that before the call was over. We *can* trace the calls – in straightforward technical terms we get the information the very second they ring in – but we're not allowed to.'

'So what's the point of us being here then?' said Vincent.

Ruben sat down in the chair next to him.

'Shit, that's hot,' he said, blowing on his mug. 'Because later on we'll request logs of mobile traffic from all the networks. And again we'll need permission from the court first. It'll take a few weeks to get hold of the logs, but they'll tell us who called. That is, assuming we get the lists before they delete them, which they usually do after a couple of months. Did I mention that we were buttfucked?'

'You said the logs covered mobile traffic,' said Vincent. 'So when you have that information you can see which locations the phones have been to by checking which phone masts they were connected to?'

'We call them base stations. But you're spot on, Mr Mindreader. We can get very close. But those logs are a nightmare, so we leave them to the analysis department, although Peder will be given a copy to get his teeth into.'

Logs of traffic. If he got access to them, he'd be able to pass them on to Benjamin. He'd love that. But no doubt the analysis department would be even harder to please than Ruben. He might be able to persuade Peder though. Or secretly copy them while Peder was snoozing. But . . . but . . . Well, the logs would have to be dealt with later.

'So we're here to note which calls may be worth tracing,' he noted. 'When you eventually get hold of your logs.'

'Hurrah! He's learning. Yep, we're here to listen. Although obviously now you're here, you can just read their minds. I think Julia is hoping so, anyway.'

Ruben laughed drily. Vincent knew it was a rhetorical question. But he was going to answer it anyway. Ruben needed to understand that they were on the same side.

'I can't read minds,' said Vincent. 'But there are things you can pick up by listening. For example, it's easier to identify a psychopath through their words. Psychopaths are good at pretending to express emotions

256

with their faces and body language, but they let themselves down with their speech. They give equal weighting to neutral and emotionally charged words. They may also mention minor events like what they had for breakfast in the same breath as they reveal a serious crime. They rarely talk about anyone other than themselves, and they like to use the past tense to distance themselves. Beyond psychopaths, we can also listen for changes in . . .'

Ruben stopped him by raising a hand.

'I'm sure it'll be fine,' he said, checking the time. 'The press conference should be up on all the news sites by now. And a short version has been posted on social media with the phone number. Let the waiting begin.'

'How long do we wait for?'

'As long as it takes.'

The first ten calls were a mixture of attention seekers and people who really wanted to help but had nothing to offer. Nothing that he considered worthy of closer analysis. After a long period of listening to twaddle, Vincent eventually gave in and fetched his own mug that he filled from the coffee maker.

Three mugs later, he decided that phone surveillance was by far the least exciting thing he had ever experienced. Ruben hadn't said much – they'd mostly sat in silence waiting for calls. Eventually, Ruben stretched with a groan.

'I'm going to bounce for a while,' he said. 'This is going nowhere.'

'Bounce? Where to?'

Ruben shrugged.

'Anywhere that isn't here. Maybe I'll play a game of padel tennis. At this hour it'll be mostly twenty-five-year-olds at the club, girls with those tight yoga pants . . .'

Ruben stood up and took his coat from his chair.

'You'll manage on your own,' he said. 'I'll be back in an hour or so. Call me if anything comes up.'

Vincent was too astonished to reply. He didn't even recover once Ruben had left him alone in the room. There was no way he was permitted to be left on his own with all that sensitive equipment. He needed to get in touch with Mina so that she would come here. She would also be far better company.

He got out his phone to message her just as the symbol for an ongoing call changed colour from red to green on the computer screen. The recorded message that announced that the person calling had reached the police tip line had come to its conclusion and the call was connected.

'I'm extremely disappointed in your incompetence,' said an irritated male voice. 'This is downright carelessness.'

Yet another dunce who wanted to complain. Half the calls had been about how the police were incapable of doing their job. Vincent began to search for Mina in his list of favourite contacts.

'Robert died on the third of May,' said the voice. 'Surely that's obvious to everyone. May the third.'

His thumb hovered over the phone. What had the man just said? Very few of the other calls had been specific and no one had mentioned an exact date. Vincent leaned over the desk and turned up the volume on the speaker beside the display.

'I'm distressed by the low levels of competence with which you're handling this,' the man continued, now sounding even more irritated.

Despite the fact that he was worked up, he still enunciated every syllable clearly. As if it were important to be accurate. The choice of words also indicated that he looked down on the person he was speaking to, placing himself above them. Possible narcissistic personality disorder. Plenty of people had called in pretending to be the murderer, but Vincent had easily seen through all of them. This one was different. His brain was raising all the red flags without bothering to explain which signals it had picked up on. He was convinced. The person who was talking was the murderer. The person they were searching for was so close he could hear him breathing. But he had no idea whether it was Rask.

'The retard might have taken a little time,' said the man with a sudden change of tone. 'But you *know* when he died. Have you really not understood what the smashed watches mean?'

Vincent had a hundred questions for the man on the phone. What did the countdown mean? Who was it all for? Why illusions, of all things? But he could do nothing but listen.

'You need to do a better job than this,' the man said, and hung up.

Vincent stared at the screen.

With the utmost caution, he moved the cursor across the spreadsheet and marked the call in red. Then he realized that Ruben hadn't left his phone number.

67

'In other words, the date is as important as I thought,' Vincent said thoughtfully.

Mina and Vincent were sitting in the conference room looking at the whiteboard showing everything they had gathered during the investigation.

'Yes,' she said, while dispensing sanitizer onto her hand and massaging it into her skin. 'Someone was very eager for us to get all the times and dates right.'

Her hands were becoming chapped, the alcohol drying them out so much that small cracks were forming. But it was a price she had to pay. She offered the bottle to Vincent; at first he looked like he was going to say no, then he shrugged and held out his hands so that she could dispense a little onto his palms.

'I just don't understand how Robert fits in,' he continued, while rubbing his palms together.

The pungent smell of spirit spread throughout the small conference room. It was a heavenly scent.

'No, nor do I. There's a natural connection between Tuva and Agnes. We've interviewed Robert's family in depth, but we've turned up nothing. Absolutely nothing. Julia has spoken to the staff at the sheltered housing unit and they didn't give us anything either. Of course, she and Christer are going there to talk to them in person to make sure, but you're right: Robert doesn't fit the pattern.'

'Mmm . . .'

Vincent spun on his chair so that his face was directed straight at the board.

'That's what doesn't add up about this case,' he said. 'There are so many things that stand out, that contradict themselves. Even I know

259

that a serial killer sticks to the same category of victim. You don't need to be a cop to know that – Google is all it takes. You could say that Tuva and Agnes had many similarities. Two young girls. But Robert . . . Robert doesn't belong there. Like that song in Sesame Street: "One of These Things". In this case, it's definitely Robert who is not like the others. What's more, he had an incredibly limited network of contacts. No social life beyond his family and the people at the sheltered housing facility. He moved in very small circles. Unlike Tuva, who met vast numbers of people every day as part of her job.'

'While I remember: we've received a tip-off about where Jonas Rask might be. One of his ex-wives heard that he was staying in a caravan somewhere not far from Stockholm, but we haven't managed to locate him yet. We're checking out sites in the area. Anyway, it feels like we might be getting close. We'll have him soon. You can ask him then.'

'Like I've said before, probability indicates he's involved,' said Vincent, turning his gaze from the board to her. 'But I don't know. I can't help feeling that Jan Bergsvik, your criminal psychologist, is talking out of his arse. It just doesn't make sense.'

His ice-blue eyes felt like they were looking straight through her. She cast down her gaze.

'People do strange things that we can't understand,' she said. 'But police work tends to be straightforward. The simple solution is often the right one. Is it really a coincidence that a man who murdered two young girls and raped even more has been seen nearby and in the cafe where Tuva worked?'

'None of the victims were raped,' Vincent objected.

'True, but Rask has been inside for twenty years. Maybe he doesn't even have a libido anymore. The act of murdering them and maiming their bodies might serve as a psychological substitute.'

Vincent looked at her in surprise.

'I know a thing or two as well,' she said, winking.

'Mmm,' he said, but she could tell that he didn't agree with her. 'You sound like Jan.'

She kicked his leg.

'It may have been Jonas Rask who called in about the date,' she said, but could feel that she was digging herself deeper into the mires of improbability with each word she uttered.

'Yes, it's quite possible. What happens next with the phone call?'

A fruit fly hovered over the platter of fruit and Mina had to swallow a few sickly sweet belches of disgust before she could reply to Vincent. She got out the hand sanitizer and poured a big dollop onto her hand. She thought about whether to go for the fly with the gel, but her chances of success were small. Vincent glanced at her quickly. Then he got up, picked up the platter and left the room. He returned empty-handed and sat down as if nothing had happened. Mina felt tears stinging her eyes. She swallowed frantically and cleared her throat.

'When do you have to go?'

Vincent checked his watch.

'My flight to Malmö leaves in two hours. So pretty soon.'

She didn't want him to go yet. They hadn't had time together properly since before the press conference. But how was she supposed to put that into words? No matter how she formulated it, she'd give away more than she wanted.

Keeping her face neutral, she said, 'Then we'd better get a move on.'

68

Kvibille 1982

'Can I come in soon? I'm dying of curiosity,' Mum laughed.

Her voice was as clear as if she had been standing inside the barn, even though she was on the other side of the door.

'Wait a minute. Not long now.'

He adjusted his shirt and frowned. He hoped he had thought this through properly – that it would go well. Mum had been so sad since Jane had left. She'd barely spoken to him at all, except when cutting his toasted sandwiches into triangles for him at breakfast and explaining how important it was to do the same thing each time. The rest of the time she seemed to be engrossed in her weeding. There was even a plan stuck on the fridge. Admittedly, it was a hand-drawn sketch in pencil on a leaf torn from the telephone book, but still . . . It was a drawing.

Malla, Sickan and Lotta had seen it and thought it was the weirdest thing ever. Apparently none of their parents did that. But he understood how important it was to be thorough. And he really hoped he had been. If there was one thing Mum needed, it was to be happy again. If this didn't help, then he didn't know what else he could do.

He cleared his throat and then opened the door with pomp and ceremony. Expectation shone in Mum's eyes as she crossed the threshold and entered his magical workshop. She took a few steps in and then came to a halt when she saw what he had built.

'But, but . . . it's absolutely . . . Ooooh!'

It was the biggest box he had made to date. It was almost up to her waist. And it had wheels so that it could be spun around and viewed from all angles.

He released the brake on one wheel and then rotated the box dramatically. The deep blue paint was still tacky to the touch.

Mum put her hands to her mouth in admiration. He exhaled. He needn't have worried. And what was more, he had one more surprise. When the final side of the box became visible it was unpainted. Instead, he had taped a piece of paper to it, on which it said *Reserved for Les Vargas*.

'I must have been a saint in a former life,' said Mum, wiping her eyes with the heels of her hands. 'Otherwise I don't know what I've done to deserve you.'

'So how does it work?' she asked when she had finished painting. 'Are you going to tell me or what?'

There were stars this time as well.

'I have to if you're going to be my assistant,' he said, opening the box. 'If you haven't changed your mind.'

'No, no, there's nothing I want more. Just think, *me* doing magic!'

The fumes from the paint made him dizzy. Perhaps they shouldn't have closed the door. But this was their secret. No one else could be allowed to see. Not that they actually ever received visitors, but still.

'First you crawl into the box,' he said. 'Really, you should be in handcuffs and inside a sack too, but I don't have a sack. Or any handcuffs.'

'Thank God for that,' Mum laughed.

'Then I lock the box with a padlock on the outside and stand on top of the lid. In the meantime you sneak out of the secret door at the back of the box and hide behind it.'

'I didn't see a secret door.'

Suddenly Mum sounded worried.

'That's the trick,' he said with a smile. 'It's hidden in the pattern.'

He showed her the invisible door at the rear of the box, concealed in the checked pattern he had painted.

'I've hung fabric from this hula hoop,' he continued. 'I'll stand on top of the box, inside the ring, holding it up around me so that the fabric covers all of me on all sides. You climb in through a gap in the fabric at the back, stand next to me and take the ring. I sneak out through the hole in the fabric and crawl in through the secret door into the box. Then you let go of the ring. Then it'll be you standing on the box and me lying inside it. It'll look like we've magically changed places. Or been transformed into each other. I'll be Mum. You'll be seven years old.'

Mum ran her hand across the secret door.

'It's very well built,' she said.

'I had the right drawings. But we have to practise it lots – the real trick is doing it quickly. Jane won't realize a thing.'

A dark shadow passed over Mum's eyes. He bit his lip. He shouldn't have mentioned Jane. Stupid, stupid little brother. Mum was still sad that his sister had gone to her friend's in Dalarna. Even if it had only been two days since she had left. Two days was an eternity. He wished that Mum would start focusing on something else. Like practising the magic trick with him.

'The box isn't very spacious,' she said as if reading his thoughts. 'Are you sure I'll fit?'

'That's part of the illusion. It's bigger than it looks.'

He showed her the drawing while spelling it quietly to himself. J-a-n-e was four letters. She would be gone for fourteen days. Four plus fourteen made eighteen. They needed to rehearse the trick eighteen times. Then Jane would come home and Mum would be happy again.

'You'll be in the box for no more than thirty seconds,' he said, 'before you crawl out and we swap places.'

'Thirty seconds, you say?'

'Tops.'

69

Vincent is sitting on the sofa in his dressing room. The voice from the phone call is still echoing in his head on repeat, just as it has done since the call came in.

The performance this evening was in the concert hall at Malmö Live.

It's always a bit tricky doing the show in concert venues – they often have to close off the seats at the very back since the people sitting in them end up too far from the stage. He wants everyone in the audience to be able to see him properly – and him them. But even with those seats taken out of action there were six hundred people at tonight's performance. Which was great for that time of year. As the weather grew warmer, beer gardens became his biggest competitor.

Not six hundred, he corrects himself. Five hundred and eighty-six. He can feel how his brain immediately wants to run away with that thought and he lets it do it while adjusting the unopened bottles of mineral water on the coffee table. All the labels in the same direction. He is tempted to send a photo to Umberto captioned #tapwater, but he refrains.

Five hundred and eighty-six.

$5 + 8 + 6 = 19. 1 + 9 = 10. 1 + 0 = 1.$

'5 8 6' is also a track on New Order's second album. It's that weird song into which they shoehorned bits of 'Blue Monday', the only listenable track New Order have ever made. And Monday is the first day of the week. The number 1 again.

According to numerology, 1 represents creativity and creation. If he flatters himself, it describes his performance pretty well. The number 1 is, however, considered to be a masculine number. He guesses that's due to its upright, phallic shape – proof that numerology was probably devised by men. A more accurately manly number would be the far floppier number 9.

Which together with 1 is of course 19, the sum of 5 + 8 + 6.

Five hundred and eighty-six.

But 1 also stands for loneliness, the separate individual – currently sitting on their own on a shabby black sofa in Malmö. He misses Mina.

Mina?

Not Maria?

Naturally, he misses his children too. His family. But yes, he misses the peculiar police officer. Very much. He hasn't even asked whether she has solved her Rubik's cube yet. Personally, he is grappling with the puzzle presented to him by the murderer on the telephone.

But you know when he died. Have you really not understood what the smashed watches mean?

Of course, it's obvious that the watches indicate the moment of death. But he can't help thinking that the murderer means something more than that. Three watches. Three victims. Two women. One man. 3321. He laughs. If he isn't mistaken, that's the headline sort code for Nordea. Probably not quite what the murderer has in mind. But he has at least been able to do an analysis of the person who called, based on his tone and choice of words. He has promised Julia that he will brief the whole team as soon as he is back in Stockholm. He knows that he is still part of the group, by their grace. Hopefully, they'll at least listen to him one more time.

He stands up, heads over to the washbasin and runs the tap until it's ice cold. He splashes his face. That's enough distracting thoughts for one night. He struggled to keep his focus during the performance. A woman in the audience called him Dumbledore, which caused a lot of laughter. But it made him think about the interview with Daniel, whose spontaneous association with magic had been Harry Potter. Daniel is an unlikely murderer compared to Rask. But he said something during the interview, something that Vincent missed at the time but which has been at the back of his mind ever since.

He wipes his face with a towel and examines his reflection in the mirror, trying to see beyond the eyes and into his own head. It's in there, somewhere. Something important. He needs to find out what it is. And they probably need to see Daniel Bargabriel again.

Daniel is standing outside the door to Evelyn's block of flats, staring up at the facade. It's late and the street is dark, but the light is on in her kitchen window on the second floor. He thinks it looks like a post-card, with that yellow *fin de siècle* facade and the solitary glowing window. He's failed completely. He knows that. But it's not so strange that he kept away from the police. He knows the score. If you're not as white as they are, then the risk of being picked up is much greater. Just ask Samir. It doesn't matter whether you've done something or not.

The angle from where he is standing down by the door is too narrow for him to be able to see in through the window, but he knows that she is sitting up there on the other side of the glass, waiting for him. He's been away from her for far too long. He thought he would be able to get the police to cross him off their list of suspects. But that Vincent, he noticed absolutely everything. If anything, Daniel is under more suspicion than ever. All because he didn't want to get in trouble. He needs Evelyn's help before this goes off the rails completely. He's guilty of nothing worse than being scared. No one can blame him for that. Just ask Samir . . .

But he doesn't just want Evelyn's help. He wants *her*. He's longing for her. They usually start their evenings in her kitchen, talking about all sorts of things, most often with a glass of wine or a beer. Evelyn usually smokes out of the open window. She barely smokes at all otherwise, but after two glasses of wine she likes to hang out of the kitchen window with a ciggie. In that stripy top with the neckline that is just the right size to slide down over a bare shoulder.

She usually says that it makes it feel like she's in Paris or Rome instead of shitty Stockholm. Especially in the spring. Then she wants to be anywhere but this city.

He's never really understood it – he thinks Stockholm is beautiful in the spring. On the other hand, he's never been to either Paris or Rome. After that talk, she usually gets a hazy look in her eyes and leads him into the bedroom. Sometimes they get started in the kitchen. She tastes of smoke and wine and spring and desire. It's a predictable routine but he likes it. It feels right. Romantic.

The early summer evening is warm. It might as well be Paris. And why not? He's burned his bridges at the cafe simply by disappearing, so why not get out of here? If he empties his accounts, he should have enough for at least a weekend for the two of them. He should have done it ages ago. She'll be so happy.

But there are things he has to explain first. Why he disappeared. Why he hasn't been answering her messages. That Tuva is missing. He hopes she can forgive him for not getting in touch, hopes she will understand that he got scared when the police came. He hopes she hasn't stopped loving him.

There are a lot of things he hopes for.

She is going to get that concerned frown on her forehead. Perhaps she'll even purse her lips. But he'll kiss her at the corner of her mouth – oh, how he longs to hold her face in his hands again! He takes a deep breath, goes to the door and begins to tap in the code when he hears a voice behind him.

'Daniel?'

Behind him is an unfamiliar man in his thirties. Dark hair, blue suit.

'Daniel, it is you, isn't it?' says the man. 'You lived with Agnes, right?'

He doesn't reply. Agnes is the last thing he wants to be reminded of right now.

'Sebastian,' says the man with a smile, offering his hand. 'I'm a friend of Agnes's. Or was. Before. Well, you know. I think we met at a party once.'

'Maybe,' he replies hesitantly.

He's convinced they've never met before.

'Do you live here now?' the man says, looking up at the building.

'No, my girlfriend lives here.'

Sebastian, as he is supposedly called, laughs. Loudly.

'That was quick work! Agnes has only been dead for, what, four or five months? Which window is hers then? Your new girl?'

'She's not new. And Agnes and me were never together. I just sublet from her.'

'Yeah, right,' says Sebastian, winking.

Daniel frowns. He doesn't like this. He doesn't need to defend himself to this man. But he's tired of being accused of stuff. Why can't this guy just be on his way? Evelyn is up there in the kitchen. She's probably already poured a glass of wine for him. Lit a ciggie. Started thinking about Paris. Maybe she's put on the stripy top that she looks so damn hot in. For his benefit. And he's still down here on the street.

'Sorry, but I'm late,' he says, beginning to tap the code into the pad again.

Sebastian puts his arm around his shoulders and drags him away from the door pad.

'Probably for the best, what happened to Agnes,' Sebastian says calmly.

Daniel's whole body goes stiff.

Vincent leans back on the sofa in the dressing room and closes his eyes. He thinks back to the interview and what Daniel said. Daniel definitely didn't know anything about magic – that much was certain. He thought

268

a double lift – when you pull two cards from a deck while making it look like one – was some form of group sex. Vincent had struggled to contain his laughter.

Daniel also demonstrated clear anxiety about them not believing him when he told them about his relationships with Agnes and Tuva. And sure, the idea that Daniel might know both of them by pure coincidence is on the face of it so unlikely that it is easy to believe that something more lies behind it. But in purely statistical terms, it is improbable that it could never occur in any investigation. All possible variants have to occur at some point. That's what people don't understand when they argue that it 'has to mean something' when they bump into an old acquaintance on the street at the same time as they happen to be thinking about that person for the first time in years.

Vincent sighs. If you correlate how many people one person meets during their lifetime with how many thoughts that person has per day, it is essentially impossible for the two variables *not* to cross paths at some point. Not in all people, but in enough of them. It isn't 'incredible'; it is on the contrary very probable.

And there were no unspoken signals in Daniel's body language or facial musculature that indicated he wasn't telling the truth about Tuva and Agnes.

Vincent opens his eyes. He isn't going to remember what he needs to like this. He has to delve into the memories that his brain didn't consciously register. Memories he doesn't know he has. There's only one way to reach them. He has to hypnotize himself.

He gets up to lock the door so that he doesn't frighten the cleaners if they come across him – for Umberto's sake. Then he lies down on the floor and stares at the ceiling. He usually uses self-hypnosis to fall asleep when Maria is lying in bed reading with her unnecessarily strong reading lamp, but this time he can't let himself fall asleep. Instead, he needs to jump up and down on the trampoline of his subconscious. Vincent looks around and registers his impressions of the dressing room.

'Chair, red, metal legs,' he mutters. 'Wardrobe, flowery, awful. Bench, blue, MDF. There's a hum in the vents. The rug under me is soft, the floor is hard, the temperature is warm.'

Then he closes his eyes.

The man called Sebastian laughs again. The laugh is friendly, but the arm around Daniel says something different.

'Agnes wasn't exactly a defender of the white nuclear family,' Sebastian says. 'So in a way you did us a favour. Just as well, us being rid of dirt like her. What do you think it was? Was it the big Syrian cock she fell for?'

Sebastian prods him teasingly between the legs on the outside of his trousers. Daniel tries to wriggle free from the grasp around his shoulders, but Sebastian has him in an iron grip. His throat is dry as the desert; he can't answer even if he wants to. This isn't happening. This *can't* be happening.

'The same cock that you're now defiling a new Swedish woman with?' Sebastian continues. 'I don't think so, Daniel. Or however it is you pronounce it in your fucking language.'

Sebastian drags him away from the door. Away from Evelyn. Away from safety, from the light. He almost loses his balance but quickly regains it. If he falls then it's over. Evelyn's kitchen window is glowing invitingly a few metres above him. He tries to force her to open it with his mind. *Look out. See me.*

Four men in black bomber jackets suddenly emerge from the shadows on the other side of the street. The letters SF are shining on their right arms like white flashes of lightning. This is nothing to do with friendly family SF cinema chain. The men's SF has a different typeface and stands for Sweden's Future.

If he wasn't afraid before, he is now. He recognizes them. Sweden's Future pretend to be a political party, but in reality they're a bunch of thugs with a logo. Josef said what they did to his cousin. A blow to the back of the head was enough for his cousin to need a colostomy bag for life. He was fifteen. And that had only been *one* of these racist idiots. Now there were five.

Apart from the men, the street is deserted. But he can still cry for help. Evelyn might hear him through the closed window.

'Evelyn!' he shouts. 'Call the police!'

His words are cut off when Sebastian head butts him on the nose. He screams as his face explodes with pure pain. His field of vision dissolves into patterns in confusing colours and his eyes fill with tears. He can't see anything, can't hear anything. Just a whining in his ears. And the pain. As if someone has struck him with a hammer. He can't breathe. Blood from his smashed nose fills his mouth and runs down his throat.

He staggers. He weighs nothing. *Do not fall. No matter what you do.* Daniel blinks away the tears and sees that the men have reached him. Two of them are clutching lengths of iron pipe.

'We heard the police released you,' Sebastian says, wiping Daniel's blood off his face with a handkerchief. 'But it's OK. We often clean up after them.'

Vincent is swimming around deep inside his own memories. He is back in the interview room. But where the brain usually sorts and prioritizes different impressions, everything that is happening here is equally important. He is overcome by colours, words and movements. It's a tsunami of impressions and it's threatening to drown him. He needs to filter. Find what stands out.

Daniel's words.

He needs to focus on Daniel's words. Especially the parts he didn't pay heed to before.

'It was Agnes and Tuva who knew each other.'

No. Not that.

'Agnes's dad is a racist.'

No. Still stuff he can remember. He needs to find the cracks, the empty patches in his memory.

'People come in all the time who are high or weird . . . And sure, we've got a few regulars among them.'

Somewhere around there. Daniel said something then.

'But most of the people who come in regularly use the cafe as their office or living room . . . the media types always have their laptops . . .'

He's close now.

'One regular is always staring at drawings in a folder.'

There it was. Drawings aren't usually kept in folders. They're too big for that. But Vincent saw drawings in a folder very recently. At Sains Bergander's.

He opens his eyes, not bothering to bring himself gently out of his hypnosis, and he feels his brain struggling to accelerate to the speed at which he is now demanding it to function.

Daniel saw a regular looking at drawings.

Vincent is willing to bet anything those drawings were blueprints for illusions. It's obvious now that he comes to think of it. Ruben was right about one thing: the murderer visited the cafe regularly to watch Tuva and learn her routines before he struck.

Daniel knows what the murderer looks like. Perhaps even what he's called. Vincent grabs his mobile from his coat, fumbling with it for a second before finding the shortcut to his favourites and pressing on Mina's number. He curses the fact that his day job has forced him so

271

far away from the centre of events. They need to get hold of Daniel as soon as possible.

One of the men swings his length of iron towards Daniel and he automatically raises his arms to his head to protect himself. Disaster. The blow strikes his raised forearms, smashing the bones in both. He screams loudly and buckles forward.

Evelyn. She must have called the police now. Can she see what is happening? Is she standing inside the window watching, too afraid to open it?

'That's enough,' he whimpers. 'That's enough. I get it.'

The next blow hits him in the side and breaks at least one rib. Probably more. He can no longer shout and it hurts to breathe. The bone fragments have punctured his lung.

He tries to back away from the men, but he's in no state to run anywhere. They look almost amused. Then the blows land faster, but it's as if the nerve endings have been overloaded with pain signals. His brain can't receive them and process them. All there is is the feeling that he is on fire.

It has to end soon.

He and Evelyn are going to Paris.

A pause in the blows. Perhaps they're satisfied now. Got their message through.

'One, two, three!'

Two of the men count and then both the pipes strike his kneecaps. He falls forward while trying to bellow, but all that comes out is a hissing. He lands on his broken arms and strikes his brow on the asphalt. Million-volt shocks shoot into his brain and white flashes cover his field of vision.

Evelyn puts her hand around his neck, the hand with the ciggie, and kisses him while blowing smoke into his mouth.

He continues to burn while the men work on him in silence. He hears the dull thuds as their boots strike his body. It's too much, the pain is being stockpiled, waiting its turn.

Evelyn's glowing window above him. So close. He tries to shout but all that comes out of his mouth is a new hissing sound. If only she would look out. Have that ciggie. But he knows that she is waiting for him before she does that.

Her top sliding down over a bare shoulder, a shoulder that promises more to come.

I'm here. See me. Call the police.

Paris, Evelyn, Paris.

An extra hard boot in his stomach and he reflexively retreats into the foetal position. The kick forces the broken ribs deeper into his lungs. Acidic bile is squeezed up through his throat and out of his mouth.

'Are you hurling on my shoe, you shit?' the man with the boot says, kicking his kneecap.

The contact makes the bone fragments in the shattered knee move and he almost loses consciousness. A dancing darkness takes over his vision. Lack of oxygen, he thinks to himself in a disconnected manner.

Why aren't the police coming?

Suddenly the blows stop. A change in the atmosphere. He knows what it means, what is coming. The thing that can't be allowed to happen.

'Your turn, Sebastian,' says one of the men. 'Let's finish this now.'

He closes his eyes.

Focuses on Evelyn.

She has a beer bottle nonchalantly dangling between the index and middle finger of one hand.

Through the pain, he concentrates on the way she tilts her head when she smiles at him.

How she looks when they wake up together, naked.

How she smells when she kisses him.

Smoke and wine.

Like Paris.

These racist bastards can never take her from him.

He holds the picture of Evelyn in his head as Sebastian leaps into the air and lands flatfooted on his head.

70

'Welcome!'

A man somewhere in his thirties giving off hipster vibes opened the glass door for them. Christer looked around. This looked very pleasant. Light, clean, cosy. Nothing like the acute psychiatric wards he visited from time to time in the line of duty. They were often bare, scruffy, filled with anxiety and distant cries echoing between the walls. But then again, this place was – as Julia had pointed out to him in the car – a supported living facility. It wasn't for psychiatric patients.

Which he knew full well. But he thought it was funny to wind her up occasionally and see her wrinkle her freckled nose. She was a good boss. While she probably didn't think so, he liked her, although he hid it well. She just needed to get the poker out of her arse on occasion.

The hipster man showed them into a small office. The desk was neat and tidy, the bookcase filled with books in straight rows. Textbooks. A Pride flag and a photo of the hipster man with his arms around another hipster man were positioned on the windowsill behind the desk, next to a dazzling pot plant. Of course. Christer's gaydar was well attuned and he had guessed as soon as he'd seen Hampus Norlén open the door.

Personally, he didn't get the thing with two penises in one bed – it was contrary to all forms of logical biology. What was likeliest? Two screws, or a screw and a nut? It went without saying. But he assumed that everybody was happy in their own way. So long as they didn't wave dildos in the faces of families with kids watching the Pride parade and kept themselves to themselves. Like Lasse had done.

Lasse.

Good God, how long had it been since then? It had to be almost forty years ago. Lasse had been his very best friend during his teenage years. They had even lived together for a while in their twenties. They had shared everything for several years. So no one had been more surprised than Christer when it had transpired that Lasse was batting for the other team. He remembered that they had hugged frequently. It had been that kind of relationship; Lasse was a sweet guy. But it hadn't meant anything. Then it had got harder when he knew. They had eventually fallen out of touch.

'We're sorry for your loss,' said Julia, sitting down on one of the two chairs that Hampus had positioned in front of the desk.

Christer sat down on the other. Hampus nodded and sat down on his own chair.

'We kept hoping,' he said, the words getting stuck in his throat. 'I suppose hope is the last thing to abandon you. Even though we feared the worst. But if what I've heard is true, then the worst we could have imagined doesn't even come close . . .'

Hampus's voice cracked and he quickly turned away and wiped his eyes.

'I'm afraid we can't make any comment on the investigation,' Julia said gently.

Silence. A big fly buzzed in a corner, trying desperately to get through the glass, not understanding why there was something between it and freedom.

'How long did Robert live here?'

Christer broke the silence and leaned forward. The chair was staggeringly uncomfortable and his backside and back were already aching.

'We've provided respite accommodation since he was fifteen.'

'We've met his parents,' said Julia. 'They spoke very highly of you.'

Hampus nodded. 'Yes, we have a good partnership with them. And Bobby is a lovely boy. Was. Calm, never violent. We've got other residents who have big issues with aggression, which is why they can't live at home. It wasn't like that with Bobby. But he often escaped and he couldn't be left on his own at home either. So combining a job with keeping a constant eye on him didn't work in the long-term. That was where we stepped in. We saw it as sharing responsibility for Bobby with his parents. Shared custody, you might say.'

Hampus smiled through his beard. Christer scratched his chin. He always ensured he was clean-shaven. Always had done. His mother had taught him that early on – no one trusted a man with a beard. And surely it had to be hot in summer, and itchy as hell. Not to mention all the food that must get stuck in a bushy thing like that. Christer shifted his gaze in irritation from Hampus's beard to the fly in the corner of the window. It was making a bloody racket.

'Could you tell us a bit about Robert? Bobby?' said Julia, seemingly altogether unaffected by the fly's loud buzzing.

'Yes, Bobby . . . What a case.'

Hampus lit up and there was a twinkle in his eye.

'Funniest guy in the world,' he said. 'We used to watch old episodes of *Jackass* together. He thought it was funny. And he loved food. We had to rein him in a bit on his intake, otherwise he'd quite easily eat two hundred kilos of scran in one sitting. I've never seen someone who enjoyed putting food in his mouth so much.'

'On that subject,' said Christer, 'his parents mentioned something about his having a tendency to put things other than food in his mouth.'

His eyes slid involuntarily to the photo of Hampus and his guy. Just as long as Hampus didn't misunderstand what he meant with that thing about putting things in mouths . . . He didn't want to come over as prejudiced.

'Yes, that was pretty weird. We were always worried Bobby might get something caught in his throat. He put everything in his mouth. Plants. Soil. Leca pebbles. Gravel. You name it.'

Talk of all the things that could be put in a mouth wasn't helping Christer in the slightest. An image appeared in his mind's eye before he could stop it: Hampus with the other man's penis in his mouth. He shook himself to get rid of the thoughts.

'And the escapes?' said Julia.

She looked cool and unaffected even though the room was warm and stifling. Christer could feel the sweat running down his spine, making his shirt stick to the small of his back. The fly turned up the volume another notch in its attempt to escape through the window.

'Yes, that was the big problem with Bobby,' said Hampus. 'He loved heading off on his own. And he was so trusting, no matter how many times we tried to warn him about "stranger danger" he'd still happily climb into a car or wander off with someone he didn't know. We had a system to ensure one of us was always keeping an eye on him, but he was a crafty bugger, so somehow he still used to get away. And always with his slingshot. No matter where Bobby was, that slingshot was with him. You have no idea how good he got at using that thing. He used to amuse the other residents with shows. He could shoot the cap off a glass bottle without even knocking it over. Totally insane.'

276

Hampus shook his head. Then he turned around and shot out his hand in a rapid, sweeping movement that crushed the fly.

'Sorry, I couldn't take it any longer,' he said.

Christer nodded gratefully.

'How did he get away this time?' he asked. 'And how long did it take for you to discover he was missing?'

'We realized straight away. It was around ten o'clock in the morning, and it was me who was meant to be keeping an eye on him, but one of the other residents slipped on the stairs so I ran there to check on her. Everything was OK and I was back five minutes later. But by then Bobby was already gone. I wasn't all that worried at first. As I said, he's always disappearing but we always find him. But . . . But not this time. When night began to fall and we still hadn't found him, I called his parents. And we agreed together to report it to the police straight away. Thank goodness you took it seriously immediately.'

'Was there anything you noticed that afternoon that was out of the ordinary? Someone you saw nearby, someone who didn't belong here? Anything that crossed your mind?'

Hampus considered the question carefully. Then he shook his head slowly and held out his hands.

'No . . . No, everything was just as usual. There was nothing that felt off. I suppose there were quite a few people and cars going by outside, but then there always are. There was nothing and no one that I reacted to.'

'Would Bobby go with a stranger?' said Julia, who had finally developed a fine line of sweat on her upper lip.

Christer was satisfied with this sign that she was, after all, human and not a robot with built-in air conditioning.

'Yes, happily. Bobby loved everyone. And he thought everyone meant him well. And I've never met anyone who didn't love Bobby. It was impossible not to love Bobby.'

He choked on his words again. Hampus looked down at his lap and clenched his hands on top of the desk. Julia stood up.

'I don't think there's anything else we need right now. But we'd like to come back to you if we have any more questions.'

'Any time,' said Hampus, standing up to shake their hands.

Christer hesitated. He pictured what Hampus's hands usually grasped. Behind closed doors. But then he took the hand. After all, it was hardly infectious. Hampus's handshake was surprisingly strong, despite his hand being soft and smooth to the touch. Christer lingered for an extra moment to show how little it worried him.

71

The room was only half full. The weather was too fine for people to want to be inside in a meeting room in the middle of the day, confessing their sins. Or burdens. Whatever you might want to call it. She had almost stayed away herself. But it was often then, just when she had begun to feel like she didn't need to go, that she found herself at the end of her tether, and she knew she needed it most. So she had come here anyway.

Mina looked around. Dolphin girl was in her usual place. The plastic had come off and a wolf was now clearly inked onto her arm with the words *Living on the edge* above it. *Carpe diem* had apparently also been deemed meaningful enough and was scrawled across her full forearm. Of course it was. Well, that was original. Perhaps Mina ought to rename her dolphin and wolf girl. Or platitude girl.

Kenneth and his wheelchair-bound wife were there – yes. And their dog. Basse? Bosse? Yes, Bosse. The dog was observing her with interest from his position lying beside the wheelchair, but he sat up eagerly when Mina's gaze met his. She quickly looked away. She didn't want the dog's attention and hoped the leash was attached to something, to stop him coming up to her. She didn't want to think about what was crawling around in that fur.

Despite the fact that summer had barely begun, it was oppressively warm. The early heatwave seemed to have no plans to loosen its grip, and beads of sweat made their way down into her waistband.

Mina resisted the impulse to stand up, walk out, drive home and leap straight into the shower. Sweat made her skin crawl with uneasiness – it was like the dirt on the inside was forcing its way up and out of her skin. In summer, she showered twice as often as she did in winter. She would have preferred to shower at least once an hour when it was hot, but that would make it difficult to get anything else done.

Kenneth waved a little absent-mindedly to her. His wife nodded in greeting. Mina realized she had no idea what the wife was called. Perhaps she should have asked. Been polite. But she wanted to avoid getting to know too many of the people who gathered here. With the dog, Bosse, that number was already one too many.

The woman in the wheelchair looked tired. Pale. And hot – sweat was running unimpeded from her hairline into her eyes. She blinked her eyes and raised her hand occasionally to wipe away the salty drops.

The voices that spoke up were drowsy. One after another they shared. Turning themselves inside out. Progress. Defeat. Tragedy. Triumph. Some were at the beginning of their journey, others had come far. Some had the bright eyes of the recent convert. They still hadn't encountered their first obstacle. They didn't yet know that the path ahead wasn't as straight as it looked at the beginning.

She envied them. Personally, she identified more with the tired determination of the veterans. It was more realistic – based on the experience of those who had already failed. And picked themselves up again. And failed. And picked themselves up again. It was the look of someone who saw a narrow and winding path ahead of them, but who had accepted that this was the path they had to follow.

Her head nodded involuntarily and she opened her eyes, which she hadn't realized were closed. Without noticing it, the heat had made her nod off. She looked around to see whether anyone had noticed that she was sitting there half asleep.

She started. Something wasn't right about Kenneth's wife. Her skin was pale and spongy and she was breathing in short, heavy gasps. Kenneth had also noticed that something was wrong and he spoke to her in a low voice, but she merely shook her head.

Mina hesitated. Then she covered the short space between them and crouched down in front of the woman. Bosse stood up happily and began to tug at the leash to get to her. Mina instinctively edged away.

'How are you feeling?' she asked, with a quick glance up at Kenneth.

'She doesn't want me to call an ambulance,' he said, his voice filled with panic.

His wife laboriously gasped for breath, seemingly unable to answer herself. But she once again shook her head. Mina pulled out her phone.

'That doesn't matter. She needs to get to a hospital. Immediately. I'll call.'

Kenneth looked relieved, but his wife shook her head firmly. Mina ignored her. Bosse panted in the heat, his tongue hanging out, but didn't seem to understand that something was the matter with his mistress, so he directed all his enthusiastic energy at Mina. She spoke briefly on the phone. She identified herself as a police officer, gave the address of the venue and described the situation. She also mentioned that the woman in need of assistance was in a wheelchair.

The others in the group had now noticed that something was happening. Dolphin girl wrung her hands and stared at Mina anxiously.

Mina ended the call. 'They're on the way,' she said.

'Thanks,' said Kenneth. 'I mean, she's not usually like this, she's always . . .'

His voice became unclear, but he continued to mumble to himself. He was presumably in a state of shock. Mina was about to place a comforting hand on his shoulder but refrained. He looked as sweaty as she felt. Kenneth's wife looked panic-stricken and her breathing was getting more and more laboured. Even Bosse seemed to have understood that not everything was as it should be. He laid his head in his owner's lap and whimpered. She patted his head clumsily while she continued to struggle with her breathing.

Mina spoke calmly while listening for the sound of sirens. It didn't take many minutes before she heard them approaching and she went out to meet the paramedics. Then everything happened very fast. The ambulance crew rushed in with a stretcher and equipment and everyone in the room stood up. They all stood stock-still, at a loss as they watched what was happening. The paramedics got Kenneth's wife onto the stretcher. He continued to hold her hand throughout. Mina went out with them and saw them lift the stretcher swiftly and efficiently into the ambulance. Kenneth jumped in too, without letting go of his wife's hand. Right before the doors shut, he shouted to Mina.

'Bosse! Please take care of Bosse for us.'

Mina stared at the ambulance as it drove away at top speed with sirens blaring. Behind her, inside, she could hear Bosse barking exuberantly.

72

A primal roar from the study startled Rebecka so much that she dropped her glass of water. Vincent tried to catch it but the glass hit the floor and smashed against the slabs. The water made a large puddle, mixed with shards of glass. He had just got home from Malmö and here things were as usual.

'Vincent!' Maria screeched, storming out of the study, her face flushed red. 'You were going to get rid of this nuisance.'

Aston, who was sitting building Legos on the living room floor began to cry when he heard how angry his mother was.

'Mum isn't angry,' Maria said, trying to calm down. 'Not at you, anyway, darling. I'm just going to throttle your father for giving your mother a heart attack because she thinks she's about to be attacked.'

Vincent was on his way out. He had called a team meeting for the first time and didn't want to be delayed by getting stuck in traffic. Hopefully they had already got hold of Daniel. Mina's phone had been switched off the night before. She had probably gone to bed early, but he had messaged that it was important for them to speak to Daniel again and that he would like to be there for the conversation – today, or as soon as they could bring Daniel in. Vincent had also messaged Sains Bergander and asked him to photograph a few blueprints for illusions and send them to him so that he could show them to Daniel. They needed to know what kind of drawings the cafe patron had been sitting there with. Daniel would be able to see whether he recognized them. He would also be able to confirm whether or not it was Jonas Rask if they were able to sort out a photo of him. The idea was exalting: 'Vincent Walder, private detective'.

But he knew exactly what had happened to Maria in the study. The production company had run off a full-size cardboard cut-out as an advert for his latest TV series. A cardboard cut-out of him. When he had brought it home, Maria had immediately christened it The Nuisance. Personally, he thought it was rather good looking. He had promised her he would throw it out, although he hadn't had the heart to do it. How many people could brag that they had a life-size copy of themselves? To be quite honest, he thought it was pretty cool. Anyway, how could he destroy it? After all, it was him. Psychologically, there was something deeply troubling about the mere thought of throwing himself away. Not long ago he had read a fascinating dissertation about me-structured psychotherapy. A recurrent theme throughout the thesis had been Ovid's story about Narcissus. Self-love and the fascination with the self was deeply rooted in human psychology. Freud himself had had a word for this fascination with self-recognition – *Verliebtheit*.

'Careful or you'll tread on that glass,' he said to Maria as she approached him at an alarming pace.

'I mean, how big is your ego?' she said. 'The fact that you even have a copy of yourself in the study! What exactly do you do with it? Do you masturbate together when the rest of us aren't at home?'

'Maria!' Rebecka exclaimed in horror. 'Come on, Aston, let's build these in your room.'

'I'm scared when Mum's angry,' Aston said unhappily.

A pained look crossed Maria's face. Vincent knew that he would get the blame for Aston too. Rebecka carefully walked past the shards of glass and the puddle to the living room. She pointedly took her little brother by the hand, scooped up as many Legos as she could and shut the door behind them. Without even a look at her father and stepmother-aunt.

'Sorry,' said Vincent. 'But I can't understand why you still get scared every single time you walk in the room. You know that it's there.'

Maria pursed her mouth.

'And I can't understand your fascination with it.'

'*Verliebtheit*,' said Vincent.

Maria stared at him.

'Throw. It. Out,' she said, fixing her eyes on his.

'Promise,' he said, getting out cloths and a dustpan and brush.

He was clearly going to be a few minutes late.

73

Mina stared tensely at the dog. Bosse didn't appear to have been washed for a long time. And it was guaranteed that he hadn't been shampooed with a bacteria-killing solution. On the other hand, he looked happy. Very happy. His tail was drumming a rhythmic solo against the asphalt, which made large volumes of dirt particles whirl up and catch in his fur.

Vincent had asked everyone in the team to a meeting after lunch. He wanted them to talk to Daniel again, since it was clear he might be in possession of important information. She'd had a missed call and a text message from Vincent earlier that morning but hadn't had time to respond. So she needed to get back to work quickly.

She looked at the dog again.

It simply wouldn't work.

She had to solve this another way. But how? She had already begged, pleaded and even threatened the others at the venue to get them to take him. But no one had wanted to do their good deed for the day. She couldn't simply abandon him. No matter how dirty and bacteria-infested he was, Bosse was a living creature.

It was at least fortunate that police headquarters was within walking distance of AA. She imagined with horror what would have happened if she had had to take the car. Would she have cellophaned the car? Tied him to the roof? Cellophaned the dog? If he had leapt into her car it would have been ruined forever.

She had to call Vincent to let him know she was going to be a little late. She got out her phone but before she could place the call a message appeared on the display. It was from Milda, the medical examiner. Intrigued, Mina clicked on the message while Bosse continued the drum solo with his tail. The tox screen results were back. They had pulled it

283

off at record speed, but she guessed that Milda had called in every favour she had at NFC to compensate for her mistake during Agnes's autopsy. Mina read the message and then put the phone back in her pocket. She *had* to get going.

She met Bosse's gaze. There was an unopened bottle of sanitizer in her pocket. If he didn't behave she was going to pour it over him.

74

Vincent was on his way through the main entrance of police headquarters when he saw a large golden retriever lolloping towards him at top speed. The thing that made him stop mid-step was what he saw next. Being dragged along on a lead behind the dog was Mina.

'Do something,' she screeched at him.

He crouched down in the dog's way. When it reached him he proffered his hand so that the dog could sniff it. If he got licked on the face then Mina would probably insist on Plexiglas between them in future. The dog yelped with happiness as it finally got the chance to sniff something. After a thorough examination of the hand, it licked his fingers – one at a time – and seemed satisfied with that.

'Do you talk to dogs too?' said Mina, panting after her double-quick entrance.

He got up and accepted the hand sanitizer that Mina had wrenched out of her pocket.

'Only with a pronounced accent. But he didn't look that difficult to understand.'

He cleaned his hands carefully, mostly for her sake. The dog looked happily up at him.

'So, a dog . . .? Is there something you haven't told me?'

'He's called Bosse and I'm looking after him and now we're not going to talk about it anymore. What's all this about Daniel?'

Mina gave him a look that clearly indicated that she intended to murder him if he so much as hinted that the dog beside them existed. He took the lead from her hand without looking at Bosse, who emitted a delighted bark. She began to breathe more easily.

'Daniel said something during the interview,' he said. 'A patron at the cafe where he worked would sit there studying drawings. I didn't realize at the time, but I think he may have seen the murderer. Possibly not just once, but several times. The next murder could be tomorrow. Or in the middle of summer. Or in the autumn. Or in fifteen minutes, for that matter. I don't know, since I haven't cracked the code yet. If a murder takes place then it'll be my fault and I don't know if I can live with that. But if we find Daniel, then with a little luck we'll find the murderer. Before he has time to strike again.'

Bosse let out a yelp as if barking his assent.

75

'No, Bosse! Not the wastepaper basket! No, Bosse, you can't have a bun! Stop it! Sit! Actually, I mean walk! We're going this way! For the love of God, you bloody mongrel! I said this way!'

Mina was attempting to lead Bosse towards the meeting room with mixed results. Vincent had given up and handed the lead back to her before they had even made it into the building. She suspected he found it more amusing to watch.

The meeting room door opened and Christer stuck out his head with a puzzled expression. His eyes widened when he caught sight of Bosse.

At the same moment, the dog caught sight of the policeman and began to wag his tail wildly. Christer crouched in front of him just like Vincent had done. What exactly was it about men and dogs? Personally, she was most definitely a cat person. Not that an animal would ever cross the threshold of her home, but if she was forced to choose . . . At least cats had some integrity, unlike dogs. By way of illustration, the golden whirlwind leapt at Christer as if he'd been reuinited with his best friend ever.

'Why, hello there, boy!' Christer said fondly. 'Aren't you a beautiful boy! Yes, you do like being scratched behind the ears. Yes, just like that . . .'

The dog eagerly licked Christer's face and her colleague genuinely didn't seem to mind. Mina watched with horror, but Vincent was grinning broadly. Eventually, Christer laboriously stood up, his knees creaking loudly.

'Don't you hate animals?' she said, baffled.

'What? No – who said that?' said Christer, smiling. 'Is this a new colleague then? The new Vincent? Their hair colour matches at any rate!'

Mina glowered at him and looked around, still clutching the lead. There was a table in the corridor. Perhaps it was heavy enough to keep Bosse in one place. She raised one table leg and shoved the loop of the lead around it so that the dog couldn't go anywhere.

'Don't ask,' she said. 'I've got to look after it for a while.'

Vincent held open the door to the meeting room and she went in.

'Christer! Are you coming?' she said.

'Yes, yes, yes. Enough nagging already,' said Christer, who had sat down to pet the dog some more.

He ruffled the golden fur one last time and then followed them into the room.

'Can't believe anyone would have said I don't like dogs,' he muttered. 'You can see with your own eyes how beautiful he is!'

The dog's gaze was both crestfallen and melancholy as Mina closed the glass door, leaving him on the outside. He turned his head uncomprehendingly back and forth, and his sad whimpering was audible through the door. She ignored him. Peder and Ruben were waiting in the meeting room. Julia was apparently not yet on the scene. Peder and Ruben had definitely heard the ruckus outside and she glowered angrily at them – especially Peder, who was now smiling broadly and waving at the dog.

'It's a dog,' she said with a sigh. 'He's called Bosse. I'm hopefully going to be rid of him soon. Right. Shall we get started?'

'We're waiting for Julia,' said Ruben.

She sat down with her back pointedly turned to Bosse, got out a pack of antiseptic wet wipes and carefully wiped her hands. She shuddered as she thought about the fact that Bosse was most likely pressing his nose against the glass behind her, leaving wet impressions on it. They waited a minute or so in silence while both Christer and Peder continued waving through the glass to Bosse.

'Is Anette feeling better, by the way? Given that you're here,' said Ruben, winking at Peder.

'Er, ye-es?' said Peder, looking at him blankly.

'I think Ruben suspected you were actually off on adventures and that Anette was just a pretext,' said Christer.

'I never said that!' Ruben exclaimed.

'No, but for those of us who know you, your thoughts are so loud we can practically hear them,' Christer said with a sigh.

Peder stuck his hand into the bag by his chair and pulled out an energy drink. It emitted a perky hiss when he opened it.

'This is as adventurous as I get these days,' he said, raising the can towards Ruben in a toast.

Julia came in through the door.

'There's a dog out here,' she started by saying, before falling silent when she saw Mina's expression. 'OK, shall we get started? Christer and I visited Robert's accommodation this morning but didn't turn anything up. Since it was Vincent who called this meeting, I'm going to hand over to him.'

Vincent cleared his throat.

'As you know, we received a call after the press conference, in which the murder date was stated to be the third of May. I think the call was genuine. I've previously discussed the fact that we're dealing with someone whose personality has two sides – a kind of Doctor Jekyll and Mister Hyde, if you like. And it was Hyde who called. He was well and truly indignant – that kind of timbre in the voice is hard to fake unless you're a method actor. What's more, the hubris of calling in matches the arrogance the murderer has previously displayed. I'm therefore convinced that it was the murderer himself who called.'

Bosse began to headbutt the glass, whimpering loudly. Mina ignored him and nodded to Vincent that he should continue.

'Was it Rask?' Peder asked.

'The recordings we have of Jonas Rask are too old for us to say for sure,' said Julia. 'Voices change over time.'

'The vocabulary would suggest not,' said Vincent. 'I've listened to old interviews with Rask and he doesn't talk like that. However, the choice of words in that call was carefully thought through. He may have had a script. And a script can be read out by anyone – even Rask. But the emphasis felt wrong.'

Bosse butted his head against the glass door so hard that it rattled, and the whimpering transitioned into a sound that was reminiscent of a wolf howling at the full moon.

'For the love of God!' Mina burst out in irritation, turning towards the glass door.

'Calm down, woman, he only wants to come in here with us,' said Christer, getting to his feet.

'Don't let him in.'

Christer pretended not to have heard her and opened the door. Bosse tore the lead free from the table leg and careered into the room like a cannonball. He immediately ran around the table greeting everyone, sniffing and licking. Eventually, he settled down between Peder and

Christer. Mina frantically wiped her hands with yet another wet wipe. She was the only one not to have touched the dog.

'Like a bloody circus,' she muttered.

'The phone call, then,' Julia continued. 'Did the caller give us any leads?'

Vincent paused for thought.

'No,' he said. 'Well, one. It's clear that he wants to be understood, if not caught. You know that I've regarded the dates as part of a message all along. Now there's no doubt about that any longer. It's very import-ant to him that we have all the pieces, that we understand the message. However, I have no idea *why* it's so important.'

Mina tried to take in what he had just said. She already knew most of this, but it was something else hearing it in one go, together with the others in the group. When she and Vincent talked together on their own she saw it as a possible theory, but in the meeting room it became reality. She could see from the others' faces that they no longer had the slightest doubt about Vincent Walder.

'It sounds like we can shut down the hotline,' said Julia. 'We've got what we needed. The other calls that came in were of no interest. Ruben? Peder? Anything to add? Have we been able to trace the call? Analysed it? Have the lists turned anything up? Have forensics found any back-ground noise that might be useful?'

'We're all over it, but I haven't got anything more specific right now. We're waiting for information from the mobile networks and a technical voice analysis for a comparison with Rask. And the analysis of the background noise is going on right now.'

Ruben sounded, as always, as if the question put to him had been an accusation.

'My turn then,' said Mina, giving a measured nod to Ruben. 'Milda called as I was on my way over. She's got the tox screen reports back. Not just for Agnes but for Tuva and Robert as well.'

She paused for effect. She wanted to make the most of it – she wanted the impact of her words to sink in.

'Ketamine,' she said.

'Ketamine?' said Ruben, frowning.

'Ketamine is an anaesthetic used in surgery,' Mina explained. 'It's available in powdered form, tablets and ampoules. It's easy to administer, even to the reluctant.'

Christer scratched Bosse's belly absent-mindedly. The dog was lying on his back with his paws in the air, his ears spread out like fans and a daft grin on his face.

'Ketamine is also what's known as a dissociative drug, like laughing gas and PCP,' Vincent added. 'Addicts usually call it Ket, KitKat or Special-K – like the cereal. But as Mina says, it's also an anaesthetic, although it's so strong it can cause hallucinations, delirium, a racing pulse and double vision. Currently, ketamine is used for medical purposes on both people and animals.'

Vincent fell silent. Everyone stared at him.

'Do I need to be worried by the fact that you're so well up on it?' Mina whispered to him.

'The short version is that it's been used to put the victims of crimes to sleep,' said Ruben.

'Addicts refer to it as falling into a K-hole,' said Vincent.

'Anyway, we have three victims with ketamine in their bodies,' said Mina, clearing her throat. 'Presumably as a way of making them more manageable. Or to heighten the nightmarish experience they found themselves in. Perhaps a mixture of both.'

'How common is it?' Julia asked.

'I called a colleague in the drugs squad on the . . . walk . . . on the way here,' said Mina, ignoring Vincent's amused expression.

It hadn't really been a walk. Bosse had more or less dragged her along on the soles of her shoes. All that had been missing was a sled. Vincent was probably trying to imagine the phone call and how many profanities aimed at Bosse her colleague had got in the ear.

'It's out on the street,' she said. 'Ketamine, I mean. It isn't all that common though. In the healthcare sector, it's occasionally prescribed as an anti-depressant. It's mainly used by vets during surgery on a wide range of animals: cats, dogs, horses, rodents, monkeys, martens, birds of prey and parrots.'

'The drugs squad knew all that stuff about animals?' Ruben said. 'Jesus, they've got a lot of time on their hands.'

Mina sighed.

'No, I googled that.'

'On your walk?' Vincent asked with an innocent expression.

'Yes. On the walk. Dear God, it's like explaining something to a bunch of pre-schoolers.'

'The kids! I'll take the kids! It's my turn!' Peder exclaimed, leaping up from his slumber.

He whacked the half-full can of energy drink, tipping it over, and a puddle formed on the table in front of him.

'I believe Peder may be producing ketamine naturally in his body,' said Ruben. 'Who the hell falls asleep while they're drinking an energy drink?'

'I give up,' said Mina, sitting down at the end of the table with a sigh.

Bosse stood up as if to approach her, but Christer took hold of the lead and held him back. Just as well; they were on the third floor and she was quite prepared to give that dog its first and last flying lesson.

'There's one last thing,' said Vincent. 'Daniel mentioned something during the interview. A patron at the cafe where he works used to sit studying drawings. I didn't realize at the time, but I think he may have seen the murderer. Perhaps not just once but on several occasions. Daniel could be our key to identifying the murderer. If it's Rask he saw, then he shouldn't have any problems recognizing him. This is why I suggested to Julia that you bring Daniel in again – right away. This could be solved very quickly.'

'I put out an alert as soon as you called,' said Julia. 'I'll have a word with uniform division, see if they've brought him in yet.'

There was a knock on the door and a man stuck his head in. Mina was unsure what the man's name was – all she knew was that he was something to do with emergency services.

'Sorry, didn't you have . . . goodness, what a handsome dog!'

'Can we help you?' Mina said coolly.

'Oh yes, of course. Didn't you have a wanted notice out on one Daniel Bargabriel?'

'Yes, we were just talking about him,' said Julia in surprise. 'We need to bring him back in for questioning as soon as possible.'

'That's going to be tricky,' said the man. 'He's already here, actually. But he's in the chiller.'

'The chiller?' Vincent said blankly.

'He's dead,' said Mina in a low voice, looking at the floor.

Even Bosse noticed something was up and whimpered.

'Just thought you'd like to know,' the man said, closing the door.

76

Vincent had taken it upon himself to go and buy some proper coffee instead of having what Ruben referred to as the 'cop coffee' in the meeting room. However, the truth was that he needed a reason to leave the building. He exited through the main door, turned the corner and leaned against the wall. He took deep breaths. Daniel couldn't be dead. He'd just met Daniel, spoken to Daniel. Questioned him.

The realization that it was all for real hit him with full force. What had befallen Tuva and Agnes was dreadful, but they had always been names on paper, photos on a computer. Robert had been someone he had read about in the papers. None of them had existed in his memory as flesh-and-blood people. He had been able to remain fairly rational and objective in relation to them. Distanced. But this was different. This was someone who had offered him a coffee. Bloody hell. He continued controlling his breathing until the adrenaline and cortisol slowly began to subside. Then he headed with heavy heart towards the cafe that Julia had recommended. They offered a police discount.

He bought coffee for all of them as well as every single bun that was left in the cafe, a gesture he knew Peder would appreciate.

When he returned, the mood in the meeting room was as low as when he had left it. Bosse was lying flat on the floor with his nose between his front paws. The dog looked at Vincent with an unhappy gaze without lifting his head. Were dogs allowed to eat buns? Christer might know.

'What did I miss?' he said, setting down the paper bags on the table and removing their contents.

Everyone gratefully accepted the coffee. When the fragrant buns appeared there was a longing yelp audible from the floor.

'You can have a little bit,' said Christer, tearing off a piece of bun for Bosse. He spoke to the dog as if he were a baby. 'But dough isn't good for you. So you can only have a little bit. Otherwise you'll have a tummy ache, won't you, my little man?'

'Do you suspect any connection between Daniel's death and the other murders?' said Vincent.

'There's a witness statement,' said Julia, shaking her head. 'We've just received a copy. People with Sweden's Future emblems on their clothing were seen running from the scene.'

'Attacks on innocent people happen more often than you'd think,' said Ruben. 'The world is an unfair place. If it's not the racists who are running amok then it's the women.'

'Of course, it'll be followed up on,' said Julia in a sharp tone and with an angry glare at Ruben. 'But I don't think we should hope for too much. And we'll have to resign ourselves to the fact that, with Daniel dead, there's no way of finding out who or what he saw. Instead we should focus on finding Rask, and trying to work out what the next murder weapon will be – i.e., the next magic trick. Not that it'll help us to prevent another murder, given the circumstances. But it would be good to know what we can expect if we don't solve this.'

'I'm not sure I follow,' said Peder, downing the portion of the energy drink that hadn't spilled out of the can. He had already drained the takeaway coffee cup. He set down the empty can on the table and immediately fished another one out of his bag.

'Are you really going to have coffee and two . . .' Mina began but fell silent when Peder turned his tired face towards her.

'I mean,' said Julia, 'what other boxes do magicians put people in so that it looks like they're dying? Are there more varieties than the ones we've seen?'

All eyes turned towards Vincent. He ran his hand over his chin, thinking. He was surprised to feel stubble scratching against his fingers. How long was it since he had last shaved? That wasn't like him. A sign of stress. He needed to remember to shave when he got home. Well, no. If he shaved in the evening he wouldn't have to do so in the morning, which was when he usually shaved. And when would he have to do it next? His whole routine would be set off-kilter.

Daniel was dead.

He had a stomach ache at the mere thought of it. Somehow he would have to remember to shave tomorrow morning.

But Julia had posed a good question. They were waiting for him. Even Bosse was looking at him with something that resembled expectation in his eyes. Or was it just the hope of getting another piece of bun?

'I'm afraid there are several,' he said. 'Illusions in which people seem to die or be maimed aren't uncommon. Quite the contrary. Right now it feels as if most of them are very common. The big classic is, of course, sawing a lady in half. Horace Goldin and P.T. Selbit quarrelled over who invented it first in the early 1920s. But the illusion originates in the early nineteenth century. In the beginning, the assistant would be split in two parts inside a box. Goldin removed the box and used a massive circular saw. Loads of fake blood. Pretty tasteless, actually. There are also versions with two assistants who get cut in half and then swap their lower torsos, or the Janet box where they are split into nine parts rather than two, and then they are pulled apart. More or less like that cut-up horse by Damien Hirst, if you've seen it. But anyway, we can expect to see some version of the lady sawn in half.'

'Anything else?' said Julia.

She looked somewhat pale after his comparison with the cut-up horse.

'Er, maybe the origami box? The assistant climbs into a box which is quickly folded up until it's far too small to fit a person.'

'That doesn't necessarily sound like something that kills,' said Christer, scratching Bosse behind the ears.

The dog had begun lapping up the spilled energy drink on the table.

'The box ends up the size of your head,' said Vincent. 'And then you obviously stick swords through it.'

'Stage illusions often seem to involve skewering women,' said Julia. 'Do all magicians really have dicks that small?'

Peder coughed into his can of energy drink as he took a gulp and Ruben's face turned bright red. He opened his mouth and looked like he was about to defend the male species before shutting it again after a look from Julia.

'Or it's about demonstrating power over life and death,' said Vincent. 'Although perhaps that's the same thing. And I almost forgot about the Crusher. The box containing the assistant is crushed in a vice until it's basically flat.'

'Charming,' said Christer. 'I think we're starting to get a very clear picture. That's a lot of boxes to search for.'

'Hmm, well it's not quite that simple,' said Vincent. 'Not all illusions include boxes. In the case of the Impaler, the assistant is balanced on the tip of a sword while lying down. It looks like she's hovering on the sword. Until she falls down onto it and the sword penetrates her body.'

'This is killing me!' said Julia. 'I was kidding before, but you can't get any more phallic than that!'

'It might amuse you to know that this particular illusion is one magicians are quite happy doing themselves,' Vincent said with a wry smile. 'I'm not sure what conclusions you want to draw from that.'

The energy drink seemed to be having an impact because Bosse suddenly shook his whole body and then happily ran two laps around the table – to Mina's obvious horror and Peder's delight. When he passed Christer for a third lap, Christer grabbed him by the scruff of the neck.

'Sit here, Bosse. Now,' he said firmly.

The dog immediately obeyed, sitting down beside Christer and looking happily up at him.

Vincent couldn't help wondering whether any of them had listened to a word of what he had said so far. Personally, he was still trying to digest the news about Daniel. But he supposed that they had become hardened in their work as police officers.

'Impaler,' said Peder. 'Crusher, zigzag girl, origami box, sword box – they all sound much cooler in English than they ever will in Swedish. "Svärdslåda" doesn't exactly have the same ring to it.'

'Was that all you had to say about the illusions, Vincent?' Julia asked him.

'Not quite,' he said, clearing his throat. 'There are obviously also the illusions where death is only a danger if the magician fails. Like the "table of death".'

He glanced at Peder, who looked almost childishly amused by the name of the illusion.

'The magician is tied to a table and has to free himself before a big panel of swords falls down and skewers him. Or he has to get out of a straitjacket while hanging upside down – preferably attached to a rope that's on fire – above something dangerous. And then there's Houdini's favourite: the water torture cell. That sees the breakout king wearing handcuffs and hanging upside down inside a water tank which is locked with a padlock on the outside. He has to get out before he drowns.'

'I like that better,' said Peder, carefully stacking the new empty can on top of the previous one. 'The person overcoming impossible odds.'

Peder was talking far more quickly now. The triple dose of caffeine was beginning to take effect.

'Exactly,' said Vincent. 'One of the reasons Houdini got so famous was that he was working in an era of economic hardship, when most people were worried about how to make ends meet. Up pops a short, Jewish man and not only challenges a shackled and claustrophobic setting – in his case quite literally – but also defeats it every single time. I think the positive message conveyed by Houdini's tricks may have saved the mental health of many following the start of the Great Depression.'

'Vincent, that was more information than I was expecting,' said Julia. 'Or could ever need. Or we have time for. But thank you. Please would you summarize it in an email, preferably more concisely? And don't share that information with anyone outside this room: the press have already dubbed our perpetrator "the Houdini murderer", the last thing I want is to encourage that sort of click-bait journalism.' She looked down at her notes before continuing: 'Could you also check with your contacts whether there is anything particular needed to build these illusions. A certain material, special hinges – try to come up with as many common denominators as you can. Then pass that information on to Peder, who can call around timberyards, wholesalers or whatever to check whether anyone has bought stuff that indicates they're building an illusion. Mina, please check out Sweden's Future and see whether they're claiming responsibility for Daniel or whether they're going to deny it.'

Silence descended on the room once again. Vincent guessed that everyone was thinking the same thing. Julia's plan sounded hopeless. There was an idea playing hide and seek in his head, but as soon as he thought he had it pinned down, it hid again. There was something in what she'd said, something about building . . .

'I know what you're thinking,' said Julia. 'It's an extreme long shot. And it probably won't get us anywhere. But with Daniel out of the picture and with Jonas Rask still at large, there's really not much more we can do at the moment. And you're good at finding needles in haystacks, Peder.'

Building.

Sains Bergander had said something about building too. About how you had to re-design the structures. Vincent suddenly realized what it meant. He had been trying to arrange to meet Sains again, ever since he'd photographed the box they'd found Robert in. But Sains hadn't replied. And he had already said once that he didn't know who had built Tuva's sword box. But Vincent had asked about the wrong things. Sains knew more. Vincent pulled out his phone and dialled right away. He was met with a voicemail message. Sains's phone was switched off. Fucking hell. He needed to get hold of Sains as quickly as possible.

77

Her panic increased more and more the closer to the flat they got. Merely being in a taxi – with a dog to boot – was the cause of enough anxiety to make Mina's breathing quick and shallow. Vincent was sitting next to her, helping her to control her breathing. Bosse was at the very back of the estate car.

'Breathe in and count to four,' said Vincent, breathing with her. 'Hold your breath for four. And now breathe out for four. Hold it again.'

They did a few rounds of breathing together. After a while, she could feel her blood oxygenating again and it was easier to think once the adrenaline wasn't rushing uninhibited around her brain.

As they drove around the roundabout at Gullmarsplan she could almost feel her clean, bacteria-free oasis of a flat getting closer. Her refuge – the place where she could feel clean, at least for brief periods. Now that was over. Her home was going to be inescapably invaded by the particles, bacteria, microorganisms and all manner of unpleasantries that Bosse was carrying on his furry body.

'Who does the dog actually belong to?' Vincent queried. 'Because I assume it's not yours.'

She shook her head firmly.

'A . . . friend . . . who ended up in hospital. I had to take care of it. Everything happened rather quickly.'

She paused. It grated to ask for help. It was a sign of weakness to be unable to cope on your own. Not being an unimpeachable fortress of self-sufficiency in every part of life. Asking for help was letting someone in. That was why she hadn't asked any of her colleagues. Asking them for help would indicate a friendliness that didn't exist. She didn't eat dinner at any of their homes. She didn't ask about their personal lives. Sometimes they told her about them anyway – it was as if they didn't even notice how she never replied, never commented, and above all gave them nothing about herself in return. She knew what opening up might lead to. But now she had no choice.

'Can . . . can you take Bosse?' she said. 'I could bake a cake for your kids as a thank you. Well, actually, I can't. But I can get one delivered to you . . . ready-bought?'

Now it was Vincent's turn to shake his head.

'I would love to,' he said. 'I'm sure Bosse would love the woods outside my house. But Maria is allergic and, given how much this dog is shedding, that wouldn't end well.'

That was the last thing Mina wanted to hear. She didn't need to turn around to see the cloud of shedded hair coming off the dog. And there were probably lots of other things living in its fur. She screwed her eyes shut and shivered.

'Don't you have anyone else you can ask?'

She turned her head away.

'It's not as if I planned for this,' she said quietly. 'I didn't suddenly decide one day to be alone. Work . . . Work is my family.'

Mina fell silent. She couldn't work out what it was about Vincent that always made her say slightly more than she had intended to. Than she usually did say.

Once upon a time she'd had friends. She'd even had a family. But life events had lined themselves up like Dorothy's yellow brick road to Oz, inexorably leading her in the only possible direction. One by one, she had pushed them away. Consciously or unconsciously, she didn't know. But work was enough – she didn't need anything else.

She shrugged and looked down at the carpet on the floor of the taxi.

'Life seems to have passed me by. I don't think I've ever had the feeling that I can control any of the things that happen to me . . .'

Vincent sat beside her in silence. She was grateful that he wasn't saying anything.

The taxi was getting closer to her home and her pulse was beginning to race even more. Bosse barked from his spot in the boot and the driver scowled in the rear-view mirror. Mina put her hand to her breast. She felt captive. Stuck. She didn't even have a last name, let alone a phone number, for Bosse's masters. They only used first names at AA, and sometimes not even that. Kenneth. And his wife. That was all she had to go on. Deep down, she hoped they would already have looked her up, intending to fetch him. That Kenneth's wife would have recovered and they'd be on their way home, eager to get their dog back. It would be easy for them to find her, she reasoned. They knew she was a police officer and that her name was Mina. It was an unusual name – she was the only policewoman in Stockholm with that first name. Perhaps they would be waiting for her at her front door? But no, when the taxi turned the corner and pulled over outside her address there was no one at the street door.

Perhaps the dolphin girl knew how Mina could get in touch with them, but how would she find her? All she knew about her was that her name was Anna.

The panic rose. Bosse barked and threw himself back and forth in the boot.

She got out of the car as quickly as she could.

'I'll take the taxi home,' Vincent said.

'What do I owe?' she said, taking deep breaths of the warm, fresh air – as far into her lungs as she could.

'This is on ShowLife Productions' tab. Not that Umberto knows about it, but still.'

The taxi driver got out to open the boot and release Bosse. The dog leapt wildly and joyfully around Mina, who in turn desperately sought to parry his jumping so that he wouldn't nuzzle her. His lead thrashed around him and the taxi driver pointedly picked up the handle with an acid expression and passed it to her. After a few seconds' hesitation, she took it.

How stupid.

How incorrigibly stupid.

Since she had no choice but to suck it up, she tapped in the door code, opened it and entered the stairwell before climbing up to the flat as the taxi conveyed Vincent away. She slowly got out the keys from her pocket and fumbled with them in the lock until she heard the click that indicated the door could now be opened. There was still time to change her mind. To keep her bubble intact. But she had put pride above the sanctity of her home and now there was no going back. Mina pressed down the door handle. Bosse was right by her side, pressing his nose into the crack, and before she knew it the door was open wide enough for him to squeeze through.

It was like an explosion in the midst of the dazzling restraint. In a few seconds, he had made his way into the living room, the bedroom, the kitchen, the bathroom, sniffing everything, brushing against the surfaces, leaving hairs drifting in the air in his wake before slowly, slowly sailing down to the floor. Mina stared at a tuft of hair that had already caught on the side of the sofa. She had gone over the sofa with tape wrapped around her hand as recently as the day before yesterday to remove as many dust particles as possible. Now particles were the least of her worries.

She closed the door behind her. She felt tears stinging her eyes and panic made her breast rise and fall heavily. Bosse seemed to sense that something was wrong. He came running back, sat down in front of her as she stood there on the doormat and cocked his head to one side. Mina couldn't bear the thought of things crawling out of him, of him crawling on her sofa, on her floor, on her bedspread, on her living room carpet, on her kitchen table, her bathroom floor, her shower, her fridge, her coffee maker, her clothes, her . . .

She opened the front door and threw herself out of the flat. Bosse followed through the open door. She closed it, sat down with her back to the door and took a firm grip of his lead. Her hands shaking, she retrieved her phone. Pride would have to be sacrificed on this occasion.

78

Vincent was marooned in the middle of the kitchen, his mobile phone in his hand. The call he'd just taken hadn't been one he was expecting. He went into the living room while trying to sort out his thoughts.

'Why the sad face?' Maria said from the sofa. 'Doesn't Mina want to have phone sex with you anymore?'

She was munching through a bag of wine gums. Sweets were fine as long as they were vegan, according to Maria. Not that she was a vegan. But it was apparently healthier. He hadn't had the heart to tell her that sugar came from a plant.

'No, I was just speaking to Ulrika,' he said. 'Your sister.'

'I know who she is.'

Maria inserted one red and one green wine gum into her mouth. She thought it tasted better if you mixed colours.

'She wants to meet,' he said. 'And discuss Rebecka. I think . . . it sounded as if she actually listened to me. About taking Rebecka to see someone.'

Maria scrunched up the bag with an aggressive rustle, but didn't say anything.

'She didn't seem anywhere near as annoyed and dogmatic as she usually does,' he continued. 'Quite the contrary. I think she's actually thought about this.'

'I don't like you seeing my sister,' said Maria. 'You know she's not over you. She hasn't even changed her last name from yours.'

He held out his hands in frustration. He should have realized this was coming.

'The name is for Rebecka and Benjamin's sake,' he said. 'You know that. And I *have* to see her now and then. After all, she is the mother of two of my three children. We need to be on the same page about certain things. I don't want Rebecka and Benjamin to be treated differently. This particular thing happens to require written consent from both their mother and me to happen.'

Maria opened the bag again and inserted three wine gums into her mouth at once. He didn't see which colours they were.

'I still don't like it,' she said. 'As the mother of one of your three children. So when are you meeting her?'

'In a month. Busy lawyer and all that. And we're meeting in town. Neutral ground. She's going for dinner with a group of friends, so we're meeting to talk before that.'

'Oh really. Well, have fun then. I won't be awake when you get home.'

'We're meeting at seven o'clock.'

Maria shrugged and began hunting for the TV remote control, which had disappeared between the cushions of the sofa. The conversation was apparently over.

Vincent sighed. Yet again a conversation with his wife had ended with him feeling that he had done something wrong without knowing what.

'Are you happy?' he suddenly asked.

It wasn't planned; he didn't know the words were going to come out of his mouth until he heard them himself. And then it was too late to take them back.

'What did you say?' Maria asked, somewhat absently.

She half turned her head towards him, but without taking her eyes from the TV where the opening credits for *Married at First Sight* were scrolling across the screen. He knew she was watching it on catch-up. She could pause it anytime if she really wanted to talk to him. But she chose to leave it running.

'It was nothing,' he said.

The truth was that he didn't know what else to say.

79

Peder was on his way home when Mina called. But he turned the car around right away. Mina asking him for help was not a regular occurrence. And her asking for help with something personal had never happened so far as he could remember. It was like Halley's comet returning after only thirty-five years. But he liked Mina. And he could hear the desperation in her voice. So no matter how much of a rush he was in to get home, Peder turned the car around. He'd never been to her home, but it was easy to find using the satnav.

'Hi.'

Mina raised a feeble hand in a small wave as he got out of the car. She got up from the pavement, picked up the plastic carrier bag she'd been sitting on and walked determinedly towards him, firmly grasping Bosse's lead. When the dog saw Peder, he jumped happily up and down with his tongue hanging out, which was like a big smile spreading across his face.

There was something about golden retrievers that filled Peder's stomach with happy butterflies. They were so frank about everything in life. If he could be reborn as an animal and he had a choice, he would without hesitation come back as a golden retriever.

'Thanks,' said Mina, passing him the lead.

Peder merely nodded. He knew better than to make a big deal out of this.

'Call me if the owners get in touch,' he said, opening the back door of the car so that Bosse could jump in.

He could see that Mina's gaze was glued to the dog in the back seat and that her hands were trembling slightly. He guessed what she was thinking. The dog hair didn't bother him one bit. He'd long ago discounted the Volvo he and Anette shared as a sanitary vehicle. Neither of them was especially tidy, and since the triplets had arrived they had completely given up. Out of the corner of his eye, he could see Bosse licking the seat where Molly had thrown up two days earlier. However, he realized it was best not to pass that information on to Mina.

'I'll be in touch as soon as they call,' said Mina.

'By the way,' Peder said, stopping halfway into the car. 'I almost forgot. I stopped by Fab Fika at Hornstull. It occurred to me that if Daniel had seen someone suspicious then maybe others there had done so too. But no one had seen a customer with drawings.'

'Of course.'

'I can understand why, given that the staff there didn't see me until I'd been standing there for five minutes. They were fully occupied chatting to each other. Customers were apparently low priority.'

He shook his head.

'Youth of today and all that,' he said.

'Your three'll never end up like that,' said Mina, smiling.

'No, it's going to be finishing school for them when I get home. Anyone who doesn't learn to bring a cappuccino to Dad within three minutes is getting the dog set on them. And there needs to be a portrait of Dad in the foam.'

He got into the car and Mina raised a hand in farewell.

As he drove off, he could see through the window that she was heading for the door to her block of flats with a decidedly straighter back than she'd had when he had arrived.

One and a half hours later he got home. He'd ended up in the worst of the rush-hour traffic and the journey had taken twice as long as usual. Bosse had slept like a log in the back seat, but as soon as Peder pulled onto the drive and stopped the car the dog sat up and looked around curiously.

The minute the door opened he flew out of the car. Peder just managed to grab hold of the lead before he absconded. And it was around that point, or thereabouts, standing on his drive, that Peder began to realize that this might not have been one of his best ideas. That feeling was confirmed when he opened the front door and encountered Anette's voice in a torrent from the bathroom.

'C'mon, I can't do this any longer. I quit – they haven't slept a single minute all day. Well, actually, they slept one minute, but they didn't sleep that minute together and I didn't get any sleep last night either – I know I was supposed to wake you up, but fuck me, you could sleep through a world war and I was awake anyway and couldn't get back to

305

sleep so I'm now on my twentieth hour awake and Molly just threw up on Meja and as soon as I'd changed them both Majken did a poo that leaked through the nappy so now I need to change her again and Jesus Christ, this isn't what I signed up for. I was going to have one kid – *one fucking kid* – on my arm, looking like those celebs on the cover of *Mama*, and be a yummy mummy, sipping a latte and eating some damn chia ball. No one mentioned all this horrible poo and sick, and if one more thing goes wrong today I swear I'm going to jump off the bloody Västerbron bridge – did you hear me, Peder? *One more thing* and I jump.'

Bosse yelped and tugged at the lead, but Peder quickly pulled him out through the front door and closed it carefully. He took out his phone and sent a message to Anette saying they'd just received an alert and that he had to go again. Then he checked an address. For a moment he considered whether to call. Then he put his phone back in his pocket.

Best not to give any forewarning.

80

Muffled but peculiar music was audible through Benjamin's door. Vincent had his hand raised to knock, but had stopped himself. He tried to understand what it was he was hearing, searching for musical references he could use in conversation with his son to maintain their relationship. He had no ambitions of being a cool dad. People who needed to point out how 'laid back' or 'comfortable' they were, especially in terms of a relationship with their children, were to be pitied. But it was always best to ease your way into a discussion about serious matters by chatting about something innocuous first.

Unfortunately, so far as Vincent was concerned, his children's interests and tastes in music were a challenge. Though most people were unaware of it, by far the best way to keep your brain in trim was to regularly expose it to unfamiliar things. While most people seemed to do the same thing the same way their whole lives, Vincent was grateful to his children for introducing him to experiences he would otherwise never have had.

He put his ear to the door and wasn't entirely sure what he made of Benjamin's music choice for the day. It wasn't that it sounded bad, but he lacked a context to place it in. The closest he could get was that it sounded like circus music – if the entire circus ensemble consisted of axe murderers. A murderous circus. Before he could stop himself, his head was filled with images of what a circus like that might look like, what it would smell like in the ring, what was on the poster. He already knew what the circus sounded like. He knocked six times on the door, two knocks in three pairs, and the feeling of the wood against his knuckles brought him back to reality. When there was no reaction from within, he opened the door and stepped inside, glancing quickly at Benjamin's desktop PC where Spotify was playing a track by the Tiger

Lillies. Three men in pale, demonic make-up wearing bowler hats and pulling peculiar faces. He hadn't been far off.

Benjamin was lying on the bed with a laptop on his belly. He had headphones on and was absorbed in a YouTube video. Presumably he couldn't even hear the music. Not until Vincent sat down on the edge of the bed did he react. Benjamin paused the video and looked up, but kept his headphones on.

'What are you watching?' said Vincent.

'It's fascinating. Imagine you're part of a troop of soldiers conquered by the enemy and rather than being captured you intend to commit collective suicide. But for religious reasons you can't kill yourselves.'

'Benjamin, do I need to worry about you?' Vincent frowned. 'This sounds like fanaticism.'

'I'm not a terrorist,' Benjamin sighed. 'It's a maths problem. Apparently it happened for real with Jewish soldiers captured by the Romans. Imagine you're one of the soldiers and you're sitting in a circle. You kill the one sitting to your left. The next one kills the person sitting to their left. And so on. Eventually, everyone will be dead. Apart from one, of course, who is forced to survive. But say you want to be the one who survives. If you know who is going to start the killing and you know the number of places, how many places from the person who starts the killing do you need to be to be the one who survives?'

'Don't you have anything harder than that to offer me?' said Vincent. 'I guess the maths behind it is interesting. When the number of people in the circle is divisible by the power of two, it's always the person who begins – the person in spot number one – who survives. If there's an odd number of people, you have to start by counting the number of people and subtracting the power of two. For example, say there's nineteen people. That means you subtract sixteen. Then you take what's left – three in this case – and double it, since it skips every second person, i.e., the ones that die. And then you add that to the starting position, which is one. One plus three plus three makes seven. So out of nineteen people, it's the person in position seven who survives.'

Benjamin shrugged his shoulders. Vincent had expected slightly more enthusiasm for his elegant answer, but since Benjamin was a teenager he would have to take it as a compliment that he was even still awake.

'On the subject of people killing each other,' said Benjamin. 'How's it going with the Houdini murderer? Are you getting anywhere?'

'Please don't call him that,' said Vincent, pulling his legs up onto the bed and leaning his back against the wall. 'There's really nothing magical about the murders. And the investigation is even less magical. I finally had something concrete to offer and now it's stalled.'

'What happened?'

'The witness is dead.'

Vincent saw his son's face go deathly white. Benjamin closed the laptop and sat up next to Vincent.

'I've tried to get hold of Sains again about the boxes,' said Vincent. 'But he's not answering his phone or emails at the moment. I know he tends to end up in his own bubble when he's in the middle of a big project. There's nothing I can do except wait it out. If I nag too much he probably won't help me at all. And the boxes are all I've got right now. Although I still think there's a message in the dates and times of the murders. If they weren't important, why would he leave behind the smashed watches? Why call in and risk being traced just to make sure we got the right date for Robert? No, there's something we're missing.'

Benjamin went over to the desktop PC and paused Spotify.

'When is the next murder going to be, by the way? How long have you got to crack this?'

'I don't know the answer to that – and you can stop being so superior. If the murderer strikes again because I'm too slow to work it out, that's really nothing to be smug about.'

Benjamin pulled up the document they had started working on after the first two murders. It was frustratingly empty apart from the basic data they had entered. Benjamin thought aloud.

'First and foremost, we don't know how many numbers are included in each piece of information in the code. I mean, we have the dates and the watches. But we also have the numbered corpses. Are the numbers part of the code? Agnes was murdered on the thirteenth of January at 14:00. So we have 13-1-14. Or maybe 14-13-1. But Agnes was also marked with the number 4. Should we include that? Is the code 4-14-13-1? Or should the four go on the end? Do you see how confusing it is?'

Vincent pointed at the screen on Benjamin's desk. He sat on something hard and pulled away the duvet to remove it. The thought that his son might have hidden something under the covers on purpose did occur to him, but his hand had already begun to move and couldn't be stopped. Under the duvet was a book with the title *Applied Cryptography*. He couldn't help smiling. It was quite clearly pornography, albeit of a rather odd kind.

'The murderer wants us to solve this,' he said. 'He wouldn't make it too difficult for us. Dates and times are the same type of information. Calendar data. But the numbering isn't. I'm still convinced that this is a countdown and nothing else. And as for the order, if you were going to give a time and specific date, what would you say? Tell me when you were born.'

'I was born on the eleventh of November at 23:03 in the evening . . . Ah, I get it.'

'Exactly. You say day, month and then time. There's your order.'

'I hear you, Master Mentalist.'

Benjamin waggled his eyebrow with exaggeration as he said the last bit.

'I don't know about that,' said Vincent. 'I'm beginning to suspect that my kids are just as smart as I am.'

'Smarter,' Benjamin said, feigning a cough.

Benjamin minimized the document and the screen went black. Images of Agnes, Tuva and Robert faded into the sound of the Star Wars theme. *Darth Vader's theme.* He spun on his chair and looked insufferably pleased with himself. Vincent didn't know whether to praise his son for the PowerPoint presentation or be concerned. Beneath the images the dates of the murders now appeared in glittering numerals together with the heading 'The Hunt for the Houdini Murderer'.

'Do you really think glitter is appropriate?' Vincent said.

'What? It's red glitter! Anyway, Dad, be quiet. Try to keep up. What we've got is Agnes's murder, 13-1-14. Tuva 20-2-15. Robert 3-5-14. I've tried processing the dates and times mathematically. Adding them, looking for sequences and so on. It turned up nothing. The idea that it might be a cipher was something you and I tested right away, so I could rule that out too. Finally, I tried translating the figures to other formats such as light, radiation or radio frequencies, latitudes, coordinates, but it gave me nothing. I'm guessing it's because the message isn't complete. You're still missing the fourth piece of the puzzle – the murder you're trying to avoid.'

'Mmm,' Vincent said thoughtfully.

He pointed at the computer.

'Stick the number sequences with the dates and times into Google.'

Benjamin did as he was told.

'That's funny. All the sequences are post codes too. For places abroad.'

Vincent eagerly leaned forward.

'Post codes? Where for?'

'Blainville, Washington and Mexico in New York. It's probably just coincidence.'

'Put all three place names in Google as a combined search term,' Vincent said.

There was something shifting in his stomach – call it instinct, call it a gut feeling – but it told him they were on the right track. Benjamin entered 'Mexico Blainville Washington' into the field and hit search.

'Let's see,' he said. 'First we have a few travel planners to get between the different places, but they're autogenerated so we can most likely skip them. Then three books. *Gulf of Mexico Origin*, *Mollusca* something, and *Mammals of Mexico*. Funny. That last book even has a specific page reference in the hit on Google.'

'That one,' said Vincent, pointing to the last one. 'It stands out. Too specific. Check it out.'

There was something familiar about the book. Far too familiar. Benjamin clicked on the links for the three books and compared them.

'You're right,' he said after a few seconds. 'Look at this. The other books seem to have the search terms all over the place in the text. But the last one has them all on one page. Page 873.'

Benjamin clicked on the link for *Mammals of Mexico* and Google brought up the PDF of the page in question with the three words highlighted in yellow. But Vincent didn't care about them. He was still thinking about Mexican mammals. So incredibly familiar. Then his gaze was caught by the page number.

'Page 873,' said Vincent, pointing to the number. 'It's a date. The eighth of the seventh. The eighth of July. And since the other murders were at 14:00 and 15:00 it's reasonable to believe that the final three means three in the afternoon. 15:00. It can't be a coincidence. I think you're right: the murderer wants to make it easy for us. Our mistake was overthinking it. All it took was a simple Google search to find the final date.'

Vincent leaned back against the wall in satisfaction. He ought to call Mina right away. But something was gnawing at him. There was something more.

The eighth of July.

No, it was something else.

He usually found it easy to search his memory banks and find what he needed. But that required him to have memorized the memory from the beginning. The eighth of July . . . there was something there, but it was too early a memory. Far too long ago. When he was little. Animals in Mexico . . .

A leopard bared its teeth at Vincent on the screen. He *had* seen the book before.

At Umberto's office.

Because . . .

Because someone had sent the book to him.

He threw himself out of his son's room and ran into his study.

'When am I getting paid for this?' Benjamin yelled in his wake. 'You wouldn't have found this solution without me!'

Vincent had a cupboard where he kept books he'd been gifted that he never intended to read but couldn't bring himself to throw out. You couldn't throw books out – that was the rule. It didn't take long to find what he was looking for. A brick of a book with a leopard emblazoned on the cover: *Mammals of Mexico* by Gerardo Ceballos. The same book he'd just seen on Benjamin's computer.

His hands were so clammy that the heavy book fell out of his grip, but he caught it and leafed feverishly to page 873. He reached the page and his breath caught in his throat. There were lines drawn all over the page in red pen. It looked as if someone had tried to make the book bleed. He leafed backwards and forwards, but no other page in the book was drawn on. Between the lines there were thicker red clumps coloured in, but it wasn't those that made him stop breathing. It was the letters next to them. The red letters. Traced over several times in a strong handwriting style. He read the message several times.

Hello Vincent,

I am most disappointed that you thought the eighth of July was the date of a new murder. Do you really not remember? You'll have to stop titting about and look harder than that if you are going to find me.

Air was still failing to make it all the way into his lungs. This was too big for his thoughts to grasp. He needed to break it down into manageable chunks to avoid going mad. Someone had sent a book with a message for him. And they had sent it at Christmas, before the first murder happened. Two months before he had met Mina at the theatre in Gävle. Long before he'd been pulled into the investigation.

Somehow it was all about him.

It had always been about him.

Without him understanding why.

And it left him terror-stricken.

312

81

Christer contemplated his bookcase, debating which of the books from the 'new' shelf he should start on. The new Anders de la Motte? Or the one by GW? The bookshop assistant had foisted a copy of the debut crime novel by that actor Alexander Karim onto him too. But after thumbing through it for a bit, he was hesitant. Time travel and all that shit. Nope, he liked his crime fiction traditional. Peter Robinson: there was a man who knew what he was doing. And Håkan Nesser. Granted, there hadn't been a new Van Veeteren for a while, but they were up to being reread, which Christer did at regular intervals.

Most of all, he preferred his crime fiction to feature male heroes. He found women in crime fiction very trying. As it happened, he found female crime writers pretty trying as people too. Lots of opinions all over the place about this and that when they didn't understand it. Of course, Leif G.W. Persson had plenty to say about most things too, if he was being honest. But what the hell – GW was GW. And his wine was good.

The majority of male heroes in crime fiction did not, however, drink wine. They drank whisky. Christer had tried to learn to drink whisky precisely for that reason. Over the course of a couple of months he had suffered through a glass of whisky every night, gradually increasing the amount of ice in order to get it down. The last time he had had a glass of ice with a minimal dash of whisky added. Then he'd given up.

But it wasn't really the whisky drinking and the probable alcoholism that appealed to him about fictional detectives. It was the gloom. The loneliness. The problems around establishing a decent relationship. He felt like he was one of them. As if he could have been there in the pages of those books, a hero in a crime series. Constantly ruminating. Constantly digging. Constantly going against the current. Well, truth be told, with the possible exception of Evert Bäckström, the blokes in crime novels worked slightly more than he was personally inclined to. Kurt Wallander, Van Veeteren, Martin Beck, Alan Banks and Mikael Blomkvist . . . Bloody hell they liked to toil away. That and the whisky were two things that Christer didn't think quite matched him.

His greatest idol was Harry Bosch. He felt he had a lot in common with Michael Connelly's hero. From the very first Bosch novel, he'd sensed that here was his twin in the world of crime fiction, his alter ego in criminal literature. He had almost become teary-eyed. It had been like finding a long-lost brother. Of course, there were plenty of differences. Harry Bosch's mother was a prostitute; Christer's mother was a prudish old woman with only a small handful of mostly platonic relationships behind her. Harry's mother was brutally murdered; Christer's died in her sleep from a stroke. Harry Bosch was a soldier in the Vietnam War; Christer had done his military service as a store-keeper with the K3 regiment in Arboga.

Nevertheless . . .

There was enough that was similar for Christer to feel comfortable with the comparison. His house, for example. His childhood home that he had inherited from his mother, located on a steep hillside with views across the Skurusundet strait. And Harry's real name was Hieronymus – named after the Dutch painter. Christer's middle name was Engelbert in honour of his mother's greatest idol, the singer Engelbert Humperdinck. Harry Bosch was left-handed, like Christer, and they were even the same height. And just like Harry Bosch, he loved jazz. To be honest, he had started listening to and learned to love jazz precisely because of Bosch's passion for the genre. It had been much easier than the whisky. Right now, Chet Baker's 'Time After Time' was playing in the background. Christer and Harry. So incredibly similar, Christer noted with satisfaction, taking in the view.

The doorbell rang. Who could it be? Christer got up from the wing chair.

Standing outside was Peder with Bosse on a lead.

'Oh it's you!' Christer said in surprise. 'I thought Mina was going to bring the dog.'

'Why did you think Mina was going to bring the dog?' said Peder, surprised. 'How did you know . . .?'

Christer didn't reply. The fact that Peder could even ask something that stupid . . . Had anyone really believed that Mina would manage to keep the dog at hers? Good God, there was an idiot born every day.

Christer stepped to one side and waved them into the hall. A large bag of dog food was already propped against the wall.

'I've bought the best dog food, two bowls and a cushion for him to lie on.'

He bent down and removed the lead from Bosse's collar. The dog immediately rushed into the living room and began to examine everything.

'But how did you know that you . . .' Peder said in confusion, his mouth gaping.

Christer shrugged.

'I was the only logical choice. But as usual, no one ever thinks of me as a first choice.'

Behind him, the record player moved on to 'Who Can I Turn To?' by George Cables.

82

Kvibille 1982

He looked at his three friends cycling ahead of him. The gravel track would lead them to the small lake where they usually went swimming. When they got there, Malla, Sickan and Lotta would hurl themselves into the water and then mercilessly tease him for not coming in. But it didn't matter. He knew they didn't really mean it when they teased him and splashed water at him as he sat in his customary position by the edge of the woods. However, the darkness in the lake was deadly serious. There could be anything down in the depths. And if you couldn't see it then how could you know when it was about to pull you down?

That was kind of how he had felt himself lately – as if something far below in the darkness was threatening to pull him down. A dark shadow inside his head. He needed Malla, Sickan and Lotta. His friends who did normal, regular things. Who treated him as normal.

'Oi! Little Yoda!' Lotta shouted back to him. 'Get a move on!'

He was wearing Jane's cast-off T-shirt adorned with a green figure that appeared to be incredibly old. He hadn't seen *Star Wars*, which everyone in his class was talking about, but he was aware of the characters and knew that Luke Skywalker or Chewbacca would have been infinitely cooler to have on his top. Even the evil one, Darth Vader, would have been an improvement. But Jane had said that Yoda was the coolest because he was the smartest of all.

'At least I'm taller than you,' he shouted back, but the girls had already disappeared round a bend.

He pedalled hard to catch up, the gravel crunching beneath his wheels. The cloak that he had been on his way to fetch when the girls

316

had come by was bundled up on the pannier rack. Yoda was for dweebs. Today he was Chewbacca.

After they had bathed, they each lay on a towel, drying off. He had stripped down to his underpants as if readying himself to swim but had changed his mind at the last minute – as they had all known he would. The sun was warm and he was starting to feel hungry. He wished he had brought along some of Mum's sandwiches.

'Do you think your mum noticed you leaving?' Lotta asked. 'We tried to be quiet, but maybe she noticed anyway.'

Oh no. His entire body went cold. He shouldn't have had that thought about the sandwiches. She probably wouldn't have asked if it weren't for him thinking of it.

'Was she even at home?' said Malla. 'I didn't see her.'

'She's resting,' he said. 'You know. So it's good we didn't make a racket.'

That was at least almost true. His friends nodded. They knew that his mother had days like that sometimes. Days when she needed to rest, days when it was better that she wasn't with them. Days when she was the one who was the dark shadow.

'Do you want to have tea at mine today?' Sickan asked. 'My mum always makes too much food.'

He could see the sunlight glittering in the drops of water on her stomach. With relief, he realized that there were too many drops for him to count.

'I don't think that I . . .'

'Your mum won't even notice you're gone,' said Malla. 'You know that. I think we should all have tea at Sickan's!'

Lotta let out a hoot of joy and Sickan burst into laughter.

'Mum's going to die!' she laughed. 'Let's head to mine as soon as we've dried off.'

He knew that his absence from home wouldn't go unpunished. It would have consequences. Mum was waiting for him. He had told her that he just needed to fetch something. Instead he had accompanied his friends. But right there and then in the patch of sunshine on the grass by the small lake, he didn't care very much about that – for the first time in his life. For a brief moment, the darkness in the lake wasn't quite as dark.

83

He poured several more fingers of Balvenie Portwood for himself. The third glass in a row. The twenty-one-year-old whisky that had been his favourite in the last few years was frankly wasted on him tonight; he might as well have been drinking surgical spirit. Or anything to calm the nerves. A small voice inside him pointed out that the calming effect of alcohol was negligible, given the paranoia that it could also awaken, but he didn't have it in him to be sensible. And he was too old to smoke grass.

Mammals of Mexico was lying in front of him on the desk in his study. Vincent had shut the book – he had no desire to see the message again. When Maria had gone to bed he'd said he needed to do a bit more work. Rebecka and Benjamin hadn't come home yet. His oldest children were clearly taking liberties. He had extinguished the ceiling light, keeping only the weak desk lamp switched on.

He spun back and forth on his desk chair. Right now he didn't know what he needed. To contact Mina? Or police headquarters? But what could he say? That he'd received a message from the murderer that could only be found if you had a brain as strange as his? He spun the whisky glass and saw the amber liquid moving slowly. Unlike Lagavulin, he drank Balvenie without ice. But the reflex to spin the glass in order to hear the ice was well embedded.

How would Ruben react if he told him that the message meant the murderer – or at least someone who knew the murder dates before they occurred – knew that Vincent was going to be involved in the investigation before there was an investigation, before any crimes had been committed? Ruben would think that the mentalist's head had finally imploded. Ruben . . . Now there was a man with demons. In Vincent's experience, alpha males like Ruben tended to be very fragile beneath the tough exterior. Not that it was Vincent's job to point that out – he would probably get a black eye if he tried. But perhaps it was time for someone to have a word with Ruben, and more importantly to listen.

He drank a little of the whisky and felt it both soothing and warming his throat. He closed his eyes and tried to focus solely on the sensations of flavour and scent for a second or two. But he couldn't. All he could see in his mind's eye was the red text in that bloody leopard book. He opened his eyes again.

Of course, the message did pose an interesting question. Namely, who could have known – or at least assumed – that he would cooperate with the police? He could only think of two people. Firstly Julia, who had been the one to approve Mina contacting him.

And then there was Mina herself.

Mina had known. Mina was the one who had ensured that he'd been sufficiently curious to say yes. Had it been anyone other than Mina who had approached him in Gävle that night, the response would have been a polite and resolute no. But Mina had been persistent.

He knocked back the remainder of the whisky and poured a refill.

It couldn't be Mina.

Wasn't *allowed* to be Mina.

The thought was absurd. He knew her. Well, he didn't really. But he imagined that he knew what made her tick. Dear God, he could feel her presence even when she wasn't there.

Mina hadn't sent the book.

But what if.

What if Mina *had* sent the book?

He went completely cold and pushed away the unwelcome thought. It was too unpleasant to linger on. Because if it were true then that would bring everything tumbling down.

That train of thought would have to be dealt with later, but in the meantime he would assume that it wasn't Mina. So who else could it be? He had a hard time believing it was from Julia. That left . . . no one. He got up and began to pace back and forth in the small room. He needed to increase the blood flow to his brain to think better. But he was too restless to lie down on the floor.

He delved into his memory, back to their first encounter.

That night in Gävle.

Mina sitting opposite him.

The conference attendees from Helsingborg in the bar.

Her straw.

His burger.

My boss has approved us taking on an external consultant.

I was advised to speak to you.

Advised. But not necessarily by Julia. And if not by Julia, then by whom? He needed to ask her. The very second he told her about the message and the book, he would be personally drawn into the investigation in a way that he wasn't looking forward to. He would prefer to wait as long as possible for that to happen. But he didn't want to obstruct the investigation either. On the contrary. He had a murder to stop.

He put the stopper back in the bottle and carried it to the kitchen cupboard. Step one was to find out who Mina had spoken to, to find out who had suggested his involvement.

Then he could tell her about the book.

The book that Mina wasn't allowed to have sent.

84

Milda knew from experience that it was just as well to set aside plenty of time for a visit to Grandpa. Grandpa Mykolas and Mum came from Greece, while Dad was from Lithuania. Milda was the name of a Lithuanian pagan goddess of love. In other words, she was like a major crossroads. Lithuanian-Greek, raised in Sweden. A peculiar combination that was difficult to beat.

What was more, she found her name's origins somewhat ironic. Love had not been bountiful in her life – at least, not if it referred to love from men. Her marriage had been nothing special, and her dating afterwards had been non-existent. Granted, she had created herself a Tinder profile over a year ago, one night when she had drunk one too many glasses of wine at home on the sofa. But she hadn't even logged in to take a look. What she had heard about Tinder didn't exactly inspire confidence. There was also the risk that she would find the kids' father on it.

'Grandpa?' she called into the house without getting an answer.

As usual, the front door had been unlocked, but she knew from many years' experience that it was fruitless trying to lecture him. His faith in the inherent goodness of humanity was commendable – but potentially lethal. Only the other week she'd had an older man on her autopsy table, killed during a robbery at his home. Two young lads had tortured him and beaten him to death – all for the princely sum of five hundred and seventy kronor.

She passed through the kitchen and living room to the back door opening into the garden. She already knew where he was likely to be: in his beloved greenhouse.

She didn't shout when she emerged onto the small wooden deck. Instead, she stopped for a few minutes and observed him before he spotted her. How many hours had she spent here as a child? In the garden of the small red house in Enskede, on the edge of the forest. The greenhouse had been her birthday present to him on his sixtieth. It was his little slice of paradise.

Milda saw him moving back and forth within the glass walls. Watering a little here and there, touching the soil with his practised fingers, carefully pinching a few dead leaves off, talking to his plants as they flourished in his care. She knew what was there. Tomatoes, chillies, peppers and courgettes. He had even managed to cultivate watermelons. Nothing was impossible for Grandpa Mykolas.

Eventually he spotted her. His face lit up and he waved at her to come to him. She felt a smile spread across her entire face and she hurried up the small slope.

'Hi, Grandpa!'

She embraced him, taking in the scent of sun-ripened tomatoes, earth and love. She knew love didn't really have a scent. But if it had, then it would have smelled like Grandpa Mykolas.

'Look!' he said, with pride in his voice. 'Look how beautiful the courgette flowers are! I'm going to pick some to fry – I know you love that. And the rest will be absolutely splendid courgettes.'

He waved his hand around his small kingdom, and she listened as he told her about plant after plant and which stage of the growing process they were at. She loved it. She knew her older brother was counting down the days until Grandpa Mykolas passed away and left them the house in Enskede as their inheritance – to be promptly sold. Personally, she got a lump in her throat at the mere thought that Grandpa wouldn't always be here, pottering away in his greenhouse. She and her brother were very different.

'How's Adi?' Grandpa asked as if he could read her mind.

Adi was the Lithuanian for wolf. It was a fitting name for her brother.

'Oh, he's fine,' she lied.

Things were never fine when it came to Adi. He always had some deal on the go that he thought was going to make him rich. It was rarely all that legal. You might have thought that a year in prison for insurance fraud would have taught him a lesson. But apparently not. Adi was incorrigible. And as the eldest son and the apple of his mother and father's eye, he was also absolutely convinced of his own excellence.

'And Vera and Conrad?'

She could tell from Grandpa's eyes that there was no point lying about the kids. So she didn't reply.

'You know that Conrad can come and stay with me any time,' he said gravely. 'A change of scene might do him good. Especially now it's the summer holidays. What's more, there's not a drop of booze in this house. He can stay as long as he likes – I'll need help anyway with my crop when it matures.'

'Thanks, but he's in rehab. He has to stay there for the whole summer. Maybe afterwards.'

The wounded look in Grandpa's eyes made her bite her lip. She had chosen an anonymous facility for her son instead of turning to her family. That wasn't the done thing in Grandpa Mykolas's world.

'I think he'd like being here,' she said, putting her hand on his. 'But he needs to be up to it first.'

Grandpa beamed again.

'Yes. Come on,' he said. 'I'll put on some coffee.'

He walked ahead of her out of the greenhouse and with slight difficulty down the small wooden staircase which sloped towards the house. It pained her to see him moving so falteringly – he had always been a strong man, constantly in motion, constantly active. But there was nothing the matter with his head – his brain was razor-sharp and after a long life as a professor of biology he was exactly the person she needed to speak to.

'Well, much as I love it when you stop by, and there's no need to have any reason to visit, I can tell there's something up. What's weighing on your heart, little girl?'

She guiltily accepted a cup of freshly brewed coffee before passing over a bag she'd brought with her. She ought to come here more often. She thought so every time she saw him. But life always seemed to get in the way.

'I had a boy on the table a while ago,' she said. 'Brutally murdered. And I found this in his stomach.'

She passed over the Ziploc bag to Mykolas, who took it with a grim expression and sat down opposite her at the small kitchen table in front of the window.

'May I?'

She nodded.

He opened the bag, first smelling it and then taking out the contents. A ball of hair. It was some of the hair that had been in Robert's stomach. She had already labelled up the majority and sent it off to NFC for analysis, as per their procedures. But she knew they had a big backlog that was painfully slow – it would be at least another month before she got an answer. There was something about both this case and this boy that – unusually – made her want to find the answer faster than the Swedish forensic authorities were able to provide. Grandpa might be most passionate about his greenhouse in his sunset years, but during her career she had never met a sharper biologist. Or zoologist for that matter.

'I think I know what it is. But I need to look at it under the microscope to be sure. Wait here. Drink your coffee. I'll be back in a moment.'

Grandpa Mykolas got up and she noted that he grimaced with pain at the movement. Milda sipped her coffee while gazing out of the window. She loved Enskede. She had grown up in Bagarmossen, which was OK, but Enskede had an old-fashioned charm and grace that always felt homely and welcoming. Or perhaps it had nothing to do with the area and more to do with the fact that it was where Grandpa lived. Either way. The old rose bushes. The lilacs spreading their sweet scent all over the neighbourhood in the early summer. The children playing in the street the way that children used to play.

A stocky man walked by and she thought she recognized him as someone she had played with as a child, but she wasn't certain. By the time she had raised her hand in greeting he had already passed by.

'Well, there we have it!'

Grandpa returned with a satisfied expression and sat down on the chair opposite. Then the same grimace once again. Milda made a mental note to force the stubborn old man to go to the doctor soon.

'Just as I thought. Genus neovison – vison comes from the French name for the animal.'

He paused for effect. She knew better than to hurry him. This was Grandpa's moment in the limelight and he was enjoying every second of it. She had not the slightest intention of depriving him of that joy. She took another sip of coffee and looked at him expectantly.

'This animal comes originally from North America – it belongs to the chordata phylum and is a vertebrate. Class mammalia, obviously. It grows to a length of thirty to forty-five centimetres, excluding the tail, which grows to around thirteen to twenty-three centimetres. The male weighs between 1 and 1.5 kilos, while the female weighs around 0.75 kilos. Those that have been bred can weigh more than those in the wild.'

Milda nodded. She thought she had a pretty good idea which animal it was. But she let her grandpa keep talking. He was in his element and his eyes were glittering happily.

324

'This animal was previously placed in the same group as polecats, genus mustela, but genetic studies have indicated such great differences that it is now placed in a category of its own. This, my dear Milda, is hair from a mink!'

He triumphantly held up the clump of hair towards her. She nodded. She had already guessed as much.

'Is it possible to determine where precisely this mink hair may have originated? Is there a species native to some location in Sweden?'

'No, unfortunately not. There are two distinct types that we usually talk about: wild mink and bred mink that are kept on mink farms. Well, I'm sure you're familiar with all the controversies around conditions on mink farms. But there's no difference between the fur of wild and bred mink.'

'I didn't even think mink farms existed any longer, to be perfectly honest.'

Milda stood up and fetched the coffee pot from the kitchen counter to refill both their cups.

'Oh, they still exist. I don't know how many or where they are, but I'm sure that's the kind of thing you can look up in the internet.'

Milda smiled slightly. Grandpa Mykolas was no cheerleader for modern technology and refused to learn the expressions properly.

'Where are the wild ones found? In what sort of environment?' she asked, taking her seat again.

Outside, a few kids had started a game of bandy and their happy yells were clearly audible through the kitchen window, which was ajar.

'Mink like to stay close to water. Lakes, watercourses, wetlands. They live on fish, shrimp, frogs and other small animals.'

Milda nodded, mulling it over. Mink hair. In Robert's stomach. What could it mean? What was the significance? Oh well . . . it wasn't her job to find that out. She would hand over what she'd found and leave the others to do the rest.

'Thank you, that was a great help.' She smiled at Grandpa. 'So, what weird experiments do you have on the go in the greenhouse this year?'

Grandpa Mykolas's face lit up. He carefully returned the hair to the bag, sealed it, and perched his elbows on the edge of the table, steepling his fingertips together.

'Well! This year I thought I'd play around with hybrids a little and see whether you can combine two different variants of carrot. Chantenay with early Nantes seemed like it would produce a pleasant result. I also thought I'd try crossing two of my roses. I believe it may be possible to make something very beautiful by crossing Rugelda and Dream Sequence. That's the one also known as Astrid Lindgren. Rugelda, as I'm sure you know, is a rugosa hybrid and Dream Sequence is a floribunda. So I think that . . .'

Milda watched him as he happily talked about his hybrids. Yet again she reminded herself to visit him more often. And to drag him along to the GP in Dalen – by force if necessary.

85

Vincent carried the two side plates of princess cake over to the table where Sains Bergander was waiting, balancing them carefully. One of the slices of cake tipped over as he set them down. He considered righting it but didn't follow through. Instead, he went over to the coffee maker, which was on a table in the centre of the room.

'How do you take it?' he asked over his shoulder.

'Black as my soul,' Sains replied.

'Well yes, considering you build crucifixes as a hobby, that seems apt,' said Vincent, heading back to the table with two cups of coffee. 'Thanks for taking the time to see me again. And sorry to pester you.'

He hadn't called Mina yet. Hadn't dared. So when it had turned out Sains was in town he'd leapt at the chance to see him and focus on something other than the book.

'It's my pleasure,' said Sains. 'Sorry I was hard to get hold of – I had a big order to finish. But at least you didn't have to come up to Sundsvall again. I'm in town to help my brother with an illusion ahead of a TV appearance. We can't quite get the size of the flames right.'

Vincent shook his head. Magicians.

He and Sains were at Vetekatten – the large cafe and bakery in Stockholm city centre. As usual, it was packed with tourists, which made it easier to talk undisturbed. Every magician knew that the best place to hide a secret was in plain sight.

He stared at the visible layers in the tipped-over slice of cake. The sponge base. Vanilla cream. Raspberry jam. Cream. Marzipan. Five layers. For fuck's sake. And then there was icing sugar on the top.

He exhaled. The sugar made it six layers.

He recalled a lecture by the mathematician Eugenia Cheng, in which she used baking to explain category theory. She would no doubt have been able to transform the slice of cake into a mathematical theorem. Usually the thought would have amused him. Instead he was wondering what Robert had looked like in cross-section when he had been cut into three parts in the zigzag girl box. Layers of fat tissue and blood. Had it been reminiscent of princess cake? With his skin like marzipan? He pushed the cake away.

'I would just as happily have come to yours,' said Sains. 'Although this is obviously very nice.'

'No, this isn't really a subject to discuss at home,' said Vincent. 'We're better off like this. And I know you're in a rush, so I'll get straight to the point. Do you remember the illusion I showed you before? The sword box?'

'The one that was built strangely,' said Sains, nodding.

Sains took a fork, pressed it into his slice of cake and raised a substantial piece to his mouth. Layers of fat and blood. Vincent screwed up his eyes. Sains was clearly unaware of the press conference, despite it relating to his profession. The price of being a genius inventor was that Sains's links to the surrounding world weren't always the strongest.

'What you don't know,' Vincent continued, 'is that the box was used in a murder. And it gets worse. We've found another two victims murdered using what appear to be stage illusions.'

The piece of cake caught in Sains's throat and he began to cough violently. Vincent hurried to fetch him a glass of water. He drank from it gratefully, setting down the empty glass and wiping his mouth thoroughly with a napkin, as if buying time to think.

'What is it you're telling me?' he said. 'Murder? For real? And who is "we"?'

Vincent glanced around to make sure no one was looking at them following Sains's coughing attack and then he took the photographs out of the folder.

'I'm helping the police with an investigation,' he said. 'The details are secret, of course, although we've briefed the media about the case. It would appear we're dealing with a complete madman. I mean, take a look at these pictures.'

He moved their coffee cups and the glass to make space and spread the photos across the table. He probably shouldn't have enlarged them to A4 format. They were a little too visible to the other patrons. But the details needed to be clear. Sains put their pieces of cake on the adjacent table. He too had apparently lost his appetite.

'Here's the box with the swords,' said Vincent, pointing. 'These are the actual swords. I don't know whether I showed them to you before. And here are four pictures showing the blade and the box for—'

'The zigzag girl,' said Sains. 'Not hard to figure out what happened in that. Awful.'

'Just seeing people getting into those boxes gives me claustrophobia,' said Vincent. 'I can't begin to imagine how the boy they found inside it must have felt.'

Sains looked at him with a strange expression.

'I think the crushing sensation would have been the last thing he thought about when being shut in the box. But you said there were three illusions – what's the third?'

'Bullet catch.'

'Oh. Jesus Christ. Thank you for not bringing a photo of that.'

Sains looked at the photos, twisting and turning them. At first glance, the pictures might have depicted innocent stage props. But the boxes and blades, their mere existence, radiated evil. No one of sound mind would make something like that.

'What do you want me to say?' said Sains. 'I haven't got anything more to offer than you got last time.'

'Perhaps not. But back then I was focusing on whether anyone had ordered a box or drawings from you or anyone else. I didn't realize that the solution might be in the actual manufacture of the illusions. At the time we only had one box to go by, so all you could say then was that it was clumsily made. But now we have two. You did say that since it requires both great carpentry skills and a sound knowledge of magic, there are actually very few people who can build illusions.'

'Yes, there aren't many of us who have mastered both aspects,' said Sains, nodding thoughtfully.

'I may be wrong,' said Vincent. 'But I can imagine that everyone who builds something has their own personal style, that they leave their own mark on whatever they do. Or in this case, whatever they build. Even if they're following a drawing, they'll still "do their own thing". Is that right?'

'Their distinguishing mark.' Sains nodded. 'We refer to it as the person doing the building leaving their distinguishing mark.'

'OK. We've already ascertained that these boxes haven't been built by a pro. So perhaps they don't have a professional distinguishing mark like a logo. But there may still be one. The two illusions in the photos were built by the same person. Can you see anything they share in common? Perhaps a detail only visible to you, something that may offer a clue as to who we are looking for? As you said, there aren't many of you who are capable of this. Whose distinguishing mark appears in these boxes?'

A party of five passed their table – Dutch tourists, all wearing identical T-shirts with prints. Undoubtedly home-made with a slogan telling everyone that they were travelling around Europe. Vincent placed his hand over the pictures, but he wasn't quick enough. A young woman had caught sight of them and stopped.

'Oh my God!' she said in perfect English. 'Are you guys building magic tricks? Awesome!'

'Thank you,' said Sains, smiling. 'Not many people would have recognized it.'

What was he playing at? Vincent wanted the woman to leave, but here was Sains engaging her in conversation. It wouldn't surprise him if Sains offered her a slice of princess cake too. Before long they'd have the rest of the Dutch around the table in their identical tops.

'Well, magic is for nerds,' said the woman. 'Got to go.'

She ran to catch up with her group, calling to Sains over her shoulder. 'Us nerds need to stick together!'

Vincent crossed his arms and waited for the Dutch to leave.

'Are you done?' he said.

'Sorry about that. But it's a rarity to get praise from anyone under the age of fifty-five. By the way, are you going to eat your cake?'

Vincent shook his head. Sains retrieved both his own and Vincent's slices, and gobbled up what was left.

'Anyway,' he said between bites, 'you're right in that if these two boxes were built by someone I know, then I would see it. But I can't see anything like that.'

Sains chewed thoughtfully.

'Vincent, you're overlooking one thing,' he said, swallowing. 'Even if it's unusual for *one* person to have good skills in the realms of both illusions and carpentry, sufficiently unusual that we can all keep track of each other . . .'

Vincent understood what Sains was trying to get at. He wanted to slap his own forehead. How could he have been so stupid?

'. . . it's not in the slightest bit unusual for *two* people to each be good at one thing,' he said, finishing Sains's sentence for him. 'A magician can do illusions. A carpenter can build.'

Vincent put his hands to his face, wanting to shut out the world for a bit.

'There's two of them,' he said into the palms of his hands. 'I've been thinking inside far too small a box. There's not one murderer working alone. There are two people working together. Which explains why I've felt like there have been two personalities expressed in the murders. One a rational planner, the other emotionally violent. I've struggled to make it all add up to a homogenous profile of the murderer without success. Not surprisingly. There was never only one.'

He let his hands fall into his lap and looked at Sains, who was still staring at the photos.

'Vincent,' said Sains slowly, 'a single person can act crazy. Commit irrational deeds of madness that are incomprehensible to everyone else but which seem perfectly reasonable to a sick mind. But two? Two people have to coordinate. Divide up the tasks between them . . .'

Sains pushed the pictures together with his fingertips as if they might infect him if he touched them too much and then he carefully put them back in the folder.

'You're not hunting a single madman,' he said. 'You're hunting two monsters.'

'*Folie à deux*,' said Vincent slowly. 'A psychosis, a madness shared by two people. And I can't find them.'

He looked out through the window at the ordinary world where people were eating ice cream in the summer sun and didn't have to think about brutal murders and indecipherable codes.

'Because I wasn't smart enough. The next life they take will be my fault. One person's stupidity and two people's madness. *Folie à trois.*'

86

She breathed in the nasal spray as deeply as she could. Then she steeled herself for the next step. She dreaded each time that she was forced – with only her willpower driving her on – to press the needle into her own skin. Julia had been advised to visualize the goal. And she tried every time. She closed her eyes. Saw a real-life baby in front of her. Didn't matter whether it was a boy or girl. Fluffy baby hair. Fat thighs. Gurgling laughter that started a long way down its throat. She connected to her desire as hard as she could.

But it didn't help. She was still scared of the injections.

Torkel could help her at home, but he could hardly leave his job in the middle of the day to come and give her her injections. *Their* injections, as the nurse so cheerfully put it. Julia wondered how the hell it could be *their* injections when it was *her* skin the needle went through. But it was just one of a thousand absurd things tied to the process they had been undergoing for the last couple of years.

She summoned up her courage again and pinched the skin at her waist, searching for a good spot, then tried to hold the needle still – no mean feat when her hand wouldn't stop shaking.

A knock at the door made her jump and she almost jabbed herself by mistake. She placed the syringe and the nasal spray on the desk, where they'd be hidden behind a framed wedding photo of her and Torkel. Then she pulled down her shirt, tucked it into her waistband and went to open the door.

'Hello. I hope I'm not disturbing you?'

Milda Hjort was standing outside. Julia weighed up her options. She needed to take the injection very soon. But Milda wasn't usually long-winded. And she had no good reason to send her away. Plus it might be something important.

'No, not at all,' said Julia, stepping to one side.

She quickly glanced at her tidy desk. To her relief, the needle wasn't visible behind the picture frame.

'Take a seat.'

Julia gestured to her visitor's chair, as if there were other options available.

She could hear how professional her voice sounded. Matter-of-fact. Completely divorced from the longing for children, from broken dreams and memories of dead foetuses emerging from her body straight into a metal bowl. Unviable, that was the word they'd used.

Milda was looking at her searchingly and Julia realized that for a brief moment she had lost control of her facial expression. When she sat down in her desk chair that moment had passed. Her gaze once again sharp, her expression focused.

'What have you got for us?' she said, contemplating Milda with curiosity.

For Julia, the goal was always first and foremost to ensure that someone stayed alive. Even in murder cases she considered that to be her primary task: find the perpetrator and ensure that no one else would die. For Milda, however, it was all about communing with the deceased. She spent more of her time with the dead than with the living. Julia doubted whether she would be capable of such a thing, but Milda had made it her life's work. At the same time, she had enormous respect for Milda. The job needed doing. The dead could talk. She had seen that time after time in the cases she had worked on. The medical examiner was an important piece of the puzzle in every investigation.

'It's about the murder of Robert Berger. And by extension the murders of Tuva Bengtsson and Agnes Ceci. But Robert is the key to unlocking a vital piece of the jigsaw, I think. I hope.'

Milda fidgeted awkwardly in her chair.

'You have my full attention,' Julia said, leaning forward.

In doing so, she accidentally nudged the wedding photo, but quickly managed to put it back in its place.

Milda cleared her throat.

'I understand Robert had a tendency to put things in his mouth,' she said. 'Apparently he was forever eating things that weren't intended for consumption. And when I opened him up, I found a large quantity of hair in his stomach.'

'Unpleasant,' Julia said with a grimace.

333

She imagined the taste of hair in her mouth and could feel her stomach turning.

'Yes, but it could turn out to be fortunate from our point of view. It's not for me to draw conclusions, I just report what I find, but it's possible that the murderer has some kind of connection to a . . . mink farm.'

Julia stared at her.

'Mink farm? Do they even exist any longer?'

'Yes – I didn't think they did either. But there are actually a number of mink farms left in Sweden, even though animal rights organizations are fighting for their closure.'

Julia was quiet.

'I'm basing this on two things,' said Milda, sitting up straighter on her chair before continuing eagerly. 'Firstly, we found traces of ketamine in all the victims – as you know. Secondly, it was mink hair that Robert had in his stomach. It could obviously have come from wild animals, but I don't think it did. You see, one of the uses for ketamine is to anaesthetize minks. I would almost go as far as betting that Robert was murdered on a mink farm. And in that case, presumably so were the others.'

Julia leaned back to digest what Milda had said. The different parts of her brain were spinning, searching for connections, pathways, truths. But so far it was all too big – an incoherent mess. The thought about the mink farm still had no natural place to settle into.

'I'll take this up with the team,' she said, standing up.

This couldn't wait. Milda got up too. Then she seemed to hesitate.

'Are you managing with the injections by yourself?' she asked carefully.

'Sorry?' said Julia, stopping mid-movement.

'I heard you were undergoing . . . a process. Are you able to manage the injections yourself, or would you like some help? I could help you.'

A lump formed in Julia's throat. She hated knowing that people knew and were talking. But there were no secrets at police headquarters; she ought to know that by this stage. She slowly reached for the syringe behind the photo frame. She handed it to Milda and pulled her shirt out of her trousers. Relief washed over her.

It didn't even hurt when Milda gave her the injection.

87

Vincent was sitting in front of the TV, remote control in hand. He knew he was already a dinosaur at the age of forty-seven. No one watched regular television these days. But he liked that the programmes were only shown at a certain time. If you didn't see it when it was broadcast, then you missed it.

Of course, most things were available to stream so it was impossible to miss anything. But therein lay the problem. He was fully aware that he was a victim of the psychological principle of availability – anything that was unavailable became more exciting and more attractive. But the modern world had shown him that the principle also worked in the opposite direction. When everything was available, nothing was interesting. And Vincent didn't have time to be dealing with things that weren't interesting.

He noticed that it was unusually quiet in the house. Benjamin's voice was faintly audible through the door, which meant that he was online. The fact that Benjamin actually had friends, albeit invisible ones, was still surprising. Aston was asleep – for once satisfied. Rebecka was out somewhere, and Maria . . . He didn't actually know what Maria was doing. He guessed she was lying in bed reading a book filled with insights about how to live a meaningful life. Maria loved books like that. She absolutely devoured them. Some people read cookbooks without cooking a single recipe. Others read fitness books without ever budging an inch. In Maria's case it was self-help books. She never applied any of the advice, preferring to move on to a new book. And then blame the book when life remained the same.

OK, perhaps that was a bit mean. But he found the library on his wife's nightstand a bit much, with every title promising to reveal *the secret of* or *the code for* something. He snorted. The people who wrote those books didn't know anything about codes or about real life.

A sound disturbed his thoughts. Something outside the living room window. He looked up and caught a glimpse of someone outside the window. Or had he? The figure had vanished almost immediately, so he couldn't be sure. It was a light evening but the trees at the corner of the house cast a shadow onto the grass outside the window. The solar-powered lights he had put up along the gravel path to the door were insufficient to light the whole front garden. He turned off the TV, went over to the window and looked out.

Nothing.

One of the bushes at the edge of the grass was moving, as if someone or something had passed by on their way into the woods. Probably a deer. He'd learned since moving out to the country that wild animals were unafraid of humans. He wondered how long it had been standing there, observing him through the window. The deer had most likely been wondering what he was doing there in the middle of her forest.

He noted two spots of grease at eye level on the window and tried to rub them off with his sleeve, but the spots were on the outside. They were the shape of two half-moons. He formed his hands into binoculars and put them against the marks. His hands fitted into the shapes perfectly. As if he were going to look out through them. Or in, he realized. Someone had stood in the same position on the other side. Someone had been standing there and looking at him through the window. And it definitely hadn't been a deer.

There was a knock on the door and the sudden loud noise almost made him let out a yell. Another knock. He went over and opened it cautiously, unsure what to expect.

Mina was standing outside.

'Oh, hello,' he said, unable to hide the surprise in his voice. 'So you're the one who's been spying on me?'

'Spying?' she said. 'No, I didn't want to ring the doorbell in case Aston was asleep.'

'No, I mean there was someone here . . .'

He began pointing towards the woods but then stopped himself when he saw Mina's expression.

'Has something happened?' he said.

He came out onto the step and shut the door behind him.

'No, I just thought . . .' began Mina, and then her voice faded away, as if she hadn't worked out what to say next. 'I thought we could do something.'

He didn't know what to say. He looked at the woman in front of

336

him. Mina might be peculiar, but at least she wasn't putting on an act, as she did for most other people. And he appreciated that. It must have taken a massive dose of courage to come to his house. To risk a no. Especially given what she'd told him in the taxi. How could he ever have believed that she could have sent the book, given who she was and what she was struggling with? He wanted to kick himself. How insensitive could a person be? A sound made him quickly glance through the crack in the door behind him. If Maria spotted Mina, all hell would break loose.

'I thought I could say hi to your family,' said Mina. 'Now that we're working together so much.'

'That's not a good idea,' he said. 'Not this evening.'

Mina took a step backwards, away from him. He could no longer see her face clearly, but the slumped shoulders told him everything he needed to know. He had badly hurt her. She had just received the no she had been afraid of.

'What I meant was, it's a good idea for us to do something,' he hurried to add. 'A great idea. But this isn't the moment to meet my family. Maria is a bit off balance today and even on a normal day she gets very jealous. If she saw you here like this when she isn't at ease with herself—'

'What do you mean, "like this"?' said Mina. 'Is there something wrong?'

Vincent looked at Mina. No, there was definitely nothing wrong. Her black hair in its taut ponytail together with her white polo neck accentuated both her features and her personality. The sum total was more than the parts in a way that took his breath away. He hoped that wasn't too obvious and he did everything he could to avoid looking at her red mouth when she spoke. What was more, he was clearly in greater need of company than he realized, given that he had just hallu-cinated someone spying on him. It had obviously been a deer.

'Do you think Maria has any reason to be jealous?' Mina continued.

There was a movement at the corner of her mouth, the hint of a smile. But he wasn't certain. It could be a shadow.

'Jealous of you?' he said, realizing that he was blushing. 'Well, she—'

'Obviously not of me,' she interrupted. 'We've never met. I meant whether she had any reason to be jealous in general. Do you usually have affairs with other women?'

And there she was – the Mina that had awakened his curiosity right on the first evening in Gävle. The almost clumsy honesty without the social fingertip sensitivity that society expected but which could be so challenging. Especially if, like him, you didn't have the social finesse that helped to oil the wheels naturally programmed into you. Mina made him feel – possibly for the first time – as if he was himself. Without needing to play a role because that was what others wanted from him. He looked at her hands. They didn't look dry. She must have moisturized them. A faint scent of vanilla reached his nostrils.

'No affairs,' he said. 'Well, I had an affair once while I was married. But it was with her. With Maria. And then I got divorced and married her instead.'

Mina nodded slowly, as if she understood.

'Let's go,' he said, closing the door behind him. 'Maria is the best mother in the world – you should see her and Aston. But generally, communication in this home can be rather . . . challenging. I'll message her and let her know you called me in. It's more or less true.'

'Although you have to promise we won't talk about work – I've thought about nothing else for months,' she said, linking her arm through his. 'Normal people are on holiday right now. Tonight let's take a break.'

The arm was stiff and the link was uncomfortable. Clearly this was an unusual gesture for her. But he appreciated the effort.

'Deal. Let's stick to innocent small talk, like my supposed infidelities and my jealous wife.'

They walked down the gravel path across the lawn in front of the house and emerged onto the winding road. It was a light evening and the heat of summer lingered in the air.

He stopped by the letterbox. Something was missing. Ahead of one of his previous shows, Umberto had had small magnetic metal signs made up with the words 'Mind-reading prohibited' as part of an advertising campaign. Vincent had attached one of them to the letterbox when he had moved there. But now the sign was gone. It was probably lying in the grass below somewhere. He had difficulty believing that someone might have taken it – he was the only one who still found the sign funny. But the letterbox seemed dull without it.

'It's very quiet here in Tyresö,' said Mina. 'It's like being in the countryside. I had to use my satnav to avoid getting lost. It feels like civilization ended miles back.'

Vincent laughed.

'There's no point concealing it, you *are* in the countryside. But I'm happy. We're happy, I mean. When I'm on tour I meet so many people. Afterwards, it feels great to come back here, where it's two hundred metres to the next neighbour. Well, you've met him – Ove with his digger. Aston has also got plenty of outdoor space to mess around in, and the bus to the kids' school stops just up the road. But enough of that – what about you? Are you happy in your flat in Årsta?'

He realized how little he knew about Mina, despite having worked together for months. And how much he wanted to know. What was that thought about the psychological principle of availability? 'Anything that is unavailable becomes more exciting and more attractive.' Enough already! He wasn't like that. Of course, Mina was an incredibly fascinating person and also very attractive. He was glad she had entered his life. But they had an adult, professional working relationship. Which was perhaps on the way to becoming a friendship. And that was more than enough.

Maria was obviously jealous anyway. It was inescapable. But then again, she was jealous even when he spoke to Liv on the checkout at the supermarket. Fifty-five-year-old Liv, married to Corinne, who worked on the dairy counter. It made no difference. He wished that Maria had some self-awareness. That at least *one* of those books could help her. Given that he had obviously failed so completely.

'Yes, I'm very happy,' said Mina, and it took him a second to remember what he had asked.

'I've actually got a work-related question,' he said hesitantly. 'But I promise it's the only one. You know when we met in Gävle, you said someone had advised you to contact me. Who was it?'

Mina stopped mid-step and turned towards him.

'Why do you want to know that?' she said.

'I promise I'll explain why I'm asking. But not now. It may be important though.'

She continued to look at him for a long time. She seemed to be weighing up what to say.

'I . . . went with a friend to Alcoholics Anonymous,' she said. 'As a support.'

It wasn't what he had been expecting. But any information he could gather was important. He merely nodded in reply.

'I met her there. She's called Anna. She was the one who tipped me off about you. All I know about her – except that she knows about you – is that she has a dolphin tattoo on her calf. And a wolf on her arm, and a few other tattoos. If you want to get hold of her, you'll have to loiter outside the venue on Kungsholmen like a stalker. I can give you the address.'

339

She maintained eye contact for a few more seconds, as if waiting to hear what he was going to say.

'Anna,' he said, smiling. 'Dolphin. Kungsholmen. Thanks. No more work now. I give you my word of honour.'

She raised an index finger in the air and stuck the other hand into her pocket. She brought out her phone. He hadn't even heard it start vibrating.

'It's Julia,' she said, showing him the display. 'I might as well take this – it feels like work is going to haunt us otherwise. Hi, Julia!'

Mina quickly fell silent and seemed to be listening attentively.

'Mink farms? For real?' Mina said after a while. 'OK, thanks for the info.'

Mina ended the call and put the phone back in her pocket, but he saw that she first switched off the vibration and then put it on silent.

'Shouldn't we work anyway?' he said, once Mina had hung up. 'That sounded important.'

Mina shook her head.

'I'm as frustrated and worried as you are about when the next murder will be,' she said. 'But we won't catch a murderer tonight. Milda, the medical examiner, found a connection between the murders and mink farms. And I saw your email on the way over about the murders probably being the work of two people rather than a single killer.'

'Yes. It doesn't change the individual psychological aspects,' Vincent said. 'But it makes them more understandable. But if there are two people then they have an unpleasantly well-developed ability to rationally plan aggressive acts over a long period of time. Perhaps a very long time.'

Mina nodded.

'But that doesn't bring us any closer to finding them,' she said. 'At least not tonight at any rate.'

He nodded and she checked her wristwatch. He appreciated the fact that she had one. It was far too common simply to use a mobile phone as a timepiece these days. It was partly that wristwatches were more elegant, and partly that he struggled with the lack of self-control that was displayed when people automatically ended up stuck on social media each time they needed to check the time.

'It's too late to send anyone out to check on mink farms this evening,' she said. 'There won't be anyone there. We'll do that tomorrow morning. Ruben can go. Tonight you and I can try and think about something else for once.'

340

'Julia's slept with Ruben, right?' he said.

'Shush, no one knows anything about that,' she said. 'Apart from everyone at police headquarters who was on the Christmas cruise, obviously. But that was like five years ago. Longer. Why do you ask?'

'Ruben intrigues me. That aura of being more God's gift to women than Björn Ranelid. There's something underneath it.'

Mina grimaced.

'You'll have to let that one go,' she said. 'Where are we heading, by the way?'

'Don't know, but it's nice out,' he said, avoiding a puddle. 'What did you have in mind?'

'I don't know either,' she said. 'I didn't even know whether you wanted to see me. But preferably away from the forest. Now that I've seen it.'

He suspected that Mina was doing her very best not to think about all the creepy crawlies that might be lurking beneath the trees and leaves. Probably best not to mention the anthill they had just passed.

'Well, if we're not going to work then maybe we . . . we could go to the cinema?' he said, blurting out the first thing that came into his head.

She laughed and looked up at him with a wry smile. Definitely a smile this time.

'The cinema? Like you do on a date?'

He blushed again. Bloody hell. He hadn't thought it through that far.

'No, of course not. Sorry. What do you like doing then?'

'I like working out,' she said. 'And playing pool. I'm very good at pool. But I'd happily go to the cinema with you. It's a long time since I saw a movie.'

She nudged him in the side with her elbow.

'If Maria is going to be horrified, we might as well give her a reason.'

They took Mina's car to the multiplex at Söderhallarna. He didn't say much in the car; it was hard to talk when he was sitting beside her and couldn't see her facial expression. This made for a quiet journey. When he paid using the parking app, he forced himself not to adjust the time until it was even instead of odd. He didn't want to do anything that might seem too strange.

Inside the cinema, they bought tickets for a film that neither of them had heard of and headed into the foyer. Behind the counters there were glass cabinets filled with big cardboard tubs of popcorn. He went over to the nearest till but stopped himself. Should he buy soft drinks and snacks? Or shouldn't he? Was that when it became a date? He wasn't sure about the rules.

He turned to ask Mina and discovered that she was no longer beside him. She had stopped a few metres behind. Mina was standing there as if frozen to the floor, her gaze fixed on the tubs of popcorn. Her face was pale. Then her eyes flickered to the side, towards the drinks machines and the straws lying there in a messy heap. The dilated pupils and the tense jaw gave away the panic bubbling within her.

He was an idiot.

Any member of staff, and countless patrons, could have touched the popcorn in the open tubs. Hundreds of people with unwashed hands had rooted through those straws. Not to mention all the ones who had already sat in the same seats they were going to occupy, or the spilled drinks that would make the soles of their shoes sticky inside the auditorium. How could he have thought she would like this?

'Mina,' he said, touching her elbow gently. 'Let's go.'

She reacted with a shudder to being touched but continued staring at the popcorn cabinets.

'But we've paid for the film,' she said.

She began rubbing her hands together as if she were washing them. They had got dry and chapped again.

'We can't leave,' she said, 'when we've paid.'

'Of course we can. We've paid to do what we want. Just because you've chosen your food doesn't mean you actually have to eat it. You always have a choice. All parents are wrong.'

Gently grasping Mina's elbow, he steered her out of the cinema. She began to breathe more easily as soon as they turned their backs on the foyer. They emerged into the labyrinth of restaurants adjacent to the cinema in Söderhallarna.

'Sit down here,' he said, pointing to the nearest cafe. 'Order something to drink. You need it. I'll be with you in a second.'

Without waiting for a reply, he ran out of Söderhallarna and into the supermarket next door, cursing his lack of consideration.

Three minutes later he was back. Mina was sitting at a table at the very back. There was a beer in his place. A Coke Zero in hers. It looked untouched.

'Here,' he said, passing across the sealed pack of straws he had just bought. 'I'm guessing you don't have any of your own with you today.'

Mina looked like she was about to burst into tears.

'Sorry,' she began. 'I don't want you to think I'm crazy. I'm trying, but it's just so . . .'

If she began crying he didn't know what he would do. There were five

342

straws in the pack. There had been seven packs on the rack. Thirty-five in total. Mina was probably no more than thirty-three years old. The difference between thirty-five and thirty-three was two. One straw for each of them. That made two. He really didn't want her to start crying.

'I see it like this,' he said. 'You're the last person in the world who is going to catch the flu. That can't be a bad thing.'

Mina smiled gratefully, opened the pack of straws and then inserted one into her fizzy drink. She looked at him gratefully and then inserted the other straw into his beer.

It wasn't excessively late when Vincent got home, but the family were already asleep. Aston usually fell asleep from exhaustion around eight o'clock. Maria liked to go to bed no later than half past nine, and the teenagers crashed an hour or so later. Personally, his most creative spell was from ten at night until two in the morning, so coming home at midnight like this was optimal. There were still two hours left when he would be sharp and effective.

But not tonight. His head was still full of thoughts about Mina and everything they had talked about. He brushed his teeth and crept into the bedroom, taking care to avoid waking Maria. If she woke up she would demand to know why he had come home in the middle of the night in her most accusatory voice and he didn't have the strength to defend himself.

He undressed without turning on any lights. Socks and underwear folded up on the floor: dirty laundry. Clothes that were still clean went on top of the bureau. Once his eyes had begun to adjust to the darkness he saw a shadow on Maria's nightstand. Her stack of books. Just like his wife, he didn't know much about how life worked. And just like his wife, he wasn't going to learn it from books. The difference was, he knew that.

But he had started learning.

Mina had started teaching him.

88

Jane was sitting on a chair in Ylva's hallway. On the bureau beside her was the home telephone. She had her hand on the grey receiver but hadn't lifted it from the cradle. To call home or not to call home? That was the question. She had been afraid that Mum would call every single day while she was staying with her friend, or even several times a day, to ask how she was doing and when she would be coming home. She had told Ylva's parents that her mother could be a little bit manic and she had apologized in advance for what she thought was going to happen.

But Mum had handled herself surprisingly well. She had only called on the first day, and then just to check that Jane had arrived and that everything was OK. She hadn't been in touch since, despite the fact that it must have been difficult for her to resist calling. But that was a good thing. Perhaps Mum had discovered that she was able to get by. Just as Jane was able to think backwards logically when reverse-engineering her brother's tricks, so perhaps her mother had realized that it wasn't Jane who had been keeping her going in spite of everything. Maybe moving out wouldn't pose any problems after all.

Nevertheless, she was sitting there holding the receiver while her hand grew sweatier and sweatier against the grey plastic. Because something felt wrong. Very wrong. She couldn't explain it – it wasn't a rational feeling. She was probably being silly, letting her guilty conscience spook her. Really, she ought to have been happy rather than concerned about the fact that Mum wasn't following her usual pattern.

And yet . . . the feeling told her that something wasn't as it should be. Something back home. She threaded the telephone cable between her fingers. If she called and expressed her anxiety then Mum would ask her to come straight home. If she didn't call, the knot in her stomach would keep bothering her.

She shifted the receiver into her other hand, wiped her sweaty palms on her trousers and dialled the number for home. It took a few seconds of spluttering and crackling in her ear before she was connected. Once it finally started ringing, the sound was as faint and fragile as if she had been placing a call to the other side of the world. After five rings someone picked up.

'Boman. Hello?'

'Hi, little brother! It's Jane!'

Silence. She knew her little brother didn't like talking on the phone. It would be up to her to guide the conversation.

'How are you both doing?' she said.

'Good. Eating breakfast.'

She smiled to herself. Everything was fine. The knot in her stomach would have to be kicked into touch.

'Let me guess,' she said. 'Mum's toasted sandwiches, cut into triangles?'

'Yes, without crusts. With sliced egg. You know that . . .'

'Routines are important.'

'. . . routines are important.'

They laughed at the same time.

'Can I talk to Mum?' she said. 'If she's done with your sarnies?'

'No, she can't talk right now.'

'Is it one . . . of those days?' she said, lowering her voice. 'Are you doing OK?'

'No, it's just that she's not in here. I'm OK.'

So Mum was at least well enough to make breakfast. Well then. The worry had been nothing more than her guilty conscience. And as long as she didn't talk to anyone other than her brother, her mother couldn't ask her to come home again.

'Weren't you building some secret magic trick before I left?' she said. 'Mum said that maybe she was going to be involved in it somehow. Are you going to show it to me when I get home?'

There was silence on the other end of the line. She pressed the receiver to her ear to hear whether he was still there. The faint sound of breathing was audible. He was reluctant to discuss his secrets. That meant there was no magic left, as he always said. But there was no need for him to be so damn touchy.

345

'Don't worry,' she said. 'Mum didn't give anything away.'

'I don't want to talk any more now. I want to eat. The toasted sandwiches are getting cold.'

'OK, little brother. See you in a week. My love to Mum.'

He hung up before she had finished. She untangled her fingers from the cable and put the receiver down. While they had been talking, she had felt as if everything was good. But now the worry returned. Her little brother had sounded weird towards the end. She ought to go home – to check that everything was OK.

'Stop it, Jane,' she said out loud to herself, with a shake of her head.

Her mother was the most manipulative person she had ever met. Mum was an expert at getting her claws right into people, until they no longer had any strength left. Those claws were apparently far deeper into Jane than she had realized. Without even doing anything, Mum had almost got her to go home. But not this time. This time Jane meant to win.

She picked up her swimming bag from the day before and went outside into the back garden. Ylva was lying on a blanket on the grass, reading a book.

'Ylva,' she said. 'How about we head over to the pool?'

'You're sooo behind,' said Ylva, getting up from the blanket.

She was already wearing her bikini.

'Last one there has to jump off the seven-metre board!' Jane yelled, accelerating towards the bicycles.

She had no intention of going home until she wanted to.

89

For perhaps the hundredth time, Ruben reached for the gear stick, only to discover that it wasn't there. And for the hundredth time he regretted not taking his own Chevrolet Camaro. An automatic? What a load of crap! He wasn't disabled or anything. But mink farms sounded like they involved mud, industrial dirt and balls of animal hair all over the place. That wasn't something he intended to do to Ellinor – as he called his car. Whenever anyone asked about the name he would reference an old action movie starring Nicolas Cage. The real reason was Ruben's own business.

Ellinor had just been in for a service and she was gleaming as if she were brand new under the tarpaulin in the underground car park. The neighbours that he shared the car park with couldn't resist teasing him about the tarpaulin, but they could hardly talk given the filthy cars they owned. He had no intention of allowing particles of grease in the enclosed air of the underground car park to get anywhere near her white paintwork.

So he'd had to take a fleet car today. It also helped to have POLICE on the car's livery when he turned up somewhere uninvited. He was quick to exploit the nervousness aroused by the car. But despite this, the day had been a complete waste of time. Just as he had suspected it might. He'd been to three mink farms so far and he was going to do a fourth before calling it a day.

At this stage, the idea was just to take a look around. To get a feeling for whether mink farms really were a place where you could hold people captive, and possibly even murder them, without being discovered. But the places he had visited hadn't had a square inch to spare. There had been minks everywhere. Thousands of them, squashed into automated systems that allowed one person to look after a thousand minks. There had barely been space for the animals themselves, let alone a discreet but murderous carpenter's workshop.

The final farm of the day was on the island of Lidön in the Norrtälje archipelago, which meant he had to take a ferry out to the island. As soon as he was aboard the boat, he switched off the engine and got out of the car. The wind caught his jacket and hair. He let it. The fresh air was badly needed. The smell on those farms had been, frankly, fucking awful. He knew that many people were agitated about the way the animals were treated – the mink industry was not a popular business among those who considered themselves informed. In a way he understood their point of view – what he had seen over the course of the day hadn't exactly filled him with joy.

At the same time, if you wanted to complain about someone having a bad time of it, then there were quite a lot of people who needed help before you started caring about animals. If you wanted to help, then you had to pick how. You could become a cop and make a difference. Or you could be a leftist and demonstrate.

After fifteen minutes the ferry reached its destination and as he got back in the car the phone rang.

'Ruben Höök,' he said, answering on the car's hands-free system.

'Hi, Ruben, it's Vincent. How are you getting on? I heard you were out following up a lead – something about a connection to mink farms?'

Vincent? Not exactly at the top of his list of likely callers. Mina must have blabbed. She seemed to think her wizard was doing a better job than the cops. She probably just wanted to get some. Wrapped in clingfilm. He laughed to himself at the image that popped up in his head.

'If I'm honest this is a complete waste of time,' he said, starting the engine. 'I'm on the way to the last place now. I hope we don't go out on field trips based on all the other contents of Robert's stomach. We'll have a lot of McDonald's to check out if we do.'

The car shuddered as the ferry touched the quayside.

'Why are you calling?' he said, as the barrier rose to allow him to drive ashore.

'I wanted to speak to you about something without anyone else on the team listening in.'

There were only two other cars on the ferry. He overtook them while checking the map on his phone. The mink farm wasn't far from the ferry. He really wanted this day to end.

'We don't know each other,' Vincent continued. 'But I've observed

348

you. Listened to how you talk. Your attitude towards women. How long ago did she leave you?'

Ruben whistled and pulled over onto the verge. The two cars he had just passed overtook him, honking in annoyance. Almost before he had stopped he'd begun digging in his pocket for his Airpods. This was too personal for someone to accidentally overhear. Admittedly it was only him in the car, but still . . .

'What kind of bloody question is that?' he said once he'd inserted the wireless headphones. 'Firstly, I've no idea what you're on about and secondly it's way too personal. Who do you think you are?'

'I don't mean to pry,' said Vincent. 'But I recognize a broken heart when I see one. I'm saying this entirely objectively.'

He didn't know what to say. He didn't want to admit it – not to himself or to anyone else. But that goddamn mentalist was right, despite his total lack of social finesse. Ruben had no desire to think about it. Not now. Not later. Women weren't to be trusted and that was that.

'Sorry for being so direct,' said Vincent, in a tone that was fortunately free of doughy sympathy. 'But I don't think you want anyone to talk to you in any other way. And I'd rather be wrong and castigated as an insensitive idiot than see you carry on feeling this bad. Assuming that I'm right and that you do.'

'Sounds like you want to marry me,' Ruben snorted, starting the car again. 'Why do you care about how I feel? Surely no need for you to give a shit?'

He'd spotted the mink farm a little way off. There was probably a track to it from the road he was on now that would lead him to a car park in front of the main building. He'd be there in under a minute.

'I don't. Or rather, I . . .'

'So you're going to be my therapist then?' he interrupted.

'Not at all,' said Vincent. 'I don't even want to know whether I'm right or not. But, Ruben . . . when you're good, you're good. That much I've grasped from your colleagues. This other thing, it seems to disturb you. Your abilities suffer.'

Ruben parked the police car and got out. At the other farms he had been able to hear the unmistakable sound of operations in full swing from the car park. Feeding systems, air conditioning, conveyor belts for transportation. Not to mention the actual animals themselves. All of that made noise. Here it was completely silent. He guessed the farm was mothballed. It was happening to more and more of them, so far as he understood. His guess also correlated with how abandoned the building looked. He could make out open water tens of metres behind the farm. It would have been almost peaceful, had it not been for the smell. It was even worse than at the other places. If there weren't animals here, then there had been until recently. Of the places he had visited so far, this was the first that might at least theoretically fulfil the requirements of a secluded murder scene.

'But above all, your behaviour has a negative effect on your colleagues' abilities too,' Vincent continued, interrupting his train of thought. 'I'm going to say what I'm about to say without any judgement. But your comments and your glances . . . the others react to them. You might think it's a funny line to take, and what do I know? Maybe it is. But I see how it sets the others off-kilter. It makes them make mistakes. I pass no judgement. It's just an objective observation.'

An objective observation? Who the hell talked like that?

'Do you mean Mina?' Ruben said.

A bearded man of retirement age emerged from what appeared to be a residence beside the actual farm. Good God, did the bloke live there? Practically on the mink farm? He could only hope the man had lost his sense of smell long ago.

'As I said, it's not my business,' said Vincent. 'But I think it's unfortunate if you as a team aren't at the top of your game, given the stage of the investigation you're at.'

At least he hadn't included himself and said 'given the stage of the investigation *we're* at'. That was something. There was white wooden garden furniture on the grass next to the house that the man was heading towards. Ruben could see from where he was standing that the paint was flaking off the furniture. A woman was sitting on one of the chairs. The man caught sight of Ruben and changed tack, heading towards him instead.

'Can I help you?' said the man, once he reached the police car.

Ruben pointed at his headphones to show the man he was in the middle of a call.

'What's more, Ruben, I'd personally much prefer to see you in a better place,' Vincent concluded.

'Vincent, just a second,' he said, before turning to the man. 'Is this your farm?'

'Mine and my wife's.'

The man pointed towards the woman.

'Or it was, at any rate. There's not much of it left now, I'm afraid. Activists broke in and "liberated" the minks. We never managed to

350

recapture them. We had to lay off Göran and Martin – our employees, that is – and shut down operations. There's still an unusually high density of minks in the woods on this island and the ones nearby. Minks are very good swimmers, see,' said the man, laughing. 'We reported it, but nothing happened. Are you here about that? It's high time the police dealt with it. I'd really like to see those activists pay at some point.'

Ruben nodded.

'Have you had any other uninvited guests here?' he asked. 'Apart from the activists?'

'Out here?' the man laughed, opening his eyes wide. 'This is a small island. The ferry you took is the only way in, unless you have your own boat, of course. We would have heard if there were someone else here. So no, no wild parties, or whatever it was you had in mind.'

The man chuckled.

'Without minks we're no longer of interest to the activists,' he continued. 'No one comes to the island unless they have business here. We're considering selling up and moving to Herrljunga. Family, y'know.'

Ruben acknowledged him and took notes. Yet another dead end. The most exciting thing to happen on this island was the paint slowly peeling from the facade of the house. But they really ought to do something about the smell.

'If you do think of anyone who has been here, then please call me,' he said, handing the man his card.

The man nodded and took the business card. Then he turned around and headed towards the garden furniture and his wife. She waved to Ruben.

He got back into the car and reactivated his headphones. He waved to the elderly couple, pulled out of the small car park and headed towards the road.

'Vincent, I'm back,' he said into his headphones. 'What exactly is it you're trying to say?'

It surprised him that he couldn't hear any irritation in his own voice. Usually, rubbish about feelings, and people trying to dig into his private life were the worst thing he could think of. But that mentalist was competent, he had to give him that. Something in Ruben wanted nothing more than to continue talking to him.

'I was starting to think you'd hung up,' said Vincent. 'Listen, I'm going to text you a phone number. It's for someone who is good to talk to about stuff like this. One of the best, as it happens. Contact her. Or

351

don't. I won't find out what you choose to do, and I don't want to know either. But you should understand that you're appreciated and liked by your colleagues. They care about you. When you're not acting like an idiot.'

Ruben was quiet as he drove back down to the ferry. Vincent's soft voice reached a place within him. He wanted to explain. He. Wanted. To. Explain.

'It's been almost eleven years,' he said. 'She was called Ellinor. It was the last time I trusted someone. Not that it has anything to do with you.'

He didn't mean that last bit. But regular Ruben was floundering inside him, protesting at this chat that went against his entire being. Although at the same time, he was unable to go any further than this. Something would break. Something he had spent a decade protecting himself from.

He ended the call and drove onto the ferry. His head was full of thoughts triggered by Vincent – of what had once been. Thoughts that he rarely if ever dared to think, which were now overwhelming him in a way that was impossible to stop. Ellinor. Ell-i-nor. She had been his anchor, his rock and his safety. She had been perfect. But he had been young and hadn't understood. So he'd carelessly lost the beauty he had. There it was. The truth he had tried to fuck away for ten years. Because after Ellinor there had been a string of pearls, Isabella and Jannika and Melissa. After Sanna, his contempt for women had been complete. And quite rightly so. If his experience had taught him anything, it was that women only wanted one thing – whatever his bank account had to offer. Which as it happened was embarrassingly low as an aim, given what he made as a police officer. But if that was what they wanted, then they couldn't fucking complain when he was done with them either. And he had gradually learned that women liked the new, boorish Ruben. It turned them on. No one asked why he was the way he was, so long as he was fun, fresh, paid the bill and fucked them better than their actual husbands. No one had wanted to know what was behind it.

Ellinor.

Until Vincent Walder had showed up. The bastard. Ruben adjusted the rear-view mirror and studied himself in it for a second. To his surprise, he discovered he was smiling. Just a little, but it was quite clearly a smile. A strange relief. There was a ping on his phone. He realized what it was. He decided to hold onto Vincent's text for a while before he deleted it.

90

Mina removed her white cotton gloves, threw them in the bin and took a new pair out of the box. After sitting in front of the computer at work for a whole day without changing gloves she couldn't bear to think about the hordes of bacteria that had now landed amidst the other rubbish. She hadn't emptied the bin since her morning coffee. More than anything, she wanted to set it alight. She pictured in her mind's eye the flames sterilizing everything within it. But that would set off the fire alarm. She pulled on the new gloves and leaned her head on her hands before realizing that the direct contact with her brow meant the gloves were unusable. She threw them on top of the old ones and got out another pair.

Then she stood up and got out a bottle of cleaning spray. It had been a whole week since she had last cleaned the walls of the room – it was high time. What was more, the act helped her to focus. But the smell of the cleaning fluid suddenly made her think of Grandma Ellen. Her safe place, her rock. The small one-bed flat by Mariatorget had always been freshly cleaned, and the smell of liquid soap had been mixed with the scent of freshly baked sponge cake just brought out of the oven. Every day after school, Mina had gone there instead of going home to the empty house. There, in Grandma's embrace, was where she had grown up. She sometimes reflected that it had been when she had been fifteen and Grandma Ellen had died unexpectedly from a stroke that the gradual descent into loneliness had begun. She hadn't really felt an affinity with any other person since then. Not even with the man Mina had lived with. Not until now. With Vincent. She looked at the spray in her hand, sighed and put it back in the drawer.

Outside the window it was high summer and the sun was shining directly in, making it almost insufferably warm in the room. But she refused to open the window. She knew the air would bring in not just coolness but also pollen, pollution, asphalt particles, cigarette smoke and all manner of dirt created down on the street. She would have preferred to be wearing a hazmat suit, but that probably wouldn't have been appreciated. She would have to deal with the sweat instead. Clothes could be washed, knickers and socks could be thrown away.

She hadn't got anywhere. Three victims. Three people killed by the same person. She couldn't believe they had been chosen at random. They were too different for that. There *had* to be a common denominator. But since Robert there had been nothing. No new murder, no confession, nothing. It couldn't be over – she knew that it wasn't. The countdown wasn't over yet.

Mina spun a half revolution on her chair so that she was looking at the wall where she had pinned up photos of Agnes, Tuva and Robert as well as the murder weapons. The illusions. The boxes. There was also a photo of Daniel and a newspaper clipping about Agnes's father, Jesper. He had denied any involvement in Daniel's murder. Granted, they had two suspects in custody, identified by witnesses at the scene. Previously known to the police, so it hadn't taken any great effort to find the culprits. The men in custody insisted they had acted on their own. She would never find out what was true or not in relation to Jesper Ceci's possible involvement. However, she had difficulty imagining that Sweden's Future had anything to do with the other murders. Admittedly, Tuva was Jewish and Robert had learning difficulties. There wasn't room for either of them in the world that Sweden's Future wanted to build. But she had a hard time believing that a political party seeking to enter parliament would systematically organize a series of murders. Daniel seemed to have been the victim of testosterone-fuelled, racist individuals who had acted on impulse. Nothing more conspiratorial than that.

On the wall, thanks to Tuva's grandparents, there was also a photo of Tuva's ex-boyfriend in London. They hadn't yet sought him out – Mina agreed with Julia that it was not a top priority. He wasn't the killer.

Vincent had explained that the murderer had visited the cafe at Hornstull several times. He believed that Daniel had seen him there. The murderer had, in other words, chosen his victims with care. They hadn't been abducted at random from the street, the way Jonas Rask used to take his victims. Rask was still at large and they had been unable to find him.

Mina stood up, went over to the wall and scrutinized the faces, as if she could compel them to answer. Why were they the chosen ones? What united them?

She went back to the computer and carefully cut a hole in the cotton at the tip of the right-hand index finger so that she could use the laptop's trackpad. It was a sacrifice, but otherwise it would be impossible to use it. Always making compromises, always making exceptions – these things were cracks in her armour where all kinds of dirt might find its way in.

Mina took a deep breath and touched the trackpad with her uncovered finger. She looked up all the information available about Agnes, Tuva and Robert in the records, as well as printing the reports from the conversations with their families and friends. She needed to start from the beginning and go through it all. Somewhere there was a connection. All she had to do was find it. And it was urgent – the murderer wasn't done yet.

It bothered her that Vincent was holding something back. He had asked about dolphin girl and it had sounded as if it were important. She didn't like not knowing, but she had to trust that he would explain as soon as he could.

Any day now, another innocent person might get trapped inside one of the dreadful things Vincent had told them about. She needed to beat them to it.

91

Vincent crossed the footbridge, heading for the Gondolen restaurant. The place was almost full when he entered, a mixture of tourists and holidaying Stockholmers thronging around the tables despite the fact it was only half past seven. Ulrika was nowhere to be seen.

'Hi, have you got a booking?' asked the maître d'.

'No, I'm not staying long. I'll sit at the bar.'

With a little luck, the conversation with Ulrika would be over and done with fairly quickly. He was going to focus solely on Rebecka's needs, ignoring all jibes about his marriage and Ulrika's sister. He had also told Maria that a restaurant was a neutral location for them to meet, and while that might have been true, it was also true that Ulrika couldn't try anything in a public setting. He didn't want a repeat of their last encounter.

He took a seat at the bar and ordered a cup of filter coffee. It wasn't really what his stomach needed. It was smarting with hunger; he hadn't eaten since breakfast. But he had no intention of staying longer than necessary. As soon as he and Ulrika were finished talking, he'd grab a kebab from the place on the corner.

He'd drunk half the cup of coffee when a glass was placed down in front of him, amply filled with red wine. Standing next to him with a similarly well-filled glass was Ulrika. He looked at her questioningly.

'You'll need it,' she said, by way of explanation.

'Oh, is it suddenly that serious?' he said, spinning the glass and making the wine splash up the sides. 'When are your friends arriving?'

He contemplated the wine as it swirled ever more slowly and ran back down into the glass like raindrops on a window.

'We've got an hour before they show up,' said Ulrika, sitting down next to him and nodding at his glass. 'Are you checking how alcoholic it is or what?'

Vincent sighed. An hour. Sixty minutes. Three thousand six hundred seconds. The kebab would have to wait for a while. He took a big gulp of the wine.

'The thing about being able to assess the alcoholic content by sight is a myth,' he said. 'Alcohol evaporates quicker than water, which means the surface tension increases and forms drops on the inside of the glass. That's what you see. A chemical phenomenon. But obviously that tells us nothing about the wine's quality or what it tastes like. It mostly looks good.'

Only 3,510 seconds to go.

'I didn't know you'd become a wine buff,' she said curtly.

'No, I don't know a thing about wine. But I know how liquids work. Right, I'd rather not be here when your friends arrive, so let's talk.'

'There's no rush,' she said softly. 'How are things at home? What are Rebecka and Benjamin actually like when they're with you?'

That was the last thing he'd been expecting. Ulrika only grudgingly talked about their children – presumably it didn't fit with her career-driven lifestyle that she was also the mother of two teenagers. Above all, she never talked about how the kids were with him, except when she had something to complain about. That she was forced to share the children with her sister was a wound that might never heal.

He looked at her, trying to see what her agenda was – what exactly lay behind the question. But the cocked head and the expectant gaze betrayed no hidden plans. Based on what he could tell, she was genuinely curious. This was far from the aggressive Ulrika he had seen before the summer. He let himself relax a smidge. Perhaps they'd be able to have a civilized conversation after all.

'Well, for starters they call your sister "aunt" all the time,' he said.

Ulrika had raised her wine glass to drink from it, and she laughed straight into it, almost making the wine splash over the brim. It was a raw laugh filled with schadenfreude, but her hoarse voice still made it sound interesting. That was what was so annoying about her. She had it all. Looks, money, drive. An incredible competitive instinct. Even when she laughed she dazzled him.

The only thing he wasn't sure she really had were emotions.

'Sorry,' she said. 'But that's what she is. An aunt.'

Over the years, he had become increasingly convinced that his ex-wife had disrupted empathy. At first he had believed that she was merely cold. Uninterested in others. But he had realized that it ran deeper than that. She was mentally incapable of putting herself in someone else's

357

shoes or empathizing with their emotions. On the other hand, she was a good actor. She knew exactly what to say to get others on her side when she needed it. That was presumably why she was such a success as a lawyer.

'I still think she prefers being called Maria,' he said. 'Other than that, Benjamin hasn't left his room for about a fortnight, and I'm beginning to suspect trolls have built their lair in the heaps of dirty laundry in there. Rebecka has loads of friends and says everything is great, so it's a dead cert that she feels awful. She still won't show her forearms . . .'

'Maybe she thinks she's bloated?'

He fell silent. There it was. The reason why it had eventually been impossible to live with Ulrika. It was one thing for her to have unreasonable – even unhealthy – demands on herself. She was a grown woman. That was none of his business. But it became a problem when she demanded that everyone around her be measured by the same yardstick. And when she eventually began making the same demands of the children, explaining how much money they ought to earn or how they ought to look to be accepted, it had been enough. That was when the rows had begun.

'If Rebecka has a body complex then she got that from you,' he said sharply. 'But it's worse than that. I didn't get the chance to say it last time. But I think our daughter is cutting her arms. With a razor. Or a knife. Until she bleeds. OK?'

He downed the wine. Ulrika wasn't laughing any longer. She downed her glass of wine too. Then she waved to the barman and ordered two strong gin and tonics. She was apparently taking the information about Rebecka seriously. In her own way.

'Well, she's not cutting herself in my house,' she said. 'That must be something you bring out in her at yours. At mine she's mostly happy.'

'Good God,' he said, staring at his ex-wife. 'How oblivious are you? What exactly do you know about your daughter? When did you last have a proper conversation with Rebecka?'

'What? We talk . . .' Ulrika protested, sipping the G&T which had appeared on the bar in front of her.

He stirred his drink, unable to conceal his irritation. If the conversation was going to continue like this, then thank God for the booze.

'So what's her best friend called?' he said. 'And don't try saying it's you. There's nothing worse than mums who wants to be BFFs with their teenage daughters.'

'Hmm, isn't it Emma?'

Vincent spun around on his bar stool, so that he was facing Ulrika.

'She doesn't have a best friend,' he said gravely. 'She has lots of acquaintances, but no real friends. That smile you see on her lips, it's not a real smile. It never reaches her eyes. How can you not see that? Or don't you want to see it, because it doesn't fit with your own self-image as a successful, fit mother with perfect kids?'

His drink was almost empty. Anger had made him down it far too quickly. He had to be careful. Had to remember he hadn't eaten.

'Jesus Christ, Vincent,' she hissed back. 'Enough already. But thanks for saying you think I'm successful and fit, I think.'

Vincent sighed. As usual, she'd managed to turn the argument upside down.

'Did I just get the blame for you not seeing what's happening?' he said. 'Is Rebecka's situation supposed to be entirely my fault? Sometimes I wonder whether you're for real.'

'Nope,' she said, moving the stirrer around her empty glass, making the ice cubes rattle. 'I'm a figment of your imagination. You're actually sitting here drinking and talking to yourself. The people at the tables behind us have already started to wonder what's going on.'

She pointed at her and Vincent's glasses while catching the eye of the barman, who immediately began to mix two more drinks.

'Hey, do you have almonds or something I can eat?' he asked.

The barman nodded, disappeared for a minute and then returned with a plate of toasted almonds that he set down in front of Vincent. It was far too small a meal, but it would have to do for now. Vincent put a fistful in his mouth. The fire of alcohol in his belly was mitigated a little.

There was a ping on Ulrika's phone.

'The others are late,' she said, after reading the message. 'You'll have to keep me company for a while longer.'

He glanced at his watch. He only had 840 seconds to go.

'Consider it a child-free evening in adult company,' she added. 'Surely you don't get those very often. Peace?'

He nodded. She was right. He might as well make the best of the situation. He did however wonder whether they were ever going to talk about Rebecka properly.

The bar gradually filled up until it was packed. Ulrika continued ordering drinks. Bit by bit, he had been squeezed closer to her and they were now sitting shoulder to shoulder. He could no longer see her as they talked. If he turned his head, his face would be an inch from hers. Far too close. He needed at least half a metre around him in his personal bubble. But there was no chance of that in this packed bar. He was on his third bowl of almonds. He inserted a few more into his mouth.

'Vincent, Vincent,' said Ulrika, her pronunciation of the first letter in his name a bit woolly.

She smiled when the barman set down a glass of Cava in front of her and a whisky in front of him. They'd long since moved on from G&Ts.

'What exactly has happened to you?' she continued, pressing her shoulder against his.

'What's happened to *me*?' he said, sighing. 'I don't know, Ulrika. What's happened to *you*? You're sitting there like some perfect doll, not wanting to look at anyone but yourself. Were you always like that?'

'You think I'm perfect?'

He glanced to the side and thought he saw a smile of satisfaction. It was hard to see clearly when they were sitting so close together. What was more, his vision seemed to have been afflicted by the same issues her speech was facing.

'Stop it,' he said. 'Of course you're beautiful, in purely objective terms, that is. And you know it. The problem isn't that, it's . . .'

She turned towards him. Close enough for her breath to warm his ear.

'You want to kiss me, don't you?' she said.

'The fuck,' he said, holding out his arms in a gesture of resignation – or at least as much as was possible in the crowded bar.

'That's exactly what I mean. You're impossible.'

He downed what was left of the whisky and put his empty glass next to hers. When she'd finished the Cava he had no idea. He thought they'd only just received the drinks. Apparently not. And he'd meant to take it easy. This was going well.

'When did you and Maria last fuck?' she said, still turned towards his ear. 'How many months ago?'

He knew better than to bite. That was Ulrika's way in, if he wasn't careful she'd start talking about how much better their sex life had been. As if regular one-hour sex sessions meant they hadn't had any issues in the remaining hours of the day.

'When did you last get some?' he countered. 'I gather you haven't met anyone new. You focusing on pickups from bars at closing time or what?'

'And whose fault is that?' she said, downing half a new glass he hadn't even seen arrive.

There was no sensible answer to that. Instead, he stared straight ahead out of the restaurant's glass walls. Thanks to its elevated position, Gondolen had magnificent views of the entire city. He loved looking out over Stockholm at night, especially from planes. When he was on his way home from a show, he would always try to work out which neighbourhoods he was flying over by studying the configuration of the dots of light beneath him.

From his position in the restaurant, he knew that he was looking towards the islands of Skeppsholmen and Djurgården, but his brain refused to assemble the pieces of the puzzle. The city's lights danced before his eyes. He was far too inebriated. He looked at his empty glass. Hadn't it been refilled again? If so, someone must have emptied it for him – he had no memory of finishing another drink. But the dancing lights below him implied something else. He really should have had more to eat since breakfast.

'So what do we do?' he said, his gaze still fixed on the summer night.

It took an effort to shape the words. Even so, they didn't come out the way he wanted them to.

'You mean about Rebecka?' she said. 'Or you mean about us?'

Obviously he had meant Rebecka. But nothing was obvious any longer. He didn't dare say anything; it was no longer possible to know what would come out if he opened his mouth.

'Vincent, you're pathetic,' she said. 'You can't think I still want you?'

'Back at you,' he said, raising the empty glass in a toast. 'I need to pee.'

He got up from the barstool and felt the world spin. Shit. He really was magnificently drunk. Oh well. No point in regrets now. He would have those tomorrow anyway. The immediate focus was making it to the toilet without embarrassing himself. With a little luck, no one would recognize him. Then he'd say his goodbyes and take a taxi home. They would have to pick up the conversation about Rebecka another day, and he really needed to get some food in his belly before he went off the rails.

He staggered into the toilet, stood by a sink and turned the tap. Once the water was cold enough, he splashed it in his face. It didn't help at all. Except for getting his shirt wet. Someone came in behind him, someone who wasn't walking straight either.

'You bastard,' he heard Ulrika say.

Before he could react, she grabbed his collar, dragged him backwards towards one of the stall doors and pushed herself against him. She pressed her lips to his and he responded. Their tongues met and they kissed like two hungry wild animals. He took hold of her hair with both his hands and she groaned faintly as he pulled her head back, away from him.

'Fuck you,' he said.

Then he opened the stall door, staggered in backwards and she locked it behind them. She unbuttoned his trousers while he fumbled with the buttons on her blouse, but she beat off his hands.

'Sit down,' she said, and he sat down heavily on the lid of the toilet seat with his trousers and underpants pulled down around his knees.

She hitched up her skirt, pulled her knickers to one side and straddled him. He was surprised how hard he was as he glided into her. He grabbed hold of her hips to keep herself in place but also to make sure she didn't get too close. She rode him with the frenzy of someone who had been disappointed and angry for so long that she didn't know any other way. There was no love when she pressed herself against him, only anger. He didn't know whether it was him or someone else she was angry at, and he didn't care. He didn't look up, didn't want to see her face. All he saw were her hips and him thrusting into her. They were going to fuck everything they'd had to destruction, everything that had been good, make it unforgivable and inescapably broken and they both knew it.

Suddenly she stopped moving. She coughed heavily once and climbed off.

She didn't look at him and he didn't look at her.

Ulrika adjusted her knickers, pulled down her skirt and buttoned her blouse while he looked down at his cock at half-mast. He heard her exit the stall and close the door.

Vincent remained sitting there with his trousers around his ankles.

Fucking hell.

Fuck, fuck, fucking hell.

92

She was on her way to bed when the phone rang. She was standing in the bathroom having just thrown away the cotton knickers she'd been wearing that day and put on a new pair for the night. Ideally, she wanted to crawl in between her freshly laundered sheets as quickly as possible – if it took too long, her new pants might feel unclean before she'd made it to bed and then she'd have to change them again.

At first she considered not answering. It was past midnight. But the phone kept ringing. Mina went into the bedroom where her mobile was charging and looked at the display. It was Vincent. It was unlike him to call so late. Something must have happened.

She inserted her buds into her ears and answered.

'Hi, Vincent, how are you?'

'Minahi,' he said quickly and far too loudly.

She could hear at once that he was drunk.

The sound of traffic blended with his words. He was outdoors. It sounded like he was walking along a road.

'Sorry, didn't mean to wake you,' he continued. 'I didn't know who to call.'

The words were slurred, as if he had cotton wool in his mouth. He was struggling to formulate his consonants. Vincent was clearly very, very drunk. She hoped he wasn't walking too close to the cars that were audible in the background.

'Has something happened?' she said, frowning.

This really wasn't like him. Vincent was always in control.

'You might say that,' he said. 'I've done something so fucking stupid. So fucking, fucking stupid.'

He paused for a long time.

She wrapped her dressing gown around her and sat down on the edge of the bed, waiting for him to start talking again. The traffic in the background faded a little. He must have found somewhere better to stand.

'I've cheated on Maria,' he said. 'With her sister. My ex-wife.'

'Your ex-wife?' she exclaimed.

All of a sudden, she didn't know whether she wanted to be part of this conversation. It was too close, too intimate. Too messy. She and Vincent had a professional relationship. The distance was just right. She liked him, and had even let him in more than she had anyone else in a long time, but that was enough. Now he was giving her part of his life that she hadn't asked for. On top of that, he seemed to have a very tumultuous personal life. But at the same time . . . He had called her. Because he trusted her. He could have called someone else, anyone really. But he hadn't. Of all the people in the world, he had chosen to confide in her. That had to be worth something. Mina talked feverishly to herself. Tried to convince herself that this was a good conversation. Between friends. But somewhere deep down she knew the truth. Jealousy had ignited a fire in her belly.

'Vincent,' she said sharply. 'Are you saying you've slept with your ex-wife?' She tried to make her voice sound controlled, but she could feel that she had the phone in a vicelike grip.

'I don't know that you'd call it sleeping,' he said. 'Mostly felt like fighting. It was just . . . anger. So, so stupid. I don't know what to do.'

He choked out the final words through the hum of the traffic and it sounded as if he were crying.

'Does Maria know?'

'No, no, if she did I would have been beaten to death by now. I don't dare go home. I've ruined everything.'

She looked at her dry hands and thought about the choices she had made herself. The choices that had made her lose her friends. Her family. The choices that had left her lonely, going to AA each week and with no one to confide in. And she was afraid of what else Vincent had ruined. Perhaps more than his family.

'How do you feel about your ex-wife?' she said.

Matter-of-fact. Cold. Sweat began to form on her palms.

'Feel?' said Vincent, sounding a tad more sober. 'For a while I thought I hated her. But it's actually just . . . nothing. Ashes. I think the feeling's mutual. It was messy, see. Very messy. For a very, very long time. Well, it's still messy. But I didn't plan to fall in love with her little sister, it . . . it just happened . . . And Ulrika and I, we weren't good, we barely even talked to each other any longer, so I don't really know why she cared. But, well, I guess it's a bit unfortunate that it was her sister that I . . .'

Vincent's slurring voice faded away. Then it returned with full force again.

'It took ten years, but she got her revenge, she got it. Fuck me . . . I didn't know it was possible to hate like that.'

Mina lay down on top of the bed and shut her eyes. The fresh sheets rustled under her dressing gown. Deep down, she understood. Her own choices hadn't been deliberate either. They had just happened. At least, she'd convinced herself afterwards that was the case. So who was she to judge? Who was she to lie there with a belly burning with pain about something that didn't even belong to her? There were no vows between them. There was nothing. Except, there was. She cleared her throat. Screwed up her eyes.

'Go home, Vincent. You and your ex-wife are grown-ups. You've done something stupid. We do that sometimes. Even us grown-ups. No one is faultless. The important thing is that you know it was wrong and that it won't happen again. You don't have to tell. Just leave it be.'

If there was one thing she had learned at AA, it was that life consisted of taking a few steps forward and then a stumble backwards. Anyone who believed otherwise was destined for disappointment. They were human, which meant they were not perfect. She had learned the truth of that mantra more times than she cared to remember.

'I feel so ashamed that you know,' Vincent said quietly. 'I don't want you to despise me. This isn't what I'm like. I . . . I like you so much, Mina.'

She opened her eyes again. Listened to the hum of the city through the phone. She was in here in the warmth of her soft bed. He was out there in the dark somewhere. But they were breathing together. Neither of them said anything for a while.

'Thanks, Mina,' Vincent said, breaking the silence. 'Sorry again for calling.'

He hung up. She remained lying there with her eyes closed and the phone in her hand. The fire in her belly was gone. But the loneliness was suddenly overwhelming. She rolled onto her side, into the foetal position.

93

Vincent was standing outside the building on Kungsholmen. He had waited two days after the encounter at Gondolen before daring to go there, to make sure he didn't still smell of booze. It felt as if he had marinated his body in alcohol. Not that it had cleaned him on the inside; rather, it had done the opposite. The shame of what had happened at Gondolen was his to bear and process. He couldn't blame anyone else. But everything had a time and place. And right now he ought to focus on why he was here.

The building looked like all the others in the district. Only a small plaque beside the doorbell disclosed that Alcoholics Anonymous had premises on the first floor. A big neon sign wouldn't have been appropriate in the circumstances. The question was what he should do now. Should he stand there in the doorway and hopefully catch sight of this Anna with her animal tattoos? Or should he go in? Was he even welcome if he didn't have his own issues with addiction? Of course, he could always fake it, but that didn't feel right.

While he thought about this, his brain toyed with the letters on the small plaque. *Alcoholics Anon* became *Nacho Colonials* after a few seconds' work. He felt pretty pleased with himself. But that wouldn't help him find Anna. He had no choice but to go inside.

In the hallway outside the venue there was a table with a coffee thermos on it. Through the doorway it looked as he had expected: a large room with a number of chairs in a circle. It was reassuring that some clichés still held true. The chairs were empty. He checked his watch. Ten minutes to go. A woman in her fifties entered the room through a side door. She caught sight of Vincent and waved him in.

'We haven't started yet,' she said. 'But grab yourself a coffee and take a seat. Is this your first time?'

366

He was about to say that he wasn't one of them, but stopped himself when he realized how that would sound. Instead, he poured coffee into a paper cup and went in.

'Lena,' said the woman, shaking his hand. 'I don't know how much you know already, but there's no need to say more than you want to. Not even your name. There's obviously a risk that other people as well as me will recognize you from the TV, but if you're here then I guess you've got more important things on your mind.'

'Hmm, OK, thanks,' was all he managed to say.

He sat down on one of the plastic chairs while he searched for the right thing to say, but couldn't think of anything. At the same time, perhaps it wasn't the craziest plan in the world to join them for a session. That would allow him to observe the other participants in peace and quiet. It might be useful to know how this Anna worked.

The room began to fill up with people who all sat down in the circle. But he saw no young woman with a dolphin tattoo on her calf. She still wasn't there when the meeting began.

He listened to their accounts of lost and regained hope, of courage and strength, but also of letting themselves down. Anna didn't seem to be coming.

'We'll take a break for a few minutes,' said Lena after a while. 'There's coffee and cake on the table as usual.'

Vincent got up and went into the foyer. He only hoped that anyone who recognized him didn't happen to work for any of the tabloids. However, Lena had been right about the fact that him being here meant he had more important things to think about. Even if she'd misunderstood the reason for his visit.

'Some coffee?'

A bearded man blocked his path and gesticulated towards the table.

'No thanks, I'm going,' Vincent said, smiling.

'Sensible choice. Not the leaving, that is. The coffee. I always bring my own. My name's Kenneth.'

The man proffered his hand.

'Force of habit,' he said apologetically. 'You don't have to tell me what you're called if you don't want to. I'm guessing it's your first visit? I think I left halfway through my first. It can be a bit much.'

Vincent shook Kenneth's hand but without introducing himself.

'I'm looking for someone,' he said. 'She has a dolphin tattoo.'

'You must mean Anna,' said the man, laughing. 'I think that dolphin has been joined by a small zoo lately.'

He fetched a plastic bag from by the coat rack and pulled out a thermos.

'She doesn't always come,' he said. 'Are you friends?'

'No, she got me a job, or so you might say. Indirectly. I just wanted to thank her.'

An older lady in a purple shawl joined them by the coffee. She moved through the room with grace, as if she were traversing a grand apartment rather than a meeting room.

'Olga,' said Kenneth to the lady. 'Do you know when Anna usually comes?'

'*Da*. Thursdays,' she said in a heavy Russian accent.

Vincent wasn't convinced it was genuine.

Kenneth nodded.

'Thursday. Try then,' he said. 'Sure you don't want a spot of coffee?'

Vincent smiled as politely as he could. This was going nowhere.

'Next time,' he said.

He would have to ask Mina for help again. He should have told her at once.

94

Sara Temeric rubbed her temples. She had been working for the police for almost ten years. First for the National Criminal Police, and then at NOA, the National Operations Department, when it superseded the former. At NOA, she'd investigated terrorist financing and had been on the team responsible for the national task force. These were weighty duties for someone who had only just turned thirty, but she had been good at her job. So good, in fact, that four years ago she'd been offered a new job in NOA with a new title and a temporary posting to New York. She was supposed to be an operations expert, whatever that meant.

She hadn't hesitated for one second and had moved to the USA. And of course she had met a man. She and Michael now had two children, Leah and Zachary, the apples of her eye. But it had been part of the deal for her that the children weren't going to grow up in America but in Sweden. Michael had had nothing against this as a plan. So the deal was for them to do a few years in the USA while the kids were really small and Michael had a chance to get established as a games developer, before they moved the whole family to Sweden. She was now effectively the vanguard and was tasked with finding a family home and an office for Michael at the same time as she bedded into her new job.

She loved her job and found house hunting deeply satisfying. She loved being back in Sweden. But she missed her family every day and longed for when they would join her.

Since she had returned in the middle of the summer, she had primarily relieved the operations analysts. In practice, this was below her pay grade, but it felt good to be involved in practical operations while waiting for circumstances around her job to clarify.

Regrettably, it also meant that she was in the unfortunate position of having to deliver surveillance analysis to Ruben Höök. She had only met him once previously before she left for the USA. But once was enough. He had quickly glanced at her and said something like 'Heist would have been better.' It was only afterwards that she found out that Heist was a brand of underwear for women who needed to hold in or lift up parts of their body.

She had always been proud of her womanly figure, but after the encounter with Ruben she had spent the rest of the day feeling like everyone was staring at her and she was overweight. Her boyfriend at the time had been obliged to spend the whole evening protesting how beautiful she was and that Ruben was an idiot who was probably turned on by anorexic school girls.

Some barbs were hard to get out. Ruben Höök had managed in five words to make her feel fat and ugly. She had never forgiven him for it. And now she had to meet him again. This time she had at any rate googled men's underwear and found a brand called Addicted that made underpants with extra padding both at the front and over the behind. *To enhance your masculinity*, as it said in the adverts. If Ruben so much as opened his mouth in a way she didn't like, she'd be making an order for a five-pack of Addicted pants in his name.

When she reached the meeting room, to Sara's great relief she discovered that Julia had called in the rest of the team to attend the presentation. She liked Julia. It was clear she hadn't got where she was because her father was the commissioner; Julia was as sharp and as smart as her dad, if not more so. And she had the measure of Ruben.

Sara greeted them all one after the other. When she shook Ruben's hand she shifted her gaze at the last moment to Peder, who was just behind Ruben. It was an ugly power play not to make eye contact with the man she was greeting and instead look at someone else, but he deserved as much. He probably didn't even remember that they had met previously. What was more, Peder had helped her to sort through the traffic data. She couldn't recall Ruben ever lending a hand.

She hooked her computer up to the screen in the meeting room and started her slideshow. A grid containing figures and columns appeared on the monitor.

'My name's Sara, for those of you who haven't met me before,' she said. 'I've been helping Analysis to trace your phone call. The network operators' traffic lists are a jungle. But as luck would have it, we have a pretty sharp machete in the shape of Peder.'

Peder smiled with pride despite the rings under his eyes. She clicked the mouse and one of the data points was highlighted with a square.

370

'This is the call you received.'

'That *I* received,' said Ruben.

'Oh really?' said Mina. 'As far as I know, you weren't even in the room when it came in. Badminton, wasn't it?'

'You shouldn't believe everything you hear,' said Ruben, gritting his teeth. 'And it was padel tennis.'

'Did you get anything out of the content, by the way?' Sara asked, turning to Julia. 'Have the results come in for secondary and background noise analysis?'

'Yes, but there was nothing of interest. The background acoustics indicate that the caller was in a medium-sized room without much furniture. There was a faint hum of traffic, so a built-up area. But no unique background sounds. We're hoping that your findings will help pinpoint the location, because based on psychological analysis provided by an external consultant we believe that the caller was in fact the murderer,' said Julia.

'One of the *murderers*,' said Ruben, rolling his eyes.

'Quite so. We're now working on the premise that two people carried out the murders. One of whom might be Jonas Rask,' Julia explained.

'I don't know if this will help,' said Sara, bringing a map up on the screen, 'but the mobile phone that made the call was connected to a base station right here in town. On Kungsholmen, to be precise. It's a pity the sound analysis hasn't provided you with any more information about what kind of place it was.'

'I assume you've checked who the phone number is registered to?' said Mina.

Peder slurped coffee from a mug with the words *Best Dad in the World* emblazoned on the side, but with the word *best* crossed through and replaced with *Sleepiest*. It looked like he'd made it himself. Or his wife had.

'Sorry, it was pay as you go,' Sara said, switching back to the columns of figures again. 'But that was to be expected. While the phone is switched on, we can track its patterns of movement by seeing which base stations it connects to. So we've checked where it's been in the last two months – unfortunately, the network operators don't keep data for any longer than that. I can tell you that this phone hasn't been anywhere – before or after the call.'

'Burner?' said Julia, who was taking notes by hand as Sara spoke, even though a summary would be emailed out afterwards.

She guessed it was a way for Julia to think.

Sara nodded. 'The caller bought a cheap phone and a SIM card to call the hotline without leaving a traceable history.'

'I assume you had to get permission for this?' said Mina, pointing at the figures.

'We applied for an SSC,' said Sara. 'Secret surveillance of electronic communication. Our prosecutor had to petition the court for it. But it came through quickly, due to the circumstances.'

'Can the tracking remain active, so that you can see if the phone number shows up again?' said Mina. 'Not on two-month-old lists but in real time? You never know.'

'I'll speak to the prosecutor. It shouldn't be an issue, given the nature of the crimes under investigation. But there's every likelihood this phone is lying smashed up in a bin somewhere.'

Sara shut down her presentation and prepared to leave. However, she didn't intend to let out a sigh of relief until she was no longer in the same room as Ruben.

'Well, well,' said Ruben in a measured tone, at the very moment she thought of him. 'In other words, Sara's little PowerPoint gave us nothing. We could be dealing with someone who lives or works on Kungsholmen – or someone who happened to be passing through but lives in Norway.'

'You do realize we're on Kungsholmen right now, don't you?' said Christer, sounding almost cheerful. 'It could be a colleague in this building. Wouldn't that be a treat?'

95

Mina stepped into the familiar room. She was starting to tire of it. Not just the venue, but the whole thing. It was the same people every time, telling the same addiction stories, sitting on the same plastic chairs in the same circle, drinking the same dishwater coffee from the pump thermos and eating the same uninspiring baked goods.

Today when she peeked into the tin on the table she saw raspberry cookies. That was at least an upgrade. One of the alcoholics might have done some baking. She looked with distaste at the crumbs already covering the white paper tablecloth. The seven people who had arrived before her had probably touched every single cookie before choosing which one they wanted. She wouldn't eat any of those that were left, even if she could blowtorch them first.

There were several new faces today. No sign of the dolphin girl, Anna, whom Vincent had asked about. Kenneth came through the door and nodded to her. She knew it was time for the obligatory small talk and she'd come prepared.

'How's your wife?' she asked, before pointing to the thermos. 'Do you want coffee?'

'Thank you for asking. She's better now. And no thanks,' Kenneth said with a look of amusement. 'You're awfully talkative today.'

She shrugged in reply.

'But while we're on the subject of her,' Kenneth said, producing his own thermos. 'She's going to be in hospital for a few more weeks and I'm not up to taking care of everything at home. I know it's asking a lot, given you've already been looking after Bosse all this time, but do you think he could stay with you for the rest of the summer? I can pay.'

She stopped mid-movement and stared at him.

He looked back with his eyes pleading. Not completely unlike Bosse's favourite expression, as it happened.

This was hard to swallow. Kenneth didn't know that Bosse currently had a far better home with Christer than she would ever have been able to offer. And this was definitely the wrong occasion to mention that. What could she even say? Hello, I've lent your dog to someone else?

'Oh, just a second, my work phone is ringing,' she said, hurrying away with an apologetic look.

'Like I said, I can pay,' she heard Kenneth say behind her.

She ran into the ladies' and locked the doors. Then she called Christer. He picked up after three rings.

'Hi, Mina, how're things? Did you leave something on your desk? I just passed by, we were heading for the kitchen, I can go back if you like . . .'

'It's not that,' she interrupted him. 'It's about Bosse.'

'He's right here next to me,' Christer said happily. 'That's why we were heading for the kitchen. I think he's saying hello, by the way. Er, Mina, why are you whispering?'

She realized that she was not only whispering but that she had also curled up into a crouching position next to the toilet seat. She got up and continued in a somewhat louder voice, although low enough that hopefully it wouldn't be audible through the door.

'I don't know how to say this,' she said. 'But I just spoke to Bosse's owner.'

There was silence on the other end.

'Oh no,' Christer said, clearly dejected. 'He wants him back, doesn't he? And just when we were going to hit town today and find some nice brushes for his coat. Maybe one of those silk ribbons too.'

Mina closed her eyes. Bosse was a big, playful golden retriever. With lively eyes and a lolling tongue. The last things she would associate with that dog were hair brushes and silk ribbons. But this wasn't the moment to tell Christer that. If he'd got it into his head that Bosse was a show poodle then that was up to him. So long as he was happy, given what she was going to say.

'That sounds great,' she said. 'Because it's actually the opposite: the owner asked whether I could keep him for the rest of the summer. I'm sure you've got plans, but perhaps we can—'

'Splendid!' Christer interrupted her.

It was the closest to a hoot of joy she'd ever heard from the otherwise rather laconic policeman.

'Bosse and I are going to have the best summer ever,' he said. 'Pass on my best and my gratitude!'

When she emerged from the toilet, Kenneth was still by the coffee. He looked at her with the same amused expression as before.

'Do you take all your work calls in the loo?' he said.

'It's confidential,' she replied, trying to put on a trouble-free smile.

It came out rather stiffer than she'd intended.

'But I can take him. Bosse. No problem. Just let me know when you want him back. After all, we see each other here. Are you offering some proper coffee?'

Kenneth thanked her over and over as he cheerily poured coffee from his own thermos into a fresh mug. She accepted it, though she had no intention of drinking any. The gesture was important – a way of keeping in Kenneth's good books. And a way of moving the conversation away from Bosse.

She went back into the meeting room with the mug in her hand and sat down on one of the chairs, positioning herself so that she could see the door. Perhaps it was time to change things. If she was so sick of the same thing happening every time she was there, then the solution was to ensure that things went differently this time.

As she thought about this, she almost sipped the coffee in the mug, but realized at the last moment what she was about to do. She quickly set the mug down on the floor under her chair and hoped that Kenneth wouldn't see.

She had already engaged in friendly conversation as a warm-up. Perhaps today it was her turn to share.

By the time everyone had taken their seats, she had made up her mind. She nodded to signal that she wanted to begin. Everyone looked at her. Curious. Expectant. Mina already regretted it. But now it was too late to change her mind. The train had already pulled away from the platform and was under way.

She stood up and cleared her throat.

Then she sat down again.

The passengers on board the train had pulled the emergency brake. She couldn't do it.

Kenneth looked at her intently.

Mina turned her head away. Her issues were hers to own. No one else's.

96

The Tantolunden park in Södermalm was full of people lounging on picnic blankets, youths playing volleyball and families with children enjoying the summer sun. There was a smell of food from the hot dog and burger stands along the shoreline promenade, and he could hear at least five different styles of music emanating from different places in the park. Vincent loved it. He always felt at his best in a swarm of people, despite the fact that it really ought to have drained him. But in a crowd, he could feel like he belonged. That he was one of them, a picnic pro who had packed his basket full of strawberries and champagne or biscuits and juice or lager or whatever it was they brought with them. He didn't actually know.

'This is a significantly better working environment than that claustrophobic police HQ,' Mina said beside him.

They were walking through Tanto, heading for the water. Vincent had suggested they stroll along the shore at Hornstull, heading for Skanstull. He'd always thought water was both beautiful and a stimulant for creativity. And there was plenty of water in Stockholm.

It also gave him something else to focus on other than Mina, who was today wearing a pair of light-coloured trousers and a blue vest. He had difficulty moving his gaze from her neckline. Despite the summer attire, she still managed to look as controlled as ever. The vest appeared to be brand new and fitted as if it had been tailored to her, and there wasn't a wrinkle in sight on the linen trousers. Her clothing might be suitable for her downtime, but there was nothing casual about Mina. Which was just as she intended it to be.

'I think better when I'm moving,' he said. 'It triggers endorphins and an elevated pulse, which delivers more resources to the brain. A beautiful view on top of that adds serotonin and dopamine, which is straight-up lubricant for the synapses between the brain cells. More thoughts per second means more opportunities for problem solving per second.'

They turned onto the promenade. Now and again a motorboat sputtered cheerily through the channel, the sun catching the reflectors on the hull.

'Thanks,' said Mina. 'I think. But that sounded a bit blokey, Vincent.'

'What?'

He'd obviously missed something. Mina must have been talking without him listening. He went back over what he'd just said, but could see nothing 'blokey' about brain cells or serotonin. Perhaps she'd misheard.

'You called me a beautiful view,' she said. 'I know you're forty-seven, but talk about objectification!'

He could feel his face going bright red and he was suddenly desperate to pee.

'I really didn't mean . . .' he stammered. 'I mean . . . it was the water beside us that I was referring to . . . you're not . . .'

He wanted the ground to swallow him up. How excruciatingly awkward! Naturally he would never express himself . . .

'Vincent,' she said sharply.

He blinked.

'I was joking, Vincent.'

He couldn't help bursting out into laughter. Slightly too loudly. But it reflected how relieved he was.

They continued along the promenade, staying out of the way of bicycles swooshing past.

'What's more, I'd never call you a view,' he said. 'You're clearly a bathing belle.'

'Oi!' she said, punching his arm. 'My God, it's incredible you've managed to have a family.'

'It wasn't easy. But you can always rent one.'

'Speaking of family . . . how's the situation with Maria and . . . Ulrika?'

It wasn't exactly a subject that he wanted to discuss. But given that he had called her in the middle of the night, he owed her a reply.

'For Ulrika, I think it never happened,' he said. 'And Maria doesn't know anything. She gets jealous if I pop out to fetch the post. She would never understand. And sorry again for calling you like that.'

Mina nodded in response. He contemplated her face. It looked a little stiff, but for once he couldn't work out her facial expression.

'How are you doing with this?' he said after a while, changing the subject. 'Being out in nature?'

'Have you seen me touch anything?' she said, waving her fingers. 'It's several metres to the nearest tree. And you know I've always got plastic gloves in my pocket if push comes to shove.'

They passed a caravan painted in bright colours and converted into a cafe, and had to wend their way through sun loungers set out in the middle of the path. Plastic palms and coloured lights decorated the scene, and calypso music was playing on a crackly speaker. For a while it felt like they were no longer in Sweden but somewhere abroad on holiday. Him and Mina.

'So what did the great mentalist want to discuss this time?' she said.

He was quiet for a few seconds, suddenly uncertain as to how to begin.

'You know when I asked you who had tipped you off about me?' he said. 'There was a reason for that. I've actually been trying to get hold of Anna without success. I'd prefer to speak to her myself, but the important thing is that we get hold of her. You see, someone has sent me a message. A message that you can only find if you are aware of the murder dates. And have a brain as screwed up as mine.'

'Yes, I can imagine you've got some . . . odd . . . admirers,' she said. 'But those dates can't be hard to find online following the press conference. It's probably all in some forum thread at Flashback.'

'I haven't made myself clear: the message was sent before I even began helping with the investigation.'

She stared at him.

'I don't understand. How . . . how do you mean?'

'At Christmas, before Agnes was found dead on the bench, someone sent a coded message to my agent with the instruction to pass it on to me. As a Christmas present. But he forgot about it, so I only got it much later. And it wasn't until very recently that I understood the message.'

'Dear God,' said Mina, putting her hand to her mouth.

They followed the path out onto a jetty over the water. He could see that she was processing what he'd just told her.

'So . . . the person who sent it guessed you would work with us before I even asked you? Now I understand why you want to track Anna down. Vincent, we need to tell the rest of the team about this.'

He was about to put his hand on her bare arm but stopped himself at the last second. He didn't want her to feel the need to wash. He stopped at the jetty balustrade and looked out across the glittering waves.

'I don't know,' he said. 'I'm worried they'll want to exclude me from the group again if it turns out I'm involved in some way.'

'It'll be fine,' she said. 'They like you.'

But she didn't sound entirely convinced.

'I'd like to stay,' he said. 'You know, police HQ on Kungsholmen . . . it has . . . a view I like a lot.'

'Now you're just flattering me, Vincent.'

97

Mina was standing with her back to the meeting room while Vincent explained to the others how the murder dates had led him to the message in the book. In purely practical terms, this was because she was writing up the facts on the big whiteboard as he presented them. But emotionally, it was because she needed a bit of extra time to gather herself together. Her hand trembled slightly against the board and she forced herself to take a few deep breaths before turning around. The book was lying in the middle of the table, open at the page with the red lines and the message.

'Vincent and I agree that the person who suggested to me that I involve him may also be the one who sent the book.'

She sat down at the table but avoided meeting the others' gazes. She could see that her hand was still shaking.

'I think it sounds completely fucking psycho,' said Ruben drily, shaking his head suspiciously. 'We're a long way from Jonas Rask now. Sorry, but you get that we live in the real world, right? Not in some bloody film or tatty paperback thriller? In the real world it isn't complicated. People kill each other at the drop of a hat, they don't pursue intricate bloody plans with codes and shit that they then hide in cryptic books about leopards. Am I the only one who sees this, or have you all joined the same cult?'

Ruben threw his pen down onto the table in frustration, leaned back and crossed his arms over his chest.

'Thanks for the reasoned input, Ruben,' said Julia in a measured tone, before turning to Mina. 'Who exactly was it that tipped you off about Vincent?'

Mina looked at her hand on the table. She prayed that none of the others would spot how much she was trembling. She lifted her gaze.

Naturally, Vincent was staring at her hand. She ignored him and answered Julia with feigned calm.

'I've been escorting a friend as a supporter to . . . their . . . AA visits in Kungsholmen. And it was there I met our tipster. Her name is Anna.'

'Fuck me, you have friends?' said Ruben, roaring with laughter.

Peder gave him an angry look and Mina noted to her satisfaction that Vincent's gaze darkened. Even Christer glowered at Ruben.

'Go on, Mina,' said Julia.

Ruben snorted.

'Anna was there and, well . . . she came to me.'

'Just like that? How did she know who you were?' Peder said, leaning forward in curiosity.

Mina could feel sweat prickling her palms. She didn't dare look at Vincent, but could clearly feel his gaze. She held out her arms and shrugged.

'She heard me talking on the phone about the case. Sometimes it can be hard to step to one side for work calls. She's often there.'

'So it's reasonable to believe that Anna sent the book to Vincent,' said Julia. 'Since she was a decisive factor in getting him onto the case.'

'Or she knows the person responsible for the message,' said Vincent.

'Regardless, we need to get hold of her straight away,' said Julia.

Mina could feel the sweat on her spine. She couldn't go to AA with any of her colleagues. That would bring the house of cards tumbling down. She would either have to make sure that she got the job herself, without backup, which was unlikely. Or someone would have to . . .

'Peder,' said Julia, turning towards him. 'Can you take this? Mina can give you a detailed description. Visit AA and find out as much as you can about Anna. Try to get a home address. And be careful. If you see her there, request reinforcements before you approach her. If Anna is involved then we don't know how she'll react to the police.'

'Wouldn't it be better if it was Mina?' said Peder. 'She's familiar with the place.'

'It wouldn't be appropriate for Mina to go there in the line of duty, given that she's been there as a supporter. We don't want to make it uncomfortable for her friend.'

'Thanks,' said Mina, and she meant it, albeit for completely different reasons to those Julia had in mind. 'Thanks.'

Her hands finally stopped trembling and she leaned back in her chair to allow her top to absorb the beads of sweat that had gathered at the base of her spine. She looked at Vincent. He smiled at her.

'Vincent, I'd like our forensics team to take a look at the book,' said Julia.

'Of course.' Vincent nodded towards the book. 'I was about to suggest that. I would, however, like to have it back as soon as possible. I won't be able to work out what the message means if I don't have the book. Because I don't know yet.'

'That's not standard procedure, given that the book may be evidence,' said Julia.

Then she sighed.

'Not that there's anything standard about this case. And I dread to think how many breaches of protocol we've already committed. But what the hell . . . I'll speak to forensics to make sure you get it back as soon as possible. Christer, put on a pair of gloves and ensure the book reaches the lab, OK?'

Christer darkened.

'I was about to take my break, can't—' he moaned, but Julia cut him off.

'It needs to be handed over immediately. By you. Losing five minutes of your lunchbreak is hardly going to do you any harm. You usually come back at least ten minutes late from lunch each day, so I'd guess the taxpayers have about' – she checked her watch for dramatic effect – 'one year, four months, one week and three days of your time at their disposal.'

Peder stifled a titter.

Christer snorted and stood up.

'No need to be sarcastic. I'll do it. Look – I'm on my way . . .'

He reached for the book but reeled backwards when Julia shouted at him.

'Gloves, Christer!'

'Yes, yes, yes.'

He turned around and went to fetch a pair.

'I don't understand,' said Vincent.

'What is it now?' Ruben snorted. 'More mysteries?'

'No, but if Christer has come back ten minutes late from each lunch break and thus accumulated time owed corresponding approximately to one year and four months, that means . . . allowing for some rounding . . . seventy thousand lunches. There's about two hundred fifty working days in a year, so Christer would have had to come back late from lunch at work for two hundred and eighty years to reach that.'

Vincent looked at Ruben innocently. Mina bit her lip to contain her laughter. She wasn't altogether sure Vincent was joking. But she suspected he was.

'That sounds about right, given it's Christer we're talking about,' said Peder.

But Ruben stood up with the same sullen expression as Christer.

'You've lost it, all of you,' he said. 'This whole thing is like something out of the *Da Vinci Code*. The simple solution is always the right one, isn't that what we say?'

'Occam's razor,' said Vincent.

Ruben stared at him.

'Whose?' said Peder mid-yawn. 'What does shaving have to do with this?'

'Send the man to the loony bin,' Ruben muttered, heading out of the meeting room.

Mina didn't even have the strength to be annoyed. She was dizzy with relief that her secret was still safe, at least for a while longer.

However, that feeling disappeared when she began to think about Anna again. Anna with the tattoos. Anna, who had always seemed so harmless. But perhaps she was more dangerous than any of them had imagined . . .

98

It was a bright and warm summer evening. There was no wind what-soever – it was like being wrapped in a blanket. The sky over Stockholm was a thousand shades of pink. Mina had heard that the sky assumed its pink colour because of air pollution, but it was still breathtaking to look at.

The girl was sitting a short distance away, with her legs dangling off the edge of the quayside. So close and yet so far away. Alone. As she was so often. A family of swans glided past with languid majesty, the parents hissing loudly when a kayak got slightly too close. The royal palace loomed up above them – that building in the Old Town with all the glamour of a prison, that always left American tourists disap-pointed because of its lack of towers and pinnacles.

Anglers standing in a row were reeling in their catches, which they put in battered plastic buckets. Mina crept closer. She had been following the girl at a safe distance since she had left her street door. But now it was tempting to get a little closer.

Her dark hair was shorter than it had been the last time she'd seen her. She must have taken off at least a couple of inches and it now stopped at her shoulders. Thick, shiny, straight. A fringe that fell over her face. As if the girl had heard her, she raised her hand and pushed her hair behind her ear. An angler reeled in a big perch and put it in his bucket. Then he added fresh bait and cast his line back in. The family of swans continued sailing past, hissing at the angler.

Mina took another few steps closer. She frowned. Stopped. Two teenage lads appeared and sat down on either side of the girl. She was too far away to hear what they were saying, and of course they might be friends she'd agreed to meet. But something in their body language suggested this wasn't the case. Mina hesitated, taking a couple more steps. She needed to get close enough to hear what they were saying.

She'd never been this close before.

Even from behind she could see clearly how the girl's shoulders were raised and stiff. A typical defensive reaction. One of the boys' hands reached towards the rucksack. Mina did a rapid analysis of the situation and approached them.

'And how are we all doing here then?' she said with a tone of authority, while presenting her police identification.

The lads looked up, first at her ID, then at her before quickly getting to their feet. They ran away, heading towards Kungsträdgården. The girl smiled gratefully at her. She picked up her rucksack and held it tightly in her arms.

'They wanted me to give them my bag,' she said.

'Suspected as much,' said Mina, feeling her entire body reacting, turning alternately cold and then hot.

'Thanks.'

The girl turned her face up towards her, fixing her gaze on Mina's.

'It's my job,' Mina said briefly, making as if to leave. But before she could stop herself, she heard herself saying:

'Can I get you a can of soda?'

She saw the girl's hesitation.

'We've got a programme in the police right now where we're encouraged to make contact with young people. So that we create good relations early on. So that we're not called pigs by your generation and . . . What do you say? It's on the taxpayer.'

'I don't drink fizzy drinks,' the girl said, standing up. 'But I'd take a cappuccino.'

Mina felt her heart begin to race with nerves and a thousand other things she couldn't identify. She shouldn't have done that. She shouldn't have asked. But what was done was done.

'The cafe over there does good coffee,' said the girl, pointing towards Kungsträdgården.

The same direction the boys had fled. Mina nodded. The boys were probably long gone. She glanced at her phone. There was nothing new from either Peder or Julia. She had this time to herself.

They strolled towards the cafe, which was full of people, but they were lucky – a small table for two was vacated just as they arrived. For once, Mina didn't care that the table hadn't been wiped down properly or that the chairs appeared not to have been cleaned in years. None of that mattered. She went to buy two cappuccinos for them while the girl sat down at the table. Out of habit, she requested takeaway cups even though they were going to drink them there. She didn't even give a thought to it.

'Thanks,' said the girl, her face lighting up when Mina returned with the coffees.

The girl took one and closed her eyes as she took her first sip.

'Aren't you a bit young to like coffee?' said Mina.

'We lived in Italy when I was little. Kids learn how to drink coffee there when they're young. I love cappuccino, but I hate disgusting filter coffee that's been stewing for too long. Isn't that what you cops drink all day long?'

The girl laughed but not in an unpleasant way.

'Sadly, that's all too true,' said Mina.

A waitress listlessly retrieved the dirty crockery that had been left on their table.

'I'm considering becoming a police officer too,' the girl said cheerily, and a big gulp of hot coffee caught in Mina's throat.

She stared at the girl.

'Why?'

The girl hesitated.

'Well . . . My mum was killed in a hit-and-run when I was little. Probably a drink driver, according to Dad. And they've never caught the person who did it. It's not right. I want to work on stuff like that.'

'I'm sorry,' said Mina.

'Well, I don't have to decide what I'm going to be yet,' the girl continued. 'But it's one of the options I'm considering. Or maybe I'll be an influencer. Spend hours getting the perfect photo of the cherry blossom here in Kungsträdgården.'

The girl pointed towards the trees, which had long ago lost their hot pink colour and were instead perfectly ordinary, not particularly photogenic trees. She pulled a mobile phone out of her rucksack. She quickly checked something on it and then put it back in her bag.

'Someone worried about you?' said Mina.

'Meh, it's just Dad. He's, well, he's a bit . . . over-protective. But he needs to chill out.'

'When you have my job, you understand why parents are over-protective.'

'Yeah, you must see a lot of shit,' the girl noted coolly while drinking more cappuccino.

Some of the foam stuck to her upper lip and Mina had to stifle the urge to lean forward and wipe it off.

She didn't ask the girl's name. She already knew it. But in order to avoid compromising herself, she always called her 'the girl' in her head.

'Most of all I'd like to be one of those investigating police officers. Not one that drives around town in a police car looking for crackheads. But I've heard you have to do a few years on the street first. Is that right? I'm honestly not sure whether I'd dare.'

'Yes, yes, that's what it's like right now,' said Mina, nodding. 'But they're thinking about changing it. Precisely for that reason. The force risks missing out on people who are good at investigating but aren't interested in or built to deal with life on the street as a police officer.'

'Did you manage?' the girl said, looking at her with curiosity.

Mina considered how to respond. She contemplated whether to be honest about what it had been like. Not the hassle or the hours or the fear – all the things that new graduates grappled with. But her own demons. The dirt, the environments she couldn't control, the pressure to hide her own characteristics from her colleagues, not to be seen as weird. It was important to belong. The group, your colleagues, were what might make the difference between life and death when decisions had to be made in a split second.

'I managed,' was all she said.

There was far too much she would have to explain. It was easier not to explain at all.

'I want to give you something,' the girl said suddenly, taking off one of the countless necklaces she was wearing. 'As a thank you.'

'There's no need – I was only doing my job,' Mina protested.

The girl held out a necklace with a black pendant on it.

'But you're nice,' said the girl. 'Not everyone in the world is. This pendant is magnetic.'

'Magnetic?'

'Apparently it's good for your body. Something to do with red blood cells. Well, I don't know. But I'd like you to have it.'

Mina wanted nothing more than to accept it, but if she hadn't already broken all the rules she was definitely about to. At the same time, she could hardly say no. At least the necklace didn't look like it had cost too much.

'Magnetic, you say?' she said, taking the item. 'Thank you. It means more than you can imagine.'

She tried to avoid showing how close to tears she was as she put it

387

around her neck. It was probably just her imagination, but she could feel the pendant warming her ribcage like a small sun. She cupped her hand around it.

'And what about training to be a police officer then?' she said.

'I'll have to see,' the girl said, draining the last of her cappuccino. 'Like I said, I've still got time.'

Mina saw a movement out of the corner of her eye. A man had come up to their table and taken a firm grip on the girl's arm. She didn't protest – she simply stood up. But the look she gave Mina was one of resignation.

'Bye, it was nice meeting you,' said the girl, turning around together with the man and leaving.

Mina also began to stand up, but a firm hand on her shoulder made her sit down again. Another man had approached from behind. He moved around the table and sat down opposite her, where the girl had been sitting. He had a nondescript appearance. Shorts and T-shirt, trainers with the ubiquitous swoosh, a Daniel Wellington wristwatch. But Mina knew better than to allow herself to be deceived by his appearance.

The man said nothing, merely producing an iPhone and passing it over. Mina knew who was going to be on the line, whose voice she was going to hear for the first time in many years. She had known what the consequences of making contact were. But what was she meant to have done? She was a police officer, after all.

She listened silently to the voice.

She said nothing, offered no reply.

When she handed back the phone, her hand was shaking heavily. The man took the phone, still without saying a word, and left. Mina stayed seated. She was trembling so much that she was afraid she would fall over if she stood up.

99

Kvibille 1982

He'd just come down from upstairs and was heading into the kitchen when there was a knock on the front door. Two knocks. He stopped mid-step, glued to the spot. At first he wondered whether his ears were deceiving him – they almost never had anyone knocking on the door. But he could see the shadow of a person through the frosted glass by the front door.

It wasn't Mum – he knew that. And Jane wasn't due home for a while. He became worried. He wanted to ask them to leave; he didn't need anyone. If he didn't budge an inch then perhaps whoever it was would give up and go away.

More knocking. Three knocks this time. And then a man's voice.

'Hello?'

The man had obviously heard the creaking stairs as he'd come down them. There was nothing else to be done. He was careful not to open the door wider than the space that allowed him to block the opening by standing in it.

'Hello, young man,' said Allan, standing on the porch steps. 'I didn't know whether you'd heard me.'

Allan from the timber merchant's. Mum's friend. Whom he'd called an hour ago – a conversation he had completely forgotten about. It might as well have been two weeks ago. Time wasn't behaving in its usual fashion.

Allan took off his green and yellow cap with the BP logo on it and wiped his sweaty brow. On the step beside him were two supermarket carrier bags brimming with food.

'I think I've got everything you asked for,' said Allan. 'Even though there was a lot. So your mum's that unwell, is she?'

389

'Yes, she can barely talk. That's why I had to call. Here. This should cover it.'

He handed over two one-hundred-kronor notes and Allan put them in his trouser pocket.

'But who's going to take care of you then?' said Allan with a troubled expression. 'Have you called the doctor to ask him to come here? Maybe I should see how she's doing – check whether I should pick up anything from the chemist in Halmstad or whatever.'

He wedged his foot against the door as Allan placed his hand on the door handle.

'She's sleeping right now,' he said, coughing. 'And . . . what if you get infected? You shouldn't even be close to me.'

Allan nodded and removed his hand. He mopped his brow again.

'You're quite right,' he said. 'I'm on my own at the yard this week and I've got loads to do. Can't afford to get sick. But at least let me carry the bags inside. You shouldn't have to do that yourself.'

'Thanks,' he said, stepping out of the doorway to avoid being in the way. 'They're going in there.'

He pointed towards the kitchen and Allan picked up the amply filled carrier bags with a grunt. A green apple fell out of one and rolled across the hall floor. He stared at the apple and put his hands to his stomach to ensure the rumbling couldn't be heard. It had been far too long since he'd eaten anything. Allan returned to the hall, picked up the apple and stopped by the foot of the stairs.

'You're sure she's sleeping up there?'

He nodded with his hand still at his stomach.

'OK,' said Allan, giving him the apple. 'Tell her I hope she gets better soon. And call me if you need anything else.'

He stayed in the doorway watching Allan leave until he was sure he wasn't coming back. Only then did he sink his teeth into the apple. Then he went inside and made sure to lock the door behind him.

Two of the things he'd asked Allan to buy were toothpaste and dental floss. He took out the boxes and put them on the table. Mum was always particular about ensuring you brushed your teeth for two minutes. He'd put on the watch he'd been given for Christmas so that he could count the seconds on it.

Two minutes. He didn't know what happened if you brushed for too long and he didn't want to know either. The dental floss was trickier. He couldn't remember whether he should use it before or after brushing. What had Mum said?

Before seemed more plausible.

Or was it after?

Oh no. He'd got into a muddle. Even though he was so careful. But two minutes was one hundred and twenty seconds. $12 + 0 = 12$. He would use twelve centimetres of floss at bedtime. Then everything would be fine.

Mum's routines were important.

We are what we usually do, she always said.

He needed to remember what she usually did.

100

Aston came running in at top speed with a mobile phone.

'Dad, I crash in the race when it rings!' he whined.

Vincent dropped the ladle into the boiling pan of macaroni and liberated his mobile from his son's grasp before Aston had time to lob it across the room.

'Turn it off,' Aston shouted. 'I'm playing *Asphalt 9* on the phone!'

'Not now you're not,' said Vincent, gesturing at his son to indicate that he should go and bother his mother instead.

The display showed that it was Mina. Finally. He hadn't managed to get hold of her all weekend. She hadn't answered any of his messages. He once again had to remind himself that the psychological spotlight effect – which made everybody believe that they were the cause of far more events than they actually were – also applied to him. But he still couldn't drop the thought that she'd been avoiding him on purpose.

'Hi, Mina,' he said as he heard Aston throw himself onto Maria with a hoot.

His son immediately became embroiled in a tickling match with his mum on the floor. Aston appeared to have the upper hand.

He turned back to the hob and began stirring the macaroni again while also turning the sliced sausages in the frying pan. They had almost stuck to the bottom. The line was silent.

'Mina, are you there?'

He could hear her breathing. But it was in fits and starts. It almost sounded as if she were . . . crying? He lowered his voice so that it was almost drowned out by the extractor fan.

'Has something happened?' he asked carefully.

It was now clear that Mina was crying. But the abrupt sobs revealed that she was struggling to regain control of her voice. He waited, letting her gather herself. The pan of macaroni boiled over without him reacting.

'I'm here,' he said. 'There's no rush.'

It was incredibly uncomfortable to hear Mina cry. He had always struggled to deal with such strong expressions of emotion – he'd never known how to behave. But this was worse than usual. Mina was always so collected, so exact. Focused. Hearing her lose control was like spying on something far too private. Something that no one was ever meant to see. The fact that she had called anyway presumably indicated how serious it was.

The water from the pan was spreading over the induction hob. The safety mechanism reacted, cutting power to the rings. Which was fortunate, given that the sausages in the frying pan were starting to burn.

'I'm not feeling so good,' she said at last, words coming in the same fits and starts as the crying. 'I haven't been able to eat or sleep all weekend.'

'Do you mean literally or metaphorically?'

'Literally. I've been awake for seventy-two hours. Longer. I'm so sad. I don't know what to do any longer.'

Water dripped off the hob and reached his feet. Only when it scalded his toes did Vincent realize he had transformed dinner into a minor disaster. He didn't even dare look at the sausages. But dinner was the least of his worries right now.

'I'm coming now,' he said. 'Are you at home? I'll be there in half an hour. Don't do anything for the time being – just stay where you are and don't move from that spot.'

He didn't say why, didn't say he was terrified of what she might get up to before he got there.

'OK,' said Mina, in a voice that didn't quite carry.

She didn't even feel up to disagreeing. But he got the door code out of her.

Vincent looked down at the wet floor. He really ought to deal with this. But it would have to keep for later.

Rebecka stuck her head out of her bedroom.

'Dad, what the hell are you doing?' she said. 'There's a burnt stench all the way to my room.'

'Rebecka – good,' he said, quickly wiping down the hob with a cloth. 'You'll have to carry on making dinner – I've got to do something.'

'But I . . . what? Argh!'

Rebecka threw up her hands in a gesture of resignation but came into the kitchen anyway.

'I'm going to buy pizza,' she said, after inspecting the catastrophe. 'Transfer the money to me. You do know the floor is wet, right?'

Vincent pulled out his mobile and sent the money to Rebecka. Then he fetched his laptop.

'What are you doing?' said Maria, getting up from the floor with Aston clinging to her legs. 'Who called?'

He hesitated. Then he took a deep breath. This wasn't going to be taken well.

'It was Mina. Something's happened. I have to go there and comfort her.'

He pulled up Google and did a hasty search.

'You must be joking. Are you winding me up?' said Maria in a shrill voice. 'Comfort? Doesn't she have anyone else she can call? It's bloody Sunday night, Vincent!'

He focused on the computer.

Maria hadn't heard how Mina sounded.

'But she called me,' he said. 'So it's my responsibility.'

He looked at his wife, who had pointedly crossed her arms.

'Maria, I was genuinely worried,' he said. 'You should have heard her.'

'Well, why don't you just go then? If you insist on being her knight in shining armour riding in on a white stallion?'

'White? The Toyota's red . . .'

'For goodness' sake. Sometimes . . .' Maria muttered with a shake of her head.

'This has nothing to do with chivalry,' he said. 'Someone close to me is in a potentially dangerous situation, physically and mentally. I seem to be the only person who knows about it and that means I'm the only one who can help. So in purely rational terms, I must. I need to make sure it wasn't because I did something wrong,' he said, turning the laptop to show her.

He had clicked on a Wikipedia page titled *How to comfort a friend*.

'Are you kidding?' Maria said with disgust. 'How Aspie are you? You need to google it to figure out how to comfort someone? Normal people just *know* that kind of thing. You say "I'm here for you if you need anything". That's the most important thing. Do you really have no genuine empathy?'

She had misunderstood. As usual. He hadn't googled to fake empathy, but precisely *because* he was empathetic. He wasn't in the slightest bit convinced that things you 'just knew' were always right. There were so many of those stupid things. Everyone 'knew' that children couldn't swim for an hour after eating because they'd get cramp. Which was a straight lie fabricated by overstuffed parents who wanted an hour off. And everyone 'just knew' that food became less nutritious in a microwave. More nonsense. Of course, he wasn't immune to such fallacies. Mina meant far too much for him to dare taking the risk. But how was he meant to explain that to Maria?

'I'm not used to comforting adults,' he said. 'And I don't want to make the situation even worse. So I wanted to see whether there were mistakes I should avoid. Like this.'

Vincent read aloud from the site:

'*One common mistake is the phase "I'm here for you, let me know if there's anything you need". The problem with this is that it is too general. The person you are comforting is suddenly required to work out themselves how you can help. Instead, you should be specific. Explain how you can help and propose that you clean or cook or sleep over.*'

'Sleep over,' said Maria, pursing her lips. 'Thought as much.'

He sighed deeply. As usual, she had completely missed the point.

'Do you know what?' Maria said bitterly. 'Don't bother coming home afterwards.'

Vincent frowned. She didn't want him to sleep over. But he wasn't allowed to come home. Good God. How was he to understand the logic of women?

101

The front door to Mina's flat was unlocked. The rug inside the door was big enough to allow you to take off your shoes on it without having to step onto the floor. At least if you were fairly nimble with good balance. To be safe, Vincent took off his shoes outside the door and carefully set them down on the rug. He didn't bother to call out for her but headed straight into the flat.

Mina was sitting on the sofa in the living room with the phone still in her hand. Given her appearance, she had been telling the truth when she'd said she hadn't slept or eaten. She was pale as a corpse, except for the dark rings around her eyes. Her posture was reminiscent of a saggy balloon. What little energy she had left was being used on crying so hard her body shook.

He placed the paper bag containing what he had bought on the coffee table. Then he went into the kitchen and found a glass. When he returned, he took a bottle of juice from the bag and poured a few inches into the glass. He guessed she didn't need a straw for her own glasses.

'Juice, yogurt, sandwich,' he said, unpacking the rest. 'A fancy sandwich at that. Avocado.'

A few crumbs ended up on the table, but he didn't think Mina cared at the moment. She merely shook her head.

'I know,' he said. 'You can't eat. I'm not going to ask you to, either. But when you realize you can, this is here. Right now I just want you to drink something. But there's no rush with that either.'

He put the glass as close to her as he could and then moved away from it, to signal how unimportant the food was to him. He hoped she hadn't been able to tell from his voice how urgent he thought it was. Mina looked like she might collapse at any moment.

Instead, he sat down on the sofa next to her and after a moment's hesitation he put an arm around her shoulders. She let him do that and curled up against his chest – despite the fact that his shirt still smelled of burned sausages and over-boiled macaroni.

She cried in silence while he stroked her head. One of the illustrations accompanying *How to comfort a friend* had shown him what to do. But he would probably have thought of it himself. It felt good. Natural.

While he waited for the worst of it to pass, he took in Mina's home. He had expected it to be all white. White furniture, white walls and white paintings. So that the dirt had nowhere to hide. Instead, the walls of Mina's flat were pale grey and her furniture was made of pale wood – at least in the living room and kitchen, which was what he could see. He was surprised by how tasteful it was. The minimalist style almost meant that it didn't look peculiar for each object to be symmetrically positioned in its own spot and for everything to be perfectly dusted. If he hadn't known Mina, he would have thought he'd stumbled into an interior design feature rather than a carefully sterilized life. There were also no signs of any interaction whatsoever with other people, as far as he could tell. No photos of relatives, no photos of friends, no calendar on the wall with dinners or coffees out noted on it.

After a few minutes, her breathing calmed down a little. At this point, he reached for the glass and passed it to her. She took it with both her hands and drank a few gulps. She paused, seemingly contemplating returning it, but then she kept it and drank the rest. He exhaled. Now at least she had a few drops of vitamins and sugar inside her. Hopefully that was enough for her appetite to start creeping back too.

'Can I ask?' he said.

'If you must,' she said in a low voice.

'I don't have to. I'll be here for as long as you think you need it. I'll let you eat and sleep. But only when you want. And we don't have to talk.'

The last bit hadn't been on the website. He'd come up with it himself. Apparently it was the right thing to say, because Mina nodded quietly. She laid her head against his chest again. Tears were still flowing but not as violently as before.

'By the way, what did Maria say when you left to come here?' she said. 'Was she jealous?'

'Is the Pope Catholic? More than anything, she thinks I'm a moron and should get diagnosed.'

Mina laughed.

397

'I think we're very much on the same page about that last bit,' she said. 'Do you know that you smell of sausages?'

It was his turn to laugh. Then both of them fell silent. Mina was clearly exhausted. It would be good if he could get her to sleep. He matched his breathing to hers until they were inhaling and exhaling in the same rhythm, synchronized with each other. She relaxed her body even more. He continued for a while longer, allowing himself to enjoy the purely physical sensation of being in sync with someone. It didn't happen often. And it had been a long time since it last had. Then he slowed down the tempo of his own breathing, checking that she was unconsciously doing the same. He continued to breathe slowly with her, lowering the tempo even further in small steps, so that her body had time to adapt. After five minutes of slow breathing, she was fast asleep.

He took a deep breath. He had never dared to comfort either Maria or Ulrika – they would definitely have had a good laugh at him if he'd tried. But with Mina it had gone well – very well, in fact. It had almost felt natural.

He carefully laid her down on the sofa without knowing what the next step was. He looked around the living room. A home always revealed details about its occupant, even if it was harder nowadays when you couldn't peruse people's records and libraries. Checking what someone had saved on Spotify or on their Kindle wasn't quite the same. However, he had learned that the most interesting information was to be found in places where people didn't realize they had left any trace. A post-it with a reminder about a repeat appointment. Magnetic words forming sentences on the fridge. Forgotten items on the bottom shelf of the coffee table.

Mina's living room and kitchen, however, bore no such signs. The paintings on the walls revealed nothing – so far as he could tell, they'd been bought at IKEA. He didn't intend to go into her bedroom, particularly not when she was sleeping. That would be far too much of an intrusion into her personal life. On the desk in the living room there was a Rubik's cube. Probably the same one he'd seen in her pocket the first time they'd met.

He picked up the cube and held it by the bottom corner between his thumb and middle finger so that he could rotate the rows using his index and ring fingers. The rows that moved did so almost without resistance. He'd been right then – it was a speed cube that was sufficiently frictionless to be solved using one hand. It surprised him that

Mina had left it unsolved. Personally, he was old school – he always began with the cross. He knew there were faster routes, but it was in his muscle memory. He absent-mindedly twisted the cube with one hand while continuing to look about him.

Also on the desk were documents he recognized, all tied to the investigation. A small, framed photograph at the far end of the table caught his eye. Hanging from the frame was a necklace. Vincent recognized it as one of those magnetic pieces of jewellery. That surprised him. Mina didn't seem the type to believe in wishy-washy New Age stuff. But then again, it wasn't his thing either.

Mina moved restlessly on the sofa. She mumbled something but he didn't manage to hear what she said. The photograph in the frame was a studio portrait of a young girl. It was only a few inches high and it reminded him of the photos they took in school, where parents paid for a bundle of far too many prints in the hope that Granny, Grandpa and the rest of the family would all be thrilled to receive portraits of the child for yet another year. A joy that he suspected the parents had grossly miscalculated.

'Nighty,' Mina muttered.

This time he heard it clearly.

'Nighty night,' he said softly. 'You need to sleep.'

'Nighty, sweetheart. I'm here,' she said again, frowning. 'Can't you see me?'

Nighty night? He could feel himself blushing. They weren't that familiar with each other. Mina still seemed to be sleeping, but more restlessly than before. He looked at the girl in the photo again. Then he carefully turned the frame over. *Nathalie, 10 years old*, it said on the reverse. He blushed even more. Mina hadn't meant him. *Natti* was a person. He put the frame back, taking care to place it in the same position as before, and adjusted the necklace. He found a pen and turned over the first page from the hard copy report on Agnes.

I'm not going to ask. But when you're ready to talk, I'll listen, he wrote on the back of the sheet.

Only then did he realize he'd solved her Rubik's cube, which he was still holding. He'd done it without thinking about it.

P.S. Sorry about the cube he added to the message, placing it along with the cube next to the sandwich on the coffee table.

At one end of the sofa there was a perfectly folded blanket. He unfurled it and laid the soft blanket over Mina. Then he picked up his shoes and crept carefully out of the flat.

102

Vincent couldn't sleep. The self-hypnosis exercise that he usually made use of wasn't working. That had never happened before. His thoughts were still in tumult. But the new letter had taken him by surprise. He was used to fan mail or emails from people who either wanted his help figuring out their lives or just wanted help for a job interview. And he hadn't given any more thought to the threatening letters he'd received in the spring. But now his stalker had written again.

He sat up with his legs over the edge of the bed and turned on the torch on his mobile. It was silly to disturb Maria. He unfolded the letter for the fifth time.

It's going to be me and you, it said. *But I understand that you can't tell your wife that. I'll take care of it.*

It was as if an invisible ice cube went down his spine each time he read it. The late hour wasn't helping him to think clearly. He needed to regain control of his brain's emotional centre, which had gone into a tailspin. If he cut off the fuel to his anxiety, it would be forced to subside. The easiest way was to solve an abstract problem. Or to read a complicated book. But his books were all down in his study. He didn't feel up to going down there. After all, it was the middle of the night.

He looked at the dark shape next to him on the other side of the bed. His wife had an ability to wrap the duvet around her body as she slept. She was wrapped up like a Greek dolmas. He knew Maria had books. Admittedly with rainbows on them, but perhaps he shouldn't be so contemptuous just this once. When he had been little, he had wished that magic existed. He had even done his utmost to find it. Now it was night-time – the time when the rules of the world didn't quite work as normal. If there were ever a time when he would find some-thing interesting in Maria's books, it was now.

He went around the bed and lit the small lamp on Maria's nightstand. The light was a glowing orb that was supposed to depict the moon. Of course. His wife grunted and turned over in bed, away from the light.

As expected, there were four books on the table. You could say what you liked, but Maria took self-improvement seriously. Theoretically, at any rate. The top book in the pile was called *Grit: The Power and Passion of Not Giving Up*. That wouldn't do. He'd actually read it, and the author – Angela Duckworth – was a sharp lady who had her wits about her. He needed something whackier – ideas that he could quarrel with.

The next book was called *How to Love Everyone Unconditionally*. The cover had an illustration of a green sprout growing out of a sunburst, the seedling shaped as a heart with yet another sun in the middle of it. There was no author named – just a reference to a website. This was more like it. This would give him something to chew over. But maybe things could get even better.

The third book was titled *Learn to Love What You Have*, while the final one was called *He's An Idiot But He's Your Idiot*. He remained standing there with the last three books in his hands.

Learn to love.

He's an idiot.

Love everyone unconditionally.

When the realization hit him, it did so with equal parts anxiety and vertigo. He had thought Maria's intense consumption of books had been about 'getting to know herself' or 'finding her spiritual self' or some other self-absorbed thing. He had teased her about it more times than he cared to remember.

But that didn't seem to be the case at all. These books spoke of her effort to understand *him*. Trying to find the route into a family where two of the children weren't hers. He had misunderstood everything. His wife was right. He is an idiot. A complete fucking idiot. She had a husband from a completely different planet. And he didn't know whether he deserved to be loved.

'Vincent,' said Maria, drunk on sleep. 'What are you doing?'

He put the books back down and adjusted the pile. Then he wiped his eyes and hoped she wouldn't notice the tears. Maria raised her head and squinted at him.

'Has something happened?' she said.

He turned off the moon lamp so she wouldn't have to see how ashamed he was.

'Do you remember when we fell in love?' he said, in a voice that didn't quite carry.

'Mmmm . . . What?'

'I told you that I was hard to live with. I just had no idea how hard. How much work it's been for you.'

'It's obviously a trying experience,' she yawned. 'Especially in the middle of the night. Won't you come back to bed?'

'But is it worth it?'

Maria opened her eyes completely.

'You mean living with you?'

He nodded quietly, without being certain whether she could see him in the dark.

'I think that depends on you,' she said. 'Do you want it to be worth it?'

He nodded again, mostly for his own sake.

'Sorry,' he said. 'I've been an idiot.'

'Well, I know that,' she said smiling. 'And sometimes I want to suffocate you with tea leaves. But you're my idiot. Come back to bed now. You can be the little spoon if you like.'

'But you don't know what I—'

'I know it's half past two in the morning,' she said, looking at the digital clock beneath the moon lamp. 'And if you don't want me to leave you, you'd better come back to bed. The alarm's set to go in four hours' time.'

Maria lay down, turned over and shuffled about in the bed, searching for the comfiest position to lie in. After a while, her breathing became heavier and slower.

He remained standing there, looking at the silhouette of his wife. The mother of his youngest son. He hadn't just given up on their relationship, he'd done his utmost to destroy it. But she had never given up. She had tried far harder than he ever had. That was going to change from now on. Not that he in any way deserved it. But if there was a small shred of their marriage left that could still be saved then he intended to do so. If she would let him.

103

A light knocking made Mina jump. She hadn't noticed Julia come into the room until Julia discreetly tapped on the corner of the desk.

'I said your name several times – you must have been miles away,' Julia said. 'Has Peder managed to get hold of this Anna yet?'

Mina spun a half circuit on her office chair. She had one made entirely from steel and chrome, without any upholstered cushion on it like the others had. Fabric was an incredible hoarder of bacteria. Especially fabric that you had your behind on for the best part of the day. Steel could be wiped down. Or rinsed if necessary.

'No, but he did get hold of an address,' she said, standing up. 'He was just in touch.'

Peder was once again having to look after the triplets. But he had sent her a brief message with the information he had pulled up before disappearing into his world of baby vomit.

'I was about to take Vincent and head over there. He deserves to come with me.'

Something told her that she needed to bring him even though she risked her secret being uncovered. It surprised her that she felt so OK with the idea of him knowing.

'Is it really a good idea to take Vincent?' said Julia. 'He's become personally involved in this, what with the book. Wouldn't it be better if you took Christer?'

Mina shook her head firmly.

'No, I want to take Vincent. It's the least we can do. It's actually thanks to him that we've made it this far. I'm more than capable of dealing with Anna if she tries anything.'

Julia smiled in amusement.

'Sure, but your colleagues did some of the work too. Don't forget that before you go all starry-eyed.'

'Starry-eyed . . .'

Mina snorted, but much to her annoyance she realized she was blushing.

'I just think it would be appropriate to bring Vincent, given his skills. It's got nothing to do with whether . . .'

'Yes, yes, there's no need to labour the point. Take Vincent with you. But be careful.'

Julia smiled teasingly as she turned on her heel and left. Part of Mina wanted to call her back and continue explaining, but she knew she would only be digging the hole deeper.

Instead, she took out her antiseptic wet wipes and carefully wiped down the spot on the desk where Julia had tapped it.

104

'So Peder hasn't met her?' Vincent asked curiously as Mina parked. 'Why wasn't she at the AA meeting?'

'Peder said no one knew why. She just hadn't shown up.'

'They're not allowed to give out addresses, are they? That's the whole point of AA. The anonymity?'

Mina nodded, applying the handbrake and turning off the engine.

'AA doesn't give out addresses, but one of the attendees knew where she lived. Apparently they were almost neighbours and often went along together.'

They got out of the car and looked around. It was a grey day and rain hung in the air. The satnav had brought them to a drab area with large blocks of flats – concrete and steel in a charmless combination that had once fulfilled the purpose of quickly providing housing for the city of Stockholm as it grew at record pace.

'Which floor?' said Vincent, squinting up at the block.

'Third,' said Mina, locating Anna's name on the entry phone by the door.

After a few seconds there was a click from the door and they entered. Mina wrinkled her nose. There was an unpleasant smell lingering in the stairwell – a mixture of old urine and something sharp she guessed emanated from the very fabric of the building.

'I know, I know, we'll skip the lift,' Vincent said, heading for the stairs.

The walls were painted a dull light green that was flaking off. She couldn't recollect how many stairwells she had visited on duty with exactly the same kind of paint. And exactly the same smell.

'Here,' said Vincent when they had climbed the stairs, pointing at a floral motif sign on the door with Anna's name on it.

A doormat was positioned outside the door, inscribed with the words *The queen of fucking everything.*

'OK then, let's roll,' Mina said drily, with a nod.

She let Vincent ring the bell. One less bacteria-infested doorbell for her to worry about. Her stomach still ached. Vincent would soon know her secret, but she would just have to deal with that later.

The door opened. Dolphin girl stared at them. For a few seconds her facial expression was neutral, as if a whole world of impressions was passing through her. Then she let out a roar that almost made Mina leap out of her shoes.

'VINCENT!'

Anna threw her arms around Vincent's neck and he staggered back. Mina's jaw dropped. Vincent stood there with a shouting Anna hanging around his neck. Mina didn't understand what was going on at all. Of course, she knew that Anna was familiar with Vincent – that was the whole reason why they were there – but this reception was not what she had expected. Nor, apparently, had Vincent. He looked confused. As if searching for something in his memory.

'Er, hello . . .' he said in confusion, untangling himself from a reluctant Anna.

'Can we come in?' said Mina. 'We need to talk to you about something.'

She could hear how harsh she sounded, but she was still trying to gather her wits after watching Anna literally throw herself at Vincent. It wasn't the behaviour one expected from a murder suspect.

'Of course, of course, come in! Sorry, gosh, look at the state of me and I haven't tidied up either. If only I'd known you were coming today of all days, Vincent, I would have got ready and made the place beautiful.'

Anna babbled nervously as she backed into the hallway to let them in. Vincent seemed to hesitate about entering, but quickly gathered himself and followed her inside.

'And here I was, frying some mince for Ingo. I'm sorry, I just need to check it isn't burning – he doesn't like it when it's burnt. He wants it to have . . . Well, he'd prefer it raw, but there's no way of knowing what's in it, so I prefer to fry it for him . . .'

Anna stopped herself and looked at Mina as if she were only now registering that Vincent wasn't alone.

'You're called Mina, right?' said Anna. 'We usually see each other . . .'

'In Kungsholmen,' Mina concluded, looking at dolphin girl significantly. 'I've been there as a supporter a few times.'

The memo was apparently received, or perhaps she couldn't think about anything other than Vincent, because Anna nodded curtly and vanished into the flat. Mina followed Vincent into the hallway, not entirely sure what they were stepping into.

The hall was nowhere near as untidy as Anna had made it sound, but it was very over-decorated. There were tapestries with words of wisdom, paintings with quotations, an enamel sign with the words *Carpe diem* and another one with *The queen of fucking everything* yet again, mirrors, artificial flowers and a plethora of knick-knacks. A cross-stitch embroidery noted that *A big cock is of little comfort in a poor home.* Anna continued to rattle around the kitchen and they slowly followed her.

'I just need to give Ingo his food, then I'll put on some coffee for you – and I think I've got some biscuits too. I can't believe you finally came, Vincent. Wait until I call Lindsy and tell her – she's been sending out soooo much negative energy and said it would never happen, that I was only imagining things and that I shouldn't have written those stupid letters, that it's all just in my head! Ha! Have you ever heard anything so stupid, Vincent, especially given, well, given that you're standing right here?'

Anna was beaming like the sun and went over to the hob where a frying pan was sizzling. Only now did Mina spot a large, furry ragdoll cat patiently waiting by the cooker. Mina's eyes began to itch and she had difficulty breathing at the mere sight of the cat. Not that she was actually allergic, but cat hair was the last thing she wanted to take home with her. The cat glanced at her and Vincent but then ignored them, since the contents of the frying pan were clearly of more interest.

'There we are, baby, time for you to eat. Mama's going to help you, it'll be so tasty, so so tasty, won't it, baby?'

Anna babbled to the cat and reached for a spoon while taking the frying pan off the heat and putting it on a mat on the table. She sat down on a chair and the cat turned to her, while its tail eagerly swept the worn kitchen floor. Mina didn't dare look at Vincent to see whether he had the same shocked expression that she probably had. Dolphin girl was spoon-feeding the cat. She had never seen the like of it before. She had met Anna at AA countless times, reluctantly exchanging a few words every now and then, listening to the testimony. But she'd had the impression that Anna was fairly normal. Maybe a little eccentric, but nothing like this . . .

407

She shook her head without being able to stop herself and then looked for somewhere to sit. This might take a while. Relieved, she noted that the flat seemed very clean and tidy. She would be able to sit down at the kitchen table. Of course, she would have preferred to get out her wet wipes to clean both the chair and table first, but she mastered her impulses when she was on duty.

Vincent sat down on the chair beside her and now Mina dared to glance at him. He was observing the spoon-feeding of the cat with fascination and seemed to be thinking intently about something. He turned his head and met her gaze. Mina nodded.

'Anna,' he said. 'There's something we'd like to clear up with you. You talked to Mina about me. Do you remember that?'

'My God, of course, Vincent! I talk to everyone about you! But you know that!'

'I do?'

Vincent cleared his throat. They had agreed not to mention the book, at least not to start with, in case Anna attempted to escape. But with every passing second, Mina was more and more convinced that Anna had nothing whatsoever to do with either the book or the message inside it. It didn't take a mentalist to see that.

'But why? And why Mina in particular? How did you come up with the idea of tipping her off about me?'

Anna continued to spoon fried mince from the frying pan into the cat's mouth as she spoke.

'It's not that surprising. There were a few of us who heard a phone call Mina received and I got the impression she needed help. And it was pretty obvious to suggest you.'

Dolphin girl talked about Mina as if she weren't there. Clearly, Vincent's showing up at her apartment was so incredible she couldn't take in anything else. Anna's eyes were radiant as she looked at Vincent, albeit in a way that didn't seem entirely healthy. Anna scraped out the last of the mince.

'Why was it obvious to think of Vincent?' Mina asked.

Anna smiled broadly.

'I'm always thinking about Vincent.'

Mina looked at the mentalist in confusion. The whole conversation felt odd. There was something else going on here that she didn't understand. But looking at it positively, at least Anna seemed uninterested in discussing how she and Mina knew each other.

'Come with me. I've got something to show you, Vincent!'

Anna leapt up and put the frying pan with the spoon in it back on the hob. She hurried across to a closed door on the other side of the hallway and waved at Vincent to follow. Both Vincent and Mina stood up and followed hesitantly behind her.

'Look! Isn't it beautiful?'

Anna opened the door wide. She pointed into the room with her whole arm, jumping on the spot with enthusiasm. Curious, Mina advanced with Vincent a step or two behind her. Then she came to an abrupt halt.

The whole room was covered in photos of Vincent. But he was most frequently not alone in the photos. It was always Vincent together with Anna. Some of the photos were selfies taken at book signings or lectures, with Anna smiling happily in the foreground and Vincent just visible in the background. Others were self-made collages in which Anna had clearly Photoshopped herself into photos of Vincent. Several of them were decorated with newspaper headline clippings. 'Celebrity love blossoms', 'Wedding of the summer' and hand-drawn hearts. Every inch of the walls was covered in pictures.

The hairs on Mina's neck stood on end as she looked around. The stuff on the walls was crazy. This level of obsession called for therapy and medication.

At the back of the room was a small table with a framed photo of Vincent from his most recent show. In front of the photo was a small metal sign with the words 'Mind-reading prohibited' on it. One corner of the sign was bent, as if it had been damaged while removing it from something.

It was an altar.

Mina looked at Vincent. His jaw had dropped, leaving his mouth wide open.

'It's you,' he said slowly. 'It's you who gets up on stage after my performances . . .'

'Of course it's me! You know that!'

Anna laughed merrily and pulled Vincent further into the room. He tried to resist, but Anna had a firm grip on his arm.

'Apparently you weren't joking when you said you're always thinking about Vincent,' Mina said diplomatically.

So much Vincent. Oh so much Vincent. Picture after picture . . .

'Anna, I have to know,' said Vincent. 'Did you send a book to me? With a leopard on the cover? Or did anyone ask you to?'

Now it was Anna's turn to look confused. Her puzzled expression was not feigned – even Mina could tell that. Mina's gut feeling had been right.

'Book?' said Anna. 'Leopard? No, I do like cats, but I've only written you letters – you have got them, right?'

'Yes, thanks. Letters in which you threaten me and my family.'

Anna didn't know anything about the book – that much was obvious. But Vincent had gone very pale. Mina needed to get him out of there. And preferably before that cat decided to be companionable. Bosse had filled her animal quota for the year.

'This was a mistake,' he said to Mina.

'It was nice to visit you, Anna,' said Mina in a friendly but firm voice. 'If Vincent doesn't have any more questions for you, then it's probably time for us to move on.'

Anna looked at her in dismay. Then she turned to Vincent.

'What? Aren't you staying? You're finally here now – you've finally come! Because you read my letters. You're going to be here now, with me! And not with her.'

Anna pointed at Mina.

'I mean, you've got a lovely place in Tyresö,' said Anna. 'But you and me don't need that big, empty house.'

'How do you know where I . . .' Vincent began.

Then his eyes opened wide.

'That sign – it's from my letterbox, isn't it?'

Anna suddenly fell silent and fingered the metal sign. Then she nodded.

'I like looking at you. Although, when she showed up,' she added, glancing at Mina, 'I had to hide. I've seen the two of you. You're always together.'

'Vincent,' said Mina, who could feel the hairs on her neck standing on end again, 'what's she talking about?'

Vincent didn't reply. Instead, he scrutinized the pictures on the walls. He looked particularly closely at the selfies of them both. All occasions when Anna had been close to him without him seeing it. All occasions when Anna could have done whatever she liked.

Mina looked at the pictures too and her gaze was caught by one of Anna lying on her stomach on a couch without her top on. Someone was doing something to her back. Oh no. The photo was unclear, but Mina knew dolphin girl far too well to fail to realize what the picture meant.

Anna saw what she was looking at, spun around with a cheery squeak

410

and raised her top so they could see her back. At the bottom of her spine she had a big pink heart tattoo. Next to the heart was a portrait of her – and another of Vincent. They looked very happy together.

'It's finally our turn now, Vincent!' Anna chirped.

Mina stared at the tattoo. Vincent backed slowly away from Anna's bare back. Then he turned around and rushed out of the flat and down the stairs.

105

The forest wasn't quite what he had expected. He'd never even been in a forest, so how was he supposed to know that it was damp, well actually, full-on wet? You couldn't just lie down here for a shag.

'Let's go a bit further,' he said, turning to her.

A branch slapped him in the face and he put a hand to his cheek.

She gave him a bored look and nodded reluctantly.

'Yes, but not much further. I'm wearing new Reeboks and I've no desire to ruin them.'

She pointed at the ground, which was squelchy and muddy. It was definitely not a surface intended for shiny new white shoes.

'I've paid,' he said by way of reminder, hoping it would be motivation enough.

He didn't give a shit about her kicks. He just wanted to get his cock inside her. Get it over with. He looked around. He needed to find somewhere dry, and fast. Before she changed her mind. His mates were hanging out on their mopeds by the convenience store at Tallkorgen, waiting for him. He couldn't come back unfucked – just couldn't. He was the only one of them who was still a virgin – as they loved to point out at every opportunity.

'Looks like there's a clearing over there – it'll be a bit drier.'

He pointed and began walking.

She followed reluctantly, sighing loudly.

'Just so you know, you've paid for regular fucking missionary and nothing extra. No blow jobs or anything like that.'

The voice was blasé. As if she were talking about the weather.

He wondered how many people she'd fucked. The thought both disgusted him and turned him on in equal measure.

His cock was uncomfortably hard and chafing inside his jeans, and he quickly shifted it a few millimetres.

She was shivering as she tottered along behind him, pulling her denim jacket tighter around her torso.

He'd found her online. His mates had helped choose. They'd been round at Adde's for a whole afternoon, searching for someone he could fuck. Someone cheap. He only had five hundred kronor – his Christmas money from Grandma. And with Lizette, that had been enough for a regular shag. Well, it had actually said a thousand on the website, but Mehmet – who was good at haggling – had got her down to five hundred on his behalf.

'Hey, look! A caravan!' he said in a shrill falsetto of relief, pointing at a ramshackle caravan parked across a clearing.

The trees were thinning out the closer they got and the ground was drier, just as he'd hoped.

His cock was now painfully hard and his breathing was shallower and faster. He wondered what it felt like. Even though he'd seen thousands of porn videos and knew in detail what happened, what it sounded like, he still had no idea what it felt like, having your cock in a cunt. But soon . . . soon he'd get to find out.

'Yes, but what if there's someone living in it?' she said, swearing as she tripped on a branch.

'It looks quiet – we'll check,' he said, crossing his fingers so hard they went white.

Soon . . . soon he was going to get to fuck.

When they reached the caravan he flapped his hand in the air. It smelled off. Probably mould or a broken pipe. But he didn't care right now. His cock was rock hard in his jeans and it didn't give a flying fuck whether the place smelled bad. A few more seconds and he would have her under him.

He opened the door and stepped in. Then he rushed out and threw up. Out of the corner of his eye he saw Lizette running away through the forest, screaming something about the police. Her brand-new Reeboks flashed in the darkness between the trees. Fuck. There wasn't going to be any fucking.

106

'Jesus Christ!'

Christer spat on the ground and got a stern look from one of the forensics team. He held up his hands apologetically.

'Hmm, well he didn't exactly look fresh . . .' Ruben said sombrely.

'No, I'm having a hard time believing Mr Rask has been running around butchering people for a while now,' Christer said, swallowing a belch.

The caravan door was open and the stench of putrefaction lay heavily over the small clearing.

'No wonder we couldn't find him,' said Ruben, shaking his head. 'But . . .'

A glimmer of hope ignited in his eyes.

'But he might have been murdered by the other murderer!'

'Aren't you the one who's always banging on about simple solutions?'

Christer took a couple of steps away to avoid obstructing the crime scene investigators in their rustling body suits. He stepped straight into a muddy puddle and looked at his shoes in dismay. He'd been given them by his mother and they had served him well – the shoes were into their second decade without looking too worn out. Mother always bought top quality that lasted. But this bloody forest was going to be their swansong.

'I suppose we'll have to see what he died of,' Ruben said, still hopeful.

One of the CSIs, a pretty young woman with electric blue hair, stopped.

'We won't know for sure until Milda does the autopsy,' she said. 'But it looks like Jonas Rask died of some kind of overdose and from the state of decomposition he's been dead at least a couple of months.'

'Which puts him out of the frame for young Robert's murder at least,' Christer muttered.

Ruben cleared his throat and turned back to the CSI. 'How sure are you about the cause of death?'

'The canula was still in his arm,' said the blue-haired woman.

'Jonas probably picked up a drug habit while he was inside,' said Christer.

He was still mourning his shoes and now the moisture was beginning to seep through them, right through and into his socks. This was the closest to the great outdoors he'd been in forever. And it wasn't inspiring him to come back.

'Tell me who doesn't pick up a drug habit inside. And he did twenty years,' said Ruben, his teeth chattering.

It was actually a warm day, but the damp and gloominess in the forest pulled the temperature down. The caravan, however, had been in the scorching sun all summer, which was guaranteed to have been a major contributory factor to what had awaited them inside.

The body was now being carried away in a black bag with a zip on it. A little fluid was dripping out through the zip and the stench hit them with full force. Christer pinched his nose shut but still had to fight against the nausea. To his satisfaction, even Ruben's face had gone a green-white shade. It had been impossible to get a trolley into the forest clearing, so the body bag was being carried away on a stretcher. Milda didn't have the pleasantest of tasks ahead of her. And the forensics team had an extensive task ahead of them at the caravan.

'Well, there we have it,' said Ruben, setting off with big strides towards the road where they'd left their police car.

Bosse was waiting for them in the car, with the window wound down and a big bowl of water on the floor. At least he'd be happy when they came back. Christer sighed at the state of things. Ruined shoes, wet socks – and yet another lead that had come to a dead end.

107

Dear God, she hated holidays. There were few words in the Swedish language she disliked quite as much, and just as few enforced behaviours she detested with the same fervour.

'You need to take a bit of time off, same as everyone else,' human resources had told her. 'It's August. Rest up. There are other investigators in the building who can man the fort for a week or two.'

That wasn't how Mina saw things. There was a reason why their team had been created. And it wasn't so they could use up their annual leave. But she strongly suspected that this eagerness for time off from the chiefs was actually the first step towards phasing them out and shutting them down. That wasn't something she intended to let happen.

Despite all their work, they hadn't even managed to locate Jonas Rask. It should have been a simple matter. Someone who'd got out after so many years inside ought to have been easy to find. Avoiding the police demanded resources and finesse. And the fact that people were creatures of habit was always advantageous for the police. But none of Rask's old watering holes had turned up anything, and they hadn't managed to find his caravan either. That had taken a randy fifteen-year-old.

Disaster.

She needed something to show for all her efforts. Something concrete. Mina took a step back and inspected her creation. The only positive thing about them forcing her to take time off was that she was able to go through everything she had on the case in peace and quiet without having to put up with colleagues interrupting her. Even if it was dull not seeing Vincent. In the last two weeks, he'd had a string of lectures to deliver – most of them not even in Sweden. Since they had seen each other at dolphin girl's, Anna's, he'd barely been in the country.

And perhaps that was for the best. Partly because she had difficulty believing that Anna could stalk him abroad, since her money seemed to mostly go on new tattoos. And partly because Mina didn't know whether she was ready to talk to him about what had happened when he had come round to hers. Soon, maybe. But not yet.

One of the long walls in the living room was covered in pinned-up pieces of paper and photographs. She had also taken the liberty of writing and drawing straight onto the wall with felt-tip pens. It would be easy enough to cover it with a fresh coat of paint later. Although she had heard that felt-tip pens needed three coats . . . But she always repainted the whole flat each autumn in a new, crisp shade of light grey – after a year it began to assume a slightly darker tone that testified all too clearly to the dirt clinging to the walls, no matter how much she scrubbed them.

She didn't care whether she was the only one who could see that the walls were getting darker. Perhaps she wasn't actually seeing it, if she was honest. But she knew it. She also found the act of painting itself to be therapeutic. Naturally she did the painting herself. There was no chance she was going to let a decorator with dirty shoes into the flat.

Tuva. Agnes. Robert.

They stared into space in her room. The photos were the same ones they had at the station – she had simply taken down everything they had, copied it, and put it back again. Since then, she had added further pieces at home. More notes. More pictures. She had drawn lines, circled some things and marked others that she considered to be particularly important.

In one corner, she had listed things she had come up with as possible and impossible connections between the victims. This offered a wealth of random words and contexts written straight onto the wall. Dentist. School. Grocery store. Related. And another ten or so words. If only people knew how easy it was to map their daily patterns. Facebook. Instagram. In certain cases, a few guesses and a follow-up phone call to confirm. If only she could work out what united them, she would be able to get closer to the truth – she knew that much.

But so far, her efforts had turned up no results. There was seemingly no connection whatsoever between the victims. Zero.

Mina tugged at her ponytail in frustration. She regretted that immediately and reached for the hand sanitizer. She dispensed a big dollop and began to rub it briskly into her hands. She took a step back. She took in the whole collage as one, before shifting her gaze to the right.

417

To Vincent's column. Obviously she had checked everything she could on him too. Especially since he'd become personally involved in the investigation. But back in March she'd chosen to trust his judgement in a sensitive murder inquiry without knowing much more about him than it said on Wikipedia. That had been a little irresponsible, she thought in hindsight, even if it had been fortunate that she had done so. Her knowledge gap about Vincent Walder had been filled in recent weeks. She still didn't have a great deal of information about him compared with the others pinned to her wall, but then he was neither a murder victim nor a suspect.

Yet.

She looked at the portrait of Vincent – an advertising poster from one of his shows. She had only known him for a bare six months, but it felt like it had been much longer than that. It was rare that she experienced that kind of connection with another person. It hadn't happened since—

She quickly pushed away the thoughts and forced her brain to focus on Vincent. His picture was looking straight at her. Sometimes it felt as if his eyes were following her around the room.

She had gone through the same factors for Vincent as she had for the others. Painstakingly working her way through the words she'd written on the wall just as carefully as she had for the others. Which meant she had also learned more about him. Which dentist he went to. Where he bought his groceries. Where he had grown up. She had even managed to get hold of a class photo showing Vincent in primary school, thanks to a company that specialized in digitizing and offering old class photos online. The photo was lying on the desk. He had been amazingly sweet with a cute gap-toothed smile which had been visible because he had been smiling so broadly in the photo.

Personally, she had hated school photos. And she had hated her classmates. All except one: her best friend Pia. So during her high school years – which had been the worst – she had quite simply crossed out the others' faces. And names.

All the names were listed in order under the picture, based on which row the pupils were in. And there was always the name of someone absent. She and Vincent came from completely different parts of Sweden and there was more than ten years' gap between them. And yet their class photos were so similar. She wondered for a moment what Pia was doing now. Their friendship had lasted for a long time, into their adult years. But Pia hadn't been able to understand the choices that Mina

418

had made. So they had gone their separate ways. And she hadn't had many new friends since then. Friends imposed. Wanted too much. Asked too many questions. Demanded that you cared, showed an interest. She hadn't felt able to commit the energy to anyone else – not until she had met Vincent. And the question was whether she really wanted him in her life. She had created an existence that worked. Where she kept the pieces of herself in place. Vincent disturbed those pieces, forcing his way in, and she had a completed Rubik's cube on her table to prove it.

Mina sighed, turned around and was about to head out of the living room to fetch coffee when her mobile rang. The display showed it was Christer.

'Hello! Bosse and I thought we'd check in and see how it's going with . . . your holiday,' he said, emphasizing that last word with slight irritability. 'Bosse is a bit out of sorts today, so we're staying in.'

He was apparently not entirely satisfied with the imposed leave. She was still struggling to get used to this new, happy Christer. Who also seemed to love animals. She had known him ever since she had arrived at police headquarters and hadn't seen him so much as smile at a goldfish.

'Do you do everything with that dog?' she said.

'Funny you should say that – Ruben said the same thing. Bosse doesn't like it when he hasn't got company. He needs the security and stability of my presence. But I guess that's hard to understand for someone who's never had to take care of anything more advanced than a yucca plant.'

'What?'

'Ruben, I mean,' he added quickly. 'The palm. Not you.'

She looked at the wall with all the pictures and notes. Her holiday. Was she going to lie to Christer and tell him that she was at a vineyard in Tuscany, on a shopping adventure in New York or on a beach in Las Palmas?

'When I say holiday, I obviously mean the investigation,' Christer added.

Mina felt as if she'd been caught with her hand in the cookie jar.

'Am I that transparent?' she said.

'Only to anyone who looks. And it's not as if I'm out sailing the archipelago myself.'

'Frankly, I'm getting nowhere,' she sighed. 'I've even started looking into the victims' parents. But I'm not finding anything there either.

They live in different places. They have different jobs. They're not related. I've been on the lookout for anything, big or small. But I'm not finding any factors that tie them together. Right now I'm mostly hoping the murderer has given up.'

She sat down on the desk, moving Vincent's class photo to avoid creasing it.

'And what about the Halland connection? That didn't turn anything up either?' Christer asked as Bosse barked in the background. 'Sorry, I'm just going to feed him.'

The loud rustling of dry food landing in a metal bowl forced her to hold the phone away from her ear. Then there was the sound of intense chewing from a happy golden retriever. Bosse was excessively happy at a base level – she didn't dare imagine what he must be like when he'd just been fed.

'What Halland connection?' she said, when Bosse had calmed down with his eating.

'Ack, well. Connection and connection. Perhaps that's too strong a word, but you have to agree that it's a funny coincidence.'

'I genuinely have no idea what you're talking about.'

Christer's sigh was clearly audible down the line.

'For God's sake. Well, it took a while for me to make the connection too, but once you've spotted it, well . . . I'm sure I mentioned it, but maybe not . . .'

'Christer,' Mina said impatiently. 'Out with it. What are you talking about?'

'Well, Agnes's father comes from Halland. You can tell right away from his dialect,' he said. 'And Robert's parents mentioned that the father had a background in the cheese industry, which makes you think of Kvibille cheese from Halland right away. And as for Tuva . . . Her grandfather is a birdwatcher and he had a big poster on his wall at home, of the peregrine falcon. That's Halland's county bird. It's all in my reports. I thought the connection was so obvious that no one could have missed it.'

She pictured how pleased with himself Christer was. It was a pity she'd have to take him down a peg or two.

'Did Tuva's grandfather have any other bird posters?'

'Perhaps,' Christer said reluctantly.

'And how many other cheese makers are there in Sweden? Kvibille is far from the only one.'

'OK, so shoot me. The connection might not be completely crystal

420

clear. But it's a feeling. I think they're from Halland. If that means anything. Anyway, I've got to go now. Bosse wants to watch TV.'

She didn't intend to ask how Christer knew that, or what a dog could possibly want to watch on TV. *Animal Hospital*? *In Nature* maybe? Or that movie *Hachi* with Richard Gere? She had great difficulty picturing Christer as Richard Gere.

What was it she'd been about to do when Christer had called . . . That was it. Coffee. She hopped off the desk, put the mobile phone to one side and took a step towards the kitchen. Then she spun on her heel. She stared at the collage. At the new pictures she had pinned up – the ones no one else had seen. She held up the photo lying on her desk. Looked at the list of names under the class photo. Then she turned it over. And read.

She could kiss Christer. He'd been right about Halland. But he'd made the classic masculine mistake of simply focusing on the men. The solution was obviously something completely different.

She knew what the connection was.

She finally knew what the connection was.

108

The rug inside Mina's front door hadn't got any bigger since the last time he'd been there. He had taken off one shoe and was balancing on one leg while trying to remove the other. Vincent didn't dare be the first person to leave a shoe print on the clinker floor. He wobbled and put his hand on the door to support himself.

Mina looked at his hand but averted her gaze when she noticed that he had seen her doing that. He knew she was already obsessing about the greasy marks his fingertips had left on the door and wondering how long she could control herself before they were sanitized away. He forestalled her by producing a pack of single-use wipes from his pocket and wiping the door. Then he looked at the pack and feigned concern.

'Hang on,' he said. 'These are the *used* wipes. That I used to wipe the handholds on the underground.'

Mina's expression transformed into one of pure horror in a split second.

'Ha ha,' she said, punching him on the shoulder – hard enough for him to realize how not *ha ha* she found it. 'Welcome back to Sweden. Have you recovered from your close encounter with your stalker, Anna? I noted that you didn't hypnotize her to forget that you existed or anything like that. Perhaps it flattered your ego a little bit after all?'

Vincent stared at her. She apparently thought that story was far funnier than he did. He had done his best to try to forget the heart tattoo, but it still kept appearing in his mind's eye when he least wanted it to.

He brushed a hand over his face and followed Mina into the living room. The flat had been cleaned with the same precision as last time he had been here. The only thing disrupting order was the chaos on the living room wall. That was new. A few paintings were lying on the floor. He guessed they'd been taken down to make space for what was now covering the wall. It seemed to be all documents and photos that Mina had access to as part of the investigation. There were some that he hadn't even seen before. Everything was laminated.

'It's happened to me before,' he said. 'Stalkers, that is. Just not so extreme. Usually it's bored housewives or young men confused about their identity, who for some reason believe all their problems will be solved if they can be with me.'

'Look at you, Casanova.'

'Not at all. If they hadn't found me they would have projected their emotions onto someone or something else. But Anna is a little different. Unlike most of the others, she isn't satisfied with letting it be a fantasy. The only thing that seems to help is to maintain as great a distance between her and me as is possible. With the help of the police, should it be needed.'

'Are you asking me to protect you?' said Mina, smiling.

'You're doing that already.'

'Ruben would love to hear about Anna,' she laughed.

Vincent looked at her wall again. He had never understood why they put everything up on a wall in all the crime dramas – except that it looked good on camera. But when he saw Mina's wall, he suddenly understood why. It was a reverse approach to making a mind map. Instead of working from a central idea and then forming branches, she already had the branches and was now searching for what tied them together. And in the middle of this creation there was a photo. He went closer and nodded at the picture.

'Is that . . .?'

'That's why I called,' she said.

Mina's voice was not altogether steady. As if she were afraid of how he would react. He didn't need to look closely at the photo to know what it was – he had seen the picture many times before. Even if it had been a long time ago. Such a very long time. He reached out to take the laminated photo off the wall, but stopped himself when he heard Mina's sharp intake of breath. He should have known better. Lying on the desk behind them was a box of single-use cotton gloves. He took a pair from the carton, put them on and then reached for the photo again. No reaction this time.

The picture was a class photo. He turned it over.

Kvibille Primary School, Class 1b, it said on the reverse. He turned it face up again. The clothes divulged that it was the early 1980s.

423

'That's you standing in the back row, right?' said Mina, pointing at a smiling boy with a gap between his front teeth, half-concealed behind a stout schoolmistress.

Vincent nodded and swallowed hard. This was the only photo from Kvibille Primary that he'd been in before he'd moved and changed schools. But he saw no similarities between the boy in the picture and himself today. How could that boy have become him? And was it good or bad that he didn't recognize himself? Didn't he *want* to recognize himself?

'I didn't know your name was Boman,' said Mina, as he read it in the list of names under the picture.

Vincent Adrian Boman.

Boman. That was a name he hadn't heard in a long time.

'The Walders were my foster family,' he said, nodding to himself. 'I took their name. I was called Boman before that. But how did you find my old class photo?'

'A little honest police work. The Walders were easy to find in the electoral register. There are only a few of them, and only one took in an orphan by the name of Vincent. The social services paperwork said the child's original surname had been Boman, and that you lived in Kvibille. The rest was easy. But that's not why I'm showing you the photo.'

Mina pointed at one of his classmates.

'This girl is called Jessica Widergård. She's Robert's mother. She looks the same. I recognized her straight away from the news reports on Bobby.'

Vincent went pale. He looked at the picture for a long time. Then he pointed at two other girls who were sitting next to Jessica.

'There were three of them. Jessica, Malin and Charlotte. Sickan, Malla and Lotta.'

'Were they good friends?' she said, her eyes widening.

'Yes, you might say that. They always hung out together. As if they were sisters. But why do you ask?'

'Because Malin Bengtsson and Charlotte Hamberg are the mothers of Agnes and Tuva.'

The silence that followed was deafening.

'Did you know them?' Mina said eventually.

'Sickan, Malla and Lotta?' he said tonelessly. 'Absolutely. The four of us spent a lot of time together the summer after this picture was taken. Before I changed schools.'

Memories he had suppressed for the majority of his life suddenly came hurtling towards him with the force of an express train. His magic workshop out in the barn. The box he'd built with the stars on it.

They were going to surprise Jane.

Mum was so happy that day.

Seven children in each row of the class photo, three rows in total. 7 + 3 = 10. The picture was taken in the spring of 1982. 1 + 9 = 10. 8 + 2 = 10. 10 + 10 + 10. Three sides of an equilateral triangle. Like Mum's cut-up toasted sandwiches. It was important that they were exact. No matter how much he tried, his thoughts led him back to Mum.

Half a minute tops.

They had got on their bikes and gone for a swim.

'I don't understand. I should have reacted to their names right away if they were in any report, but I haven't seen them anywhere so far as I know. I don't understand.'

'Because they haven't been part of the investigation. Charlotte passed away shortly after giving birth to Agnes. Malin is Tuva's mother, but she left for France with her husband when Tuva turned sixteen. She hasn't been back to the country since. Jessica, Bobby's mum, you've read about in the report. But it's not surprising that you didn't give it any thought, because she's no longer called Widergård. Like all the others she changed her name when she got married. As you have, for that matter. Changed surname, I mean.'

He stared at the photo. His old friends. The summer when they had gone swimming. The others. Not him. He had sat there looking at the lake. And he felt how the dark, deep shadow was big enough to reach into the present day and consume him.

'Anyway,' Mina continued, 'this class photo proves that the victims' mothers knew each other. And now you're saying that they also knew *you*. That you played together. That can't be a coincidence.'

Mina stood right in front of him and rather incredibly placed her hands on his. She was deadly serious right now.

'Vincent, what's your involvement in this?'

'Me? But . . . Do I have to be? There's guaranteed to be other people who also knew them. Give me ten minutes and I'll prove that Malin, Jessica and Charlotte all bought sweets in the same shop. Or snogged the same boy in their teens. Or worked at the same place in adulthood. Are you going to cross-examine anyone who might have met all three?'

Mina removed her hands, taken aback by the attack. He hadn't meant to hurt her. He had just been so unprepared for what she said. And what she hadn't said. Yet.

'Sorry,' he said, reaching out his hand towards her.

She didn't take it.

'You're right,' he said. 'It's unlikely this is a coincidence, given that I'm helping with the investigation. None of their other potential mutual friends is doing that. I just don't want you to think that I'm somehow involved in this, that I know something I haven't told you. Especially given the message in the book. I really don't understand what all this means.'

He pointed at the class photo.

'Unless . . . Do you think I'm the fourth victim? Or rather, my son Benjamin? Are you going to find him compressed into an origami box with a number carved into his forehead?'

It felt as if he was standing outside his own body and watching himself. As if it was all a film. But Mina shook her head.

'I think your role in this is a completely different one,' she said, standing up and going over to the desk. She fetched a laminated sheet from the desk and handed it to him. It was an article from an old issue of the *Hallandsposten* newspaper. The article was a double-page spread, complete with a sensational headline ending in exclamation marks. However, the majority of the space was taken up by a photo. He had only seen it once previously before his foster parents had thrown out the newspaper. But he would never forget it. The picture showed a young boy standing in a farmyard. It was impossible to tell which farm it was, but Vincent knew. A bigger newspaper would have chosen a different photo – or omitted it altogether. But the editor at *Hallandsposten* hadn't had any objection to publishing photos of children. The eighties had been a different time.

Behind the boy, striped police tape denoted a cordoned-off area. And behind the tape, in front of a barn, there was a glimpse of a box painted in stars.

The boy was looking straight into the camera. His gaze contained all the grief and pain in the world. Vincent recognized the look without difficulty. It was still the same every morning when he looked in the bathroom mirror.

'How many of your colleagues know?' he whispered.

'None as yet,' Mina said.

He paused for a long time.

'Why didn't you say anything?' she said. 'Seriously, fuck you.'

426

She tilted her head backwards and blinked, but he'd heard the emotion in her voice.

'What am I supposed to think, Vincent? I trusted you.'

'I was a child, Mina.'

The tears were openly flowing down her cheeks now, and she brushed her face with the sleeve of her jumper.

'I make it a rule never to trust anyone,' she said. 'But I made an exception for you. And I got the others to trust you too. Fuck you for showing me I was right. Surely you realize that you'll be our prime suspect as soon as I tell the others?'

Vincent looked down at the floor.

'And what do you suspect?' he said. 'Do you think I murdered them?'

Mina snuffled and gathered herself together. She studied him with a look that was nothing but professional.

'That's a good question,' she said flatly. 'Did you?'

109

The summer evening was darker than it should have been. Clouds that hadn't been there when he'd driven over to Mina's were now covering the sky. It looked like it might rain at any moment. Vincent was struggling to concentrate on the drive home, but fortunately there weren't many other cars on the roads. People weren't back from their summer holidays yet. Lucky for them, given how he was driving.

At the same time, he didn't want to get home too quickly. Once home, he wouldn't have the headspace he needed to process everything that Mina had said. Maria had already sent a text warning him that Aston wanted to build a 'gigantic-enormous Lego spaceship' and that she was benevolently delegating this to Vincent. Or as she put it: 'to you boys'. Maria often said it was important for her to feel equal. That apparently did not include building Lego with her son. Not that it bothered Vincent. She didn't know what she was missing.

This time, however, it meant he took the long route home to clear his thoughts first. Perhaps he would drive by the car park at Partihallarna where they'd found Robert. See whether that got his thoughts going. On the other hand, it might not look good if he visited a crime scene, now that he was on the way to being a murder suspect. Mina had probably already called Julia and told her everything. He wondered who they'd send to take him into custody if she had. Christer? No. Not Christer. Ruben. Of course they'd send Ruben. A light rain began to fall and he switched on the windscreen wipers.

Mina's information was a box that needed to be unpacked in the right order. He needed to start from the beginning. His classmates: Malin, Jessica and Charlotte. Or Malla, Sickan and Lotta. His friends when he was little. Who had then become the mothers of Tuva, Robert and Agnes. But surely that didn't have to mean it was about him. Right?

The rain increased in intensity and he sped up the windscreen wipers. The patter on the car roof had a slightly hypnotic effect; his thoughts wanted to fly away but he had to make an effort to line them up in a logical order.

What if Mina's discovery was not specifically about him? Was someone murdering the children of all his old classmates? And why their children in particular? Why not the offspring of the other class in the same school year?

No, not the children of all of them. The countdown spoke its own clear language. There were only going to be four murders. And the killer was keeping something in store for when when the countdown reached zero – he was convinced of that. Something that tied Malin, Jessica and Charlotte together specifically. Had they had a common enemy? But once again, if they'd had a common enemy then they ought to have been the ones who'd been murdered, not their children, who hadn't even known each other.

And who was the fourth person – murder number one – if it wasn't him? Because despite the book with the message from the murderer, he was still not prepared to accept that it could be him, Vincent, who was the common denominator. Admittedly, the four of them had been a fixture for a brief period. A summer. But when he had moved away from there, they must have found someone else. The fourth person *could* be him, but it wasn't certain. It could be another friend. After all, they had spent a long time without him and only a short time with him. They hadn't been that important together. He couldn't make it add up.

What was more, there was no one in the present who knew about his past. Following the newspaper article, his foster family had done everything they could to bury what had happened. And they had done a good job. He was honestly surprised that Mina had managed to dig it up. Vincent Walder hadn't existed then. In Kvibille he'd just been plain old Vincent Boman.

Boman.

Bo-man.

Wait

wait

wait

He floored the accelerator and sped into a roundabout. Someone honked angrily at him. Then the heavens opened and the rain began to pour with full force. It wasn't important. Nothing was important.

Except the dates. He knew what they meant. He needed to double-check with Benjamin, but he had cracked the code. He saw the numbers in the air in front of him, hovering a few inches above the bonnet and glittering in the rain as they were transformed into letters. And what they revealed filled him with horror.

110

She was sitting on the cold floor, staring at her wall. The picture of Vincent was staring back at her. She had pinned the newspaper article above the class photo in the middle of the spider's web that she had built. Mina had her Rubik's cube in her hand - the one that Vincent had solved for her. She tossed the cube back and forth between her hands. She was tempted to twist it, but didn't dare. She wasn't sure whether she'd be able to get it back to its finished state. As if she would be triggering an unstoppable chain reaction by a gentle twist, where each subsequent attempt to make it right again would only create more and more disorder. Just like her life.

Seven-year-old Vincent Boman was looking at her from the wall with sorrowful eyes.

She had confided in him. Good God, he'd been here while she was *asleep*.

The cube flew from one hand to the other.

He had been allowed to get to know part of her innermost self. And all along he had been lying to her.

The cube flew in an arc through the air, back to her other hand.

If only he'd said something about it. About what had happened to his mother. He claimed he'd suppressed it. That he couldn't remember. And she wanted to believe him. But she didn't know whether she'd ever be able to do that again.

Why couldn't she just have settled for being alone?

She looked at the cube. Then she threw it as hard as she could at the wall. The cube hit young Vincent on the forehead and broke into several pieces. She wrapped her arms around her legs and began to rock back and forth, sitting there on the floor as she quietly cried.

111

Vincent hurtled into Benjamin's room without knocking. His son was, as usual, lying on the bed with headphones on and his computer perched on his ribcage. He jumped when Vincent stormed in.

'What are you doing?' Benjamin said, shutting his laptop. 'And look out for my books on the floor – you're leaving a puddle!'

Benjamin was right. Water was running off Vincent. He hadn't bothered to remove his outerwear but had headed straight into Benjamin's room. He had been drenched by the rain on the brief stretch between the garage and the front door, and he could feel water dripping from the tip of his nose. He reached for a towel that was slung over the back of the desk chair, but Benjamin stopped him.

'You really don't want to use that one.'

Vincent withdrew his hand. He wasn't going to ask.

'The murders,' he said, taking off his jacket. 'Pull up the dates.'

'That again,' Benjamin sighed, slowly getting out of bed and heading over to the desk where the computer was. 'You know that uni starts again this week, right? I've got quite a lot of lectures to be concentrating on.'

'I need to see all the dates in front of me,' said Vincent, not caring about his son's objection.

'OK, but can you dry off first?' Benjamin said in annoyance, moving a few painted *Warhammer* figurines to a safe distance. 'You're soaking everything.'

Vincent quickly fetched a towel from the bathroom while Benjamin opened the Excel spread.

'Do you remember the first time we tried to crack the code?' Vincent said on his return.

'You mean when we translated the dates to letters? 1 is A, 2 is B, and so on. The simplest cipher there is. And it got us nowhere.'

'Let's do it again,' said Vincent, rubbing the towel through his hair. 'In numerical order.'

'If that's what it takes to get you to chill out, fine. But I don't understand why.'

Benjamin pulled up the pictures of Agnes, Tuva and Robert showing the dates and times.

'The first murder, Agnes's so-called suicide, took place on the thirteenth of January at 14:00,' said Benjamin. 'So 13-1-14. That gives us M-A-N.'

He changed the numbers under the image to letters as he spoke.

'Tuva was murdered in the sword box on the twentieth of February at 15:00. So 20-2-15. That gives us T-B-O. And according to the anonymous tipster, Robert was chopped up on the third of May at 14:00. Ergo 3-5-14. Which makes C-E-N.'

He changed the last figures and pushed his chair away from the desk so that Vincent could see properly.

'M-A-N-T-B-O-C-E-N. Still doesn't mean anything. But we knew that.'

'It doesn't mean anything because that's the order of the murders,' said Vincent, standing on the towel in an attempt to minimize the puddles on the floor. 'The chronological order. But the *numerical order* is the other way around. Agnes had the number four carved onto her. Tuva a three. Robert a two. Put them in numerical order, i.e. two-three-four. Robert-Tuva-Agnes.'

Benjamin swapped Robert and Agnes on the screen and looked at the new combination of letters.

'C-E-N-T-B-O-M-A-N. I still don't understand it,' he said, frowning. 'It's still nonsense.'

'Far from it,' said Vincent. 'It tells us when the next murder – murder number one – will take place. On the twenty-second of September at 14:00. In a month's time.'

Benjamin looked at him in astonishment.

'How do you reach that conclusion?'

'Because the twenty-second of September at 14:00 makes 22-9-14. The letters V-I-N. And murder number one should appear first in sequence, before the others. Don't you see?'

Vincent stretched across Benjamin in frustration and tapped in the letters V-I-N on the keyboard. The keys got wet, but that was too bad.

'One, two, three and four. Four murders,' he said.

V-I-N-C-E-N-T-B-O-M-A-N glared at them from the screen.

'Vincent Boman is my real name. The murders have been a message to me all along.'

112

Why couldn't the bloody Sunday drivers on Essingeleden learn to keep out of the way? Ruben shifted down to second. Admittedly, it was a Thursday, but the point still held. What business did they have being out on the roads? He shifted up into third again and wondered whether he'd make it to fourth if he pushed it. But things up ahead didn't look too good. A white Toyota Auris had just changed lanes and was right in his way.

'There there, Ellinor,' he said to the car. 'Calm down.'

He imagined the engine growling in frustration. Unlike the real Ellinor, the car would never let him down, never one day say that it had had enough of him. He ran his fingers over the top of the dashboard and noticed the dust. He ought to clean her.

Then he changed his mind. He ought to be on the Autobahn by now, but instead he was heading to police headquarters. The murder inquiry had been at a standstill for far too long. All the leads had turned out to be dead ends. And now there were apparently others looking at what little they had come up with. He didn't know whether their so-called team even formally existed any longer. The rest of police HQ were probably laughing at his incompetence. It was embarrassing that for the foreseeable future he would be associated with an infamous but unsolved spree of serial killings. But the final straw was being summoned to a meeting by that pathetic excuse for a magician, Vincent Walder. The guy was a civilian. And a complete fraud. He had no right to call a meeting, especially when they were all on leave.

Ruben put his hand on the brown envelope on the seat next to him, to reassure himself it was still there. It had come in the post. No return address. At first its contents had made him choke, then he'd begun to laugh before finally being pissed off. Whoever had sent it, it was obviously someone who knew about Vincent's involvement in the investigation.

The contents of the envelope painted the mentalist in a whole new light. Ruben now knew that Vincent had deceived them all. But apparently the mind reader didn't think that was enough – he wanted to rub the lies in their faces. That was what the meeting would be about – Ruben was absolutely certain of it. Bloody Vincent Walder. To think Ruben had started to believe the guy was OK, that Vincent genuinely wanted to help him. He would never forgive him for that.

He patted the envelope next to him again.

'Vincent Walder, you're going down,' he said grimly, pressing his foot on the accelerator.

The Toyota ahead would just have to get out of the way.

113

Ruben was first to arrive at the meeting room. He picked a chair opposite the whiteboard where he suspected Vincent was going to give his presentation. Ruben wanted that bastard in his sights the whole time.

Peder sauntered in shortly afterwards, sporting what could only be described as a full beard. Apparently he hadn't laid eyes on a razor since the start of his holiday. Confusingly, Peder also looked tanned and alert. Ruben's surprise must have been visible on his face, because Peder winked at him.

'We've been staying with my parents for two weeks,' he said, smiling happily. 'So right now, life's a dream. It's amazing the difference two energetic sixty-year-olds can make to your mental health. Well, mine and Anette's, anyway. It may be a few years before we're allowed back. Dad looked a bit haggard on the last nappy change. But I've even started reading a book. Well, almost. I've considered which book to start reading at least.'

With a contented sigh, Peder sat down next to Ruben at the same moment Christer and Mina came through the door. They were mid-conversation. Mina's eyes were red-rimmed, as if she had been crying. Or else she had started using that dehydrating sanitizing gel on her face too – it wouldn't have surprised him.

'I promise,' said Christer. 'It's no problem at all. As I said before, I'm more than happy to have him. I've even bought Bosse a nicer lead with jewels embedded in it. Obviously they're not real diamonds, but they glitter nicely when we're out walking.'

'I'm going to owe you a year's salary after this,' Mina sighed, taking a seat beside Peder.

Christer laughed and sat down on Ruben's other side.

'Nice necklace, Mina,' Peder said suddenly. 'I think I've seen ads on TV for it. It's one of those magnetic things, isn't it?'

'Well, aren't you attentive?' Christer said with another laugh. 'Have you had some sleep?'

'Yes, it only took a few hours' total coma to get my concentration back.'

'It was a gift,' Mina said curtly.

Ruben realized that for some reason it wasn't something Mina wanted to talk about. But Peder was apparently so happy about his new-found mental agility that he didn't spot the signs.

'I thought Vincent would be coming with you,' Ruben said, changing the subject before Peder asked anything else about the necklace.

'Why?' snapped Mina. 'It's not like we live together.'

'I wonder sometimes.'

Mina glowered at him in response. Vincent was apparently out of favour. Well, that was something. He was about to say a few choice words about the mentalist when Julia and Vincent arrived.

'Good, you're all here already,' said Julia. 'Let's start right away.'

She was wearing a summer dress that ended just above the knee. Maybe not the most suitable attire for the head of a police investigation, but Julia had been forced to take time off too. And Ruben wasn't about to complain. He could easily picture the rest of those toned legs, all the way up to the arse. He knew exactly what it looked like underneath the dress. And damn it, if he wasn't mistaken she was wearing a thong today. That should have been enough for a very pleasant fantasy for the remainder of the meeting, but Vincent ruined it all. There he was, pretending to look nervous, the conceited bastard. But Ruben was in no rush. He was going to wait for the right moment. The earlier conversation between them had probably been a trap, a way to try to worm his way in and find out how much the police knew.

'Shouldn't we call in those dopes who've been managing the investigation in our absence?' he said. 'Because surely we're not officially back from our "holiday"?'

'I want to tell you about this first,' said Vincent, fidgeting. 'The fewer people who know, the better.'

'Is it to do with the tipster from AA?' Ruben asked.

'That went nowhere,' said Julia. 'It turned out she was an admirer of Vincent's. She didn't know anything about the book.'

'For God's sake.'

'There's no easy way to say this,' said Vincent, clearing his throat. 'I've always claimed there was a code or a message in the information

437

about the murders. Now we've found it. It was staring us in the face all along.'

He wrote *Agnes-Tuva-Robert* on the whiteboard.

'This is the order the murders occurred in,' he said, pointing to the names. 'But if we instead take into account the numbers carved onto the bodies, the order is this.'

He rubbed out the names and instead wrote *Robert-Tuva-Agnes*. Then he put a question mark in front of *Robert*.

'The question mark represents murder number one. The last one in the countdown, but the first in the sequence. If we translate the day, month and time of the three murders into letters, with one meaning A, two B, and so on, this is what we get.'

Vincent drew an arrow underneath the names and wrote *CEN-TBO-MAN* on a new line beneath them.

'This gives us two pieces of important information,' he continued. 'Partly, it gives us the date of the next murder. Which is good. But if it's right then it also implicates me in a way that I'm afraid I'm unable to explain.'

Vincent cleared his throat, visibly troubled. He was a good actor – Ruben had to give him that. He was going to let Vincent continue the charade a while longer.

'There's one more thing,' said Vincent. 'My name used to be Boman.'

He wrote *VIN-* under the number one so that it was in front of the other letters on the board.

VIN-CEN-TBO-MAN. Ruben let out a low laugh. He was impressed despite himself. He hadn't thought Vincent would dare go so far. It took balls of steel. Or delusions of grandeur. Ruben knew which it was.

'But it says Vincent Boman there!' Christer exclaimed, a second after the whole room had realized the same thing. 'What on earth?'

'Assuming I'm right,' said Vincent, without paying any heed to Christer, 'the final murder will therefore occur on the twenty-second of September at 14:00. Because 22-9-14 gives us the letters V-I-N.'

'Anette's birthday!' Peder cried out, looking suspiciously like he had just woken up.

The energy he'd acquired from two weeks' rest had apparently deserted him.

The others stared at him.

'Yes, well, the twenty-second of September is my wife's birthday,' he said, blushing.

'And I happen to have an important doctor's appointment then,' Julia said ironically.

438

'But I don't understand,' Peder continued. 'Why do the murders spell out your name?'

'Ruben, I think we're officially back on duty,' said Julia. 'And then some. I'll let the chiefs know.'

'The name isn't the only connection to Vincent,' said Mina in a strained-but-neutral tone. 'The mothers of our victims are Vincent's old playmates.'

Ruben smiled when he saw how bright red Vincent's face went. He was probably wishing the ground would swallow him up. That disclosure couldn't have been part of his plan, no matter how good an actor he was. It was quite simply *too* compromising. Vincent's friends. Jesus Christ! Well done, Mina. Vincent was in the shit now. And Ruben hadn't even opened his mouth yet.

'Believe me,' Vincent said, without meeting anyone's eye, 'I have no idea what this means. Somehow these murders are about me. The book was only the beginning. I've been trying to think who might be after me like this, but I can't think of anyone. At most, I have a few jealous colleagues on the lecture circuit, but no *enemies*. That's the kind of thing people have in books or movies. Not in reality.'

'Sounds like someone is out to get you for no reason,' Ruben said, pouting with his lower lip. 'Poor Vincent.'

Then he took the envelope out of his bag and set it on the table.

'Although I have another explanation,' he said. 'Which is that it was Vincent himself who committed the murders. And that his ego is so big he hid his name in the murder dates as a game. But when we didn't find the message he got restless about the fact that we weren't as smart as him and he had to point it out to us.'

'Ruben!' said Christer, looking at him in horror. 'What are you saying?'

'I've read up on magic a bit myself,' said Ruben. 'And I've learned that the best magic trick is to hide something in plain sight. Vincent, tell them about Al Koran and his ring.'

Ruben could tell that Vincent understood. He had him now.

'Al Koran was a famous magician,' Vincent began slowly. 'He was known for a trick where he linked together borrowed wedding rings. One of the rings, however, was his own. According to legend, he began the trick by demonstrating a trick ring with a secret opening, and then he said that was how the trick was usually done but that he would never use such deception himself. Then he went on to use exactly that method. And no one could understand how on earth it worked, despite

439

the fact – or perhaps precisely because – he had revealed the method. But I don't understand what this has to do with the investigation.'

'You mostly certainly do,' Ruben said, turning to his colleagues. 'I think Vincent has just pulled an Al Koran on us. He's revealed how the trick works and is relying on the fact that we will not therefore believe it was done by him. Despite all the evidence to the contrary.'

'Ruben, these are very troubling accusations,' said Julia. 'What evidence do you have? It had better be something better than a ring trick.'

'Come on – you lot must have the memories of goldfish!'

He raised his voice in frustration and pointed at Vincent with his index finger and at the letters on the whiteboard with another.

'Our good friend Vincent likes nothing more than using his own name when manipulating people! "An artist always signs his works" – does that ring any bells? The man who wrote VINCENT WALDER one hundred times on the walls without remembering it, just to stroke Vincent's ego?'

Vincent's face had gone chalk white.

'That experiment was about explaining fanaticism,' he began weakly, but he stopped when he saw the way the others were staring at him.

Ruben loved it.

And he wasn't done.

He'd saved the best for last.

He opened the envelope and put the contents in the centre of the table where everyone could see it.

'I received this in the post,' he said. 'From an anonymous source who clearly doesn't want us to get caught in Vincent's trap. Before you ask, yes, I've checked and the article is genuine.'

MAGIC ENDS IN TRAGEDY! read the headline in the old newspaper article from *Hallandsposten*. Christer, Peder and Julia leaned forward curiously. Ruben managed to spot Mina glancing briefly at Vincent. Apparently the clipping wasn't new to her. She was very good, was Mina.

'On a farm near Kvibille, a playful illusion suddenly became deadly reality,' Ruben read from the first paragraph of the article.

Then he fixed his gaze on Vincent again.

'It's no surprise Vincent knows so much about how to kill people with illusions. Our good friend Vincent *Boman* has had a lifetime's experience of killing people in boxes.'

114

He had gone downstairs to the kitchen extra early. It was hard making Mum's breakfast and it took longer when he did it. He knew it had to be *exact*. Ritual, that was what Mum had called it. He put two slices of bread in the toaster, checked that the dial was set to 3.5 and waited. Beyond the kitchen window, the sun was already shining. But it had risen some twelve minutes later than a few weeks earlier. The summer holidays were almost over. And today Jane was coming home. Today, *everything* had to be exact.

When the bread popped up, he carefully lifted it out of the machine using a meat skewer to avoid burning himself. Then he meticulously cut off one crust on the slices of bread by carefully pressing down with the knife, just like Mum had shown him. Then the other edge. When he cut the third crust, the toast crackled. He stopped with the knife raised in the air. The slice of toast had broken. And the crack was a whole centimetre in length. That wouldn't do. He threw the bread in the bin and started over. Two slices of bread in the toaster, set to 3.5. After several seconds of contemplation, he lowered the dial to 3. The toaster had already warmed up. He didn't want to burn the new slices.

It took three attempts before he managed to cut a toast sandwich into perfect triangles. Finally. Step one complete. He threw away one of the halves lying in front of him.

Three sandwiches.

Three sides to a triangle.

The third edge which was cracked.

Three times three was 9.

But three times three times three was 27. And 2 plus 7 was also 9.

No matter how he counted, 9 was always the same thing as a triangle.

He put his head in his hands and pressed his fingers to his temples. Nine plus his own age made sixteen, which was Jane's age. The difference between him and Jane was thus nine – a triangle. Him, Jane, Mum. That was their triangle.

A triangle that had cracked on the third edge.

Stop. Stop. Stop.

He understood why Mum's rituals were so important. As long as you did everything the exact same way, your thoughts couldn't take over. And there was something he had forgotten. What was . . .

Coffee. He had forgotten to switch on Mum's coffee maker. He filled the glass jug with water and then put it back on the hot plate while wondering which had come to his mother first. The rituals, or the thoughts that the rituals were there to stop. Or perhaps they were the same thing?

By the time Jane reached the farm in the evening, it was much later than she had planned. But it wasn't as if anyone had made an effort to help her either. It really said something about how little her mother actually cared about anyone other than herself. Mum had just needed to get all the threats out before Jane left. After that she hadn't even bothered to get in touch.

Jane climbed onto the porch steps and pressed down the door handle. Locked. Since when had they locked the front door? She rang the doorbell angrily. This was too much. If they weren't at home she would be furious. She'd be off again tonight.

The door was unlocked from inside and her little brother opened it wearing his pyjamas.

'Why aren't you answering the phone?' she said, putting her rucksack down in the hall with a thud.

Her little brother looked puzzled.

'Phone?' he said.

She put her hands to the base of her spine and stretched backwards. She'd had to walk the final stretch and was exhausted. When she'd packed the rucksack, she hadn't expected to have to carry it that far.

'I called from the station before I got on the train,' she said. 'And again when I got off at Halmstad. And then again from the bus station in Kvibille. I thought maybe you'd want to come and meet me. Some help carrying this would actually have been appreciated.'

Her little brother glanced towards the kitchen and she followed his gaze. The telephone receiver was lying off the hook on the kitchen counter.

'What the hell?' she said.

'Must have forgotten to put it back,' he said falteringly.

'My God. Same as ever here, I see.'

She shook her head and headed into the kitchen.

'Well, now I'm home,' she said. 'Although it's only for a few days. I assume Mum explained?'

She opened the fridge and took out everything she could find. Ylva's dad had made two sandwiches for her to eat on the train. That had been the last thing she'd eaten. An eternity ago.

'Explained what?'

She sighed and pointed at a chair by the kitchen table. Her little brother sat down. She opted for the one next to him, put what she had found in the fridge on the table and took his hand. It was cold and a little moist.

'I'm moving,' she said. 'I'm going to sixth form in Mora. It's not Stockholm, which is what I really wanted, but at least it's not . . . this. Do you remember my three Ts?'

'Theatre, Theme-parks, Traffic?' her little brother said with a frown.

'Mora at least has two out of three,' she said. 'And when you're not already from Mora you can board at the school. Ylva's dad has helped me with all the details, all Mum has to do is sign a document to consent to me living there.'

Her little brother's eyes filled with tears. Bloody Mum forcing her to do this. She'd really hoped Mum would have plucked up the courage to tell him before she got home. Her little brother wasn't good at processing change – he needed to be prepared a long way in advance.

'In how many years' time are you moving?' he whispered.

'Not years. Now. I'm only home for four days. Then I'm going again.'

'But Jane, you can't!'

He flung his arms around her neck.

'A triangle can't only have one edge,' he cried against her cheek. 'Then it's just a line. Then it falls over. I don't want to fall over, Jane. Please, please. I don't want to fall over.'

She pushed him away and looked into his eyes.

'What are you talking about?'

'The triangle,' he sobbed. 'You. Me. Mum. It can't just be me. You're older, you know how to get by, but I . . . I . . . I promise to follow all the rituals exactly. *Exactly*. I've been practising so much. Please don't go.'

The knot in her stomach that she'd had when she'd called home almost two weeks ago returned. She'd been worried something was wrong at home. Then she'd convinced herself that there was nothing to worry about. But something *was* wrong. More than that, something was dangerously wrong. Her little brother was scaring her.

'Where's Mum?' she said, carefully loosening his grip.

He pointed towards the kitchen counter without looking at her. The whole counter was covered in carefully cut triangular sandwiches. Hundreds of them. Perfectly toasted.

'Those are Mum's sandwiches,' she said. 'Where's *Mum*?'

She was starting to get really scared. The sinking feeling in her stomach had become a black hole.

'On the counter,' he said. 'Do you remember? "We are what we do" – like she always said. And I've done it so many times. And *exactly*. Every time. So she'd be there.'

It felt like insects were crawling on the back of her neck. She stood up and backed away from her little brother, who was still looking at the floor.

'Mum?' she shouted into the hallway without getting a reply.

She ran upstairs in a panic and opened the doors to all the bedrooms. Mum wasn't in any of them.

She ran back downstairs towards the front door. Her little brother was still in the kitchen, crying. She ought to stop, to hug him, to say everything was fine, but there was no time. And everything wasn't fine.

She had to know.

It was dusk outside. They only had electric lighting on the porch and outside the barn. The darkness was lightened up by the stars which had begun to appear – enough that she could see the big lawn standing out in relief as a field of shadows. But it appeared to be empty. No Mum.

The woods at the far side of the grass were forbiddingly black – she couldn't go into them until it got light.

'Mum!'

She shouted again. Maybe Mum was at Allan's. She liked hanging out at his place. Perhaps she had forgotten that it was today her daughter was due home. But why didn't her little brother say so if that were the case? And why was the phone off the hook?

What were they playing at?

In the worst case, her mother had had a panic attack and was lying somewhere out there in the darkness, unable to get up by herself. She might need help. Of course her little brother would be frightened if Mum had had an attack. He was obviously in shock. That explained his behaviour. After all, he wasn't that old.

She ran to the barn. In the light outside she stopped and took a deep breath. Something smelled. A sweet and . . . suffocating smell. Last summer her brother had eaten his packed lunch in the barn and left some of the food to slowly cook in the summer heat. The stench had been disgusting by the time they found the food. The smell reminded her of that. But this was worse.

Much worse.

She opened the barn door and immediately put her hand to her nose and mouth. The stench made her eyes tear up. It smelled of urine and sweat and decay and death. The light only reached a short distance inside – most of the building was in darkness.

She blinked away the tears and realized that the darkness was moving.

And it was *making sounds.*

What she had thought were shadows were actually flies in a huge, concentrated mass. Thousands of fat bluebottles buzzing in agitation as they flew and clambered over each other. The swarm was bigger than she was. Acidic bile filled her mouth. She had to get out of there before she threw up. She lunged for the barn door just as part of the cloud of flies thinned slightly, allowing her to see the contours of what was attracting them

It was a box.

A blue box with a big padlock and stars painted on it.

445

115

Hail was beating against the tarpaulin above her head. She had suggested they meet at TAK – the outdoor restaurant on the roof of the Gallerian shopping mall. There was something about being that high up. The air was always easier to breathe. It was as if the dirt stayed down below.

But they had only just got their noodles served in takeaway boxes when the hail came. They hurried under the tarpaulin covering the kitchen and bar area of the restaurant, together with the other patrons. The white pellets poured down with the fury of someone who had been kept waiting far too long. She shivered and looked at her bare arms. They were covered in goosebumps from the cold. She almost wished Vincent would offer her his jacket, but she knew he wouldn't do that. Especially not now that things were so tense between them. She hadn't exactly sided with him during the meeting at police headquarters. She had been too shocked at what he had revealed.

'Vincent, I've got to know,' she said.

He stopped looking at the hail shower in fascination and turned towards her.

'I'm only going to ask this once,' she continued. 'But you've got to be honest. Do you have anything whatsoever to do with this? You don't have to say what, just . . . well, do you?'

She could see how wounded he was by her words. The otherwise upright posture slumped and the spark in his eyes disappeared. But she had to know. Once and for all. He turned away from her and was silent for a long time. Then he took a step forward into the hail. Away from her.

'If I did,' he said, 'do you think I would have said yes to joining the investigation? Or do you think I would in fact have run in the opposite direction as quickly as I could when I met you that first evening in Gävle? Of course I don't have anything to do with it.'

The hail caught in his blond hair and on his shoulders where it melted and began to trickle down his back.

'Sorry,' she said. 'I had to ask.'

He turned around and looked her in the eyes.

'Did you?' he said. 'Did you really? I thought we knew each other better than that. I thought that we . . . that we . . .'

She nodded to him to continue, but the mentalist fell silent. She went into the hail and stood next to him. No one had ever died from a little frozen water. They surveyed the wet rooftops together. Without realizing what she was doing until it was too late, she entwined her hand with his. Bloody hell. She hadn't meant to. She held her breath while awaiting his reaction, but he didn't withdraw. Instead, his hand squeezed hers.

'That we understood each other,' she said, finishing his sentence.

He nodded quietly.

Then he squinted into the hail and suddenly jumped.

'Jesus!' he said. 'For one moment I thought I could see Anna over there.'

She looked in the same direction but it was hard to see the other patrons clearly through the hail.

'It wasn't her,' he said, shaking his head. 'Now I'm apparently hallucinating my stalkers. Wonderful.'

The hail stopped as quickly as it had begun. The patrons began to tentatively emerge from beneath the tarpaulin and they let go of each other.

'And what about now, then?' she said, looking at the water-damaged noodle tub in her other hand. 'Do you want to run in the opposite direction now?'

He found a bin where they could throw away the remains of their lunch. Then he retrieved a bottle of hand sanitizer from his pocket and handed it to her. His gaze was still wounded.

'I'll run where you tell me to,' he said. 'I thought you knew that.'

116

'According to Vincent's theory, we have a date when the next murder is likely to take place. And since the other murders occurred in Stockholm, we have reason to believe it will happen here.'

Ruben looked at Julia sceptically when she stopped.

'How many times do I have to say that we should bring Vincent in? Stick him in the cells as a material suspect – then all we have to do is wait a few weeks until the twenty-second. He may have accomplices we're not aware of – have you asked him about that? Have you asked him whether he knew Rask? We still don't know anything. It's like searching for a needle in a haystack. And the only person who knows anything, you don't want to question. Is it just me who can see what's happening? How much more evidence do you need?'

Mina glowered at him. Her own feeling of hopelessness in this situation wasn't improved by Ruben's attitude.

She felt overwhelmed. Somewhere out there was a person, alive, occupied with their daily activities, friends, work, convinced that life ahead of them ran into the infinite horizon. Happily ignorant that it would all be over in a few weeks if she and her colleagues didn't manage to stop it. And the worst of it was, Ruben might be right.

But she knew Vincent. He was brilliant, but he took ten minutes to tie his shoelaces to make sure it was right. And she had his word that he was innocent.

Vincent had at least understood the gravity of the suspicions directed at him. He had cancelled all his other engagements for the rest of the month and promised not to leave town. And he was no longer part of the investigation.

Julia continued calmly.

It was one of the things Mina really appreciated about her boss. She kept her cool in all situations. Even when Ruben was behaving like an arse.

'I've spoken personally to the chief of police and been promised extra resources on the twenty-second of September,' Julia said. 'We don't know where, you're right about that. But to date the victims have been found in a certain type of location in Stockholm. They've been well-known public locations rather than randomly chosen backstreets.'

Peder raised his hand and Julia nodded.

'It's been different places each time,' he said. 'So perhaps we can take a chance and rule out those places that have already been used? I mean, we don't bother using resources to watch Gröna Lund, the park outside the China Theatre or Partihallarna?'

'Good thinking, and I think you're right. It's obviously a risk, we may be wrong, but I think it's worth taking that risk. We won't watch those locations. But what places does that leave us with that are very Stockholm-specific? Known sites?'

She held up the pen to start writing their suggestions on the white-board.

'The Kaknäs Tower, the mushroom on Stureplan, the park at Humlegården,' Mina said.

Julia made notes in her barely legible handwriting.

'Sergel's Square, the palace,' Ruben said without enthusiasm.

'Junibacken, Djurgården, the Vasa Museum,' Peder added as Julia continued to write them down.

'Hornstull,' said Peder.

Ruben snorted.

'Hornstull? On Södermalm?'

He said 'Södermalm' like it was a dirty word.

'Horns . . . tull,' Julia vocalized as she wrote it on the board.

'Why are we not supposed to give a toss about Söder?' said Peder.

'Well, who the hell gives a fuck about Söder? And Hornstull? What's there?' Ruben said.

'Oi, class, pull yourselves together,' Julia said severely.

Mina rolled her eyes. Ruben was such a snob. Which was the height of irony, because she happened to know he'd been born and raised in the sticks in Rimbo, and not in Stockholm's leafy Vasastan as he liked to make out.

'The Royal Dramatic Theatre,' Christer said, nodding to himself. 'I've got a strong feeling about the theatre. If I were a murderer, I would definitely have left a body on the steps there. Very impactful.'

449

'We don't know whether impact is what the murderer is going for, or whether there's some kind of personal connection to these places.'

'Or whether the places are part of some kind of code,' Mina interjected.

Ruben sighed.

'Fuck me, that's enough,' he said. 'Vincent showed us a hidden message. One that he had put there himself. But not everything is a cipher or morse code or hidden message. Let's do some good old-fashioned police work instead of wasting our time on a load of hocus pocus.'

'The Royal Dramatic Theatre.' Julia added it to the board, taking a step back.

'The problem is,' said Mina, 'the places where we found the victims were secondary crime scenes. The actual murders took place somewhere else. I agree that this surveillance will increase the chances of finding the murderers. But only after the murder takes place. We still have a murder to prevent.'

'And we're going to do that with every means we have at our disposal,' said Julia. 'But this is at least a start. I'll get to work on allocating resources, set up a rota and so on, and if you think of any more places we should assign officers to, then note them on the list here on the board. I'm also going to ask Sara Temeric in Analysis to initiate more active monitoring of the mobile network from now on. Of course, we'll also have a greater police presence on the streets of the city. And all ideas on what we can do before this list comes into play will be gratefully accepted.'

'Needle in a haystack, like I said,' Ruben muttered. 'And the needle is called Vincent Walder.'

Julia turned around and stared angrily at him.

'Your attitude is not helping! Aside from your brilliant suggestion that we take Vincent into custody, what else would you have us do? Sit there twiddling our thumbs waiting for the phone to ring?'

'We could interview his old teachers and classmates,' Ruben muttered. 'And that Jessica woman, Robert's mother, was one of his playmates. Why don't we talk to her again?'

'Because Vincent isn't a material suspect!' Julia screeched. 'There's nothing tangible tying him to the murders. What is it that you don't understand about that?'

Ruben's cheeks went red and he avoided her eyes.

Mina wished she'd brought popcorn. Seeing Ruben being told off was one of her favourite pastimes.

'Perhaps you could assign Ruben to oversee the surveillance on Södermalm?' Christer said, and Peder stifled a chortle.

'Bunch of jokers,' Ruben muttered.

He quickly exited the room the moment others stood up. Mina lingered for a moment, looking at the board and the list that was only going to grow. Ruben was right about one thing. It was like trying to find a needle in a haystack.

117

For the first time in ages no one in the family was at home. Aston was at school, Benjamin had a lecture on campus in Kista, Rebecka was seeing a friend and Maria was at yoga. Which was just as well. That meant they didn't have to see the police car parked on the opposite side of the street with a view of the house and the driveway. He wasn't a suspect – not officially – but when Ruben had insisted, he had agreed to be watched anyway. After all, this was the day he had told them the next murder was going to take place. The twenty-second of September. If nothing else, it might prove his innocence when at the end of the day he hadn't actually murdered anyone – no doubt to Ruben's great disappointment.

Ruben could have opted for an unmarked car. Vincent guessed that was the norm when carrying out surveillance. But no, Ruben wanted to be visible. Damn it, it even looked like the white police car with its blue and yellow livery had just been washed. Ruben must have been so disappointed when he discovered that Vincent didn't have any neighbours. Vincent waved to him through the kitchen window. When Ruben turned away, Vincent gave him the middle finger instead.

The fact that no one else was at home meant that he had the whole house to himself. He could watch porn on Benjamin's computer, finish building Aston's Lego models, bake cookies for Rebecka or dance around the living room naked without anyone caring. Or not. Well, not that last one. Dancing naked was more Maria's thing. Not in reality, of course, but she probably wished it was.

He got out the album *Telekon* by Gary Numan and put it on the record player in the living room. The first time he had heard music that wasn't for children when he had been little, it had been songs by Gary Numan, Kim Wilde and other artists from the British New Wave scene. They had just started playing them on Swedish radio. When, as a five-year-old, he had heard the song 'I Die: You Die' for the first time, he'd had nightmares all night. It was comprised of sounds that came from no instrument he knew of. Notes and harmonies that were anything other than sweet and familiar. At first it had scared him. Then it had fascinated him. His absolute certainty about what music was, based on the extensive life experience of being a five-year-old, had turned out to be completely wrong. And if that was the case with music, then what else might it apply to? The world was completely different to what he had thought. Everything was possible. And there was no safety net.

Even now, whenever he heard that music it put him in the same state of mind. And right now, that was exactly what he needed. He needed to think outside the box. Because even if he was going to disappoint Ruben by not committing a murder today, *someone* was going to do it. *Someones*, he corrected himself. He didn't believe for one moment that Rask had been one of the murderers. And he doubted Anna was involved either.

He bent down in front of the aquarium, but the mudminnows stayed away. As if they knew something was afoot.

He turned up the volume of the music and went into his study. With the whole house at his disposal, the study was still the place he preferred to be. There were no surprises; he knew exactly where everything was and what everything was for.

Above all, it was his. No one would be annoyed that the books in the bookcase were sorted by colour rather than alphabetical order. Or that there was a portrait of him as a zombie – a gift from a famous cartoonist who was also an admirer – standing on the shelf amidst the other, fancier awards he had received.

Vincent lay down flat on the thick green carpet to think. He had tried to go through all the pieces and see where he himself fitted into the puzzle, but no matter what he did, he couldn't make it add up. His head was a maelstrom and it was no longer possible to keep his thoughts in check. His thoughts were swirling so violently that he felt as if he were going to fall, despite the fact that he was already lying down. He stretched his arms in an attempt to subdue the dizziness and felt the fibres of the carpet under his hands as he focused on his breathing. The dizziness dissipated slowly. All the pieces of the puzzle had been identified. But he still understood nothing.

It was pure luck that none of the other detectives were as convinced

453

of his guilt as Ruben. Not that he blamed Ruben – he would have thought the same thing had the tables been turned. But all it had done was buy him a little time. Sooner or later, his involvement would come out in the media. Then Mina and the others would be unable to protect him any longer, no matter how innocent he was.

He focused on the weak yellow glow from the ceiling light above him. He had dimmed it before lying down. Now it looked like a floating golden-yellow globe on the ceiling.

The media would eat him alive. The Houdini murderer was the mentalist Vincent Walder. He would be declared guilty for sure. Guilty of three murders. Or four, because there would be another before the day was out. Then the police would have no other option. It was only a matter of time. And presumably he didn't have much of that left. So what exactly did he have?

He started from the beginning for the thousandth time, to see whether he had missed something.

Vincent closed his eyes and picked out three boxes in his network of thoughts. Inside each box were several layers of reasoning, possible conclusions and potential patterns. But for now, he settled for looking at their labels.

Box one: *the victims' mothers: his old playmates*. So the murderers knew, in other words, where he had grown up and with whom.

Box two: *the victims died in faulty illusions: just like Mum*. So the murderers knew what had happened to his mother.

Box three: *the murder dates spelled out his childhood name*. See box one.

He opened his eyes again and fixed his gaze on the golden globe.

Everything seemed to point to his childhood.

It was easy to draw the conclusion that the murderers must know him; perhaps they had even grown up with him. But that was a psychological thinking trap. It was so easy to believe that everything revolved around yourself. To believe that you were the origin of everything that happened. Everyone thought like that to some extent – it was impossible to avoid it, since we were all at the centre of our own universe. But thinking it didn't make it so.

All the information about him as a young boy was available online. It wasn't even hard to find – you just had to know how to look for it. The murderers didn't need to have any personal ties to him at all – merely a functioning internet connection.

But if the murderers didn't know him, then he couldn't see any

454

motive. Why would a stranger do all this? To flatter him? To challenge him? His ego might be big, but not big enough to seriously believe an explanation like that. Stalker madness didn't usually extend any further than fantasies like Anna's. Granted, Moriarty had created murder mysteries for Sherlock Holmes just to see whether he could solve them. But that had been a work of fiction. There was very little mist-shrouded mysterious romance to what had happened to Agnes, Tuva and Robert.

The golden globe throbbed and suddenly increased in intensity. The dimmer clearly needed replacing. He sat up on the carpet with his legs stretched out in front of him. He changed tack and toyed with the idea that the murderers actually knew him. Not that he could come up with anyone of his acquaintance who could carry out such deeds, but, all the same . . . Gary Numan seemed to concur in some perverse fashion out in the living room as he hit the refrain of 'I Die: You Die'.

But so what if he knew the murderers? He could still find no motive. And the fourth murder was going to happen today.

A fourth box of ideas suddenly appeared in his head. He couldn't remember having made it. But there it was, clearly visible in the row beside the other three. He closed his eyes and peeked inside the new box. It was completely empty. His subconscious was clearly trying to tell him something. Four boxes, four pieces of the puzzle, of which one was empty.

Aha.

Of course.

The puzzle was incomplete, despite everything. There was important information that he had missed. A final, fourth piece of the puzzle that would reveal all. The LP in the living room ended. He could hear the needle scratching the edge of the label. He let it carry on.

The fourth piece of the puzzle wasn't the final murder, as he had thought. He knew exactly where it was.

It was in his home.

118

Mina had just changed into clean clothes and put on Nathalie's necklace when the doorbell rang. She jumped. The doorbell never rang. No one visited her. Ever. Unless . . . could it be Vincent? Had they entered a phase of their relationship where he felt able to spontaneously stop by? No. Especially not today – not with Ruben on his tail. It didn't sound like Vincent. It must be a salesperson. Some kid who wanted to flog football socks or tulips.

Or Jehovah's Witnesses. Well-kempt young men in white shirts and black ties with God's glory shining in their vacant eyes. Like small, nasty brainwashed robots.

She opened the door. Standing on the other side was Kenneth.

'Hello!' she said in surprise. 'You're here?'

'Hello to you too! I thought I'd pick up Bosse. Sorry it's been so long. As luck would have it, I was able to look your address up in the phone book. A friendly neighbour let me in downstairs.'

Relief mingled with guilt. Relief that she'd finally made contact with Bosse's master. But guilt, since Kenneth thought she had their dog at hers.

'I was beginning to think you'd gone underground,' she said, trying to buy some time. 'I don't think I've seen you at AA since the summer.'

'We've been going on different days,' he said. 'Has everything been all right with Bosse?'

Kenneth looked at her eagerly and then looked around for the dog. Mina could feel her face forming into a stiff grimace as she replied.

'Hmm, well. Bosse's fine. But he's not here . . .'

'Well, where is he then?'

Kenneth's expression was confused. Mina shrugged apologetically.

'It wasn't working for my schedule for me to have him. I really did want to. But I'm afraid it just wasn't possible. I've got an amazing colleague who offered to help out. So he's at Christer's.'

'Oh right, at Christer's,' said Kenneth, his expression still one of confusion.

'How's your wife feeling?' Mina hurried to ask.

'Sweet of you to ask. Yes, things were a bit touch and go there for a while, but it turned out to be just a mild stroke – they stabilized her quickly, so she's been at home resting up over the summer and early autumn. Now she's well enough for me to be able to take care of Bosse again.'

'I'm glad to hear it,' Mina said. And she meant it.

The obvious affection between Kenneth and his wife had touched her, and she had wondered many times in the last few months how they were doing.

'Where can I find . . . Christer?' Kenneth said, raising a quizzical eyebrow.

Mina pulled out her phone and began to scroll through her contacts.

'He lives by Skurusundet. If you head for Värmdövägen you'll spot the strait after about 10 kilometres. Take a right just after the round-about and then it's another five hundred metres. It's a brown house on the right, looks like a hunting cabin.'

She only knew this because in a recent attack of guilty conscience she had driven out to Christer's with a big bag of dog food and left it outside his front door.

'Here's his number – you can call him for the address and . . .'

'That's a lot to take in. Why don't you come with me and show me?'

The voice was pleading and Kenneth's eyes were as big as Bosse's. Mina glanced through the window and down to the street. A beaten-up van was outside the main door. It looked like it had seen better days. She could only imagine what the hygiene rating inside was like.

'I'd really appreciate it. We did leave Bosse with you and you said you'd take care of him for us . . .'

Mina wriggled with discomfort. This was completely the wrong day for this. But Christer would drive her to police headquarters afterwards. Kenneth was applying pressure directly to her guilty conscience, and she couldn't see how she was going to deny him this favour – no matter how much her entire body and soul protested against getting into that dirty van. She reached for her denim jacket.

'OK, I'll come with you and show you.'

She locked the door, squeezed past him and went down the stairs and out the street door, and walked briskly towards the van before she had time to change her mind. Kenneth hurried along in her wake and went to the driver side where he unlocked the van. Mina opened the passenger-side door and took a deep breath. It was as she'd feared. She took another breath. And then she got in.

119

Vincent got up from the carpet and fetched the book. The big book that someone had sent to Umberto at ShowLife Productions at Christmas, to make sure he got it. The one with the leopard on the cover. He had got it back from the police after a week. They would have liked to keep it longer, but he didn't think the solution was in carrying out chemical analysis on the pages of the book. They would presumably find nothing other than his and Umberto's fingerprints. If there was a solution then it lay in the message itself.

The message was guaranteed to have come from the murderers, but last time he hadn't given it much thought, since it wasn't connected to the other pieces of the jigsaw. He had interpreted it as nothing more than the murderers teasing him. Perhaps he hadn't looked at it properly. He opened it to page 873, the one that Benjamin had come up with. He still hadn't worked out what 15:00 on the eighth of July stood for. If it stood for anything, that was. As before, it rang a bell, but it was so faint that he might as well have been imagining it. Sometimes there was no pattern, even if you were convinced that you could see it.

The message on the page stared at him just as cryptically as last time.

Hello Vincent,
I am most disappointed that you thought the eighth of July was the date of a new murder. Do you really not remember? You'll have to stop titting about and look harder than that if you are going to find me.

'Titting about'. That was strangely slangy compared to the rest of the message. Why not simply 'messing about' or 'wasting time'? He ignored the message, examining the rest of the page instead. The aggressive lines and the coloured-in red clumps. He now realized that the latter marks were actually more structured than clumps. They had clear edges, but the shapes were strange. The whirlwind in his head began to take on a solid shape. A summer memory he hadn't thought about for many years. It had been obscured and suppressed by what had happened later that summer. A memory of a blanket on grass.

Mum's birthday.

When he'd been called Vincent Boman.

Mum's favourite dress.

A card.

He looked at the lines of the page again. Some of them weren't solid but merely dashed. It was impossible . . . It couldn't be. *Mustn't* be. His hands trembling, he carefully tore the page out of the book, almost ruining it as his hands were shaking so much.

Fold it like a paper plane.

He didn't want to see the figure taking shape inside his head, and he shook his head to get rid of it, but there was no way out. He had to know.

Mum's favourite dress had been leopard print.

A leopard on the front cover of the book.

He'd had a deck of cards in his hand.

He folded the dashed lines inwards and the solid ones outwards, and with each fold the red shapes began to merge together.

'*Remember this day: three o'clock in the afternoon on the eighth of July, because you'll be telling your grandchildren about it.*'

That was what he had said. At three o'clock on the eighth of July: 873. Mum's birthday. He hadn't celebrated the day for almost forty years.

When he had finished folding, he stared at the result. The same thick, blood-red letters repeated three times.

T T T

He let out a yell and crumpled the page into a ball. Then he picked up the book and threw it at the shelf, making his awards fall to the floor with a rattle. The zombie portrait fell down and the glass fell out of the frame. T T T. He'd heard those letters repeated far too often in his childhood not to know what they stood for.

They were also the places they'd found Agnes, Tuva and Robert. Agnes in Berzelii park beside the China Theatre. Tuva outside the Tivoli at Gröna Lund. Robert in a car park. Theatre, Theme-parks, Traffic.

Jane.

The murderer was his big sister. It was completely preposterous, but it was also the only explanation. He had to get hold of Mina. Fast.

460

120

'Sorry, I . . . I should have said something. Bosse . . .'

Mina struggled to find the right words. Apologizing was one of her weakest skills, and something she sought to avoid as much as possible. As a result, the sentences felt huge, weird in her mouth. But Kenneth came to her rescue.

'Don't worry about it,' he said. 'He's been taken care of, that's the main thing.'

'Thanks,' said Mina, sounding curter than she'd meant to.

In order to smooth things over, she embarked upon something she generally sought to avoid. Small talk. There were few things she detested as much as having to converse without any particular aim. But right now it served a kind of purpose. The dirt in the van was creeping all over her, metaphorically of course, but what difference did that make? It felt as if invisible particles were moving across her skin. In order to fill the silence, she could at least detract a little of the focus from the slowly rising sense of panic within her.

'How did you and . . . your wife meet? Sorry, I've just realized I don't know what she's called.'

'Jane. She's called Jane.'

'Jane. Lovely. Well, how did you and Jane meet?'

Mina could hear how clumsy and unaccustomed she sounded in what was supposed to be light conversation. Most people mastered this art form. She thought she had it in her too. She had never had the inclination to practise.

'We met at the bottom.'

'The bottom?'

Mina looked at him. It wasn't the answer she'd expected. Which

461

meant her interest was immediately piqued in keeping the conversation going. Kenneth kept his eyes on the road as he answered.

'I found her on the street. Almost beaten to death. She had . . . problems. Her life hadn't been easy. Nor had mine. I had problems too. But it's like when two minuses make a plus. Something happened when I saw her lying there. Her jaw had been dislocated. One eye was so swollen it wasn't even visible. She had three broken ribs and a broken leg. Fractured right arm. And someone had kicked her so hard in the back that her spine was damaged.'

Mina nodded.

'So not scoliosis,' she said.

Kenneth shook his head.

'We come off soon,' Mina said, and he switched on the right indicator.

'People generally don't want to hear the truth. So we lie. It's easier that way,' he said.

'I understand what you mean,' said Mina, looking out of the window.

She did the same. Lied. To everyone. It had always been easiest that way.

'I called an ambulance. Went with her to the hospital. Since then, it's been us two.'

'And you found your way to AA . . . Does it help you? With your . . . problems?'

'Yes, it does. That and things we do ourselves. Sometimes you have to be proactive. You can't just sit there, waiting for things to happen. For things to change. Sometimes you have to take things into your own hands.'

'I understand what you mean,' said Mina. And she really did. 'Are you from here? Stockholm?'

'Yes. And no.'

He didn't say more. And she didn't ask.

'How long do you have?' she said instead.

Kenneth didn't even shudder. She regretted the question as soon as she'd asked it. But it was as if she lacked the filter that others had – the one between their brains and mouths. It was another reason why she avoided conversation. It usually ended with people taking it badly.

'How did you know?' he said, his gaze still fixed on the road ahead.

'I didn't know for sure until you just confirmed it. But it was a good guess. You've got yellow whites in your eyes and a yellow tinge to your skin. Just like my Grandpa who died of liver cancer. And there's an empty Nexavar jar on the floor. My Grandpa took that too.'

Mina cautiously prodded an empty pill jar lying on the floor with her toe.

'A few months, if I'm lucky,' he said. 'Too many metastases. I'm not taking Nexavar any longer.'

'I'm sorry,' she said.

They were silent for a while.

'I have to do everything for Jane,' he said. 'It's all I can give her. It's all I can do. To give her everything she needs.'

'Great,' said Mina.

She twisted in her seat and supported herself on her hand. This was starting to get too personal, too human. She could feel something sticky against her hand. A sweet wrapper. Disgusted, she tried to remove it but it stuck to her fingers and she felt her nausea increase. She finally got the wrapper off. She looked up.

'You should have turned off there,' she said, pointing at the exit they had just passed.

But instead of slowing down, the van sped up.

'You missed the exit,' said Mina, turning towards him with a frown.

Kenneth didn't answer. He merely pressed his foot down on the accelerator even harder, the speedometer now showing they were doing one hundred and fifty kilometres an hour.

'What are you doing?' Mina shouted, staring at him.

Eventually he turned his head slowly towards her and spoke calmly. 'You're coming home with me.'

Then he turned his eyes back to the road again. Mina sat immobile for a few seconds, then she pulled her phone out of her pocket. Before she could stop him, Kenneth wrenched it from her hand and threw it out of the gap at the top of the window. And it was at that moment Mina realized she had made a mistake.

A big mistake.

121

Her little brother was sitting on the living room sofa with his knees pulled up. He'd wrapped his arms around his legs and was crying. The tears were staining his top and the sofa cushion underneath him. She could barely hear what he was saying.

'She got into the box,' he sobbed. 'I locked it with the padlock. Then I was going to fetch my cloak. The one you made for me. I ran to the house. Then I got hungry. I ate three sandwiches with one slice of cheese and half a slice of ham on each. And I drank . . .'

'What you ate and drank isn't important!' she shouted, unable to stop herself.

'Yes it is!' he shouted back. 'The radio was on in the kitchen. It was a programme about manic depress . . . man . . . like Mum is sometimes. So I listened to it. Then Malla, Sickan and Lotta came. They had a picnic with them. We cycled over to the lake and went swimming. Then we had dinner at Sickan's.'

It felt like she needed to throw up again.

That bloody cloak. If she hadn't given it to him, he would have stayed in the barn. Nothing would have happened. It was all her fault. Well, no. That thought belonged to old Jane. Not this time. Not any longer.

'Didn't your friends wonder where your mother was?'

'Yes, they asked for her and I remembered she was in the barn, but they thought we should sneak off so that she didn't see. Mischief, they said.'

Mischief. Jane could murder those girls.

'When did you remember you'd left her in the box?' she asked, forcing herself to sound calm.

464

She sat down next to her little brother on the sofa and he leaned his forehead against his knees.

'In the evening,' he said quietly. 'When it was time for me to go to bed.'

'*In the evening?* But how could you forget something like that? *You* of all people?'

'But I didn't forget! It was dark out! It's scary.'

He suddenly looked up at her with defiance in his gaze.

'Anyway, she could get out! There was a . . . I'm not really allowed to say. A magician never reveals his secrets, but . . .'

'I'm going to hit you.'

'There was a secret door. The whole trick is based on her being able to sneak out the back. I thought she'd done it – that she crawled out as soon as I didn't come back and then perhaps she'd gone to a friend's or something. Or was weeding the dandelions. I don't know.'

She gulped hard. He was only seven. And he wasn't like most other seven-year-olds. She had to remember that. But still. There was a limit.

'Why didn't you go and check?' she said. 'When she didn't come home?'

'I was afraid. Maybe she'd be angry. Or hurt after waiting in the box for too long. I didn't want to be told off. But Jane, I don't understand – why did she stay in it?'

'Because your bloody secret door didn't work!'

Her little brother recoiled hard. Then he frowned.

'Didn't work?' he said. 'I don't think I got my calculations wrong . . . But wouldn't she have knocked?'

Sometimes he was so dumb. It was a miracle he hadn't got caught in the barn door by his cloak and strangled himself.

'How do you know she didn't knock?' she said. 'You were gone. And then you didn't go and check! You avoided the barn for almost two weeks. Because you didn't want to get told off. What were you *thinking*? She might have been knocking for hours. Or days!'

A small part of her wasn't completely satisfied. Perhaps it wasn't as simple as she wanted to make it. Was it really that certain that it was completely her brother's fault? The image of Mum on the lawn was still crystal clear in her memory. She could hear the words as clearly as if they had been said a few seconds ago.

If you leave I'll kill myself.

Surely no one killed themselves by starving themselves to death, not to mention slowly *cooking* themselves in a sauna-hot wooden box? No.

At least, not as a deliberate plan. Mum probably hadn't sabotaged the door on purpose. But when she had realized she was trapped . . . Had part of her given up then? Had a voice inside her said that it was for the best? That they would cope better without her? And then she had just . . . waited?

Jane shook her head so hard it hurt. The thought was barbarous. It was impossible to do that. Impossible. Surely? She looked at the boy sitting next to her on the sofa and made up her mind. It was his fault. Her disturbed little brother who hadn't even gone to check. If he hadn't been so stupid then everything would have been different. That was how it was – no other way.

The doorbell rang.

'Who do you think it is?' her little brother sobbed.

She looked up at the ceiling, blinking away the tears. He had ruined her life. There wouldn't be any sixth form in Mora for her now. Without parents, she'd end up in a foster home and she knew how well *that* would go. If there was anything her years in Kvibille had taught her, it was that she wasn't like the others. Teachers rolled their eyes when she finished her work too quickly and asked questions they didn't under-stand. None of the boys in class fancied her – apparently no one wanted to be with someone who could think so much. Even the girls in class went quiet when she showed up, as if they didn't know which language to use. She couldn't help it that they were so incredibly dense.

But in Mora it would have been different. There were other people like her there. Other smart people. Ylva had told her that. She would have been normal there. No need to keep quiet – on the contrary, she would have blossomed.

A new life.

She got off the sofa and went to open the door to the police. She had called them an hour earlier. The new life was over before it had even begun. She hated her little brother so much. So very, very much. Him and his damn friends.

122

Kenneth drove the van onto a patch of gravel in front of a big, grey building. She recognized it from the photos she'd seen when researching ketamine. They'd been right. It was a mink farm. Kenneth switched off the engine and turned to her.

Without any warning he gave her a slap. A scare tactic. An effective way of making victims compliant and easier to manage because they couldn't predict when it would happen again. She knew all that. But knowing it didn't prevent the tactic from working. She was shocked that the old man had such force in his blow. Cortisol and adrenaline exploded throughout her body, making her feel terrified.

'Wait there,' he said, opening the door on his side and getting out.

She fought against the adrenaline and fear that was preventing her from thinking clearly. She had to rely on her instincts – and that all her years of police training had programmed reflexes into her that would ensure she survived.

Kenneth went round the bonnet to open her door. When he was right in front of the van, she considered whether to throw herself out of his side, but he would presumably make it back round before she managed to get away. Instead, she quickly took off her seat belt and drew up her legs. When Kenneth pressed down her door handle, she kicked straight out as hard as she could. The door flew open and hit his head and upper body. He shouted and fell backwards heavily into the gravel. She hoped it hurt.

She threw herself out of the van and ran past the dazed Kenneth. The smell that hit her was overwhelming. She had expected the smell of animals, but this was . . . this was something else. Something sickly. She put her hand to her mouth.

There only seemed to be one route away from the gravel, and that was the track they had just come along. She began to run towards it, but only managed a few steps before a loud bang echoed between the trees. She spun around. Sitting in her wheelchair in front of the grey building was Jane. She took aim at Mina with a pistol. Mina cursed her stupidity. How could she not have thought about the fact that Jane would be there?

'Don't do anything stupid,' said Mina, slowly raising her hands.

Jane's practised grip on the pistol revealed this was not the first time she had handled a weapon. She might be old and in a wheelchair, but Jane's aim was straight as an arrow.

'I might say the same to you,' said Jane gravely. 'You've seen what I can do with one of these.'

'Agnes?'

Jane nodded in satisfaction.

'Good deduction, officer. Straight in the mouth. You should have seen how surprised she was.'

Mina needed to disarm Jane and fast. Jane was clearly a good shot. But it was one thing shooting at a stationary target and quite another to hit a moving one. Especially one moving towards you. Mina's only choice was to rush at Jane while zig-zagging and hope that she didn't keep up. A gunshot to her arm wasn't exactly something she was looking forward to, but she'd be able to take it. As long as she got the pistol away from Jane.

She slowly lowered her arms while maintaining eye contact with Jane. She couldn't show any muscle tension in her legs or stomach, no shifting of her centre of gravity, nothing that would reveal she was readying herself for a spring. Once she started running, it needed to be over almost before she had begun.

A hard thump on her back suddenly threw her forwards. The gravel scraped her knees as she fell and landed with her face in the small stones. The air was forced out of her lungs and when she tried to inhale again all she did was rasp. She heard steps and a pair of feet appeared in front of her eyes. It was impossible to raise her head to see who they belonged to. She was fully occupied trying to get air into her lungs. Not that she needed to see – she knew whose they were. So stupid.

'I think this one's a bit friskier than the others,' Kenneth chuckled from above her.

123

The fifth time he called, he got exactly the same message as the first four times. A friendly voice explained that it was not possible to connect to the number dialled. Mina's phone was switched off.

Admittedly, Mina was a very private person, but the only time he knew of when she actually turned off her phone was when she went to the meetings that she thought no one knew about. And even there she seemed to forget about it quite frequently. Otherwise she was always reachable, thanks to that old-fashioned dedication to her job. She might be at one of those meetings, of course, and therefore have her phone off. But not today. Not the day that was going to end with a fourth murder if they didn't stop it in time.

And yet she wasn't answering.

Vincent had no rational explanation for the fateful feeling that overcame him and so he should have been able to ignore it. But it stubbornly dug into his brain's amygdala, drowning out the rational frontal lobes.

He needed to call one of the others. The problem was that apart from Mina he only had numbers for Ruben and Julia. Ruben was sitting in his car a few metres away. And Ruben would never believe him and would assume that Vincent was attempting a ruse in order to leave the house.

He called Julia instead, but only got her voicemail. He hung up before it had finished talking. He looked at Ruben's car through the window. This was about *Mina*. If something happened to her, he would never forgive himself. He wasn't even going to let her get a headache if he could prevent it. He quite simply had to get Ruben to believe him.

Before he had time to open the front door, the phone in his hand rang. It was a number he didn't recognize. Requesting a video call. The only person he knew that liked video calls was Aston, but his son didn't have his own phone. He hesitated, then he answered.

'Yes? Hello?'

The picture that appeared on his phone made him struggle for breath. It was Mina. She was in a wheelchair, her hands lashed to it. Her hair, always so perfectly presented, was hanging in wisps and her face was dirty. She was wearing the necklace he had seen on her desk and the white polo neck was black with grime. There was a long rip in one sleeve. She had fought someone. Violently, it appeared. And lost.

An older man was standing next to her. As soon as Mina realized the camera was running she began talking quickly.

'Vincent,' she said. 'I don't know where I am but it stinks of . . .'

She was interrupted by a hard slap from the man. Vincent realized he'd seen him before. It was the man he'd met at the AA meeting. Kenneth.

'Do you know how bloody stupid it is to hit a cop?' Mina yelled, tugging at the ropes holding her down. 'I can put you away for life!'

Kenneth merely chuckled. Then he pulled on a rope attached to the wheelchair and coiled it around Mina's torso. Mina whimpered as the rope was tightened, as if the pressure from it hurt a lot, and she stopped moving. The person holding the phone switched to the selfie camera and he looked straight into the eyes of an old woman. She looked sick. Her face seemed to have shrivelled up and was smaller than it ought to have been. Her skin was hardened and cracked, as if she had lived outdoors for most of her life – a life that didn't appear to have been very kind to her.

Then he saw her gaze – and he recognized it. The gaze was as intense as it had always been. His eyes opened wide when he realized who he was looking at. How had his sister grown so old?

'Hello, little brother,' she said. 'How are you doing these days?'

'What have you done to Mina?' he shouted.

'Hush. No manners,' Jane snorted. 'A hello would have been nice. But you don't seem surprised to see me, so I assume you finally solved the puzzle in the book. Admit it, you appreciated that detail!'

His sister chortled with satisfaction.

'By the way, we heard at AA that you harassed your admirer, Anna,' she said. 'That was cruel. She was always talking about "the amazing Vincent Walder". The ideal match for easily duped people. Kenneth merely had to say that someone might need to put Mina on the right track and she did the job for us and suggested you. And we had come up with a whole plan for how to get you involved, too – completely unnecessary. It was barely even fun when it was that easy.'

'Let Mina go,' he hissed between his teeth.

His sister's face still took up the whole screen. He needed to see Mina again to check that she was OK.

'I understand,' said Jane. 'You want to get started right away. Fine by me. We'll have time for small talk later. But first we've got a few rules of the game. I'm sure you understand.'

'What are you talking about? What do y—'

'Don't interrupt when the grown-ups are talking!' Jane hissed. 'You haven't changed a bit. Always needing to be the centre of attention. I'm sure you've got lots of questions for Mina: where is she, how is she feeling, and all that jazz. But I promise you this – ask one more question and she dies immediately. And Mina, the same applies to you. Say another word and this will be over before it's even begun.'

Vincent was silent. It sounded like Jane was serious. What had happened to his sister? She had been so smart. Now she was psychotic. Mad. He had difficulty comprehending that the woman on the phone was the girl he had once amused with card tricks on a blanket.

Jane switched cameras again so that he could see the man taking Mina's chin in a firm grip. She lunged back and forth with her head, trying to get out of his hands, but it didn't help. The man compressed her cheeks.

'Is that understood?' said Jane.

The man moved his hand up and down, making Mina nod without saying anything. But the panic in her eyes couldn't be mistaken. At the same time, it was a sign that she hadn't given up.

'It's OK, Mina,' he said, trying to convey: *I see you, I can see you're hurting, but they don't know what we have, how we connect.* 'We'll do as they say.'

Mina's eyes gazed into his.

We'll get out of this. I trust you. Us.

'But now I'm hiding. How impolite,' said Jane. 'And here I am, accusing you of having no manners. You've met Kenneth before. My husband and partner.'

The man who was still holding Mina's face bowed, with a smile towards the camera. Jane backed away and the picture panned out. Mina appeared to be sitting behind a workbench. Lying on the bench was a sword. Vincent immediately recognized the type. A Condor Grosse Messer. The same sort that had penetrated Tuva. The handle of the sword was attached to a clamp which was in turn attached to a hammer drill. That explained the marks he'd seen on the sword handles when he'd visited the forensic lab. The hammer drill looked like the kind used to remove asphalt from roads, but smaller. Jesus Christ. They had stuck the swords into Tuva using a hammer drill. He couldn't even imagine how much it must have hurt.

But it wasn't the sword and the hammer drill that most captured his attention.

It was the five numbered, upside-down paper bags standing in front of Mina. Each was big enough to accommodate an upright eight-inch nail under it. Vincent's entire body went icy cold.

'I'm not heartless,' said his sister. 'I know how important Mina is to you. Oh, don't look so surprised. Anna has told us how often she's seen you around town. Apparently you've been courting all over the place. In Rålambshovsparken. On Fjällgatan. At that rooftop restaurant. Even at hers. So don't play indifferent. I should think no one matters more to you right now than her. And do you know what? You're going to have the chance to save her.'

Kenneth chuckled.

'Or kill her,' he said with a cold smile.

'Isn't it funny how it's always the assistant that comes off worst?' said Jane, leaning into shot to look Vincent in the eyes. 'It's the cute assistant's job to be shut into cramped spaces and tortured. But you know all about that, little brother. By the way, do you know how we met Mina? Do you know about her little . . . problem?'

Jane fixed her gaze on Mina. She didn't meet Jane's eyes.

'She's a coward. Do you know that? Do you know how cowardly Mina is?'

The question was rhetorical and Jane didn't seem to be expecting an answer.

'She's sat there,' she continued. 'Time after time. Week after week. Listening to everyone else open up. She's heard everyone else share. She's shared in their pain, their struggle, their stories. But what about her? She hasn't shared shit. Well, now you have the chance, Mina. What is it you'd like to say? What is it you're going to share? This is your audience. Could be your last chance. Who knows? So take it now.'

Mina's expression didn't flicker one bit.

'I'm going to remove one of the bags. One without a nail under it. Unless you share.'

Jane's voice was calm. Completely free from emotion. Kenneth's hand moved towards the table with the bags.

'Mina. Do as they say,' said Vincent with forced calm.

472

Five bags meant there was a 20 per cent risk of hitting the nail, whichever one was chosen. One bag less increased the risk to 25 per cent. He needed every last per cent on his side.

Mina slowly raised her head. She looked straight at Vincent and took a deep breath. Her nervousness and anxiety were wasted if it was his reaction she was afraid of. He already knew what she was going to say.

'I'm . . . I'm called Mina. And I . . . am addicted to pills.'

'There we are. Now, that wasn't so difficult, was it?'

Jane smiled. A surprisingly warm, open smile.

'Wasn't that nice, Vincent? Why did it have to be so difficult? She's not that bloody special. No better than any of the rest of us sitting in those sessions. Isn't that right, Vincent? Just a regular fucking addict . . . Sitting there with her nose turned up . . .'

'I already knew,' Vincent said, interrupting his sister.

Jane's schadenfreude was replaced with a sour expression and Mina looked at him in surprise. Jane seemed about to say something else but he was no longer listening to her. He stared at the bags and felt the sweat breaking out all over his body. He looked at Mina. Then at Jane. Thoughts bounced against the inside of his cranium, breaking loose and escaping with screams. He and Jane and Mina were three sides to a triangle, a perfect triangle where the toast didn't crack because then Mum had to throw it away but there were also five bags, 3 + 5 = 8 – which led nowhere.

stop it

but eight plus Kenneth (why was his sister's husband called Kenneth, surely no one was called that?) was nine and nine centimetres was 3.5 inches

stop it, stop it

and 3.5 was the setting on the toaster if it hadn't already warmed up to make the triangle perfectly crispy but the edges always broke just like him and-and-and—

STOP IT.

'I was seven years old, Jane,' he said. 'It was an accident.'

Something hard appeared in his sister's gaze.

'Do you think this is just about Mum?' she hissed. 'You're as child-ishly selfish as ever, little brother. Enough talk. It's time.'

She disappeared out of shot and he could see Mina and the paper bags clearly again.

'You're only making matters worse for yourselves,' said Mina, tugging at the ropes again.

Once again her words were ignored. Kenneth grabbed her head, this time the back of it.

'You know the rules, little brother,' said Jane. 'After all, it is your favourite trick. Pick a number.'

He swallowed hard, concentrating on his breathing until he felt that his thoughts were his again. He had to do as she said. He couldn't afford to lose himself. He didn't doubt for a moment that they would kill Mina the very second he didn't follow their instructions. But at the same time, how was he supposed to choose?

'How do I know you haven't put nails under all the bags?' he said.

'Pick a number now,' Jane said threateningly. 'Otherwise I will.'

He concentrated. Five bags. Five positions. When people were asked to pick from five objects in a row, they most often picked the object in position number four, but position two came in a solid second place. The psychological theories about why this was were many, but everyone agreed that it was true. If Jane was unaware of the phenomenon and had placed the nail without any particular consideration then there was a good chance it was in position two or four.

But if she did know about it, then she would have put it in one of the other positions to increase the chances of Vincent picking the nail, since she knew that he would avoid two and four if he thought the nail was there.

That was if she didn't expect Vincent to see through the dummy manoeuvre and realize that the nail wasn't under two or four. Then she might have put the nail under two or four on purpose, counting on him picking one of them in the belief that the nail was under one of the other three.

Provided there weren't more nails, that was.

Bloody hell.

He hadn't seen his sister since he was little. But she had always been smart. Smart all the way. On the other hand, she had never seen him as particularly smart. That was why she'd been astonished by his tricks when they were children. Even if afterwards she always claimed she'd worked it out. She never believed that he would be able to outwit her. Presumably she didn't now, either.

'I choose bag two,' said Vincent, holding his breath.

'What happens next is completely and entirely your fault,' said Jane. 'I want you to know that.'

Kenneth slammed Mina's head down hard over bag two. The chosen bag crumpled as her forehead hit the table.

'Ouch!' Mina yelled.

Kenneth pulled her up by the hair. She had a glowing mark on her brow. But no nail. Vincent exhaled.

'Beginner's luck,' said his big sister. 'Pick again.'

He dared to ask a question.

'Mina, are you OK?'

She shook her head. Tears were running down her cheeks. There was tension in her facial muscles.

'Do you know where the nail is?' he said.

She shook her head again. The resistance he'd seen in her eyes had almost been extinguished.

'I'm warning you, Vincent!' said Jane. 'Don't ask any questions unless you want Kenneth to use the sword instead. Choose. Now.'

'OK, OK. Wait. I pick . . . bag one,' said Vincent.

He had no idea, no way of knowing. More than the fact that statistics were on his side. With four bags left there was a seventy-five per cent chance that his chosen bag was empty. On the other hand, there was a twenty-five per cent chance he'd just killed Mina.

Mina let out a cry when her head hit the workbench again. The bang as her forehead hit the wood blared through the phone. Kenneth pulled her back upright immediately afterwards. Her whole body was shaking in spasms. She was crying uncontrollably and was no longer meeting Vincent's gaze. The mark on her forehead was dark red. But still no nail.

'Are you having fun, Vincent?' Jane laughed. 'Now it's starting to get exciting! Three to go. The audience is holding its breath! Pick.'

'Stop it,' he said quietly. 'That's enough. You'll give her concussion. I'll do whatever you want. But please stop. I can't handle any more.'

He blinked, feeling tears running down his cheeks.

'Pick!' roared his sister.

'No!' Vincent shouted back.

'As you wish.'

Jane waved at Kenneth, and without warning he thumped Mina's head down onto the table over bag five. Mina only managed to emit a whimper. Once again, she was yanked back upright. This time her forehead left a bloodstain on the table. She appeared to be bordering on unconsciousness. The crying had stopped and her shoulders were limp. Mina was staring straight ahead but her eyes had lost focus. There was nothing in her gaze to reveal whether she was still there or whether she had fled somewhere he couldn't follow her. The mark on her brow was bleeding, dripping down into her dark, beautiful eyes. But it was still just a mark. There was no nail in her head.

Vincent stared at the two bags left. Numbers three and four. Fifty per cent chance. Right now, Mina was equal parts dead and alive.

Schrödinger's assistant, he thought, unable to stop himself. Her existence was indefinite. Until he chose and condemned her to one of two possible futures. He, Vincent. He couldn't have that power – he couldn't hold her life in his hands – it was too much.

He looked at her, at the policewoman he had come to know better than anyone. Better than he knew himself. Her dark hair, beautiful features and distinct nose. The fulsome lips and chapped, tied-up hands. Mina was still staring expressionlessly into space, but her eyes were the most intelligent he had ever seen.

She had put a straw in his beer.

She had taken his hand.

She had cried on his shoulder.

She had trusted him.

And now he was going to let her down.

He needed her in order to keep himself in reality. In the real reality. Since Mina had come into his life, everything had changed, more than she knew, more than he could ever explain. When she was with him, the deep shadow within him, the very shadow of his brain, no longer had any strength. Without her, he was . . . The thought couldn't even be completed.

Two bags. One choice.

She would live.

She would die.

It was impossible. He needed some way of knowing, some way of understanding where the nail was.

'And now, a big drum roll,' said Jane dramatically. 'The great mentalist will make his absolutely final choice within five seconds.'

Mina blinked, seeming to return to reality. She looked at the bags in front of her and shook her head when she realized what the situation was. Her eyes met Vincent's. He probably looked as panic-stricken as she did.

'No,' she mumbled over and over. 'No, no, no.'

He thought more quickly than ever. *The great mentalist* was what Jane had said. But a mentalist was also an illusionist. And they had more tricks up their sleeve than the audience knew. Invisible wires. Duplicates. Mirrors. And . . . Yes. *YES!*

He bit his cheek to avoid showing how elated he was. It might just work. And it was all he had.

'Is it OK if I get a little closer to the bags?' he asked as neutrally as he could.

'Ah, a little drama. Why not!' Jane laughed. 'We'll get to see her brain matter up close!'

'Vincent,' said Mina in confusion, 'why would I want . . .?'

Then she fell silent.

We'll do this together. We have to trust each other. We'll make it.

'Lean forward, towards bag three.'

She did as he said.

'Good. And now bag four.'

Mina leaned forward again. *There.* Vincent made an effort not to show any micro expressions of emotion on his face. Mina's position meant that she hadn't seen what had happened. Jane and Kenneth didn't seem to have noticed anything, but Vincent had clearly seen the magnetic pendant on Mina's necklace move by a millimetre when it got close to bag four.

As if reacting to metal.

A twenty-centimetre nail, for instance.

'Three!' Vincent shouted. 'I choose bag three!'

'Remember it was you who chose, little brother,' said his sister. 'Goodbye, Mina.'

Mina took a deep breath and screwed up her eyes. She resisted with all her might, but Kenneth was stronger. He pushed her head forward until her forehead was resting over the top of bag three. Then he continued downwards, slowly but surely. The bag crumped under the weight of Mina's head being forced onto the bench. Kenneth put both hands on the back of her head, as if it was being pushed against a nail that needed to be pressed through the skull with force. A gurgling sound escaped from Mina's lips along with saliva, and spasms made her body shudder. When Kenneth eventually let go, she stayed lying there with her forehead against the table. Her head appeared to be glued to the wood. Mina was completely still.

Much, much too still.

124

She ran down the corridor at police headquarters. Finally something was happening. Michael and the kids had arrived from New York in early August. They'd spent three weeks of vacation time together and gone on a road trip around Sweden. And then the kids had started school. Sara had thought they would get used to life in Stockholm very quickly. But she'd been wrong.

She took the long staircase down into the atrium two steps at a time, crossing the atrium before running onwards. She didn't want to waste time calling Julia – this was too important not to do in person.

The Stockholm she had returned to was completely stationary compared with the pulsating city of New York. The kids still missed their American friends and Michael was talking about moving to California, since the games company he worked for had teams out there. It was starting to sound more and more like a good idea. But she could at least do this final thing before quitting the force.

Sara didn't dare wait for the lift to arrive promptly, so she ran up the three flights of stairs to the floor where Julia had her office.

She had been waiting patiently to find out what her new role would be now that she was back home. There still seemed to be no one who was quite sure. When Julia had asked her for help in the spring she had gratefully accepted. It was at least something to keep her occupied in the meantime. And for the same reason she had said yes again when Julia had renewed her request. This time the work had been more intense. She had spent the last week working day in, day out to monitor traffic on the mobile network in real time. To start with, she'd had Peder's help. His keen eyes missed nothing. At least when they were open. After he had nodded off twice in the middle of their surveillance work, they had agreed it would be better for Sara to take over. Naturally, there was far too much information passing over the network for her to be able to sort through it in a meaningful way. But now she had smart software to do it for her, which knew what she was on the lookout for. Not that she had thought it would turn anything up. In her experience, phones were only used once in these contexts. Then they were chucked to make sure they couldn't be traced. She was rarely wrong at work. She was far too meticulous for that to happen. But this time she had actually been wrong. And it was the best thing that could have happened.

After months of silence, the murderer had finally used their phone.

125

Vincent stared at a lifeless Mina on the screen. It was hard to see properly, his hand was shaking so much. He had hoped that Mina's magnetic necklace would respond to the nail. And it had done. Perhaps. The movement had been so small that it might have been Mina imperceptibly moving and making it sway. Maybe the nail wasn't even magnetic. Most nails weren't.

But what was he supposed to have done? One out of two. He might well have picked the right one simply by taking his chances. Instead of the wrong one. It was so horribly unfair. He really had tried.

Mina's head stood out against the pale wood of the table. It stood against the *pale wood*, because . . . Because there was no blood.

No blood at all.

His heart skipped a beat.

Mina slowly raised her head. Her gaze met his in the camera.

They had won. But it didn't feel that way. Far from it.

'My goodness,' Jane laughed. 'That's not like you, little brother – saving your assistants.'

'You're sick,' he said. 'Disgusting. There wasn't a nail, was there?'

In response, Kenneth removed the final bag. Bag number four. The most common one to choose by far. The nail was standing upright from a wooden board with the spike sharpened so that it shone. When Mina saw the nail, she threw up right over the table.

Jane twisted the phone away from the bench and Mina so that Vincent could see the rest of the workshop. In the centre of the room there was something that looked like a giant aquarium on its end.

'We had been saving this one for you,' she said. 'For today. I honestly didn't think she was going to make it. Now we'll get to put her in it instead.'

'Wait a minute, I did as you asked!' he shouted. 'Let her go.'

'Of course. If you come and take her place. I'll message you the address. It normally takes one hour and forty minutes to drive here – provided you catch the ferry on time. We'll put your friend in the tank now. In ninety-five minutes, we'll start filling it with water. It takes five minutes to fill it to the top. I advise you not to miss that ferry.'

Kenneth began to push the wheelchair containing Mina towards the water tank. Mina tugged and struggled to get loose, but it was no use.

'And Vincent,' said his big sister, looking right at him, 'if there's even a hint that anyone other than you is coming, or if you don't come alone, then I'll shoot her in the face.'

He shouted Mina's name as loudly as he could, but Jane had already hung up. Vincent looked out through the kitchen window. Ruben was still parked up in his car on the road on the far side of the lawn. Vincent's own car was parked on the driveway. He couldn't get to it without being spotted by Ruben. The question was how to pull it off. Ruben couldn't be allowed to realize he was leaving the house. If the police followed him it would end in disaster. He wished he could make himself disappear in a puff of smoke, but that was more Tom Presto's thing. If he'd been clever with his hands he could have built a silhouette of himself using a hat and coat and left it behind the curtains. He laughed grimly at the idea. It was probably the kind of trick that only worked on TV.

But a copy of himself.

He actually had one of those.

He ran into the study. The life-size, cardboard cut-out of him wasn't hard to find – it was propped against the wall behind some boxes. The cardboard had got a bit soiled after the production team had taken it on a bar crawl when he couldn't join them himself. But it was far better than a hat and coat. The figure was him. *Verliebtheit.*

At least for five seconds, until Ruben realized he wasn't moving.

He needed to reinforce the illusion. He glanced quickly at his watch. Two minutes had elapsed since the phone call. He needed to be in his car in no more than three minutes' time. He spent thirty seconds putting on the same clothes the cardboard cut-out version of him was wearing. Then he ran out of the house, across the lawn and over to Ruben, who lowered the police car window when he spotted Vincent.

'Hi, Ruben,' said Vincent, putting his index finger in the air sufficiently high up that Ruben had to look upwards, his eyes automatically drawn to the finger.

'Now, you are going to do . . . this,' said Vincent, quickly moving his finger down while lowering his voice an octave on 'this'.

Ruben's gaze followed the downward motion of the finger until his eyes closed automatically. Vincent quickly put his hand to Ruben's neck to ensure he kept his head gently leaning forward. Ruben would never forgive him for this.

'Relax and breathe deeply,' said Vincent. 'With each breath you take, you're feeling more and more relaxed. Deeper and deeper.'

He waited a few seconds until he heard Ruben breathing deeply and rhythmically.

'In a few seconds, you'll see me in the kitchen window,' he continued. 'We're going to play the angry game. Do you understand?'

'Yes. The angry game,' Ruben mumbled in the monotonous tone of one who was easily hypnotized.

'We're going to stay completely still and stare at each other,' said Vincent. 'The first one to blink loses. You've never seen someone who can stay as still as I can. But the more I stay still, the more determined you are to win. Do you understand?'

'You are still,' Ruben murmured. 'But I will win.'

Vincent removed his hand and raised Ruben's head. His eyes were still closed. He could click his fingers to get Ruben to start and open them, but he'd never really liked that finger clicking thing. It was so . . . unsophisticated.

'Ruben, look at me,' he said instead, stating it as a command.

Ruben blinked at him in confusion.

'Good, well that's agreed then,' said Vincent. 'Good chat. I'm going to think over what you said. It'll be a quiet night in for me.'

It was important to continue talking immediately after implanting a suggestion, in order to prevent Ruben's brain from trying to figure out what had just happened.

'Hmm, yes,' Ruben said, trying to gather himself. 'I'll be keeping my eye on you, Vincent. Don't try anything.'

Vincent jogged back to the house, checking the time. The whole thing had taken ninety seconds. One minute left. Once inside, he crouched beneath the kitchen window and positioned the cardboard cut-out in the window, turning it to face the police car. He saw Ruben sit up straighter.

He crept out via the terrace door into the back garden while sending a message to Benjamin asking him to pick up his little brother from school.

Vincent came round the corner of the house and followed the wall to his own car, which was parked in front of the garage. The car was between him and Ruben. He crouched behind it, so that he was hidden in case Ruben were to look in his direction. Ruben would hopefully have all his concentration aimed at the kitchen window for a good while to come, but he couldn't afford to take chances.

Vincent carefully unlocked the car, opened the passenger-side door and wriggled over to the driver's seat. Then he quietly reversed onto the street, just a few metres from the police car. The gravel crunched under his tyres, but Ruben didn't react. Vincent didn't dare drive past the police car and break Ruben's field of vision. It would have to be the other way instead. Once he was round the corner so that Ruben could no longer see him, he floored it. He had to google his route while on the move. He couldn't lose his grip now. He had to keep focused. Keep thinking one step at a time. But just one.

Mina.

Jane.

He couldn't think about the cramped water tank. Couldn't think about the fact that he was driving as fast as he could to let his big sister lock him in a glass box full of water. Couldn't think about the fact that Jane was going to let him drown, couldn't think about the fact that he was racing towards his death with the accelerator to the floor. Cars honked at him as he overtook them, nearly close enough to scrape their paintwork. He pushed the accelerator down even further.

Mina.

Jane.

126

Sara caught her breath for a few seconds outside Julia's door. Then she knocked and entered. The room was empty. That wasn't what she had been expecting. She thought everyone would be on site, today of all days, on high alert. She knew that Christer's office was further down the corridor and she went there. The door was wide open, but his office was also empty. What was going on? Perhaps they'd been called out. If so, they needed her information even more.

Cheerful laughter and music was audible from a few rooms down: the unmistakable rhythms of Bob Marley. What on earth? She hurried to the room where the sound was coming from and was stopped dead in her tracks by the sight that met her eyes.

Peder was reggae dancing to 'No Woman No Cry', leaning back and raising his knees. On his chest he was wearing a baby carrier, in which a baby was happily babbling away. Lying on the floor were another two babies on a thick blanket. They were displaying equal parts delight and terror as they were drowned in slobbery kisses from an overexcited golden retriever. Christer was holding the lead and doing his best to make sure the dog didn't eat the children. Peder caught sight of Sara, stopped in the middle of a particularly exuberant leg lift and blushed from ear to ear.

'Er . . . you see, it's my wife's birthday today,' he said, embarrassed.

Sara didn't reply. She was too busy trying to take in what she was seeing.

'Her present,' Peder continued in response to the unspoken question, 'or, well, her demand actually, was to go out for lunch. Alone. And then to get her hair done. Alone. And then to nod off in the corner of some cafe. It's been on the cards for a long time. So, yes. Hmm.'

He nodded towards the triplets as if this explained everything.

'I gathered from Julia that today was an important day,' Sara said. 'Full mobilization. She can't have been referring to your wife's birthday.'

Peder cleared his throat, even more embarrassed, and switched off Bob Marley on the computer. Christer pulled the retriever away from the babies, who were gurgling with laughter on the blanket. The dog immediately looked deeply unhappy.

'That's correct, we're on full alert today,' said Christer. 'We're on standby, like you say. According to Vin— I mean, we have information suggesting another murder may take place today. The squad cars out on the streets are on the highest state of alert. But since we don't have anything else to go on for the time being, Peder and I are manning the fort here. In case something comes in that requires us to act quickly.'

'Then you'll want to hear this,' said Sara. 'Do you remember the phone we traced in the spring? The one from Kungsholmen that called the tip line? You thought it was probably your murderer.'

Peder and Christer nodded attentively. The triplets and the dog seemed to sense the seriousness that had descended on the room, as all four went quiet at the same time.

'Julia asked me to monitor that number this week in case it was reactivated. Which it just was. The phone was switched on for ten minutes and one call was made. But this time the call was made from the Norrtälje archipelago.'

The baby in Peder's sling began to whimper anxiously. He carefully enveloped the small, chubby hands in his own.

'Norrtälje?' he said. 'What was the call about?'

'Don't know. We can't listen in; that requires a different warrant. Julia never asked me to obtain one.'

Sara had a sinking feeling in her stomach that she had made a fool of herself. She should obviously have asked Julia what they needed. It took time to obtain a warrant – it was necessary to plan in advance. But it wasn't easy to get to grips with the procedures if you didn't work on them day in day out. Of course she should have double-checked. Three months into her new job and still no better than a rookie.

'It's not your fault,' said Christer as if reading her thoughts. 'Julia should have asked you, but she's had other things on her plate. Do we know more than the fact that the call came from the archipelago?'

'Much more,' Sara said, relieved. 'We know who the call was placed to. Someone called Victor . . . sorry, *Vincent* Walder.'

Peder and Christer looked at each other in shock. Sara didn't understand – she hadn't thought they'd react so strongly. Or react at all, to

485

be honest. There was clearly more going on here than Julia had told her about.

'Bloody hell,' said Peder quietly before turning to her. 'We know him.'

'I'll call the task force right away and ask them to dispatch the flying squad,' said Christer. 'Come on, Bosse, we've got work to do.'

'Ruben is already at Vincent's,' said Peder. 'I'll contact him and then try to get hold of Julia. Thanks, Sara. Good work.'

She couldn't help smiling as Peder and Christer disappeared to carry out their duties. It was these moments she lived for. When she knew she had made a difference. When all the hours of slog suddenly produced results in the real world. She and Michael might put off the move to California for a while longer.

127

She looked at the bag on the bed in resignation. She had pointed out
– several times – that they didn't need to pack as if they were going
abroad. Uppsala was only around an hour away. And they weren't going
to stay any longer than necessary. But Torkel liked to be prepared. So
well prepared that you'd have thought he was one of those survivalists
on Netflix. Without even opening the bag, Julia suspected its contents
would see the two of them through a small war. And if they stayed at
home it would see them through several years of subsistence. Above
all, they had enough toilet paper to keep a whole county going for a
fair while. What sort of muppet hoarded toilet paper? Ah well, she
supposed he was *her* muppet.

And when it came down to it, he couldn't do much else during this
phase. He wasn't the one who was going to have a vacuum cleaner hose
shoved into his body, it wasn't his eggs that were going to be sucked
out by the dozen to see whether there were two or three that were
usable.

The only meaningful thing he could do was pack her bag. She couldn't
reproach him for doing so with a vengeance.

However, she was annoyed at his attitude right now. She wasn't just
his wife and the potential mother of their future children. He refused
to accept that she actually had a job to do too.

'They can manage without you,' he said from the hallway. 'Come on.'

She heard him take the car keys from the hook by the door.

'I don't know how I can say this any more clearly,' she hissed. 'I'm
heading up an investigation, in charge of a team – I'm involved in every
aspect. And today is the day we have to stop a murderer from claiming
his fourth victim. Don't you understand how it would look if I wasn't
there?'

She was close to tears. How could he be so petty and not understand? At the same time, she had stuck more needles in her belly and breathed in that bloody spray more times than she cared to count. It had to come to an end. Torkel came into the bedroom. He was struggling not to show the frustration that nevertheless shone clearly out of his face.

'You've said it yourself many times,' he said. 'You're one part of a highly skilled team. The others will manage. They know what they have to do. Surely it's not up to you personally to stop the murder?'

'Thanks for your vote of confidence,' she said, backing away from him.

Torkel sighed and sat down on the bed. She knew that her low oestrogen made her more irritable, but sometimes he was just so damned stupid.

'What you *can* do,' he said. 'Is this. Give us a chance. It didn't work last time we tried. I know the timing is disastrous. But this date has been blocked off in the diary for weeks. If we don't go to Uppsala University Hospital today then you'll have to start again from the beginning with the injections and the whole circus for several weeks. Just to get back to this point again. Is it worth that?'

She sat down next to him and wiped her eyes with her sleeve. Then she slumped her shoulders in resignation.

'No, it isn't worth it,' she said. 'But you're asking me to choose between creating a life – a life that might not ever really exist, we don't know for sure – and trying to prevent another life being ended, a life that definitely exists today. It's not fair.'

There was a vibration from under her bum. She had sat on her phone. She stood up and pulled it out. There was a message from Peder on the illuminated display. Two words. Two puny words that made her decision for her.

'I've got to go right away,' she said. 'Give me the car keys.'

Torkel passed her the keys without arguing.

'Kiss, darling. We'll talk more later,' he said while she put on her jacket.

She read the message again on the way out to the car.

It's Vincent.

128

An irritating, muffled ringing sound interrupted his concentration. As if someone had set an alarm somewhere in the distance. Last week or something. Ruben furrowed his brow.

He couldn't be disturbed – if he moved even an inch then Vincent would win.

Vincent was standing so still. Ruben was trying really hard.

He couldn't fathom how it was possible to stand as still as that mentalist was doing in his window.

But Ruben didn't plan on losing.

He fixed his gaze on Vincent even harder.

The sound went off again, much sharper now. Odd. By comparison, it had sounded like it was coming through cotton wool last time. Now it was more like a sharp knife cutting through his ear.

He squinted at Vincent.

Something looked different.

Something wasn't right.

It rang a third time. Ruben blinked as if waking from sleep. Really deep sleep that you struggled to emerge from.

Although he knew he hadn't slept. Not a wink.

He had been staring at Vincent the whole time and hadn't nodded off even for a second.

But there was something about the shadows on Vincent's face over in the kitchen window that didn't add up.

Why not?

The phone rang for a fourth time and he had to tear his gaze away to locate it on the seat next to him. He put it on speakerphone as he answered.

'Ruben Höök, what is it?' he said in irritation.

'It's Peder. The murderer has just called Vincent. I know you consider him a suspect and this obviously points in that direction. But he may also be in trouble. Christer has deployed the flying squad – sit tight and don't do anything until they arrive.'

Ruben hung up. He thought for a moment. He looked across the street towards the house. Then he got out of the car. He hesitated and stood there for a few seconds leaning against the car door. Then he ran across the lawn, heading for the window. Vincent's cardboard cut-out stared placidly back at him. Ruben could have sworn the cut-out was smiling.

129

He pulled up on the patch of gravel in front of the mink farm. Kenneth was waiting for him. The bastard even waved at him. Vincent hated him. He parked and got out. The stench of decay was powerful. It seemed to be coming from the main building. Something had happened at the farm – that much was clear. But right now he didn't care one iota about that. He wanted to murder Kenneth – to eradicate him from the surface of the earth for what he had done to Mina. But he knew there was no point in venting his fury on the bearded pensioner. If he did, he'd never see Mina again.

'Where is she?' he said instead.

Kenneth turned his back to him and began to walk away. Vincent had no choice but to follow. At the far end of the building there was a small door, through which the man disappeared. With his hand to his mouth, Vincent stopped in the doorway. The sunlight outside made it dark inside. There could be anything inside. It could be a trap. But Mina was in there.

The room inside turned out to be a workshop – the workshop he'd seen during their video call. The water tank was standing in the middle of the floor. Mina was sitting at the bottom. He ran over to her and hammered on the wall of the tank. He crouched so that he could see her better. The blood on her forehead had begun to dry. There was going to be one hell of a bruise there. She seemed otherwise unharmed so far as he could tell. But she wasn't moving.

'Mina,' he shouted, with his mouth pressed to the glass.

'We gave her something to make her sleep,' the man explained while closing the door. 'She put up too much of a struggle.'

The reassuring autumn sunshine outside disappeared and was replaced by the cold glow of fluorescent tubes. A generator was humming away somewhere.

'But I'm sure she'll come to when we start filling it with water,' said Kenneth, reaching his hand out towards Vincent. 'Your phone.'

Vincent stood up. He hadn't been certain when he'd only seen the tank on the phone, but now there was no doubt. The glass box was an exact copy of Houdini's water torture cell, built to accommodate one person with no room to spare. In the original, Houdini had been hung upside down with his ankles tied. Soon it would be his turn to do the same. There was no other option.

He worked to control his breathing. He couldn't show how frightened he was. He handed his phone to Kenneth, who carried it towards a large container in the corner.

'There's no need to add any water,' Vincent called out to him. 'I'm here now. Just like you asked. Take her out.'

The water tank was decidedly better built than the other boxes they had found the victims in. As a matter of fact, it looked genuine.

'This is the only one we haven't built ourselves,' said his sister.

She rolled out of the shadows and over to the tank in her wheelchair and patted the glass walls.

'We saved it for last,' she said. 'Only the best is good enough for you.'

'But how . . .?'

'We actually got the others from you,' she continued, throwing something onto the floor at his feet.

It was a thin book that he hadn't seen since he was seven years old. A book titled *Hobby Series 12: Build your own magic!*

'Those drawings don't work at all,' said Jane with a bitter laugh. 'Not that we wanted them to, but still. Anyway, we bought this one off that illusionist, what's his name? Tomas Pesto? Presto?'

A big knot formed in his stomach. 'I don't know where that tank is gathering dust now' was what Umberto had said about Presto's water tank. And Vincent hadn't asked him to look into it further. What a fool he had been. If only he had, then Mina wouldn't be lying at the bottom of it now.

'But don't you worry,' his big sister continued. 'Presto explained how the illusion works. The hatch, the lock and all the bolts that need to be adjusted to keep it shut can also be lifted off like one big lid to allow the magician to get out. Incredibly smart. Anyway, Kenneth has welded it shut. I guarantee there is no way out.'

He stared at his sister. She looked so decrepit – so old and fragile sitting there in her wheelchair. Her skin was pale and grey, and she shook slightly when she moved. It was hard to believe she was only nine years his senior.

'But why, Jane?' he said.

She looked at him with eyes that smouldered the same way they had when they were both children.

'You took my life away from me,' she said. 'The summer when you killed Mum. That was the last time I was alive. Do you know how many foster homes I was in after that? Should I tell you about the guy who whipped me with a radio aerial while his wife watched? About the drunkard dad we hid in the toilet to get away from? About my first boyfriend who took me to a party so that his friends could rape me? About the pills? The needles? I've been living in hell since that summer. But you – the cause of it all, the one who killed our mum – have been able to move on and have a happy life. A *career*. Where's the justice in that?'

Vincent's brain was working so hard it hurt. He couldn't take in what Jane was saying – his thoughts were still stuck on what she'd said before.

'Those drawings don't work at all.'

He picked up the book from the floor. Sains had said something too the first time Vincent had visited him. What had he . . .? That was it.

'Plenty of the classic designs have been drawn up wrong on purpose. If you're going to build an illusion, you also need to understand how to change the drawing so that it actually works. Otherwise the trapdoor won't open. Or whatever it might be.'

So he hadn't made a mistake. He had done exactly what the book said. And he had been only seven years old – a child – terrified that Mum would get angry. But that wasn't going to appease his sister. Not any longer. Jane's hatred had been fuelled over far too many years for him to be able to extinguish the fire with the mere truth. And what was more, she was right. If he hadn't built those boxes then none of the rest of it would have happened.

'I swore there and then,' she said, 'that even if it was the last thing I did I would take from you what you took from me. But I haven't been strong enough to do it by myself. Not until Kenneth came into my life. He's the first person who understood me.'

Kenneth reached out to her with his hand and she took it tenderly. Vincent saw from the corner of his eye that Mina was moving. If he bought her enough time to allow her to regain consciousness, perhaps they could resolve this situation together.

'But why all the others?' he said. 'Why did you – the two of you – murder Agnes, Tuva and Robert – if it was me you wanted revenge on?'

493

He tried to look around surreptitiously for a weapon. Something he could use to stop Jane and Kenneth. By the far wall was the workbench where they had tortured Mina. But it appeared to be empty. No sword. They hadn't taken any risks.

'You know who their mothers were,' said Kenneth. 'Jane's told me about your friends. They were also guilty of your mother's death. The four of you share that guilt. It's just that your share is biggest. They took Jane's mother from her. We've taken their children away. Karma.'

'What's more,' said Jane with a chuckle, 'no one would have cared if we'd killed some middle-aged women. But their kids . . . Oh, Vincent. Their kids. Young women and disabled boys? The media loves it. Taking out the young and innocent was the worst thing you could have done, Vincent.'

He was startled. He must have heard wrong.

'Me?' he said, shaking his head.

'I did say I was going to take the same thing from you that you took from me,' Jane said. 'You took the life I could have had away from me. So I'm going to erase yours. When they find you dead in the water tank they'll also find a letter. From you. In it, you'll explain that you made the world a better place by cleansing it of vermin.'

He still didn't understand. Jane was clearly delirious.

'Come on, don't be so slow,' Jane said in irritation. 'Agnes was busy mixing races. Tuva was a Jew. And Robert had special needs. All things you hate. At least, that's what you say in the letter. Your confession, taken in combination with you leaving your own name as a clue in the murder dates, will be enough to condemn you and see you hated for generations to come. No one will want to even say your name. You'll be struck out of the history books as a hideous stain of shame. It'll be like you never existed.'

'The police didn't discover the clue with the name,' he said. 'I had to point it out to them.'

Jane burst out into yet more laughter.

'Oh, little brother! You're doing my job for me! And of course they believed you when you pleaded your innocence?'

'Not quite.'

There was a glitter of crazed happiness in Jane's eyes and he looked down at the floor. How could he have been so stupid?

'So that was why you sent the newspaper clipping to Ruben,' he said. 'To help put the police on the right track with the code.'

'Newspaper clipping?' said Jane, looking at him blankly. 'I don't know what you're talking about. But you're right that sometimes you have to give a little nudge to the powers that be who uphold law and order. For example, by getting a rabid admirer to suggest to them that they work together with you.'

'Dolphin girl.'

Jane let out a satisfied snort.

'Yes, sometimes you get lucky,' she said. 'She and Kenneth heard the same call when Mina was talking to her boss. We realized what a perfect opportunity it was for us. Kenneth didn't even have to suggest it to Mina – he just mentioned it to Anna . . . My God. Some things come together so easily you can tell it's meant to be.'

Mina. Vincent glanced towards her again. She had stopped moving. He needed more time.

'And how would you have explained away Mina if you'd killed her with the nail?' he asked.

'According to the letter, "your great work" is concluded by you taking your own life,' said Kenneth. 'But when Anna told us how much Mina meant to you, we couldn't help ourselves. Anyway, a name like Dabiri means she fits the pattern perfectly. You hate Muslims too, you know.'

There was a change in the atmosphere. Something shifted. He could feel that the conversation was drawing to a close.

'I can see what you're thinking,' said Jane. 'You're thinking that the phone I called you from has been traced. That the police know where you are and are on their way here. That's true. I want them to know. I'll even call to make sure they come. As many of them as possible, to enjoy your final performance and your passage into the afterlife. They'll arrive right after you've drawn your final breath.'

Last chance.

'Mina, wake up!' Vincent shouted, pounding as hard as he could on the glass.

Her eyelids flickered and it sounded as if she said something. Then she was still again.

Kenneth grabbed hold of his shoulders and dragged him away from the glass box.

'Pull yourself together,' the old man snarled.

'Enough talk,' said Jane, rolling over to a ladder propped against one side of the box. 'It's time, little brother.'

He looked at the ladder. Looked at the glass box. It was made for one person.

'First you take out Mina,' he said.

'I need your help with that,' said Kenneth. 'You get in and lift from the bottom, I'll lift from the top.'

He had no choice. It was going to happen now. No one was going to come and rescue them. He stood on the ladder. The opening in the glass box gaped at him, threatening to swallow his entire being. Too cramped. Far too cramped. And it wouldn't end there. Maria would believe the letter. Benjamin, Rebecka and Aston would hate him forever. They'd have to change their last names. The press wouldn't listen to Mina's assertions that he was innocent. Not when the evidence was so overwhelming. But his family might. That was the only hope he had left. That his family would listen.

He focused on Rebecka, Benjamin, Aston and Maria as he took the final steps and climbed into the tank. They might not hate him. Maybe not. Once he was in the glass box he crouched and brushed the hair off Mina's face. It was hard – there wasn't enough space to bend forward. The only way to reach Mina was to bend his knees while keeping his upper body upright.

'Mina,' he said tenderly, patting her on the cheek. 'You need to wake up now. You need to help me if we're going to climb out.'

Mina mumbled yet again, drunk on sleep. What exactly had they given her? He hoped it wasn't ketamine.

'Wake up now, Mina.'

A scraping sound above his head made him look up. Kenneth had pulled the lid over the tank. He heard something rattling above the lid. A chain. Of course. Jane tapped on the glass to get his attention.

'Surely you understand that she can't be allowed to live, little brother? She could ruin everything.'

Jane took out a pen and a folded piece of paper.

'I'll have to add a line to the letter,' she said. 'About why you're choosing to die together with her. To make sure that even after death she can't get into Muslim heaven or something. The ironic thing is that Mina saved my life. If she hadn't called the ambulance when I collapsed at AA, we wouldn't have been here today. You'll have to thank her for me.'

She wrote a few lines, folded the paper back up and inserted it into an envelope.

'Jane!' Vincent shouted, striking his fists against the glass as hard as he could. 'You're my sister! We had a deal! Mina was going to live!'

'Your sister?' she said, staring at him with her cold, intense eyes. 'That Jane died over thirty years ago. And her little brother is going to die today.'

He pounded on the lid above his head, but it was hopeless. Kenneth climbed down off the ladder and went over to the wall where a hose was attached to a tap. The hose ran across the floor to the tank. The hose began to murmur as Kenneth turned the tap. A few seconds later, water began to appear at Vincent's feet. He raised a foot in reflex before his brain grasped that it was impossible to avoid the wet. But the water had to be coming in somewhere. With a little luck he might stop the hole. He feverishly searched the bottom of the box without finding anything. It was presumably hidden behind a valve. Good design.

'We're even, Vincent,' said Jane from beyond the glass. 'Well, we will be soon. We're going to call the police now. It'll take them half an hour to get out here by boat from Norrtälje. When they find your body and Mina's, as well as your startling confession, it will finally be over. You'll have to excuse us for not sticking around until then.'

She smiled faintly and attached the letter to the outside of the glass at face height so that he could see it clearly. Then she sighed deeply as if she had relieved herself of a heavy burden, and let Kenneth wheel her out of the workshop. If it had been a movie, she would have uttered a witty, well-formulated line in parting and Vincent would have found an ingenious way of escaping the tank at the last second – or someone would have passed by and smashed the glass just when all hope was lost.

But none of that happened.

All that was audible was the bubbling of the water slowly rising and someone saying his sister's name as an old man pushed a woman in a wheelchair out through a door into the sunshine.

130

The cardboard cut-out depicting Vincent was folded in half – that was the only way to get it into the car. When Christer had asked him what he needed it for, he'd merely muttered something about evidence and continued to shove it into the back seat.

To be perfectly honest, Ruben didn't really know why he was taking the cardboard cut-out with him. Except that it reminded him of Vincent's stuck-up mug, which kept the adrenaline levels in his body elevated since he was furious each time he looked at it. What Vincent had done to him was unforgivable. Vincent might as well have tied Ruben's shoelaces together and pulled his trousers down.

None of his colleagues had dared laugh – at least not so that he could hear them – but he could see it in their eyes. The great Ruben Höök. Led up the garden path by a stupid mentalist. He looked around to make sure that no one was looking his way then he socked the cut-out on the face before shutting the back door. Bloody Vincent. Again.

He went over to Christer, who was standing by the flying squad van a bit further up the road.

'Did you have to bring the whole flying squad?' he said acidly to Christer. 'By tomorrow the whole of police headquarters will know about this.'

'We didn't know what the situation was,' said Christer. 'With the information we had, it could very well have been the case that Vincent was about to become the next victim.'

'Don't you get that he's taken us in? I said from the beginning that we should bring Vincent in. If you'd listened to me, this wouldn't have happened. Remember that when you find his next victim.'

Peder and that woman from analysis, Sara Something-or-other, got out of an unmarked car. Peder must have dumped the triplets with his wife. So much for her birthday.

The last time Ruben had met Sara she had treated him like he was nobody. He had no idea why; he couldn't recall ever having met her before. Must be a dyke. Wouldn't surprise him in the least.

'Do we have any idea where Vincent is right now?' he said to Peder.

'Not exactly,' said Sara. 'A mobile call connects to the nearest base station. Vincent received a call that we traced to a base station on the island of Gräddö in the Norrtälje archipelago. So we're guessing that he's there somewhere. But the problem is that the base stations out in the archipelago cover much bigger areas than they do here in the city. Had it been in town, we would have known which street he was on. Right now we've got rather a lot of islands to choose from. Tjockö, Edsgarn, Lidön . . .'

'Lidön?' Ruben interrupted her. 'That can't be a coincidence. I was there – at the mink farm.'

He looked from one of them to the other.

'I know exactly where he is.'

131

The water had reached the top of his shoelaces, soaking his socks and filling his shoes. Don't think about it. Don't think about the water that will only take five minutes to fill the glass box. The box that has four sides – six if you count the top and bottom – it's too cramped, he can't be there and he *can't* be there with Mina.

He has to help Mina.

Four and six makes ten which is one and zero, man and woman, him and Mina. It's a mathematical function of the water tank. He needs to get them free. Five minutes to fill. The fifth wheel. Five fingers on each hand. Between two celestial bodies orbiting each other there are five points where an object can be held in perfect balance by the gravitational power of the bodies, where the pull from both is equal and thus there is no movement. Two bodies. Him and Mina. With a perfect balance between them. As long as there are two of them.

Since Mina is sitting down the water is soaking her trousers, legs and back. She frowns and mumbles something without opening her eyes.

'Mina, you have to wake up!'

He bends his knees, his upper body still bolt upright since it's so tight, trying to put her arms around his shoulders to raise her, but he can't get a grip. It's impossible. The box is so cramped that they can't both stand up even if they are pressed together. One of them has to be below the other.

One of them has to end up underwater first.

One of them has to die first.

Mina suddenly takes a deep breath and opens her eyes. There is shock in her eyes.

'Vincent! Where are we what's happening why . . .'

She bends her neck to look up and hits the back of her head on the glass.

'Ouch!' she shouts, gasping for breath as a reflex.

'A locked room,' he says without being able to stop himself. 'Four glass walls. Letter number four is D. Five minutes. Letter number five is E. Four and five make nine. Letter number nine is I. That makes D, E, I . . . Latin for "of god". No, that's not it. Shuffle them: D, I, E. Die.'

His brain is in free fall. His thoughts are pounding feverishly against the walls, he is trapped but all he did was follow the instructions, he's always just followed the instructions to the letter, it wasn't his fault, he was only seven years old . . .

'Vincent!' Mina shouts, hitting him hard on the thigh. 'Stop it!'

'Sorry,' he says. 'Sorry for everything.'

Jane takes in the water and the archipelago while Kenneth wheels her down the path behind the mink farm. It's very beautiful on the island – especially today.

She's grateful to him. She can't claim to have had a good life, but Kenneth at least made it meaningful, towards the end. He didn't have to care about her. But he understood. Perhaps because he was so close to the end when they met. He's helped her obtain redress – which is the greatest declaration of love she could ever have received from anyone.

They reach the jetty and Kenneth stops. The water is lapping peacefully against the wooden posts supporting the jetty and a seagull cries out to its friends in the distance. He puts his hand on her shoulder and she pats it lovingly without turning around.

'It'll soon be over,' he says.

'I know,' she replies. 'Thank you. Without you it would have dragged on unbearably.'

They don't need to talk any longer. He doesn't need to ask whether she really wants to. He hasn't asked that question for a long time. They're past all that. Not that they have a choice anymore.

He gets out a roll of silver tape and wraps it around his left hand and the handle of the wheelchair. Loop after loop after loop. It's important for the hand to stay attached. She helps him to tape his right hand. Only when he is done does she look up at him. But he doesn't meet her gaze – his has already disappeared into the distance.

He begins to roll her along the jetty. Slowly at first. The planks of wood creak under the wheels. The further out they get, the more he picks up pace. She holds onto the seat to avoid falling out. When they reach the end of the jetty, he doesn't stop. Instead he leaps, letting the wheelchair continue straight into the air.

Kvibille 1982

'Vincent? The door doesn't seem to be working like it should.'

She presses against the hidden door her son showed to her, but it's stuck. Immovably stuck. Or perhaps she's doing it wrong, maybe she's pressing on it from a strange angle, it's hard to tell when she's as good as bent double. Clearly, you have to be stick thin but as flexible as a hinge if you're a magician's assistant.

'Vincent, where are you?' she calls out again.

She tries to push open the lid, but it's stuck too. He's obviously locked it with that padlock. Vincent said he was going to fetch something. It's probably a surprise for her. That's what it'll be. He knows the door can't be opened. It's his way of making a joke. Any moment now he's going to unlock the lid and present the assistant's costume he's made for her in rainbow colours. Or something else. She needs to remember not to shout at him too much.

But it's taking a long time for him to come back. Far too long, given how uncomfortable it is sitting bent double in the box. She changes her mind. There's going to be quite a telling off after all. This is not one of Vincent's better ideas.

Finally she hears a sound. Voices. They're not in the barn, not yet. Outside. She can definitely hear Vincent. And he's not alone. There are several voices. Girls' voices. They're laughing. Vincent is too. Then they hush each other. As if they're up to mischief.

'Don't be such a coward about swimming, Vincent!' someone shouts. 'Come on!'

Then the voices begin to fade.

'Vincent!' she shouts, hammering the box wall in front of her.

Much harder this time.

'Have you come back, Vincent?'

Mina gives him a sharp look. He merely nods in reply, too ashamed to say anything. She tries to stand up, and is forced to press herself against him to fit. It's just about possible. The water reaches their thighs. Their ribcages are pressed hard against each other, squeezing the air out of their lungs. He can't look at her. She's standing too close. But he can

502

feel that she is there. Not only because she's pressed against him but also because she . . . is.

$4 + 6 = 10$, which is $1 + 0 =$ him and Mina. Two bodies in orbit. A small object, a fragile understanding, in perfect balance between them. But that's not what he says. He's not an idiot.

'We can't move if we stand like this,' he says in a strained voice. 'And that means we can't get out.'

'Tell me that you know how we can get out,' she says with the same effort.

'I know how we can get out.'

'Do you mean it?'

'No, I've got no idea. All I know is that we don't have enough strength to smash the glass from the inside. That only works on TV. We have to come up with something else.'

'There's a lot of water, Vincent.'

'I know. Sorry.'

'Stop apologizing and think instead. You're good at that. Sometimes.'

The water reaches their stomachs. They have two minutes left at most. But she's right. And his thoughts are his own again. He ignores the water, ignores the glass box, tries to think.

Hang on a second. Take a step back.

The glass box. Unlike Agnes, Tuva and Robert, this isn't a home-made box. They're in a professional water illusion. And those always have layer upon layer of secrets. Presto may not have revealed all to Jane. There are ways to get out and there are also . . . ways to get air in.

Snorkels.

A water illusion always has hidden tubes leading to the outside that the magician can breathe through. He pounds his forehead hard against the glass in frustration.

'Vincent?' says Mina, and he hears the worry in her voice.

But he can't forgive himself. He should have thought of it far earlier. The box is still stopping his brain from working the way it should. It's so cramped. In around a minute, the air will run out and he needs to find the tubes fast.

Assuming Jane and Kenneth haven't removed them.

For a second, it feels like flying. As if she is weightless, or she is falling upwards. Then the wheelchair strikes the water with a big splash. The chilly water takes Jane's breath away. She knew it would be cold, but not this cold. She's still holding on tight to the seat as they begin to sink.

503

The sunlight vanishes almost immediately. The seawater is dark and she can see nothing ahead of her. It wasn't supposed to be like this. She lets go of the seat, turns around and searches for Kenneth's arms in the darkness. He's still taped to the sinking wheelchair and can't respond to her touch. She pulls herself up his arm and away from the chair until she can hold him. He presses his upper arms around her in an insufficient embrace.

They were going to meet their end together.

Sink entwined into the blue.

Dignified and calm.

But it's pitch black and it's cold and it hurts.

Hurts so much.

She screws up her eyes against the chill and tugs at Kenneth, trying to pull him upwards, out of the dark. She can feel him desperately trying to release his hands from the wheelchair, but they're stuck down with the tape.

Loop after loop after loop.

The chair continues to drag them down. She tries to think. Panic strikes when she realizes that she can no longer tell which direction they are moving in, or even *whether* they are moving at all. The dark of the water has consumed them. There's nothing left to reveal what is up and what is down.

Kvibille 1982

'Vincent, Vincent, Vincent,' she whispers, her lips pressed to the wood.

At first she shouted until she was hoarse, waiting for the voices to come back. But they never did. Now she can only hiss. So she whispers his name until she can no longer do that.

The heat inside the box is like a sauna, sweat leaving her hair straggling and dripping from the tip of her nose. She can feel how wet her back is, even though she can't reach it with her hands to check.

If the box had been made from thin fibreboard then she might have been able to kick out and destroy it from the inside. But Vincent has done his homework. Allan must have given him good quality materials from the timberyard. And the joints have been nailed and glued.

The lactic acid in her limbs is screaming at her. If she doesn't get to straighten her legs out soon she's really going to lose her mind. It's an inhuman feeling to sit like this for hours. Or however long it's been. It could be days. Years.

'Someone help me,' she whispers.

She's going to shout that too. Soon. Just as soon as she's gathered her strength.

Vincent takes a deep breath and then bends his knees as much as he can. Then he reaches for the bottom. He runs his hands along the edges underwater. Nothing along the floor. The finger of his pinkie catches something in one corner, around a centimetre up. There it is. *There it is.* Jane didn't find it after all.

He carefully prises open the tube. Of course the snorkel is at the very bottom. The magician hangs upside down in the box, which means the floor is closest to the head. He stands up again, spitting and spluttering water. It's up to Mina to use her mouth now.

'Are you sure it's not possible to break the glass?' she says quickly, spitting as the water slops against her lips.

The desperation isn't far away, he can hear it in her voice. He nods in reply and looks at the letter from Jane, his final message for posterity, pinned to the outside of the glass. He would do anything to smash the glass and tear the letter into tiny pieces. He doesn't want his family to start hating him.

'There's a snorkel down there,' he says. 'You have to take it.'

'There's no need for you to be the knight in shining armour, I'm the police officer,' she says, coughing again into the water.

'You're shorter than me,' he says. 'I've probably got another half minute up here to try and find a solution. Then I'll come down. And then we'll have to see which of us is the strongest.'

'Ha ha ha.'

But Mina does as he says and dives down to the snorkel just before the water reaches her nose. The movement makes the water splash and he screws his mouth and eyes shut. He's never bothered to practise holding his breath. Of course, he could share the snorkel with Mina, if it weren't for the fact that the manoeuvre to change places would take longer than the amount of air they had in their lungs. And they would need to swap places straight away again. He tries to control his breathing.

The water is tickling his lips and he shuts his mouth, pressing his lips together. He breathes in fits and starts through his nose. It already feels like he can't get air. No air left in the tank. He thumps hard on the lid just above his head. *Let us out, please let us out. That's enough.* The sound of his fists against the metal echoes in the space outside but otherwise there's silence. He can't cope with this. Not any longer. He can't be smothered in this tiny space. When the water passes his upper lip, he slams against the glass walls in a panic. He can't give in to the panic, if he does he'll have lost, but he can't hold it at bay any longer.

Panic.

Something about panic.

The water reaches his nostrils, he lunges upwards and takes what he realizes is his final breath. He has as long left as it takes for his lungs to be exhausted. Someone tugs at his trouser leg. He looks down and sees Mina pointing at the snorkel, but he shakes his head. There's no time. His body is already exploding. He should have practised holding his breath. All his focus goes on not opening his mouth. He can't see clearly, blinking in response to the water in his eyes. If he lets go at the last moment then it's over. His body is on fire he's on fire his brain wants to stop now

panic

panic . . .

. . . *lever.*

Umberto. What was it Umberto said? His field of vision begins to flicker. Something about a lever. All sound disappears as the water covers his ears. A lever that wasn't there. A panic lever. He's isolated in the water. Enveloped. On the other side of the glass is an empty room. Air. Life. The lever wasn't there because Tom Presto took risks. He presses his hand against the glass. Salvation on the other side. On his side nothing but death. But the Tom Presto Vincent met wouldn't play with death. On the contrary. He'd refuse to place his life in the hands of someone else. Vincent can no longer think. His brain shuts down, he's sinking into a primal darkness. He strikes wildly out at the water but his movements are dull, lacking force. He relaxes his cheeks and his body reflexively draws water into his lungs. Umberto's French collector was wrong. Tom would definitely have had a panic level. Not just on the outside. It would be . . . *on the inside of the tank.*

The perfect balance between two bodies is smashed into a million pieces when they complete their orbits.

It doesn't take long.

It feels like a mere second's dizziness.

The rest is just like falling asleep.

The body that Jane is clinging to is jerking about in violent spasms. She doesn't want this any longer. She wants to live. This wasn't how it was supposed to be.

She lets go of Kenneth and tries to swim upwards. Let's him sink to his fate on the seabed. She knows that she's far too deep and that her legs are useless. She can only swim with her arms.

It's taking too long. She might not even be swimming in the right direction. Perhaps she's just going deeper down. But she doesn't want it.

After three strokes, her lungs explode.

It wasn't like this.

It was like this.

Kvibille 1982

She doesn't know who she is any longer. All she knows is that it has hurt for so long. Her limbs are screaming. The heat. The thirst. She sucks on her bloody fingers to get some liquids into her. The fingernail she long ago scraped off against the wood that is still holding her prisoner. It seems like so long ago. She curses the world and then she begs for forgiveness.

'Vincent, Jane. This is for the best. I'm not going to shout at you anymore. You'll be better off without me. I know that. I've always known that.'

She doesn't know it, but she's probably not saying this aloud.

Then she says nothing more.

132

'Was it you who built the box?'

An unfamiliar woman was standing in front of him with a notepad and pen in her hands. She was talking in an eager, almost greedy tone. He didn't answer. It sounded as if she already knew. Anyway, he didn't know her. He looked at her hands again. A pen was a line. A dimension. A notepad was a square. Two dimensions. The box he had built was a cube. Three dimensions. The fourth dimension was time. But right now he was moving outside of that. He had been standing in the farmyard for an eternity. Or a second. Someone had talked to him. Or perhaps not.

A policeman whom he thought he had met before – it was probably the same officer who had helped Mum when the car had broken down outside the shop – took the woman by the arm and led her away.

'Leave the lad alone,' said the policeman. 'He's not even meant to still be here. But the woman from social services is late.'

The barn door was cordoned off with police tape and the star-spangled box was standing in the yard, having been rolled out. It was lucky he had put wheels on it – it would have been too heavy for them to carry otherwise. But he couldn't understand how he was supposed to get into his workshop now – where he had all his secrets. Just as long as they didn't start rooting through them. That'd make him really upset.

'I'm from *Hallandsposten*,' snapped the woman, twisting herself out of the policeman's grip. 'The public has a right to know.'

He looked at his shadow on the gravel. It was starting to get long. He was just his shadow. The very core shadow where the light never penetrated. And he was one-dimensional. He wasn't visible from the side. The woman bent down towards him.

'How does it feel not to have a mother anymore?' she said, putting her pen to paper.

He couldn't understand how she could see him. He was turned to the side. And what did she mean, no mother? Mum was there, in the kitchen. Mum was there in how he brushed his teeth. We are what we do, his mother always said. He can be her whenever he likes.

'Jesus, that's enough,' the policeman said angrily to the woman. 'This is the scene of an accident – either you leave or I'll arrest you for obstructing the police in the course of their duties.'

Before the policeman had time to react the woman produced a camera and took a photo. The flash made him blink.

'You forgot to smile,' she said. 'But that's good. Serious children look good on film. Wasn't there a sister too? Perhaps she'll be more talkative.'

The woman vanished across the yard. The policeman stood in front of him and put his hands on his shoulders. He blotted out the sun.

'It was an accident,' said the man. 'You know that, right? No one blames you. It'll be OK. You and your sister will be placed in new homes, but the important thing is, you must understand that no one thinks that what happened was your fault.'

'Will we live together?' he asked anxiously. 'Me and Jane?'

'I don't know, Vincent. It depends whether someone is willing to take you both. So maybe not. But you'll both still live close by. I'm sure you'll be able to see each other as often as you like. This is only temporary. I can understand if everything seems weird right now. But you're both smart kids. The pair of you will grow up to be strong and put this behind you. You've got each other. You're a family. Everything will be forgiven.'

133

Mina was sitting on the bottom of Houdini's water torture cell trying to gather her thoughts. The water had suddenly gushed out of the tank and onto the floor below – as if the bottom had dropped out. Water continued to pour into the tank from the hose but it poured out just as quickly.

Vincent was standing lifeless above her. He had slumped over with his forehead and knees against the glass, but the confined space was holding him upright. She had seen him flailing around in wild panic when his air ran out. He'd come close to kicking her in the head. While he'd been kicking and pounding he must have found a lever or button that emptied the tank.

But they still needed to get out of the bloody thing. She didn't know whether Vincent was dead, but he definitely would be very soon if she didn't give him immediate resuscitation. He had said the glass couldn't be broken. But shame on anyone who gave in. She took off a shoe and began to strike the heel repeatedly against the glass. She ensured that each blow struck the exact same point. It took fifteen hard blows. He was right, it would have been impossible to do it in water. When the glass shattered she protected herself reflexively with her arms. Vincent fell forward but her body was in the way and stopped him from landing headlong with his face among the shards of glass.

She climbed out of the water tank, pulled Vincent away and carefully laid him out on a glass-free area of the floor. He was lighter than he looked. Or perhaps she had got stronger. She looked at him. The mentalist. She was the one who had dragged him into all of this. Because Kenneth had got Anna to suggest it to her. She had swallowed the bait, hook, line and sinker. Then Vincent's sister had almost killed her, and now Vincent himself might be dead. She wasn't going to let him get away with it. The water had probably washed away all the bacteria from him by this stage. She raised his neck to open the airway, took a deep breath and put her mouth to his.

134

Vincent was still too exhausted to help her. He was lying on his back, gasping for air. Mina had no idea where Jane and Kenneth were, or when they were coming back. It surprised her that they hadn't stayed to watch her and Vincent die, but perhaps they didn't feel they had to. They thought they had achieved their goal and perhaps that was enough. Now it was just a question of whether they had fled or whether they were still nearby.

She tried to think clearly.

Her brain was in acute flight mode and she had to fight her desire to run away. Partly, it was that she couldn't leave Vincent. She had saved his life. According to some old Chinese proverb, that meant she was now responsible for him. There was also the fact that, if she ran, she might end up running straight into the arms of Jane and Kenneth.

She looked around, fighting off the nausea triggered by the rotten, sweet stench still filling the air. She had to call for help. Which meant she had to get hold of a phone. Kenneth had thrown hers out of the van window – it was smashed into a thousand pieces far away from here. They'd probably taken Vincent's too, but if they hadn't taken it with them then it was surely around here somewhere. She searched the workshop bench, which was the only piece of furniture in the room, but found nothing.

'Vincent,' she coaxed, turning towards him.

He was still lying on his back, his eyes rolled up so that the whites were visible. His breathing was shallow and stuttering and he seemed to be struggling to regain consciousness.

'Vincent!' she said more firmly. 'Did you see where they put your phone? It's not here on the bench and I can't find it. Might they have taken it with them?'

She felt hope sinking in her breast. Of course they had.

But Vincent laboriously raised his right arm and pointed towards the corner of the room. There was a large container standing there. The kind you filled with rubbish and then paid someone to cart it away. She hadn't even noticed it; a container summoned far too many emotions around dirt that could never be washed away for her to want to take in its existence. But Vincent continued pointing.

She reluctantly went over to the container. The rotten smell got stronger the closer she got. The contents of her stomach came up her throat, acidly burning her mouth before returning in the other direction. Panic gripped her more tightly with each step she took. She didn't want to see what was in the container. Didn't even want to brush past it. She didn't want to be in the *same room* as the container.

She turned around and looked pleadingly at Vincent. She saw that he was trying to talk, but still didn't have the strength. Instead he raised his hand again and pointed for a third time at the container. Bloody hell. Bloody, bloody hell.

She thought she heard something outside. She stood stock-still to listen, but could hear nothing but silence. No one was coming to help them. It was up to her.

The container was tall – too tall. There was no way she'd be able to get up to look in it by herself. She looked around. The ladder leaning against the water tank had fallen down when she had smashed the glass. It was now wet and slippery, as well as covered in glass. Unusable. Standing against the far wall was another ladder. It looked much older, as if it hadn't been used in many years, but at least it wasn't glittering with shards of glass. She went over to the old ladder after another longing glance towards the door.

The ladder was covered in spiders' webs. Not just webs, she spotted with distaste. Spiders. Loads of small spiders were crawling over the ladder and clambering around the intricate webs. She found a few centimetres that weren't as festooned with sticky white threads, and full of horror and disgust she grabbed hold of that part of the ladder. When she pulled it away from the wall, she discovered the source of all the little spiders. A big, fat, hairy mother spider that had been sitting on the back of the wooden frame strolled straight across Mina's hand.

She screamed out loud. She couldn't stop herself. The scream echoed between the walls and she felt her heart pounding with terror as she stared towards the door. Had they heard? Would Jane and Kenneth come back now and discover that she and Vincent hadn't died in the water tank?

But there was nothing.

No one.

Silence.

Her heart still pounding, she picked up the ladder and carried it over to the container. Her whole body was itchy from her scalp to her feet, and she pictured her entire body covered in tiny spider babies that would almost certainly lay their eggs under her skin or something equally awful.

She thought about a YouTube video that Ruben had once shown her out of some perverted need to disgust her just for the hell of it. It had been about the botfly, a South American insect that laid eggs under the skin that then hatched into larvae. In the video, you saw someone pull a big, floundering larva out of the scalp of another person.

She'd had to fight off the urge to be sick, determined not to give Ruben the satisfaction. Somehow she had mastered her revulsion. Just as she was doing now, with all the willpower she was able to summon.

She carefully set down the ladder by the container and tried to make as little sound as possible when the wood hit the metal. Several of the small spiders had come with it during the move and skittered around anxiously when the webs came loose in various places.

But Mina was barely thinking about the webs any longer. The smell was unbearable when she stood this close to the container. Tears formed in her eyes and the stench stung her nostrils. No matter what it was, something that smelled like that must definitely be filling the air with bacteria and microorganisms that were now swarming around her, past her, over her. *Inside* her.

She forced herself to focus on the task at hand – the goal. When she glanced at Vincent, she saw that he had managed to sit upright with his head hanging between his knees. He began to sob. Then the rest of the water he had swallowed came up and he vomited onto the floor.

She could feel her mouth filling with bile again. She swallowed and swallowed. She couldn't throw up now, not again. If she did, she wouldn't manage to do what she had to. Throwing up was the absolute worst thing she could imagine. Worse than *botfly*. Seeing all the disgusting things that were inside her, the thought of which she spent every waking moment suppressing, always gave her a total panic attack. Once was more than enough. During flu season, she sanitized three times more often than usual, and swallowed ten whole white peppercorns every

514

day just to be sure. While the thing with the peppercorns wasn't actually scientifically proven in any way, her mother had always done that and Mina had avoided stomach bugs for the last decade.

Three bars up the ladder. The crown of her head was level with the edge of the container. She couldn't see what was in there yet. But the smell had, if possible, become even stronger and ranker. She pulled up the collar of her top over her nose as an inadequate shield. A few baby spiders ran over the back of her hand, but compared with the heavy, rotten stench she was able to ignore that.

One more step up.

Another one – and she peered over the edge.

The container was full of cadavers.

Minks.

Thousands of dead minks were staring up at her in varying degrees of decomposition. And they were moving. She knew why. The cadavers were filled with so many gases, worms and sticky flies that they made the dead flesh move. She couldn't stop herself but instead leaned to one side and allowed the breakfast cereal she hadn't brought up last time to splatter onto the concrete floor.

Tears began to flow. Her heart was beating in her chest in triple time, and she could feel the palms of her hands clammy with sweat. The panic attack threatened to take over completely, but she knew that if she let in that feeling even for a millisecond she wouldn't be able to hold it together any longer.

She looked over to Vincent. He looked more stable. He was sitting up and looking at her, with a little more colour in his cheeks. Perhaps he'd be up to walking? Perhaps they should just leave and take the chance that Kenneth and Jane had fled and were far away?

But she knew they couldn't. It would be a while before Vincent could move quickly and he wouldn't be able to offer any resistance at all if they needed to defend themselves.

They needed backup.

She needed the phone.

She put one foot on the edge of the container. She tried to ignore the gaseous, rotting animal corpses below her. She refused to think about the millions of carrion insects and flies' eggs. Instead, she desperately summoned up images of rainbows and unicorns, summer meadows and cute kittens.

Then she jumped.

135

When the Norrtälje police arrived, they found Mina and Vincent on the workshop floor. Mina had used the hose running to the glass box to rinse herself off as best she could, but clumps of blood and animal remains that she didn't even want to think about were still stuck in her hair. As soon as she got hold of something sharp, she was going to cut off the lot.

Her clothes were lying in a corner, ruined forever. She had torn them off, shrieking loudly. But at least she had found Vincent's phone, sticky with blood. And it had worked. As soon as she had finished the call she'd thrown it to the floor in disgust and drenched it with the hose.

Vincent hadn't said anything about that. Instead, he'd given her his clothes. They were far too large and soaked through, but at least they were free from spiders, worms and animal guts. Vincent was sitting there in his underwear. A pair of Björn Borgs in a Hawaiian print, she couldn't help noticing.

Norrtälje had sent two officers, both women. When they saw Mina and Vincent, one of them turned around in the doorway.

'We need blankets!' she shouted to someone in the yard. 'Quickly!'

'We received a call from here,' said the other policewoman. 'And just after that, one from the police in Stockholm.'

She crouched beside Mina with an anxious look.

'Yes, it was me who called from here,' said Mina, snuffling. 'You got here really quickly.'

'You called?' said the officer, looking surprised. 'I thought the voice sounded much older. Stockholm were rather confused, but according to the person I spoke to there, there are meant to be two dead bodies. Something about a hate crime and a suicide. And a letter. Do you know anything about that?'

Mina didn't know what to say. She looked at Vincent.

'Jane and Kenneth rang the police before they left,' he said apologetically. 'There wasn't time to mention it.'

136

They passed the exit for Arlanda Airport and carried on north. After Arlanda, the traffic always thinned out. Right now they were almost alone on the motorway. But she knew that it would get busier the closer to Uppsala they got. Christer had been in touch while Julia was in the car and said that the police were on the lookout for Vincent but that it had been passed to the police in Norrtälje. It was no longer their case. She didn't need to come in.

Christer had added far too knowingly that he obviously had no idea why she was at home, but perhaps she had something more important to be doing, today of all days. She had called Torkel and turned around straight away, grateful that her colleagues at police headquarters were the worst people in the world at keeping secrets.

She squeezed his hand on the wheel. He squeezed back without taking his eyes off the road.

'Thank you,' she said. 'For putting up with me. Fuck these hormones.'

'Hey, you're the hotshot detective,' he said, smiling. 'You had a tough choice to make today. I'm sorry I didn't make it any easier for you. But there's one thing you should know.'

He took his gaze off the road for a second to look her in the eyes.

'I love you. And I think you made the right choice. We would have had more chances to have kids. But what kind of father would I be if I didn't let you protect someone already out there, a person who is someone else's child? Sorry I was so stupid.'

'It's OK,' she said, putting her hand on his thigh. 'I didn't pick you for your intellect, you know.'

Torkel burst into laughter and she laughed with him. The laughter felt like a dam bursting. Tensions that had been simmering for months, ever since she had once again started hormone treatment, finally left her body. And Torkel seemed to feel the same way. They were heading for something new. Together. She wound down the side window to let in the chill September air. The wind resistance whirled around her face and hair. It felt boisterous, playful. She smiled and closed her eyes. The wind was full of life.

137

Vincent hadn't shown up for the press conference. Mina could understand that. The media had leapt onto the news of his connection to the murders with the same fervour displayed by piranhas encountering a dead cow in a river. It was in everyone's best interest that he kept out of the way.

Julia stepped up onto the podium. Some of the details had already leaked, the media having mixed up unconnected fragments of the truth with what the journalists had added from their own imaginations. 'A possible scenario' as they liked to call it.

The hubbub began to quieten down and everyone's gazes turned expectantly towards Julia. Mina was standing at the side of the stage, concealed behind a drape. Even she hadn't been able to escape the press. She couldn't understand where they'd got hold of the pictures. She'd always been careful to stay out of the public eye and didn't even like standing in front of the camera in her personal life. Nevertheless, they'd managed to dig up some old black and white photo in which she looked dreadful – taken at some raid where she wasn't even aware of the photographer's presence.

'We still haven't located the murderers, but they have been identified as Jane Boman and Kenneth Bengtsson. As members of the press corps have already noted, Jane is the sister of the mentalist Vincent Walder.'

'How long has Vincent known that the perpetrator was his sister?'

One of the most forward reporters from *Expressen* asked the question straight up.

'Please ensure you raise your hand and wait to be called on,' said Julia curtly. 'It'll be chaos otherwise.'

It was only now that Mina noted that the commissioner of police in Stockholm, Julia's father, was standing at the back of the room watching his daughter on the podium. He looked proud. Mina knew that Julia and the team were a complicated issue for him, so his proud expression raised Mina's spirits. Julia deserved his approval.

'But to answer your question,' said Julia. 'Vincent was not aware that it was his sister until he and our colleague Mina Dabiri were taken hostage.'

'Why? What was the motive?'

The same reporter again, and once again without raising his hand. Mina could see that Julia's patience was about to run out.

'*Please* raise your hand. It's true that the motive is tied to the incident that you've pulled apart and put back together again in the press in recent days. I'm referring to the accident that occurred during Vincent and Jane's childhood. Their mother, Gabriella Boman, died in tragic circumstances and for various reasons Jane held Vincent responsible for that, as well as the course that Jane's life took after the accident.'

Another reporter waved their hand in the air.

'Why the illusion theme? Isn't it a bit unnecessarily complicated?'

'What can I say? My experience is that murderers aren't always rational when it comes to methods. As I said, the reason behind the murders and the way they were carried out are linked to the circumstances around Gabriella Boman's death.'

'Is Daniel Bargabriel's death connected to this in any way?'

'Daniel's death is not tied to this case beyond the fact that he knew two of the victims. On the other hand, I am able to tell you that we have today taken into custody two of the perpetrators we believe were involved in Daniel's death and we expect charges to be filed by the prosecutor shortly.'

Mina felt a pang of sorrow for the young man who had died as a result of Jane's lust for revenge, even if it wasn't Jane who had killed him. It was so unnecessary. So much waste. But hopefully, Sweden's Future would be hit hard by the scandal, which would see them sink like a stone in the next elections.

Julia continued to field an onslaught of heated questions. Mina slowly withdrew, letting Julia's voice – the one with all the answers – fade into the background.

138

Dry dog food rattled into the metal bowl. Bosse came running as soon as he heard the sound and began to eat with the table manners of a small earthquake.

'Good boy,' said Christer.

He used the edge of the table to support him as he sat down on the floor. It wasn't entirely straightforward, but a bit easier than usual. The walks with Bosse were beginning to pay dividends. He leaned his back against the kitchen drawers and stroked the dog's fur. Eat your heart out, Harry Bosch.

'Your masters seem to have gone missing without trace,' said Christer. 'They're nowhere to be found on the island. No one saw a boat leave either. They definitely didn't take the ferry. The whole thing is a mystery. Of course, the police in Norrtälje are dragging for bodies, but they probably won't find anything. It's deep out there.'

Bosse stopped eating and looked up at Christer with a quizzical expression. He must have heard from his tone that something was different.

'I know you're sad,' said Christer, scratching Bosse behind the ears. 'But I thought we'd take a long walk when you've finished eating and then buy one of those squeaky balls that you love to chew to pieces. A glittery one. I don't think they're coming back, you see. I think it's you and me now.'

Bosse let out a curt bark and then licked Christer's face from his chin to his forehead. The dog's breath was keen with the scent of the dry food. A little company was no bad thing, thought Christer. For the umpteenth time, his thoughts drifted back to when he had been young. Back to Lasse. Frankly, it was a scandal that he didn't have a clue what Lasse had been up to since then. Someone that he had once known so well, who since then had lived a whole life of his own experiences and adventures that Christer knew nothing about. He felt almost envious, without being entirely sure what he was envious of. But it wasn't too late to change that. After all, he was a policeman. And there was social media these days. Surely it wouldn't be all that hard to find out what Lasse was up to.

As Christer sat there on the floor with Bosse's fur under his hands, he felt something shifting deep down inside him. It was faint to start with – at first he wasn't even sure it was there. But as it grew, he became increasingly convinced. It was a brand-new feeling. Something he'd never felt before. He wasn't certain, but he thought it might just be happiness.

139

Milda was still sitting at the dining table. Vera and Conrad had, as usual, eaten at record speed. Then Vera had settled down in front of the PlayStation while Conrad had gone to fetch his homework. Now he was sitting opposite her, absorbed in a book on social studies and diligently taking notes on the computer.

Her Conrad. It had been a tough summer for him. But the residential treatment centre seemed to have had an almost magical effect. Since he had returned, he had not only refrained from his previous mischief, but he had also gained a new attitude to both life and school. Vera had also noticed that Conrad had been much happier during the autumn. And now here he was, even doing his homework of his own accord.

Of course, Milda knew she couldn't get her hopes up too much. She had thought in the past that Conrad had got his life in order. And then he had reverted to his old ways after a month or so. But this felt . . . different. She didn't dare think it, she knew she oughtn't to, but this time it might be permanent. They all deserved that.

Especially now.

She didn't need to fetch the letter from Adi to remember what it said. The letter hadn't actually come from her brother but from his lawyer. She snorted. More likely some mate he'd met through his dodgy dealings – or even in prison. Lawyer? Well, sure. Unlike Conrad, Adi hadn't changed one bit. He was still going his own way and that way was one where money was all that mattered.

And money was the problem at hand. She and Adi had jointly inherited the house she lived in. Adi had let her live there with Vera and Conrad in an uncharacteristic gesture of generosity when the kids' inadequate father was unable to do the right thing. However, she knew the generosity wasn't genuine. Adi was after Grandpa Mykolas's house in Enskede, since it was both bigger and in a better location. When Grandpa died, Adi would claim that Grandpa's house was his, since he'd given away his half of the house that Milda lived in.

But the feigned generosity was apparently spent. She couldn't blame him – he had the law on his side. It was just so sudden. She had thought they would talk about it first. But Adi had notified her – through that lawyer – that if she wanted to stay on she had to buy him out. Otherwise they would have to sell the house. Or set it off against her share of their future inheritance from Grandpa. She didn't have long to pay.

Selling was out of the question – the money wouldn't stretch to a decent new home, and she couldn't put her children through that. And she would never be able to get a big enough mortgage to pay Adi – not given the state of her finances at present. Conrad's treatment over the summer had taken place at a private clinic – and had been very expensive.

At the same time, there was no other way to get hold of the money if she didn't want to rob a bank. She looked at Conrad's head bowed over his textbook. She and her family needed a miracle.

140

Ruben hesitated. He was so far outside his comfort zone that he really ought to have brought his passport and been vaccinated in order to be here. For a moment, he contemplated not bothering. After all, he had a good life.

Or did he?

Yes, he thought he did. He had a job that was no more demanding than he allowed it to be. Especially now that the new team had proved their expertise and been granted leave to continue. As part of that, he didn't have to work under the same restrictions that had previously been so irritating. And as a bachelor he had the freedom to do what he liked. No kids to be picked up after lunch from nursery and no looking after them while they were sick all winter. He snorted. Paid leave to look after sick kids – what a bloody innovation. Peder would have to quit as soon as the triplets learned to walk.

He had it all. A city so brimming with willing, horny chicks that it was like a round-the-clock, full-service car park for his penis. And no one ruining things by staying afterwards.

No one nagging him about the dishes and cleaning, or not enough flowers on Valentine's Day.

No one to eat dinner with in front of the TV, to snuggle up to in the evenings, no one with blond hair that always smelled of timothy grass and who got tiny, tiny freckles everywhere in the summer . . .

No one . . .

No one like Ellinor.

Ruben quickly picked up the note where he'd scribbled the phone number and dialled before he changed his mind. He took a deep breath.

'Hello. My name's Ruben Höök and I'd like to make an appointment.'

141

Anette looked at him with an expression he hadn't seen in a long time. He automatically assumed that she was joking. It was only when she began to unbutton his shirt that he realized she was serious.

'Have you noticed that the triplets are asleep?' she said softly. 'All three of them. At the same time.'

Peder reached for the remote control on the coffee table and switched off the TV before sinking back into the sofa again. Anette inserted her hand inside his shirt and began to caress his skin.

'You're right,' he said, listening to the silence. 'All three of them are actually asleep at once. We should buy a lottery ticket or something, given what a rarity that is.'

'Or we could spend our time doing something else,' Anette whispered into his ear.

She stood up and held out her hand. He took it and let her lead him to the bedroom.

'Are you sure?' he said, when she continued to undress him.

At first she didn't answer. Once he was down to his underpants, she crept into bed. After a bit of rummaging around under the duvet, she pulled out his top and trousers and threw them at him. Then she patted his pillow.

'I'm absolutely certain,' she said. 'If we go to bed now, we might manage half an hour's sleep before they wake up.'

Peder looked at the pillow and then at his wife. He didn't see how pale she was, he didn't see the bags under her eyes. All he saw was how much he loved her. Peder fell asleep almost before his head hit the pillow.

142

The small picture of Nathalie was moving slowly across the map on her mobile display. Mina had photographed the framed picture she had on her desk to use as an icon. The photo bore almost no resemblance to the girl's appearance today, but it was the most recent picture she had. On several occasions she had been tempted to photograph Nathalie from a distance, but her own sense of self-preservation had taken over each time. She didn't dare contemplate what might happen if she were discovered.

Mina hadn't known that she was planning to plant a GPS tracker in Nathalie's backpack until she had done it. But when they had drunk coffee in Kungsträdgården it had been the first time in many years she had been that close to the girl, and she didn't know when it would happen again.

At first she had thought that the men guarding Nathalie had seen what she had done. When they had come and fetched the girl, Mina had almost wet herself in fear. For real. But if they had found the tracker then the threats in the phone calls would have been much worse. It would have been the last time she set eyes on Nathalie.

What it did mean, however, was that Mina didn't dare get close to the girl for a while. She couldn't stand on the platform of the underground station at Blåsut and watch Nathalie going to school. She couldn't wait outside the door in Östermalm or follow her movements around town. It would be a while before Mina could see her in real life again.

But that didn't matter.

She had the girl in front of her, in her hand.

The app allowed her to see exactly where Nathalie was and she could fantasize about what she was doing, who she was with. The little portrait was currently stationary and the map showed her to be in Östermalm, which probably meant Nathalie was at home. If Mina zoomed in then she'd be able to pull up the address, but she already knew it.

Of course, she wasn't going to spy. Natti had the right to a private life. But she would continue to check in every now and then.

Check that everything was OK. That the men in the sunglasses were taking good care of her.

'Hello, sweetheart,' she said, stroking the screen with her fingertips. 'I'm going to make sure nothing happens to you.'

143

Vincent took the *Glitter Pussy* mug out of the cupboard, filled a tea strainer with tea leaves and poured water from the kettle over it. Then he set the steaming mug down on the kitchen table in front of his wife.

'There you go, darling,' he said. 'You look like you need it.'

'Is it green tea?' she said.

He hesitated for a second.

'No,' he admitted. 'It's chai.'

'Thank God,' said Maria, blowing on the mug. 'I'm so sick of that dishwater. I think it gives me a stomach ache.'

A while later, dinner was on the table. Sausage stroganoff with chorizo and chilli flakes in the sauce, brown rice, salad and kale crisps. The kale crisps didn't really go with the rest, but he knew that Benjamin loved them. He pretended to spill some sauce on Rebecka's mobile when she sat down near the frying pan.

'*So* lame,' she said, moving her mobile half a centimetre.

Then she looked up from the screen and laughed.

'I mean, it's lucky we don't have neighbours who live nearby. If my friends had seen you coming home in a police car – completely soaked through as well – I would have died! Sometimes you make me wonder, Dad.'

Vincent smiled.

'Yes, it was clumsy. I'm not going to walk so close to the edge of the quayside next time.'

Maria looked at him searchingly over the top of her mug. Though he hadn't talked much about the investigation, no one in the family had been able to avoid the newspaper headlines. But she said nothing. Instead, she set down the mug of hot tea and helped herself to the food.

'What do you say, darling?' he said. 'Perhaps we should invite your parents over next week? I've got a late birthday present for your father.'

Maria began to cough heavily and put a napkin to her mouth to contain the stroganoff.

'Have you had a bump on the head?' she asked between coughs.

But he could see that she was smiling behind the napkin.

He let his gaze continue on around the table, surveying his family. Rebecka was eating with one hand while messaging with the other. Her multitasking was actually impressive – if you chose to look at it like that. Aston was, as usual, counting the pieces of his food, which had been cut up for him by Maria, against her better judgement. Vincent knew full well where Aston had got it from – he could hardly blame his son. Benjamin was eating with his gaze elsewhere. He was at that age when girls – or boys – ought to be his primary focus. But Vincent knew that Benjamin was more likely thinking about a new mathematical problem. Perhaps one he'd found on YouTube. Hopefully it was one that encompassed less death this time around.

'Mum, I love you,' Aston said suddenly.

'And Mum loves you,' Maria replied, smiling.

'But I love you too, Dad,' Aston continued, looking gravely at Vincent.

'So you're a private detective now or something, right?' said Benjamin, who seemed to have returned to reality.

'You shouldn't believe everything you read on the *Aftonbladet* website,' Vincent replied quickly.

'But, I mean, was she really your sister?' said Rebecka. 'I didn't even know I had an aunt.'

He shook his head and wiped his mouth with a napkin.

'Those murders weren't about me,' he said. 'They were about people who haven't been around for a very long time.'

'How long will we be around?' Aston asked anxiously.

Vincent couldn't help ruffling his son's hair, although he knew Aston didn't like it.

'This family is going to be around for as long as we want it to be,' he said. 'For better or worse.'

144

Julia gathered together the papers on her desk and put them in a plastic folder. When she stood up, Mina and Vincent did likewise.

'Thanks for coming in one last time,' Julia said, shaking Vincent's hand. 'It feels good to tie this up a little more formally without a media presence. But I promise you that from now on you'll be shot of us.'

Vincent laughed. Mina thought it didn't sound altogether happy. Julia held out her hand.

'You can leave your pass with me.'

'Yes, of course. Well, thanks,' said Vincent, passing her the plastic card. 'It's been . . . bewildering.'

'I'll walk him out,' said Mina. 'So that he can get through the barriers.'

They left Julia's office and walked down the corridor. They walked quietly side by side. Mina didn't intend to be the first to say something. She had no idea how to do this kind of thing. What was more, she wasn't sure her voice wouldn't break.

'So that's that,' Vincent said at last.

'Yes. I suppose it is,' she said.

She hesitated.

'Jane was right,' she said. 'About me being a coward.'

'You're not a coward.'

'How . . . how did you know?' she said, glancing at Vincent out of the corner of her eye. 'Was it something about my body language or something else you managed to discern about me?'

Vincent rubbed his nose.

'You drag your right foot a little when you walk, and then you lift your left shoulder slightly. Plus you blink twice as much as a normal person. Those are clear signs of neurological damage from addiction to pills.'

Mina came to a halt.

'What! I do?'

She looked down at her right foot in shock. Vincent laughed.

'No, I'm just kidding. Don't worry. I saw your sobriety coin when I was at your flat. Obviously, I didn't know for sure that it was pills, but alcohol didn't seem very you, given your passion for Coke Zero. Well, if we overlook the hand sanitizer, that is – I gather it can be 85 per cent. Do you partake of it?'

'Ack, enough already!'

Mina punched him gently in the side. They fell silent again. They took the stairs down to the foyer and she used her pass to let him out into reception. She escorted him through the barrier. The exit from police headquarters was a few metres in front of them on the other side of reception. Only a few metres to go until it was over. Vincent suddenly stopped and looked at her.

'Sorry,' he said. 'For my sister hurting you. I haven't been able to sleep properly since then – I see you trapped in the tank every time I close my eyes. And it was all my fault. I've tried to think of a way to make it up to you, but nothing seems good enough.'

Then he smiled weakly.

'At least short hair suits you,' he said.

She ran her hand through her new haircut before managing to stop herself and rubbing her fingers against her jeans as if they had been infected. Hair was still an infection zone as far as she was concerned. It didn't matter how many times she had washed it since the container.

'Yes, it would have saved me both the trauma and a haircut if you'd mentioned the minor detail that the police were already on their way ...'

She glowered at him but didn't manage to inject any real anger into the look. He smiled in embarrassment and held out his hands apologetically.

'Well, I was barely conscious,' he said. 'And I would never have believed that you'd jump down into that awful container. Sorry. But like I said, the hair suits you.'

Mina gave him a final glance, then she chose to let it go.

It was water under the bridge. And she was quite happy with her new hair, if she was honest about it. Mina thought about what Vincent had said about his sister and shook her head.

'We're here now,' she said. 'We survived. They probably didn't. And they won't be able to murder any more innocent people.'

He nodded quietly. Then he glanced towards the exit.

'You're right about that. And as Julia said, now you're shot of me.'

He offered his hand in farewell. It was the last thing she wanted. After everything they had gone through, it couldn't end with a measly handshake. She had given part of herself to Vincent. He was the only person who knew who she truly was. You didn't shake hands for that. It meant you were connected forever.

But all the same . . .

They weren't in a romantic drama and she wasn't fifteen years old. They were standing in reception at police headquarters on Kungsholmen on a regular Wednesday in October and she was on duty. Once Vincent had left, she would go back upstairs and deal with her neglected inbox.

She wasn't connected to anyone.

'Likewise. As Julia said,' she said, taking his hand.

She had no idea how long they held hands for. Ten minutes, a year, half a second.

Then he broke off the handshake and turned towards the exit.

She began to head back towards the barriers.

'Mina, wait,' he called out suddenly, running towards her while digging in his inside pocket. 'Here!'

He passed her a sealed pack of single-use straws. She smiled as she took them, but had to blink away the tears. Then she dug in her own pocket.

'For you,' she said, tossing him her Rubik's cube. 'Be careful with it, the pieces are quite loose.'

Vincent smiled back when their eyes met.

Then he turned around and left through the doors with the colourful toy in his hand.

She was struck by the momentary impulse of wanting to use her hand sanitizer. But she decided to leave it.

Acknowledgements

You don't write a book like this alone. Not even two people are enough. We have had the pleasure of having extremely knowledgeable people around us who have ensured that we haven't made any really big mistakes in terms of the factual stuff. Some of these people deserve particularly thunderous rounds of applause.

Kelda Stagg MSc, a crime scene investigator with the Stockholm Region Police Authority has guided us away from our preconceived notions about forensic medicine and how bodies that are found are dealt with during an investigation. Instead, we have learned a lot about everything from who is present at an autopsy to what eye fluid is actually for.

We've also benefited from the great assistance provided by Teresa Maric, an expert based in the Investigations Unit at the National Operations Department (NOA) of the Swedish Police Authority, who explained phone tracing and information analysis to us at such a fascinating level of detail that we could have written a book just on that. All accurate descriptions of these areas of police activity are credited to Kelda and Teresa, while all errors are our own.

When it comes to the history of magic and how to build illusions, we absolutely bow down before the expertise that inventor and magic builder Andreas Sebring has selflessly shared with us. Andreas is the Sains Bergander of real life, to the extent that the workshop mentioned in the book is in fact a description of Andreas's own.

The magician and breakout king Anders Sebring also merits special thanks for a crucial conversation about how to get out of things you're not supposed to be able to get out of.

Although we have tried to be as accurate as possible with reality, we have also consciously taken a few creative liberties as authors to help the narrative flow better. For example, we have moved the mink farm on the island of Lidön both in terms of era and geographically. The farm closed many years ago and it wasn't by the water's edge either. There are actually six balconies at Gävle Theatre, not eight. There are several other, similar examples in the book where we have been somewhat free and easy with the facts. But if we had described reality every step of the way, the book would have been much longer than it already is – and rather duller too.

The biggest metaphorical bouquet of flowers goes to our amazing team at Bokförlaget Forum: our publisher Ebba Östberg, our manuscript consultant John Häggblom and our editor Kerstin Ödeen. We have laughed and cried together in frustration, but they have never given up, not even when we were prepared to do so. Without the devotion of the entire Forum team, this book would not be half of what it is today.

Copious thanks are also offered to Joakim Hansson, Anna Frankl, Signe Lundgren and the whole team at Nordin Agency, as well as Lili Assefa and the team at Assefa Communication, who believed in this series right from the start and managed to convince the world of its merits in an almost magical fashion. We're not quite sure how they pulled it off. But we are dumbfounded with admiration. We think ninja swords may have been involved.

Camilla's personal acknowledgements
As an author, it's completely impossible to write books without enormous support on the home front. My incredible husband Simon is the best spouse – and the best author's spouse in particular – that you could wish for. I'm also grateful for the unfailing support of my children, my friends and the rest of my family. Thank you for your cheerleading, which always gets me across the finishing line.

Henrik's personal acknowledgements
Thank you to my beloved wife Linda for your invaluable feedback on the manuscript when the book was at its most broken, for listening to me as I harped on about Vincent and Mina for two years and not actually finishing me off, and above all for never losing faith in me and putting up with me even when I don't deserve it. Thanks also to my

sons Sebastian, Nemo and Milo. If it weren't for you, none of what I do would be meaningful.

Finally, we want to thank all you readers who have given this series a chance. We love you all. And we hope that after reading this first part you're as excited about meeting Vincent and Mina again in the future as we are.